The Memory of an Elephant

Peter Webb

Grosvenor House
Publishing Limited

This book is published by
Grosvenor House Publishing Ltd
Link House
140 The Broadway, Tolworth, Surrey, KT6 7HT.
www.grosvenorhousepublishing.co.uk

This book is a work of fiction. Any resemblance to
people or events, past or present, is purely coincidental.

A CIP record for this book
is available from the British Library

ISBN 978-1-83975-177-6

Dedicated to:

*My family and the dogs that have
shared their lives with us:
Susan – Shandy – Kim – Mollie – Patsy – Sweeper –
Teacup – Saucer – Toby – Ceilidh – Larkrise – Toffee – Bracken
– Bailey – Fennel – Tigger – Milo*

Thank You For Your Love And Friendship

Also by Peter Webb:

Ladies of the Shire

The Quarry

Acknowledgements:
My sincere and enduring thanks to:

Rosemary Gaches:
Without your anecdote all those years ago this story never
would have taken shape

Marjorie Webb:
For your support and persistence in keeping me
on the right track throughout the story development and for
your ability to rein in my more outlandish ideas; The Memory
of an Elephant is a tribute to your skills and patience

Ben Rowe:
For, once again, your sterling work on the creation and
development of the artwork for this book;
couldn't have done it without you

Dawn Flynne:
For Publicity and Marketing for the past ten years; thank you

**Muneaki Kinoshita, The Kyoto Seishu Netsuke
Art Museum, Kyoto, Japan:**
For kind permission to use the netsuke image

**Akira Yamamoto, Sagawa Printing,
Kyoto, Japan:**
For reproducing the netsuke image

Image & Design Credits

~

Two Years Later...

"...and we'll go live to our Africa Correspondent, Marcus Gerber... Marcus, first reports in say this incident happened during a rest day; is that correct? What can you tell us?"

"...Yes Patrick. I've been covering the African Trade Talks in Gaborone where leaders of the industrialised nations have gathered for discussions surrounding the refunding of the region's mining and agricultural assets, called after the country defaulted on payments to the World Bank made to shore up the country's degraded economy earlier this year. Yesterday and today were rest days after a week of six sessions of gruelling and sometimes fractious negotiations. A small number of the delegates took the opportunity to fly out and attend an organised tour of a sanctuary...

'Archie... Oh, Lord... Archie! You need to come and see this...'

"...for elephants orphaned by the continued poaching in..."

'Archie!'

~

THE MEMORY OF AN ELEPHANT

Sunday – Apologue

A woman and a terrier walk along a country lane the sides of which are hemmed in by a tall stone wall which casts further shadow on this already fast-darkling evening. From behind her out of trees arched over the lane a black, bull-barred Range Rover Sport glides silent, smooth and dark from its woodland womb. The lagging terrier trots to the woman's side just as a squeal of tyres announces the vehicle changing down, finding extra grip in its acceleration, and only now does it light up, stabbing the inky black and illuminating both woman and dog in the splash of the beam. Realising its intent, she attempts a scramble back up the wall to her left which falls tight to the lane, the moss denying her the climb, but not the dog. She slip-slides back down and makes to cross the lane to where a grass verge and ditch meets the opposite wall that is lower, calling the dog to follow. The vehicle blisters along, the terrier halts mid-lane disorientated like a lamped rabbit and the woman makes the first move back to remove it from harm. The distance too far the approach too fast, she gives the dog a look of farewell as two point one tons of whooshing metal whacks into her, smashing body and soul onto the metalwork. The vehicle's savage braking releases her, sending the rag-doll replacement of a former life cartwheeling down the lane until her body slithers to an eventual, twitching halt. The Range Rover tail-wags to a stop and backs up to illuminate the bloody mess, exhaust steaming. A man, snub-nosed shotgun in hand, gets out as, from inside the vehicle, a hissed voice follows him.

'Quick search...and no guns!'

He stands over the body and watches with dead-pan interest as her spot-lit life seeps away; he bends and rummages through the coat, removing a mobile phone. The glint of an ivory netsuke hanging by a leather strip from her belt attracts his attention; an intricately carved baby elephant cradling an acorn through the centre of which is drilled a worm hole. Another single strand of leather is passed through this hole and looped through that are several other strips of leather, some plaited and all of different colours. He cuts the netsuke free then slices through and discards the other leather strips. At the same moment he pockets this prize the terrier locks onto his leg and he yells out, whacking down at the dog's head with the shotgun in overbalanced shock. The terrier yelps and skittles back to the top of the wall where it stands defiant. It is closely followed by the pattern of BB shot striking the wall just below its feet, pellets ricocheting up to rake across the dog's face. The terrier yelps and tumbles off the wall, into the wood and out of sight.

'I said no guns!' The driver joins him and the two men drag-carry the corpse across the lane. At the grass verge they leg-and-a-wing it back once then fling it into the ditch.

The vehicle doors slam, the car lights up and it purrs rapidly away down the lane.

After a short pause, the terrier appears atop the wall, one eye bloodshot, a red slash across the black muzzle, blood seeping freely from its mouth. The dog slips down the wall and trots nose down along the bloody smear to finally stand at the edge of the ditch. He looks into it with side-cocked head, panting, grinning, waiting for signs of life until he slowly moves down the slope to his companion, accompanied by a low whine...

Sunday – Prologue

'Thing is you see, fox aint no hyena Jasp; what my country call impisi?' The jet-black terrier's gaze never leaves hers. 'Foxes, they're chancers...like jackals, but impisi? Killers they are. Would've flipped this tin sheet off, rolled him and gobbled the arse straight off; jaws like a vice, couple of bites and gone... Yeah, best part of the kill the arse...for leeu too.' The dog's gaze was unaltered. 'Leeu... Lion.'

The terrier wags its stump of a tail at a woman, sun-and-weather faced, crouching stick in hand by the crabbed human corpse in its makeshift grave. An age-worn corrugated tin sheet part covers the couched body, a discarded thick branch lies nearby.

'You're not getting much of this are y'?' Jasper dabs at the grave's edge with his front paw. 'Yeah yeah, I know, it was you found him, I know.' She scruffs his ear. Jasper lolls his tongue and follows her gaze as she looks around. 'And no fox covered him over with this stuff that's for sure. Them Irish an' them Chinese all with their fighting dogs, they did it... I wonder where his dog went? Buried under him I guess, poor little mite...' She instinctively puts a hand to her trench coat pocket to quieten the buzz from a vibrating mobile phone, her under-breath voice full of annoyance, 'Jesus Lin leave us be! When we're back at camp, I'll call then, if we've got a signal.' She scrubs the terrier's neck with grubby fingers, her splintered nails rearranging the dog's wiry ruff, then clicks her tongue at him.

'Tch-Tch!'

The terrier reacts, the call to get sharp well drilled into him. 'This is what you get for choosin' to live in the world Jasp. We want no part of it, eh?' She looks back into the woodland. 'Yeah, them fellas....' The terrier drops down on his front paws and gives a yap. 'Shush, isiwula! Don't want folk knowing you've found this.' She scans left and right then back at the grave. 'Best not hang around, not if the pay-off's being stuffed into a pauper's plot with nothing but a tin sheet for a headstone.' She pauses, looks at the corpse and shakes her head. 'Ought we to leave him summat eh? Leave him summat for his journey home?'

Around her waist is a woven leather belt. From this, secured by a thin strip of leather, hangs an ivory netsuke, an intricately carved baby elephant cradling an acorn. She unties a leather strip hanging from it and offers it to the dog.

'Here, give a lick.'

The dog sniffs, licks, and she drops the leather onto the corpse. 'A gift from me.' She looks at the dog. 'Cockerleg.' The terrier lifts a hind leg and squirts a jet of urine onto the disturbed soil. 'And one from Jasper here.' The dog turns its head deeper into the wood and gives a whine and the woman stands quickly and freezes, following the dog's gaze. 'You heard it too?' She shivers and tosses the stick away. 'C'mon, let's slope off, things are not right here.' She eyes the falling dusk. 'Usathane about, he just walked over my grave.' She draws the tin sheet back over the corpse. 'We'll be safe back at camp; stones will 'ave cooked supper by now.' Placing the large branch gently back on top of the sheet she tongue-clicks the terrier.

'Tch-tch!'

They set off, weaving slowly through the autumn-stripped trees, both living in their shared but separate worlds, the terrier lifting a right hind every now and then. They approach a tall stone wall bordering a lane which slices through the woodland and slow to a standstill. 'Careful time.'

A full minute of silent study ends with the woman dropping to one knee, placing her hand on the terrier's head and fixing a stained finger to her chapped lips. 'No noise Jasp. Fella back there riled them thugs somehow and look how he ended up.' She holds up her right hand. 'Tch-tch! Sit and stay.'

The dog sits, watches, his tail sweeping a tiny section of the woodland floor clear of leaves as the woman climbs stiffly to the top of the eight foot high wall, slipping and slithering on the green ice of moss in her efforts. Her stare along the lane is followed by a tongue click and tap of her thigh. The terrier is up the wall in a single scrambled bound where he stands, pants, grins, wags, looking as smug as it's possible for a dog to look.

'Ziqhenya, you wait while arthritis kicks in.' She pauses then they descend in a half scrabble, half slide down the wall's slippery-wet face, chunks of moss accompanying them.

The woman and a terrier walk along the country lane. From behind her, out of trees arched over the lane, a black, bull-barred Range Rover Sport glides silent, smooth and dark from its woodland womb...

Sunday – Epilogue

The vehicle doors slam, the car lights up and it purrs rapidly away down the lane. The dog slips down the wall and across the road and verge to stand at the edge of the ditch waiting for signs of life; he slowly moves down the slope, a low whine his only companion.

Matt switches the lights of the Range Rover to main beam and rests his hand on the door frame. '...An' I told you no guns!'

'The bloody dog bit me leg Matt, what was I supposed to do!'

'Club it.'

'I did.'

'I mean to dead.'

'Too fast for me. It was up on that wall like a rat up a drainpipe, how else was I gonna sort it?'

'Well I just hope the shot was worth it.'

'Well fuck you very much for your concern.' Chris presses the paper handkerchief to the wound.

'For what? You sound off that gun so I have to help you drag the corpse to the ditch dressed like this! I was goin' out tonight on a date, remember? That's why the suit. I didn't get dressed up just to mow her down did I? Now I'm late already.'

'I don't see why we couldn't just have chucked her into the back of your motor. Take her to the wood yard and into the furnace.'

'Don't talk so daft! In case you've missed it she's fresh-dead an' there was no time to collect a plastic sheet thanks to you!' Matt changed gear with excessive force. 'There'll be traces of her left all over us as it is.'

'But, she'll be found in there.'

'She will, but time and distance all help to confuse. You're sure you left her tidy?'

'Yeah, just that phone.'

'Nothing left?'

'Just the phone, I said! Ow, me bloody leg...!'

'It's just a nip. I've seen dogs with far worse fight on an' win. An' that fellah she found under that tin sheet, the one them Chinks killed and those Irish just chucked away...'

'They didn't do it on purpose!'

'Convince me. I want him bagged up and shifted, tonight.'

'Tonight?'

'Yeah Chris, tonight.'

'But...'

'Tonight. Your shit, you scrape it up.' Turning onto the main road Matt accelerates away. 'What happened to the dog?'

'Buried with him I guess.'

'He was a lot of things, buried wasn't one of them.' Matt shakes his head. 'Check for the dog when you shift him.'

'It'll be there, them Irish said they'd sort it.'

'An' you believed 'em? Fuck's sake... Shift the lot then burn your clothes an' chuck the shotgun in the mere. I want nothin' even remotely traceable left from this little lot.'

'It's just a shotgun, Matt...'

'In the mere.'

Chris flips open the shotgun to extract the one empty cartridge case. 'Well, what about your suit then?'

'I'll be burning this too, all three hundred quid's worth of it, and that'll make me even later...' Matt eyes the empty cartridge Chris is holding. 'Black Feather? Where'd you get them from?'

'Aiden. He brought a crate full of 'em with him when he came over. Gave me a couple of boxes.'

'I thought you didn't like him.'

'I don't.'

'Huh. Well chuck the empty in the mere as well.'

'What about the mobile?'

'I'll check it then lose it.'

Chris presses the tissue to the still-leaking bite. 'It's a cheap and cheerful model, like a burner...'

Matt ignores Chris' efforts at conversation and talks over him. 'I'll report back to the Gaffer when he gets home on Tuesday, but my guess is he won't be happy so tidy up that corpse proper this time. I'll drop you at the kennels an' see you tomorrow, I've had enough of your company for one day.' Matt changes down as he approaches the wide gates and notices Chris lift the pad a little to inspect his leg. 'Get a dressin' an' some antiseptic on it, you'll live. Just watch the blood don't drop...'

'On the seats, yeah, thanks.'

'And watch your hands on the dash an' the seat belt.'

'Jesus, it's like bein' in a car with me dad.'

'If only you knew who he was...'

Monday

Mayflower Rise and Pool Heath were misnomers.
There was no pool. There was no rise. There was no heath. And as for it being a mode of transport for a persecuted people to escape starvation and go in search of a better life? No chance.

Built in the mid-sixties with bricks formed from crushed privation held together with a mortar of hopelessness, the whole venture was supposedly constructed to reflect the white heat of technology. But Mayflower Rise was just another working-class collective, another pigeon-hole for the proletariat glued together in the day when architectural cubism had penetrated every possible orifice of aesthetic design. No personal space was allowed to infiltrate these areas of mass habitation, no differentiation of private or public, no designated, carefully nurtured soft-play area allowed any influence on this act of vandalism perpetrated by the stack 'em high sell 'em cheap ethos of sixties social engineering.

Linden Lea stepped out of flat number fifteen on the first storey, closed the door and breathed in the scent emanating from the scarred and neglected communal refuse bins banned to the basement, their reek rising up like a determined fart. *Ripe is that,* she thought as she reacted to the opening of a door two flats along and nodded at the elderly, dressing-gowned lady lighting up.

'Morning Amy.' A cough and a wave returned her greeting as Lin set off along the walkway. *One-woman neighbourhood watch she is; misses nothing...and not long for this world by the tone of that cough.*

Lin descended the steps and passed the odd patch of neglected, unkempt rhododendron on her way to the bare-earth track which crossed what had started out as a communal grassed area but was now the scabbed, divoted home pitch of the grubby-kneed tykes from adjoining flats. This scrub area was surrounded on three sides by identical flat-faced buildings, each wall bearing a pock-marked, air-gun-pelleted sign confirming that no ballgames were allowed.

Lin avoided a stooping mongrel releasing the remains of last night's bin-scavenged kebab back into the wild. *And a good morning to you too*, ran through her head as, never halting in her progress, she called out.

'This shitting dog? Belong to anybody? Anybody?'

Her lone voice reverberated off the walls and echoed across the blandscape, only to die in the silence of its return as she set out along Cleveland Road which ran to Chorleton centre. A girl on a mission, she took out the cheap and cheerful mobile phone from her pocket and looked at the screen. *I know texting's beyond you Rene, but pressing the pre-set button to return my call? No one's that busy.* Lin hunched her shoulders, the outward expression of her displeasure. 'Jobcentre then...'

'... And do you think it's a job that would suit?'

'Absolutely; yes, absolutely.' Lin hoped her voice sounded earnest but not desperate. 'It's my field, it's what I'm good at.'

'Up to a point Lin. Your African experience is all very positive, but your extra-curricular stuff...' Angela Thorne, Employment Technician to the great unwashed, raised an eyebrow. 'The bee protest thing?'

Lin paused. 'Well, I think that shows commitment, determination...an understanding of how the environment works...'

'Yes, it does and Chorleton certainly enjoyed the spectacle, but this is a job working for a company that does research and development into...' she read, 'crop diversification and specialist foods.'

'Genetically modified cereals you mean?'

'Yes.'

'Then say it Angie, it's OK, I'll not throw a fit, I'm a vegetarian not a nutter. My only surprise is the company are placing the ad here, a job centre in the middle of nowhere.'

'Thanks.'

'No offence, you guys are great, just...here, y know?'

Angela nodded. 'I think they wanted to show they were in support of places outside of London.'

'And it helps them get their diversification grants.'

'Bit harsh Lin.'

'Doesn't make it untrue though does it? Look, I know you've almost given up on me...'

Angela sighed. 'This'll be eight months of effort on our part and,' she looked through the file and counted, her lips moving silently at first, '...nine, ten, eleven; eleven job interviews arranged, four you never attended the rest coming to nothing. We all know you're more than capable, so yes, I would say there's a level of frustration amongst the staff.' She smiled. 'This is a job centre and we're on first name terms Lin, that should give you a hint.'

'I've got nothing to say to that except I really do think this one could be it. Alright, yes, it could be said I'm in the opposing camp to Braxhams, but do you not think they'd feel the benefit of a voice from a different background? All the stuff I've done, apart from the bee thing, has been focussed on getting food to the hungry. I've done agricultural college, worked on farms here and in Romania and done three years of summer voluntary work at Kew in their seed bank site. I stopped going there 'cos of money, nothing to do with unsuitability just a lack of cash...and we've no need to include anything about the protest...or any other sensitive matters on my résumé, do we? Surely what I've done, the good stuff, it's got to count for something?'

'Yes, it does.' Angela sighed. 'And no, we don't need to be forensic about the detail...' She paused, considered, decided. 'OK right, I'll put you up for it, but you'll have to be on your best behaviour, alright?' Lin nodded. 'This is a first for us, a company as big as this coming here to recruit. The last thing we need is for them to think we're sending them unsuitable candidates, or ones that don't turn up.' She checked the details. 'I'll print these out. Wednesday, three-thirty. OK?'

'Yup.'

'It's at their London head office. You good for the travel fares?'

'Absolutely. Thanks Angie, really. I'll give it my best shot; I'll even get a decent outfit to wear for it.'

The printer whirred as backdrop. 'Can you afford one?'

'Well OK, a new coat then.'

Angela got up and handed over the sheet of paper. 'Here. I'll ring them and let them know you're coming, and please Lin, show up...on time?'

'I will, honest I will.' She folded the paper into her pocket. 'Thanks.'

'Good luck.'

'Luck's not needed, just a willingness for them to be creative in their appointments.'

Angela smiled. 'Creative? This is an agricultural multinational we're talking about Lin not the National Theatre.'

Lin began to leave. 'Then they'll not know I'm acting will they?' She saw Angela's expression. 'Joke, honest.' The job centre door sealed her to the street. 'God, I hope I can pull this one off...go and see Sarah.' She looked into her bag and rummaged. 'Have I got enough for a pint...?'

~

6

o o o An' even now, I can't believe you trusted 'em to do it anywhere near right!'

'I had no choice seein' as how my Chinese is below par and everyone else had buggered off.'

Matt's expression hardened. 'You can drop the sarcasm, alright?'

Matt and Chris were standing in a large tractor barn the inside of which was spotlessly clean. Directly opposite this building, across a large concrete yard which housed a fenced off exercise area, was a disused cattle barn which had been bovine-free for many a year. Forming the third side of the rectangle were eight detached, brick and barred kennels each containing a single puppy of different parentage, age and temperament; the final kennel in the line abutted onto a small windowless shed. A tall, metal fence and spike-topped gate completed the corral.

Parked in this yard was a well-used Series 3 long wheel-based Land Rover, poor cousin to the pristine, black, supercharged Range Rover Sport V-8 parked inside the barn. Matt was dressed in blue coveralls, the legs of which were tucked into a pair of green Hunter wellingtons. On a square of carpet nearby were placed his pair of highly polished alligator skin shoes. A fitted kitchen ran along one wall of the barn and next to a stainless-steel sink stood a tall rubbish bin, alongside of which was a standpipe with hose attached. Matt turned on the tap and began to wash the previously applied suds off the Range Rover.

'Before I left the match site I told you to sort out that bloke's corpse an' his dog. You. An' you knew where we'd gone.'

'I did but not that fast! One minute we're havin' a bit of sport, next I know there's me left with a corpse, a gang of pissed shamrocks to organise, and the Gaffer to get to the airport for his shootin' trip. It was like gluin' a busted jelly back together! They offered to dump the body an' I said yeah. Told 'em if they did it I'd see 'em right. Paid that one with the peach-fuzz moustache...Josh, that's him. Shelled out a thou up front to split between 'em, a thou of my own I'll have you know. Things were bad enough as it was, an' I couldn't very well tell the Gaffer I was gonna be late could I?'

'Would've taken you all of twenty minutes, plane wasn't 'til half nine, bit of inventive drivin' you'd 'ave made it.'

'Should never have happened in the first place, Gaffer gettin' them Chinks involved.'

'Who d'you think the whole event was put on for? They weren't just folk he'd dragged in off the street they were his guests, his business guests! Form, Chris, it's all about form.'

'Form be buggered, he just wanted to put on a show, be the big I-am, slither his way even further up their factory arseholes. When those bodyguards started in on that chap them Irish had no idea what were goin' on, you an' me neither.'

'Too busy watchin' their dog.'

Chris' temper rose slightly. 'I'm not on about the scrap, I'm on about that chap turnin' up with his corgi and them bloody Chink bodyguards goin' ape-shit on him! Next thing I know he's dead an' that corgi's up the road like shit off a shovel.'

'If that's the way they do things in China then that's the way they do things.'

'But this is England Matt; we don't do that sort of thing over here!' His anger turned to sulk. 'Then I'm told to clean up the mess; their mess.'

'We were the hosts so, yeah, it was down to us to clean up. Y' don't invite folk round for dinner then tell 'em they've to clean the bog before they leave do y'?' Matt moved round the vehicle, sluicing as he went. 'An' the corgi? It's gone?'

'Gone.'

'You sure?'

'As in 'I can't find it'. It ran off. Wouldn't you?'

'With them Irish after me, I would. There's no logic to 'em, the fuckin' idiots. They think they're back in the Troubles, shoot first ask after. The corpse?'

'Went straight into the grinder, along with two sacks of deer heads guts and skins from the deer park cull last week. Hunt knacker cart called this morning so hound food by now.'

'No trace back to here then, and you sluiced out your car?'

'Yeah.'

Matt looked out to the yard searching for understanding, 'Jesus H. Christ this has been harder work than needed. What were that chap doin' round them old pigsties in the first place anyway? There's enough no trespassin' signs about. What is it with the folk of this country that think they can wander where they like with their bloody maps and socks? Then her, that bloody woman we whacked on the lane, wanderin' about the woods like she owned 'em... Like Piccadilly-bloody-circus round here.'

'What about where she were stayin', her camp-site? She'd no backpack when you clobbered her.'

Matt shook his head. 'No, but with three keepers on the case it shouldn't take long. Aiden says he'll be out and about as well, so if he comes across any piles of sticks or such I've told him to bring everything back here to get rid of.'

'Aiden's an 'alf-wit, he couldn't find his own cock.'

'Matt half-smiled at Chris. 'You really don't like him do y'?'

'An' you do?'

'I put up with him, he does a good job.'

'For a dog trainer. For anything else he's a big-headed prat who's all mouth and trousers, there's no bravery in him.'

Matt sighed large and restarted his cleaning. 'Your clothes are burnt?' Chris nodded. 'An' the shotgun's in the mere, right?'

'Yeah, but I don't know for why. They won't match the bullet, it's a shotgun.'

'I've said I want nothing to come back to here, that's why. You don't seem to realise how lucky we've been.'

'Lucky? Jesus, if this past couple of days have been lucky...'

'They have! Our luck Aiden was out checkin' setts for bait; our luck he saw that woman sniffin' round and called it in; our luck he could clock which way she were goin' and bloody lucky we were home and could get across to her just in time! An' all this from your fuck up on fight night.'

'I'd not the time, I've said! It was a scrum an' I'm certain-sure you were nowhere to be seen.'

'No I weren't! Aiden needed to get Derringer stitched up an' I 'ad to get everyone away from the scene in case he was followed. I'd enough to do!'

'An' me! I weren't here havin' tea an' biscuits was I?'

Matt's face and sudden slowed speech advertised his mood-shift. 'This has been a wrong 'un from the start Chris, the last thing I want from you right now is sarcasm, right?' Matt drew the hosepipe back to the tap with unnecessary force as he curled it into a circle of neatness. 'When the Gaffer told us to set that match up I said it'd go tits. Too rushed I said. Would he listen? No, he has to have his way. I said we'd have a job sortin' out safe competition that fast. "Find someone," he says. "Those Irish have been pestering for a bout," he says. "Get them". Just like that. I told him I need more time to vet them properly, but no, he wants it an' he wants it now. "Affairs of State, Lamb, Affairs of State". he says. Affairs of state my arse.'

'Best you could do in the time though weren't it, an' that Rebel were supposed to be Derry's best-of-the-best.'

'Dog looked the part...' Matt collected a carefully folded chamois leather, held it under the tap, wrung it out and began to wipe down the car, 'Pity it showed up with a pair of tossers.'

'True. Derringer'd turned it twice.' Chris thought for a moment. 'Where'd they take it to get that shoulder stitched?'

'Gyppos' camp out at Carlington; Aiden's recommendation. It weren't much, just a tear.'

'Why not use the Loveridges?'

'Nah, that car-breaker lot are permanent and too close to home. Gyppos will be on the move in a couple of weeks, as usual. They're gonna keep it for a few days 'cos the Irish had to get back to London. Only reason that dog's still alive is 'cos the rematch is on.'

'How y' gonna keep in touch?'

'Burner. Willis took one across.'

'Oh. Still a bit risky though, the rematch.'

'It is but the Gaffer wants it; already got the dates them Chinks are back in the country sorted. No patience. Thinks his class makes him untouchable, arrogant sod. Forgets that what we're doin' is illegal and when it goes tits-up-in-a-ditch we're the ones left to shovel it up.'

'That's why I handed on the burial...'

The reminder relit Matt's smouldering injustice. 'There's a laugh!'

'Could've been worse...'

'You really think leavin' a discreet burial job to a band of half-wits then havin' to mow down that lass 'cos of it could've got any worse?' Chris began self-consciously inspecting the now scab-dried remains of Jasper's attack, avoiding eye contact as Matt bent close to inspect the vehicle's bonnet. 'Tch! I can still see traces of the dent she put in this, thought that bull-bar would've kept her clear...bugger. I warmed it up and used a plunger but...I still see a trace. I'll get a hair-dryer an' some ice on it, then another cut an' polish...' Matt continued to wipe down the vehicle. 'Right, on to matters more pressin'.'

'Like my money?'

'Your donation to the stupidity charity you mean? Kiss it goodbye, I'm re-directing it.'

'What for?'

'I've just said! Them Chinese fellas! They're due to come back for the rematch at the end of the month; some deal goin' on, some government initiative. Christ knows why but they were impressed with the entertainment.'

'That dog won't do well next time neither.'

'Against a front-ender like Derringer? No he'll not, an' they know it.'

'Then why send it back into that lot? That aint sport.'

''Cos them Irish want a way in to the bigger fights, an' they don't come bigger than goin' against the Gaffer's line.'

Chris pondered on this before shaking his head. 'Well I think sendin' it back in, that's just stupid.'

'No Chris, what you did was stupid. What they're doin' is cruel, but as stupid as you were I don't want 'em thinkin' we're an easy touch for a grand, not after doin' nothin' for it, so your money's goin' as a down payment.'

'On?'

'The results of my check on that phone you found.'

'Got friends has she?'

'Friend; got a friend.' Matt finished wiping down, squeezed out the shammy and draped it out carefully over the tap before unbuttoning and stepping out of the coveralls, revealing an immaculate tie-shirt-suit combination. 'Only got one number on it; Linden Lea. That made things easy, Pay-Gee didn't though.'

'Ah, right. So...?'

Removing a black plastic bin liner from the shelf and holding the coveralls well away from his clothing, Matt lifted them high before curling them gently into the bin liner. 'Contacted the network provider, told 'em the tale of the old iron pot, said it was a lost family phone, for the kids...blah, blah, amazin' how trustin' folk are. Ran a range trace for me, helpful souls. That narrowed it down a bit. Took a while, but I finally tracked down her council; she's got tax problems. They were a bit cagey with the personal stuff so I traced things back through the electoral register. Lives in some backwater called Chorleton, out Buckingham way, about thirty miles from here.'

'Not near her dead mate then?'

'Nah, thank God. Anyway, this Lea girl called the evenin' we bowled our lass over; call was missed.'

'Or ignored.'

'Or ignored.'

'Friend? Girlfriend?'

'Makes no odds, outcome's the same.' Matt removed a roll of electrical tape from the shelf and sealed the bin liner as he expanded the point. 'There were two other calls from the same number over the past week, same area, so, we have to ask ourselves, what did they talk about? Was that her first visit to that corpse or a revisit? Had that dead lass seen us, seen them Chinks in action doin' that butchery, dumpin' the corpse, seen the scrap?'

'Well, I dunno...we don't know.'

'Exactly. We don't know, that's why it can't be left, that's why I look at all the angles, plan for the worst hope for the best.' Matt placed the bin liner on the work surface. 'Supposing this Lea does know and blabs, can you imagine it for the Gaffer, for us more to the point? We'd all be down the nick faster than shit through a goose. Can't run that risk.' Chris nodded his head in agreement. 'They can't bury for shit, but one thing them Irish lads can do is frighten folk; lot of practice they've had. They're gonna acquaint her kneecaps with a gun muzzle, buy the other phone off her with a couple of thou and say how things will lay out should she ever consider talkin'.' Matt took a soft cloth from the shelf and began to polish the car's headlights, then stopped to gain confirmation. 'You sure there was nothin' else on her?'

Chris gave only the very slightest of pauses. 'Yeah...yeah. She were clean, just the phone...then that dog...we couldn't hang about could we?'

'Not after your clay shoot, no.'

'One shot Matt; it was just the one.'

'I just hope it was enough to send it off to die.' Matt indicated the bin liner. 'See that?' Chris nodded. 'Sealed, into the furnace when I'm done here an' the phone with it. That's what tidy looks like.' He continued polishing, working his way round the various lights, mulling things over. 'An' our little run-away. She's just some outta work drifter caught up in a speeding car mishap. Happens all the time, lack of coppers means most are never solved. Just this little problem of our lass in Chorleton to sort. I've got the address. Gaffer only got back from his hunt yesterday; went straight down to London so I had to talk that little shit Quinn through things.'

'Gaffer's trip go well?'

'Apparently. Shot himself another cheetah.'

'Another one?'

'Yeah, different spots or summat accordin' to Quinn...' Matt shook his head. 'Mental... Anyhow, we've got the go-ahead. Gaffer said he'll monitor things, Police Commissioner an' such, but he wants our end of it done clean an' quick. Said it were a good choice using them Micks 'cos if things get serious an IRA revenge feud can be flagged up to the press; they'll print any tale that's got blood-and-crumpet mixed in with a terror threat.' Matt swapped the cloth for another and began to buff the chrome work, looking along it every now and then to fix the available light from differing angles as he checked for traces of missed marks. 'That old fella they did for and the burial you fucked up is another thing though. Gaffer's a bit twitchy about how much might have leaked out, and that bastard Quinn's got his own agenda, as usual. Gaffer wants me to get some background on the corpse and wants to chat it through with us tomorrow...an' you know what a chat with 'im can turn into. We just concentrate on this, get it right, we might get a bonus and not a bollocking. When I'm finished here I'll make a call or two... Your thou is the down payment for the scare and I've sorted out another thou for 'em from petty cash. OK?' He didn't wait for an answer. 'I'll set things up with our Miss Lea for Wednesday evening, after we've seen the Gaffer and got confirmation.'

'Quick as that'?'

'Can't be left, an' if them Irish want any chance in the dog-fight world they'll make the time an' do this one proper.'

Chris made a move to leave. 'Right. That it?'

'Not quite. You'll not have heard but Badger's to stop fightin'. He's to be yarded so get over an' help Aiden.'

Chris stopped. 'Oh Christ, do I 'ave to?'

'You do since Gerry's gone,' Matt smirked. Think of that as y' bonus.'

'But...when I took on the cleanin' an' exercise stuff with them pups I thought that'd be all I was doin'. I don't mind all that, the early starts an' such, I like the pups...an' you, you've been happy with what I done so far, haven't y'? You an' the Gaffer?'

'We are.'

'Then how come I've gotta get involved...?'

''Cos things 'ave changed. I told you that when we were organising Gerry's departure. We're the team now; just us. No more outsiders, Gaffer wants to keep it all in-house from now on, 'specially with them RSPCA do-gooders gettin' all self-righteous again, stirrin' things up in the red tops, promotin' their bunny-huggin' agenda.'

'Been problems before, we've always weathered it.'

'Up 'til now yeah.' Matt looked out into the yard, shook his head and sighed. 'Whole world's gone soft. All these bloody David Attenborough programmes are to blame, an' that's why we're all in-house now. Less chance of leaks if we see to all of it ourselves, right?'

'But Aiden's an outsider aint he?'

'He is, but he's a class act so...'

'Well, yeah, but them dogs, it's the way he treats 'em.'

'Trains 'em y' mean.'

'Trains 'em then, just, he's so bloody strict with 'em.'

'Different requirement now. Remember what it was like before?'

'Yeah... I do...'

'Well then. Our dogs are fitter, healthier and fight better 'cause of him.'

'But he's a bossy little fucker an' it's just 'cos he's got the Gaffer's backin'.' Matt folded the polishing cloth and placed it back onto the shelf before removing his Hunters, placing them regimentally next to the standpipe then stepping into his shoes. 'And he's a Yank.'

Matt stopped in his dressing. 'Oh, so now we're down to it are we? It's not because the man we've got knows his chops so our dogs are fitter, nor because we treat 'em with a bit of respect, not even because we're winnin'; it's because he's foreign?'

'Well, he is.'

Matt stood for a little while looking at Chris before sighing and shaking his head. 'Y' not big on debate, are y'? Aiden was brought in precisely because he is American, do you not see that? Because he's never figured on anyone's radar, and them Southern Yanks know what's what in the fight game. You think he came all the way from America and we'd have no idea of his pedigree?' Matt began to tidy the shelving, putting items square along it, lining them up, wiping down surfaces with kitchen roll before dropping the used sheets into the bin. He stopped and nodded in the general direction of the horizon. 'I put in the work, just like those sties. They were the perfect place for them scraps. Got 'em all nicely set up. Electric, water piped in, nice walled boxes, good size an' good concrete floorin'; even put in a boiler for the drinks. Now? Now I've got to start all over again.' He sighed at the prospect.

'I could have a scout about, there's that disused quarry a bit away from here.'

'That's exactly why I do it. First place them tree-huggers look. You'd not be there minutes before Blue Cross, RSPCA an' a gang of coppers would be there, all of 'em yellin' about dogs' rights...' He shook his head in disbelief. 'They call us cruel. I mean, what do they think they're for eh? Dogs? These folk, they call themselves dog lovers then give 'em a slow death by overfeedin' 'em, breed 'em so close they can't breathe nor walk proper...poor buggers. No idea most folk... No, you leave the scoutin' to me. There's a shell of a building near that excuse for a burial site.' Matt began to fuss with the crease in his trousers, leaning against the wing of the vehicle for balance, then left without further comment.

Chris watched him go then took out the ivory netsuke and stared at it.

'Well, I've got my bonus so, bollocks Matt.'

Tuesday

'Gum!'

Detective Chief Inspector Archie Arnold halted, one hand holding a sheaf of papers the other on the handle of the office door, before turning back toward the imposing desk. 'Sir?' He folded back a misbehaving lank of hair from his forehead, the fingers of his right hand a makeshift comb.

Chief Superintendent James Campbell nodded towards the tea trolley on which were a cup and saucer adorned with tea dregs and spillage, and a plate dressed with Hob-Nob crumbs. 'The used chewing gum in the spoon holder. You dropped it in there, thought I didn't notice.'

'I wrapped it.'

'Wrapped or not our catering staff, such as they are, don't want to have to deal with your masticated remains. The removal of it for our short chat is appreciated, your disposal method is not; please take it with you.'

Archie walked back to the tea trolley, dipped his two fingers in the spoon holder and retrieved the wrapped gum. 'See?'

'Not interested Arnold, take it with you and dispose of it elsewhere.' Archie retraced his steps to the door as Campbell picked up his pen to resume his desk work. 'And I'll have your report on that search warrant debacle by Thursday, won't I?'

Archie turned back. 'Yes Chief; what's a bit more paperwork between friends?'

Campbell looked up, his tone dismissive. 'I called you in to impart the need for further procedural efforts on your part; a further post-mortem on your filing oversight will only worsen things. Get the paperwork done.'

'That's it is it? You're just going to bollock me.' He waved the papers aloft. 'Not even listen to my side.'

'I've work to do Arnold and so, it seems, do you...' Campbell saw the set of Arnold's face, sighed and put down his pen. 'Right, you have my undivided attention for,' he looked at the wall clock, 'four minutes. CPS says the case was a mess...'

'There's rich...'

'A mess; namely, you neglected to hand over what turned out to be an incomplete search warrant but continued with the search despite this little oversight.'

'Which resulted in the discovery of exactly what we'd been looking for; namely a large quantity of drugs which led to an eventual prosecution and the break-up of a significant drug marketing operation, so I guess CPS are right. A mess all round.'

Campbell's face showed annoyance at Arnold's attitude. 'No one is disputing the success of the operation just the manner in which it was carried out and of how close it came to being abandoned.'

'It was one sheet of paper Chief, one sheet that I happened to give him late...' Archie saw the expression. 'Yeah, OK, and the one I'd added the details to, but only because information was late arriving.'

'And which turned out to be the very sheet you failed to pass on to the owner of both premises and goods.'

Archie shrugged. 'Drugs not goods, and I didn't fail, I was just a bit late. Got it in the end didn't he?'

'And that, if I may say, is a prime example of your often-cavalier attitude to policing!' Through the part-opened door Campbell's raised voice was heard in the outer offices and heads ducked in apparent industrious endeavour. Campbell adjusted his agitation and thought for a moment or two before continuing in a more level tone. 'DCI Arnold...despite our frequent run-ins you...you are a damn good detective. Your clear up rate is the highest in the district and some of your successes have surprised even me, someone who's been in the force for some thirty years. However, you run the risk, not for the first time, of fouling it all up by your continued willingness to play fast and loose with the system; it will be your downfall believe me, and I will not hesitate to follow the book should it require it.' Archie was about to interrupt but Campbell held up his hand and continued. 'Your neglect compromised this operation and, in the eyes of the law, was on the cusp of rendering the search and seizure unlawful and the case forfeit.'

'I gave him the forms!'

'Waving a warrant in the man's face as you barged your way onto his property does not count as giving! That warrant had my reputation affixed to it! To compound matters you added the full address to your schedule by hand but failed to transfer that information onto the schedule given to the occupant. Do you not recall any of your case law sessions? Bhatti? Croydon Magistrates' Court? Ring any bells?'

'"A copy of the warrant, including particulars of the premises to be searched must be supplied to the occupier as a mandatory requirement: the wording of section fifteen bracket one is plain and non-compliance renders entry, search and seizure unlawful". Chief, this was the culmination of three months prep work, we were on the clock.'

'The accuracy of your memory does you no favours detective, if you knew it you should have acted on it. A month; that's how long you'd had the warrant.'

'Exactly, a month! The magistrates were picky about the original application as it was 'cos that slippy little sod had set up his main house near that school so he was dealing around places of high human density; y'know, families and kids? We were at the edge of the warrant's life, last thing I wanted was to have to go back to court for another. We'd forced them to gather all their kit together in one place but they only made their move on the day before it ran out and the magistrate was insistent the locals, the kids, needed to be clear before any raid; I saw a window of opportunity and decided to go in then and there. All came in a rush. Form-filling was the last thing on my mind.'

'It's a mandatory requirement Arnold not an afterthought! You had no one else on your team who could've handled it? DC Reeve for instance?'

'He'd enough on with that break-in at the football club; stole the only trophy they've ever won, and his sister, Gabrielle, she'd come down for the week-end so... We got him in the end though, didn't we? That's what counts.'

'That's not the point! We were about to scrub three months of investigative work...'

'My work.'

'Paid for by the taxpayer and that I have to account for!' Campbell sighed before leaning forward. With elbows propped on the table and chin resting on intertwined fingers, he thought for a few moments before continuing. 'There were only two things that stopped this becoming a full-blown internal investigation; one, the fact that by some diligent and creative office work, backed by the sympathetic support of an out-of-county magistrate and some questionable but effective interview techniques, you extracted a full confession from which you'll most likely get a conviction.'

'And two?'

'Because of my intervention on your behalf. The ripples went all the way up to the Assistant Commissioner.' Archie's expression spoke volumes. 'I thought that would give you pause for thought.'

'What did he say?'

'He laughed... What do you think he said! If I say he was less than pleased then you'll have a measure of it. However, I apprised him of the facts and, with a little embellishment to safeguard my own position should this backfire, I got him to appreciate some of the nuances in the case, but he put me on notice. He informed me that he would expect you to face the full disciplinary measures and the concomitant blemish on your record should you pull such a trick again and that, as your commanding officer, I would be the subject of discussions: Me! So, consider yourself informed and duly warned.'

'Right. Thanks Sir... Who else knows, about the AC I mean?'

'The DC, you and I, and that's the way I want it to remain; clear?' Archie nodded. 'Last thing I need is this becoming open gossip and kick-starting an investigation and the possibility of a blemish on my record.' Once more Archie opened his mouth to speak but was talked over by Campbell. 'Now, enough of this. Think yourself lucky, get that form filled in and ensure the statements from your attending officers corroborate. That'll be all.'

'Yes Chief.'

Archie unwrapped a fresh stick of gum, pocketed the wrapper and began to chew. Folding back the wayward quiff again he closed the door and re-entered the unusual quiet of the team office. DC Adam Reeve looked up from non-existent paperwork and grinned.

Archie scanned them all. 'Enjoyed that did we? Listening to me having my balls chewed off?' He moved to the pinboard decorating one of the windowless walls. 'Right, where are we with this fag-smuggling lot?'

Reeve and a couple of the other team members got up and joined him at the board...

~

For the upper echelons of English society living in a class-based system, pedigree is all; for both the three-times-married-three-times-divorced Lawrence Alexandre Perceval Brightwick de Roazhon, 19th Viscount Vichendelle and Middlecombe and his English country seat, Bliss Bank Hall, their pedigrees were impeccable.

Apart from that disagreeable French episode during the Reign of Terror, the Anglo-French de Roazhon family line stretched unsullied from the Lords Bellême of the fourteenth century to the present day. Longevity had been maintained by pragmatic family alignments, occasional bastardy, a willingness to gamble all when selecting sides and sheer, blind luck. Selecting the right side when Henry the fifth took his victory at

Agincourt gained the family kudos with the English nobility; selecting the right side when Henry the sixth pruned the upstart white rose put the family on the right side of church and state during the Charles the first reshuffles; aligning their trade efforts with European industry during two world wars increased the family's international status and fortune, raising it to its present-day beau ideal.

To reflect the family's elevation to the ranks of the haut monde the construction of Bliss Bank Hall, on what was now the Bedfordshire-Northamptonshire border, was completed in seventeen thirty-two with no expense spared. From an empire on which the sun never set the labour of the world's disenfranchised and the intimate delicacies of its finest craftsmen had been purchased, bartered or stolen to create this monument to territorial vanity. The finest specimens nature could produce were fashioned by England's finest craftsmen to dress the Hall and its environs with an artistic finery that became the exclusive diversion of the favoured few. The adventures of profligate, gambling offspring or sexually diverted patriarchs had shepherded many such houses into the arms of the nation's trust, but for this estate such proletariat gawking was in the land of elsewhere; this family, this estate would never bend the knee to populist demands. A willingness to do business with anyone who had the money to facilitate such trade became the Brightwick de Roazhon modus operandi. Bliss Bank Hall and its owners could rest easy under the arched protection of its wyverns rampant and the family motto *Potissimum Suo Custodiat Te* which, roughly translated read, 'after a night out on the piss, always have enough money left to pay your taxi fare home'.

Inside the Hall's nineteenth century Spanish oak-panelled trophy room Matt and Chris stood quietly, respectfully almost. Chris' hands were folded across his genitals like a cane threatened schoolboy; Matt had one hand in his jacket pocket, his thumb hanging over the edge like a page marker, his other held a folder which twitched occasionally showing that even he was just a little ill at ease. From a not too distant room the kind of laughter only the privileged can release intruded on their studied silence until, with a suddenness, one of the matching oak doors hissed open. A caparisoned butler floated into the room, approached the two men but spoke directly to Matt.

'His Lordship will be with you shortly Mister Lamb, but he has asked me to offer you refreshment in the interim.'

Matt's reply was swift, abrupt. 'No thanks.' As Chris opened his mouth to say something Matt trod on the line. 'And he wants nothing either.'

'Thank you, Sir.' The butler left without a sound, the door whispering shut behind him.

'I wanted a drink,' commented Chris.

'You'll have nothin'. You've not done one of these serious sessions before; I have.'

'Never had cause.'

'An' we know why there's cause now don't we?'

Chris pursed his lips at Matt's comment. 'Yeah, 's'pose.'

'No suppose about it. You've had a clear two-and-a-bit years here and apart from that upset with Gerry you've been kept clear for the most part. Not this time though, front line for you. Gaffer'll wanna know every detail so he knows whose head to lop off if needed an' he'll do it, without a second's thought. He aint got where he's got by lovin' the people. Not a drop of sentiment in him, none; three marriages prove that. All I want is to get this thing sorted as fast as possible then get out.'

'I was only gonna ask for water. I'm dry.'

'Nerves...an' just watch what y' say. He'll have that Quinn with him. Had my meetin' with him earlier,' Matt flipped the folder, 'to put this little lot together. Had to fight me corner all the way. You think the Gaffer's trouble? Got nothin' on Quinn. Slippery as a shit-house rat an' uses every chance to make me look bad. Bastard would sacrifice his granny for a shillin'; hates me...feelin's mutual.'

Listening to the sounds of distant merriment Chris looked around a room dedicated to the hunter's braggadocio. From every wall at every level stared the stuffed heads of animals, plaque-mounted and mute, their living grace and beauty subjected to the interpretation of the taxidermist's imagination. Below these decapitations were further testimonies to the unequal contest between hunter and hunted. Glass dioramas filled with exotica: birds, reptiles and mammals, many clinging to a plaster branch for dear death and wearing their grimace of eternity, each glass eye staring unseeingly at other glass-topped cabinets wherein nestled serried ranks of birds' eggs. Scattered throughout the room were the historical engines of their demise: shotguns, punt guns, rifles and traps, contraptions of capture varying in antiquity and severity. Draped at intervals on the floor were the scatter-rugs favoured by the unthinking wealthy; polar bear, brown bear, tiger and wolf, legs akimbo, heads resting on chins, eyes unflinching in the glare of ceiling-mounted spotlights. On the only bare stone wall in the room were the cunningly fastened pelts of varying species of big cats, each stretched flat, spread-eagled and snarling. Chris spoke in hushed tones.

'Has he shot all these then?'

'If not him then his dad or his grandad.'

'But not the eggs; he's not shot them eggs.'

Matt smiled in spite of the situation. 'Well spotted. No, not the eggs.'

Chris stared again at the pelt-bedecked wall. 'Shot them though?'

Matt followed his gaze. 'Yeah.'

'That one you said he shot on that last trip, is that up there?'

'Not got it back yet.'

'From where?'

'Wherever he shot it.'

Chris thought for moment. 'How's he do that then?'

'What?'

'Get it back to here. Aint there some laws or other?'

'In the Diplomatic Bag.'

Chris was quiet again. Then eventually, 'What, like a duffel bag y' mean? Customs would be on to that.'

'It's a special bag.'

'Smell-proof is it? Lined?'

Matt was quiet for a lot longer, weighing up the effort required in either keeping quiet or trying to explain. Eventually he sighed and answered, 'Yeah, it's like a smell-proof duffel bag thing.'

'Oh right. What's he want so many for?'

'Couldn't say, loves 'em I suppose, loves collecting 'em anyway. Like them eggs. He's got hundreds but loads of 'em are the same.'

Chris frowned. 'Jesus...how these rich buggers amuse themselves.'

'Never understand it me. Only good egg's on a plate, scrambled and with some bacon.'

In the silence that followed this evaluation Chris scanned the room some more until his gaze alighted on one side of the huge fireplace. A stuffed, Staffordshire bull terrier, its lips drawn back into a snarl, eyes wide and ears pinned flat returned Chris' stare in glacial recognition. 'Bloody hell, that's Cruiser aint it?!'

'Yeah.'

'Blimey. I reckon the bloke that stuffed him must've been on drugs 'cos he never looked as fierce as that when I saw him, not ever. Couldn't knock the skin off a rice puddin'.'

'That's why he's been stuffed.'

'To teach him a lesson.'

'No idiot, 'cos the Gaffer still wants 'im about. Cruiser was his favourite.'

'Favourite. Right... Well y' wouldn't want t' be in his bad books then would y'? Barely been dead a couple of month an' 'ere he is back again, 'cept this time he's stuffed. Can't have had time to get cold.'

'Plenty of time, freeze-dried he were.'

'What, like frozen peas y' mean?'

'Yeah, summat like that...' Matt looked at Chris. 'Do we need all this?'

'What?'

'This bloody pub quiz.'

'Well, you keep tellin' me to pay attention. It's just hard to believe with all the killin' he's done that he'd have such a soft spot for Captain Useless over there.'

Matt's voice dripped derision. 'Used to sleep on his bed and everythin'. Ate with him at the bloody table, better food than most folk, then he'd slope off an' shit it round the house. Hallway and boot room were his hot spots Gemma said.' Matt sighed. 'Nah, stuffed and in front of that fire's best place for him.'

'Who's Gemma?'

'New head of kitchen, nice lookin' lass...' Chris looked nonplussed. 'Just started, a few months back.'

Chris thought for a moment or two before realisation dawned. 'Oh, hang on, her. Oh yeah, right. Saw her when I was fetchin' bones from the chiller the other day. Yeah, nice looker... She married?'

Matt raised an eyebrow. 'No, an' I'm workin' on first refusal. That's who I had my date with when we had to do a test drive over our happy camper on Sunday.'

'Oh right. Is she settled here d'you think? They never seem to last long. It's the isolation gets to 'em I heard.'

'Don't know. She's got a sister, said she's comin' across for a visit soon, maybe that'll help...' Matt saw Chris' expression. 'Don't get your hopes up, you'll do better tryin' Cruiser over there.'

Their relaxed chat came to an abrupt halt and both men stiffened slightly as the side door opened. Lord Brightwick, and a couple of paces behind his PPS, Randal Quinn, entered. No preliminaries, straight to it, Brightwick stretched out his hand as he approached. 'You have something for me Lamb?' He took the folder. 'This all?' Matt nodded. 'The police have yet to find the poor lady?'

'Yes Gaffer.'

'Our meeting is timely then. A name for your victim?'

'Not yet; provin' hard to chase up.'

'And you thought it best to leave things as they were?'

Matt looked firstly at Brightwick then at Quinn and his eyes narrowed a little as he quickly worked out who was really asking this question. His eyes stayed fixed on Quinn. 'I did, we were strapped for time and that lane's a regular shaggers' bolt hole, traffic up and down it like a dog's hind leg.' Matt turned to Brightwick. 'Two reasons clinched it: my need to avoid leavin' traces in my motor and to be off from there as fast as possible', he turned to Quinn, 'before anyone turned up to disturb us. Tragic hit-and-run.'

Quinn smirked. 'What was to stop you packing some plastic sheeting and then cleaning up your car on one of your seemingly interminable valeting sessions?'

'Easy from back here aint it Quinn; shows what you know. No matter how hard you scrub there's always summat you miss. If we'd had a bit of notice then, yeah, I would've done things different, but as things were we had to think on our feet, so we did, so no plastic.'

Brightwick could see this conversation was taking a downward spiral and that personal animosity was driving it. 'The playground is the place for squabbles such as this, we'll get on to the reasons for your hurried solution shortly.' Chris shifted a little uncomfortably as Brightwick continued. 'Her woodland camp has been found and tidied up I hear.'

'Yes, Gaffer. Yesterday. Aiden eventually found it stashed inside a hollowed-out tree trunk topped with some fresh bent bramble; took some findin'. Just a backpack with some clothes in it, scruff-stuff, an' a kit bag full of hippie things, leather bracelets and necklaces, nothin' of value. Oh, and there was a tin plate an' a mug. All disposed of now.'

'No letters, no social security information?'

'Nothin' Gaffer. Only that ticket thing.' Matt indicated the folder Brightwick was holding. 'In there.' Brightwick took out the dog-eared card at the top of which were printed the words, RMS ST HELENA. Underneath this was an ink line-drawing of a steamship and at the bottom were the words, PASSAGE TICKET WALLET. He scanned the heading then opened it.

'Empty?'

'Beats me too. Hard to trace a name and history from that, but at least she's off the grid as far as your super-spy government's concerned so some good there.'

'Unless she's a terrorist, Lamb, unless she's a terrorist. You've seen this Quinn?'

Brightwick passed it across and Quinn gave it a cursory glance. 'Yes Minister. Certainly not current judging by the state of it.'

Matt took it from Quinn. 'Only reason you'd keep a piece of tat like this is sentiment.'

Brightwick nodded. 'Agreed. She's of mixed parentage I gather?'

'Half-caste, yeah.'

Brightwick raised his eyebrows at Chris' contribution. 'Thank you, Phillips. So, from your questionable description of her parentage and this wallet we can deduce that at some point she or someone close to her has maybe crossed from Africa.'

Matt nodded. 'Strong possibility.'

'And she has a friend?'

'She does.'

'Name?'

'Linden Lea. Lives in Chorleton. Sortin' things out now.'

'So I've been informed. First things first.' Brightwick slipped the wallet back into the folder then scanned the other handwritten sheets. 'Stanley Mason...and dog, a corgi?'

'Yes Gaffer.'

'I like corgis. Her Majesty owns a number.' He turned to Chris. 'This Mister Mason. Disinterred and used as dog nourishment I'm informed.' There was a silence. 'Dug up and fed to hounds?'

'Oh, yes Gaffer.'

Brightwick held up a card. 'This?'

Matt developed the theme. 'Mister Mason's bus pass.'

'Bus pass?'

'It's for old folk, pensioners,' Chris began helpfully. 'For cheaper travel on the buses, that go...into...' His voice tailed off as he saw he was reeling off unwanted information that no one was listening to.

Matt talked over him. 'It's where I got most of the information from before I followed him through the electoral roll. Penfore Close, Wynington... He's a widower so that plays out well for us.'

Brightwick tapped the card on the folder, 'As for your country lane events, I'm not entirely happy with them, but, right decision, lack of preparation and an unfortunate outcome. Quinn said you and he had a meeting yesterday to discuss options, your arrangements concerning the friend?' Brightwick looked at his watch. 'You have my undivided attention for the next six minutes, make the most of it.'

As Matt began the group dropped easily into official mode, something they were well practised at. 'I've broken down the jobs into three boxes: search of Mason's place, Irish lads and the payoff of the dead lady's friend, their travel plans. They're comin' up by train.'

'From?'

'London, Wednesday evenin'. I texted them on their burner. Aiden went down on Monday afternoon,' Matt nodded at Quinn, 'soon as our meetin' was over.'

'With cash?'

'Yeah. Travel money, a second burner and the retainer envelope with the girl's address in it.'

'Price?'

'The promise of the rematch and two thousand. Half from petty cash...' Matt flicked Chris a look, 'half from elsewhere.'

'Delivered to?'

'The Irish Centre in Reading. Them Irish will collect from there.'

'Transport for the task?'

'Hire car.'

'From?'

'Newbury. Aiden's usin' cash an' a set of false documents from the stash we've been gifted by them Chinese fellas.'

'Why Newbury?'

'Good as anywhere and far enough away from us. Small affair, happy to do cash, don't go through the books that way.'

'The working man's off-shore accounting system. Sufficiently discreet?'

'We've not used 'em before and never will again. Aiden's dropped the car outside Chorleton station, keys inside the wheel trim and the rest of the cash for the job in the glovebox. Irish will pick it up from there, motor over, have their chat with that lass, pay her off then drop the car back at the station for Aiden to collect and return to the hire company early Thursday mornin'. That way he don't have to see them again. Keys through the letter box an' away.'

Brightwick considered the information for a few seconds before nodding. 'All seems in order. You're sure these Irish gentlemen will make a good fist of persuading this lady? They do have fuck-up form.'

'Yeah I know, but the re-match should cut it and I left them in no doubts about how serious this lot was.'

'And the friend, she's persuadable?'

'I had a chat with her local council. Turns out she's behind with her council tax, probably the rent too. That means she's probably been out of work for a good while and on her uppers so the money should clinch it. Friendship or not, that sort of money when you're broke cuts a lot of ties.'

Brightwick nodded then snapped the folder shut and looked at his watch. 'And now, quickly on to the hit-and-run lady and the late Mister Mason. Do we need to be proactive in the matter?'

'In what way Gaffer?'

'Is there any risk of either of these events returning to confound us, that Mister Mason's appearance wasn't by accident, that he had foreknowledge?'

'Highly doubtful. He'd not been seen about by anyone on the estate and if he'd known anythin' beforehand he'd 'ave arrived with a posse of cops.'

'True. Well, myself and Quinn have done all we can to minimise any aftershocks with the Chinese delegation, let's just put their bodyguards' reactions to his arrival down to poor timing and our bad form.'

Chris shook his head at this. 'Hardly ours Gaffer.'

'Ours Phillips. Business is won and lost on knowing the little peccadilloes of those with whom you're dealing with.'

'Well I thought it was way over the top; not the English way.'

'We aren't paid to like them Phillips, we're paid to work with them.'

Like a dog with a bone Quinn picked up an earlier thread. 'Regarding Mason, Sir. Widower he may be, but we have to consider he was dear to someone. Are we not being foolish in the extreme if we believe for one minute he's not going to be missed by someone, him and his dog.'

'We are. His dog, Lamb?'

'Ran off in the scrap. Not turned up yet.'

'Did those Irish gentlemen not catch it?'

'Not that we've heard Gaffer, and I don't want to phone 'em and leave a trace.'

'Good point, but, loose ends?'

'Yes Gaffer, we're on it.'

'Good.' Brightwick looked once more at his watch. 'Time is pressing. The follow up of Mister Mason?'

'Goin' there this evenin' to do a search. Needs to get done, find out if he knew anythin' else.'

'Quite, report back on your findings. We must be assured we can cater for any surprises you uncover. What I would like is some insurance on this.'

Quinn nodded. 'Agreed, Sir.' He turned to Matt. 'Suggestions, Lamb?'

Quinn's attempt to wrong foot Matt was wasted. 'We'll do a search then set up an accidental fire for future use.'

'Good. Attention to detail Phillips, thinking ahead, that's what will allow us to operate with impunity.' He turned back to Matt. 'And finally, the rematch, where are we with that?'

Quinn was in fast. 'You'd suggested the twentieth of this month Sir.'

'So, less than ten days away.'

'Yes, Sir.'

Matt spoke over him. 'I was wantin' to talk about that, Gaffer.'

Brightwick looked at the door from behind which the rising chatter of satisfied guests leaked. 'Now?' Brightwick sighed deeply. 'Very well; briefly.'

'Perfect as they were, I say to continue usin' the sties is just askin' for trouble.'

'Good point. So, alternative suggestions please.'

'Postpone it.'

'Absolutely not!' Brightwick sighed in impatience and frustration. 'The Chinese delegation are pivotal to my businesses, both there and here. They are the ones we work with the most, the ones who make and supply the false documents which play such an important part in my import-export business. But before any of that can be put in place they come first to test our security, our hospitality and our ability to work with discretion...in short, our commitment to their cause and our ability to keep the heads of their government and their leading trade delegates satisfied, amused and out of the public eye. There is much at stake. This is about entertaining clients central to government policy initiatives which are about to be put into the public arena; about jobs and security and all events must run smoothly. They must, I've gone to considerable effort and expense to cater for it; powdered rhinoceros horn for the drinks, the importation of the tiger parts for the Hǔbiān tāng...' He turned to Quinn. 'Where are we with that?'

'The powder has arrived through the usual pathways; the tiger parts have proved a little more troublesome.'

'But they will be here?'

'Absolutely Sir, just not via the diplomatic bag. We're using other routes.'

'That's how advanced we are Lamb, and I want the rematch on the twentieth to complement it.'

'Providin' I can find a place.'

'Find one. All will culminate at the reception here on the twenty-first, which is timed to run alongside my appearance on the Gov.UK Show on Sunday the eighteenth, just two days after the Prime Minister announces...' Brightwick and Quinn spoke together, 'the new trade deal with China.'

'Timing Lamb, it's all about the timing.' Brightwick made his way to the door, closely followed by Quinn. 'And find that corgi; I don't want to hear you've fucked up again Phillips.'

With that they were gone leaving Matt and Chris to stare at the door. The butler re-entered. 'I'll see you two gentlemen out if I may? This way sirs.'

As they left Chris whispered to Matt. 'Which one of them Chinky thugs was Hoobin Tang then?'

Wednesday

DCI Arnold, the collar of his open-necked shirt showing a lack of familiarity with an iron, stepped out of the car, his silk tie knotted but pulled down to dangle ineffectually. He swapped a stale piece of chewing gum for a fresh stick, wrapping the old gum in the paper sleeve, and resumed his rapid chewing without missing a beat.

'Evenin' Martin, where is it?'

PC Martin Coombes pointed down the lane to the hastily discarded and totally ineffectual arc lights. 'In that ditch, tucked well down. Comes over the top like a banshee.'

Archie looked around the site then at his companion, DC Adam Reeve, who was leaning on the open passenger door. 'Like a banshee Adam, so not subtle like us lot then?' The fast-glooming location had been transformed from quiet country lane and trysting place to a scene of crime. Vehicles bearing differing police logos were parked in the lane. The area was cordoned off, a generator and floodlights installed along with a mobile operations room, a forensics laboratory made operationally ready and, in a single nod to civility, a small mobile canteen had been set up and was in imminent danger of boiling a kettle. He sighed. 'Where are we operating from?'

'Penngorse.' Archie shook his head, Reeve elaborated. 'Country station, five, six miles away; near Callow Green.'

'Cutting edge of policing then. Why not our base at Northampton? It's got all the kit. I'll wager Penngorse struggles for a phone connection.'

'Especially seein' as how it's due for closure next year.'

Archie rolled his eyes. 'Right. Thanks.' He indicated the handkerchief wrapped round Coombes' one hand, a half-eaten tuna-mayo-on-white in his other. 'Banshee nailed you did it?'

'Yeah, me and WPC Arne. We were first on the scene. Barely saw it was a body before the dog was amongst us; must've been under the clothes or summat. Jet-black it is. I only saw it 'cos it were snarling and the moon lit up its teeth. Forensics wanted to set up their butcher's shop.' He pointed, 'They only got those two arc lights to there before it saw them off as well.'

Archie looked across at the blazing arc lights, one laying on its side and pointing roughly towards the ditch, the other erect and helpfully lighting up the leaf-lost branches above. 'They won't do a lot of good there, not unless we're spotting owls. Where's WPC Arne?'

'Went to A&E. Only nipped me but really nailed her, on her leg.'

Archie looked at the group of forensic workers huddled well clear, their conversation, like their courage, hushed. 'Who's running SOC?'

'Jay Millar's CSM.'

'Sweet. Not managing this crime scene very well is he? Did he get nibbled?'

'Not quite.'

'Shame.'

DC Reeve pulled the discussion back on track. 'So, Martin, a dog and a...?'

'Well... A body.'

Reeve glanced in the direction of a car containing two people parked on the verge. 'What about that pair?'

Coombes smirked. 'Them? Not a lot of use. He jabbered summat about the dog appearing when they first parked up, yapping and bouncing round the car. Bloke gets out, the dog runs along the road and disappears into the ditch. He follows and barely gets a glimpse of what's in it before the dog comes out, chases him back to his car then dodges front and back of it to stop him leaving, clever little sod. He phoned us, the bloke not the dog, it's not that clever; he phoned us 'cos she started screamin' for him to watch the dog, not to run it over like. That's when he realised it wasn't gonna let him go anywhere and he made the call to us.'

Archie smiled. 'Bet he was thrilled when you hoisted that hazard tape round him then.'

'Thrilled. Said he tried to report it straight away, "Honest, Guv", bad signal on his mobile, said he was only tryin' to drive away to find a better location so's he could call it in... "Honest, Guv".'

'And she's not got a phone?'

'She has. Her signal was iffy too.'

'Convenient.'

'He said he saw the body about five 'o clock but it could've been earlier.'

'So somewhere between four and five.' Reeve pursued the line. 'Not much from him and nothing from her then?'

'No. She seems a bit traumatised, but I suspect it's not by our situation but by hers. Our trained WPC might've helped had she not been savaged. Dog didn't give up 'til me and Arne arrived, that's when it slunk back into that ditch. We went over there, like walking into a bloody Ninja movie. Talk about fast.' He held up his wrapped hand as evidence. 'Mister Millar's cavalry turned up and tried to get things rollin' with them lights, but it wasn't havin' any of that either. Now it only comes up for air and blood.'

'You didn't think to warn forensics then?'

'We did! I said it was a bit frisky. They said they could handle it, well Mister Millar did, said he'd owned a dog as a kid.' Coombes shrugged. 'That went corkscrewed real fast. Millar was on the blower straight away, injured pride I'd guess. Called up the RSPCA and the firearms lads as back-up 'cos it's been classed as a dangerous dog.'

'Firearms; right. What sort of dog is it?'

'A terrier.'

Archie ceased his machine-gun chewing and almost laughed as he looked from the constable to Reeve. 'A what?'

'A terrier.'

'You're joking right?' Coombes shook his head. 'I thought we were talking a fighting-weight Bull Mastiff at least!'

'Size and sense don't come into it. This little sod's a fruit-loop. Made up of tail and teeth, everything between is missin'.'

Archie looked across at the arc lights again. 'Does it have a collar, a name-tag?'

'I think I saw a collar yeah, but, a name tag? Are you serious? No one's got anywhere near close enough to see that.'

Archie continued to look in the direction of the arc lights. 'Victim's got a guard of honour and we've got an uncorrupted crime scene then. Do we know how long it might have been here?'

'Dunno; for as long as the body has I guess. Won't let anyone near enough to find out.'

'Poor little sod.' Archie took stock. 'Have Traffic been informed?'

'Yup, but they'll be late. There's been a multiple shunt on the M40, twelve car pile-up and the fog's as thick as a smoker's cough. They've called in the troops from three divisions to cover it so they could be some time.'

'Their lateness nothing to do with the staff cuts then?' Archie resumed his chewing and flicked the hazard tape up and over his head. 'Give us your sandwich.' He took both halves from Coombes even before it was offered and spoke to him as he put the one half in his trouser pocket and handed back the empty pack. 'Go and tell Jay I want absolute quiet. Adam, hold off the traffic cowboys if they turn up, and calm the firearms lot down too. I know how they work, they'll just as likely shoot me.' He folded back his wayward flop of hair. 'And see if you can get some more grub from the canteen.'

Coombes shook his head. 'You'll regret it.'

Reeve smiled. 'Best leave him. Ex farmer-cum-backwoodsman. He reckons he can communicate with 'em.'

'What, like doctor whatshisname?'

'Doolittle. Yeah, just like him.'

Coombes moved across to speak to the forensic team as Archie walked to the edge of the nearby ditch, picking up a wind-dislodged branch a couple of feet long from the roadside on the way. Testing its elasticity as he went, he slowed as he approached the outer circle of the ineffectual arc lights, unplugging the one illuminating the tree before moving across to the other. Once there he hunkered down behind it before removing his tie, fashioning it into a noose and attaching it to the end of the stick. He turned his jacket inside out so that the sleeves showed white before placing it just to the side of the light then flicked the old gum into the ditch as a calling card. This action released a low growl from the ditch's bowels. Archie pressed the back of his hand to his lips and sucked in air, the squeal this caused mimicking the sound of a rabbit in distress.

After several seconds Jasper appeared slowly over the top of the ditch like a sniper; head low, flight-fright-fight reactions on red alert. Archie squinted, *That's one black dog.* He squeaked again and gently slid the warming jacket a little further out of the beam's pathway, illuminating the terrier some more as it continued to slink forward down the beam towards what appeared to be an easy supper. Archie, picking up the stick as the terrier drew closer, could see the scabbed and dried blood on his mask. *Poor little mite.* He pressed his lips harder to his hand now, making the squeal higher pitched as Jasper moved slightly to the side in an effort to see beyond the light. Archie twitched the jacket's sleeve with his foot to gain the terrier's fullest concentration and Jasper locked on to the half-seen movement.

Even though Archie was up and over the arc light in an instant the terrier reacted just as fast and purely by instinct, rising up on his hind legs and snapping at ghosts. This reaction only served to help Archie as the outstretched neck and head allowed the noose a free run over the dog's head. The passage of the tie over the dog's muzzle re-opened the wounds, adding to the terrier's distress as Archie jerked the noose backwards completing capture; now Jasper showed his full disapproval. Snapping, snarling, jumping and twisting the enraged terrier lunged at Archie as, like a badly rehearsed heelwork-to-music duo at a silent disco, they pranced and puckered, side-stepped and frothed for several seconds. Unable to get close to his captor, Jasper, even with his gaping face-wound, attempted to take his temper out on the branch.

'Hey hey, steady now lad, steady. Not gonna hurt you.'

Jasper responded to Archie's soothing tones by letting go of the branch and lunging at him. Archie danced back away. *Nice. That worked. Try again...you know how this works Archie Arnold.* 'Steady now lad, steady.' Archie clicked his tongue at the dog. 'Tch-Tch!' He saw a momentary change in the terrier's demeanour, almost a full-stop and he clicked again and saw a flash of recognition in the dog's eyes. *Know that sound do you? There's lucky.* He clicked again and the terrier stopped chewing but continued growling, cocking his head to one side and looking from Archie to ditch, ditch to Archie.

'Let's just draw breath, eh? You and me? Here.' He took out one portion of the sandwich, bit it in half and tossed a chunk at the dog's feet. 'You must be starved.' The scent of tuna billowed up and the terrier jumped forward, snaffling up the sandwich and growling throughout. 'That nice eh? Nice? I'll bet. How long you been here? Eh? You poor sod. Is that your owner down there is it? Tch-tch!' The terrier took a pace toward Archie's outstretched hand which now held a further portion of the sandwich "S'alright, not gonna hurt y', been hurt enough I reckon. What'd you do to that nose eh? Come on... Tch-tch!' The terrier gave a little whine and a wag of his stump, then took another step toward Archie. 'Let's get you sorted out eh? Good lad.' Jasper's head dropped a little and he clawed along the ground towards the outstretched hand; when the terrier jumped forward to snatch the food Archie felt the kiss of teeth. Wolfing it down Jasper stood, emitting a distant rumble, surveying the situation, juggling his options.

Archie sat down.

The terrier looked almost taken aback.

'Nothing to fear here lad, really. Tch-tch!' Archie threw another small section of sandwich to the terrier and waited patiently, talking steadily in the same reassuring tone. 'You not wanna leave your partner eh? I know.' He shifted slightly. 'Let me share summat with y'.' He leant forward a little and tossed the rest of the sandwich to the dog. 'I know that feelin', believe me. I've been there so...you and me both. Thing is, if you come with me you're not bein' disloyal y'know. We need to put things right, but we can't do it from here and you can't help in that state, do you see...? Come on. Help me help you, eh?' Archie slowly stood up and gently made his move towards Martin's car, coaxing the terrier with him. The dog looked back at the ditch and Archie squatted down. 'I know, I know, it hurts. We'll be back I promise, but you'll be no help to anyone if that cut goes bad will y'? Here.' Archie took out the second half of the sandwich, bit a piece off and threw it, noticing he was fast running out of bribes. 'Tch-tch! Come on lad, come with me.'

As their distance from the ditch increased so the group of cowed forensics staff regained their courage, moving back to the ditch and abandoned arc lights with a purpose.

'Open the back door Martin then call dog support at Balsall Common. Tell 'em an injured terrier needs seein' too. Food Adam?'

'Yeah. Ham on brown. Where d'you want it?'

'Toss it on the back seat.'

'Can't we just get a local vet in? Be easier.'

'Nope, he's our only material witness to all this an' he's not well. I want to make sure he gets the best.'

'Witness?'

'Witness, trust me. Watch him close enough and he'll talk.'

Archie and terrier drew closer to the car as PC Coombes, in the process of making the call, saw Reeve open the box and toss the ham sandwich onto the rear seat. 'Jesus, he's gonna wreck my motor.'

'Get ready to close the door Adam, gentle now.' Archie climbed backwards onto the rear seat and slid along it, shoving the ham sandwich towards the terrier. He held out the last square of the tuna sandwich. 'Here y' are fella, surf 'n' turf; in y' get. Tch-tch!'

Jasper paused at the door, scenting the interior of man-and-tuna layered with a background hum of ham. Lifting his front legs onto the sill the terrier stretched forward as far as he could, his back legs still refusing to commit as Archie drew back both hand and food before tossing the tuna into the footwell. The terrier, leaning forward to his fullest extent, drew his back legs up and over the sill and into the car to retrieve the food. Archie then offered the first of the ham sandwich. 'Door.'

Reeve stepped forward and gently clicked the door shut just as Jasper leant forward to take it from Archie's hand. 'Good lad.'

After a slight reaction to the sound of the closing door, Archie could see and sense a shift in the dog's attitude. Unwrapping a fresh stick of gum from his pocket, he began chewing and tossed a quarter of the ham sandwich to the terrier. 'Look, supper continues. In y' get Martin, but slowly.' Jasper swallowed the last of the sandwich then sat for ham seconds, swaying slightly. Archie folded back his wayward flop of hair and obliged. After finishing, the terrier sat once more in the footwell before dropping flat. 'You must be exhausted. No sleep 'til rescue, eh?' He surveyed the damage. 'I'm surprised you can eat with that mouth; that's some cut.'

Coombes closed the door and started the engine. 'There'll be blood and snot everywhere.'

The terrier reacted to the tone of conversation and engine noise by letting out a low grumbling growl. 'No no, steady there fella, nothing to hurt, just a grumpy policeman.' Archie threw another chunk of sandwich which Jasper began to eat but with less energy this time, not even bothering to rise up fully. Archie part lowered the window. 'Adam?' Archie indicated the couple still ensconced in their vehicle. 'See what you can get from those two. Another WPC would be good. There's a few arrivin' on scene with the search team, get one of them. I'll drop him off then come back, shouldn't be more than a couple of hours. What's the time now?'

'Time you had a watch...'

'Time you had a new joke.'

'Just gone six.'

'Right, back by eight, then we'll see what you and forensics have come up with.' Reeve lowered his face to the part-opened window. 'Oh, an' get me coat will you, it's...' In a flash the terrier was up out of the footwell and onto the back seat alongside Archie, snapping and snarling, blood-stained spittle peppering the window.

Reeve jumped back with a yell and Coombes moved hastily forward in his seat pressing his chest against the steering wheel and setting off the horn as Archie put pressure on the stick causing Jasper to drop to the seat still growling and snapping. 'Now then fella now then. Tch-tch! He's alright, steady now, he's not gonna hurt you.'

'I wouldn't get the chance,' Reeve's distant voice floated in through the window. 'Jesus but he moves fast.'

'See if you can do the same. My coat?'

Reeve walked to the scene of capture and retrieved the damp and scuffed coat that had been dumped aside by the forensics team as Coombes' voice came shakily from the front of the car. 'Christ, I was expecting him up and over the seat then.'

'Reeves' fault. Daft sod's got no understanding of the canine mind, shoving his face into the gap like that.'

'Never mind the canine mind, I nearly had a bowel movement.'

'I'll keep control here you just keep control there. He'll soon settle.' Archie reached through the open window and took his coat from Reeve's distant, outstretched grasp. 'If Traffic deign to turn up tell them to leave things 'til I get back, I want a scout round first.'

'They'll love you for that.'

'My case so they'll do as they're told.' Archie fussed at the terrier as it lay down in the seat well once more. 'Alright lad, everybody relax. Here, some more ham. Did you get through to Balsall, Martin?'

'Yeah, duty vet's on his way in, they're settin' up and waitin' for you.'

'Right. Home Coombes, and don't spare the horses.'

The firearms unit turned up just as PC Coombes' patrol car moved along the lane and out of sight...

~

*W*ould you employ me after that car crash of an *interview? No, I wouldn't. So, definitely no job.*

A minor station bleached its way past Lin's window as the train gathered momentum for the final push in the hope that this time, one time, it might arrive on time; something told her the dice were loaded against it. She took the headed letter from her battered, mock-leather briefcase and re-ran the day's events as if a revisit would change the outcomes. It didn't. *This is as close as you'll ever get to working at Braxhams. That interview panel looked like they'd seen one candidate too many and I was it. Felt about as welcome as a debt collector...a black one at that.* She closed the briefcase, snapping the one remaining clip reluctantly into place and looked out onto the tail end of this overcast and thoroughly beaten day; a day where only fools and entire tomcats were out with any relish. Finally her gaze shifted onto the leopard-print coat draped across her knees. *And I bought this new rain-bloody-coat for it; what a waste.* Lin attempted to put the letter into the coat pocket; the fit was inadequate. *And who is it making these fashion things anyway...more to the point who are the idiots who buy them?* She tried to force the letter downwards, crushing it out of shape in her silent, frustration-fuelled fit. *You Linden! You're the idiot who buys them. Neither use nor ornament these pockets, nothing fits...oh, bugger it!* She let go and the letter began to uncurl, protruding from the pocket like a tongue. *About as useful as that interview.* She remembered those soulless faces gazing from across that table in a room bereft of art and pity. *That cup of coffee I should never have accepted.* She winced inwardly as she re-ran seeing the contents spread across tabletop and paperwork when her sleeve caught it as she expanded lavishly on her scientific abilities. *Like a bloodstain that coffee...the life of my interview draining away right there. Ah well, your loss Braxhams... Ha! Just as sure as my flat will be when I tell the council I've no money for council tax...again.* She took out her mobile and scanned the screen. *Why is it you only get in touch on your terms Rene? One call ages ago to ask what I know about Rutland then nothing for a week. Why? To worry the life out of me, that's why.* Lin sighed and pocketed the phone. As happened whenever she felt stressed her hand went instinctively to her netsuke, an intricately carved baby elephant cradling an acorn through the centre of which is drilled a worm hole and which was attached round her wrist by a leather strap. Fondling this comforter with her free hand she gazed around the carriage, pushing back into the angle between wall and seat back. *I'm just a wild animal really; mistrusting all, guarding my territory.* Gazing round she assessed the other passengers. *Just like everyone else in here.*

In her present, melancholic state Lin's thoughts meandered on. *What I wouldn't give for a regular wage. What regular wage? Enough left over after food shopping to buy a regular pint on a regular basis would be nice. Jesus but I've got to get some money from somewhere soon.* Lin shook her head and settled back to doze. *Soon be back in my sunny hometown of Chorleton-cum-Deadend-in-Backwater. Thank Christ the rich folk from London still retire to their country estates round there otherwise the station would've been slammed shut years ago and I'd be searching for a non-existent rural bus service right about now.*

These half-doze musings on the unfairness in her personal life and on social injustice in general were broken when a movement flickered across her slatted gaze. One of the occupants had moved to Lin's side of the carriage to stand just ahead of her, one hand gripping a seat back, the train's motion causing him to sway like a babyless mother. He stared through the unscrubbed window into the unscrubbed landscape, trying to separate the outer blackness from the inner grime and spoke to no one in particular.

'Is't 'Allam next?'

Lin noticed the man's effort to cover the mediocre beginnings of a pale moustache with his hand, as if he was afraid of having it stolen in the rough and tumble of everyday conversation. *No prizes for guessing where you're from.* As his face was turned more Lin's way, she thought it would be churlish not to reply.

'Hallam? Yea.' She nodded at the bleak vista. 'Should've been fifteen minutes ago, but, y' know...railways?' The man grunted, stroked his lip again and moved to a seat behind her. *Thank you. You're welcome. All the way from Ireland just to fail your good manners starter-for-ten...and you stink of alcohol.*

Trackside houses, part-hidden behind poorly maintained shiplap fencing, gradually became more visible and more frequent as, like a reluctant weed-trapped pike, a jaundiced Hallam was reeled in. Now the density of housing increased and along with it the designer curtains of suburbia. Fire-ash, garden hackings, the occasional corpse of unwanted white goods some naked and bruised, some respectfully shrouded with old carpet, dressed the embankment. Lin shook her head at the sadness of it all. She pressed the recall button on her phone and listened to it ring out and play the 'not-available' message. She closed the connection. *Oh, come on Rene!*

As the train protested to resting at Hallam Halt Station Lin rose from her seat, collecting her raincoat and taking her other briefcase, courtesy of Lidl's, off the luggage rack. Chorleton was the next stop, her stop, but with the myriad little kinks in the line between Hallam and Chorleton she always found it safer to stand and grip a seat back, luggage in hand as the journey progressed rather than try and wrestle with her belongings as Chorleton grew closer; the last thing she needed was to be sent bustle-over-bonnet into the laps of strangers. The man with the face-fuzz looked away from the window to take in her movements. After the briefest of pauses he moved further down the carriage before taking yet another seat just beyond a large middle-aged woman.

Lin looked at the only other man sitting in the carriage and something in his appearance, his relaxed manner, made Lin think of the universal guy on the Friday night door at any one of the clubs or pubs in the dance-and-drink hot spots. She recognised the type; didn't look up to much but had 'on the door' written all over him. She placed her raincoat and bag onto the seat and held on tightly as the train bellyached its way out of Hallam Halt. Her eyes closed. In five minutes she would be back in Chorleton and today would mist into crisps-and-domino small talk in the company of friends. *Thank Christ...*

~

DC Reeve opened the passenger door of the squad car and Archie got out, gum-chewing as if his life depended on it as PC Coombes switched off the engine.

'Thanks Martin.'

'You're welcome.' Coombes closed the driver's door and immediately left them to join a group of other officers gathered by the mobile canteen.

Archie watched him go. 'Don't let us keep you.' He turned to Reeve. 'Anything from forensics yet?'

'Bits, they're still workin' on it.'

Archie looked at his watch. 'Jay's got fifteen minutes before I rattle his cage. Tea for two?'

'I will if you will. How's the dog?'

'Doin' alright. After we'd got him doped-up I left him with Bob. Says he knows you.'

'Bob Lord? Yeah. Each time I've been back to Ashford to give a talk to the new recruits he was there to talk about the dog unit and its H&S routines. Good vet. If anyone can fix that dog up it'll be him. Best hands in the business.'

'Best hand.'

'Got him did he?'

'No, but I'll open a book on it, even with the loss of that one shattered tooth. Bob had to sedate him before he'd even let them do an inspection. I managed to trade on his cupboard-love and calm him sufficiently to get a towel wrapped round him so's they could give him a tranquillizer... We were getting on famously during the drive over there, but now? I doubt he'll ever trust me again.'

'Dog's got summat about him then?'

'He has; 'cept for a name.'

'Nothing?'

'Nope. Collar was a leather one, home-made by the look of it. Nice bit of plaiting work and the bright red stood out well against the black, but no name tag or microchip, an' he weren't about to let anyone rummage around to find one either, not while he was *omnibus dubitandum*. Had to be done though, gash was a lot worse than I first thought, infected too, poor little sod. It took some firm stitching and he's on a course of industrial strength anti-b's to sort him out.'

'Car must've given him a wallop then.'

'Nope, not the car.'

'Then what? What did Bob say?'

Archie glanced over to the tent-covered ditch where forensic shadow play was continuing. He smiled and changed the subject. 'I'll fill you in later. Two teas Steve please.' Steven Warne began to sort teabags into mugs as Archie removed his chewing gum and wrapped it in his handkerchief. 'Right, where were we?'

'Before we were so rudely interrupted? Dead in that ditch.'

'Got that bit. What do we know?'

'Bad news, good news?'

'Bad.'

Reeve opened his notebook. 'Current forensics' report states: *Female, mixed race, deceased...*' He paused dramatically then closed the notebook with a flourish.

'That bad, eh? How long's she been there?'

'Not sure, days possibly.'

'Well, the state of the dog's injuries should help with the timescale. Bob's gonna send samples over to the lab for culture smears and microbe testing.'

'You were right then, the dog can talk.'

'In a way yeah.'

'That'll be useful then 'cos Forensics won't be moving the body for a good while yet.'

Archie shook his head. 'No wonder that poor little sod was hungry and scared.' He looked across to where the lovers' car had been parked. 'I see our extracurricular couple have been dismissed. Anything more there?'

'Bits, not much.' Reeve opened his notebook at a fresh page and read, 'Got here, saw the dog...'

'Different kind of dogging then.'

'Mrs Christine Turley and Mr Robert Allen. Both married, unfortunately not to each other. They drive up here. Terrier does his bit, Allen gets out and follows it to the ditch. Soon as he's clocked the contents, the dog goes from Jekyll to Hyde...or Hyde to Jekyll...whichever, it turns into a different beast, snapping and snarling.'

'Beginning to sound like an episode of Lassie. What do we know about the area?'

'Not a lot. Our local blokes know it as a bit of rat run for the commuters hereabouts and a place of country sports, various types. Couple of the lads said a fair chunk of the surrounding land is owned by a...' Reeve paused and concentrated, 'Bright wick dee Rose a hon, I think. Notable character, government that kind of thing. Full information's on its way from Northants.'

'Until that arrives?'

'Not a lot. He's an entrepreneur, opens his estate for his mates to come and slaughter some pheasants and such in the winter. Local lads have had to turn out on the odd occasion to give chase to poachers. Do you want to interview him?'

'Shouldn't think so, but he'll need informing for sure, maybe an interview at some point. They get a bit touchy if they're lumped in with the suspected proles. For now have one of the local lads let him know as a courtesy. No rush.'

Adam scribbled details. 'Right.'

'So our hero had his ego deflated as he beat a retreat back to his car.'

'Yeah, dog tore his trousers in the process!'

'That's my boy.'

'Allen did all the talking, and I mean all of it. I tried to get him to stop so's we could hear her side of it. I took Kanga with me...'

'Who?'

'Kanga. Kanjara. WPC Desai. Took her with me as per rules and also 'cos she's good at it, but even her feminine wiles weren't able to get any more from Mrs Turley except how terrible it all was. But then, what's to tell? She stayed in the car throughout.'

'Regular Samaritan she sounds. They've both got phones.'

'Yeah, but in their defence the signal hereabouts can be really iffy. He says he just wanted to get Mrs. Turley home, something about conflicting family timetables, that and the dog's attempts to redistribute his legs across the surrounding countryside. After a few dummy runs to try and leave she gets into a flat panic about the dog, gives him GBH of the earhole that he might run it over, so he takes the lesser of two evils and on the blower to us to get things sorted.'

'She's a bit of a spitfire then.'

'Yeah. We took statements and logged their calls. They're both in to see us tomorrow at the station to fill in any gaps but my guess is we've got all we're gonna get. She was right unhappy about the second interview; face like a gurning toad when they left.'

'And the call to us was at?'

'Seventeen forty.'

Archie sighed, 'Right. And the good news?'

Reeve winked at Archie. 'Got lucky there. Kanga thinks she might know her, our lady of the ditch.' He saw Archie's reaction. 'Not who she is or anything, we should ever be that lucky.' He turned to the gathered officers. 'Kanga! Here a minute.'

'How come, all the way out here, you know her?'

'Because I pay attention, like you should've done with that search warrant.'

'Don't, OK, just...don't.' Archie watched as WPC Kanjara Desai walking towards them, his face a study in concentration. 'I'm gonna have to start payin' attention too.'

Archie sugared his tea. It was as they began to move towards Kanjara that Steve rapped on the counter with his forefinger. 'Er, eighty pence please.'

They stopped and Archie looked at Steve, at Reeve, then back to Steve. 'You are kiddin', right?'

'No, I think that's right.' Steve pursed his lips and gazed into the sky as if trying to solve the theory of relativity. 'Two teas, er, forty pence each, that's...er...that's...eighty pence. Yeah, eighty!' He smiled at them in triumph.

'Comedy aside, we're out on site and you want us to pay forty pence for tea?'

'No, I want you to pay eighty.'

Reeve stepped in front of Archie with a pound coin. 'Here, before this escalates into a full-blown enquiry.'

'It's not the money Adam, it's the principle of the thing...'

The arrival of WPC Desai stopped Arnold's complaint as Reeve made the introductions. 'Kanga, this is my boss Detective Chief Inspector Archie Arnold, he's a one-off.'

'Hi, evening.' Archie sipped from his mug in displacement activity.

'Right Kanga, tell him what you told me.'

'It's like I said to Adam, Sir...'

'Archie.'

'Sir?'

'If his name's Adam then mine's Archie.'

'Yes, Sir...Archie.'

'Can I call you Kanjara?'

'Kanga.'

'Oh, right Kanga. On you go.'

'Well, Archie, it was when Adam asked me to help with the interview, with the couple in the car? After I'd heard about the black dog then heard the victim was of mixed race it clicked. I'd heard some chat in a couple of the villages, about how a mixed-race woman and a black terrier had been seen in the area for about a month now.'

'You know round here?'

'Not this exact location no, but I'm from these parts so I know a good number of the people in the villages. Heard of this estate too, only from chat of course, no invites yet.' She smiled. 'The locals are slow to trust round here, but if you live long enough in the county you develop a burr in your speech, so they recognise me as one of their own.' She saw Archie's look. 'Despite the tan; I'm second generation.'

Archie realised the interpretation. 'What? No, that's not what I was thinking, really.' Archie saw her look and felt charmed and scrutinised in equal measure. 'I was thinking that if my present and singularly ugly companion knows you so well how come I've not met you before?'

'The fact you're in Northants HQ and I'm out here in the sticks. I've got a little cottage out at Weirholme-Stantonbury.'

'All the way out there? Blimey, that is in the sticks.'

'Suits me fine Adam. Not a great one for crowds.'

Archie nodded. 'We've got something in common then. And you've got local knowledge?'

'Some. I try and walk some of the villages round this way once a month, on my days off.'

'Bet your husband loves that.'

'Not married, despite my parents' best efforts.'

Archie looked intrigued. 'So, hang on, on your day's off you...?'

59

'I pick one; a town or village. Market days are best. Chat to folk, cup of tea and such. You hear all sorts. That's where I picked up on our victim.' Archie exchanged a glance with Reeve. 'The Butterworths. Elderly couple live in Horsemill Lane, centre of Callow Green. They've lived there all their married life, market-traders, run a plant stall, and they mentioned this woman when we last chatted. Said they'd seen a nice dark lady, their words not mine, with a black terrier at a few of the markets. Said she sold home-made bracelets and ethnic jewellery, said the dog was very friendly too.'

'Tell that to Bob.'

Kanjara looked puzzled. 'Tell what?'

Archie smiled. 'Later. Go on.'

'Most elderly folk want to chat given the chance, makes them feel part of the world, all we have to do is listen, so my guess is others will know the victim too 'cos the Butterworths said she made an impression; not pushy or creepy. Anyhow, as I was in the area, I checked up on her. Nothing serious, no line-of-inquiry stuff but just 'cos she'd come onto my radar. Turns out she was a big reader.'

'In what sense?'

'At the local library. She'd wile away long spells in there.'

'Did she take out books?'

'You're thinking library card?' Archie nodded. 'I did ask. They said she used the reference section, that's all. That and the magazines. Seemed almost like she didn't want to leave a trail. Librarian said she used their power to recharge her mobile.' Archie and Reeve reacted. 'The librarian knew of course, they even let the dog sit with her, gave it a bowl to drink out of.'

Archie looked across at the tent. 'Jay should be in possession of the phone then. Best news we've had to date. Right Kanga. Tomorrow, follow that library lead up then go back to talk to that old couple, see what else they know; report back to me when you're done.'

WPC Desai looked from one to the other in a bemused fashion. 'But, won't you want to...?'

'You've done the spade work you follow it up, this is a team effort. I've already had your CV from Adam here.' Reeve and Kanjara exchanged looks. 'So do what you do. Adam, as soon as we get that phone start a scan on it. Contract paperwork, calls, gotta be summat on file.' He turned back to Kanjara. 'Next shift?'

'Tomorrow. Two 'til ten.'

'OK, full report with me by tomorrow evening, right?'

'Yes, Sir...Archie, I'll do that.'

'Good. Thanks Kanga, you've been brilliant.'

Kanjara smiled at Archie. 'Thank you. Nice to see you again Adam.'

'You too Kanga.'

She left to join the other police officers who were suiting up for a crawl-search of the lane. Reeve watched their preparations for a moment or two then turned to Archie and imitated him. 'Bet your husband loves that? Full report with me by tomorrow evenin'? That was about as subtle as dysentery was that.'

'Nothin' of the sort, credit where it's due.'

'Yeah right! Told you she was good.'

'Not the word I was going to use.'

'We're not talking about the same thing here, are we?'

Archie smiled. 'Probably not. Right, back to the case. Corpse thoughts?'

Reeve paused, considered. 'If she was dossing around here and for that long she'd know the area fairly well. Know that the traffic's infrequent and of the slow, cruising-for-privacy variety, so when the unexpected happens, like what caused those tyre marks, you're not expecting it.'

'Yeah. Something big, and unlike everything else along here moving at a fair lick. Bruising positions on the body might reveal a rough vehicle size. OK, I'll give the road the once-over...'

'Search team will do that.'

Archie was in fast. 'I'll do it. You told 'em to hold up a bit?' Adam nodded. 'Good, just something I want to check for myself first.'

'They'll get jealous.' Reeve eyed the central, taped-off area. 'And Jay will get really cross if you go in there without his say-so and a suit.'

'You'll have me crying soon, and his fifteen minutes are about up.' A police dog unit van pulled up and emptied out. 'Ayup, here comes the cavalry. Get across and tell them to wait. I'll go and have a word with the wonderful Mister Millar after my walk along the lane.' He gave Reeve his mug. 'And take that back. I'm buggered if I'll help that tight-fisted sod out with anything.'

Reeve spoke over his shoulder as he returned to the canteen. 'You're not over it yet then?'

Archie grunted in reply, removed the stale gum from his handkerchief and popped it back in his mouth. Brushing back his quiff he slipped under the tape and began a leisurely stroll, hands behind back, head bowed. After a short distance he stopped, inspected a darkened area on the lane then moved on to a point opposite the white forensic tent. Stooping down he studied the barely visible blood marks which crossed the lane, now helpfully marked by numbered yellow plastic cards. Archie walked back to the start of the skid marks, also helpfully marked out by forensics, as he thought things through. *Impact point there...knocked away down the lane to...* He pin-pointed the last resting place, *there...so, where'd the dog go?* Moving back to the blood trail that led to the tent he closed in on the wall. The dislodged moss told the tale. *That's his nail marks, got to be.* Archie slowly surveyed the wall's upper edges. *Hold up... Dog's not done them, too deep, stones are chipped...that'll be the shotgun pellets then. That's what came out of his gum...along with that tooth. Hmm, a metal detector might be worth a punt.* As he picked up a stone to place it at the base of the wall in line with the marks, so his eye was caught by something out of place; a brown leather strip which he picked up, turning it over slowly in his fingers. *That's not a frosted worm, that's leather.* He noticed the neat ending. *And cut with a knife...ah, traded in ethnic stuff...right.* A further search found two more sections of leather and a damaged, plaited leather strap resting where the wall met the lane. He smiled. *Hello my little Hippie.* Removing the remaining sticks of gum from their outer wrapper Archie dropped the leather collection into it, put it in his pocket then grabbed two stones from the base of the wall and placed them where he had found the leather strips. Across to the tent, Archie got down on his knees and surveyed the grass verge for a few seconds then spoke loudly at the tented ditch.

'Has anyone got anything they'd like to share? Anybody? Millar! Anything?'

~

Like a wooden spoon in a pot of stew the slowing of the train as it approached Chorleton stirred all the ingredients in the carriage. Lin opened her eyes at the noise of the lady rising from her seat. The man with the wispy moustache stood up too and they both moved unsteadily to the doorway at the back of the carriage. Lin swayed in the aisle as she picked up her bags, noticing that on-the-door-man had taken a sagging backpack from the rack above his head, carelessly carrying it along the carriage on his way to join the other two.

Lin slung the raincoat over her arm with a devil-may-care swipe and set off to join them, striding confidently towards the exit. Stepping on the trailing belt of the raincoat she was pulled earthwards like a fresh-roped steer as she staggered then crumpled unceremoniously to the deck in one easy movement. Her briefcase, jarred from her grip, fell onto its edge and snapped open and its contents of pens, papers, pads, an empty yoghurt pot, licked lid and plastic spoon were projectile vomited across the floor. Lin began to rise rapidly onto one bruised knee, trying to look as if she had never actually reached the floor as all heads turned her way. She smiled widely through her discomfiture. 'Sorry... Cabaret's just started, ha-ha!'

There was no further reaction from the two men, both of whom had slipped back into self-life, far too intent on being the first off the train.

'Are you alright dear?'

Lin smiled at the lady. 'Yes fine, sorry.'

'As long as you're not hurt.' She took a step towards Lin, 'Can I help?'

Lin covered further embarrassment. 'No!' She realised how that sounded and tempered her voice. 'No...thank you, I'm fine. Just not concentrating...trains huh? Thanks, sorry.'

'Well, if you're sure.' The lady smiled then turned a dagger's look at the two men, leaving Lin to scrabble around for her bits and bobs before finally clipping the briefcase closed. It was just as she was about to stand up that she saw it, just to her right and under a seat; a circular wad of bank notes. Rolled tightly and secured with a broad, brown, elastic band their end reminded her of age rings in a tree trunk. Lin's involuntary breath came out as 'Oh!', but she covered it by rubbing her knee so as to deflect attention. There was no need for concern, all were turned away, positioned on the starting blocks of escape. Lin stretched out a hand, closing it tightly over the bundle. *Heavens-to-Betsy but this is solid, this is serious money.* Her slight movement uncovered the figure twenty as she stood up, wrapping the overcoat round the hand that gripped the bundle, her heart starting to do a rumba and her right leg feel on the verge of giving way.

Stand up Linden Lea you daft bitch...stand up! She grabbed onto the back of a seat, steadying herself and staring unblinkingly unflinchingly, straight ahead. *You've just come into wealth, now's not the time to peg out.*

~

J ay Millar, complete with one-piece white suit and hood, stepped out of the tent from where the odd camera flash gave a momentary glow. In his gloved hand he held a blob of gum which he brandished. He looked at the kneeling detective. 'And your prayers are answered. This will be yours I imagine, and where the hell is your suit?'

'I'm wearin' it.'

'Your protective suit you idiot!'

'Oh that one,' He looked towards the forensics' truck. 'Erm...'

'You do realise the deliberate contamination of a crime scene is an offence?' He looked Archie over. 'Your lackadaisical treatment of a Windsor knot is offensive but your carefree abandonment of this,' he held up the gum once more, 'is just plain criminal.'

'You'd never have found that or anything else had I not gone in and sorted out the dog for you.'

'Don't change the subject, I very much doubt the disposal of chewing gum was central to your mission which, I may add, you carried out impeccably.'

'Thank you and you're wrong, it was central to the mission. Can I let the search team loose?'

'Yes, but not the taped-off area, not yet.' In the background more generators were being positioned, and gradually the Incident Site Infrastructure Team began to lay out a string of arc lights along the lane. Jay shook his head. 'We've only done a preliminary sweep. Things have been blurred by the passage of time as it is, but I don't want any extra contamination.'

Archie stood and called out, 'Right Adam un-van the hounds, but not the taped-off section!'

Reeve waved by reply then passed the green light on to the search team leader who grumbled, ''Bout bloody time!' as he and the dog-men dispersed to begin their work.

Archie turned to Jay. 'So I repeat, but for me what would you have done?'

'Waited for firearms like you should've.'

'What, and let them shoot it for being faithful? The John Gray Society would be outraged at our lack of charity.'

'Charity and Greyfriars Bobby aside there are rules and procedures for these incidents. Health and Safety. You know those rules as well as I do but continue to flout them, vis-a-vis your recent search warrant debacle.'

'What? How the hell did you hear about that?'

Jay smirked at him then looked across at the blood trail. 'Just keep your movements around the impact site to a minimum and not...'

Archie completed the sentence, his face showing not a flicker. 'In the taped-off area, yeah, got it.'

'And at the first opportunity adjust that tie and put on a bloody protective suit!'

'And look like a sperm? No thanks. So, name and address of victim, identity of her assailants?'

'In your dreams. Where would be the fun in that for you?'

'OK, I'll settle for time of death.'

'Time of death was sometime between when a reliable person last saw her alive and now.'

'I always held you in such high esteem, scientist and all that.'

The line of arc lights fired up, lighting the whole length of the lane as Jay shrugged in answer. 'I'm just a lost soul wading through a heady mix of blind luck liberally dosed with exact science and casual brutality.'

'What is the point of you?' Archie sighed in resignation. 'OK, what can you tell me? Anything at all?'

Jay also sighed and looked back into the ditch, his flippancy gone. 'Another diamond day in the force; I do love my job but there's some days I don't particularly like it... OK. First assessment, rudimentary at present. Deceased has been here four possibly five days, plus or minus a day.'

'That's what I'd call rudimentary too.'

Jay ignored him. 'The point of impact was around where the second set of skid marks start; Traffic will confirm when I allow them in. She was knocked down the road with some considerable force travelling nine metres from point of impact, hitting the tarmac surface several times on her journey and ending up just opposite here. That's all the researched assessments, on to conjecture now. Possibly she was sufficiently compos mentis to drag herself to this ditch. You'll have noticed the cards marking the blood trail, what's left of it?' Archie nodded as Jay looked back at the tent. 'Contusions on the body are muddled due to her method of travel after impact which means help in sizing the vehicle from the bruising may be hard to determine. Whether the car driver witnessed her last hurrah, watched her complete it even, is a moot point.'

'Couldn't have missed her. Vehicle overshot so it had to back up, double skid marks show that, and the headlights would've illuminated the state she was in.'

'Yes, I saw those marks too.' Jay sighed heavily. 'I do try to look on the positive side of things, give the humanity in us the benefit of the doubt, but as much as it pains me to say so, I think you're right.' He shook his head slowly. 'However...back to science. The frosts we've had over the last few days make things a little hazy. My feeling is a VH test will reveal a little more information, cool conditions and such, but...' Jay looked at Archie's expression. 'VH test? Vitreous humour test.' Archie's gaze was unflinching. 'A look at the goo in her one undamaged eye.'

'Oh, right.'

'Shall I continue, or will I totally confuse you?'

'Sarcasm; lowest form of wit.'

'But the highest form of intelligence. Right, determining TOD... Time of death?' Archie nodded. 'Good. Determining TOD will be helped by the fact that half her head and the one good eye were out of the water in the bottom of the ditch so the VH test may, I restate may, yield some helpful truths. The water in the bottom of the ditch is full of old leaves and such, but the edges have good vegetation growth. As most of her body is out of the ditch water we should be able to get some helpful chlorophyll information due to her compression. I'll be contacting the university flora bods later.'

'Any ID indicators?'

'Of mixed-race certainly. By the state of her hands, her lack of sartorial elegance and her body ornaments I'd say she was a lady of the road; bit of a Hippie.'

'Just what I said.'

'What?'

'Nothing. She wearing any wristbands? Leather, home-made?'

Jay looked sideways at Archie then at the ditch, like a man waiting to be ambushed. 'Yes. How did you know that?'

'Oh, you know... Age?'

Jay's face wore an I-smell-a-rat expression. 'Dental will help with age, but given her lifestyle? Living rough ages one prematurely so possibly thirty-five coming on mid-fifties is my present best guess.'

'What happened to this exact science you said was involved?'

'Gone, along with cuts in the policing budget so eagerly pushed through by our brainless Home Secretary who, if rumour be true, is soon to usher us into the world of private law enforcement.'

'Glad to hear you're not bitter about it all then.'

'Don't get me started.'

'When can I have more, about her that is, not about the state of British policing?'

'When we get her home.' He turned to the ditch. 'She took the full impact Archie and she's been here a good while so, all in all, a wee bit of a mess and these aren't the best working conditions. It'll be at least another one-plus hours before we can move her so I can't be more precise until then.'

Archie looked back along the lane. 'We agree there was no reaction from the driver until after contact?'

'Nope, not even the reaction to do something to help...phone for us before buggering off at the very least.'

'Just left it to those two poor saps in the car, them and that dog.'

'Which was very much alive and taking no prisoners when we arrived, as you noted.'

'Guarding the pack.'

'A very dead pack.' Jay saw Archie was deep in thought then cottoned on to an earlier remark. 'Assailants?'

'Sorry?'

'You asked for the name of her assailants.'

Archie looked back at the skid-marks. 'Oh... Yes, I did. You're late picking that one up.'

'And I'd say you were early. Bit of an assumption at this juncture, wouldn't you say?' He paused. 'Hello, hello, hello, do I sense a level of detection going on here?'

'Let me run some stuff past you Jay, and hear me out, OK?' Archie pursed his lips and thought a little before continuing. 'For starters, and in my humble opinion, only one of two things happened here. One, it was an accidental hit-and-run and the driver left in a panic, or two, it was a deliberate hit-and-run and the driver and his mate left after making sure she was dead. Me? I'm thinking scenario two.'

~

*R*egular meals; use of the launderette; repairs to my laptop...council tax! These were Lin's thoughts as, at one and the same time, she heard herself say out loud,

'Has anyone dropped any money?'

A stunned silence followed.

~

*J*ay frowned. 'What? No, no. Early indicators say she's just a drifter, certainly never figured on any oligarch's hit list, just a lass and her dog living rough and finding themselves in the wrong place at the wrong time.'

'You're a detective now, are you? Jay... Look at those skid marks; they're what, twenty-five plus metres long? That length of skid says the vehicle was going near-on fifty miles an hour when it smacked into her.'

'Something from all that time in formal training did stick then. That is indeed the braking distance of a vehicle travelling at that speed.'

'Definitely in the frosty conditions we've had over the last few days.'

'So, classic accidental hit-and-run. Driving too fast in icy conditions on a narrow lane, woman suddenly appears in the road, the driver barely knew what he'd hit. Braked, came to a halt, paused in realisation...'

'Backed up and paused in realisation.'

'Backed up and paused in realisation, then set off in a panic and at speed in the original direction of travel.'

'Really? What about thinking distance?'

'What?'

'The time needed...'

Jay sighed. 'I know what the term thinking distance means Archie, I'm head of forensics. What of it?'

'I've had a little more time than you and I've been able to walk the tyre line, so I'll overlook your ignorance...'

'What...in the taped-off area? I thought you were telling me this from guesswork...! You'll have contaminated the whole lane! Are you completely without scruples?'

'Yeah, but I've got some chewing gum if you want one.'

'Don't be bloody facetious DCI Arnold! Before we could actually start our work on what I've already said is a degraded site it took us an hour to maintain and ensure the integrity of the scene, we avoided all extraneous contact with the central area, and that damn dog didn't help either. Now I find you've been wandering around it like a lost soul, and without a protective suit on!'

'Sorry Jay, really. Sorry.'

'This is a crime scene Detective Chief Inspector, a tragic crime scene of some brutality not your personal playground! Treat it and her memory with a little respect!'

'Point taken, sorry. But look, if you do find anything of mine, and that's highly unlikely, then you've got me on the DNA database so you shouldn't have any trouble eliminating me.'

Jay shook his head in annoyed disbelief. 'Yes, we do have you on file, yes, but...it's not the elimination it's the time it takes to make it!' His voice softened a little. 'Look...look, I know how hard you work, and I admire it, I do. We've worked together on many cases and you're the one who gets results when everybody else passes, but please, just try and stick to the rules even for a short time? Make these hateful jobs a little easier and the time we have to spend on them a little shorter?'

Archie nodded. 'Sure Jay, do my best. Apologies again, really... Oh,' he reached into his pocket and took out the gum wrapper. 'Run this lot through your system will you, see if you can't get a match to her...' Jay was standing in open-mouthed disbelief. 'You look like a Port Logan cod.'

'A what?'

'Never mind. Here.' He gave Jay the wrapper. 'I just want to see if she's on these leather strips, as well as me and Mr. Wrigley.' Jay looked at the wrapper. 'Go on. Open it.'

Jay tipped out the contents into his rubber-gloved palm and stared. 'I don't believe this.' He sighed deeply. 'I'm afraid to ask...' He shook his head as if to clear it. 'OK, where did you find these?'

'Over there. I marked the spot with some stones so's you could find it easily.' Archie pointed then looked back at Jay with a pleased expression. 'You can swap them for your plastic cards when you've time.'

'You marked the spot with...a stone.'

'Stones.'

Jay paused, collected his thoughts. 'Right. And you think they belong to madam here?'

'It's just something DC Reeve said came back to me when I found them. Now you've come up with the thought that she was a bit of a Hippy independently of him.' Archie saw Jay's expression. 'What? I thought you'd be pleased.'

'Pleased? Right. Yes. Thank you.' Jay turned to the tent. 'Maurice?' A head popped out of the tent and Millar handed across the gum wrapper and leather strips. 'Bag these please.' He saw Maurice's expression, 'Don't...just bag and number them.' A puzzle-faced Maurice Parr re-entered the tent as Jay sighed once more. 'Move on. Tyre marks, you were saying.'

Archie pointed. 'Back there, another set of skid marks.'

'Yes. They were measured, checked and noted.'

'Both sets the same span?'

They are. That's where he first saw something, the dog perhaps?'

'Maybe.'

'Saw something, not quite sure, dabbed the brakes, slight skid in the frost, definitely saw her, slammed them on, too late and here's me.'

'What if they aren't the marks made by a set of dabbed brakes, but the marks made by a dabbed accelerator after the driver changed down, the better to move forward; fast? Think about it. This lane? Who drives down this lane at seventy?'

'No no, not seventy. We've just agreed it was fifty.'

'Hear me out, OK?' Jay nodded and folded his arms across his chest in his best, OK go ahead and impress me pose as Archie continued. 'My guess is no one, not even someone who knows this lane well would scoot along here at anything more than thirty, thirty-five tops.'

'Any more would be suicidal I'd say.'

Agreed. And anyone who used this lane regularly would know that, and the driver did.'

'What?'

'Know this lane; strangers would travel slower than fifty.'

'Ah, back to fifty now...'

'Yes, because he hit her at fifty.'

'Yes fifty, agreed...'

'The long skid's easy then, it's just those tyre marks thirty yards back from the point of impact, they're the real puzzle. So, either he was driving around these lanes at seventy and managed to slow to fifty in those thirty yards before he hit her...or he was doing thirty and accelerated to fifty to hit her. No other explanations.'

'You think?'

'A woman and a dog sighted that close in headlights? Come on Jay. No, he knew. Those first marks are from an act of acceleration or I'm Snow White. That lass and dog were the bullseye of his target. He was doing thirty right up 'til she came into sight then he made fifty, hit her and came to a halt. That's why the separate sets of skid marks, one accelerating one braking.'

'You keep saying 'he'. What if it was a woman?'

'Nope. Judging by the acceleration marks, the masculine change down, the pilot was a man, as was his passenger.'

'He had a passenger!'

'He did, and it was his accomplice that stepped out to make sure she was dead, that the contract was complete.'

'You've been reading too many detective stories.'

'Jay...listen. When we got here, thanks to the corralling instinct of that terrier and your diligent hoisting of the hazard-tape...'

'Which you ignored.'

'Yes, but thanks to you the ground around the body was totally uncorrupted.'

'Yes. We approached along the ditch.'

Archie paused and looked at the edge of the grass by his feet. 'And this is where you reckon she crawled to the ditch, right?'

'Yes, that's her line of entry. She crawled to the top then rolled down here into her final resting place after the vehicle had left the scene.'

'See that treeline?' He pointed as Jay nodded. 'Runs west-south-west so the tree cover would've been shading this area each day, possibly for the whole day. You reckon she's been dead two, three days?'

'Possibly more, but for conversation's sake yes, about that.'

'I'd say the frost's been on this grass for the past week.'

'Our friends in the Met Office will confirm the local macro-climate, but yes, I'd say that was entirely possible.'

'And frost burns grass when it's subject to pressure.' Jay nodded, now fully engrossed as Archie continued, 'When I got here to sort out that terrier there were only two sets of prints burnt into that grass, the terrier's and that chap's from the car. Thing is, Jay, the blood trail...'

'Is there on the road, leading to the verge and ditch.'

'But not here.' Archie pointed at the grass between him and Jay. 'And the grass, still erect and I'd guess you've found no blood on it either.'

'No, but her blood was on the downslope.'

'But not here, at the front.' repeated Archie. So, how come our fatally wounded hit-and-run victim crawls to the edge of the road, at death's door, and yet miraculously finds enough energy to leap from the lane's edge into the ditch without touching this patch of grass?' There was a silence as Archie let it sink in. 'My gut instinct is she was flung in there.' Archie looked at the tent. 'How long before I can have an ID on her?'

Jay was about to speak when a voice came from the tent.

'Mister Millar?' Maurice was reaching up from the tent, a plastic-bagged kidney donor card in his hand.

Jay took the bag. 'How about immediately? Is immediately too soon? God bless the organ donor system.'

Before he could read it, Archie had taken it. 'This is detective work; you just stick to sorting out what organs can be harvested for the benefit of humanity.'

'State of her and the time gap? Not much.'

Archie flicked the bag over in his hand. 'There's another of her dreams destroyed then.'

'You're all heart, Archie.'

Archie read the name on the card. 'Renata Lea. Unusual name. Rough-living Renata, the Hippy with a social conscience. Anything else on her?'

'Not as yet. This is painstaking work that takes long and meticulous...'

'Mister Millar?'

'Yes, that's me.'

Maurice handed up further plastic-bagged scraps of a life. 'These were in her trouser pocket Sir...'

'Thank you.'

'The tiepin was in the ditch, near her feet,' continued Maurice.

'Not too much now or our shining detective will have nothing to take a wild stab in the dark at.' He handed Archie the bag containing two photo-booth snapshots and the tiepin which had a model of an elephant at its centre, the middle of its head bearing a stone of some kind.

'Thanks...whoa, that's heavy! It's like holding a rock...is it gold?' He spoke past Jay. 'Nothing else Maurice?'

'Nope.'

'All pockets checked?'

'Yes.'

'No mobile then?'

'Er, no.'

'Right.' Archie looked at the photos then back to the ditch. 'Is it her?'

Jay took the photos and inspected them. 'Hard to tell. If pushed I'd say a tentative yes. Mixed race certainly. Hair's a little shorter than in the photo but could be an old one. Facial features are similar, but, in her present condition...'

Archie took the photos back. 'They come in fours.'

'What?'

'Photo-booth prints, they come in fours. Someone's got the other two.' He turned the bag over and saw the water blurred inscription on the reverse side. 'Hard to make out. What's that say? "forget", is it?'

He turned the photo round and they both inspected it then Jay attempted a translation. "...forget what...we...forget what we...like"? Is that it, "like"?'

'Think so, and is that "Love...or Lip...Lin...? Lim..."? Too smudged. "Love" definitely, and is that some X's?' He looked at

Jay. 'Her name's Renata, says so on her donor card so who's this Lip, Lim or Lin? You sure you can't be more specific on any facial resemblance?'

'If she'd got much of a face left I'd tell you.'

'Bit too much information there Mister Millar.' Archie paused. 'Oh, hang on. It's "look like"! It says, "forget what we look like"!' Archie thought for a while then his face showed realisation and he flicked the bag. 'Tell you what, if this isn't photos of the victim then it's her twin! She's got a twin!' He held up the photo. 'This could be exactly what our victim looks like but it's not her it's her twin, and her twin's got the other two photos of her twin...they swapped places in the booth!'

'Could be, yes, but at present I'll not commit.' Jay looked at the tiepin. 'And this? Aren't they supposed to bring luck or long life or something?'

'Wisdom, mental strength. Ganesh in the Hindu religion, usually rides a mouse.'

'You never cease to amaze, DCI Arnold. Is it hers?'

'Possibly. The Hippy angle fits, eastern religions and all that.' Arnold turned the pin over in his fingers. 'But still, an odd thing for a woman of the road to have, and if it's gold I reckon it's worth a bob or two so why keep it and live in penury? Curiouser and curiouser.' He looked up as Reeve approached. 'And here's another conundrum. I gather from your expression an imminent solution to our roadside puzzle from the search team isn't exactly imminent.'

'Would've been better off talking to their dogs.'

Jay picked it up. 'Talking of dogs, how is our canine witness? Do we have a microchip? Name tag?'

Archie smiled. 'No, but it wasn't all a blank. Our dog is as well as can be expected, particularly after being shot.'

'Shot?' Reeve awaited confirmation.

Jay paused for a second. 'You slithy little toad; you knew that all along! I'm Crime Scene Manager, you should have shared that with me the moment you got back!'

'I was a little busy sorting out the causes Jay, but now we're all together, I'll tell you both, saves me repeating myself. You'll know I took him to Balsall Common?' Jay nodded. 'They stitched up that tear in his muzzle and removed the splintered canine tooth from his gum...together with a ball of BB shot.' Jay and Reeve both reacted. Archie could see Jay's expression and sought to clarify. 'Tooth and shot have been bagged and sent over to your place for a look-see, Jay.'

'That was good of you.'

'Would be good to know what the shot's made of asap.'

'Lead?' ventured Reeve.

'Possibly. That's the reason for Jay.'

Reeve was puzzled and looked at Archie. 'Why wouldn't it be lead?'

'Ducks.' Archie elaborated. 'Wildfowlers.'

'What?'

'Wildfowlers; folk who shoot ducks by the sea.'

'We're not by the sea.'

Jay joined in. 'There's been a ban on lead shot being discharged on the foreshore for some time. The ducks were mistaking the pellets for seeds, eating them and dying of lead poisoning...'

Arnold tailed on. 'So they've been experimenting with other types of shot over the years.'

Reeve nodded. 'And you think this may be something other than lead?'

'Like I say, that's the reason for Jay. Would be useful if it was, narrow things down a little.'

'It would. I'll inform Ms Cresson when she arrives, but right now I have a corpse to decipher.'

'Oh, and something that might help you with that. Over the other side of the lane you'll find the marks left by the rest of the BB shot. Can't miss it. I've placed another pile of stones at the base of the wall. A run round with a metal detector may well pick up some strays if it was lead.' Miller stood open mouthed as Archie turned to Reeve. 'I'll explain about the skid marks later.'

Reeve, still slightly confused, nodded. 'Oh, OK...'

Jay turned to rejoin his team in the ditch. 'One day you'll slip up and there'll be no safety net Arnold, you smug git.'

'Got results though didn't it?' Archie handed over the bagged donor card and photos to Reeve. 'Our hippy camper here. A Miss or Mrs Renata Lea, and in all likelihood she's got a twin sister.'

Jay's head reappeared from the tent. 'Conjecture. And I want those photos back before you leave.'

Reeve scrutinised the photos. 'Renata? Unusual name. Spanish or Mexican?'

'Possibly. That would account for her colouring.'

Jay's voice drifted up. 'Nope, even from this view and in this state I'd say she is of part African parentage.'

Archie smiled. 'He does have his uses you know.' He handed over the third bag with the tiepin in it. 'And there's this.'

Reeve took it. 'That's some weight there. Is it gold?'

'Yeah, think so. That, the photos and donor card are all that remain of a life lived.'

'The photos, are they of her?' Reeve squinted at the blurred writing. 'Or her twin?'

'I feel proof positive beckoning, provided our forensics team can get its arse into gear.' Archie turned and addressed the tent. 'I hope you're listening to this Millar, you dinosaur.'

'With bated breath,' the tent replied.

Archie turned back. 'To be honest Adam I don't know what we've got here, a part of the story or the whole of it. One thing's for sure, this was no accident.' Archie exchanged old gum for new in his time-honoured fashion and flicked back his unruly forelock. 'Right, you and me stood here won't buy the baby a new bonnet. You'd best get back to base. Brief the team and set them to piecing stuff together...oh, and get an OS map of this area up on the board will you? One to fifty-thousand, pinpoint some detail on it; footpaths, buildings and such.' He dropped the level of his voice. 'Take the photo and donor card with you, I'll hold on to the tiepin for now.' He took it from Reeve.

'Is that allowed?'

''Course, my say-so. Show those snaps to Kanjara on your way out, see if it rings any bells, and get her a copy to show the Butterworths tomorrow. I'll await the graveside results here and have another mooch about, see if I can't find out where our lady was lodging...and why she was worth the killing.'

~

*W*as that me? Lin almost turned round to see who had shopped her. *Of course it was you! What do you expect? Honesty sticks to you and Rene like ticks on a hippo, 'course it was you!* Through the gradual animation of her fellow travellers, her thoughts tumbled on. *Our bloody Nan's got a lot to answer for. Feisty grandmas do that. Before I knew what-was-what, I'd swapped a life of freedom and sunshine for silent farting and napkins at lunch.* The hand holding the money twitched, sending a signal up her arm and reinforcing her conscience. *Now here I am giving up this small fortune when maybe I should've just kept shtum.*

Meanwhile back in reality-carriage, her impromptu announcement had created a full-scale search. Two members of her audience began a systematic check as Lin watched, almost amused. *Christ, you'd know if this wad was missing without a search, your jacket lapels would be level for a start.* Then she noticed on-the-door man was far from active. His hand was resting on the lower pocket of the bag, his attention directed straight at her. *Ah, bingo!*

'Yeah, I 'ave.' He gave Lin the stare of a man who cowed cobras for a living, his words thick with meaning and Guinness. 'I've dropped some.'

Now Lin was in a bit of a quandary. *OK. If it's yours then you should have it back, but I've not seen you move until just.* 'What is it?'

Lin could see he was uncomfortable, like an interviewed politician who thinks he's dodged the bullet of a tricky question only to get hit by the ricochet. A glance told Lin she had everyone's attention as he answered.

'Come again?'

'You know. Is it in a container, a wallet...purse? Is it loose change, a note?'

The man paused and stared at her, seemingly weighing up her honesty too. Then his eyes flicked across to the other man and something in the return gaze alerted Lin as he said, very slowly and very deliberately, 'No, it aint loose change. In a band. Quite a few quid.' He paused for a split second then added, pointedly, 'Brown, wide, made of rubber.'

The man's eyes never left Lin's and she, in turn, held his stare, a half-smile on her lips. *This is what you get from someone who was reared by a feisty grandma and played with elephants as a kid.* She instinctively reached for the ivory netsuke as she continued her inquisition. 'What denominations?'

The silence that followed was palpable as the train squeaked to a halt, seemingly joining in the hiatus in the carriage. The man could see quite clearly by the set of her jaw that this finder was determined to get it right, that an answer was required and much depended on it.

At last he spoke. 'Danny boys.'

'What?'

'Twenties.'

'Oh. All?'

The man blinked once and replied flatly, 'All.'

'Hang on.'

Lin released the netsuke and turned slightly away from the group to open up her sweaty palm. A quick flick through the bundle told her four things: *It was fixed by a wide brown rubber band. It was a lot of cash. It was all in twenties.* And finally. *Linden Lea, you're the mompie.*

She turned back and held the wad in her closed fist, so the amount was difficult to see by the others. 'Sorry if I seemed suspicious, only it's not as if it was a couple of quid, y' know?'

'Bang on.' He looked straight at her, taking the money and slipping it back into his jacket pocket.

'Just needed to be sure.' Then she added, shrugging her shoulders as she did so, 'My Nan, she...' Her voice tailed off.

The two men exchanged a further glance. 'Y'r Nan...? Yeah sure,' replied the man eventually. 'Sure.'

They know each other, definitely, thought Lin.

Then all turned as one and made their way out through the doorway, the excitement well and truly over. At its threshold the now considerably richer man turned back to Lin. 'Thanks... I didn't catch your name.'

'That's because I didn't give it.'

He smiled insincerely. 'Huh, no, so y' didn't. Well thanks, you're a wee blade, Miss.' He turned and stepped off the train.

Lin didn't believe a word of it. *Luck of the Irish was me findin' it you ungrateful bastard. Anyone else would've been down the road and into the pub.* She shook her head and stepped out onto the platform in time to see the three passengers well ahead, all walking in time to their well-waged drum. *Wonder where the hell they all live? Strangers here that's for certain, 'specially those Irish... Ah, who gives a toss.* Lin followed what passed for a crowd in Chorleton out through the station entrance and into a small chippings-coated car park. Here her fellow passengers splintered, the lady on foot towards the village centre, the two men to a car parked in the shadows. Lin's interest was pricked again and she stood in the shadows to watch. *Commuters? I've not seen them here before; I mean never.* She jangled the loose change in her purse. *Sod this. Spar shop at the garage for some bread and beans, then on to the Lion...*

~

6

o o o A n' the photo will help with the enquiries Jay, so...'

'Yes, but you of all people should know that letting your assistant take it back to Northampton is tampering with evidence from a crime scene, which is also a criminal act. It wasn't tagged, neither was the donor card.'

'But it was bagged, an' I told Adam not to open it.'

'You did?'

'Well not directly, but he knows the game and it'll only be a criminal act if you think it is. I'll get it back to you as soon as, I promise.'

'Just make sure you do.'

'I will. Now, after that semi-bollocking can I have a better look round without ruining your delicate work?'

'Where? I want to keep tabs on you.'

'Christ, it's like being in front of the headmaster. I just want to scan the general woodland and see what's what.' He saw Jay's look. 'What? You've swept the area and OK'd it, the search team are doing this side, your man with the metal-detector is sweeping the wall marks so I thought I'd do a preliminary sniff about in the woodland at the back of it, keep out of their way... and yours.'

After some thought Jay nodded. 'Right, you can...providing you put a suit on and keep that gum in your mouth.'

'Oh great.' He looked at the van. 'Do I have to?'

'No suitee, no lookee.'

'Isn't that just a little bit racist?'

Jay smiled. 'Only if you think it is.'

'Right. Can I use one of the torches in there too?'

'Yes, providing you sign for it.'

'Why, are they yours?'

'Sign for it!'

'Yeah, yeah...'

Five minutes later Archie appeared in the truck doorway, white-suited and booted, a torch in each hand. At the ditch's edge Jay and two of the forensics team were lined up from where they sang the opening two lines of Every Sperm is Sacred then gave him a round of applause. Archie bowed and stuck two fingers up at them before walking off along the lane.

Clipping the two halogen torches onto the suit and after paying the nearer set of skid marks a little more attention, Archie checked the lane's edge carefully. Moving along at a snail's pace he swayed occasionally to adjust the fall of his shadow under the arc lights as he surveyed the wall, until eventually, he stopped. *Bugger, missed it...bloody shadows.* He turned and retraced his steps until, almost as if he had reached the end of a leash, he stopped dead. From this direction the dark marks of the wall's disturbed vegetation stood out well under the cold glare of arc light. *More scuff marks in that moss...too steep for foxes to slide down, they'd just jump; too much damage for a cat...badgers? Nah, idle buggers, they'd look for an easier way. I wonder...is this you, lady? Is this where you got onto the lane?* Tossing a stone on top of the wall in line with the marks, Archie looked for a way up and saw a low-hanging fir branch. Counting the steps over to it he climbed partway up the wall, reached out, grabbed the branch and was over and on the other side of the wall in a trice, jumping down neatly into a decent stand of elderly brambles.

'Ahhh...! Ow! Bugger, damn...bugger!'

Torch on, he snaggled his way along the inside wall, the bare branches lifted into stark relief by the arc lights on the lane until, curses and thorns later, he was back level with the balanced stone. The scuff marks caused by a climber were clearly visible on this side too, and a look along the torch beam into the woodland confirmed his first thoughts. *That's a track. Faint, but even in this light, a track.* He knelt and looked along the line. *Busy woodland. So, she gets to here, climbs over and, bang! Coming from where though...? What would Brock do? Line of least resistance, that's what.* He plotted the line, unhitched and turned on the second torch and moved deeper into the woodland and the dark, following the track's natural lines until the trees thickened and the undergrowth thinned. He gave up and came to a standstill. *Bugger; oh, for a bit of daylight.* He dropped to his knees and set the torch beams along the ground, but every gap between the trees seemed to offer an easy way through. Archie now lay at full stretch like a snooker player on a rest-free shot, looking along the beams again through the serried ranks of saplings; that was when he saw the out-of-place angle. *What the…?* A long look eventually deciphered the curled edge of a corrugated tin sheet standing like an alert ear on the woodland floor. Archie picked up the torches. *Where the hell's that come from? Must be a building nearby.* Arriving at the tin sheet he studied it. *Rust well started.* He dropped to one knee, concentrating the beam so his gaze could home in on a darker stain that discoloured the even tan. *Old rust?* He bent down further in study. *No, not rust…blood?* He scanned the nearby ground then delicately lifted the sheet just enough to peer under it. *Not been here more than a few days. Odd bit of ground ivy's not gone pale, leaves are still damp from the moisture drawn up…no mouse runs.* He looked around. *Was she starting to build a shelter, cut herself on the sharp edge? Right. Scout round.*

Using the tin sheet as the centre Archie began walking in slow circles, widening his distance with each circuit. The broken branch of a silver birch sapling drew him in. *Not deer, no top bite. Something's bust this off, or someone. When she dragged the sheet through, or when it was flung here maybe?* He looked through the woodland, the silent swish of the torch beam sending a couple of roosting wood pigeons rattling away to a less disturbed sleeping place. Stepping on a little further he came to a sudden stop. *These leaves are darker,* he picked one up, *and damp. Squirrels have scratched around a bit. Two piles of fox-shit there, couple of days old…and those old leaves, they shouldn't be on top.* Already close to the woodland floor, he dropped even lower, folding back the hood of his suit and smoothing back his wayward quiff, chewing ferociously as he looked over the torchlit ground until his eye focussed on the shadow of a dip, its edge showing as a dark line. *That ground's been moved about, and not that long ago either.* At the edge of the depression he picked up a large leaf. *A sweet chestnut leaf...* He moved the torch beam around the tree canopy. *Where there's no sweet chestnut trees.* On the ground uncovered by the leaf's removal the torchlight illuminated a leather strap, fixing his gaze like a laser as his eyes widened in disbelief. *What the f...?* He picked it up gently between finger and thumb, twisting it round to inspect it. *Need Jay to see this.* He replaced the strap and sweet chestnut leaf to their original positions. *That tin sheet didn't get over there by itself so...from where?*

Archie moved cautiously until he saw the blur of an overgrown and dilapidated building ahead. Scanning the area he spotted the tall sweet chestnut tree. *Castanea sativa...that leaf's home...* He looked upwards to the remains of the roof. *The tin sheet's home too. Got to have been carried by someone to over there, wind didn't blow it.* The enclosed area held a scent and Archie's nose twitched at the strength and pungency. *Bloody hell but that stinks. Summat dead and rotting round here.* He skirted the building's skeleton, reaching an old yard wall that contained a scrub-filled gateway, the hinge-post standing drunkenly, grasping on to past memories of a useful existence. At the foot of the post the glint of a set fox-wire showed in the beam. *Perfect spot.* He stooped, pinched it closed, entered the building and moved along between the back wall and the greedy woodland, the stench growing stronger. After a few paces he stood still, drawing in lungfuls of foetid air. *There, by that busted feeder.* He moved to the wall-mounted wooden troughs wrapped in fronds of bramble and, in the double torchlight, spotted the reason for his journey. *That a fox?* He bent and looked closer, then leant back in realisation. *Oh, you poor little sod. What you doin' out here in this cold, eh? You poor little sod.* He gently brushed the coat of what had once been a small dog then stood and considered. *Dogs here, dogs there. Has this one been shot by a keeper and flung here? No, they'd chuck it on the main road, make it look like an accident...* He looked towards the tin sheet then back to the canine corpse and shook his head. *Definitely need Jay.*

Back on the lane Archie flashed his torches across to the forensics tent and called out. 'Jay! Jay?' Millar appeared from the ditch. 'Can you spare me a second or two?'

'Lost your gum?'

'Funny. Seriously now. Can you have a look at a couple of things, help me out a bit. Have we got a ladder?'

'Why?'

'It involves some climbing and in your soft condition you'll need one.'

Jay ignored the dig. 'What, now?'

'If you want to be part of the solution, yes. Get yourself a torch.' Archie smiled. 'And sign for it...'

~

The Red Lion, Cleveland Road, Chorleton was celebrating a near miss.

God was in his or her heaven, or at least in the Cranford Brewery boardroom on the day an aggressive takeover bid by a large international consortium was staved off after the shareholders voted to continue in the hostelry business. Had conglomerates inc. won the vote, this old-established country town pub would have ceased to be. It would have been turned into a mock-wood, mock-plastic, mock-Viking ship, and renamed The Norseman. Instead of Sarah Wilmott and her family plying the locals with drink from the Red Lion's renowned guest-beer cellar, customers would be drinking any one of ten varieties of totally indistinguishable ice-cold lagers. But now, after the initial euphoria following the vote, continuity settled like blazing logs in the pub's winter fireplaces and Cranford Greene Bitter continued to flow through the taps. For the locals it was a bullet dodged.

The sight as Lin rounded the corner was one of comforting familiarity and her stride increased in length, speed and determination as she approached the pub's entrance. She dodged her way through the flock of determined smokers huddled around the doorway, each one inhaling as if their life depended on it. In the deepest shadows of this nicotine alcove a sizeable woman stood smoking with the nonchalance of someone who had spent a lifetime getting it just right. Lin, oblivious to all but the impending drink, pushed against the door and the pub's sphincter opened to release the welcome flatulence of hospitality.

'Evening Lin. Usual?'

'Please Sarah, can you line up a chaser too?'

'Which?'

'Scapa?'

'Crikey, splashing out.'

'It'll break me, but...'

Sarah Wilmott, barmaid to the masses and daughter of the pub's owners, took down a straight pint glass from the shelf above the bar and began to tease out a pint of Dawlish Breweries' Summer Blush Bitter.

'Long day?'

'Long, fruitless and now, with that chaser, really expensive.'

'Bad as that?'

'Worse.'

Sarah smiled at her. 'I'll do the malt at cost.'

'Oh Sarah...' Lin was embarrassed by the whole situation. 'Thanks. I'm really sorry to be such a disappointment.'

'You aren't a disappointment and it's fine.'

'Is it? Oh well, while I'm on a roll, could I borrow your cash-and-carry card for tomorrow please?'

Sarah took her handbag off the back shelf. 'If Mum finds out about this I'll be in real trouble you know that don't you? Not you, me.'

'I've got to have more sustenance than bread and beans. Tell her I stole it.'

'Mum knows you too well. She thinks you're a paragon of honesty and virtue.'

'Obviously not all that well then.' As Sarah passed the card across Lin looked around the bar. 'No one else in yet?'

'Tim was here earlier.' She gave a knowing look. 'Asking after you. Saw Eleanor and Lisa this morning over at the Farmers' Market. They said they'll be in this evening.'

'Oh yes, Wednesday. Many there?'

'Good few, and I got some excellent chorizo. Lisa said she'll try and drag Vasiri away from his computer. Apart from that,' she looked around the bar, 'what you see is what you get.'

'Cut-price night then.' She took the pint as Sarah poured a single shot of malt. 'Can your kindness stretch to a double at cost?'

Sarah laughed. 'Ha! Yeah, just this once.' She filled the silver measure a second time. 'You weren't kidding then, about it being worse.'

'Never more serious. Is that paper available?'

'Yeah.' Sarah turned and took the discarded Oxford Mail from the back counter. 'Here.'

Lin turned and walked to a window seat. 'Back in a sec.' She put paper and pint on the table, dropped her luggage on the floor, flopped the coat off her shoulders and onto the back of a chair then returned to the bar to pick up the glass of malt. 'Now the day's getting better. Thanks Sarah.'

'No prob. New coat?'

'Yeah. For all the good it did.'

'Home thoughts from abroad, eh?' Lin looked puzzled. 'Leopard print?'

'Oh yes, yeah.'

'And the job?'

'Extinct, just like leopards will be in five years' time.'

'There's cheerful.'

'Sorry. Miserable bitch dialling out. Thanks Sarah.' Lin lifted the glass. 'Really, thanks.'

'When you're a millionaire you can pay me back.' Sarah turned to serve another couple, saving Lin further embarrassment. 'What can I get you?'

Lin took a sip of the malt on her way back to the table then she sat, fumbling in her coat pocket for her mobile phone only to look at the blank screen. *Nothing. You can't possibly have lost it Rene, surely not.'*

She put the phone away, opened the paper and began to read, fussing with the netsuke and releasing a huge sigh as the committed smokers began to drift back into the pub to partake of their other drug.

~

Jay and Archie were squatting by the tin sheet which was encircled by white material. Away to their left a large square tent covered the depression, the lights inside silhouetting two of Jay's forensic team like a child's party shadow play. A small generator thrummed some distance away, several floodlights were dotted around the site and two others glowed eerily through the trees from the direction of the dilapidated building.

'Whatever it was it was killed elsewhere then brought to there; barely any blood.'

'But definitely a burial site?'

'No question.'

'Recent?'

'Difficult. Two, possibly three days...possibly more.'

'Around the time of our ditch inhabitant though?'

'Possibly.'

'I thought this was an exact science?'

'It is when it's backed up by laboratory research. Out here it's just another wild stab in the dark.'

'Which is what I reckon happened here.'

'Big jump DCI Arnold, big jump.' Jay looked at him. 'Yes alright, I'll concede the possibility. The stains in the soil do indicate blood, as does your find on this tin sheet, but you'll have to wait until I get all and sundry back to base for confirmation of species.'

'But if the two lots of leather match...?'

'That further corroborates your initial suggestion, yes, but I repeat, it has to run through the procedures.'

'If it's not human then animal...?'

'Vegetable, mineral?' Jay looked at Archie's puzzled face. 'Never mind, before your time, and you'll still have to wait for the test results.'

Archie looked towards the old building. 'What if the blood over there matches the blood here?'

'If.' Jay finished scraping samples from the tin sheet. 'What if they're different blood types? This could be from someone or something just brushing past that's totally unconnected to that found in the depression. Might not even be blood, just a colour coincidence.'

'Don't believe in coincidences.'

'Then you'll find disillusionment and heartache will be your constant companions.'

Archie stopped chewing. 'Need to know Jay, need to know.'

'Do you have no patience?' Jay thought for a moment or two. 'Tomorrow, possibly Friday. Nice find Archie. Excellent detective work, particularly these marks on the tin. As a reward I'll do my best for tomorrow.'

The chewing of gum resumed. 'Thanks Jay.'

'Ms. Cresson!' Anita Cresson, slight of build, small of stature and also white suited, poked her head out of the tent. 'Bring some zip-locks, temporary marker posts and a marker pen please.'

Anita soon joined them, handing the white plastic markers and pen over Jay's shoulder. 'Evening Archie.'

Archie folded back his flop of hair. 'Hi Anita. How's tricks?'

'Not as clever as yours apparently.'

Jay cast a glance Anita's way. 'Careful you two, familiarity breeds attempt. What file number are you up to Miss Cresson?'

'L-Lima zero-one-two. Site Four.'

'Right, this is M-Mike zero-zero-one through to,' he scanned the area, 'Zero-zero-seven. Site Five.' She began to note the information down on an i-Pad. 'And can we make sure they're photographed in the next few minutes please?'

'We can.'

'Can you also swap these temps for yellow cards and tape but only after...' Jay stopped as he saw Anita's look.

'Thank goodness you're here Mister Millar. Never having done this before it's so reassuring to have it fully mansplained to me.'

'Point taken. Apologies.' He turned to Archie. 'I used to strike fear into the hearts of my underlings, but now...? Anything else you'd like to show us detective, save us the trouble of doing any further searches?'

'Would it be OK for me to have another look at the dog? I came away fast so's not to mess the site up.'

'There's a first.'

'What?'

'You asking for permission. Yes, as long as you put that hood back up, but don't get in the way, we're still in the process, you know?'

Archie pulled the hood up-and-over as he indicated the depths of the wood. 'Yup, right. Perhaps Anita would like to accompany me, keep me out of mischief?'

'Over my dead body.' Jay looked around. 'Or two possibly. Make do with Maurice.'

'Poor substitute.' Archie winked at Anita as he left. 'Me and Maurice it is then.'

After a few seconds Jay looked back at the tin sheet. 'Do another scraping would you Ms. Cresson, as a back-up to mine.' Jay took out a small notebook and began to sketch the site.

Anita gently scraped the material into a zip lock before standing to watch Jay for a moment or two. 'Photography.'

'Pardon?'

'Photography. Photographs? They've invented the camera, gone digital, and now...? I-Pads! No more waiting at the chemist.' She indicated his notebook, 'Or relying on an artist's impression.'

Jay gave a shy smile. 'Old habits. Helps me fix it in the memory...old habits. Apologies for my remark of earlier, about familiarity, you're over twenty-one, etc...'

'Very chivalrous, but yes, definitely over twenty-one.'

'It's just... He's good you know, Archie. Amongst the best I've ever worked with and I've been doing this for some years, but when it comes to the ladies? He's got a bit of history there if HQ locker-room gossip is anything to go by.'

'Very good of you to take such an interest Mister Millar.'

'I'd do the same for anyone in my team.'

'He's not married I gather.'

'Not anymore no...' Jay saw the look in Anita's eye, a look of surprise mixed with intrigue and he closed down, taking the zip-lock out of her hand. 'You want to know the details then ask him. Not mine to share.'

'Curiouser and curiouser. Until you'd started talking I'd got no interest whatsoever, but now?'

'That's it, pile the guilt on my narrow shoulders.' Jay put the finishing touches to his sketch in silence then closed the notebook. 'All done. Back to work now Ms. Cresson, banish all sordid thoughts through honest labour.'

'Easier said than done. These camping trips will never be quite the same again.' She disappeared inside the tent, closing the flap behind her.

Jay watched Archie approach. 'Any other startling finds?'

'You've had a look yourself?'

'I have, I just want to hear what you've gleaned that may be extra.'

'I'd say that poor wee fella over there was a corgi, Pembroke type.'

'You recognised the breed?'

'I do, and two other things. It didn't die there, or of old age. Maurice let me have a close-up. My guess is the dog was flung in there much like our lady in the ditch.' Archie exchanged old gum for new.

Jay wrinkled his nose. 'Disgusting habit.'

'You've said.'

'For all the difference it's made. The dog...what did your close-up make of its possible demise?'

'Been mauled about by another creature, probably a dog, and also by an amateur butcher.'

'Agreed.'

'My guess? Your chaps won't find a microchip.'

'We concur. Pembroke-type corgi, microchip possibly removed, and the sufferer of several bites caused by a bigger canine.'

Archie ceased chewing. 'Are we talking bigger as in Labrador size or bigger as in wolf size?'

'Last wolf in the UK was killed in sixteen-eighty.'

'Ewan Cameron, Perthshire, yes, but this one?'

Millar smiled at him. 'Very good. 'Twas indeed that noble Scot. However, this one was killed about a week ago so not by Mister Cameron's wolf, but not a Labrador either.'

Archie resumed his chewing. 'No, a Lab would've licked it to death. Mastiff?'

'Possibly. We'll be able to narrow it down a little when we measure the bite size.'

'If the micro-chip's gone that means whoever did this didn't want the dog's owner identified.'

'If. At present that's conjecture.'

'Doesn't make it wrong though does it?' Archie nodded in the direction of earlier findings. 'Those fox scats might contain traces that'll double-down on whether it was a human corpse who last lodged under this tin.'

'As macabre as it is, yes. The nourishment Reynard took over the last few days may well contain human DNA. Possibly.'

'You'll be inspecting it?'

'We will,' Jay held out some zip-locks, 'Providing you collect.'

'On it.' Archie held up his used gloves. 'You got fresh gloves?'

'Ms. Cresson!' Anita reappeared from the tent. 'Some gloves please, for our resident sleuth.'

Anita ducked back into the tent then reappeared holding out a pair of surgical gloves. 'Thanks.' Archie smiled at her. 'Prophylactics for the paws.'

'Do you want help putting them on?'

Jay interjected. 'Enough! Work to do!'

A grinning Anita took Archie's old gloves off him and returned to the tent as Archie pulled on the new gloves and moved round the site collecting the piles of fox faeces, vocalising his thought process as he went. 'So, two corpses then. One in a ditch, one in a grave. Chap out for a stroll, walking his dog, knows the woods, not on a bus route and no abandoned car so local. Meets up with a stray...a stray wandering about on keepered land? But, if the big dog killed the little one, who does for this fella?' He handed across the plastic bags to Jay and spoke with authority. 'Four things come to mind Jay.' Archie counted them out with raised fingers. 'One, our corgi didn't meet its end by a fox snare. Two, if it was keepers did this, they'd not have left it there, they'd have chucked it on the road, blamed traffic. Three, with your preliminaries about bite-size it wasn't savaged by fox or badger. Four, I've not met a dog yet that's capable of performing surgery on itself. I reckon the poor sod was killed by a distinctly unfriendly bullmastiff, that or a pit bull. They're the ones with as near the bite-size of a wolf.'

'Where do you pick all this up from Archie, that's what intrigues.'

'Nowhere...everywhere. You learn something new every day if you pay attention.' He peeled off the gloves and handed them to Jay. 'And we've enough here to get us started. Right, having been instrumental in the evidence gathering I'm gonna get out of this ridiculous suit, check on progress then track back along the lane the way our killers came, round to the other side of this woodland see what stories it can tell. I'll rely on you and your team of ghouls to fill me in on specifics...tomorrow, if it please your highness.' Archie pushed back the hood, rearranged his flop of hair and began to leave. 'Call me if anything else turns up.'

'What, you mean like another body?'

'Something like that Jay, yeah. Tarra.' With the briefest of waves Archie left the scene.

~

Tim leant forward in his seat and fixed Lin with a stare. 'You did what?'

'I gave it back.'

'Have you lost your senses?'

'No! It just didn't seem right to do anything else.'

'That's the daftest thing you've done since your fruit escapade.'

'That wasn't daft, it needed to be done, the bees...'

Tim smiled at her. 'And your determination is laudable, but I'm not talking bees I'm talking bread, cash, and in your situation you gave it all back.'

'Of course.'

Tim shifted in his seat and picked up his pint. 'Can you believe this Lenny?'

Eleanor picked up the cross-questioning that had been taking place ever since Lin had mentioned about the train journey. 'With our Lin and her gran? Yes, I can. You forget, I knew Nanny Betty from way back. How much was it Lin?'

Lin looked around the table at her transfixed audience feeling very exposed. 'I...I didn't count it.'

Vasiri leaned in. 'How thick again?'

Lin demonstrated with her part-closed fist. 'About so.'

'All in twenties?'

'From what I could tell... You're not making me feel any better about this Vas, you know?'

'Neither should I. Me, I'd've kept it. There must've been a thousand or more quid there.'

'It wasn't mine to take. Anyway, it turned out it belonged to a chap who looked like he'd earned it working for a living, an Irish fella, so...'

'Lot of money for digging trenches.'

'That's very racist Vas, even for you.'

'We're allowed to be Lin, you and me. The colour of our skin gives us certain rights.'

'No it doesn't.'

Eleanor cut in. 'Never mind the semantics, the money, the man...?'

'I'd have felt wretched with every pound I spent Lenny.' Lin stood up. 'Tell you what, as it's been my bad I'll get the next round in.' She looked into the chasm of her purse. 'As long as it's halves.'

Vasiri patted Lin's coat on the bench. 'Can only afford halves but can afford to kit herself out with a new wardrobe.'

'One coat equals a wardrobe? That could only be a man talking.' Lin clipped her purse shut. 'Had to buy it Vaz.' She took the crumpled letter from the coat pocket and waved it in his face. 'Interview and all that. Good impressions? Wasted, it turns out.'

Vasiri took the letter and uncreased it. 'Don't know why you wanted to work for Braxhams anyway, they're just another arm of big agribusiness.'

Lin was regretting the turn in the conversation. 'I know, I know, but...it was in their research department.' She looked at their disbelieving faces. 'I just thought if I got in there I could make a small difference, you know? Change things from within.'

'And get well paid for it too.'

This last hurt Lin and she reacted. 'And why not, eh? I mean, what's wrong with that? I'm behind with my council tax by two months, I've been surviving on baked beans, white bread and scrape for the past fortnight and I'm sick of always having to scrounge off you lot, can't you see that? I'm just trying to get a bit of dignity back into my life...so, I went to Braxhams.'

Eleanor leant across and put her hand on Lin's. 'With your background you should be in the thick of it, full-time in conservation and then changing things... Your bee protest; there! That's just a sample of what you can do. The make-up, the fruit? Brilliant!'

'I didn't do the make-up, Jenni did it for me.'

'And it was excellent.'

'So it should be, it's her job... I know I've got skills I can offer but no one's buying Lennie...'

'I know.' Eleanor tried to calm the moment. 'You try, which is more than we ever do. You're a vegetarian crusader and what with your African background and all that...' Eleanor's voice faded as Vasiri gave her a withering look.

Lin stood, snatched the letter from Vas and began to rip it up, her emotions breaking her speech. 'It's not background Eleanor it's my history! My family's, mine and Rene's, you all know that!'

There was a long, embarrassed silence until Vas spoke again. 'You still not know where she is?' Lin shook her head. 'No phone calls?'

'Nothing.'

Eleanor joined in. 'How long since you last saw her?'

Lin sighed. 'Months... Months, a year at least. Look... Sorry all, it's just a bit fresh...my interview, no contact from Rene, and then this.' She picked up the newspaper from off the bench seat and dropped it onto the table. 'This shit doesn't help.'

The group gathered round and read the headline. "Roazhon Foods Secure China Deal". Vaz looked up. 'What's this to do with you?'

'Roazhon Foods? Do none of you see the connection?'

There was a short silence, then Lisa suddenly tapped the tabletop with her finger. 'Oh...hang on. Roazhon Foods...your bee protest!'

'Well spotted.'

Vaz twisted the paper round. 'Oh OK. I get it. They're the company that forged that tie-in with that drug company... Mistral Pharmaceuticals; something about a pesticide they were testing?'

Tim joined in. 'Yeah, yeah, I remember some bits about it now. Not a pesticide, it was herbicide! They'd been using a... what was it Lin?'

'A neonicotinoid.'

'That's it, a neonicotinoid! They sprayed cereal crops with it, and it killed millions of bees. Was it his farm, his fields?'

Lin nodded. 'Ha! Not likely, no, but it was in the US and now Roazhon's lobbying on behalf of Mistral to get it licensed in the UK.'

Vaz pointed to the photo accompanying the article. 'Is that him? Your bee nemesis?'

'The one and only.' Lin sat down again. 'He says here that using blanket sprays would increase yields and feed the starving millions. Ha! His cattle millions more like.' She dropped the torn shreds of the letter onto the table. 'Look, see? Now it's all gone.' She stood again. 'Drinks...halves.'

Tim reached into his back pocket, pulling out his wallet and a mobile phone. 'Leave it Lin. I'll get these.'

He offered her a ten-pound note but Lin's eyes latched on to the mobile, glad of the shift in focus. 'I was going to say no, but if you can afford one of those.'

Vasiri saw it too. 'You robbed a bank?'

'No. Why would you assume that? It's the new job, ah...sorry Lin.' He smiled at her. 'The new job requires me to have one and I chose this. I need to be available pretty much all the time, internet, e-mails, conference calls and stuff, so I got one with the most bells and whistles. Means I'm contactable all the time, GPS tracking...'

'It's called Big Brother.'

'No Lisa, it's called connectivity. They're an international company and they pay for the calls so I thought I'd splash out on the latest model.' He looked up. 'This isn't helping you Lin, is it?'

'It's fine. I'm pleased for you Tim, really I am.' Lyn took her basic mobile from her pocket and held it alongside Tim's. 'And I've got one too, all it needs now is for Rene to call me back and it'll be doing exactly what it's supposed to.' She took the money. 'And with you so flush, I think I'll just help myself to that tenner. Thanks Tim.'

Lisa offered her another five pounds. 'That'll run to some nibbles, I skipped tea tonight.'

Lin paused and looked round the table. 'Where would I be without you lot?'

They all spoke over one another. 'Employed.' 'At the AA meeting.' 'Richer.'

'Thanks Lisa but...' Lin gave the five-pound note back. 'I skipped tea too and I think I can cover the rest.' She collected the glasses and made her way to the bar. 'Same-old-same-old Sarah, pints please, and can I have three packs of crisps, two plain, one salt and vinegar, a pack of cheese thingies. oh, and two packs of pork scratchings as well?'

'An evening of fine dining ahead then.'

'Indeed. All we want is a tumbler of meths to wash it down and the meal will be complete.' Lin gazed around the room. 'Busy tonight.'

A woman got up from the far end of the seated area and moved over to the bar as Sarah began to line up the drinks before removing snacks from under-the-counter boxes and top-of-the-counter card holders. 'Yes, well, busier than usual, but if it weren't for you regulars... That's sixteen forty Lin, please.'

Lin put the note on the counter then sorted through her purse for change as Sarah turned to the other woman. 'Yes love, what can I get you?'

'I'll have another half of the Mayflower please, and I'll get those as well.'

Lin turned toward her, the look of the misheard fashioning her face. 'Sorry?'

'Your drinks and snacks, I'll pay for those as well. You're the lady who ended up out of pocket on the train earlier, yes?'

Lin's inbred suspicious nature held sway as she feigned ignorance. 'The train?'

'Yes. We were on the same train.' She handed over a twenty-pound note. 'You found a considerable number of these if I'm not mistaken.' Sarah looked at Lin for a second or two to gain permission then took the note. 'Not much by comparison, but

I think your honesty deserves some form of reward, and the gentleman you returned the money-roll to wasn't going to do that.'

'Erm...yes.' Lin opened up a little. 'So, you were the lady in my carriage.'

'Yes. My sister works up on the big estate.' Lin nodded. 'In the kitchens. She's house cook. I'm on my way to spend a few days with her, holiday sort of.' She could see Lin was looking to be away. 'Your friends are getting thirsty. Best get back to them.'

'Yes...and thank you. That's very kind.'

'My pleasure.' The woman was already moving back to her chair as Sarah closed the till drawer.

'Your change?'

The woman looked back. 'Have one yourself dear. Alright?'

'Yes, er...thank you.' Sarah and Lin exchanged puzzled glances and Lin moved back to the table with the drinks on a tray.

Eleanor picked up her pint first as Lisa made a grab for the bags. 'Pork scratchings, excellent choice.'

Tim watched her for a second. 'If you've not eaten yet they'll give you chronic indigestion, you know that don't you?'

Lisa carried on eating. 'Don't care, they're scrummy.' She turned to Lin, speaking with mouth full. 'Who was that lady you were talking to?'

Lin gave a surprised Tim his ten pounds back. 'Who was it said, 'the reward of a thing done well is the having done it', or something like that?'

'Emerson.'

'Thanks, Vaz. Well, he was wrong.'

~

Walking to the forensics truck, Arnold climbed the short set of treads and retrieved his shoes. He was almost back at the car when his mobile rang. 'DCI Arnold...'

'Archie?'

'Oh Adam, hi. Sorry, I didn't spot the caller ID.'

'You still at the cemetery?'

'Yeah.'

'And you got signal again? Amazing.'

'Yeah, but it's only 'cos I'm close to the forensics truck. Jay got Bedford IT to put up a booster aerial because he's important people so here it's not too bad. Everywhere else is like Dances with Wolves but minus the Indians...and the wolves according to Jay.'

'Relief all round then. Minus the Indians? So, Kanjara gone too has she?'

'Funny. No, she's still with the search team.'

'That'll please you.'

'You're reading far too much into this.'

'Yeah, right. Anything more for the pot?'

'Bits.' Archie reached the passenger side of the car, released the locks and put his shoes down. 'Have you briefed all those who missed my last call?'

'As far as I can. You want to go on speaker with this one as well?'

'No, couldn't stand a repetition of the constant criticism. Just relay it, OK?'

'Yeah.'

'Right. Update. They're looking for a discarded micro-chip from the dog as we speak, not holding my breath. But, sunny side up, the supposed bloodstain on the tin sheet may well be blood. We'll know tomorrow. More cheery news from you I trust?'

'Yup. We've got a positive ID on the girl in the photo.'

'Excellent! Tell me all.'

'Her and the girl in the ditch, they're not just sisters...they're twins.'

Archie punched the air. 'Knew it!'

'Linden and Renata Lea.'

'Wow. OK.'

'And the surviving twin's a bit whacky as well.'

'Whacky? What was it brought her to our attention?'

There was a short silence before Adam spoke. *'OK, brace yourself. Not the thing you want to hear right now, I know, but, do you remember, three or so months past, some lass got herself reported in the Brackley Advertiser which got picked up by the Oxford Gazette, The Beavis Beat column? It was about a stunt she did in Enville village square, headline was 'Mystery Buzz About Bee Woman'?'*

Archie spoke like a man waiting to be ambushed. 'Right. Go on.'

'Well, Beavis also mentioned he'd tried to get her onto that daily radio programme of his on Radio NorthOx-Xtra. Made a lot of her reluctance to be interviewed.' Reeve heard the continuing silence and let it hang.

'No, I didn't know that...not one of the faithful. I didn't realise you were a fan.'

'I'm not. Clive, that bearded chap in the garage at HQ, he's got his radio tuned to the local stuff, so I hear it sometimes when I'm there...'

There was a silence full of memory on both ends of the phone before Archie continued, 'No, missed that one. What of it?' He unzipped and began slowly shrugging off the suit as he listened, the phone changing hands to accommodate.

'If you'd seen the article you'd remember, trust me. The photos were of a woman dressed in a see-through body stocking; face painted to look like a bee. Covered herself in fruit then invited people to help themselves so she was gradually revealed. When all the fruit was gone it uncovered her naked body which was painted to look like a skeleton, very realistic. A protest about the use of pesticides and what the death of millions of bees would do to our food supply and humanity.'

'She's not wrong.' Archie stopped undressing and turned to face the car, the wrinkled suit around his ankles as if caught in flagrante.

'No. Well, whatever, those photos Jay found in her pocket aren't of the victim they're of her twin, hairstyles give it away, one short one long. Pictures in the Gazette were of our lass lying down and decked out in plums and pears, bit of pineapple here and here, and a couple of our lads recognised her.'

'Miss nothing even remotely female do they?'

'Nope, and neither did Beavis. Made a lot of her gender and race, tried to dig into her background, that's probably why she gave him the F.O. about the radio thing.'

'Yeah.' Archie rested his elbows on the roof as he gazed into the woodland. 'Well, given his past MO and his warnings about immigrants flooding our shores etcetera, in her case naked immigrants, he'd take it all personally.'

'Yup, but to be fair to Beavis, even though I know you don't want to be, it seems there wasn't much else to gather. From foreign parts and suggestions that she'd come over as a kid, but anything helpful from her was in short supply.'

'That it?'

'Pretty well.'

'Pretty thin.'

'Yup. Oh, and there's nothing on the NCDB about her either.'

'Right. Anything on our victim's missing mobile?'

'Working on it. Nothing on the major network supply lists for contracts so she was probably on Pay-Gee and that makes life difficult 'cos it doesn't include the intrusion into your life of an all-singing-all-dancing piece of kit.'

'Maybe they chose pay-gee precisely because of that. No forms, no records.'

'But why? What's to hide? They're obviously low-profile; even the Gazette struggled with that one.'

Archie turned round and continued disrobing, heeling off the wellingtons then standing on the excess material of each leg to draw them over his socks. 'Pair of rebels then. Like sister like sister.'

'Would seem so.' Reeve paused before committing. 'And, talking of the Gazette...'

Archie sat in the passenger seat to put on his shoes, cradling the phone between cheek and shoulder again. 'I sense trouble.'

'Not wrong. They've been on the phone to here.'

'You mean Beavis has been on the phone.'

'Yeah. Sorry to keep bringing him up.'

'Like a bit of sick.' Reeve gave space for Archie's reactions, until eventually Archie cleared his throat. 'Right. Sorry Adam.'

'Me that's sorry.'

'No. I need to get over it.' Archie shook his head for clearance. 'Right, the Gazette... Beavis.'

'They've got wind of the kerfuffle and he wants to know what we can tell him.'

'Nothing, we can tell him bloody nothing! Jesus, how do they find out so fast?'

''Cos they monitor our frequencies, you know they do.'

'Yeah, yeah. Probably listening in on this call too. Right. We need to keep this quiet Adam, tread very carefully.' Archie stood and began tying his laces, lifting each foot onto the door sill. The intricacies of the task got the better of him and the phone slipped from his shoulder grip, bounced off his foot and onto the ground. 'Bollocks!' He snaffled it up. 'You still there?'

'Yup. What happened?'

'Dropped the phone, I thought I might have cut you off. Thing is, what the Gazette and Beavis don't know is it's the lack of information that's the story here.' He thought for a moment. 'Right, good work on the ID Adam. You got an address?'

'Yup. Gazette reporter got it off her, er...fifteen, Mayflower Rise, Pool Heath, Chorleton. About eighteen or twenty miles from where you are.'

'Then surely the sisters must've met up?'

'Gotta think that, haven't you?'

'Unless neither knew where the other was, that or they'd fallen out.' Archie looked at his watch. 'Twenty-past...' He was silent for a few seconds.

'You still there?'

'Yeah sorry, just thinking.'

'*Thought I heard something.*'

'Ha! Right, we can't leave it. Local press will be all over it by the morning if not before, and the nationals will soon follow when they sniff a partially dressed woman is part of the story. Last thing we want is for one twin to read of the other twin's demise in the gutter press.' He paused again. 'Right. Sorry to drop this on you Adam, can you make your way over to Chorleton, break the news and get what you can out of the sister?' He heard the silence and knew its meaning. 'I know... sorry.'

'*No, no that's cool.*'

'Liar.'

'*Yeah. Right, and you?*'

'I'll get on to the Gazette...to Beavis.'

'*Now it's my turn; you sure?*'

'Yeah. We've got previous so I guess he's mine. I'll stall him, get him to let me have whatever background they've got...' Archie's voice tailed off.

'*Look, Archie...do you want me to do it?*'

'No...'

'*''Cos I will, y'know.*'

'I know you would, I know. No, you've enough on with the twin. That'll be shitty enough. Me meeting up with him would've happened at some point anyway; the jobs we both do, bound to. I'll tell him I'll make a statement tomorrow afternoon but just to him, like a scoop. Right, onward. You get over to Chorleton.'

'*Right.*'

'We'll not get support from Family Liaison this time of the day so best take a WPC with you.' He scanned the collection of police. 'Kanjara?'

'*Yeah, spot on.*'

'Text me the address an' I'll pass it on. In the meantime, I'm gonna take a peek over the other side of the woodland, might give us some more ideas. I'll ask Kanga to contact Family Liaison on her way over to you. They can help pick up the pieces tomorrow.'

'*Right.*'

'Oh, and do the neighbours as well.'

'*Will do.*'

'And, thanks again Adam...on Beavis I mean.'

'*Anytime.*'

Archie shut down the call and, gathering his scattered memories alongside his discarded clothing, dropped them all into the boot. Pocketing the phone, he retraced his steps into the woodland. Jay was still there deep in thought and Archie watched him for few seconds before breaking his concentration. 'Jay!'

A startled Jay dropped some of the cards and looked across at Archie. 'Some warning would help, creeping up on a fellow like that!'

'Sorry. Is tomorrow still good for the results from your ghoulary?'

'If my heart holds out yes. Early.'

'For real?'

'Ms. Cresson and I have decided to work through. The lady's body is going to be moved across to the facility within the next half hour, we've done all we can for her on-site. Rest of the team can finish up here. If you call in early we'll have a preliminary sheet filled in by then.'

'Sure? You'll 'ave had no sleep.'

'Neither will you.' Jay bent and retrieved the dropped cards. 'We know time's not your friend on this one Archie.'

'What a team.'

'The very word, team.'

'Thanks Jay, you're the best.'

'Tell the Home Office that will you?'

This last caused a smile as Archie returned to the lane where he spotted Kanjara standing with another couple of the search team at the canteen. One arm was resting on the counter, a plastic beaker of tea in her hand, the white suit unzipped to the waist. 'Kanjara?'

'Evening Sir.' chorused the group.

'Evening each.' Archie's text-alert sounded. 'Could you spare me a moment please?'

'Sure Sir...Archie.' She left her two companions, both of whom mouthed the words, 'Kanga? Archie?' and exchanged knowing nods and glances.

'Look, do me a favour would you, well two actually?'

'As long as they're both legal.'

'Ha! Look, I know the evening's getting on and this is not what you came here for, but I'd like you to support Adam. He's going over to break the news to the sister of the deceased, it can't be left 'cos the Gazette's sniffing round. And can I also ask you to contact Family Liaison before you clock off? They'll be long gone but leave a message with the details.'

'Yes of course.'

'The signal's good by the forensics truck so stick around there when you contact them, it's not the sort of conversation you'll want to be cut off in the middle of.'

'Yes, thanks.'

Archie flipped open his mobile. 'That's the address.' He turned the phone towards her and she wrote the details in her notebook.

'I know that estate. Sixties build, seen better days.'

'Thought you might.'

'I'll get across there now. Right, goodnight Archie.'

''Night Kanga, go steady.' Archie watched her for a few seconds before clicking through the numbers on his phone. The name BeavisGazette came up. He looked at it for some seconds before clicking the call button. The ring tone sounded and Archie sighed long and loud before a voice on the other end spoke.

'Hello, Beavis Beat, Robert Beavis speaking.'

'Hello Robert, sorry about the hour. It's Archie...Arnold.'

The silence at the other end of the line spoke volumes and for several seconds there was nothing until the reply came back, flat and distant. 'Hi Detective Chief Inspector, what can I do for you?'

'Wasn't sure you'd still be awake.'

'Like you, always on duty.'

'I've heard from my staff you've been bothering them. Can we chat briefly?'

~

Thirty-six, Penfore Close, Wynington was thrown together in a time when no expense was spent. Backing onto a mine-waste dumping ground the whole place leaked damp, a damp that seeped in through the cat-flaps of pensioner ladies and rotted the prefabricated concrete used to construct these headstones to the dispossessed.

Matt and Chris stood quietly outside the frosted half-glazed back door of the bungalow's Formica-topped, tile-floored kitchen; the Neighbourhood Watch sign fixed on the glass a seeming mockery. Chris' surgical-gloved hands held his mobile phone, its light beam aimed tightly at the door lock. Over Matt's shoulder was a small cloth bag, his one hand-held the door handle the other a screwdriver. From somewhere out front and nearby came the laughter only a carefree drunk can release. Chris shut off the light and they froze, waiting for the noise to fade before he switched it back on. Matt freed the last of the screws from the door plate then, flipping the latch open with the screwdriver blade, the two men slipped into the kitchen and Matt placed the shoulder bag onto the work surface. Chris stood in silent vigil as Matt illuminated the kitchen with his head torch, halting it momentarily on the mains box positioned over the low-level fridge before flicking the beam on to the gas stove.

'Perfect.' Matt stepped over to the stove and angled it slightly away from the wall. Lifting the slack of the flexible metal-and-rubber gas pipe onto the top of the stove he set the alarm button on his wristwatch and whispered to Chris. 'Two minutes thirty. Camera on?'

Chris held up his mobile phone and nodded.

Matt pressed the count-down button and they crossed the kitchen, slipping into the hallway like smoke. Matt pointed ahead. 'You do those two rooms. Photo any specials, check for smoke alarms. I'll do in here.'

They split up, rummaging as only professionals can, then met in the hallway as Matt checked his watch. 'One-fifty. All good?'

'Yeah. Definitely him, photos of that corgi all over the place.'

'In there too. I'll do the other room you do the hallway. Check that hallstand, collect any post and meet me in the kitchen.'

They split up once more then rejoined one minute later at the kitchen doorway. 'Fifty seconds. Letters?'

Chris nodded and patted his pocket. 'Just the one.'

'Smoke alarms?'

'Nope.'

'Tight-fisted council; good.' Matt pointed to the kitchen cupboards. 'You up top, me below and white goods.'

They searched towards the back door; the watch alarm sounded. Matt silenced it, opened the door and re-set it. 'Pick me up fifty yards down the street in four minutes. I'll set the fire trap.'

'What you usin'?'

'The usual. Some chemicals, lighter fuel, a low rate capacitor.'

'Blimey, you still old school then? When did you last use one of them then?'

'Six, eight years ago? Served me well over the years, last one in my box anyway, so... Should give you a full two minutes to get clear before the power blows it, the gas pipe will do the rest, just don't hang about after you've flicked the switch.' He held up a small rubber bung. 'If it's you who sets it off all you'll need to do is pull this out of the gas pipe here. Right?' Chris nodded. 'I'll leave the door off the latch.' Chris left as Matt re-started the four-minute countdown, switched off the power and began to lay the fire trap.

A final check and Matt stepped outside, replaced the doorplate and handle and pressed the door firmly closed onto a wodge of Blue Tack. Wiping down as insurance, he slipped out of the yard gate and along the street to where Chris was waiting, engine running.

Matt stepped in as his watch alarm went off.

'Away.'

They were gone.

~

'**F**ifteen Mayflower Rise, Pool Heath...' DC Reeve leant forward and looked through the windscreen. 'There's welcoming.'

All was clothed in grey with just the odd square of lighted, curtained window scatter-gunning the expanse of neglect. Even the majority of fluorescent ceiling lights along the walkways had given up, leaving inkspots of trouble for any late night homecomers to negotiate. He sighed as his eye swept across the brooding surroundings. *Christ. What a dump.* He looked at his phone. *Mayflower Rise? Who the hell names these places?* Odd clumps of neglected, unkempt rhododendron dotted the ground below the balconies. *And that's what passes as soft landscaping out here in the cultural wasteland; just hiding places for muggers.* A car rolled up behind him breaking Reeve's train of thought. He got out. 'Evening again Kanga.'

'Evening Adam.'

'Glad he chose you. Turning out alright this, despite the mission.'

'Nice of you to say so.'

'Might not seem it, but you've got Archie's seal of approval.'

'I'll thank him when I see him tomorrow.' She paused, smiled. 'He seems alright.'

'Archie? Out of the top draw, and I can tell he likes you.'

'You've already said, and this is becoming embarrassing. We're here because? Sister to...?'

'Because someone has died, sister to the deceased. My guess is Miss Lea has no idea yet. Done a live one before?'

Kanjara nodded. 'Once.'

'You've done the training course though?'

'I have. As much use as a celery shotgun on a bank job.'

'Yeah. PowerPoint's a wonderful thing in the snug safety of a lecture room. What was the live one?'

'Six-year-old kid out with his eight-year-old sister who was supposedly looking out for him. He drowned in a duck pond. Harrowing wasn't the word.'

'Jesus... Well that should prepare you nicely for this. This'll be my sixth an' they just keep on giving.' He smiled thinly.

'Lucky you. I've contacted Family Liaison and left a message which they won't pick it up 'til the morning.'

'That'll be well after the papers come out. The last thing Archie will want is his 'pal' Beavis from the local rag crawling all over it.'

'They not get on?'

'Let's just say they've got form; previous.' Reeve closed up. 'Not my story to tell.' He looked around for the non-existent cavalry. 'Can't be left I s'pose can it?' Kanga shook her head and Reeve rubbed his palms together. 'Right well, best get cracking, delay won't revive the corpse.' He snatched a glance at his watch. 'Gone eleven now so she may not thank us for the wake-up, even before we tell her the whys and wherefores.' Reeve scanned the flats. 'Fifteen...so...over that side and up on the first balcony.'

They moved from the dubious safety of the intermittent, widely spaced streetlights into the dubious safety of the intermittent, deep shadow of the poorly lit buildings.

'Oh, fuck it! Sorry Kanga.' Adam lifted his foot up. 'Why is it they never smell 'til you step in them?' He attempted to wipe the firmly squished dog turd from off his left shoe onto what passed as grass but only succeeded in smearing it further along the sole and upper. 'Pity they don't make glue like this...bloody hell but that stinks.' Kanga stifled a laugh. 'Tell you what, when we get there you go in first. I'll hover in the hallway. If she doesn't throw up at the news she'll throw up at the smell.'

'Neat bit of footwork there Adam.'

'No, really, I'll be right behind you as support, promise. It'll be better coming from a woman anyhow...'

'Yeah, right.'

Just before they reached the wide, dark steps, Reeve found a hollowed-out bike rut that held some water and he slipped his shoe into it before re-wiping it on a patch of grass. Kanga looked back down the steps at him and sighed. 'What are you like?' She moved up and along the walkway, Adam climbing the steps behind her, before she halted in front of a badly chipped, once green door. 'Fifteen, Adam.'

Reeve arrived on the balcony. 'Give it a knock.'

She did so, her action causing the door to swing back. 'It's open...' She stepped across the threshold. 'Hello? It's the police Miss...?'

Two shots blasted out from the hallway in quick succession and Kanga half staggered half fell back to the balcony wall then flopped backwards, over the edge and away down the drop. Reeve was rooted to the spot; no breath; no movement; then he rushed forward.

'Kanga! Kanjara...Kanga!'

His quick glimpse over the balcony wall to fix on her crooked position amongst the spindled shrubbery coincided with the exit from the flat of a black-clothed man wearing a skull face mask. He exploded onto the balcony firing once more as he crossed the door's threshold, hitting Reeve in the chest. Reeve dropped like a pole-axed horse, the force of the bullet knocking all the wind out of him before sitting him down; after a short pause he dropped onto his back. The pain was searing, all consuming. The man's backlit shadow fell across him as Reeve lifted his hand then focussed on the raised firearm.

'Hel...' The fourth shot went into Reeve's head and darkness took him.

Along the balcony walkway a door opened and an elderly lady stepped out, illuminated by the stab of light from her hallway.

'Go back to y' bed granny! Nothin' to see here.' The man waved the gun and she stepped rapidly back, closing off light and pity.

Like a yawn spreading through a crowd, other distant doors opened as the querulous shouts of residents replaced the blasted airspace as the man made a rapid retreat along the balcony, down the steps and away as the darkness took him.

~

Lin watched as Sarah collected their empty glasses, dropping discarded snack packets into a plastic rubbish bag draped over her arm. After a short pause Lin ventured, 'Well, that's dinner finished courtesy of the mystery woman over there.' Sarah continued tidying. 'Oh, OK. Well, I suppose that'll be closing time.' She glanced at the bar clock. 'Eleven o'clock...barely. Seems the suggestion from management is we'd best all be making a move then.'

The group grunted agreement as Sarah spoke. 'Glad your sensitivity monitor's on and working, and just look at the muck in here.' Sarah picked up the tattered remnants of the letter and homed in on the heading. 'Braxton's?'

'Remains of my failure at joining the ranks of the employed.'

'But, Braxton's Lin? Aren't they pesticide manufact...?'

Eleanor stepped on the conversation. 'We've done that one Sarah, OK?'

'To death,' added Vaz.

Sarah looked round at them. 'Oh OK, got it. Their loss I'd say Lin.' She dropped the torn shreds into the bag, 'Best place for it.'

'Yeah, right. I'll tell myself that when the tallyman calls next Friday.'

This shut down anything further and the group gathered up their belongings. Tim looked across at Lin. 'I could always walk you back, you know, to yours. Only twenty minutes away, I could do with the exercise, if...?'

He had that look, Lin recognised it. *And why not? Apart from the free round it's been a shitty day. Comfortable missionary sex with someone I can trust, whose history I know...what's not to like?* She looked across at Tim. *An absolute no-hoper as far as being my life partner but caring and thoughtful as an occasional sex partner.* She smiled in return. 'Yeah, you could. I'd be glad of the company, save me from getting murdered in my bed.' They both laughed. 'But only murdered.'

Sarah rolled her eyes. 'I'd say get a room, but...' She returned to the bar with the loaded tray.

Lin handed her briefcase and carrier bag to Tim. 'Hold this a sec, I just want to thank our anonymous benefactor for the drinks of earlier.' She moved round the curve of the bar to where the woman was still seated, her drink all but finished. She looked up as Lin came over.

'Still here, dear?'

'Yes, well, just going. I only wanted to thank you for my drink of earlier, for our drinks.'

'My pleasure. As I said, I think your honesty earned it. You're local then, from round here I mean?'

Even given their vague acquaintance and the woman's generosity Lin was still guarded with her reply. 'Erm, yes... yes-ish.'

'It's nice and quiet here, isn't it?'

'It's alright. You, you're not local?'

'No, I'm up here visiting my sister, remember?'

'Oh yes, of course.'

'You live nearby Lin? Linda, is it?'

There was a slightly expectant silence then Lin locked fully into her default setting. 'Yeah. Well, must be off. Thank you again...I've got friends waiting.'

'Yes, so I see.'

Lin turned away. 'Goodnight.'

'Yes, I'm about to leave too dear, still got a bit of a journey to do so I'll say goodnight also.'

'Not big on thanks or tearful farewells are you?' Sarah whispered.

Lin made a sour-lemon face as she whispered back, 'Wants to share too much.' Tim was standing by the door with the group of friends, his backpack slung carelessly over one shoulder, Lin's bags in his hand. 'Right, well, we're away then.'

Sarah called over. 'Oh Lin? You've not forgotten about tomorrow? You and me, Cheetham Street market, afternoon tea, on me.'

'No. Three o'clock still good?'

'Will you be up? Not you Tim, Lin.'

This brought stifled laughter from Vaz. ''Course I will cheeky.' She waved the card. 'I'll have been to the cash and carry before that. We'll be up by nine...' She looked at Tim, 'eleven.'

'Easy by three then, and make sure you bring that card with you otherwise Mum'll be on my case.'

Lin placed the card in her pocket. 'I will. Thanks again for that, a lifesaver. 'Night.' Sarah picked up the glass cloth and mouthed, 'Jammy bitch'. Lin put her tongue out in reply as the woman, without finishing her drink, also got up and left by the side door, rummaging in her handbag as she went. Lin took her plastic carrier and briefcase off Tim and they stepped into the chill night air. She shuddered. 'Lord but that's come on cold.' The group agreed, snuggled chins into coat lapels and began to go their separate ways, calling good nights to each other until Lin and Tim were left in the car park. In the half light of the pub sign Lin caught the whiff of cigarette smoke. Looking across she could see the lady leaning against the tall, blue-brick wall that formed the boundary of the pub car park. She was fully engaged in a fag-and-phone conversation. 'There's that woman again, on the phone.'

Tim, who was fully preoccupied with the promise of events to come and would have missed a herd of wildebeest crossing the car park, looked at Lin then followed her gaze. 'Oh yeah. Probably on the blower for a taxi. She'll have a long wait, Des only has two cars,' he looked at his watch, 'and the Working Men's Club bingo kicks out around this time.'

As they turned away and began walking along the road Lin threw another glance over her shoulder. 'Wonder where she's from?'

'Well if she's drinking out here of a Tuesday night then I'd reckon from round here.'

'No, she was on the train.' She looked at Tim. 'Do you not listen to anything I say? She's on a visit she said, I told you all earlier. Up at the big house, sister or something...wonder why no one's picked her up by now? Why stay out here this long...? Oh, who cares? Let's get back to Pool Heath for some tea, toast and Marmite and a bit of warmth, I'm feeling chilly.'

'I'll just settle for the bit of warmth.'

Lin shoved Tim playfully on the arm and he exaggerated the force, stumbling into the gutter and gripping his upper arm. She laughed at him. 'Man-up you wimp, there's no way that hurt.'

'No, I know, I just like it when you get physical with me.'

They both laughed as they linked arms and walked away from the lighted embrace of the Red Lion car park and the still-smoking, still-talking woman.

~

Driving away from the hit-and-run site, Archie's eyes flicked from lane to the speedometer and back as he gently pressed the accelerator. *Thirty...five...eight...forty...five... Bugger, not even on full beam, fifty...three... Nope, no good.* He eased back and the car slowed to a more sedate twenty-five. *No way. There's no way you could drive at that speed, not along here and definitely not at night.* He slowed even further as he arrived at a junction and came to a halt. One lane cut sharply away to his right, the other carved a disappearing arc to his left. He considered. *Going right takes me to the opposite side of the wood at the rear of the hit-and-run site and the tin sheet grave.* He looked along the left-hand road and swapped old gum for new. *Yeah, go left, let's just see what's about.* He began driving steadily, beam on full, gear in third.

The lane ambled on, well clipped hedges to his left, woodland to the right with the odd, well maintained field gate bearing the no entry labels of twenty-first century's continuation of the nineteenth century enclosure act. *Our government man must own all this.* Driving further along he came to a wide track which dissolved into the inked horizon and he pulled up at its gravelled entrance. *Are those buildings away up there?* Archie switched off the engine and opened the window. *Is that a dog?* He stepped from the car and walked a short distance before stopping once more to listen. *Yup. Dog or dogs. Hunt kennels? Nah, not enough noise. One starts they all have a go. No gatehouse so this is maybe a back entrance to the home farm.* He walked back to the car. *Let's go back and do the other lane.*

Archie set off until he reached the junction again and drove straight on, following the bend. After three hundred yards, he slowed to a stop once more, turned engine and lights off and stepped into the night, torch in hand. A very dim glow deep in the woodland set him to drawing a mental map. *That'll be the arc lights of the burial site and that corgi, so, I'm at the back of that building, opposite side of the hit-and-run lane...* He considered for a moment. *Odd the keepers haven't been sniffing around, see what us coppers are up to.*

Scanning the verge, he noticed a wide line of damaged grass leading into the woodland. *Ah OK. So, human gone for a piss? Wide track so mob-handed if they did.* He moved slowly along the trampled vegetation for a few steps until his beam alighted on a large patch of low leaves scatter-gunned with the odd, faded flower. *Butterbur, nice scent...* The large, heart-shaped leaves spread away from him and a cursory search with the torch allowed him to pick out the bruised foliage that trailed further into the woodland. *Definitely more than one person, or...has something been dragged through here...? Hang on... These tracks are going both ways...what th' f...? Jay needs to see this.*

His musings were cut short as his mobile sounded, its modernity seeming distinctly incongruous in these rustic surroundings. *Bloody hell, a signal, out here!*

The caller ID flashed Northants HQ...

~

The fast rising and swelling sounds of passing emergency sirens overtook further comment. Lin and Tim watched as the vehicles continued to race past them, police cars, blue trucks, ambulances.

'Blimey, summat serious by the looks. Spend your life living through nothing, then this.' Further vehicles careered by as Tim stopped to watch and Lin carried on walking. 'Over your way Lin, certainly down towards Pool Heath. I'll bet the Goddard boys have been peeling lead off church roofs and selling it for scrap again.' Another flurry of sirens ripped past. 'Wasn't their youngest, whatshisname, wasn't he up before Cheltenham magistrates the other week? Saul isn't it? Something about a prize ram and a willing van driver?'

Lin slowed down then stopped, calculating direction and distance. 'Yeah, I think so... Whatever it is, it's not all that far from mine.'

Tim caught her up and they re-linked arms as the level of blue light interference bleeding into the skyline ahead grew. Tim's voice was drenched with disappointment. 'We may not even be able to get to your place, that level of activity.'

Lin's sudden pull on his arm slowed their pace. 'There's something not right here Tim.'

'What?'

'Not right. Those lights...' They moved on more slowly now, each step increasing the feeling of dread in Lin's chest. At the top of the rise Pool Heath was spread before them, a vista of flashing blue; Lin halted. 'That's not near my place.' She focussed. 'That is my place!' The sudden noise of a helicopter startled them both, its spotlight picking them out momentarily. House lights began to flip on in bedrooms as the noises became something too urgent to ignore and Lin saw the ripple effect of suburban life wakened from slumber. 'Tim...there's something really not right.'

After seeking them out for a second time in its circle of stardom the helicopter lifted away with determination, the searchlight dancing over the rooftops like a skimmed stone.

'That was for us.'

'What Lin...what was?'

'That helicopter, all that action, it's for us...for me.'

Tim smiled nervously at the sudden urgency in her voice. 'Delusions of grandeur Lin. 'Course it's not.'

Lin was still staring at the blue-lit action scene. 'That's at my block Tim...we have to go.'

Tim was well out of his depth now. 'Go? Where, w...why?'

'Round the back way, by James's Butchers, back down Tunland Close.' The noise of the helicopter returned closer.

'Are you serious? We'll as likely get mugged round there and all the police in the district are occupied round this side.'

'Will you just do as I ask for once?'

'Alright, alright, if it makes you happy. Just don't expect me to be all brave when a gang of thugs step out from the shadows.'

Turning back, they walked quickly down the cut-through that led between back gardens and out into the sealed end of the partially lit cul-de-sac that was Tunland Close, the helicopter distant but insistent. Barely thirty yards had been covered along the close before three squad cars rounded in front of them swinging left, right and centre in order to block off the road, their banks of headlights illuminating Lin and Tim as surely as two lamped rabbits. Lin turned away as, with the engines still running, six police officers leapt out and squatted, using the open doors as cover. Without a second's thought she took the mobile from her pocket and pushed it down the front of her pants.

'Drop the bags! Hands over your heads and face down on the ground! Now!' The startled duo stood their ground, screwed to the spot in confusion as the voice followed on in more measured tone. 'Make no mistake as to the seriousness of your situation. Now, drop the bags and lie flat on the floor, hands behind your head. Now!' Running footsteps from behind caused Lin to half turn again as she heard the helicopter sweep away. The voice from the car rose in threat and urgency. 'Face front! The bags and rucksack! Down now!'

Tim spoke in a panicky tone, 'Jesus Lin, they've got guns.'

The footsteps ceased some way behind them as Tim began to off-load his rucksack. 'Slowly! Slowly with that! The bag Miss. Down. The briefcase!' Their bags hit the floor. 'Now, on the ground, face down! Cross your legs!' Almost before they were prostrate, armed police officers were on them from all sides as bags and baggage were subjected to the passing nose of an electronic sniffer device.

'Right, up!' They were peremptorily patted down and the nearby officers visibly relaxed although firearms were still part-levelled their way. 'Who are you, where are you going?'

'I'm Tim.'

'Second name is?'

'Blake, and this is L...'

'Sarah, I'm Sarah Wilmott.' Tim stared at Lin, mouth slightly open. 'We were just making our way home...'

They spoke together, 'to his place.'

'to my place.'

Lin clarified, 'Our place.'

'All clear Sir.' The officer held up the sniffer device.

'Do them.'

He scanned them and looked at the readings. 'Clear Sir.'

'Open them up.' As the bag search was initiated the senior officer turned back to Tim. 'Pockets.' Tim took out his mobile phone and wallet. 'That it?' Tim nodded. He turned to Lin. 'You?' She fished out a few coins from one of the coat pockets. 'That all?'

'Yes.'

'No mobile? You must be the only person on the planet without one then.'

'I've got one 'course, but it's broken, back at our place.'

'Your place. Which is where?'

Tim hesitated, mouth still ajar as the lies tumbled on, Lin speaking confidently. 'Sambrook Terrace.'

'Number?'

'Forty-four.'

'Coming from?'

'The Red Lion.'

'Red Lion's back there on the Cleveland Road, Sambrook Terrace is over there, you're here, in Tunland Close. Why are you going this way?'

'Saw all the lights, thought we'd take a look, get a bit closer.'

'Bit round the houses...'

The officer holding the plastic carrier bag interjected. 'Bits of shopping, Sir, milk, baked beans, bread, jar of Marmite.'

'The briefcase?'

Another officer shook his head. 'Pens, a notepad, empty yoghurt pot, couple of books and some artwork Sir.'

The senior officer turned to Lin. 'Artwork?'

'Just sketches...for work.'

'Which is?'

'Freelance writer, work from home.'

'Not in the pub?'

'Help out occasionally but decided a while ago it's not for me. Seen how hard Mum and Dad work.'

He paused, his lips pursed in frustration. 'Do either of you have any official ID?'

A wide-eyed Tim nodded at the rucksack. 'In there, that front pocket. My bank card's in there, and my British Library card. It's got my photo on it.'

'And you? Nothing?' Lin shook her head. 'Not even a bank card?'

'Need a bank account for that, never had enough money to warrant one.'

'Rely on the bank of mum-and-dad do we?'

'Summat like that.' Then the thought occurred. 'Oh, hang on...' she rummaged in the pocket of her coat, 'I might have... This is their cash-and-carry card, Mum and Dad's. Any good?'

'This the best you can do?'

'At such short notice, yeah.'

'Careful, don't get cocky Ms... Wilmott.' He called across to another member of the team who sat in the rear of a vehicle, a laptop balanced on his knee, a portable printer on the seat beside him. 'Have the photos of the flat's occupant come through yet?'

'No Sir, not great reception here.'

'They've been sent though?'

'Yes, Sir, five or more minutes ago.'

'Super-fast bullshit.' He handed the cards over. 'Right, run these details through data, at least we'll get something.' He turned once more to Lin and sighed, 'Address Sarah Wilmott?'

'The Red Lion, Cleveland Road.'

'You're going to Sambrook Terrace. Your place, you said.'

'Well, when I say our place, Tim's mum lives there. We've a room which we use.'

Tim's face remained stoic, his heart rate anything but. The name change, card production and Lin's implacable narrative in the face of this armed authority was scaring the hell out of him.

'You two an item then?'

'Childhood sweethearts. Right through school, inseparable. My folks wanted better for me, still not resigned to it, that's why the room. We're known locally as Sas-and-Tim, aren't we Tim? Never say one name without the other, do they?'

Tim was also winging it, but not well. 'Yes...well, yes, Sas... and Tim.'

Lin covered it with a forced laugh. 'So, all these police, where's the fire?'

The senior officer's voice hardened. 'No fire, Miss, and no laughing matter either.'

'Oh, I'm sorry. Anyone hurt?' No reply followed. 'Well, I hope whatever's happened it will turn out well, for all parties.'

'Not likely Miss.' Lin was about to pursue the opening when the policeman who had been checking ID's came back to them. 'All checks out. Timothy Blake, Sarah Wilmott. All addresses good and ID, such as it is, is solid. Both locals.'

'Still no photos of the lady from the flat through?'

'No Sir.'

Lin forced a smile. 'Technology eh? Alright when it's working.'

'Indeed. Apologies to you both. All very necessary. Now, I'd suggest you give the area a wide berth tonight. All ahead is cordoned off for the incident. If you want to go to Sambrook Terrace you'll have to skirt around the edge of the common, and watch out how you behave yourselves. Those guns pointed at you earlier?' Tim and Lin nodded. 'Locked and loaded.'

They took back their belongings. 'Yes officer, and thank you. Good to know we're being looked after. Come on L...Sas, let's get off home.' They walked through the gathered officers towards the alleyway.

The noise of a working printer reached them. 'Sir?'

'Yes?'

Tim took Lin's hand and he felt her stiffen.

'Photo's coming through Sir.'

Lin's grip tightened further. 'Run!'

'What?'

The officer stood up holding the freshly-minted photo. 'Sir...!

'Run! Run like fuck!'

The shout came fast. 'It's her Sir, she's the girl. It's her flat!'

'Grab her! Stop them!'

The relaxed officers were galvanised into action. 'You two, follow them! The rest round the back, cut them off!'

Like the shrapnel from a hand grenade the party split in pursuit. The cars screeched carelessly away, bouncing over kerbs and grass verges as they sped off.

Tim and Lin reached the end of the cut-through. To their right was another narrow track yet to be graced with street lighting and known locally as shag alley. 'Your rucksack! Chuck it up the road!'

'What?'

'Chuck it, that way!'

'But my cards...!'

Lin wrestled the rucksack off Tim. 'Chrissakes Tim, chuck it!' She lobbed the bag away. 'This way!'

She grabbed his arm and they sped off, disappearing round the bend at its mid-point. In time with their disappearance the two, armed officers reached the end of the alley and peered into its darkness.

'There!' The one pointed to the discarded rucksack. 'He's dumped it, look!' They weighed the options. 'Could've split. I'll go this way you get along the road, stay on headset!'

Reaching the alley's end, Lin and Tim scampered across the road and onto the common where they crouched under some gorse cover to regain their breath and listen for signs of pursuit. It wasn't long before they heard a voice nearby answered by the faint crackle of a police radio.

'Open ground...could be anywhere. You?'

'*Negative.*'

'Right, I'll log it in and wait, slow search needed an' I won't be able to cover it on my own. Get clearance for a sweep...some help too, the chopper.'

'*Will do. Out.*'

Lin and Tim were still regaining their breath, but this did not stop Tim from firing off his whispered question. 'What the fuck Lin! My card's gone...and what was all that Sarah and Sas shit about? You never lie, never...'

All the events of the day had finally come together for Lin. The people on the train, the money, the lady in the pub, the armed officers and blue-light activity; all of it arriving in a rush. 'It's like what happened to Mum and Dad; clings on, like a burr on a badger's coat.'

'What?'

'At my place!'

'Lin...you're not making any sense. Your parents...what...? You told me they'd passed away...what the fuck are you talking about?'

Lin's mind was racing now with thoughts way outside of Tim's understanding and her impatience showed. 'He said it was bad for someone and they'd got guns Tim! Why do that unless there's a danger to life, or do you still think it's about a bit of missing lead? The photo that came through! He said, "Her flat"! It was at my flat!'

Tim was losing patience. 'What was!?'

'Not now! We've got to get away from here!' Distant sirens and renewed activity convinced Tim of this fact. 'Come on, over to the main road. There's a bus due. We'll get into Worsley then try and figure out what to do next.'

'How do you know there's a bus...?'

'Not now Tim! Come on!'

They gathered themselves together and set off, dodging from cover to cover until they reached the main road. The sound of a distant helicopter reached them, its light scything the common just as the number forty-six reveller's bus to Worsley hove into view. They clambered on board, Tim paying both fares. He followed Lin to the rear of the bus and they sat.

The bus pulled away.

'Right,' said Tim. 'Explanations Lin, and now!'

'What, nothing?'

Archie was speaking rapidly, decisively, the earbuds firmly inserted as he sped along the back lane and on to the main road that would lead to the hospital.

'The flats all full of blind and deaf people are they? She saw him! Did she give a description?' Archie's initial reaction was tempered as he repeated the information coming through.

'Dark...the wrong glasses on. Great. He spoke!' He stiffened a little. 'Did she know what type? Foreign. Like what? Italian...or Irish, she thinks. Wearing a face mask, right. But she saw the gun, and thinks he was maybe Irish...yeah, or Italian...' He sighed again. 'Right, well get her down the station, play some accents at her, try and pin it down. Who's on scene from our lot? Poor sods. Right, ask Pat and Martha to get what they can from the other neighbours. Empty? What, both sides? Jesus. Well, just get Pat to relay whatever she can back to me as it comes in, real-time. Put a general alert out at all exits, airports, rail... they have? Good. I want that fucker found, the sister too, she figures in this somewhere.' He groaned. 'What do you mean, had her? How the hell did that happen...?'

Archie listened, shaking his head as Barry Richards, Duty Sergeant at Northants HQ related the tale of Lin's escape.

'Jesus Barry, what the hell were they, asleep? Don't make excuses for them. The ARU are a bunch of armed professionals and she's just a slip of a girl! Chrissakes. Well, tell them from me to unload their fuckin' guns, I want her in one piece and willing to talk not scared shitless and mute or worse, dead. Is DS Truman about? OK, put her on... Hi, Debbie. Can you get a handle on this ARU fuck up? Get on to bus depots, coach and rail stations, taxis. Is ballistics on the scene? ... Right, good, well tell them I want the make and model of the firearm by yesterday. Yeah, every available person except DC Canning ... No. Tell her to pick up Adam's files, get up to speed on the story and follow up his narrative. I'll want a briefing with her as soon as I get back. Any more background on the sister, apart from her ability to evade our crack armed unit that is? Tim Blake. Nope. Anyone else know him? Find him. What type? iPhone seven. OK, phone records, put a trace on it. A rucksack? Send it across to Penngorse once forensics have finished with it. Was there ID for her? A what? ... a cash-and-carry card? Jesus this gets worse. Well they've both got to be on the usual files, electoral rolls and such, get the team onto it... Good. And this Sarah Wilmott, our girl used her name so knows her. Find her and get reasons ... The Red Lion, I guess ... Adam? No

I don't, nor Kanga. Two down and it's bad they said. I'm on my way there now. I'll want the whole crew in the office for when I've finished ... Hour, hour and a half, 'til then crack on. Break down all the information we've got, hit-and-run, car, area, library, known witnesses. Box it off, split the workload amongst them. I'll want a complete family tree of events and timelines when I get in. The sister? Well that bee stunt should yield something, oh, and someone get on to Jay. Get what we've got so far over to him and tell him I'll be early ... straight after the hospital, then get someone along to Callow Green first thing, a WPC in preference. Redmond? Yeah, she'll do, and send PC Graham with her, he's local. A couple named Butterworth, tell them I'll get Kanga's notes across to them after I've seen her...' He stopped, aware of the suppositions he was making. 'If she can talk. No, I've no idea. What?' He groaned inwardly. 'Beavis, right. Figures. We talked earlier, I gave out a few sweeties but events overtook us ... yeah. I've already asked him to rummage through the Gazette's back numbers, sort out the bee stunt information and send it across to you lot. Has he not?' Archie thought for a few seconds. 'OK, well get back onto him and push it along, tell him I'll free some time up for a radio piece but it's not an official request, tell Beavis it won't be until after I've spoken to him again, in person. As far as anyone else is concerned the hit-and-run and shooting at the flat are two separate incidents ... Yeah, as soon as I know anything so will you.'

He clicked the headset button to shut the call down and pulled the earphones out in one movement. Renewing his gum, the slight increase in traffic at the town's edge caused his frustration to rise.

'Come on! Come on!'

~

The estate car windows were steamed up, canine nose prints adorned the rear and side windows like caravan club stickers and beyond the back seat a very large, bruised, rag-eared, bite-scarred bull mastiff cross gazed longingly over the seats of the hire car parked in a lay-by. Jimmy and Josh, the object of his gaze, nursed a bottle of Knappogue Castle malt between them.

'Why didn't you just skittle off out the back?'

'Out the back...? Jesus Jimmy, to where? Had you not noticed it was on the first floor of a block of flats? Skittle off to where?' Josh took a pull at the bottle. 'Went arseways, whole thing. All we was supposed to be doin' was givin' her a talkin' too...'

'An' some money.'

'Fuck that, that were for our trouble! A talkin' to an' maybe a clout would've been enough, now look at us.'

'Us? You shot 'em!'

'Us! This all comes out we're both in the shit.'

'I'm not takin' the fall for this Josh! You should've got y'self out of it; we could've come back.'

'Always rely on you for support... I'd nowhere to go Jimmy, I said!'

'Well you should've took stock first, fired off into the ceilin', cleared the door, made off through it.'

'She was in the door Jimmy! In it! Only way out was past her, and she weren't about to move unless I moved her.'

Tempers were rising but Jimmy was not about to let things drop. 'Then you should've fired over her head, shouted Allah Akbar or summat, that would've shifted her, but no, not you. You blow her over the drop then set about that other one. No need for it.' He stopped, his disbelief and anger fully obvious.

Josh looked hard at Jimmy. 'I bet you're a hundred percent right in hindsight. It's a wonder I was there at all seein' as how you're so much better at these things than me.'

'Someone had to stay with the dog didn't they?'

'An' that should've been me!'

Jimmy's voice dripped with sarcasm. 'Bugger that. It was me said we should've left the mutt with them Loveridge lot 'til later.'

'What, in that breaker's yard? You're bloody jokin'.'

'No I'm not! Collectin' him meant we sure as hell couldn't run the risk of havin' him watch us melt into the twilight an' start soundin' off 'cos he wants to come with us, and this all because you've made a fool of him from the off. Your choice was collectin' him, my choice was to stay with him, right?'

Josh paused now, flummoxed at Jimmy's rapid twisting of their predicament. 'Well...it were me in there not you, so you'll just have to face that. I'd not been there two minutes, not even time to shut the door, I was still nosin' around for the bedroom. I'd a second's glimpse at the cut of her, saw the uniform, she called out 'copper' an' I knew two things straight away; we was in trouble and them bastards always travel in pairs.'

'An' I said you should've checked, y' gimp.'

'Don't you gimp me. Checked what? Ask her for her ID an' a dance? I was expecting some hippie to walk in! How was I to know coppers would be payin' a visit?'

'I would've thought coppers droppin' by would've been obvious as her sister's been found dead. What did you think, they'd send her a postcard?'

'Your smart mouth's gonna get you into trouble with me one day, y' know that?'

'What, even more trouble than I'm in right now?'

The two men were swivelled in their seats, squaring up to each other as their acrimony deepened. It was only the whine and yap from the dog as it sensed the developing threat that diffused the atmosphere. ''S'alright, Rebel, good lad.' Josh faced Jimmy. 'See, you're upsetting him now.'

'Jesus, you an' that feckin' dog. We should've left him with them travellers. The bites were healin', all he needed was rest to get him fit for the rematch.'

'An' he'd've got that when this lot hits the headlines for sure, they'd 'ave put him down fast; not his fault, none of this...'

Jimmy snatched the bottle away from Josh. 'You need to slow down on this stuff and stop talkin' the maggot.' Rebel yapped again and Jimmy turned towards him, real venom in his frustrated voice. 'Oi! Shut it y' loser! Lie down and shut it!'

Rebel whined and lay down, licking his front paws in displacement activity.

'No need to take it out on him, not his fault is all this!'

'You've said and no it's not; we already know whose.' A short, high-pitched woof bordering on a comment came from the depths of the car and Jimmy took the bottle back. 'An' there's the agreement.'

He took a swig as Josh sighed and voiced what they were both thinking. 'Do we tell 'em, Matt an' his mates, about the shooting, I mean?'

'You mean you're thinkin' they don't know already?'

'Right, stupid.'

'First sensible thing's come out of you tonight. Right, we need a plan. Your gun.'

'What about it.'

'We need to dump it.'

Josh looked at Jimmy for a few seconds before replying, 'You what?'

'You need to dump that gun.'

'Not for a heap of coin I won't.'

'You're carrying around the evidence to a double cop murder. Dump it I say.'

'This gun's been with me for twenty years now, with me da for ten before that. You chuck yours!'

'My gun didn't do no shooting.'

'Not gonna happen... All the trouble it's seen, if you think summat like this is gonna change me opinion of it you'd best think again.' Josh's determined tone closed the subject. He took the bottle back and swigged. 'Jesus, when I think of what could've been...rainin' soup an' we'd got forks.'

'An' two dead coppers.'

Josh swigged again. 'One copper, two...hung for a sheep as a lamb, an' they're not the first, not for either of us.'

'First on the mainland pal, and things play different here.' This brought about a longer pause of realisation. 'What do you think?'

Josh screwed the cap onto the bottle with finality. 'We need to cop on. Let's just bolt back over to Derry, first boat an' away. What d'you think?'

'I think we'll be lucky to get as far as Liverpool before one or other catches up with us. They'll have the main ports and airports staked out if we don't get a move on.'

'Cairnryan then?'

Jimmy thought for moment. 'We've used it before. Worth a punt. We got the cash, maybe they won't be expectin' us that far north; we've got the drop on 'em, maybe get an hour or more start.'

'What about the car?'

'Hired. No trace on it. Pick up some fuel and screwdrivers from an all-nighter, get to Dumfries, swap some plates, dump the car near the ferry and go on as footies.'

Josh half turned to look through the dog guard. 'What about Rebel?'

'Two Irish fellas walkin' a bitten dog on a ferry, are you serious?'

'But...'

'Fuck the dog Josh, it's to Hell or Connaught for us; we top him! He's already lost a front tooth in that scrap. We can get another dog.' Jimmy flicked the key and the car burst into life. 'A second life's a rarer animal.' He indicated Josh's meagre moustache, 'An' you wanna shave that off. It'll be a marker for the cops an' you look stupid with it.'

He footed the accelerator, the car wheel-skidded from lay-by to roadway to gone-away...

~

The late bus pulled into Worsley depot on time, a rarity made possible courtesy of it being mid-week and no displays of violence from the smattering of drunk and disoriented people travelling on it. The only disturbance came from a gaggle of dishevelled girls getting on at Ransom village, their declarations of undying love for each other swiftly followed by synchronised alcoholic snoring. Lin and Tim gazed out of steamy windows having completed their urgent, whispered conversation during the journey. Tim's face was drawn, surprised, scared; Lin's focussed and alert.

'Well OK, so let's say it was your place...'

'We've done this Tim. It was.'

Tim sighed deeply as he spoke, 'OK. So it was your place. OK... But...' Tim noticed they were the only ones left on the bus. 'We'll have to go, the driver's looking at us. Last thing we want is to be noticed.' As they got off the bus the driver joked they would have to pay again if they wanted to stay on any longer. 'Gosh that's so funny, so original,' replied Tim.

Lin managed to tug at his arm as she hissed, 'Jesus Tim! Noticeable?'

Walking through the waiting area they made a rapid exit through the sliding doors of the bus station and entered what was euphemistically referred to as the tumult of nightlife in Worsley. Lin looked around. 'We stand out here too, we're the only sober and sensibly dressed ones on the street. Unforgettable. Half this lot will be in that canal come morning.'

'OK. So now what?' Nothing came back. 'You don't know do you?' Tim sat down heavily on one of the metal benches that were a comment on the council's misunderstanding of aesthetics and their surrender to modern vandalism. 'You don't do you?'

'I will if you'll just shut up a second!' She saw his lost expression and sat next to him. 'Sorry Tim...sorry. I'm making this up as I go along.' Lin paused then laid out her thoughts. 'First thing we have to do is find somewhere we can spend the night.' Tim's face brightened. 'What is it with men? My flat is a major crime scene Tim! All concerned think I'm implicated, and because you've run with me, you too. If that doesn't concentrate your mind on other things then nothing will.'

Tim looked around the immediate area. 'Travelodge?'

'Money?'

'I've got some cash; my bank card was in the bloody bag you chucked as bait.'

'Is there one near Worsley? A Travelodge.'

'Not sure, they seem to be everywhere...' The distant sound of sirens shut down their conversation momentarily until Tim carried on. 'Christ... We're in deep trouble, well you certainly are. Why your place?'

Lin didn't answer. She was too busy concentrating on the now not-so-distant sirens until, after a few moments she laid it out. 'They'll be checking all the ways out, train stations, taxi ranks...' she looked around, 'Bus stations... We've got to get away from here, I need time to think.' Now blue slashes accompanied the ever-louder sirens. 'Christ, they're on their way here, and I'll bet it's not a random check! How did they...? Oh shit, the phones!'

'What?'

'Mobile phone tracking! That copper said, when they stopped us!'

'They're tracking our phones?'

'Not mine, yours!'

'But...'

'Mine's a pound shop chuck-it, yours is the NASA model. You need to get rid of it!'

'My phone?'

'Yes! They know it's us! Chuck your phone and go, come on!'

It was all too late.

The first police car rounded the high brick wall that marked out the bus station perimeter. Lin ran towards the town centre only to have another squad car sweep in blocking her path. She took out her phone, tossed it down a drain and turned back towards the bus station and possible escape, glimpsing Tim's reflection in the glass frontage as he dodged towards a red-bricked dip that led to the canal tow path. The police, some armed, now surrounded Lin. She stopped running and flopped to the ground as ordered, hands over her head in submission. 'Fuck it.'

The wall rose above Tim as he ran down the dip. Looking back he saw Lin disappear amongst the blue lights and uniforms. He slowed involuntarily, feeling helpless. 'Fuck it.'

'Stand still!'

The rapid approach and call of two policemen added impetus to Tim's stride and with one last look in Lin's direction he sprinted away from the two, full-English-challenged policemen. 'Jesus, Lin...' Away along the canal, throwing his phone into the cut, Tim put space and possibility between himself, Lin and his pursuers.

~

Once upon a time in A&E, or Casualty as it was called back then, the mid-weekdays occasionally gave staff a breathing space. A chance for these overworked public servants to catch their breath before the arrival of the weekend and another clutch of determined-to-die halfwits. Not now. Now even weekday late nights were filling up with the symphony of the stupid; tonight was no exception.

Casual damage requiring casualty care caused in the main by the casual over-use of booze and drugs was always treated but not always tolerated by the Accident and Emergency Staff at St. Margaret's Hospital, Worsley. They did their job of course, Hippocrates oversaw that, but sometimes, particularly when the Friday and Saturday night rush was on and at its peak, just sometimes, one or other member of the nursing or doctoring staff would lose a little of their sleep-challenged self-composure. At those times the desire to give the next drunken, bleeding oaf a slap followed by a short lecture on just how much of the NHS budget they were needlessly wasting would become all consuming. They never did of course. Another staff member always talked them down or covered for five minutes whilst the exasperated went outside for a fag, calmed down, put their life back on track. Sad life it may be, oftentimes full of blood and temper, but it was all part of the bloody treatment, all part of their journey to the real doctoring they had signed up for all those bloody years ago.

It was into this melee of self-inflicted injuries that the wailing ambulance pulled that night, complete with its cargo of gunshot victim; a gunshot victim who was a serving police officer to boot. Now the casualty staff were given a genuine if unhappy reason to bypass these hysterical, drunken arses and do a meaningful act.

There was something almost balletic in the structured preliminaries carried out by the forewarned, fully staffed and fully equipped rolling gurney as it barged out through the department's swing doors and coalesced with the ambulance to form a chorus-line of activity. Instructions were exchanged between the carers, one relinquishing control the other taking it, their conversation cut to the minimum. Decisions made at the scene continued to be assessed and implemented on the journey of WPC Kanjara Desai from ambulance interior to hospital interior. Lines, drips, information and control were swapped and exchanged during a flow of movement that saw the patient's journey proceed without so much as a stutter. Disconnected numbers and disjointed medical sentences became the trauma team's call-and-response as the gurney was propelled into the Trauma Unit. Notes were taken by a dedicated nurse, iPad focussed and as close to the action as intrusion would allow. And, at the centre, the patient; a sack of injuries and possible outcomes integral to the process and yet divorced from it.

Doors swung to, shutting out some, ensconcing others, its threshold marking the point of change from what had been an act of primitive human cruelty intent on destruction into a scene of human endeavour focussed on an intent to cheat heaven.

~

'Martha, we could do with moving the body. You finished?'

DC Martha Carron turned to Mark Rogers, Senior Pathologist for Heaton and Chorleton District. 'Mark? Are we done?'

Mark nodded. 'All that can be.' He called to two of his staff. 'David, Carl? Could you...?' The two orderlies carried the thick, black plastic bag into the screened off area and the whole scene came to a silent standstill. The rasp of the zipper drew a line under phase one of the investigation as they quickly dismantled the structure, opening the body up for collection.

Martha stepped back. 'Thanks. OK Pat, we're done.'

DI Pat Kershaw lifted the tape to allow entry for the mortuary attendants. With the utmost delicacy the bag was placed onto the stretcher and carried down the flight of stairs to the waiting black van in absolute silence...

Then the scene slipped effortlessly back into full professional mode. 'Mark?'

'Yes, Pat.'

'You've notified Mister Millar?'

'Yes. He knows what to expect.'

'Thanks.' Rogers went about his business as DI Kershaw scanned the balconies where dressing-gowned, slippered and indifferent inmates, their folded arms draped over the walling, gawped with idle interest at events, swapping personal tales of family loss and past traumas for cigarettes and tea. Pat turned to Martha. 'Bet they saw nothing.'

'To a man.'

'Right. You carry on with the lady two doors down. Get what extra you can then take her to the station, see if you can get a definitive on the accent. I'll start off a house-to-house on the rest of it, see what else can be gleaned from the silent majority.'

Along the balcony and down the steps, Pat made her way to the gaggle of constables gathered by the Mobile Incident Unit truck. 'Right, listen up! You know the reasons we're here?'

A mumbled collective, 'Yes Ma'am.'

'Good. OK. House-to-house on those two blocks.' She pointed to the flats at right angles to the SOC site, 'If they aren't up knock 'em up. I want an answer from everyone even if it's only "I was asleep", and I want all completed questionnaires with my unit by O eight hundred, that's eight o'clock this morning. Good?' All the constables nodded and murmured assent. 'Right, on with it!'

The half dozen officers moved with determination to their task. Pat climbed the steps back to the balcony and knocked on the first door...

Thursday

Archie arrived in the hospital car park and stepped out onto the tarmac.

'Oh shit.'

He slipped the gum from his mouth and pocketed it as he moved swiftly towards Adam's sister, Gabrielle, talking rapidly as he approached. 'Jesus Gabbie, what the...? I'd no idea you were here. I'm sorry...I'm so, so sorry. I've only just got here myself. You should've let me know, they should've let me know...'

'I just got a call from your front desk. They told me Adam had been badly injured and to come here.'

'Front desk? Not from HR?'

'No, from Julie, Julie Parker. She's one of the staff there. I know her, she heard the chatter and...'

'Jesus...'

'What have you heard Archie, what have they said?'

Thinking on his feet, Archie kissed her on the cheek. 'I know as much as you, probably less. I got a call from HQ when I was at a hit-and-run site. All they said was there'd been a shooting over at Chorleton and to come here, that's it.'

'She told me it was bad... It is isn't it?'

'I don't know how bad Gabbie, honest. A WPC went with him to the flat and shots were fired, that's all I know.' Archie was stalling, scrabbling for time to think. They went through the main hospital doors and along a blue-tiled corridor. 'So sorry Gabbie, they're like a rabbit warren, these places.'

'And you, you must be hating it too.' Archie gave her a sideways look. 'Hospitals were never your favourite place, certainly not this one.'

Archie looked into Gabrielle's eyes. Their knowledge of past conversations and history filled the void with unspoken clarity. 'No, not my favourite. Look, whatever it is let's do this together eh?' Gabrielle nodded and gripped Archie's hand tightly.

Scanning the blue overhead signs which mile-posted their progress they strode purposefully and silently along the corridor until it ended at a set of rubberised swing doors allowing entry to a large, seated area. Before them were spread the joys of an A&E waiting room. In various stages of undress and relaxation were its late-night inhabitants, the flotsam and jetsam of a typical mid-weeknight of re-acquaintance with booze, ineptitude and domestics. Archie steered Gabrielle expertly along the yellow lined trackway to where two large men stood guarding another set of double doors. He waved his warrant card as they were nodded through to the relative peace of the treatment area and approached a nurse.

'You have one possibly two colleagues of mine here.' He waved his ID card again. 'Detective Constable Reeve, Adam Reeve, and WPC Kanjara Desai.' He half turned and put his hand on Gabrielle's shoulder. 'This is DC Reeve's sister, Gabrielle.'

Realisation filled the nurse's face. 'Yes we do...er, I believe Miss Desai is still in surgery.'

'And Adam?'

The nurse wrestled with the needs of information and truth. 'Not got the full picture Miss Reeve, so forgive me if I...'

Archie stepped. 'Where do we need to go?'

'Along there, follow the signs for the theatre. It's about a two-minute walk.'

'Thanks. Come on Gabbie.'

In the theatre wing, Chief Superintendent James Campbell stepped forward to meet them and Archie began introductions. 'Evening Sir, this is DC Reeve's sister, Gabrielle. Gabrielle, this is my Super.'

'Ah, Arnold...hello Miss Reeve. I'd not been told you were here.' Another man joined them. 'This is Mister York, he's the surgeon who's been overseeing the...overseeing the treatment here.' Campbell looked decidedly uneasy. 'This is Gabrielle Reeve, DC Reeve's sister.'

Mister York nodded. 'His sister. Right...'

Archie was in fast again. 'Like me, she was told about the incident but has no idea of the details. Could you...?'

Much to Archie's relief Mister York picked up the cue beautifully and barely missed a beat. 'Yes of course. Hello Miss Reeve.'

'Gabrielle, please.' They shook hands.

'Gabrielle, yes.' Mister York turned to Archie. 'And...?'

Supt. Campbell completed the introductions. 'DCI Arnold. He's worked with DC Reeve for what, seven years now?'

'And a half, yes. Hello Mister York.'

They shook hands and Campbell continued in hushed tones. 'You've come a long way for this Miss Reeve, I just wish someone had said...' He turned to Mister York. 'You'll be wanting some private time and an update on your brother, I imagine?'

Gabrielle nodded. 'Yes please. Is he here? Can I see him?' Mister York and Supt. Campbell exchanged glances. Gabrielle missed it, Archie did not.

'I do believe there'll be time for that. I've had a long conversation with the on-scene medical people... ' Mister York moved towards a side room. 'I think it would be best if we go in here Miss Reeve, give us space to talk.' He indicated to a nurse who had been standing nearby throughout. 'Sister?' At the same time CS Campbell motioned to a WPC standing a little way up the corridor and she joined the group.

Gabrielle saw their approach and her face leached colour as she turned to Archie. 'You'll come too Archie?'

'If you want, yes.'

'Of course, you've seen more of him than I have these past few years.'

'Needs must Gabbie.'

'Yes yes, of course, yes, I only meant...'

Archie's phone rang and he saw the Northants ID flash up. 'I have to take this, Gabbie. Sorry.'

'Of course, you do that.' Gabrielle rested her hand on Archie's arm. 'You'll come in though, after?'

'Be right behind you.' Archie guessed what might be coming and held up his mobile. 'Right after...' He opened the phone, grateful to break one connection for another and heard the door close. He let go a long, long sigh before moving down the corridor and opening the conversation.

'What you got, Mary? Oh shit, I knew it...Jesus Adam, and poor Gabrielle...' Archie paused for what seemed like an age until Mary's voice dragged him back to the needs of the job. 'Yeah, sorry Mary, just... Tell me what you've got. They have! OK good, what time? Where...? Got that far did she? And the bloke with her? ... How the hell did they manage that? ... Along the canal.' He shook his head. 'Oh well, that explains everything then...I mean, the canal, perfectly understandable they lost him there, straight line and hemmed in by water and walls as it is; fuck's sake.' He sighed in exasperation. 'Right, right, but she's safe? ... Good ... Yeah, I'll be straight over after I finish up at the hospital; I'm there now, with Adam's sister ... Yes! After our phone call just pop along to the front desk for me will you? There's a Julie Parker there, she's one of the office staff. You tell her from me that if she ever makes a personal phone call over something like this again ... She phoned Gabbie, Mary! I got to the car park, she was already here! You tell this Julie woman, she ever pulls a stunt like that again she'll be walking, got it? ... Right. Me...?' He looked at his watch. 'Twenty-five to three now so, forty minutes tops. Super's here ... Yeah, joyful. WPC Desai? Well, it isn't a flesh wound ... No ... Our runaway? Just make her comfortable, and put a WPC in with her ... No Mary, I said no one else; wait for me. The woman at the flats who saw the shooter, any good on the accent? ... Irish. Definite? ... Just pretty sure...OK, well, it's a start. Get Pat or Martha to ring me as soon they've finished, and get back on to all ports and airports, concentrate on folk travelling out to Ireland ... Thought you would, well done. Yep, forty minutes.' He closed the phone and turned to CS Campbell. 'Mary's just told me...'

~

The office creaked of old wood and leather and smelt of cigars. Lord Trivett of Allingborough took the drink being offered by Brightwick.

'Yes, but we both know that's the sort of muddled, unclear thinking that will keep this bill from moving forward don't we Mark?' Brightwick sat on the leather chesterfield, glass in hand. 'What's beyond doubt is that the scientific element of my Rare and Exotic Animals Research Bill will add to the sum total of our knowledge of these endangered species, immeasurably.'

'Well clearly there are some on the other side who don't see it that way.'

'Three times it's been sent back with their piddling amendments.'

'Proves my point Larry, and I'd hardly call the doubts surrounding one of the central tenets of your bill a piddling amendment.'

'It's because of such ping-pong diplomacy we end up where we are now, us two sat in my office at,' Brightwick glanced at his watch, 'a quarter to two after a late-night sitting with only a seriously abused bottle of malt for company after having voted on the...?'

'Cosmetic Surgery Standards Bill.'

Brightwick's voice dripped sarcasm. 'The Cosmetic Surgery Standards Bill.'

Trivett sipped his malt. 'We could have left after the sitting Larry, no one was holding a gun to our heads.'

'We could, but where would be the help in that. No point going home, I have to go up to Sheffield tomorrow...later today and spend time with the factory workers of Gladding's Steel; joyful. This malt will dull the senses a little.'

'Government initiative?'

'Yes. Trying to breathe life into the corpse that is the Northern Powerhouse; state sponsored support for the Commies in our midst.' There was drinking silence before Brightwick slotted back into his default position of late. 'Tell me Mark, what do I have to do to get my bill passed? I'll do anything, anything that doesn't further dilute it that is.'

'As was noted on its last return there's still some concern over the inclusion of killing the very mammals whose population numbers already put them in a precarious state.'

'Sampling Mark, sampling. Population sampling. Not killing. That's the sort of emotive language that's dogged it from the very start, muddled unclear thinking, d'you see?'

'Killing, sampling, still means the population of a threatened species has its numbers further depleted. The feeling is held by some members that it's just for the sport.'

'Not for the sport Mark, for the research!' Brightwick saw Trivett's look. 'If you aren't yet convinced then how do we square the circle of a deer park, hmm?'

'I don't follow.'

'Blythebrook Park, Bedfordshire? Your family seat at one time, yes?'

'Ah.'

'Yes, ah. A gift to the nation that now sells the venison of its deer park in order to generate income.'

'Not personal income.'

'No, but Trust income nonetheless. If we were to let emotion run riot we could call this exploitation, but we choose to be more nuanced in our language do we not? That way we allow our brave English history to flourish, a history forged by our ancestors Mark, yours and mine.' Trivett nodded. 'Just like your deer park, my bill, particularly the sampling procedure, is an integral part of the scientific research and of raising the much-needed money to support it, not just a means to some sport! Such work has benefitted conservationists and helped formulate further safeguards for other species by providing significant extra funds from the granting of hunting licences which, in turn, get ploughed back into the safeguarding of those very same creatures. Where would we be without that, hmm? Where would the local population be?'

'What, like the Japanese maintaining their ability to scientifically sample dolphins in Taiji each year through their system of corrective lobbying at the IUCN Conference?'

'Yes exactly, and don't look so surprised, naïvety doesn't suit you. Look at the information gained from allowing them to sample and study those dolphins.'

'It's for the meat Larry, they kill them for the meat. What possible, usable research could be gleaned from what is essentially a bloodbath in a charnel house?'

'Mark...' Brightwick sighed. 'Mark, language; it's all in the framing of the language. Using words like bloodbath and killing only shifts the argument from the temporal to the emotional. It's part of their ancient culture. How would this country react if an outside agency told us we could no longer eat roast beef because the way cattle are slaughtered lacks dignity? Where is the difference? Dolphins are driven into a cove and humanely slaughtered, cattle are driven into abattoirs and humanely slaughtered.'

'The difference Larry? They're dolphins!'

'Semantics Mark. Species are irrelevant. Eating beef is part of our culture, eating dolphin part of theirs, and when it comes to the choice of food I don't think we have the right to tell another nation how to frame what is part of their culture.'

'Like fox-hunting?'

'If you like. The chase is part of our heritage, our culture, part of our national identity.'

'And the people of this country, they stopped that heritage, didn't they? And look around, it hasn't caused the end of civilisation has it?'

'The key word here Mark is, they, the uninformed they. And of whose civilisation do we speak? Certainly not mine! Yes. It was a change brought to life internally by they, the people of this country, ill-informed though they were. But we, the enlightened we, know the necessity of curbing fox numbers and the most effective way of undertaking it, and we will see that change reversed before the end of this Parliament.'

'Didn't happen with the Animal Fighting Sentencing Bill did it?'

'Another piece of unnecessary legislation, just like the whispers I'm hearing about a bill to give all animals sentient-being status. A waste of our time and efforts.'

'You may scoff but those very same wastes of time and effort finally outlawed bear and bull baiting. Both are illegal Larry, have been since eighteen thirty-five, that and the passing of The Cruelty to Animals Act, an act that was an early recognition by the people that animals feel pain and experience fear.'

'Brutish reflexes, certainly not sentience.' Brightwick leaned in. 'And because something is illegal doesn't make it wrong does it, otherwise how would we prosecute wars of convenience, hmm?' Trivett opened his mouth to speak but Brightwick talked over him, the emphasis in his words seeming more threat than statement. 'The hunting of foxes will resume, Mark. And as with the Japanese and their ancient cultural practices with dolphins that has enormous research benefits, aids the continuation of a healthy dolphin population and helps feed a nation, so the benefits of my bill will be clearly seen once the people are given the correct information couched in the correct terminology.'

'And if the people exercise their democratic will, demand a revocation of such practices even in the face of the correct terminology?'

Brightwick smiled indulgently. 'Mark, my dear fellow... Democracy is too important to be left to the people.'

'So all that deliberation by the ICJ, who have consistently said lethal research should not be part of the conservation tactic, that was all just misguided democracy was it, a further waste of our time and effort?'

'The International Court of Justice is just another desk-bound body that has no understanding of the difficulties involved in safeguarding a threatened species in the field, and how could they? How often do leopards stroll across their antique rugs?'

'I suspect less frequently than people walk across leopard-skin rugs.'

Brightwick was annoyed and paused, mastering his persuasive skills, his expression adding both gravitas and concern to his words. 'Mark, trust me. I have nothing but the best interests of the many threatened large mammal species at heart, they are uppermost in my thinking. I want them to survive. If there were another way, I'd be the first to champion it, you know where my heart lies in all this. But, although I have searched I've come to the conclusion that in order to gain a thorough understanding of the health and future of any wild mammal population, the definitive method of study has been and always will be the sampling and thorough dissection of selected members of that population and that can only be achieved, sadly but necessarily, by the termination and removal of selected individuals. Take the ridiculous spectacle created by the burning of thousands of tons of elephant ivory. Will this bring all those poor, slaughtered individuals back to life? No. It's just a ruse used by the environmental lobby to grab some headlines and justify their charitable status. A way of justifying their continued raid on the public purse, a gesture that is full of sound and fury but signifying nothing. Why not accept these animals are dead and release their ivory, their legacy, back into the world of research and commerce? At least let them have the dignity of adding to the furtherance of artistic endeavour and the feeding of impoverished families.'

'The vast majority of that ivory was gathered illegally Larry. Why not just dart them, investigate their heath under anaesthetic? Why, when it comes to the research, do we sink to killing them?'

'Think of the stress when compared to a clean kill…and think of the cost of such a programme. Do you honestly think the Treasury would donate funds to such an undertaking in these times of necessary austerity when the same can be achieved at a fraction of the cost? Costs that would be offset by accredited volunteers offering their services for free, experts willing to part-fund any expense incurred in the sampling of the population?'

Trivett smiled thinly. 'By accredited volunteers and experts, I imagine you are referring to hunters such as yourself?'

'Among others, yes. I've already stated my willingness to help with this research.'

'That's good of you.'

'Always willing to serve the greater good, and to do this we have to be forthright and clear in our thinking.'

'Impôt du sang, Larry.'

'Unhelpful and emotive Mark. Not a blood tax, just a collectable levy from those such as me who are willing and wealthy. Such work would save the Treasury and the British people unnecessary and costly expense, freeing up such funds for use in the Health Service and Community Care; a win-win outcome if ever there was one.'

'Now who's being emotive...? May I?' Brightwick waved a hand and Trivett poured another generous malt for them both and sat back in a leather chair. Tired of the argument wherein viewpoints would never be understood, Trivett changed the subject. 'How are things in China?'

'My things or Government things?'

'Both?'

'Well... Government things are progressing well. The Chinese delegation that came over few weeks back...'

'You hosted them didn't you?'

'Yes. The PM was good enough to include me in the planning and execution of the entertainments surrounding their visit.'

'You had them at your place, Bliss Bank?'

'The main heads of the delegation? I did, yes. Just a couple of days. Some time for them away from the cut and thrust of politics, a chance to relax in the English countryside.'

'A wise move, given your personal interest in the region; your feedlot enterprise?'

'Well yes, but I would like to think I was chosen on merit not just on the convenience of my business contacts.'

'Feedlot enterprise going well though, is it?'

Brightwick shifted slightly under the spotlight of Mark's fishing. 'Can't complain. Still a lot to put in place, you know how slow on the uptake our Chinese friends can be. It's all still at the head-bowing stage, a little hush-hush at present. I don't want the Chinese to feel I'm telling tales out of school so, forgive me if I seem...'

'Guarded? Certainly, Larry. Diplomacy always begins with trust, I can quite see the need, but...you'll keep me informed of any useful market developments?'

'Of course, you'll be the first. They're just a little shifty when it comes to the big decisions.'

'Yes. Their footwork over Hong Kong left much to be desired.'

'Ah. Foreign Office still not over it then?'

'Not by a long way but then, if rumour be true, they do say, when it comes to perceived slights, the Foreign Office have the memory of an elephant.'

'If rumour be true. Well Mark, you can tell them from me that nothing but good came of my contact with their delegation. They enjoyed the sightseeing and sundry entertainments I put on for them.'

'A popular man and becoming more so I hear. Colleagues tell me you're about to go on the television shortly. That subversive Gov.UK programme.'

'Yes. Interrupts one's Sunday, but I'm a slave to the cause Mark, as you well know.'

Mark smiled thinly, unconvincingly. 'Well, I shall give it a passing glance. You on the other hand, just be on your guard. It's run by a load of bleeding-heart liberals with an agenda to suit.' Trivett stood up. 'And, speaking of agendas, I must use the little boy's room, if you'll excuse me a moment Larry.'

'Of course.' Brightwick's mobile rang as Trivett left. 'Quinn. No, I'm still at the House having drinks with Mark Trivett. Why, is there a problem?'

~

Closing the door after a stunned and ashen-faced Gabrielle had been escorted out by the WPC and the nurse, Desmond York offered Archie a seat then sat back down. 'Can I firstly thank you for your support during my session with Miss Reeve, it really was much appreciated. Right, you've heard the sanitised version, but I know, as this is a criminal investigation, that you require more. I'm sure you'll be familiar with much of what I'm about to say, so let me tell you where we are at present concerning Ms. Desai. I want there to be no misunderstandings. The case is complex, the outcomes uncertain and I don't deal in conjecture.' Archie nodded. York drew in a deep breath. 'Your colleague, WPC Desai...'

'Kanjara, Kanga.'

'Yes, Kanjara.'

Archie took out some fresh gum. 'Is it OK if...?'

'Of course. Whatever gets you through it. As your Superintendent or department has no doubt informed you, Kanjara was shot twice with a handgun,' he glanced at the wall clock, 'some four and a bit hours ago.' Archie nodded. 'It was a point thirty-eight calibre. One bullet went through her front upper chest, left side, the other entered her front left shoulder. Three pieces of good news, from our perspective at least. Both bullets passed right through, and although some slight damage to the upper right lung was sustained and the bullet broke two ribs, no vital organs or nerves were compromised by either projectile. Also, according to your on-scene forensics expert,' he consulted his notes, 'a Doctor Mark Rogers, all bullets were copper-coated, so compression and surrounding tissue damage was less than with bullets of the hollow-nosed variety.'

'Any of the bullets...?'

Mister York was ahead of him. 'Been recovered? One has. It's been sent on to your forensics' lab.'

'Excellent. So,' Archie steeled himself, 'damage report.'

'Kanjara was treated at the scene by the paramedics for a collapsed lung and we undertook a bronchoscopy here to re-inflate it and do repairs to the ribs, a procedure which was entirely successful. She's out of surgery and in the HDU...High Dependency Unit?' Archie nodded. 'We'll be requiring her back in surgery, probably within a day or two, for a reinspection and also to determine when the wounds should be closed, but all that will be done under a local anaesthetic. Where we are a little unclear is what damage her fall did.' He shuffled some paperwork, his displacement activity understood immediately by Archie who stiffened a little in his chair. 'Her landing spot amongst the shrubbery cushioned her from the full impact, but only to a degree. There's severe fracturing of the pelvis and lower spine as well as considerable nerve damage which has given our resident orthopaedic surgeon some grounds for concern in his, albeit early prognosis.' York eventually filled the chasm of uncertainty. 'What he is certain of is there'll be some level of mobility issues in the foreseeable future.'

It took a few seconds to register. 'You're saying...what? She may not walk again?'

'Not quite, but, and this is a worst-case scenario and a very early prognosis you understand, there is the possibility that her mobility will be compromised, at least for the time being.' York sat back a little in a silence that was abuzz with possibilities. 'Now, I imagine you have other questions too.'

'Yeah...' Archie cleared his throat, his head spinning a little. 'Got the news and was straight across here, then this...this walking thing, along with Adam. Forgive me if I seem a little unfocussed.'

'Not at all, only natural. Take your time.'

Archie stopped chewing, the gum seeming like putty in his mouth. 'This might sound, erm...a bit callous, but...Reeve. How...how...?'

'Quickly?'

Archie swallowed heavily. 'Yeah.'

'I understand you were close friends.'

'Very.'

'Then I understand this is doubly difficult for you. I've not seen the deceased, but in my experience, which spans twelve years in the armed forces and includes two tours in Afghanistan, I would say her brother knew little or nothing. The shock to his system would have shut down all external pain parameters and levels of understanding within a second, a fraction of a second. He may have had a flash of external realisation, but otherwise, very little.' York glanced at the clock again. 'I imagine he will have been moved from the scene of the shooting to your facility for autopsy by now.'

'Not here?'

'No.'

'OK...' Archie held the pause for a long time, digesting the information, collecting himself. 'And Kanga? Leaving aside the walking thing, what's her chances?'

'Well, as I mentioned, the bullet was a solid projectile, so in a strange way, with that and her cushioned fall she was very lucky.' York put an upbeat tone into his next few lines. 'Can I just say this, Detective Chief Inspector...'

'Archie, please.' The chewing restarted.

'Can I just say this, Archie. When she came into this hospital your colleague was placed into the hands of some the very finest practising surgeons in the country. All her signs, all the measurable indicators on the MGCS...'

'That's the dead or alive scale you use.'

'Rough and ready description, but yes, the Modern Glasgow Coma Scale. On that her figures totted up to ten. Considering the shock, wounds and blood loss, that's an excellent starting place believe me. The whole team, from the scene of the attack to the operating theatre, I couldn't have assembled a better group for this incident if I'd hand-picked them. It was our combined expertise which took charge of Kanjara and she couldn't have wished for better care.'

There was another long silence in which Archie had to fight back the desire to well up. After a few deep breaths he felt in control enough to speak again. 'Does Kanga know? About her predicament I mean?' York shook his head. 'And about Adam?'

'Not yet, no. The subject of possible movement restrictions will come later, and from us, but...I'd prefer if you inform her about your colleague.'

Archie nodded. 'Best coming from me, and sooner rather than later. Saves everyone tiptoeing round the subject. Have her folks been informed?'

'I believe your Commander said he'd tried to get in touch, but they're not in the country at present.'

'Oh, OK. So, can I see her, is she able to talk?'

'Are you hoping to extract a statement?'

'It would really help with things so, yes.'

York considered for several moments before replying. 'Yes, you can see her, but very, very briefly, and your eagerness for a statement will have to wait. She's on a high dose of pain relief and sedation and should be asleep; if so I do not want her woken. Understood?' Archie nodded and both men stood up. 'I'll have the sister in charge show you the way. Could you just wait here a moment please?' Mister York returned with a nursing sister. 'This is Sister Waldeck. She's our Critical Care Coordinator with day-to-day responsibility for the HDU and has full control of the situation in all things Kanjara. Please feel free to contact me at any time Archie. The sister will give you my secretary's number. I'll keep you as informed as I can.' He left them.

After a brief pause Sister Waldeck smiled at Archie. 'Jenny, please.'

'Jenny. Right, thanks.'

'Forgive me, but...I've a feeling we've met before.'

'Don't know, how long have you been here?'

'Fifteen years in the hospital, ten on this ward.'

Archie shifted slightly. 'Yes, well, the sort of cases we deal with it's possible.'

'Of course, but my memory is of something more personal?'

Archie shrugged. 'Not to my knowledge.'

Sister Waldeck could see Archie was becoming uneasy with the conversation's direction and content. 'No, of course not. I see a lot of people, could've been anyone really, all blends into one sometimes...' She adjusted back to ward sister manner. 'Right. Would you like a cup of tea first?'

'No, I'm...no, thank you.'

'Then let me take you in and you can see her for yourself.'

They had reached the door to the HDU when Archie's mobile rang. He glanced at the caller display. 'I have to take this, do you mind?'

Sister Waldeck smiled. 'Not at all. I'll go in and see how she is.'

'Thanks.' Archie answered the call. 'Hi Jay ... What, now? OK, I'm just going in to see Kanga so let's say half an hour, forty minutes? OK...' He paused, not knowing quite how to broach the subject. 'You'll be in receipt of Adam then? ... Right, oh, and Gabrielle's here ... She got a tip-off from someone at HQ apparently ... Never mind, it's being dealt with ... No, thank God. The surgeon, Mister York, he did it. No, I'd no idea ... She was here when I arrived Jay! ... Yeah, shattered. Can you give her a call? ... Excellent, thanks Jay. Yeah OK, forty minutes.'

He shut down the call, wrapped the gum, took a deep breath and entered the room as Sister Waldeck turned from the bed. 'She's sleeping.'

The door swung to behind Archie, exchanging random scents and echoes for the reek and bleep of intensely close monitoring.

~

'**M**orning Jay.'

Jay Millar looked up from desk and paperwork. Archie was leaning against the office door jamb, chewing nonchalantly, stance belying emotion. Jay looked at the wall clock. 'You made good time.'

'Sounded urgent.'

'Yes I know, but still...' Jay motioned the clock with his head.

'I know. Are they both here?'

'They are.'

'Then just a few minutes? Just a breath, before...' Archie indicated the autopsy room with a nod.

'Yes, if you want.'

'Just gives me a bit of time to adjust with this one, y'know?'

'I do,' Jay shifted the focus slightly. 'Anita should be closing up our lady about now. I hear they have the deceased's twin in custody?'

'Yeah. Picked her up over at Worsley bus station. Some get-away transport, eh?'

Jay smiled. 'And it was definitely her flat?'

Archie looked up from foot contemplation. 'It was. You didn't deal with it?'

'No, with your need to get on I was spared that cruelty, and anyway, too much going on in the woodland. Mark Rogers attended; you know of him?' Archie nodded. 'He's a good man, we were at UEA together. He did some sterling work at the flat, bullet found and such.'

'So I was told.'

'It's with ballistics now. They're running them through the database as a priority. Results should be in by mid-morning.' Jay's look conveyed his empathy with the situation. 'Look Archie, not to labour a point, but can I just say how dreadfully, dreadfully sorry I am for all this, he was my friend too.'

'I know. Thanks Jay.'

'And you say Gabrielle was at the hospital when you got there?'

'You not phoned her yet then?'

'Been a bit busy, I will soon.'

'Of course, I didn't mean... Yeah, she was. I think she knew the minute that consultant called across the nurse and Campbell the WPC.'

'Mister York you said, Desmond.'

'Yeah.'

'I know him a little, and by reputation. Top of the range I'm given to understand. And how is Miss Desai?'

'Asleep when I went in, came to very briefly so I only exchanged a couple of words with her...told her about Adam.'

'Wow.'

'She asked, so yeah; wow. She doesn't know about her potential difficulties yet either.'

'Difficulties?'

'Mobility difficulties.'

Jay's face said it all and there was a silence of some moments before he replied. 'Again; wow. OK... Well, poor comfort that it is, in an effort to not let the grass grow, Anita and I have kept the pressure up. Thing is, I have to sign off the official reports, hence my presence at this desk so...can I ask a huge favour?'

Archie knew what was coming and braced for it. 'Anything Jay, ask.'

'I'd really rather not face a second session with Gabrielle, my phone call will be traumatic enough so, the initial ID of Adam...?'

'Me?'

'Please.'

'Er...OK, yeah, sure.'

'Thanks Archie.'

'No prob. And the pellet from the dog's gum?'

'Balsall Common sent it over here.'

'Bypassing ballistics.'

'No rifling marks on a pellet so no need. For such as this we have our own resident expert on site; one Ms. Cresson. How is the dog by the way?'

'OK given his ordeal by firing squad and Bob's needles and pliers. Pellet might prove useful then?'

'Might, yes. Had a quick look. Anita will give it more time after your...visit.' Jay held up the sheets of paper he had been working on. 'I've got Mark's on-site report. He's coming across later to assist with Adam's autopsy and to swap stories.'

'Some story, eh?'

Jay glanced at the sheaf of papers. 'Yes. But the ID still needs to be done.'

'Yeah, 'course.'

He replaced the papers. 'Have you talked to the twin yet?'

Archie adjusted his slouched position and hauled himself upright. 'No. I wanted to get the full story from here before I confront that one. No matter how much trouble she's caused she deserves an accurate truth.'

'Quite right.' Jay pointed to a bank of single metal cabinets along the wall of the corridor. 'Right. Pop your stuff in there, put on a gown and boots and grab a mask. I'll finish up here then we'll go in.'

As Archie changed clothes Millar pen-scratched and paper-shuffled until he put away his fountain pen and looked up at the suited and booted detective, the mask still under his chin. 'You'll do, come on.'

Jay collected a white lab coat from the back of his door and slipped it on as they walked down the short corridor towards the autopsy room, filling Archie in with events so far. 'We've managed to pin down the time of her physiological death which, give-or-take, was between fifteen hundred and twenty-one hundred on Sunday last.' Jay paused at the door, casting a quick glance through the small thick window. 'Not pretty, OK? Not to any of the senses.' Archie nodded. 'I know you've seen most of it before, but time, events and nature have had their way in this particular case. What with the force of the collision, her days in the ditch and us, just...not pretty.' Jay opened the door and the familiar sight of the beige, ceramic-tiled autopsy room filled Archie's view.

On the stainless-steel table at the centre of the room, positioned over the collection tube and sump, was the laid-bare corpse of the hit-and-run victim. On another table placed well to the side was a zip-shrouded shape, and as much as he tried Archie could not help his eyes being dragged to the bragging indecency of it. He placed his hand on the door jamb for steadiness and immediately lifted the mask to his face as emotion and the pungent scent of researched death hit him. Jay's over-cheerful voice deflected the moment.

'Anita, you have a visitor.'

Anita Cresson, masked, goggled and plastic-aproned, looked up from replacing major organs into Renata's upper body cavity. 'Morning Archie.'

'Mmmm...'

Anita recognised the reaction. 'Just stand yourself still there for a moment or two, it'll pass.' The sincerity showed in her eyes, even through her goggles. Jay put on a plastic apron and moved to one of the side tables on which were placed a number of clipboards with pre-printed sheets fastened to them. He busied himself with reading. There was a long-drawn-out silence of stoic contemplation before Archie could look up at Anita again. She had completed her task and was now beginning to suture the Y-incision. She glimpsed his movement in her peripheral vision. 'OK now? Get this done and it'll be all to the good.'

Around the momentary star of this drama were gathered the bit-part players to Renata's last act; the body sketch sheets marked with the tattoos of injury, the sample jars all containing various fluids and segments of a life. One wall was dressed with a large whiteboard on which were written various notes, graphs, formulae and calculations. Above the table was an adjustable LED light and on a tripod to the right of the table stood a video camera, its companion slung overhead, both winking with a callous, unembarrassed, red eye. Each camera fed a separate monitor, and together with a centrally mounted overhead microphone, they were ready to detail the closing karaoke all autopsies require.

Jay approached the table. 'Good for this?'

Archie nodded, took another step forward then halted. 'Close enough. Talk to me.'

Jay restarted the recording and switched on the microphone. Looking up at the room's wall clock he faced the camera. 'Zero four thirty-eight. Resumption of investigation into case number,' Jay glanced at the sheet uppermost on a nearby clipboard then back to camera, 'three three two four slash zero nine. Present in the room are CSI and Pathologist Anita Cresson, Detective Chief Inspector Archie Arnold and Senior Forensic Pathologist Jay Millar. This addendum concerns further discussions surrounding the initial autopsy outcomes for the benefit of DCI Arnold.' He began moving round the table, picking up a clipboard and using the attached body sketch as a comparison map, indicating the regions and points of interest much as a travel courier describes the historical highlights of a famous city. 'These positions correspond to the injuries sustained on the body at impact and give us an approximate height of the front end of the vehicle...'

Jay's words became a buzz and fast-faded as Archie's eyes were dragged back to the covered corpse. Anita was the first to spot his change in focus and her hand movement alerted Jay who paused and allowed a few seconds to pass before speaking again.

'Archie? Archie.' Archie's difficult journey back from his thousand-yard stare to the present showed and Jay put the clipboard down. 'Do you want me to take Mister Reeve into the ante room?' Archie said nothing.

Anita took a step toward him. 'Archie, would it help if we removed Adam?'

Archie shook his head. 'Move him? No...no. It lets me know why I'm here.' He looked directly at Anita then down to the part-sutured corpse. 'Sorry... Could you just repeat Jay, please?'

'Right.' Jay picked up the clipboard and continued as Anita, whose concentration was fixed on the final suturing, still had room for frequent checks on Archie. 'These marked positions on her upper torso, here and here, correspond to the injuries sustained on the body at impact and give us an approximation of the upper height of the vehicle's front end. The severe fracturing of both lower legs indicates the height of impact from the road's surface. The secondary cause of death was the massive, and I mean massive, damage to the rib cage, lungs, heart and pelvic structure.'

'So, not a hatchback then?'

Jay noted the change in Archie from devastated friend to seasoned detective. 'Correct Archie, not a hatchback.'

'A taller vehicle. An off-roader possibly?'

'Almost certainly when our estimates are added to Traffic's details.' He picked up another clipboard. 'Ah, here...track width of sixteen ninety.'

'So a larger than average vehicle travelling at high speed. No tyre-tread information?'

'None, but at those speeds, on that surface and over that amount of time, not expected. We've taken rubber samples, but I hold no hope.'

'Right.'

Anita finished her work. Covering the lower part of the corpse with a sheet she stood back to allow Jay full access.

'Neat suturing Ms. Cresson.'

'She deserves nothing less.'

'As do we all.' He turned to Archie. 'Conjecture now. Given the speed at impact...would you do the honours again Ms. Cresson? Given the speed at impact our hypothesis, taking the injuries and our measurements into account is that she was stationary at the moment of collision and positioned,' Jay manoeuvred Anita using her as the dummy, 'just so. At impact the lady was folded, forward and over.' Jay folded Anita at the midriff. 'This caused the side of the victim's head to make contact with the bonnet where, I hasten to add, there will be a corresponding dent on the vehicle. This resulted in the wide fracture of her skull and massive trauma similar to one being struck, just the once, with a baseball bat...wielded by a gorilla.'

Archie winced at the description. Anita stood up and moved closer to Jay, speaking softly 'Nice metaphor Mister Millar.'

Millar shrugged. 'Needs must Miss Cresson. If it's any consolation I would suggest that, at this juncture, our victim was already out of life, certainly out of senses.'

'The head injury. That's not from her travels down the road then?'

'The absence of deeply embedded road debris at the site of the skull fracture would suggest not.' Millar paused before closing in on the whiteboard and its formulae. Archie held up his hand.

'Just, steady on there Jay. I'm a simple chap who you're about to make look even simpler in the eyes of Anita here with your calculations and such. Summation please, and best guess.'

'A further opportunity to lord it over the proles missed. Shame. Right.' He considered for a moment or two before answering. 'Best guess?' Archie nodded as Jay moved back to the corpse. 'The deep gouges on the cheek and forehead together with the abrasions on the hands and their concomitant inclusion of lane debris, these were caused by our victim's progress, post-impact, along the lane, but in my humble opinion, the colossal chest, pelvic and organ injuries were not.'

Jay paused and held Archie's gaze. 'Then she must've made a hell of a mess of the front of that vehicle... Oh, OK. There's something you're not telling me Jay, isn't there?'

Jay smiled. 'Because you don't want technical.'

'OK. Just a little, and as long as it doesn't contain smug.'

Jay moved back to the board. 'This is detailed and important stuff Archie, but I'll do my best.' He underlined a set of figures and letters in red. 'This is a formula we use to calculate HIC, Head Injury Criterion. Using both the injury's severity and position, and by comparing it to a set of pre-determined results we can deduce the vehicle's impact speed and the consequent loading onto the victim from that impact. It also gives us an approximation of the vehicle's front-end design pattern. Good so far?' Archie nodded. 'Now, most vehicles have some amount of give in them, either through deliberate design or poor build quality, so on contact with a body, that body is manoeuvred, much as you saw Ms. Cresson's was, into the vehicle's front end and bonnet. These surfaces distribute the loading and crumple with contact, softening the blow before the victim travels across the bonnet and through the windscreen.'

'No glass.'

Jay looked across at Anita. 'Sharp as a razor; correct. No glass. Not at the scene or in the victim. This, massive vital organ damage plus the fact she was catapulted along the lane for such a distance and with such ferocity instead of through the windscreen, this gives us our anomaly. My best guess you said? I would suggest the vehicle had some form of bull-bar on its front, made of metal and slightly higher than the bonnet, which meant she was only ever going to be propelled away from the vehicle.'

'Whoa... Definitely metal?'

'From our modelling, yes. Plastic bull bars, polyethylene and such, are a cosmetic touch designed to act like a cushion. More pedestrian friendly they give sufficiently to allow the object a slowed down mode of travel across the bonnet. Metal ones are rigid. They alter the geometry at the front of the vehicle, protect it and, crucially in this case, transmit all the force away from the vehicle and on to the object of the collision.'

'A lot to process here Jay.' Archie paced a couple of times then stood still. 'OK, let me... The blood at the burial site?'

'Not hers.'

'Then whose?'

'We don't know. Not on our database so possibly a fine upstanding citizen.'

'There's no reports of missing persons in the area, I checked earlier. And nothing more on the corgi?'

'Nothing to tell other than what we discussed on site. No name tag or chip and nothing to connect them at present.'

'Gets worse. Those leather scraps I found?'

'Better news there. They were hers and, yes, she was there at the burial site, but the bloodstains belong to someone else entirely.'

Archie paced again then stood still in order to concentrate. 'Two corpses within a three-hundred-yard radius of each other, one fresh one stale, and a dog plus some scraps of leather.'

'You really do think all this is connected, don't you?'

'My best guess now? Our hit-and-run discovered the corpse in the wood, someone killed her, shot her dog then, for some reason, went after the corgi and the twin...' Archie suddenly patted his pockets. 'Ahhh shit...! The dog!'

Anita looked from one to the other. 'The corgi?'

'No. Her dog. The one I rescued you all from...damn! I left my phone in the locker.' He saw explanations were needed. 'I passed up on a call from Bob at Balsall Common just before I left the hospital. I need to get a dog lead from him and ask him to drop the dog off at Penngorse; bugger! Stupid.'

'Lot going on Archie, considering.'

'No excuse. Need to call him back. Thanks both, I owe you several...' He noticed Jay's expression, 'I'll do the ID later, if that's OK. Sorry.'

'No apologies necessary, no rush, later will be fine.'

Anita added her voice in support of Jay's. 'Another time Archie.'

Archie's reluctant gaze finally rested on Adam Reeves' black-bagged body. '"You should reach the edge of virtue, before you cross the border of death". That right Jay?'

'"Limits", Archie, "limits of virtue".'

'"Limits", that's it, yeah...' Archie left the room, his voice receding as he gently closed the door. 'Yeah. "Limits"...'

The short walk back to the locker to change clothing did nothing to conquer the emotions that time, scent and sight had caused to well up in the autopsy room. The enormity of it all, the finality of it all and the release of memories long buried suddenly became very real and Archie slid down the cabinet door to a hunkered position, his head resting on his knees. This was how Anita found him.

'Archie? He felt the arm go over his shoulder. 'What can I do to help?' Archie shook his head. 'Nothing? Is there nothing I can do?' Archie stood up taking Anita with him, his height gradually counteracted Anita's until her arm slid free. Both stood in silence until she spoke again. 'Well, just ask, OK?' Archie nodded. 'I'll go back in then, if you're sure you're OK?'

'Yeah.' He winked, 'I'm good. Work to do.'

Anita smiled at him. 'Me too.' She turned to head back.

'Oh Anita?' She stopped. 'That ballistic stuff? As soon as you know anything.'

'Yes, of course.'

'And...' Anita looked across the void of the pause, 'thanks for rescuing me, in there and out here.'

'That's alright Archie, anytime.' She re-entered the autopsy room, its closing door sealing both into their tasks.

~

Chris, in overalls and wellingtons, a bass broom in his hands, came out of one of the puppy kennels. 'What? When?'

Matt, in sharp suit and hand-tooled shoes, a gold Rolex showing on his wrist, leant across onto the passenger seat of his Range Rover and spoke earnestly through the opened door. 'Now! Right now!'

Propping the shovel against the outer kennel wall Chris closed the door behind him and walked to the edge of the concentrated arc lights that showered the kennels. 'He wants to see me?'

'Us. Quinn wants to see us.'

'But,' Chris looked at his watch, 'it's only half five. Never mind Quinn, what th' hell you doin' up this time of the day, was the bed on fire or summat?'

'Cut the lip, stop askin' questions an' get in, this is fuckin' serious!'

'Can I not change first?'

'No y' can't!'

'But...' he lifted one foot to inspect the sole of his boot.

'Will you just get in!'

Chris grumbled his way onto the passenger seat. 'Well, just don't blame me if y' motor stinks of puppy shit for the next month.'

If Chris was unsure about the seriousness of the situation any such insecurity was dispelled by the instruction to get into a vehicle Matt treated almost like a religion without a thorough clothing inspection. He sighed. One minute he was into the daily routine of kennel cleaning, daydreaming about one day leaving this all behind him and getting his own place, the next he was on his way to a serious meeting with someone he would rather not spend time with. It occurred to him that a place of his own might be here quicker than expected.

Matt screeched out of the yard and along the lanes at indecent haste as Chris opened tentative conversation. 'What's he want?'

'Have you not heard? Do you not listen to anything else on that radio of yours but local crap?'

'It aint crap.'

'Crap! Them Micks are all over the nationals and you, you're listening to some tosser tellin' you about a sale of dustbins at Fendwick's hardware store!'

'Micks? What, our Micks?'

'Who else's? They topped two coppers last night!'

This concentrated Chris' mind wonderfully. 'Jesus...when?'

'Around the time we was givin' Mason's place the once-over. Quinn phoned me at half-four.'

'Jesus, what took him so long to get in touch?'

'Couldn't get confirmation, he had the media blackout to get past. Even then it was thin, then he had to contact the Gaffer who was still in London drinking with his pals. Quinn said he could only give him the barest details and had to wait 'til the Gaffer could make his excuses and find a quiet place to go ballistic. Then Quinn rang me to tell me how we've buggered up. We've buggered up?'

'Gaffer comin' back too?'

'Not any time soon thank Christ. Got to go up to Sheffield straight from the House apparently, so he's staying in London. Quinn's feeding him developments as-and-when but you can just imagine his reactions.'

'Jesus. Two coppers?'

'Yeah, two.'

'Christ, this used to be a peaceful spot here. Odd bit of persuasion, occasional dog scrap... Now? Ever since the Gaffer upped the stakes with them Chinks it's all gone tits.'

'Do you think you've had nothin' to do with all this then?'

'Well...'

'That woman findin' that bloke dumped in that comedy burial site by what turns out to be a couple of cop killers kick-started this little shit storm.'

'That's it, blame me!'

'Cap fits.' Matt increased his speed a little more as the lane widened. 'Now, shut up and let me concentrate or we'll be tits up too.'

Chris gazed moodily out of the windscreen as the hedgerow and interspersed trees flashed by in the headlights, Matt concentrating on the need for haste, both men mulling over just what it was that had brought them all to this point...

... Chris came to Matt's full attention twenty-eight years earlier when, although known locally as a bit of a cissy because of his softness towards animals, Chris had supported Matt with the fallout from a particularly sensitive gambling disagreement in the Prospect of Whitby, the two young men taking down six renowned, outsider opponents in less time than it takes to tell; when it happens to one on your patch it happens to all. Matt showed his thanks for Chris' help by speaking of the people he knew in the game, of his plan to move away and get rich and had said, should circumstances allow and life go as planned, Chris could always look to him for employment. Chris nodded, thought, *Jesus, you think a lot of y'self don't y'*, dismissed it as post-scrap euphoria and they went their separate ways; in Chris' case by travelling through the fickleness of Britain's penal system, in Matt's, by travelling round the fickleness of Britain's dog tracks...via a short stint as a guest of HMP.

For the greater part of the next twenty-one years, Matt graduated from small-time bookie to the go-to man for a wager at Walthamstow Stadium during its greyhound heydays and it was here that he came to the attention of a trio of seemingly odd bedfellows: Lawrence Brightwick de Roazhon, the east-west Vladkov brothers, whose business portfolio extended from the mining of gold, oil and diamonds by cheap labour, the supply of high-end London property for tax offsetting purposes, and into the supply of high-end girls for entertainment purposes, and finally the East-End Lander family from Shadwell, abattoir owners and meat suppliers to the masses.

For the Vladkov and Lander families there was kudos to be gained from rubbing shoulders with the likes of the de Roazhon's of this world; for de Roazhon, his empire-building was complemented by melding the Lander's meat-trading abilities and the Vladkov's ready supply of cheap labour with his own high density livestock enterprises in both the USA and China. What caused this coalescence of the questionable and Matt's eventual servitude to Brightwick were the two highly rated winning greyhounds, Slippery Bob and his eventual nemesis, Westmade Rival.

A fast-improving, six-bend specialist, Rival had regularly run a close second to Bob, only missing out by a short head in their last meeting; that is nought-point-nought-one of a second in racing parlance. With the Greyhound St. Leger approaching and both dogs entered, Matt saw the opening for a killing, but to do so meant he would have to play both ends against the middle and ensure the killing was not of himself. With the odds on Rival running at three to two Matt used several of the nom de plumes invented early on in his bookie career, via the bogus bank accounts he had set up in their names, to place several major bets against his own dog and onto Rival. However, with the call as to which dog would win being so close, insurance had to be put in place; the odds had to be ever so slightly loaded in Rival's favour.

As a part-owner, via a gambling debt, Matt was allowed entry to the kennels up to forty-eight hours before any race, albeit under scrutiny. So it was, with concealed pin in one hand and a matchbox containing a suitably starved deer tick the size of a grain of rice in the other, Matt looked in on Bob in the company of racetrack kennel man Melvin Clarke. When Melvin stepped out for a cigarette it was the work of just a few seconds for Matt to prick the pin high up in the gap between two of Bob's rear left pads, retrieve the tick from the matchbox with tweezers and press it onto the tiny wound. Tucked tightly and neatly between the folds it only took a few moments for the ravenous tick to latch on. Missed in the inspection on race day, Slippery Bob, carrying the hopes and considerable wagers of his investors, was entered to trap four carrying an unregistered passenger. He ran well, but not well enough; Westmade Rival won by half a length.

The post-mortem on the race was immediate.

'How was Bob's appetite?'

'What was his temperature?'

'Had he emptied bowel and bladder on time?'

'Had he been over-exercised on the day of the race?'

'Was there anyone hanging round the kennels on the day of the race who shouldn't have been?'

Melvin answered each question thoroughly, right up to the point Matt stepped forward.

'The place was clear when I stopped by the day before the race.'

'What time was this?' asked Brightwick.

'Just gone eleven.'

'Why so late?'

'Time. Busy day ahead. Good luck pat. Clarke was with me all the time.'

With the strong possibility of a slow and painful end to his career, Melvin nodded.

'I was.'

No obvious reason for Bob's defeat could be found at the track kennels and the dog looked and moved well, albeit slightly toed, which was put down to the particularly stiff race he had just undergone. No distress, eyes clear, no ear pain, temperature good, all joints sound, all nails in good order and recovery time as it should be. Four days later the post-race urine tests came back as clear and it began to look like Slippery Bob had just been beaten by the better dog on the day. It was not until Bob had been back at the home kennels a further two days that the reason was found. Ixodes scapularis, now bloated to three times its original size on the blood gorged from his well-fed host, threw Bob's gait and only a cursory inspection was needed to discover the culprit. After the tick's removal and destruction and a suitable antibiotic salve applied to the wound, the whole operation being filmed for distribution to the interested parties, honour was seemingly satisfied and tighter controls for track-side kennel hygiene were stepped up as plans were made for Slippery Bob's comeback race. So far so good for Matt.

Six weeks and two races into his re-training, Slippery Bob showed signs of lethargy, went off his food and began to run a temperature. This time the vet was called, tests done and it was quickly established the dog had contracted Lyme Disease from an infected parasite. After this initial diagnosis Bob's decline was fast, so fast that little could be done. Liver and heart damage, even though slight, were detected and his racing career was seemingly in jeopardy, as was his ability to go on to stud. Even given Bob's race record the decision was made to cut the syndicate's losses and rely on his stored semen for a slight profit from the mess. So far so good for Matt.

It was while Brightwick was at dinner in the House one evening with Gordon Elliott, the Lord Braceforth of Lynne, owner-chairman of the high street, track side, and online betting company BetScribe, that the chummy conversation inevitably turned to things racing.

'Sad to hear about that dog of yours Larry. Slippery Bob was it?'

'Yes. Thank you, Gordon. Bad business all round.'

'Hell of a dog, lost me some money over the years. Deer tick wasn't it?'

'How well informed you are. Yes. Well, when we say tick, it was the disease it carried that did the damage.'

'Was it not treated?'

'First inspections and tests threw up nothing adverse, but now, obviously, it would seem we were not showing the dog due diligence.'

'Shame. I assume you lost on the race too, personally I mean?'

'All the syndicate did, both race and dog; not best pleased.'

'All the syndicate? Really?'

Brightwick picked up on the emphasis, put his knife and fork down and leaned towards the centre of the table a little. 'You've heard differently?'

'Nothing specific, just, I heard Corals got stung with a block of high wagers on the winner...all of it laid in the forty-eight hours leading up to the race. I thought to myself, someone must have known something.'

'When you say high wagers...?'

'In total?' Brightwick nodded. 'Twelve thousand in differing amounts, two thousand was the highest.'

'At?'

'Three-to-two.'

'Twelve thousand; that's...a thirty thousand return, depending on when you paid the tax...' Brightwick sat back in his chair. 'Do we know the name of this clever high roller?'

'Not one, eight.'

'Eight? Really?'

'That's why it wasn't picked up on; all different postcodes.'

Brightwick leant in again. 'You're saying these eight punters, all from differing parts of the country, had the same intuition in the same forty-eight hour period that a dog already beaten into second place on four occasions by the very dog he was racing against would reverse the result? All eight? Really?'

Braceforth nodded. 'Coincidence?'

'I think not. Aliases?'

'One way to do it.'

'And they didn't check?'

'Too late in the day, where would you go that close to the race?'

'The timing is all. So, do we have a list of the aliases used?'

'No, but give me a few days and I can possibly get some of them.'

'That would be most helpful. Is there anything I can help you with?'

'The next online gambling investigation?'

'Consider me an ally Gordon. Always willing to fight the nanny state.' Brightwick indicated the plate opposite. 'The fish?'

'Not bad, a little dry. Your steak?'

'Excellent.' Brightwick poured wine into his companion's empty glass. 'This twenty-thirteen white Burgundy will help it slip down...'

Four days later Brightwick was in possession of the list of aliases, and two days after that, Quinn, with a little official help, furnished his boss with the name of the clever high roller: one Matthew Lamb.

A short phone call, followed by a meeting and short chat with Brightwick, convinced Matt of two things: that the Vladkov and Lander factions would fight each other for the privilege of killing the person responsible for the premature demise of Slippery Bob, and that he, Brightwick, was without scruple and more than willing to pass this information on if Matt did not do exactly as requested. Matt, ever the pragmatist, suggested they should arrive at a compromise. Brightwick agreed and laid out the terms. Matt would enter His Lordship's service and, using his newly discovered canine skills, do whatever was needed to make Brightwick's newly started canine venture a success. Taking out and brandishing the miniature tape recorder used to document their recent conversation, Brightwick then promised to keep their secret safe. From that point on Matt had become Brightwick's Canine Sporting Facilitator.

As the dog-centred venture grew in importance due to the visiting clientele and their sporting peccadilloes, the staffing needed to be increased and Matt, to his credit, repaid the debt owed to Chris, who was glad of it, mainly because a couple of awkward situations he was involved in were on the cusp of developing into major embarrassments.

Once out of London and into the self-contained world of Bliss Bank Estate, Chris was absorbed into the day-to-day events that accompanied the demands of a high-flying government minister. Chauffeuring duties; help with peripheral arrangements for the game hunting trips his boss was fanatical about both at home and abroad; helping Matt and Gerry with the canine sporting events that were becoming increasingly important in cementing relationships between Brightwick and the visiting Chinese trade delegations. But all was not well, all was not going as planned.

Feeding and training, such as it was, was conducted by Gerry, but there was little else in the way of a strict regime, so the home dogs often failed to win, something not appreciated by Brightwick. It was on a government fact-finding trip to the southern states of America, in order to gain further knowledge into the bulk rearing of cattle, that Brightwick had first been introduced to Aiden Youngman the Third.

Americans, always eager to enable growth in the special relationship both political and commercial with the UK, had entered into diligent research prior to Brightwick's arrival and they quickly discovered his love of all things hunting and shooting, but more important to them was his involvement in other less well known, less-than-legal canine sporting activities. Eager to make a claim and stake a claim, his hosts organised a visit, sanctioned by Clem Mortimer the US Senator for Alabama, to one of the more reputable canine sporting establishments, Sagebrush Kennels.

Shown around by one of the three canine managers, a Mister Aiden Youngman the Third, Brightwick was greatly impressed with both the set up and Mr. Youngman. Aiden was no tattooed thug but a clean-cut, all-American, sensitive man who thought only about what was best for his charges; that those same dogs were involved in competitions of a violent nature only seemed to deepen his feelings for them. He wanted his combatants to be a reflection of his abilities, to acquit themselves with honour, for the contest to be fair and for the result to be a deserved one. To that end only the very best would suffice and this attitude appealed to Brightwick de Roazhon's Ryder Haggard upbringing and mentality. What he saw in Youngman was that quintessential quality that had built a nation and saw the Englishman rise above the common herd and set him on a march to civilise the world, a quality Brightwick saw as sadly lacking in today's modern, slack-jawed society where mediocrity was the new perfection and no one ever finished second lest it upset them. In truth he saw Youngman as a son of England, as near a member of the Virginia Company as four hundred and fifty years of distance would allow.

Their shared beliefs in pure lines and an obvious respect for both the dogs and the sport forged a swift and pragmatic understanding, and Brightwick let it be known that he would greatly appreciate using Mr Youngman's expertise to advance his own sporting endeavour. As far as Aiden's present employers were concerned, if advancement along both the US and UK corridors of power were facilitated by this plan, then all to the good. Terms of employment and travel arrangements were swiftly made, a five-year contract drawn up and signed and, thanks to good friends in the UK Foreign Office and US Homeland Security, visas, residency documents and the necessary permits were fast-tracked for a smooth transition. Within six weeks of the deal being struck Aiden Youngman joined the staff at Bliss Bank Hall under the official title Head Stockman at the newly named Calvary Kennels, with a generous salary to boot. His arrival was swiftly preceded by Gerry's sudden removal from the dog team. Now, with Aiden in charge, the relaxed atmosphere changed markedly, much to Chris' annoyance.

Six weeks after his arrival, courtesy of other good friends in the Foreign Office and UK Customs and Excise, licences and documentation were swiftly expedited and fresh young canine stock were imported from the USA. Calvary Kennels was set to move from strength to strength, the wins quickly overtook the losses and now, unlike former relaxed times, clear lines of responsibility were put into place to ensure this success continued.

Social interaction with dogs both young and old was discouraged, routine cleaning was carried out in silence with no pet names used and no attempts at fraternisation. The feeding regime was under Aiden's strict supervision, sourced and butchered by him, no treats were allowed lest they upset the delicate dietary balance, and definitely no toys lest they softened the dogs' demeanour; even raw bones for jaw strengthening were left with the dogs for just one day lest they became playthings. To increase response times and fitness, four tumbrels, two catch-up treadmills and two continuous current swim pools were installed; tug-bars and a practice arena were constructed and fitted out with training aids, and any live-bait needed was supplied direct to Aiden courtesy of the Loveridge family, for a price. All post-match injuries and retirements were handled in-house by Aiden, with the occasional assistance of a reluctant Chris. Within this smooth-running operation Chris was given kennel cleaning duties for the puppies and although, to some, that may seem like a demotion, to Chris with his history it was like a birthday present. The months that followed dropped into a routine, right up until now...

... Matt and Chris were speeding along the country road, both locked into their own Bliss Bank tumbrel, both feeling the heat.

'We've got Quinn to bullshit first then the Gaffer. He's not back 'til tonight but as soon as he lands we'd better be ready for it or we'll be thrown t' the wolves.'

The rest of the breakneck drive was undertaken in further grim silence as each man wrestled with the reasons, the tales... the possible outcomes.

~

'Linden Lea, which chat suite is she in?' Archie's question as he entered and stood on the grubby vinyl-floored lobby of Penngorse Police Station was greeted with a momentary pause by Desk Sergeant Robson before recognition kicked in.

'Ah, morning Sir. Er, suite?' Robson looked confused.

'Yeah. You know, soft furniture, coffee machine...for the relatives, the witnesses?'

'Oh yeah, them. No, not here.'

'So where is she then?'

'Interview Room Two.' Robson pointed. 'Down the corridor there.'

'Interview room...' Archie sighed at the news. 'Christ.'

'Really sorry to hear about DC Reeve Sir. Only met him the once, but...let's make sure we get the bastard.'

'That's the idea.'

'How's Kanjara? Anything to say?'

'Out of it, pain-killers and such. She's based here, right?'

'Yeah, three years now. Good copper.'

'She is.' Archie nodded towards the corridor. 'Who's with Miss Lea?'

'WPC Williams, Amoya. Fairly new, been here eighteen months.'

'Was she chosen on purpose?'

Robson frowned. 'Er, no...she was just who was available.'

'Blind luck forging the right choice.'

'Eh?'

'Nothing. And no one's talked to her yet?'

'No one Sir. I popped me head round the corner when she first got here, offered her a tea, she just gave me a shake of the head.'

'And nothing's come her way from the media?'

'Not from here. I can't vouch for her time with ARU though.' Robson handed a file across. 'Here Sir.'

Archie took the brown folder containing a couple of sheets of paper. 'Bit thin.'

'She's refused to comment apart from name, rank and serial number. Knows her rights it seems.'

Archie looked at his watch. 'Six o'clock. She must be knackered. Did she seem stressed?'

'A bit, wanted to know why she was being kept. I told her there were some details we needed to double check but that she wasn't to worry, that someone would see her soon, the usual tactics. She's aware there's serious stuff going on though.'

'She'll know it wasn't a cat up a tree. No one come in from her side?'

'Not yet. She made a phone call.'

'From her mobile?'

Robson checked the daybook again. 'Not got one. Made it from the desk here.'

'Bugger.'

'Thirty minutes ago, so just before I came on.'

'To?'

Another day-book scan. 'A...Sarah Wilmott. Red Lion.'

Archie twisted the day-book round and read. 'And you think she knows her rights?'

'Yeah. I've a feeling she doesn't entirely trust us.'

'No shit. Her and eighty percent of the adult population then.'

'Yeah, but it's got to be coming from past experience I'd say 'cos from first reports she's not on anyone's books.'

'No, she's not. No call to family?'

'Nope.'

Archie shook his head. 'I don't suppose Bereavement or Family Liaison have been in touch?'

'No sign yet.'

Archie sighed. 'Excellent, all cogs whirring here then. Right, thanks. Staff canteen, open all night?'

'No canteen. You can make tea in the back kitchen. Down and first on the right, milk in the fridge, tea bags in a tin above it marked tea bags. Use any mug but the one that's got "Keep Calm and Arrest Someone" on it, that's the Station Commander's. If you want food there's a twenty-four-hour greasy spoon and truck stop round the corner.'

'That'll do, send out for three bacon sarnies will you please, all on brown.'

'You payin'?'

'Not again...' Archie fished in his back pocket and put a ten-pound note on the counter. 'Make one well-done will you?'

'That'll be short.' Archie looked at him. 'Three bacon sarnies. Ten pounds fifty. You're fifty pence light.'

Archie shook his head and produced a fifty-pence piece, tossing it on the counter which was all the comment needed. 'I can get tea without paying though, right?'

'There's a visitors' contribution box in the main office if you want to help out.'

'Seriously?' The Desk Sergeant nodded. 'Great. Oh, Balsall Common will be delivering a dog here later.'

'A dog?'

'The one found guarding the hit-and-run victim.'

'Oh, right...er...we don't have any facilities. Where do we keep it?'

'Use an interview room, you use them for everything else.'

'Will it have been fed?'

'It will. I take it there'll be no kennelling fee?'

'Only if we have to clean up after it.'

Archie ignored this and walked down the corridor before turning into a small kitchen where he began to sort tea things. As he waited for the kettle to boil he flicked through the sparse notes from ARU. *Desk Sergeant wasn't kidding. Name, address...no call to family; why's that? Used Ms. Wilmott's name as her cover when she was first picked up then used her as her first port of call. Why d'you do that Ms. Lea...eh? Why lie? Afraid? Once bitten twice shy, is that it?* The kettle announced its intention. He placed the filled mugs onto a well-stained tray together with some well-ignored sugar sticks and a one pint, well-sniffed plastic milk container liberated from the small counter-top fridge. At the door marked Interview Room 2 he balanced the tray along one arm, his finger-ends wrapped over the front edge and tapped on the door with his free hand before stepping back. WPC Williams opened it and Archie gestured for her to join him in the corridor, nodding at the tray. 'Morning tea, Amoya, is it?'

The door creaked to behind her. 'Yes. Thanks Sir. How's Kanga?'

'You two worked together?'

'A few times, and us girls, particularly us girls, have to stick together.'

'I bet. She's sedated and out of it, but as well as can be expected considering. News is thin at present.'

'Except on the TV, and no doubt in the papers later.'

'That'll be conjecture not news.'

'I'm so sorry to hear about Detective Constable Reeve.'

Archie nodded. 'Yeah...yeah.'

He stood with the tray looking like a displaced waiter and Amoya put her hands under it. 'Here, let me have that Sir.'

'No, I'm good, it acts as displacement activity. Help yourself though, make it a bit lighter.' Amoya added a little milk then picked up the mug. 'Bacon butties are on their way. Has she said anything?'

Amoya shook her head. 'Only that she doesn't understand what's happened.'

'I'll bet. And you weren't able to get anything else?'

'Wants to know why she's being detained here, done nothing wrong, that sort of thing. Made a phone call about half an hour ago.'

'Yeah, I heard. Knows about the shootings though?'

'I suppose, she muttered about stuff coming through the police radio on her way across here...'

Archie sighed. 'It's a pity the ARU haven't learnt to isolate them yet. But she doesn't know anything about her sister?'

WPC Williams shook her head. 'Not that I'm aware of. Media was all locked down in here before she arrived as per your instructions. I reckon she thinks she's here because of the goings-on at her place and no one's disabused her of that.'

'You two just been in there in shared silence then?'

'Pretty well. After first asking about the people involved she's just sat there, self-contained like, almost as if she's meditating.' Amoya looked at her watch. 'Nearly an hour now.'

'Right.' Archie straightened up. 'You done one of these before?'

'Training only.'

'Then brace yourself. This tea's going cold, the newspapers will be hammering at the doors before long and we've no porter to stall 'em.'

'No what?'

'Nothing.' Archie motioned towards the door. 'In we go.'

WPC Williams led the way.

~

⁶Who? Sarah? What...what time is it?'

Sarah slipped in through the part opened door as a tousle-haired and fresh-from-sleep Vasiri closed it behind her. 'Seven o'clock. Have you not heard?'

Vasiri rubbed his eyes with fisted hands. 'Heard what? All I heard was you hammering on the door like the drug squad... Seven o'clock?'

'There's been a shooting at Lin's flats! It's all over the morning news.'

'Seven in the morning... A shooting?'

'Is there an echo in here? Yes! It's made the headlines, where've you been Vaz, in a cave?'

Vasiri pointed towards his bedroom then indicated his level of undress and state of his hair. 'No, I've been working then sleeping. Look at the state of me...what shooting? Is Lin OK?'

'Yes, yes. She phoned this morning; said she'd been arrested.'

'What, for shooting someone?'

'No Vaz...'

'I didn't even know she had a gun...'

'Shut up you idiot and listen! She hasn't shot anybody! Someone else shot some policemen at her flats last night.'

'Then why have they arrested Lin?'

This was happening a bit fast for Vasiri, Sarah could see that. 'What time were you in bed?'

Vasiri looked at his watch. 'A bit under forty-five minutes ago.'

Sarah sighed. 'OK. Last night. There was a double shooting of some police at Lin's flats and because of that Lin's been arrested and is down at Penngorse nick...can you get dressed?' Vaz stood, mouth agape as Sarah continued, 'She rang and asked me, us, to get over there, take a change of clothes and act as support... get dressed will you? 'Course, I can't get into her place, it's all taped off so I sorted some of my things, we're about the same size...Vaz! Get dressed! I tried to ring you, but your phone's switched off.'

Vasiri thought for a second. 'Er...no it's not, it's on vibrate.'

'Then why didn't you pick up.'

'I leave it in the kitchen. I do most of my work overnight on the net Sarah, you know I do, USA time differences and all that. If I silence my phone it means I don't get disturbed.'

'Then at least carry it with you. It's a mobile phone, the clue's in the name...and will you please get dressed!'

Vasiri moved into the bedroom. 'Is Tim involved?'

'Not that I know of.' Sarah did not leave it long before she pushed the door open. 'Will you bloody well hurry up!'

Vasiri snatched his up trousers. 'Hang on! Can you just...?'

'Vaz, I know what you look like part naked, we've been to the swimming baths together, remember?'

'When we were about seven, yeah.' Vasiri pushed his sockless feet into slip-on shoes.

Sarah grabbed him by the arm, hauling him to the door. 'Let's go!'

'My jacket...'

'Get it!'

'My phone, it's...'

She went into the kitchen and came out holding the mobile. 'Here...'

'How did you know it was in there?'

'Not another word from you. Car! Now!'

~

Brooms Road car park was busier than usual, courtesy of it being the second of a three-day whisky festival hosted by the good men of the Royal Burgh of Dumfries; this suited Josh and Jimmy's purpose well. The surfeit of cars left overnight so that owners had sufficient time to reduce the alcohol in their bloodstream to an acceptable level made for a good choice, and also gave Josh and Jimmy an above average chance of getting a head start in the discovery stakes. With the hire car number plates tucked underarm and screwdrivers in hand, the two men ambled along the rows of vehicles. A long look around, using the lighting of a cigarette as a distraction, confirmed all was clear.

Their bad-tempered journey had so far precluded any niceties, but they were so used to this particular routine that conversation was, thankfully, unnecessary. Down on one knee, Jimmy at the rear Josh at the front, they soon had the number plates replaced. A short walk to the next selected car ended in another changeover before they returned to their hire vehicle and fixed the fresh plates to it thereby completing the double whammy of confusion. The duo sped away from the scene, out along the river, over the bridge and safely on to the road to Stranraer, to Cairnryan and to home. Jimmy settled into the journey.

'Fuel?' Josh's moody resignation showed in his tone.

'Just over half a tank.'

'Barely enough. How far?'

'Hour and fifteen, hour and a half, enough to get there without stopping.'

Josh looked at his watch and rubbed his moustache vigorously. 'We'll miss the half past sailing then.'

Jimmy nodded, his efforts at lightening the mood showing distinct signs of wear. 'We will, can't be helped. Just get the next sailing, right? We'll be home free...'

Josh mimicked him. 'If we get the next sailing...right?'

'Jesus but you're a cheerful fella...we're away aren't we?'

~

'What time are you an' Cashman in tomorrow?'

Kenzie Jardine paused at the doorway of the Portakabin and turned to the black-and-white Cocker Spaniel seemingly glued to his leg. 'Sit up Cash.' The spaniel sat rigid, it's tail disobeying. Kenzie looked at his watch. 'In...six hours forty minutes from now. You?'

'Day off.'

'Jammy bugger.'

'Hardly worth while you two going home is it?'

'Always worth it.'

'Glenluce or Faye?'

'Both.'

James Lamont smiled at him. 'I'd feel the same, 'bout Faye anyhow. How come you got picked for the early shift again?'

''Cos I was out of the room when the vote was taken.'

James closed the port log. 'That'll learn y'.'

'Y' think so? That's how much you islanders know, my third early shift in a row.'

'Union wouldn't allow it.'

'And if we had one worth its salt plus a full contingent of staff I'd be the first to complain, but as things are now double shifts are the new eight hour day.'

'Means it's you here doin' the job though. I hear you had some more success the other day, those Samoyed puppies, or should I say yet more Samoyed puppies?'

'Aye.' Kenzie turned towards the dog that had maintained its place sitting at the doorway. 'Well Cash did, didn't y' lad, eh?' The spaniel half lifted its backside off the floor, its rump seemingly forced to hover by the movement of its tail. Kenzie held up a flat palm of instruction. 'Sit on it clever clogs.' The dog sat again, the downward pressure trapping the tail and stilling Cash's outward expression of happiness.

James smiled. 'Always seem to get the excitement on my days off.'

'That's because you always seem to get days off.'

'So do you, the difference is I take 'em.'

'Aye, well, you've seen enough of it to know there wasn't any excitement. Poor little mites they were.'

'Did he hear or smell 'em?'

'Bit of both I think. Lodged in amongst a delivery of used cooking oil from Albania. Fifteen, forty-five-gallon drums of the stuff so not an easy perfume to fight against.' He saw James' expression. 'Canny eh? Drums at the far end of the trailer, wall of waste-paper bales boxing them in.'

'Is that where they were from, Albania?'

'That was the truck's state of origin, but hard to tell. Eastern Europe definitely, but they could've been from almost anywhere on the trip, anywhere that's got breeders who want to avoid the expense of chips, jabs and quarantine.'

'And the driver did a divert through Ireland as well.'

'To collect the bales of paper, aye. The trace-back clocked the driver going via Slovenia too...' Kenzie paused. 'How many countries would that be?'

'Depends on the route. At least seven.'

'So they could've been loaded onto the truck from any one of the stops. Slippy sods.'

'Aye. As the rules change so does the footwork. How'd Cash find 'em?'

'Joint effort. The paper bales were three deep, but the stacker had been a bit sloppy and left a gap between a couple of bales 'bout halfway up, and you know what he's like about scuffling his way into gaps.'

'Aye. I always thought he should've been a terrier.'

'He'd just lifted his nose towards it and the driver took a half step forward. Shouldn't have done that. He's as daft as a brush most of the time, but if he senses it's me under threat...well, you've seen for y'self.'

'I have. Like when that Romanian fella, him with the false papers, pushed you against the truck then tried to make a run for it. I was glad he was on the end of those teeth an' not me.'

'Aye, when he goes in, he goes in. That three-week session we did with the firearms unit at Pollok Park really sharpened him, as if he needed it. They just see him as a spaniel, they don't realise he's an animal with a fierce understanding of pack protection and there's no brakes when he goes in. The chaps at Pollok were amazed that he faced point-blank gunfire and followed through; I wasn't.'

'And our mate with the cooking oil?'

'Soon got the message. He'd barely taken a step before Cash was part-way up his leg, teeth pressed up against his thigh, nose pointing at his dangly bits an' givin' that low rumble. The bloke freezes, but his eyes? I knew we were on to somethin' right then. Called McKinnon across from the gate and suggested the chap stayed with him if the life of a eunuch wasn't in his plans. I lifted Cash up to have a sniff at the gap in the bales, said 'Ganja Puppy' and he pushes against me belly with his back feet and slithers away in search mode. I was a bit worried 'cos you never know how secure this stuff is, but then he starts to yip, you know, that noise he makes when he's not sure what but knows that something's wrong?'

James smiled, enjoying the tale's unfolding. 'Aye.'

'That was enough for me. McKinnon walked him off to the office, I got Derek over with the forklift, the rest's in the report.'

'What was the final count?'

'Twenty.'

'In how many barrels?'

'Three.'

'Jesus...for what, up to four days?'

'Probably. At least three.'

'No wonder some were dead. Were they even weaned?'

'Just. Another designer breed for the moneyed classes.'

'Hang on.' James stopped to think. 'Twenty? In three barrels?'

'Well, three dead so seventeen in all.' Kenzie could see James' head working. 'The barrels were adapted to three-stories Jim. A floor and ceiling welded into the middle section of each, cooking oil top and bottom.' James' eyes widened. 'Pup sandwich. Took us an hour and a half to open 'em up.'

'Breathing holes?'

'They'd popped a few pin holes under each of the ribs and glued fragments of coloured hessian over them; crude and, it turns out, ineffective.'

'So that means no border security checked the load on the way across. Are you serious?'

Kenzie nodded. 'Yeah. Either short-staffed like us or fully-staffed and easy to bribe, but then at what, twelve hundred a pup? Easy money.'

'Well that's a new one on me.'

Kenzie looked at Cashman. 'First for us too wasn't it boy, eh?' The spaniel's hind legs moved slightly as its tail formulated an escape plan.

'Important thing is you saved a few. Dogs' Trust took 'em?'

'Yeah, again. God alone knows how these buggers gather so many together.'

'Could've been a collection trip. Different farms en route, different gangs workin' together; if there's money to be made someone'll find a way to make it.'

'An' as we all know, cutting staff in the Excise Office here is exactly the right way to tackle it.'

'They're not cutting staff they're streamlining potential.'

'Fuck that. They've halved the inspection crew here in the last three years and I'm the only dog man now.'

'But we've got carbon dioxide sniffers an' heartbeat monitors now, so...'

'And with no recruitment for the extra staff needed to operate them we're expected to multi-task. We can only pull aside one in seven trucks now y' know; one in seven...'

'I know Ken, I work here as well.'

'...And with twenty percent cuts year-on-year that number's set to increase. The last twelve months there's been six days when we've not been able to pull aside and check a single freight vehicle; six days, not even one truck. What did someone once call us here?'

'"The unlocked door to Great Britain."'

'Aye, that's it. The minute they spot we're under pressure they rush through their shipments; arms, drugs, slaves...dogs. Bloody joke it is.'

'Blood pressure Kenzie, blood pressure.'

'The devil with that Jim!' Cashman could sense the level of agitation in his master's voice and whined quietly, rising up to a sitting position, ears slightly back now and very alert. Kenzie saw it and moved back to the dog. Squatting down in front of him he took an ear in each hand and rubbed them gently. ''S'alright Cash, just Dad getting all riled up, but not at you.' He looked deep into the well of the dog's eyes. 'If they were to see a fraction of the stuff we see, eh? Animals near extinct in the wild arriving here dead or as near as makes no difference. Skins, horns, exotics...an' puppies.' Kenzie pivoted back on the soles of his boots. 'I've lost count of the dead pups he's found.' He turned back to the dog who wagged his tail and ran a friendly tongue across Kenzie's forehead. 'Good boy.' He stood and turned. 'I've been doing this job for nigh on twenty-five years Jim and the abject cruelty of folk still surprises me.'

'I should never have started his one...you take it all so personal.'

'When it's me has to shovel it up it is personal. Just glance at any page in the daily log. It's a wonder there's anything left the amount they slaughter or catch each year. They've impounded six tons of pangolin scales so far this year, and you'll have heard about Sheerness?'

'Yeah, came through on the daily briefing. Eighteen tiger cocks inside a shipment of bananas, actually inside some plastic bananas! Custom-made and buried right in the middle they were.'

Kenzie almost laughed. 'Aye. And you know what they were for? Tiger cock soup! Can you believe these people?'

'I can, but you gettin' all riled up won't sort it. Just don't tell your missus it were me what started the discussion.'

Kenzie's mood lifted a little. 'You've no need to fret on that account, you can do no wrong in Faye's eyes...oh, bugger!'

'What?'

'I forgot that tenner I owe you, from Sunday last; sorry Jim.'

'That's fine, you'll not be leavin' the country over it.'

'No, couldn't afford to. You and Megan still good for a fish supper on Friday? I'll bring it along then.'

'At the Cock Inn...?' James paused. 'There's topical then... yeah, eight o'clock, you can buy the first round with that tenner, unless you get grafted on for a second stint here of course.'

'I'll tell them to stick their shift.'

'No you won't, and that's why you look like someone's sucked the blood out of you.'

'I don't.'

'Yes you do. Tell me, where are you off to now? Straight home is it?'

'Via a ride out along the perimeter.' Kenzie saw the look. 'It's on the way.'

'To Glenluce? Bloody long way round. Jesus Ken, just give it a miss for once. Go by the seventy-five and you could be back to that lovely wife of yours in twenty minutes. Just watch those roads. That recent rain and this drop in temperature will make 'em like a skating rink.'

'Since when did you become my mother?'

'Since you stopped acting like a grown-up.'

Kenzie smiled and walked towards the door. A click of his tongue and the command, 'Heel up' brought the dog swiftly round. 'Come on Cash, let's leave this old letch to his dreams.'

The dog fell in alongside Master, tight to leg, tail wagging, out into the chilled morning air. James' voice followed them. 'Door!'

Without stopping Kenzie flicked his hand backwards. 'Close it Cash.' The dog slipped back and put his front paws on the door, the weight pushing it shut, before returning to heel. 'Good lad.'

James' muffled voice reached them as they walked to the van. 'You wanna sell that dog to a circus and retire on the proceeds!'

Kenzie looked down at the spaniel both of them taking such pleasure at their togetherness. 'He's got a point, I could y'know.' He opened the driver's door. 'Load up!' Cash jumped in and across to the passenger seat as Kenzie scanned the port yard then sighed. 'He's right y'know. Long day...long week. Sod it, let's go straight home.' The dog yapped.

Kenzie got into the driver's seat, clipped the dog into his travel harness and they were away, out of the port's main entrance and along the A75 towards home.

~

T he journey along the A75 had passed without incident and without comment. Castle Douglas and Newton Stewart had been successfully negotiated, and apart from the two men adhering to past habits of lifting seatbelts across their shoulders but not clipping them into pace, the better to allow for a swift exit if the enemy turned up, Jimmy made sure that speed limits and traffic instructions were faithfully followed. It was just after they had left Dunragit that Jimmy broke the brooding silence. 'Nearly there.' Nothing came back. 'Eh?' Still nothing. 'Jesus, you look like you were weaned on a gherkin, are you still moonin' about that bloody dog?'

Josh shifted slightly in his seat. 'Just leave it will y'?'

'You are. You've got your puss face on.' He sighed at having to go over what had obviously been an acrimonious discussion of earlier. 'Rebel had to go, can y' not see that?'

''S'pose...'

'Then stop bein' such a gimp about it.'

Josh turned in his seat. 'I'm not bein' a gimp alright! It's just he was...'

'A dog f'r feck's sake, he was a dog! We didn't shoot him did we?'

'No.'

'No. You was acting the maggot over it so I agreed to set him loose didn't I?'

'On th' feckin' motorway!'

'As much chance there as anywhere. There's no way we could've taken him with us, don't y' see? Two brogues with a battered pit-bull-cross tryin' to buy ferry tickets off the peg? Police are wise to us by now so they are, thanks to you turning that flat into a shootin' gallery, so there you have it, no choice. We can't draw attention, not if we want to get away, an' we do cos we're sittin' on two dead coppers.'

'But Rebel...'

'Will you cop on! He's gone, so are we with any luck, now shut it or I'll drop you off on the road t' join him!'

'Y' mean you'll try...' Josh reached into his inside pocket.

Jimmy knew what was in there and stabbed the brakes to stall this movement, the car scrabbling for grip on the patchy black ice before it was wrenched sideways and the front end slammed into the ridge fronting the grass verge. This first shock wave caused them both to lurch forwards, in Josh's case fully into the windscreen, Jimmy managing to brace himself on the steering wheel as the passenger door was ripped open and the air bags deployed. Jimmy's head was whipped to one side and whacked onto the door frame, Josh's head was flipped straight back onto the headrest and the gun, dislodged from his grip, was sent cartwheeling onto the rear seat before the vehicle twisted ninety degrees to bounce and slither, boot first, into the deep ditch, ending up with just one front wheel protruding from it.

Their pent-up disagreements to the fore, fighting each other, the air bags and their injuries in their efforts to gain the upper hand, their violence was reduced to near horizontal fist and foot movement as they grabbed, gouged and flailed in their fury. Any semblance of accuracy in this first flurry of blows was compromised by the lack of sight out of Jimmy's right eye because of the blood running into it and the poor breathing of Josh through his nose because of the blood running out of it. Even so, the two men fought with random spirit as they tumbled out through the crumpled doorway and into the ditch before scrambling up onto the road. Here, in undiminished anger, they charged like prop forwards, grabbing at each other, rolling and spitting as a pair of rival Highland toms would. After several seconds, using each other as leverage, they managed to scramble upright where they attempted to continue to trade blows. Jimmy's unsure footing caused him to fall short in his punch allowing Josh to land an unexpected but brutal thwack to the side of his head; Jimmy was knocked to the ground as Josh overbalanced on the ice and tumbled head first back into the ditch.

The snowfall of post-fight silence descended on the scene. Only the gasping breath of the exhausted and bloody participants spilt into the autumn air as they sat waiting for the next move.

Josh finally clambered out of the ditch and sat at its edge. 'That'll be the next sailing gone away then.'

Jimmy nodded at him. 'Gone...like that feckin' dog.'

T ogether once again in the lighted trophy room, Quinn and Matt were face-to-face in what had quickly become an acrimonious debate.

'It was two police officers Lamb, at the girl's flat! Two! And her and those Irish men still free!' Quinn spread his arms and shrugged in a hopeless gesture. 'Good God... The Minister was prepared for the possible loss of our lady friend, could have covered that, but...two police officers?'

'At the girl's flat, yeah, I heard. You repeatin' it aint gonna make the number any the less nor make it go away.'

Quinn raised one hand in a dismissive gesture and looked from Matt to the far window. 'Just how in hell are we supposed to cover this?'

'Because it's our job! What we have to do now is close ranks, sort stories and make sure, if it does come back here, that we've all the blocks in place to build a believable tale.'

'Of course it will come back here!'

'Why will it?'

'Because of that police constable who was here earlier, informing us of the hit-and-run.'

'Just a courtesy call. If there was any suspicion, they'd 'ave been down here with force. Trust me, I've first-hand knowledge of 'em.'

'And the Irish? They were here on this estate with their fighting dog!'

'And who knows that?' Quinn looked at him and blinked. 'No one, that's who. They were last minute arrangements. I know that 'cos I made them and anybody who saw them here is either dead or back in Chinky-land so what's to tell? Nothin', that's what. If them pair have any sense, an' I know we're talking

Micks here, but if they've any sense they'll've legged it back to Ireland.'

'But what if they stumble and get picked up? Don't try and tell me they'll keep quiet, not with a double police murder on their hands. They'll most likely do anything to soften the blow and that will mean using us as a trade-off!'

'Two Micks, each with a terrorist past, up against a peer of the realm? No chance. What you have to do is make sure we've got their credibility well and truly fucked even before they're found, if they're found. The Gaffer and you can do that; it's what you're good at. Raise the fear of them being a rogue element, of a fresh terrorist threat from Ireland, that kind of thing. And make up what you can't prove just like the red tops do; should be easy. Everybody over there's broken some law or other, you just need to muddy the waters. Until then we know nothin'. We, that's me and Chris, we'll make sure there's no physical traces to be found here.'

'Muddy the waters, right.' Quinn had calmed a little. In spite of the dislike he held for Matt he had to admit there was merit in his ideas, but he still wanted to make his position felt. 'Where is your assistant? He should be here.'

'He will be. I sent him to the kitchens, the chiller.'

'What, now? Why?'

'To get some bones for them pups.' Quinn looked at him in surprise. 'While you an' the Gaffer are away swannin' it in London things still have to go on here, Quinn. You heard any more from him by the way, any of his crack-brain ideas come back?'

The dig registered but Quinn decided not to react. 'No. He knows of course. I'll phone him to keep him up to date, but he's not back from Sheffield 'til late, then he has to go back to the House. I'll not get a full response until I meet with him again. Right, your plan?'

'The sties. We sweep 'em clean, and I mean clean. Me, Chris an' Aiden...'

'That's not what he's employed for.'

'Who, Aiden? Fuck that. If we don't get this sorted he'll have no employment, none of us will, we'll sink without trace; he's in. And in case them Micks do get caught and blab about us, about them Chinks, the pups have to go. That's why Chris is in the chiller. A bone apiece gets 'em to stand still and make an easy target. Blazer, Dreadnought and Derringer we can pass off as guard dogs, the rest go; and we cancel the dog fight.'

Quinn was in fast. 'We'll do no such thing and that comes from the top. The pups can go, yes, I'll support that and we can breed more, that's why the working stock will be needed. The Minister has no intention of having his kennels decimated or his forthcoming plans altered, certainly not after all the effort and money he's invested.'

'Jesus! Even with all this shit flyin' about he still wants to risk it?'

'You have no understanding of just what's at stake here do you?'

'If you pair were to tell me then I'd know, but you're both so bloody guarded about it all!'

'A full-on tantrum is not what's needed right now.' Matt's hackles rose along with the temperature in the room. 'You need to concentrate on your scrubbing duties.'

'I do?' Like in a wrestling match they held eye contact until Quinn finally looked towards Chris who had just entered the room. Matt's gaze never faltered as he spoke slowly, deliberately. 'Scrubbing duties; right Mister Quinn, I will. Thank you for giving me a reminder of my place here. Well, I'd be very grateful if you an' the Gaffer could see your way clear to dragging the brushwood behind us, help cover our tracks. We all do our jobs right and no one else needs to die...right?'

The tone and intent were obvious, and not for the first time in Matt's company, Quinn felt distinctly uneasy. 'Absolutely. Yes of course. And the man's bungalow? Do you have plans for that?'

'Torch it now you mean?'

'Yes.'

'I've readied it, but it stays built until we've no choice and we can handle the flack that'll come from it; one crisis at a time.'

Quinn shifted the focus to Chris. 'Right Phillips. Lamb will tell you the detail. Suffice to say that everything rests on us all doing a first-class job, understand?'

Matt was eager to be away and tried to wrap things up with Chris. 'Bones?'

'In the car.'

'Right, let's...'

'An' summat else. Possible problem.'

Quinn vocalised their trepidation. 'What? What else?'

Chris answered Quinn but looked at Matt. 'Gemma.'

Quinn paused for a moment, his expression telegraphing his bemusement. 'Gemma...? You mean Miss Connor?'

'Yeah.'

'Our housekeeper and cook? That Miss Connor?'

Matt joined in. 'What about her?'

'Not Gemma, her sister.'

'Her sister...?'

'Yeah. I was in the chiller gettin' bones just now an' I heard 'em talkin', Gemma and her sister Andera.'

'Andrea.'

'Yeah, Andera. They was just round from the chiller door, them an' a couple of the kitchen crew. This Andera came up by train from London and she told this tale about an 'alf-caste girl finding a bundle of cash and returning it to a Mick on the train.'

Quinn's eyes grew wider by the second. 'All the staff was impressed, marvelled about how they weren't all terrorists, some were good. She saw it all on the train, Andera did.'

Quinn was aghast. 'This Andrea was on the same train?'

'She was.'

'But...good Lord, that means someone else knows, and that girl's still on the loose!'

Matt stepped in. 'Stop y' frettin' Quinn. Nobody knows anybody in all this, there's no connection between them or to here, they're just strangers on a train.'

'Strangers who might be the only people in the universe who can identify the Irishmen in a police line-up!'

'If they get picked up.'

'Well shouldn't we at least talk to the Connor sisters?'

'Let sleepin' dogs lie I say'

'But what if she talks?'

Matt was getting to the end of his patience. 'About what? Jesus Quinn, you'd have to be psychic to add this lot together.'

'Well...I'll have to inform His Lordship. What his reaction will be I don't know...all we need after a sleepless night.'

'Us too, Quinn! Well, tell him or don't tell him, this one's past my attention span.' Matt turned to Chris. 'Right, for now we'd best get our boots and scrubbing brushes then collect Aiden on the way, we've got a cleanin' job to do.' Quinn stood for a moment or two until he turned on his heel and swept out through the door. 'One day I'll have that little shite-poke so I will.' Matt turned to the door. 'Come on.'

~

There's nothing like the smell of cold congealing fat for making a room seem uninviting and uncared for, particularly with the sadly neglected moss green walls underlining it. The centrally positioned laminate table in Interview Room Two at Penngorse Police Station was dressed with what the English laughingly referred to as breakfast, the remains of which were pushed to the side like unwanted relatives at a family gathering. Grouped around the three grease-stained white paper bags, two empty one full, were five mugs, each decorated with twenty-first century graffiti and holding tea dregs in their tannin-stained interiors. Keeping them company were two discarded paper napkins and a part-finished pack of Rich Tea biscuits. To the side of the mugs, scrunched to an origami state no Japanese practitioner could copy, were two gum wrappers. Both Archie and Lin rested their forearms on the tabletop, Archie's hands folded into gentle fists, Lin's close to her chest and clasped in mock prayer. Her face reflected the emotional intensity of the recent conversation and Archie sat quietly, respecting her silence and inner turmoil.

WPC Williams entered, speaking quietly but unable to avoid disturbing the eggshells left by recent disclosures. 'Sorry Miss Lea, Sir...there's no mugs left, can I just...?' She gathered the mugs, the chink of their removal serving to emphasise the previous silence. 'Back in a couple of minutes with fresh tea.'

Almost from the very start of their conversation he was aware he was asking Lin to enter rooms of historical importance she would rather leave locked, but these things had to be done and Archie smiled, gaining relief at the out-breath her interruption had provided. ''S'alright Amoya. Thanks.' He twisted back towards Lin, eager to further the conversation but not wanting to be pushy. 'So, the wrist bands you're wearing, Renata made them?'

'Yes, she did.'

'And the netsuke?'

'No... That's another story...' She rolled her fingers over the bands in a near caress. 'It's what I'd grab from a house fire. She gave them to me the last time we met.'

'Which was a year, eighteen months ago you said?'

She saw his expression. 'I know...but, not big on get-togethers Rene and me...Just...family stuff, history, you know?'

Archie nodded in understanding. 'Know it well. We'll have to touch on that later if you feel able, but for now a bit of background would help me get some sort of understanding on events; that OK?' Lin nodded. 'OK. You've told some bits already, let's get a little context. You've friends locally, Tim for a start, and you also gave a false name and address to the ARU... Armed Response Unit. Sarah was it?'

Lin coloured slightly. 'Wilmott. Yes, sorry about that.'

'What made you do that? It's not as though you'd done anything wrong.' Lin shook her head. 'Then why?' She remained silent. 'For all they knew you were armed and dangerous and they'd got guns too, loaded guns. You knew that and yet you still ran off.' Lin tensed a little. 'And from their reports it seems you knew the shooting was at your place.'

'At the flat?' She looked at him for a moment or two, making decisions on the hoof, deciding just how free she could be. 'Yes, I did. I...felt it. Usathane walked over my grave, the Devil, like the night Rene failed to get back in touch.' She saw no alteration in his gum-chewing, not even a flinch. 'I just joined the dots, do you see?' She smiled a little self-consciously at Archie who still held the same look of deep concentration. 'Rene was always bad at contact, but this time? This time was different.' Silence followed as Archie gathered his thoughts, allowing Lin more time to study his face. *He's seen some stuff this one, and not all of it good... a gentle heart in a room of beasts, and what's with the gum...?* Her thoughts were interrupted as Archie began.

'OK... Some of this is rhetorical, other stuff you'll be able to help me with... Let's be realistic about all this. Why your place? Was that a mistake or was it actually for you? Forgive me, but you're hardly dripping art treasures and gold bullion, just an unemployed lady who wears home-made leather wrist bands and paints herself as a bee. You're living a low-profile life in a backwater town and yet, in the space of three days, your twin sister is the victim of a hit-and-run, a masked man breaks into your flat and shoots two police officers, and you run from an armed unit. Where's the common thread in all this? Begs the question of whether you've got any bad connections...to your home country?'

'Well spotted. Can't hide it even after all these years.'

'South Africa?' Lin nodded. 'Twang's still there in the background. Accent gets thicker when you're angry or on the phone to friends and family I'll bet?'

'To my sister it did.' She held his stare.

'OK. Erm, your mum and dad are...?'

'Both passed...' She looked lost for a moment. 'Long time gone.'

'I'm sorry to hear that. Your family came over to England when?'

'Eighty-nine and they didn't, we did; Rene and me...all that remained of a family. Came across by ship.'

'How old were you?'

'Thirteen.'

'Thirteen and on your own?'

'Not quite. We had a guardian of sorts, but we might as well have been on our own. She was only in it for the free documents.'

'And am I right in thinking your distrust of the police, your reactions, they come from your time back home?'

'Early years coming back to haunt me.'

'Ah. Right. So, you came across to the UK... Was there no one you could stay with over there?'

'Not if they wanted to live.' Archie sat up further at this and waited. 'What few friends we had left, those brave enough to identify themselves as such anyway. They managed to squirrel us away until they could convince the relevant authorities that shipping us off would save them the embarrassment of international damnation if they did anything else; God knows how they managed that.'

'Jeez... OK, let me... With a guardian you said?'

'So-called.' She half-smiled at the memory. 'A loskind looking for an easy trip to the UK.'

'Loskind?'

'Sorry. Like the accent I drop into slang; old habits. Erm... slut, slapper.'

'Oh,'

'Cunard, the shipping line, they insisted on it...that we travelled with an adult I mean, not necessarily with a slut.'

Arnold smiled. 'Not very sensible, entrusting two minors to that kind of influence? Was there no one more suitable?'

'No. Suitability didn't start 'til we arrived in the UK.'

'Who was that with?'

'Nanny Betty. Dad's mum.'

Archie paused and exchanged old gum for new, offering one to Lin who refused it with a smile and a shake of her head. 'I know, just a habit, helps me concentrate.' He folded the silver paper around the old gum and added it to the pile. 'OK. So, here you are, you and your sister... Were the options of staying in South Africa really that impossible?'

'For us, yes.' She sighed as embers long turned to ash now glowed brightly under the fan of Archie's questioning. 'We were persona non grata through our parentage alone, so when it came to the choice of travel companions suitability was of little concern. Probably hoped she'd toss us overboard.'

Her lack of emotion showed, and Arnold noted it. 'Right...but I'm still confused about how this connects to where we are now... OK. Your folks are...?'

'Killed by poachers; same place, same day.' Her statement interrupting him was as abrupt as Archie's reaction and it took a while for her to add to it. 'My backpack of ghosts...' She sighed. 'Erm... Mum's family were members of a political movement in the forties and fifties that was affiliated to the Torch Commandos?' Archie shook his head. 'Germ of the anti-apartheid movement, or Communists as the west likes to refer to them. Made themselves a lot of enemies. The indigenous people, my mum's lot included, they had the audacity to say they wanted to manage their own country and its resources, remove it from the grip of the whites.'

'Found an echo in your bee protest then?'

'I was never so brave... Their involvement marked them out as an enemy of the state, mine just got me a line in a local rag by a reporter who was only interested in my colour, the size of my tits and my outfit.'

'Beavis? You're not special, he treats everyone like that. Was your mum involved in all this then?'

'And how. She was an only child, grew up secretive, self-reliant, well, with that as your background who wouldn't? Idolised grandad and that made her feisty.'

'I've heard that phrase said of you.'

'I take it as a compliment. My mum in me, and my nan.'

'OK.' Archie drew in a deep breath. 'Elephant in the room; you're from South Africa but, y'know...?'

'Coffee coloured? Mum's family were originally from Nigeria, they moved south for the work and that's where she met Dad. My guess is he'd no idea what he was getting into; soon got educated. As if belonging to that family of communists wasn't enough, my mum marrying a white man just underlined their undesirable status for anything and everything. Jobs, housing, medical care...friends even. Gone native they called it, betraying the Commonwealth. All state help shut down, all travel, social rights, welfare...the works.'

'Must have made life difficult for you and your sister, even as kids.'

'Oh yeah. When the nationalists go on-point they really know how to put the fear of the state into you.'

Archie paused, digesting the sheer volume of information. 'So you lose both parents then you get shipped over here to a new country and a new school full of new faces and you two full of old fears...and with your colour? Must've been a breeze.'

'Yeah, a breeze.'

Archie sighed and shook his head. 'Big stuff for small girls.'

'Mum raised us to cope.'

'Didn't you wish for it to be quieter? I mean all this angst and fear, did you not resent it?'

'No. Mum and Dad were, are, my complete heroes. Rene's too.'

'All that baggage though.'

'It laid the foundations for us to deal with what followed.'

'There's more?'

She raised her brows, nodded and looked at the uneaten food on the table. 'Sorry about that. There's the difference you see. You might not think it, but that's what's comfortable about living here. If this was happening back there, the South African police would've known I was veggie, it would've been on my file and you'd be force-feeding me meat right now. They knew everything about us, every little thing.' She sighed. 'You sure you want all this?'

'Only if you feel able. It's surprising how crimes are solved.'

'And demons are killed by the sunlight of sharing... OK.' She launched into it. 'Back then much of the ivory poached in South Africa was sent out from Durban. Mum and Dad challenged that ivory trade, and when they did that they challenged the three p's: poachers, police and politicians. All their friends thought them dwankie, mad. Told them what they were doing was a direct threat to the pay packets of the rule-makers and enforcers, that it would only be a matter of time before those three p's would come to some arrangement, an accommodation, and it'd turn into a race to see who was keenest to finish the job. Poachers beat the police to it and got in first. Mum and Dad knew all that but did it anyway.'

'Jesus... You seem so accepting of it all.'

'Now? Yes, but back then? Not at all. Never cried so much and so hard for so long, not before or since. Thought I'd go dwankie...Rene did in a way.'

'Not surprising. We had ideas here in the UK of how bad things were, inklings. Marches and protests by those who paid attention, Corbyn, Tariq Ali, Hain, one of the Kinnock's, I think. I even did a couple myself, but I was never so brave either. Career, life, working for the state, it all got in the way...for what good it did. All of us became wiser after the event, but it's never quite the same as when you're living it. Your folks must have been very isolated.'

'We were the unit. Us and a couple of other brave souls. The poachers could operate with virtual impunity, courtesy of the kickbacks they paid out. Still can. The police were just a private security force employed by politicians who already despised my mother for daring to be a socialist, for daring to be black and marrying white, and Dad for his betrayal. Then Mum and Dad upped the ante and opened their elephant orphanage, Iranti ti Erin...Memory of Elephant in Mum's language. It's still an orphanage now, still taking in the babies of slaughtered elephants; nothing changes.'

'You didn't go back?'

'Ha! Back to that? To those memories, that hatred?'

'What, not even after Mandela took control?'

'Wasn't all sweetness and light even then, not for years. Don't get me wrong, Mandela was the man, but to make it work he had to sup with Usathane, and the change of government didn't suddenly rid the country of the bribery and corruption, of the poachers and rogues. No, the old guard were still very much in play in the bush. Going back there, Rene and I wouldn't have felt safe, not with our parentage, our history, not after the things we'd witnessed. Then, when things did truly settle...well, I couldn't afford the bus fare to Witney let alone Wartburg; nah, let sleeping dogs lie.'

'Truth and reconciliation depend on who you tell the truth to and about, is that it?'

'Something like that, yeah. Thing is, something like Iranti ti Erin costs a lot to run, so Mum decided to advertise it to the wider world as a charity along with the reasons for its necessity. That's when ill-disguised punishments turned to outright hatred. On a hiding to nothing my folks were, they played right into it...and we lost them.'

Lin stopped, looking towards the opening door and the arrival of WPC Williams carrying a tray with three well-balanced mugs of tea. Amoya crossed to the table and placed them down. Archie looked into his mug as she spoke. 'Ran out of milk. Yours is black Sir; sorry.'

Lin looked at her. 'Story of our lives Amoya.'

'Fast Lin, you're fast, I'll give you that. OK, back to it. You said, about the lives of your mum and dad...you said you lost them.'

'Not lost so much...stolen more like. Bravest people I knew, will ever know.'

'Lost them?'

'They were murdered, Amoya, back in South Africa when Renata and I were kids.'

Amoya put her mug down slowly. 'Wow... I'm so sorry. What did they do, your parents?' She looked self-consciously at them both.' Sorry Sir, I didn't mean to butt in, I was making tea...just...'

'I know. It took me like that.'

Lin turned to Amoya. 'Mum and Dad opened up a rescue centre for baby elephants left after their parents had been poisoned, snared or shot by poachers...' Lin sipped at her tea before continuing. 'Anyway, as I was telling your boss, after the orphanage opened up it didn't take long for Mum and Dad to be seen as an even bigger dam to the river of profits being made from the ivory.'

'Big money involved?'

'I've seen men with so much they could commit suicide by jumping off their wallets, even then it's never enough. Nothing exercised their minds as did the rustle of cash being removed from their pockets.'

Archie picked up on it. 'And that's why you ran from the ARU.'

'Seems silly to say but, yes. After the shooting at my place and now, with the death of Rene... One thing I've learnt, nothing bears a grudge like a slighted politician, and no matter where you are in the world, the supporters of apartheid are a special breed when it comes to that, I can tell you; still are...and Mum and Dad made an awful lot of very powerful people very pissed off.'

'And what about you and Renata through all this?'

'Loved it. Baby elephants to play with, how could you not? There were three of us...' She stopped, caught by her use of the past tense so easily, and fished in her jacket pocket, pulling out an old photo in a plastic wallet. Three girls and two baby elephants stared out of the picture. 'Rene and me and Khanyisile, Momma Lesedi's daughter, and we had the time of our lives. That's Khanyisile, she still works at the reserve. Her mum delivered me and Rene.' She paused and collected herself. 'We only understood about Mum and Dad's sacrifice later. Back then we just ran around in the sunshine with half-ton friends, played together in the lake at the back of the house.'

'And how about now?' asked Amoya. 'You say the orphanage is still going?'

'It is, sad to say. Things are safer now, but back then, an orphanage like ours, like Iranti ti Erin? It flew in the face of government denials, but, like I said, through it all Mum and Dad knew exactly what they were doing and where it might end up, but they did it anyway. It was only when they showed us why Iranti ti Erin was necessary that we really understood.'

'Showed you? What, you mean...?'

'Once.'

'Wow. That must have been traumatic.'

'Made a memory for sure.'

'How old were you?'

'Rising ten.'

Archie's eyes were wide open at this. 'Jesus... How?'

'Family outing.'

Amoya's eyes also widened at the matter-of-factness of it all. 'That's what I'd call extreme parenting.'

'Just parenting. Too much made of my little darlings these days. You see something like that, something that's so wrong, it teaches you right, d'you see?' Lin laid out the details in her head, then spoke. 'They'd got a tip-off, bush telegraph, no time to lose just grabbed us and away, and we found her...' Lin was back there, they could both see it in her eyes. 'That beautiful, dedicated mother slaughtered and butchered, her gentle face smashed, one tusk hacked out with a tapanga, the other still attached by bloody strips of meat left in their panic to get away before anyone arrived; her tiny baby close by, stunned into immobility by the brutality, and all that...blood. Those men were in a hurry, so...Dad had to deal with it... You see something like that, it sorts out your priorities; fast. Mum and Dad talked us through it afterwards, made sure we understood what had happened and why they did what they did...that was our introduction to Africa's slaughterhouse.'

The concern showed on Arnold's face. 'What about the baby?'

'Amahle.' She lifted the photo again and pointed to the smaller of the baby elephants. 'That's her, on the left. Couldn't leave her there, impisi would've made short work of one so small. Loading her into our truck was...entertaining. Rene sat with her, soothing, talking as we took her back to the reserve; she's still there. She was our constant companion, well, Rene's really. She took charge. Amahle doted on her, followed her everywhere, even tried to get into bed with her once; smashed it!' She laughed at the memory. 'As much a sister to Rene as I was. Khanyisile said she pined for months after we left, literally months. Stood outside the bungalow, dropping her trunk into Rene's bedroom, drawing in huge trunkful's of air so as to catch Rene's scent... Poor little Amahle...'

~

Kenzie saw the two men from some distance away, picked out in the headlights. 'Odd time to be walking to the port Cash, eh? Stupid way to be dressed at night as well, all in black. Should at least have a high-viz chest stripe, that or some reflective tape on their shoes. Well, if they want the half-past it's gone.' Cashman placed his front paws onto the dashboard and stared out of the windscreen then whined once and whipped his tongue round his flews. 'Agreed eh?' Kenzie slowed down and lowered the window as he drew level. Now the spaniel placed both front paws on Kenzie's nearest leg, his gaze piercing and fully concentrated as the two men stopped walking. Both of them seemed unwilling to get too close, but even at this distance and in this light the bruising on their faces showed. Kenzie smiled at them.

'Evenin'. You to the ferry?'

There was an awkward silence before Josh answered. 'Who wants to know?'

Kenzie was taken aback by the brusqueness of the reply. 'Er... no one, just, y' know...?' Now he was stationary the marks on their faces and hands showed more clearly. 'You both OK?'

'We are.'

Kenzie realised that conversation concerning health and temper was not required. 'Aye, well, OK. I was just going to say, if you were for the ferry then you've missed the half-past sailing that was all.' Cashman took another step across to Kenzie's other leg, the seatbelt tether halting further progress as he leant forward and began drawing in the evening air.

'That right?'

'Aye. I mean, if you've an open ticket it'll be fine, but otherwise, with a fixed-time ticket you may have to buy again...' Kenzie could see he was talking to people who were not listening. 'Can I offer you a lift to the ferry port, if that's where you're going?'

Cash continued to pull in further scents, his senses and learned memory working overtime in order to decipher a level of information denied his human companion. Dousing the present scents of master and car interior with a lick of his nose, he prepared to receive the new chapter of understanding drifting towards him. The ever-present saline-spiked air and traffic scents were overridden as Cashman concentrated. *Sweat; urine; faecal matter; stomach-acid droplets on breath...a sweet smell with a background of soil and solvents, the same smell as in Master's cabinet at home and in some of the clinking containers inside the lorries that came into the port, the scent of a dog, and blood; dried; two types, and...?* It was then the aroma of lead styphnate from a fired gun reached him. Cashman immediately recognised this scent as a threat he had encountered several times in searches over the years and at the training centre at Pollok Park. Kenzie recognised the signals from his dog, not the detail, just his level of arousal. Outside the car the two men attempted to shut things down and move on.

'An' who says we're to the ferry then?'

Once again the shortness of the reply was not lost on Kenzie. Cash's ears lifted slightly as he leaned to the window and let out a low, deep growl which set all of Kenzie's senses to red alert. 'Er, no one, I just thought...' He pushed against the dog's chest. 'Get back, Cash.' The dog leant back a little, but the low rumble continued.

'That your dog?' Jimmy slid his hand behind his back and gripped the nine-millimetre pistol tucked into his belt as Kenzie nodded in reply. 'Nice dog. You work there then, you two? At the ferry port?'

There was something in the way the question was framed that made Kenzie alter his reply. 'You don't need a lift then?'

'Nah, we're just walkin', y'know, takin' the air.' Josh took a couple of steps towards the vehicle. 'The dog, a sniffer is it?' Cashman leaned forward again, the former low rumble lifting to a full growl as the scents grew in strength. Josh halted. 'Bit sharp is he?'

'Knows his job, but no, daft as a brush usually.' Kenzie shut down the conversation. 'Well, enjoy the stroll then, g'night.' He closed the window, slipped the car into gear and set off.

Josh looked across at Jimmy. 'Feckit... They work the docks, him an' that feckin' sniffer dog. If he goes on that way he'll find the car, feckit...'

Cashman, still rumbling, stepped back onto the passenger seat and revolved slowly, watching the disappearing men in the glow of the rear lights. Kenzie, too, took a long look back in the wing mirror until they were lost in the darkness. The thrum of the road was backdrop to the silence in the car until Kenzie spoke.

'Summat not right there Cash.' The dog barked and continued to stare rearwards. The next few moments were conducted in silence until Kenzie had almost driven past the ditch-delivered vehicle before it registered. 'What the...?' Slowing as rapidly as the conditions would allow and turning back round using the headlights for a sweep-search illumination, he drew alongside it. With the engine still running he unclipped the dog, put his hazard lights on and went over to the abandoned vehicle, Kenzie torch in hand, the spaniel leading the way.

Going round the vehicle, Cashman began to piece together the trails and scents. 'Anybody there?' Kenzie called out, then he waved a hand. 'Get in Cash. Seek on!' The dog jumped down and began a search along the ditch in the direction indicated as Kenzie shone his torch along its other side then into the car's interior. 'How the hell did it get here Cash, eh?' The dog rejoined him. 'Nothing?' Cash wagged his tail then closed in on the car. 'Ganja-puppy!' The spaniel hopped up into the car and began a detailed check of the interior. Kenzie shone his torch back along the road, his face creased in inquiry, but Cash was busy with other puzzles. *There they were again, the same scents as earlier...*

The spaniel's querulous yip alerted Kenzie. 'What is it, fella, eh? What y' got?' Cashman scratched at the rear seat. Kenzie looked back up the road. 'It's those two isn't it? You knew it too, didn't y'? Good lad.' Shining the torch inside, Kenzie's eyes locked onto the smears of blood decorating one of the airbags. 'Oh Christ, and on their way to the ferry too. Out y' come fella. Heel up!' Cashman jumped out of the wreck and followed Kenzie to the car as he fired up his mobile. 'Need to call James, get him to alert the port police.' Kenzie opened the passenger door and the spaniel jumped in as he buttoned the pre-dialled number and walked round to the driver's side. He opened his door as James picked up.

'Hi Jim, it's Kenzie, I'm just along the seventy-five...' Cashman barked. Kenzie followed his arrow-straight gaze along the road. There was no mistake, two men were trotting, swiftly and with purpose, towards them. 'We gotta go Cash.' Kenzie tossed the phone onto the dashboard, got in and slotted reverse as the two men increased their speed, one of them reaching into his belt.

'Oh shit...'

Cashman barked.

The windscreen was punctured as the first bullet entered through it, zipping between Cashman and Kenzie before blistering its way out of the rear window.

~

'Poor little Amahle...'

Lin stopped, struck by the reality of it all and Archie could see she was lost in its depths. 'It must've had a lasting effect on you all.'

'Definitely on Rene. That scene, the brutalised mother, it just made her withdraw. We were born only an hour apart, but Rene was definitely a late lamb. Always the creative one, gentle, living in the sunny stories of her own making, and loving her time with the locals and with Amahle, but seeing that scene of such bloody savagery? That really stuck, I mean really. She was never the same after that. Then, when Mum and Dad were murdered...' Lin waved a hand in despair. 'Her heart broke a third time when we had to leave Amahle behind, but we had no choice. That's when I knew we'd lost her.'

'Lost her, as in?'

'As in everything. Nanny Betty, people, the world... Me... She closed down on the trip over here and when we arrived things just went from bad to worse. She got into trouble at school, truanted at every opportunity, Nanny Betty was at her wits' end, I mean, she'd gained us but lost a son so was struggling with the constant reminder, and Rene. Everything was on sufferance for Rene, everything. The only things she could relate to were animals...trying to gain forgiveness for leaving Amahle I suppose... I'm not making any sense, sorry... Animals...the strays she picked up, Jasper for one.'

'Well, if it helps Jasper's being delivered here later, by our canine unit. He picked up an injury, so...'

'The car hit him too did it?'

'No Lin…no. I should have said earlier, when you first mentioned him. He was shot, just a ricochet, but he needed a bit of veterinary care so we dropped him off at our dog place to get sorted out.'

'Yet more guns.'

'Just a clumsy attempt to finish an already botched job, luckily it was human error that saved Jasper.'

She looked up at him. 'These aren't humans. Is Jasper alright?'

'He's OK, but he's minus a front tooth now. Got a gap when he grins…well, when I say grins, snarl covers it better.'

Lin smiled thinly. 'That'll be Jasper, he's a toughie. She got him from a dogs' home. The only room she had was for strays, occasionally for me.' Lin smiled a little as the memory came back. 'When she was little she was forever coming home with some creature or other she'd found, some waif or stray. It used to annoy the hell out of Nanny Betty, but she put up with it, tried to make a connection with her through them and back to her son, I guess. All for nothing really. She used to say, "The only thing I want from society is for it to leave me the fuck alone". The day after her sixteenth birthday she left, took the remains of her cake and sloped off. Only ever checked in every now and then, to reassure folk. She did her own thing from then right up to the last.' Once more she paused and gathered herself up to continue in spite of it all. 'The last time we met up.'

'Eighteen months ago?'

'Yeah. I bought her some fresh clothes from a market in Leicester. That's where she was camping at the time. Good day that. I was getting some odd bits of work so I could afford to buy us some lunch, had our photos taken in one of those booth things.'

'I've seen them.'

'What, the photos?'

'Yeah. They're with Forensics but I'll get them back to you when they're done with them.'

'Thank you. The others are in my bag, be good to reunite them.'

'Can I see them?'

'Yeah, 'course.' Lin fished in her bag and produced the photos. 'Here.'

Arnold looked at them and the writing on the back. '"So I don't forget what you look like". Right, that's another mystery cleared up. The writing on the other pair, we couldn't quite make it out, now I can.' He gave them back.

'Oh, yeah, I scribbled a line on both. Well, that's when I first met Jasper. She'd had him about a year. Yet another infrequent visit of mine, but what are you to do? She was never in the same place for more than a few months at a time and for most of that time I've been without money...for what seems like forever.'

'I'm not judging Lin... Well at least now you'll be able to meet up with him again.'

'Good. I got her a mobile phone on that last visit too, got us both one.'

'Pay as you go?'

Lin nodded. 'That broke me pretty well. It was her one and only nod to twenty-first century technology, and she only did that for me. I managed to scrape the payments for calls together so's we could keep in touch. Well I did, she was never very good at anything like that, I bet she never even charged it.'

'No, she did. At the local library.'

'Oh...Rene. Such a rubbish sister...she never made any calls, hardly ever answered mine.'

'We were aware she had a mobile from other lines of enquiry, but it wasn't with her when we found her.'

'Could've lost it. Never did get the meaning of the word mobile, not unless it referred to herself. Maybe she left it at wherever she was camping.'

'When we find out where that was we'll know.'

'Not yet?'

'No. Search squad are on it, so hopefully soon.'

'Tell them they need to look very carefully. Wherever it was it'll be hard to find. Rene may have been bad at some things, but bush-trekking? She was a past master at it.'

'Right, I'll pass that on.' Archie paused. 'Look, there's no easy way to say this. Can I ask you to do an official identification? You're the only one...sorry.'

Lin nodded. 'Yes, of course. Where and when?'

'Not far and now?'

'Sure.' She paused. 'The wrist bands. How did you know Rene made them?'

'I found some on the lane, where the incident took place. The dog's collar, did she make that herself too?'

'Plaited leather?' Archie nodded. 'Then yes. And the netsuke, can I have that as well?'

'The what?'

'The elephant netsuke. It's a...'

'No, sorry, I meant I know what a netsuke is; what netsuke?'

'Rene's'. Lin pulled back her sleeve. 'Exactly like this one. I'd just like to have it.'

'Exactly the same?'

'On an acorn, yes. Rene and I had one each, and then Khanyisile, she wanted one too, wanted to be our other sister, so another was made...the only three in the world. ' Lin stopped and stared at the table for a few seconds. 'I'm going to have to phone her soon, Khanyisile. Not looking forward to that.'

Archie nodded. 'Yes, always hard being the messenger.'

'Oh no, she'll already know. The details of Rene's future, that's what she'll want.'

'Future?'

'Yes. Erm... When these three netsuke were made we had a ceremony, all three of us, when we were six and Khanyisile was five.'

Amoya leant in slightly. 'What, like a joining ceremony you mean?'

'Yes, a birth ceremony. Did you?'

'Not me, but I know about them from my grandma.'

'Well ours was a homespun affair using some of the birth rituals. Momma Lesedi, she dropped the netsuke into a bowl of milk, pricked our fingers and dipped them in, then we each drank in turn, three times, then she poured the rest on the ground. Our blood was used to give the milk extra strength. Milk from the breast is the giver of life, blood of the nurturer, a gift from an earth mother to mother earth. That ceremony joined us as three sisters and made those ivory netsuke our connector, they're sacred to us.' Lin looked troubled. 'Did you not find one?'

'Not at the scene no. Could she have left it at her campsite?'

Lin slipped off the netsuke. 'This? No. Rene would never go anywhere without it, never.' Archie took it. 'Even when I bought her the mobile she said, "Why do I need this, we've got our connector"?'

'What, like, a route through to each other?'

Lin nodded. 'Exactly. Mum taught Rene and me in the old ways.'

'Which was?'

'That we're all connected, all of us, all life on this planet. Invisible threads interconnect us...like spiderwebs, a platform we all stand on, all of life, so when something happens to one it happens to all. We're each at the centre of our web of beliefs, our own core and we're responsible for seeing it doesn't become fractured by things like carelessness or cruelty.' Archie and Amoya listened in silence, both captivated by the tale. 'Over the centuries we've rejected this connection with the earth, become clever, lost our roots. That means, sometimes, to help us rediscover this connectivity, we need reminders, signposts to get back to our core. That netsuke was our signpost, Rene's, Khanyisile's and mine, our way back to each other if ever we became lost; that's why she'll know about Rene.'

Amoya frowned. 'But... wasn't an elephant killed for them?'

'No. That's just it. Mum and Dad got the ivory sent from the caves at Mount Elgon. It's in Kenya, where the elephants go to get salt, rock salt. They have to dig it out and sometimes they'll get a tusk broken off; our netsuke were carved from a found tusk. Momma Lesedi, she was the tribal sangoma and midwife

who delivered all three of us, she carved them, took her ages.'
Lin frowned. 'So, no netsuke then?'

'Nope. Are you quite sure she would've had it with her?'

'Absolutely. You'd have to cut it off her.'

Archie's face showed sudden realisation. 'Well, I'll be... What did I say, about crimes being solved in strange ways? I think someone did just that...cut it off her I mean. Just needs a few more slip ups like that and some progress will be made'

Lin sat thinking for a moment or two before speaking. 'Can I ask a favour? It might help you too.'

'Ask away.'

'It'd really help me to see the site of the hit-and-run, for when I talk to Khanyisile. Would you take me? It'll help me make my own connection...collect something from the land there if possible, and maybe take Jasper too? Animals might tell a different story, but it's still the truth.'

'That they do.' Archie considered the implications, weighing up Lin's character. 'Yeah, OK. It might even throw us a lifeline on this one. I've got a couple of things to see to first, Jasper an' that, so if it's OK, Amoya will take you there and I'll meet you both later. Oh, and...' Archie fished in his pocket and pulled out the tiepin. 'While we're on the subject, did this belong to your sister?'

She took it from him. 'No. Not that I know of, why?'

'It was found close to her in the ditch, it was one of the things that intrigued me about all this in the first place, this and her situation.'

'Well, I say no, can I say it's very unlikely? Rene was never a believer in possessions and by the weight of that it isn't a bit of costume jewellery. If she'd had it she would've sold it.'

'That figures.'

Lin handed it back. 'Sorry.'

'No that's fine, just a coincidence then, I guess...' He pocketed it as the door opened and the Desk Sergeant came in.

'Sorry Sir, but the young lady's two friends have just arrived, got some clothes and such. Would it be alright if...?'

'Your friends?'

'Sarah. My weak lie to the police with guns.'

'Ah, OK.' Archie smiled. 'I think we can allow you a change of clothes at least. Do we have showers here?' Robson gave him a look as he left. 'Take that as a no then.' He turned to Lin. 'Sorry. Spartan doesn't come into it.'

'S'alright, just a sink-wash and some fresh clothes will do.'

'I'll take you along to the ladies.' Amoya led the way. 'Do you have somewhere to stay? Your place will still be out of bounds.'

Lin stopped. 'Oh, so selfish... Your colleagues, how are they?'

'One didn't make it.' Lin gave him a look that demanded more. 'Adam. Adam Reeve. One of my team.'

'Goodness me, I'm so sorry. The other?'

'Kanga. WPC Desai. Not sure. There's...complications.'

'Oh dear, please pass on my thoughts and wishes to his family and wish the lady a speedy recovery.'

'I will, thanks. You share a burden of loss with Gabrielle and she'll be touched, I know.'

'His wife?'

'Sister.'

'Oh Lord. Connections, do you see?'

'I do. And, at the risk of repetition, once we've cornered Jasper and done the crime scene, we'll head over to Jay at Forensics, for the ID... Sorry, this just keeps getting worse.'

'Got to be done.' Lin followed Amoya to the door. 'And to think things all started out so well.'

'How was that?'

'Tonight, well, last night now. I found a money roll that contained enough for me to be able to swank my way into a five-star hotel, only to give it back.'

'Really? Where was this?'

They reached the door and Amoya opened it. 'On the train home last night. An Irishman dropped it...'

Archie stopped chewing and moved towards them. 'What money...? Irish you say?'

'Yes.'

'Local man?'

'No. Not to here anyway, neither was the woman on the train. None of them were, not to my knowledge.'

'That train goes to?'

'Out to Ollerton, but they all got off at my stop.'

Archie's focus was pin sharp. 'All of them?'

'Yes.'

'Were they all Irish? Not Italian?'

'Well the man who dropped the money definitely was Irish, we exchanged words about it. The other man didn't speak, but they left together so... The woman definitely wasn't Irish though because she bought me a drink in the Lion, we had a bit of a chat. Said she was up visiting her sister, said she felt sorry for me, all that money.'

'How much was there?'

'Not sure, a thousand at least. The two men got into a car in the car park, the only car. Odd that.'

'Odd?'

'Well, yes. If their car was at the station it suggests they drove there and parked it for their outward journey and yet I'm certain they weren't local, accent as thick as that would stand out round here.'

Archie nodded. 'And the woman?'

'She was waiting in the car park for her sister I suppose. Either that or waiting for a taxi.'

'The men, which direction did they drive off in?'

'Towards the town centre, along the Cleveland Road....'

Archie fixed her with a stare. 'Would you recognise them again?'

'Absolutely.'

Archie took hold of Lin's arm and led her back to the table. 'Amoya, get a tape recorder in here, if they've got one, and let Lin's friends know she'll be a little while yet. Get on to the local taxi firm too...' He looked at Lin for confirmation.

'Des Jacobs, Jacobs Taxis. Local monopoly.'

He continued his orders to Amoya. 'Get him in with his passenger list and destinations for pick-ups from the Red Lion last night.' He addressed Lin again, 'Time?'

'Erm... around eleven-ish?' Amoya nodded and left.

Archie took out his mobile phone, selected a number and called out to the disappearing Amoya, 'And get Robson in here, I want that woman found!' The phone connected and he put it on speaker as he pulled out a chair and Lin sat back down. 'Hi Pat, who's there?'

'The gang's all here, you got something?'

He placed the phone on the table. 'Yup. Gather 'em round, put me on speaker and get someone to send across mug shots to here, anyone Irish and heavy duty; I think Miss Lea may have met our shooters.'

~

6 I don't see why all the pups have t' go.'

The tall arc lights dotted around the yard illuminated the kennels and their inmates, the shadows of the two men painted large on the concrete floor. Matt stopped short and laid things out to Chris. 'A line up of kennels filled with cross-dogs of mixed age. What do you reckon a tree-hugger or the cops are gonna make of that, guide dogs for the blind?'

'Tell 'em they're just house pets.'

'Them two eldest have got cropped ears and tails... House pets they aint.' They began to walk along the kennels. 'An' not a ringer for gun dogs neither.' He stopped and looked into kennels three and four. 'Decision's been made. You've got the bones and they're all to go, just scrub out well after.' They moved on toward the end kennel.

'But, all of 'em? Even the littlies?'

'You're hung for a sheep as a lamb, we can get replacements when the shit settles. '

'Bloody waste if you ask me.'

'Then I won't. You're too soft with these dogs, always said it...'

Inside the last kennel a six-month old brindle cross with a white blaze on its chest had been bouncing up on hind legs, shadow boxing and squeaking at the bars ever since Matt and Chris had arrived. Now, as they drew closer, it could hardly contain its excitement and the squeak turned into a high-pitched yap as it bounced higher on hind paws in an effort to attract attention.

'The fuck's up with this one?'

'That one? Mad, I think. Does this every time someone comes to the kennels.'

'Aiden's not mentioned it an' he's the first to nip soft things in the bud.' Matt stopped, looking from pup with thrashing stump-tail to other inmates and back before noticing the pup's adoring eyes for Chris. 'It's you aint it?'

'What?'

'Don't get coy with me. I know when a dog forms a bond, I've been doing this long enough. It's you! He's pleased to see you. You've made him a pet haven't y'?'

Chris' face reddened a little. 'No, no...not a pet, just...' His voice failed.

'Just what?' Matt's face showed all the signs of the frustration he was feeling. 'Can I not leave you to do anything as asked! Well that one's to go for a start, first in line, and you're the one who's signed its warrant.'

'But...'

'No!'

'I was gonna ask Aiden if I could buy him, as a pet, y'know, for when I drop out of here, have me own place, maybe me own dog that I'll look after meself. Not a fighter just a pet, y'know, like Chipper.'

'Who?'

'Er...'

'Chipper...? His name's Marksman! Jesus, you've renamed him?'

'Yeah, well I was thinkin' if I can buy him...'

'No! Shut it! That one first! Your fault.' Matt looked around for help. 'Jesus Christ Chris... We aint no Mickey Mouse affair here! We take this seriously. You? You've buggered that up right and proper with this one. What chance do you think he'd stand in the ring, eh? Wouldn't even make a good teaser. What's he gonna do, whine 'em to death?' He looked again from pup to Chris and sighed. 'People would ask if we do anything cruel here. 'Til now I'd 'ave said no, we don't. These dogs are better looked after than most humans. We've refined it. No dogs are tortured here. They're not overfed, dressed in costumes, bred not to breathe or stand up proper. They fight 'cos they want to, an' with some dignity too. And when they're too old or get damaged we don't let 'em suffer or run about on wheels, we put 'em down ourselves. No cruelty involved. Short and sweet. What you've done here, that's cruel.' Chris was about to speak, but Matt turned and moved back to Chris' Land Rover. 'He's gone, as soon as you're back from cleanin'. We've enough kit, right?'

A crestfallen Chris followed him to look in the back of his vehicle at the pressure washer, buckets, cleaning fluids and brushes of various sorts. 'Yeah. Is electric and water still on at the sties?'

'Water is, no electric. I've already shifted the big generator and the cabling. We'll have to use that little Honda genny for the pressure washer so cold water only. Boiler's goin' in the skip soon as we get there. We got the cutters, crowbar and hammers?'

'Yeah, and I chucked in some screwdrivers too.'

'No time for delicacies, smash and grab, we need to get on.'

'Will we have time?'

'Have to. Grab that genny from the tractor shed.' Chris set off as Matt's voice followed him, 'Then we'll collect Aiden.'

Chris raised his voice as the distance between them grew. 'Does he know we're coming?'

'Dunno. My guess is Quinn will 'ave bottled out so it'll be a nice surprise when we get there, an' there's no way he's side-steppin' this one.' In the shed, Chris collected the generator, traipsed back carrying it by the top bars and loaded it into the rear of his vehicle. 'Now, let's grab Aiden and get the strippin' an' cleanin' done. We got fuel for the genny?'

'Yeah. tank's full.'

'Oil good?'

'Yeah. You got the key?'

Matt patted his pocket. 'Yeah. You drop me off at the house, we'll finish the cleaning, then you drop the kit off and sort out these lot.' Matt pointed at the still bouncing and yapping pup, 'Startin' with that one.' Opening the door of the Land Rover, Matt paused and sighed. 'Look at the crap in here!'

Apart from the torn seats and the worn and stained steering wheel and gear stick, the under window shelving was stuffed full of chocolate wrappers, old fast-food bags and, on the passenger side, several of the Black Feather shotgun cartridges Chris had blagged from Aiden. The floor was decorated with dried mud, further sweet wrappers and a couple of polystyrene burger boxes. Matt stepped back. 'Have you ever cleaned this out, I mean ever?'

Chris looked over Matt's shoulder. 'Couple of weeks ago, yeah.'

'Couple of months y' mean. You'll need a JCB to clear this lot. How am I supposed to travel over to collect mine in this?'

'We can always swap the kit over into yours.'

'An' ruin it with the stink of that Jeyes fluid an' that genny? I don't think so.'

'Well then.' Chris moved round to the driver's side. 'You'll be alright, nothing's gonna hurt you in here.'

Matt climbed in trying his best to hover above the seat. 'I'm not so sure. Jesus, it looks like you're growin' a cure for summat in here.' He paused and pushed a brown something onto the floor from the central seat. It bounced twice before settling. 'An' what th' fuck's that?'

Chris glanced as he climbed in. 'Battered onion ring.'

'A what?'

'Onion ring. Some of us don't get time to do a cooked meal a lot of the time y'know. I 'ave to make do. That was last night's tea, that an' a kebab.'

Matt looked across at Chris. 'A kebab...? Christ, there's no hope for you is there?' Chris twisted the key, the engine fired up and they set off, the local news channel blasting away. 'You wanna get this shit-hole cleared out, an' either turn that radio down or off!'

The sound of a hysterically barking puppy fast faded.

~

Cashman's hysterical bark swelled in volume and speed accompanied by the sound of a second bullet crashing through the windscreen as Kenzie reversed rapidly, all his skills under test as he made distance between him and the fast-approaching duo. This bullet grazed the head of the spaniel, piercing one wildly flapping ear and exchanging bark for yelp. The gun flashed again and Kenzie increased the car's weave, sending the mobile off the dashboard and him into the path of this oncoming bullet which entered his upper arm, slamming him round and back into the seat. The spaniel was now hysterical with both the pain in his ear and his desire to indulge in defensive violence, his barking and snarling filling the airspace in the careening car, his face up against the windscreen, spittle, froth and blood smattering and streaking the punctured glass. Kenzie's disabled arm forced him to switch the wheel with his one good hand, decreasing the depth but increasing the speed of each change in direction; it also made Cashman's need to stay upright and repel this frontal attack even harder...and the men now fired a gun apiece.

Josh and James, running as fast as a lifetime of Guinness would allow, felt it was wise to sacrifice accuracy for quantity and had adopted the rapid-fire method in order to bring this cartoon of a chase to a successful conclusion. Their barrage of bullets penetrated radiator, nearside headlight and shattered the windscreen. A hailstorm of glass scatter-gunned into the car just as Cashman was swept off the dashboard and onto the floor by Kenzie's particularly extravagant swing of the steering wheel. Undaunted, the spaniel was back on the seat, over the dashboard, out of the gaping frame and onto the bonnet in a heartbeat.

'Cash!'

Straight into trained reactions, Cashman was across the bonnet, the car's swerving action sending the dog tumbling and rolling across the tarmac and making him an impossible target for either of the shooters. Almost without pause from his final somersault the spaniel set off towards James at full tilt, fully focussed but silent-running in a fight where all bets were off, all reasons or avenues for flight cancelled, no quarter asked or given.

In a panic for the spaniel, Kenzie slammed the brakes on bringing the car to a screeching halt before snatching it into first gear, depressing the accelerator and aiming straight for Josh. James shifted his aim from car to Cash.

Standing his ground and fast-firing at the approaching swerving vehicle, Josh had seconds to fire off four further rounds from the semi-automatic pistol into the car's interior and grill before attempting to avoid contact with the vehicular missile. Two of these bullets found their mark, one passing through the bonnet and dashboard before grazing Kenzie's left knee, the other making its way unhindered into the shoulder of his already damaged arm, shattering bone and ripping flesh, embedding tatters of cloth into the seat back before shredding its way onwards and into the rear door. The searing pain and shock knocked Kenzie backwards, forcing him to release the wheel and harden his pressure on the accelerator... Josh had left it too late, there was nothing he could do to avoid the inevitable.

Cashman was also committed to the inevitable. Trials of strength and positional point-scoring were dumped in favour of a decisive attack; disable then kill were the only items on the list. With six feet to go, and in perfect timing with the arc Josh's body described as the nose of the car carved him high into the air, Cash launched himself at James in his distracted aim. The bullets skipped and bounced around the dog, the ricochet from one tearing through his front paw and removing two pads and a strip of leg skin just before the spaniel crashed into James. Taking hold of his gun arm, his jaws working overtime on his now screaming victim, Cashman flipped his head from side to side in machine gun movement.

James's screams drowned out the dull thud as Josh, still gripping the gun, hit the road and bounced along it, the car skidding to a halt just a few feet from him. Despite the pain, Kenzie scrambled out of the car as best he could, rolling over and trying to get upright with his one good arm.

Even with the degree of difficulty, James swivelled the gun onto Cashman, pressing the muzzle against the dog's rib cage. Their eyes met for a second before he pulled the trigger, the dull click of an empty gun sounding the starter for Cash's race to grab James by the throat. James punched out with his other arm to fend off the attack, the dog dodged it and took in a portion of James' neck which he began to shake. Through the pain James screamed out.

'Jesus, Josh, help me...! Shoot the fucker!'

In a haze of blood and last gasps, Josh levelled the gun at Cashman. Kenzie launched himself forwards as Josh fired, just the once, before the weight that was Kenzie landed on top of him, knocking the gun from his hand and a last gasp from his broken body. The force and shock as the bullet hit Cashman punched the dog off James as Kenzie scrabbled across and picked up the dislodged gun.

The two men stared at each other, the shroud of silence seeming almost indecent. Kenzie focussed on the lifeless body of Cashman, levelled the gun at James and was the first to speak.

'You stay just where you are!'

James lifted his head and saw the carnage that was Josh. 'Me mate...?'

'Dead. Make a move and you'll be with him.'

James slowly pointed the gun at Kenzie and pulled the trigger. The dull click from the empty pistol was drowned out by the crash of Kenzie's nine millimetre going off.

The gun's fading reverb was overtaken by the sound of approaching sirens as the two dockyard security vehicles, their flashing blue lights contrasting perfectly with the distant orange glow of the port, sped towards the scene. The sight of Cashman's lifeless body filled Kenzie's view as his head sagged to the floor...

~

'I should really have you in the back in a seat-belt, y' know that don't y'?'

Jasper looked across at Archie as he drove the car along the main road. The red leather collar matched the red streak on his muzzle and the thick, black webbing lead, a gift from Bob and much more suited to holding back an eager-to-get-acquainted German Shepherd than this diminutive terrier, was clipped to the collar and tied to the seat adjuster.

'I'm a copper, right?' The dog gave Archie a yeah whatever glance before turning to the infinitely more interesting spectacle of what was passing by the side window. 'Right well, just so's you understand who's in charge here, don't think this is gonna become a habit, and you, just be on your best behaviour. We're off to meet your prospective owner so no snappy-snarly like you were with me OK? Jasper?' The terrier maintained his inspection of the passing countryside. 'Glad we've got that settled.' The hands-free set rang, Jasper cocked his head to one side at the sound. 'You expecting anyone? That'll be for me then.'

Morning Archie, and how are you?

Archie rested his elbows on the steering wheel as he unwrapped a stick of gum, the scent of sweet mint causing

Jasper to watch him very closely. 'Unable to sleep Jay, just like you. What you got for me?'

'*We're bypassing all the usual niceties that separate us from the animals of this world then.*'

'Strip us down and we're just another beast of the field. Nobody listens anyway, not these days. I picked up a companion here that gives me a more honest reaction than most of the people I've come across.'

'*So I heard. You're still able to drive then?*'

'Yeah. He was a bit dazed from the work they'd done on him, the anaesthetic, so that slowed him down a bit.'

'*How is he?*'

'Yeah, good. Perked up a bit now, even let me take him out of the cage at Bob's; I carried him to the car.'

'*He's loose in the car with you?*'

'Yeah, well, loosely tied up.'

'*Very trusting of you.*'

'Nah, he's alright. He's a knowing little sod and his face looks like a welder's bench, but apart from that, all good. I think we got the introductions written off when I teased him away from that ditch. Just need to get him in tune with the lead, my bet is it'll be like walking a kite. So, the ballistics report?'

'*Yes. We've come up with some interesting stuff.*'

'Let's have it then.'

'*OK...*' Jay paused. '*You're driving?*'

'Yeah.'

'*Then you may want to pull over.*'

'No, I'm fine, you're on speaker...'

'*Not a request Detective Chief Inspector. I don't want to be responsible for further losses amongst our finest through lack of concentration. I'll wait.*'

Archie sighed. 'Yeah right. Hang on.' He turned to the terrier. 'It's like having a vicar in the car.'

'*And this Holy Father says you're to pull over.*'

Archie smiled at Jay's retort. 'Oh good, here we are. Hang on Padre.' Jasper bounced from side door to dashboard via the seat as Archie slowed and coasted to a halt in the lay-by. As he pulled on the handbrake Jasper's tail wagged and he let out a low whine. 'Not stopping for a walk, we're stopping for a chat.' He folded his flop of hair back. 'Right Jay, this'd better be good.'

'Are you sitting comfortably? Then I'll begin. The bullets from the flat, NABIS has got a tentative match on them.'

'Excellent work.'

'Don't get too excited, it's only a preliminary result, but it looks like they're from one of the many guns linked to the loyalist kill-squads in Ireland.'

'Jesus... From when?'

'Here's the thing; if their preliminaries are correct, nineteen eighty-eight.' There was a long silence until Jay spoke again. 'Thought that'd give you pause for thought.'

'Eighty-eight. Blooodeee hell. Lots of coincidences here, Jay, and...'

'You don't believe in coincidences.'

'Nope. Here's my twopenn'orth. The lady's neighbour said the man that did the shooting was Irish...or Italian, and the sister met two Irish chaps on her train just before the shooting at her flat. One of them dropped a bundle of cash.'

'You're thinking hit money?'

'More than likely.'

'Careless. How does she know...about the cash, I mean?'

'Because she was the one who picked it up and gave it back.' Now it was Jay's turn for silence. 'Thought that'd give you pause for thought.'

'She, gave back her hit money...to the hit men?'

'That's what I think, yeah, so what with that, the old lady at the flats and now your news, that's three strikes and out for me. We've sent off what we had to all the ports and airports, all the known leakage points, but now, with your news, the team will need an update. You've got all the stats, could you do it?'

'Sure. Is it to Pat?'

'Yeah, or Martha. How about the pellet from the dog?'

'Ah, that's where we go international and have the wondrous Anita to thank. It's not lead, it's a composite of tungsten with a polymer binder.'

'Lead alternatives, aren't they? I remember our conversations about ducks by the ditch. Not wanting to pour cold water on her findings Jay, but she's just discovered something that's available over the counter at every good gun shop, so not a lot of use there.'

'This is true, but you're missing out on the brilliance that is Ms. Cresson, particularly in any discussion involving ballistics. These pellets are not UK made and not recent.'

'Ah. I take it back. She is good isn't she?'

'Makes me think she needs to get out more, but yes, she has an eye for detail. According to her first pass these are some several years old and from the USA.'

Archie's chewing speed increased. 'Wow. OK.'

'My dedicated assistant is running electron micrographs as we speak so we should be pedigree-perfect within the hour.'

'Why the US?'

'Because of those first results. American pellets were manufactured using a particular grade of tungsten-based polymer which, according to our tables and Anita's remarkable memory, is typical of early American, lead-shot alternatives.'

'They changed them? How helpful.'

'Yes, wasn't it. The originals were too expensive to manufacture and lacked the stopping power of lead, and because of this lack of slaughter-power they switched to bismuth, but not before batches of the polymer mix had been released for sale.'

Archie shook his head. 'Nothing exercises the wit of man like seeking a better way to kill does it? So when was the switch?'

'Late nineteen-eighties.'

'Rare as rocking-horse shit then. Do you have a list of the cartridge makes that carried that type of pellet?'

'We will have during the day. It just needs further work for us to be positive, and it may not be exhaustive.'

'No, but it's a start point. Great work you guys, really.'

'I'll pass on your praise, but don't get ahead of yourself on this. Taste not of the Pierian spring. Where are you now?'

'On my way to the hit-and-run site via the back lanes. I'm meeting up with the twin.'

'At the site? Is that allowed?'

'Absolutely. You've signed off on it haven't you?'

'Yes-ish. I've got to go back later today. I meant you taking her there. Won't that be a bit...raw?'

'Her suggestion and she impressed me when we chatted so...'

'You're the judge of that. Well just remember, although I'm absent there's still some continuing on-site work to be done. I'll be back there with a couple of folk from Queen Mary's University. They're coming over to give a further opinion on the vegetation found on the corpse and you'll find a couple of uniforms in attendance. Her last resting place is still taped off, so preserve the site's integrity, and heed their restrictions as if they're mine.'

'Point taken boss.'

'And the terrier, what do you intend to do with it?'

'Dunno. My hope is the sister will want it, if not it'll be the dogs' home I guess.'

'Couldn't stay on with Bob to be re-homed then?'

'Nope. Tax-payer transparency, the cuts and all that.'

'Indeed. Oh, I thought you'd like to know we've got Gabrielle staying with us for the remainder of the week, probably until the funeral.'

'I don't suppose there's a date on that?'

'No. We've completed our initial examinations...'

'Shouldn't think there's any doubt about cause of death, Jay.'

'No, but the coroner may want the evidence held over until there's a significant chance of an arrest and conviction.'

'No pressure then. OK, thanks Jay, you'll keep me in the loop about the ballistics pedigree?'

'Of course, and mind you treat my crime scene with a little respect.'

'My word on it.' Archie closed the connection and turned to Jasper who had been following the conversation, trying to work out whereabouts in the car the disembodied voice was coming from, head to one side in perplexed fashion.

'Moving it along Jasper. Right, sit still a bit longer while I make a couple more calls. When I've done that we'll just take a run round the lanes on our way over to see a friend of your late mistress, someone you've met before, see if we can't find you a new home, eh?' Archie stared hard at the dog. 'And remember, you bite her and that'll be any chance of comfort gone, right? You getting this?' The terrier, after scenting Archie's mint-flavoured breath, continued to stare out the windscreen. 'Suit y'self...'

~

Chris pulled onto the grass-flecked cobbles of the pigsty yard just behind Matt's vehicle and Aiden, voicing his disapproval, rolled out of the passenger door of the Land Rover almost before it had stopped.

'Man, but that stinks in there.' Chris got out and began unloading the clean-up tools and kit. Aiden eyed the collection as Matt joined them. 'Er...are we all fixin' to do this?'

'We are, you aren't.'

'Good...'

'Yet. We two, me an' Chris, we're starting the clean-up. You're goin' back to that camp site to do another search.' Matt talked over Aiden's reaction. 'Then, once you're sure there's nothing left to find you're coming back here to help.'

'I've already done it.'

'And you're doin' it again.'

'Why?'

''Cos I say so that's why. This job's gone tits up too many times for my liking.'

'I don't get you.'

'Tits up? You know belly up?' Aiden nodded. 'Then that's what it's done. I've been dragged into the office more times in the last three days over what should've been a simple job than I have the whole time I've worked for the Gaffer, an' it stops right now.'

'Don't put any of this on me man.'

Matt turned full-face to Aiden. 'It's on all of us, man! We don't get this right we'll all be...'

'Tits up?'

'Don't get smart. You may be the dog's bollocks with the Gaffer about his livestock, but out here you're just another hired hand and I'm the boss...where you goin'?'

Aiden had moved to the driver's side of Matt's vehicle. 'I was...'

'You're havin' a giraffe, right?' Aiden looked at Matt, flummoxed. 'Get yourself into that Land Rover and over to the campsite.'

'I gotta get back in that junk-yard?'

'Unless you want to walk.' Aiden lingered by the Range Rover. 'Not gonna happen.' Matt nodded at the Land Rover. 'That one, and don't come away until you're sure there's nothing else to find. You remember where it is?'

Aiden moved sulkily to Chris' vehicle. 'Sure do, I cleaned it up, remember?'

'An' I said do it again!' Aiden could see the fire in Matt's eye and closed down. 'I want every part of this shitty mess signed, sealed and delivered and us be away in three hours.' Matt turned to Chris. 'Let's get on, and make sure you take my two pairs of coveralls and my Hunters in.' He turned back to Aiden as Chris began offloading. 'You still here?' Aiden turned, his hand on the door handle.

'Do you want it done fast or done right?'

'I want both and for you not to take all soddin' day about it! The quicker you're back the quicker we're finished and I'm out of your company.'

'Well thank you too. You all done?' Chris grunted in reply as Aiden opened the door before turning back to Matt. 'Y'ever think you get y'self all bowed up about others when maybe it's just your people skills need a-fixin'?'

Matt studied Aiden for a few seconds before giving his considered reply.

'Fuck. Off.'

~

6 The dog...Ss...spaniel...?'

Blue lights from the scattered emergency vehicles manfully scythed the road and surrounding shrubbery giving a disco feel to the shoot-out at Cairnryan. Two ambulances were central to the action, one already loaded with the corpses of Josh and Jimmy, and an Air Ambulance helicopter chopped its background symphony to an already cacophonous scene.

Kenzie needed on-site treatment before he could be moved and, from his swooned state, he had only just awakened to the facts of his injuries, the pain and the choreographed mayhem around him. Even so his first thought was to relive the closing seconds of his ordeal and ask the question. The paramedics tending his shattered shoulder and stemming his blood loss cast glances at each other; it was enough, he knew all was lost. After this there was nothing. He closed down, allowing the professionals to get on with their work. His head was full of images and his heart full of longing, there was no space left for pain. It was the arrival of James Lamont at his side that stirred Kenzie's focus back to a landscape he didn't want to contemplate.

'He's gone Jim. Cash. He's gone...'

Jim nodded. 'I know. Coppers said. I asked as soon as I got here.'

'Where is he?'

'Still on the road, I've been a bit busy of late. I'll move him to the verge as soon as the photos are taken.'

'He shot him; the bastard shot him.'

'He won't ever do that again; you saw to that.'

'Too late.'

'Aye. Not for the want of tryin' though Ken, eh?'

'Too late... Who the hell were they?'

'Prints came back not two minutes ago. Irish, both of 'em, had a record Arthur Thompson would be proud of. Word's gone out to all forces so somebody'll claim 'em, this isn't their first. Car was nicked from Dumfries...' Kenzie began to cough and James stood. 'Enough. These lads need to get you away to South Glasgow. Chopper's waitin, so are the surgeons.'

The two paramedics and a helmeted flier lifted the stretcher. As it reached waist height, Kenzie took hold of James's forearm. 'Cash...?'

'I'll see to him, never worry.'

'Can they keep him on ice, 'til I can organise stuff...?'

'Aye. I'll go and sort him now then chat to the chaps who run the chillers.'

As they carried him away to the helicopter Kenzie called back. 'Treat him well Jim...'

~

Archie could see the police car up ahead, parked on the site previously occupied by the mobile canteen and Steve Warne's failed attempt at customer service. Inside were Lin and WPC Williams, and as Archie drew up to the front of their car so Jasper's growl grew deeper and more intense.

'Christ dog, you're not out of the car and already you're making enemies; will you just behave!' He leant across and removed the lead from the seat adjuster. Jasper took immediate evasive action and uttered a further growl. Archie leaned back in his seat. 'Now look, this isn't gonna work if we can't settle on who's in charge. If you aren't fussed with it being on in the car then don't be when you're out of it. I'm doing nothing that'll hurt you, I'm just trying to keep you secure on this lane. You may remember it's not the safest of places, hmm? Good boy Jasp, tch-tch!' Archie held up his hand with the lead in it to show his intent but to his surprise the terrier responded by sitting. 'Ah, so that's it is it? Good lad. Thank you Renata.' He clipped the lead on. 'Good boy. Let's go and see the ladies. Tch-tch!' He called across. 'Sorry about the hour you two...and the temperature.'

'Not at all, I love this time of the day.' answered Lin, her breath streaming.

As Jasper's paws hit the floor so he was at the extent of the lead, but after his initial surge forward there was a pause and he lifted one front paw off the ground, scenting briefly before bounding off towards Lin uttering small yaps of excitement, his tail working overtime in anticipation of a joyous reunion. Archie could only follow, arm at full stretch. Lin dropped down on one knee in readiness for the welcoming onslaught, but it was only as he got to within a couple of metres of her that Jasper's progress stuttered to a stop.

'Hello Jasper, hello boy!' Lin put out her hand for Jasper to sniff.

It was the voice that confirmed this was a changed mistress. His original eagerness became tempered, his greeting more circumspect, a question mark accompanying his now subdued pleasure and his realisation that Lin's scent was only a silhouette of past remembrance. Jasper pulled back, the tip of his nose brushing Lin's knuckles as his tail stiffened and he let out a soft growl. Archie recognised the signs.

'You might want to adjust your welcome gesture Lin.'

Lin withdrew her hand a little but continued to fuss the terrier. 'Good boy Jasper, good lad. It's me, Lin, remember?' She looked closely at his muzzle. 'You poor thing. Is that where he was shot?' Archie nodded. 'Oh, bless...' The terrier's tail twitched and he looked into her face trying to decipher the conflicting signals nose, eyes and ears were receiving, a low whimper floating from his closed mouth.

'Knowledge not recognition. That's one confused dog.' said Archie.

Lin was unable to reply. It was Amoya, taking a step forward and dropping down to the terrier's level that varnished over the moment. 'Poor little chap...' Now here was a clear-cut pathway to reaction and the terrier withdrew further, lifting both volume and top lip as he lowered the tone of his previous throaty growl. Amoya stood slowly. 'Oh, right.'

'Wise move, don't for a minute think he's not serious.' Archie rolled the gum to the front of his mouth and smiled at the chutzpah being shown by one so small in the face of all this confused bigness. 'I could weep for this chap, I could honest.' Lin was still squatting, her hand now resting on her knee. 'Lin. Miss Lea? Are you OK?'

It was a few seconds before she spoke. 'I remember when I first met him. I said to Rene, "You'll be safe with him hartlam". Got that wrong. Rene said he was black-and-white when it came to friendships. Treat him right he'll be a friend for life, give him cause to take offence, become a threat to the pack and there's no second chance; she said he'd got the memory of an elephant to back it up too...'

Archie twitched the lead slightly. 'Don't be such a misery you. Tch-tch!' The terrier's reaction was immediate as he turned and took a couple of steps back to Archie, slackening the lead a little. 'That's one sound you do seem to recognise, eh Jasp?'

Jasper wagged his tail uncertainly a couple of times as he looked around at the trio then up at Archie. Lin smiled. 'There's a memory. That was the noise Rene made when she wanted him to pay attention, how did you know about that?'

'I just got lucky.'

'Well, he's taken a shine to you, not something he does lightly.'

'Don't know about a shine, I reckon he's just deciding which horse to back.' Archie turned to look down the lane at the taped off area and the two uniformed officers. 'OK, in sequence, let me give you the layout of the events here followed by the events at your flat.'...

...After a long and thoughtful pause Lin was the first to speak. 'And you believe all this is connected; Rene, me, your officers; that it's not by accident but by design?'

'At first I thought your sister was just unfortunate, you know, wrong place wrong time? Then your family history back at the station, that set me to rethinking, but there were elements that just didn't gel. Now? For me there is a connection involved in all of this, but it doesn't directly concern you, Rene, or your past. What happened here and at your flat was deliberate, planned; the phone call I got on my way over here convinced me of that.'

'But, if our past has nothing to do with this, then why her, why me?'

Archie paused for a moment. 'Couple of tidy-up things first. Was she involved in any drugs at all?'

'No. Rene...? No. I mean, she was an earth-child, a bit of a hippie, but no. The only dealing she did was in ethnic trinkets she made herself. Rene was a lot of things, smoked a bit of dagga when she was younger, who didn't, but as for dealing. She'd seen what it did to folk back home, we both had, and we knew it was all tied in with the smuggling of ivory and rhino horn; Mum and Dad laid that out for us very early on. Our mum would've skinned us alive if she'd even got a whisper we were involved in any of that, Granny too.'

'OK. Has she ever spent time in Ireland?'

'No, not to my knowledge, I mean...limited as our contact was, she would've told me, if not before then certainly after.'

'Right. Well whatever it was she became involved in or saw here, and I've a good suspicion what, it was something she wasn't meant to. Events just snowballed from then, and it was your connection to her that made you a problem. Fortunately for you, unfortunately for them, Adam and Kanga got there first.'

Archie's statement, coming as cold and crisp as the morning, caused Lin to snatch at her breath as past events and present information rapidly caught up with her. Her initial reaction to the news of her sister's death had been quickly overtaken by the need to give accurate feedback to Archie and Amoya, but now, stood here, there was nowhere to hide from the awfulness of events and the domino effect they had set in motion. Lin's silent tears were not only for her own loss, but the loss of a son and brother to a family and the confusion of a small terrier. She squatted down once more, holding out her hand to Jasper as the tears ran down her cheeks to drop as wreaths of remembrance onto the verge-side grass, causing a small black terrier to close in to the proffered hand and give it a cursory sniff and lick, his tail-twitch the simple outward sign of his limited understanding of the intricacies of humans. Lin smiled at the contact. She took the offer of a handkerchief from Archie, before looking up at them both. Archie rested his hand on her shoulder.

'Do you want to go down there or is this close enough?' Lin looked down the lane and at the two foot-stamping officers.

Amoya stepped to her side. 'You know you don't have to do this, not if you don't feel up to it.'

Lin wiped her nose. 'No, it's important...' The terrier came into her focus again, its face scanning hers for meaning as Lin stood up. 'For everyone. I'm alright.' She opened the handkerchief fully to blow, looked at the discarded gum and turned to Archie. 'This'll be yours then.'

'Oh...bollocks! Sorry, I didn't mean to swear.' He smiled and shook his head.

The tension dissipated. Amoya handed Lin a fresh paper tissue from a pack in her pocket. 'Here, try this.'

Lin returned the handkerchief to Archie who pocketed it and pointed down the lane as distraction. 'So, given the facts so far, it begs the question what was your sister doing here?'

Lin thought for a moment. 'Nothing of Rene's has been found has it, her things?'

'Not a stitch. All the immediate area's been searched and we found nothing.'

'That's because she was travelling light, earth is the queen of beds. Siphelele, our Zulu bushman, he took us camping, told us that when we were, oh, six, seven years old, and Rene spent more time with him than anyone. Unless she was moving base she'd have very little with her; everything else would be hidden at camp, and if your searches are anything to go by it's not round here.'

'You think?'

'I know. I packed it in when we came over here, not a big enough country for me, too regimented; not Rene, she was always off and away, but I still know how it works. She'd always travel light but have a base, a kitchen, somewhere to call home.'

'OK.' Jasper picked up the vibe from the group again and Archie took the moment. 'Well, only one way to find out.' Jasper's intent swelled to meet the scents of remembrance as they walked along the lane and his nose swept the valleys and plateaus of the verge. It was only as they approached the taped area that his approach slowed; Archie could feel it through the leash. 'Dog knows what's coming.'

Lin looked at Jasper. 'Me too.' Amoya took Lin's arm as they reached the tape and came to a halt.

'Sir.'

Archie reined the terrier in and stood a little away from the officer. 'Constable.' He showed his warrant card. 'DCI Arnold and WPC Williams.' The constable noted this down in his visitor log. 'I've had my instruction from the CSO not to make too much of a mess. Jay Millar?'

'Yes, Sir.'

'Mister Millar tells me he'll be along later today.'

'Around lunchtime so we've been told.'

'And with some other folk in tow. This is Miss Linden Lea, sister of the deceased, she's come to give us some further insight.'

'Mornin' Miss.' The constable looked at the terrier that had entered under the tape to the full extent of the lead and was testing the air, nose working overtime. He bent towards Jasper slightly. 'Nice dog...'

'He is but don't think about patting him, he's not keen on the uniform.' The offer of friendship was swiftly withdrawn as the officer stood up. 'This is the deceased's dog, also come along to give his opinion on events.' The officer took a second to assimilate this. 'Can you just give us a few minutes please?'

The two constables moved away, allowing Archie to lift the tape for the quartet to enter. 'Jasper first?'

Lin was glad of it. 'Yes.'

Archie relaxed his grip on the leash and Jasper moved into the ditch, his stump-tail erect, metronomic, his ears raised stiffly, nose skimming the ground, hackles lifted to their utmost. The terrier halted, sweeping the bank like a metal detector before doing a half turn, his nose remaining rooted to a spot of interest.

This was it.

The unmistakable distant scent of Rene.

This was where Mistress had lain, her past life now as much a part of these grass blades as the autumn moisture that dressed them.

He let out a quiet whine and Archie squatted, his scent drifting down to Jasper who looked up, making connections. After a pause the terrier climbed up the bank to stand at its edge alongside Archie who gently rested a hand on the terrier's shoulder causing his tail to twitch a couple of times. 'I know fella, I know.'

Here, at the edge of such cruelty, Amoya had to work hard to quell her immediate reaction which was tears of rage. 'Lin...I'm just so, so sorry.'

But there were no tears from Lin now. 'Me too, but now? Now I just want the chance to inflict the same level of brutality on the bastard who did this.'

Amoya stared at her for a moment and saw the look in her eyes. 'And I believe you would too.'

Archie scanned the site. 'So, if this wasn't her destination that means she was going elsewhere, probably to camp, and we've not found it yet.'

Lin's eyes settled on Jasper. 'Did you do it with him? The sweep?'

'No, he was over with Bob Lord getting patched up.'

'Do you think he might help?'

'Worth a punt. Dogs like order, work well on routine, maybe she was camped hereabouts long enough for him to run on auto pilot.' Archie flicked the lead gently sending a ripple of attention the dog's way. 'Jasper? Tch-tch! Come on, let's walk.' Jasper set off in earnest and Archie gave him full leash.

A hundred yards from the hit-and-run site the high wall to their right ended in a right angle, forming a barrier between the woodland and a field of barley stubble. A tumble of stonework beckoned entry and without any hesitation Jasper left the lane, scrabbled over the fallen masonry and set off along a tight trackway between wood and wall. Archie turned to his two companions. 'This lad knows exactly where he's headed.'

~

Released from the smell of stale grease, Aiden took the short walk along the riding which still bore the bruising from his earlier visit. Weaving his way through the lattice of silver birch and scrub oaks he tracked his original path towards the ancient badger sett he had checked before he had stumbled on Renata's campsite.

'This way, f'r sure...'

Gradually the small clearing came into view, a little further to his right than he thought, but definitely there.

Let's get this waste of time outta the way and skedaddle... He slowed slightly, *but not so fast that they won't have finished by the time I get back.*

~

J asper led the trio onto the riding and Archie reigned the terrier in. 'Steady on Jasp, you'll have my arm out of its socket.' Tall grasses and goldfinch-stripped thistles bedecked the edges of the riding where a Land Rover was parked. 'Is that a keeper's motor down there?'

'Do you want me to have a look?'

Jasper pulled towards the vehicle. 'Thanks Amoya, but it seems he wants to go that way anyhow so we'll all follow.' Jasper's nose was tilted to the side, the terrier dwarfed by the unkempt growth until, twenty yards short of the Land Rover, he veered off to the left. 'No. Hang on Jasp. Tch-tch! I know you know which way to go, I can see the track, I just need to take a peek at this motor. Lin, could you hold him a minute?' He handed the lead across. 'Won't be a sec.'

B reg? Not often you see them about. Moving to the vehicle Archie took a note of the licence plate number and folded back his forelock as he peered inside then tried the door handle. It was unlocked and he muttered to himself. 'So, Detective Chief Inspector, did you believe a crime was in the process of being committed or that this vehicle was intimately connected to one? Yes, Sir, I did. The vehicle was unlocked, parked in or near a scene of crime and I had every reason to believe, blah blah blah.' He opened the door and began a visual search of the interior. The first thing that registered was the smell, the second was the mess, the third was the three Black Feather cartridges resting on the open shelf under the windscreen. *That's a strange one; could that be...?* He looked around the general woodland then reached in, pocketed a cartridge, clicked the door to and walked back. As he approached, Jasper stood on his hind legs and yipped.

'Looks like a keeper's vehicle, not sure...' Before he could finish Jasper begin to growl and Archie saw a man moving through the trees towards them. 'And here he is...' Archie raised a hand. 'Hello!'

Aiden stopped short at the call and looked out onto the ride. *What the...?* He saw the uniform as, stepping out onto the ride, he addressed Amoya. 'Is there a problem Missy?'

Archie could feel Amoya bristle even from where he was standing as her opaque reply came back. 'I don't know; is there?'

Archie half smiled at her reply and at Jasper's continued growl which had become deeper, lengthier and more threatening. He took out his warrant card. 'I'm Detective Chief Inspector Arnold, Northants CID and this is a WPC Sir, not a Missy anything. Can I ask who you are and what you're doing here?'

'I might ask the same. You're a long way from home and this is private land.'

Archie ignored it. 'And you are...?'

'Aiden Steerholm-Youngman III. I work here.'

'On this estate?'

'Where else?'

'And who's the one that's a long way from home? America, southern states if I know anything about accents.'

'Dixie through and through.'

'And you work here doing what exactly?'

Aiden smiled, as close to a sneer as it was possible to get without offending. 'Estate Livestock Manager.'

'And you're here because?'

'In this piece of wood?' Archie nodded. 'I'm checking on a couple of biggish trees that suffered this fall. Rain we've had of late waterlogged their roots and those strong winds we had last month, they've shook 'em to a widow-maker... Will do for the fires up at the house, after we've felled 'em and they've dried some.'

'That's the house belonging to?'

'Lord Brightwick.'

'Right.' Archie shortened Jasper's lead. The terrier had been testing its reach, its strength and his growl for the past few seconds. 'And he owns all this?'

'And plenty more.'

'I see.' Archie smiled in friendly enquiry. 'And if I may ask, what brings you, an American, all this way from his home country?'

'Work, money.'

'That all?'

'That, and a chance to make a name. How about you? What brings y'all here, on a place where you could become creatures of interest for the keepers.'

'We're following up on a hit-and-run that took place last week, just on the lane that runs through these woods...well, you'd know that.'

'No. Can't say I do. I keep away from such doings.' Aiden looked across at the still-growling Jasper, the dog's gaze intent and piercing. He gave a smile that held all the warmth of an icicle 'Dog looks sharp. Wouldn't wanna pet him.'

Lin shook her head. 'Not unless you want to lose a hand.'

Aiden smiled that smile again. 'Right. Thanks for the warning Ma'am.'

'My pleasure. You're working for Brightwick did you say?'

'Lord Brightwick. Yes Ma'am.'

'A Lord no less. Big agricultural man is he?' Aiden frowned at the conversation's direction. 'Does a lot of spraying does he? Crop spraying?'

'Not here Ma'am. All the ground's organic, for the huntin', it's what's best.'

'In America though? He sprays these chemicals in America?'

'Couldn't say Ma'am, not my job, Livestock Manager remember?' It was after a few moments staring at Lin that Aiden looked at Archie. 'Anybody get banged out, in the crash?'

'Not a crash, a hit-and-run.'

'Bad then.'

'Yes. A lady died.' He nodded towards Lin. 'Her sister.'

'Sorry to hear that Ma'am. So, if the mishap was up the road aways...'

'Hit-and-run. I said.'

Aiden's eyes narrowed slightly at Archie's tone. 'Apologies. So why're y'all around these parts?'

'Well, it turns out the victim may have been living rough, in these woodlands as a matter of fact.'

Aiden was in fast. 'No way, would've been found and moved on within the day.'

Lin was in equally fast. 'Really?'

'Yeah lady. The keepers hereabouts, there's three of 'em and they miss nothing.'

'You're not one of them then?'

'No siree. I've said twice now, I'm Livestock Manager.'

'As in...?'

'As in livestock.'

'OK. Well...is it OK if we just continue our look around?'

'You got a search warrant?'

This brought Archie up short. 'Do I need one?'

Aiden looked at Archie and they held each other's stare before he replied, 'Well, yeah. These woods, they got a lotta birds. I think His Lordship would want to know before you began snoopin', scarin' the game; so would the keepers.'

'So, a warrant then.'

'A courtesy call.'

'OK. Well, we'll head back to the road and get one. Wouldn't want to upset the boss.' Jasper stood his ground, his stare fixed on Aiden. Archie looked at them both, this man and this terrier, locked into a stare of statements, one still smirking quietly the other still growling quietly. 'Jasper, come on.'

'That his name, Jasper?'

'Yeah.'

'Bit of a fighter is he? Sounds it.'

'Don't know, he's not mine. He belonged to the lady who was killed on the lane, the one that runs through your woodland, the one you've heard nothing of.'

Aiden gave Archie a challenging stare before turning to Lin. 'So, yours now then?' Lin nodded. 'Cool. D'y know, we could use a decent terrier on the staff. You ever have a want to sell him, I'm sure he'd be good on small stuff, rats and such.'

'He's not for sale.'

'Pity. I'm sure he'd give a good account of himself, in the right company. Well, must be movin' on. Y'all make sure you get a warrant if you wanna come back here, all legal like.'

'We will.'

Aiden tipped his hat. 'Have a nice day, y' hear?' With that he walked down the ride to the vehicle as the trio and reluctant terrier began to retrace their steps.

Amoya leant towards Archie as Lin handed him the lead. 'There's something really not right about him, Sir.'

Lin nodded in agreement. 'Jasper knew it to.'

Archie frowned. 'And so did you. You seem to have a fixation on him, Brightwick?'

'Not a fixation. Just some things fell into place when Brightwick's name came up. Now I know for certain who we're dealing with.'

'Is this something I should know about?'

'Not really...' Lin sighed. 'Just, that bee protest I told you about, and that company he's connected with.'

'Mistral Pharmaceuticals.'

'The same. Their chemicals, they've had a devastating effect on the US bees and now there's moves to license some of them in the UK. I was just making a point with my bee thing.'

'Did Rene know anything about this?'

'Doubt it. All outside our meetings, so not really.'

'Not really or no?'

Lin paused for a fraction before answering. 'No.'

'OK. I don't want to play the heavy parent card Lin, but you should tell us everything. Connections like this can lead to home, you know?' Lin nodded. 'Right, and I agree, there's something in the air surrounding this Brightwick fella and those around him.' They heard the Land Rover start up and pull away. 'You two head back to the lane. Amoya, let those two constables know about Mister Youngman and put in a call to DI Pat

Kershaw from me. She runs my team in Northants. Tell her I want a full workup on this Lord Brightwick, his staff,' he looked at Lin, 'and Mistral Pharmaceuticals. And tell her to organise a search warrant for here.'

'And you?'

'I'm going back with Jasper.' The terrier looked up and Archie spoke to him. 'You're spot-on about him boy and you'd not finished your walk yet, had you?'

~

'Did you make sure the Telegraph, Guardian and Independent were fully briefed?'

'Yes, Sir, they know what questions to ask.'

'Is that disagreeable Socialist oik Pritchard amongst them?'

'Afraid so Sir.'

'Well just try and keep her under control.'

'You'll have to let her ask at least one question Minister otherwise she'll write a complaint piece.'

'Not for the first time. Right, just the one. What's the police officer's room number?'

'Two. Do you want to make a statement outside the hospital or wait until you can gather Mister York and Chief Constable Strathallen together inside the hospital?'

'We'll wait. Desmond was immovable about me going in to see her with the press I understand.'

'Absolutely Sir.'

'Do you think a personal call would have helped?'

'Not from his tone Sir, no.'

'No...he always was the officious sort. Well, maybe low-key is the preferable route, given our connection.'

'That's how I feel too Sir.'

'And her room would be quite small, to fit us all in I mean.'

'Usual NHS size.'

'Quite small then. And my statement about the shooting?'

Quinn took out a sheet of paper. 'Here Sir.'

Brightwick took it and began to read out loud, skipping through the text.

'"Thank you for attending...Mister Desmond York, Senior Trauma Surgeon...NHS at its finest...life-saving surgery on the injured officer..." good. "Commander Strathallen...officers are conducting enquiries into this dreadful affair...just a few doors down from where we are gathered a young and determined police officer has been fighting for her life..." I think I might just change that to young and dedicated.' He red-penned and scribbled his addition before continuing, '"...young and dedicated police officer who is fighting for her life...who... miraculous work carried out by..." Yes, very good, reads well. I'm just a deeply concerned politician paying my respects to our brave law officers and the work of our splendid NHS.' He scanned the rest of the sheet and read out the odd line as the car travelled the final half mile to the hospital. '"Erm...da, da...must remember that not everyone fared so well...do everything in our power to assist..." Good.' Brightwick folded the sheet. 'What we need is a little time alone with Strathallen, find out what he knows and how far they've progressed.'

Quinn nodded. 'I'll see what I can engineer Sir.'

'Do that.' They arrived in the hospital's private parking area and Brightwick slipped the notes into his pocket and adjusted his jacket sleeves. 'Right, let's feed them the lines.' Stepping from the car Brightwick approached the press. 'Good morning and thank you for attending at this hour. Now, I'll be giving a prepared statement and I'll be glad to answer any questions, but only when we're convened with the Chief Commissioner and the leading surgeon who attended the brave policewoman who was so very nearly taken from us. That way you'll get a fuller picture. She is, after all, the reason for our visit. If you would care to follow me.' Brightwick led the way up the short flight of steps and into the hospital foyer where Mr. York, Commander Strathallen, a nursing sister and a staff nurse waited to greet him.

'If you'll just wait here.' Quinn shepherded the reporters away a little as Brightwick strode forward.

'Desmond! So pleased it was you in attendance for this nasty business.'

Mister York took the proffered hand. 'Nasty business indeed Lawrence.'

'Well if anyone can handle things it's you.' Brightwick's face creased with concern. 'The other policeman, I hear he wasn't so fortunate.'

'Indeed not. Died at the scene.'

'Ah yes. Terrible...terrible.' Brightwick stepped across to the Chief Constable. 'Gregory. Good to see you again too, even in such tragic circumstances.'

They shook hands as Quinn joined them, focussing closely on Strathallen's reply. 'Yes, Larry, tragic indeed. How are you?'

'Very well, but more importantly,' he turned back to Mister York, 'your patient, how is she?'

'Surprisingly well all things considered.'

'She's awake? Able to talk?'

'Yes, but only for a limited time.'

Brightwick focussed back on Strathallen. 'Has she been able to shed any light on matters?'

'Not a great deal; all happened so fast and in the dark.'

'Yes...yes, I see. Well, should we...?'

Mr. York nodded towards the gathered press. 'Certainly not up to such an intrusion as this, Lawrence.'

'No, absolutely not, they're not invited. I would ask a favour though Desmond. I would be so grateful if just I could look in on the lady, give her recovery a boost.'

'Just you?'

'Of course. Whip the rabble back. I just thought my presence here would reassure the officer and might also increase the possibility of finding the people responsible for this heinous crime.'

'Very well, just you, and for just a few seconds.'

'Of course; you're the man in charge, but anything that helps the police in their investigations can only be good, you'll agree?' Without waiting for a reply Brightwick turned to Strathallen. 'Where are we with that Gregory?' Anyone else but Quinn would have missed the inflection, the inquisitorial glint in the eye.

'We've made some progress Minister...' He paused. 'I have a short statement which I'll give out.'

'But you can brief me further, off the record?'

'A little yes, but only that which has been verified so far.'

'Of course, Gregory, of course, and I'll be eager to hear about it. Quinn will put the time aside for us to chat. Now...' Brightwick turned to Quinn who took up the narrative.

'We were wanting a room Mister York. One where we can gather for press questions and photos afterwards, a place not so public?'

'I see.' Mr. York turned to the sister. 'Is there one that can be put at their disposal?'

'Near the patient's room.'

'As Mr. Quinn says Sister Bray, near to Ms. Desai's room.'

'There's the Consultation and Bereavement Room just down the corridor Mr. York, that's quite large, but...'

Brightwick spoke over her. 'That will be perfect.'

'Yes, Sir, but we do try to keep that room open for relatives and...'

Quinn added his weight. 'Yes nurse I'm sure, but given the gathering of press, the Minister's presence, and his willingness to enhance the reputation of this hospital and the excellence and professionalism of its staff, surely we can use it for the brief period required?'

Sister Bray looked at Mr. York. 'Sir?'

Mr. York held Brightwick's stare for a few moments before answering. 'Yes, of course, Lawrence. Sister Bray, could you see to it that the room is made ready.'

'Yes Mister York, of course...' she half turned to Quinn. 'And it's Sister.' Quinn looked nonplussed. 'My position. I'm a Sister.'

247

'Indeed you are.' Brightwick broke in, exerting all his charm. 'And we thank you for your service and cooperation. No ceremony needed Desmond. This is purely a domestic briefing.'

'Thank you Lawrence. You have your room, but for twenty minutes only, then I would like it returned to its proper purpose. The sister will see this timetable is strictly adhered to.'

'Understand you perfectly Desmond, hospital regimes, a need for a peaceful environment to aid recovery...and all that.'

'"And all that" are the most important factors here Lawrence.'

'Of course they are... Quinn, collect the press would you?' They made their way to a lift, leaving Quinn to organise the gathered press. Brightwick placed a hand on York's shoulder as they walked. 'You and Christina really must come round to dinner again very soon, it's been too long, you too Gregory, you and your charming wife. I'll have Quinn contact your secretaries and suggest some dates.'

'That will be my wife Christina then; my secretary.'

'Will it...? Will it really? Then yes, Quinn will contact Christina.' The lift arrived and Brightwick stood back from the open doors. 'Shall we?'

~

Archie followed Jasper quickly across the open ground as he entered the woodland. There was no deviation, no hesitation in the dog's progress through the zigzag of saplings and round the odd, autumn-weakened briar patch. After a couple of minutes Jasper slowed as they arrived at the edge of a small glade.

'Jasp! Jasper, wait.' Archie held up his hand. 'Tch-tch! Sit.' The terrier sat. 'Good boy, good lad. Just hold on there, I don't work as fast as you. Stay?' He saw something in the dog's expression and said, more authoritatively this time. 'Stay.' Jasper settled. 'Simple stuff Rene, bless you. Good boy Jasp.' Archie dropped the lead in front of the terrier, refreshed his gum then took a couple of paces into the glade and stood still, chewing methodically and scanning the fallen leaves.

He could see straight away that someone else had been here, and recently. The wet, deep brown leaves lying on top of the dry, sandy coloured ones told a tale of movement as easily discernible as a billboard to the observant. *Pound to a pinch of pig shit this was our American cousin mooching about here.* He looked around. *No suspect trees hereabouts, definitely nothing worth logging.* He dropped down low, folding back his wayward quiff, and looked along the floor. *Nothing out of place...* Then he saw it, yet another colour change in the leaf covering and he spoke out loud. 'Ha! I'm right. Someone's been here before us and had a good rootle about, eh, Jasp?'

He dropped lower and was suddenly aware of the cold wet nose pressed against his ear. 'I thought I told you to stay.' The terrier wagged his tail. 'What?' Jasper yipped. 'Yeah OK, I'll let you have a look-see.' Archie unclipped the lead and allowed the terrier to range around. A handful of stubby dry sticks were lying under a part-flattened bramble. The darkened tip of one stood out and he bent to pick it up. *This has been burned...part of a fire maybe, a campfire.* His attention was pulled back to the terrier.

'What you got there, lad?' Jasper looked up then returned to his excavations. 'Good lad, what is it?' The terrier continued to shovel the vegetation, ash and soil behind him, the debris flying away to patter around Archie. 'What you got?' More leaves and dirt followed until the terrier was nearly a foot down and Archie heard the click of stones and Jasper emerged triumphantly with a charred, foliage-wrapped parcel in his mouth, a rabbit's head poking out of the end. As Jasper lifted it from the hole so the head fell off and bounced on the ground. 'Not often they come out of a burrow cooked.'

Archie put his hand onto the leaf wrap. 'Share?' Jasper's grip tightened, he lifted his top lip and a soft growl filtered out between grilled teeth. 'Not gonna share?' The growl continued and Archie tightened his grip. 'Dead. Drop it. Down...leave?' Jasper continued to hold on and looked over the disputed carcass with raised eyebrows at Archie. 'Give.' Jasper's grip changed and Archie toughened the tone. 'Give.' The terrier slowly released the carcass and Archie bent to pick up the head and unwrapped the contents. *Skinned and wrapped in sweet chestnut leaves; not from here so, imported.* He placed the rabbit portions on the ground and dipped back into the pit to uncover two distinct sections. Another leaf-embalmed item was exhumed. *Looks like a horse mushroom. Well charred...oh, hang on, two ovens, she was a vegetarian; right...* 'Clever. These are ovens and this is your campsite Jasp. This is what that Yank was sniffin' around for. Loose trees my arse, he was looking to find this campsite.' His thoughts ran on as he looked around. *Why? Keepers asked him to...? Nah, if they're worth anything they'd have done it themselves and according to our American pal they miss nothing; so, why him not them?*

He looked at Jasper whose eyes were still firmly fixed on the rabbit remains. 'Didn't have you with him did he mister clever-clogs. Right, no warrant needed now. Official crime scene. Sorry, pal, can't have any of this back, evidence. Phone calls to make, if I can get a bloody signal, get Jay's team over here.' He looked at his watch, *Oh hang on, he should be here soon, excellent timing.* 'Right.' He turned to the terrier. 'This is gonna be hard to understand, Jasp.' Archie placed the carcass and mushroom back into the pit then scuffed the soil and leaves back over it before re-clipping the lead. 'Tch-tch! Come on you...Jasp? Come on.' The terrier looked long and hard at the cooking site before responding as Archie checked his phone. 'Jesus, no signal, again...on the lane maybe. Let's go, Jasp.' The terrier followed... reluctantly.

~

⁶'Bring the hose over here and sluice this wall down...an' where th' fuck's that Yank?'

Chris grabbed the hosepipe. 'Sat in my motor with his feet up waitin' for us to finish, I'll bet.'

'Nah. Couldn't stand the stink.' Matt looked towards the door. 'Will all the tat fit in the back?'

'Yeah, there's not that much. Boiler's the biggest thing.'

'Took me days to get that system up and runnin' and minutes to tear it all down...what a waste.'

Chris pinched the hose pipe's end together to increase the force of flow and began to spray the wall they had finished scrubbing with the soft brooms. Matt shook his head. 'Jesus... Why'd y' not pick up a spray nozzle?'

'Because I thought we were gonna be usin' the pressure washer, we brought the genny.'

'Changed me mind, I want the place to look clean, not spotless.'

'Waste of time bringin' it then.' Chris sprayed the jet of water left to right across the wall, the spray bouncing off the angle between wall and floor, arcing into the air and back at them.

'Bloody hell, careful with that, you'll have me soaked!'

Chris altered the angle of the jet. 'You've got coveralls and boots on.'

''Cos I've got decent clobber on underneath.'

'Should've worn scruffs, like me.'

Matt picked up a bass broom and began to work it back and forth on the floor. 'You've only got 'em on 'cos you've nothin' else to wear. I take a bit of pride in meself.' Chris was about to reply but Matt shut him down. 'Enough of the banter, we're one man down as it is.' Matt leant the broom against the wall, walked over to the doorway and picked up the can of Jeyes Fluid. Removing the cap he poured a generous amount of the black liquid onto the floor, leaving a white trail in his wake. 'Let's scrub this sty and move on, there's another to sort out yet an' time's runnin' on.'

~

P at Kershaw closed the door to the incident room and took the coffee from DC Dougie Brand, one of the several Serious Crime Squad members gathered round the desk. 'Thanks Dougie.' She scanned the map alongside the whiteboard then looked round the room. 'Right, no sleep up 'til now and no sleep until conclusion. I echo Archie's statement, I want these bastards found, and fast. So, in fullness to the memory of DC Reeve here's where we are at present.' As she talked she pointed out headings and photos scribbled and pinned on the whiteboard.

'We know the number and nationality of our assassins, the pedigree of the firearm used, and we know the rail journey and the local route the shooters took. All roads out are on high alert, at last, and we've drafted in extra staff to run all the angles.' Pat looked round the room at the number of new faces interspersed with the regular crew. 'These lads and lasses are new to SCS and the way we operate so give them guidance and whatever support they need. I want no solo flights and no hierarchy tantrums on this, understood?' She smiled at them generally as they muttered agreement. 'Right, what we haven't got yet is the connection between our gunmen, the hit-and-run and the Pool Heath shootings and, need I add, anything even resembling an ID. But as you've all had the past couple of hours to flex your collective-detective muscle I'm hopeful that'll be remedied.' She looked round the room. 'Or not. Right, for the newbies, let's start and fill in the picture. Further information on the shootings. Dougie?'

'Not much more. From the neighbour's description Irish probably, Northern most likely. Enquiries at the various Shamrock Clubs and watering holes frequented by our Irish friends locally have revealed absolutely nothing. Shut like clams.'

'They know the consequences of chatter.'

'Forty years on and little's changed.'

'Bit more than that. Sixteen-ninety, if memory serves.'

'Thank you for the history lesson, Arnue.'

'Just sayin'.'

Dougie finished up. 'Shotgun used at the hit-and-run is commonplace. Probably shortened in the barrel as suggested by the patterning on the wall, that or very open choke. Our next line of enquiry was to start looking at recent passenger arrivals from Ireland, but it's a big ask. Thirty-six million visitors a year, three and a half million from Ireland. We've honed it down. Male only. Northern Ireland only, still runs at nearly a quarter of a million. We're in touch with Border Security and waiting on figures...their staffing cuts will only add to the wait. We don't expect them to get back to us until this evening at the earliest.'

'My, this Home Secretary's got summat to answer for, eh? Right. The owner of the land where Renata Lea was run down. Debbie, Phil?'

DS Deborah Truman moved to the second whiteboard.

'Lawrence Brightwick de Roazhon, pronounced Britik-de-Roan according to our tame snob Phil over there.' DC Philip Grainger smiled, doffed an imaginary hat and bowed. 'Lord Brightwick is the nineteenth Viscount Vichendelle and Middlecombe, CBE, Minister of State for Industry in our present, beloved government. Larry to his friends. Anglo-French, country seat is Bliss Bank Hall in the fair county of Buckinghamshire, our next-door neighbour since the county amalgamations in the last economy drive. Owns all the land round the hit-and-run site, most of the county in fact, as well as a moor in Sutherland, several square miles in the Central Highlands, forestry in County Clare and a fair chunk of several US states.'

Phil Granger smiled. 'Yes, but he only keeps Sutherland for the grouse and Kentucky for the horse-breeding.'

'As Phil says, for the grouses and horses. We've yet to interview him because, as his very officious and very guarded PPS Randal Quinn informed our visiting constable, "This has nothing to do with us and he's a very busy man".'

DS Mary Beckett shook her head. 'And we aren't.'

Pat spoke over her. 'Well I can say without fear of contradiction that a dead copper takes precedence, Lord or no. Do we have anything further about the lady on the train?'

'Good title for a film that.'

'Phil, enough! Mary, anything?'

'The chap who did the driving is coming in later today...'

'Don't wait chase him, better still go and bang on his door, I want an answer for this one in the next half-hour.' Mary nodded as Pat spoke on, 'As for our esteemed member of HMG, I know Archie wants the interview pleasure, but there's nothing to stop us running a stick along his bars. Phil, your territory.'

'Noted.'

Pat continued. 'However, when Archie does go over to Bliss Bank for the fireside chat one of us will have to skittle over and be support. We'll draw straws for that.'

Phil's voice dripped sarcasm. 'Surely we don't suspect a peer of the realm, do we?'

Pat sealed it up. 'Joking aside, it's a worthy point of Phil's, at last. I'll spell it out. Everyone, we suspect everyone. No amount of letters after a name is an excuse, so just you remember that.' She looked at Deborah. 'Anything to add?'

'Just a few notes for Brightwick's file, might help with your background searches Phil. This guy is a serious shooter, and by shooter I mean hunter and by serious I mean serious. Travels all over the world to do it.'

Dougie settled himself onto the corner of the desk. 'Shooting what?'

'Anything and everything.' Deborah consulted her notes. 'He's in the Guinness Book of Records for shooting the sixth highest number of grouse in one day to a single gun, only beaten by others of his ilk, er...the Lords Walsingham and Ripon to name but two, according to Debrett's...oh, and he also holds the record for shooting the most diverse number of Indian ground wildlife in a single, twenty-four-hour period, again courtesy of...'

They all joined in. 'Debrett's.'

'Christ.' Doug shook his head. 'So, he goes off to sunny places and...?'

'Shoots whatever he sees? Yes.' Deborah referred to her tablet again. 'Lion, kudu...chee-tal, bles-bok, whatever they are, er, tiger, water buffalo, hippo, giraffe, leopard, elephant...' She looked up. 'When do you want me to stop?' She flipped the scroll-screen. 'The list goes on...and on, oh, and he's completed the African Big Five eight times.'

'Big five?' asked DS Beckett.

'Lion, leopard, rhinoceros, elephant, buffalo all in one day.'

'Oh, that big five.'

Deborah nodded. 'Yeah, I know Mary, you can't plumb the depths of man can you? Anyway, what with all this gallivanting around the globe on the slaughter run, his winter shooting parties over here and his government and business interests, it makes him...'

They all spoke together again, 'A very busy man.'

Pat continued, 'Business interests Deb?'

'Sits on a lot of government committees, mainly environmental matters, and has international businesses, mainly livestock. Also a major player in Mistral Pharmaceuticals, a company based in the US but peddling their wares on just about every continent, particularly in Africa, with what they call their fifth generation of herb and pest controllers. He's also a frequent member on fact-finding visits to Africa, China and America.'

'Taxpayer-funded junkets. Anything else?'

'Like I said, when do you want me to stop? Part-owner in cattle feedlots in the US, Kenya, China. Fast-food industry stuff. Herds of beef cattle for processing in...' Deborah consulted the screen again, 'Nebraska, Colorado, Oklahoma, Alabama and Texas to name but a few, each feedlot averaging two-thousand head. He's also looking to move into the Chinese beef market, a new venture a couple of years in the making. A real mover and shaker by any stretch of the imagination.'

Mary indicated the whiteboard. 'OK. Cut to the chase. Does his hectic social calendar write him off for anything even slightly connected with the times of either the hit-and-run or the shootings?'

Deborah nodded. 'He was in London at the time our victim got run over and when the shootings happened.'

'Doing what?'

'Parliamentary business; votes and such, so airtight.'

Pat walked to the board and scanned the photos of Bliss Bank, of Brightwick and of the hit-and-run site before addressing the room in general again. 'Fine. Right. What about the people who work for him Marissa? Start with the general domestic and estate staff.'

DC Marissa Canning indicated her computer screen. 'Deb and I have been working our way through the list. Quite a few. We figure someone must have seen or heard something, the gamekeepers at least, all three of them.'

'What about others?'

Marissa scanned the list. 'He's got his own personal secretary, Quinn, and an office manager, Willis, there's nine in-house staff, an Estate Manager and secretary, six gardeners, a home farm that employs seven, four foresters, a water bailiff... Let's just say the place is self-sufficient and I doubt his Lordship has to raise a finger, inside or out.'

'I'd suggest that's all he has to do.' Pat turned back to the whiteboard and considered again. 'Right, redefine. House staff, that's your priority Marissa. Debs, Dougie you're to concentrate on the shooters at the flat. Who've you got with you?'

Dougie motioned to some of the assembled crew. 'I've got these two here and access to any number of rank and file for the general research, which is a bit scarce at the minute on account of that mass pile-up on the M6 round Brum.'

'Oh yeah, I heard about that on the radio this morning. Fifteen vehicles weren't there? Something about a dog running across the motorway?'

'Yeah. I picked up the details when I got in. Two dead and a tail-back of twelve miles.'

'Did they get it?'

'The dog? Yeah.'

'What was it?'

'Dunno. Some mongrel that got kicked out 'cos it grew too big probably.'

'Bloody strays. Right, well, keep the demands up on the shooter angle. What do we have on Brightwick's personal staff...?' The door opened and a uniformed officer came in holding up a report sheet. 'This looks serious. What is it, Ameet?'

'Reports of a shooting Guv'nor, in Stranraer near the Cairnryan ferry port. Couple of Irishmen opened fire on a port security chap and his dog. Both gunmen are dead.'

The room stiffened as Pat followed on. 'Irish...?'

'Yes Guv'nor.'

'The security chap?'

'Badly injured.'

'Our all-points bulletin got the ARU involved at least then.'

'No armed officers at the scene Guv. It was their port security chap did the killing.' He checked his notes. 'A Kenzie Jardine. Him an' his dog, they sorted it out. The dog stalled 'em, Jardine shot one and ran over the other.'

'Bloody hell. The dog?'

Ameet shrugged. 'Dunno Guv'nor, I heard dead...'

'Poor sod.'

'Same type of gun used on Detective Reeve. They're fast-tracking a match now, but first word is it's Irish.'

'What's the odds?' Pat shook her head. 'Christ, one minute we're treading water the next we're drowning. That it?'

Ameet checked the sheet. 'James Lamont, that's Jardine's co-worker, he's the point of contact. That's his mobile.'

He gave the sheet to Pat. 'Right, thanks Ameet. Arnue go with him, collect any extra info then pack a bag, you're off up to Glasgow. Interview this chap Jardine asap if he's fit enough, Lamont if he's not.' She turned back to the room. 'This'll be our two lads who did the shooting out at Pool Heath, and maybe the hit-and-run too...and we owe this bloke Kenzie a drink. You've got the number Arnue so call ahead.'

'Will do.' Arnue was already partway out the door.

'And don't forget the malt!' Arnue raised a hand both in recognition and farewell as Pat turned back to her team. 'Right, changes called for. Senior Officers, we spread the workload. Newcomers, this is a baptism of fire but that'll not be an excuse for missing anything, understood?' Collective nodding. 'Right, Phil, do the initial follow-up on the ferry info. Sailings, security, I want to know chapter and verse on the events. Deb, drop your Lordship searches for the minute and get on to Dumfries and Galloway, make them fully aware of our interest. Marissa? Leave the staff for the minute. Archie's asked for all intelligence surrounding the hit-and-run site, houses, farms, buildings and such. That was mine, but I need to do a board update then get onto Jay and get him to coordinate the post-mortem and the NaBIS ends as soon as stuff comes in. Do an OS map scan, put some notes with it on building positions and use, then get it across to Archie on our group WhatsApp. Co-ordinates would help too. Dougie...?'

Dougie was already at his desk. 'NaBIS in Glasgow boss; all over it.'

'Good. I want a copy of their report as soon as the ink's dry. I'll get in touch with Archie when you collect the details. The rest of you, divide up the spoils and pick up any slack, I need you all at the top of your game, this is moving fast enough to overtake us if we're not on it and I don't want anyone involved to get clear.'

To chants of 'Yes Guv' and 'On it, Guv' the team dispersed to their various spaces. Pat began to transfer the information from white page to whiteboard.

~

Jay scanned the sheet. 'Is this it? Anita nodded. 'Sparse, thank goodness. Right, a call is required, you'll oblige?'

'I will. I'll just finish up the last of the samples I've collected from Adam.'

'Of course. I'll pop back to the office and get on to NaBIS again, they should have the confirmation results from Dumfries and Galloway by now. It would be good to have the bullet matches documented.'

'It would.' Anita returned to the central table upon which was placed the part-covered corpse of Adam Reeve.

'Then I'll get over to the hit-and-run site and meet up with our University chums.' Jay thought he saw a slight hesitation in her first step. 'Anita? Do you want me to stay? Give a hand?'

She smiled at him. 'You really are kindness itself.'

'Not really, I just...'

'No, you are, and you want this thankless task as much as I do. I'll be fine. I'd like to make sure things are done properly, decently, for myself...no offence to your abilities.'

'None taken.' Jay paused to watch as Anita began her work then turned and left, muttering quietly. 'Ever the painstaking professional.' He entered the office, picked up the phone, checked his computer and tapped in the number.

'Hello? NaBIS Strathclyde? Yes. This is Professor Millar, Head of Forensics and SCO Northants and Beds. Could you put me through to Doctor Saunders please? Thank you.' Jay stood quietly, a ballistic report sheet to hand. 'Hello, Doctor Saunders. This is... Sylvia? Right, thank you Sylvia. It's Jay Millar, Jay, please. I spoke earlier to one of your lab techs...' He looked at the sheet heading. 'A Paul Royston? Yes, about the ballistic results from Cairn... Indeed ... Yes, from Ireland to Cairnryan via Bedfordshire and about forty years ... a much-travelled bullet indeed. Do you have the detailed projectile results? You do. Excellent! Just let me get my pen...'

~

J ames Lamont looked round the reception at Glasgow Infirmary A&E Department and sighed. The slumped and sloshed people littered the open area as he stood at the desk awaiting the attention of the receptionist. 'Cut out the drink and drugs you'd have an empty space here,' he said to no one in particular.

The receptionist looked up. 'Pardon?'

'Nothing. Busy still I see?'

'No more than usual.'

'Oh, right.'

A further silence followed until the receptionist put aside the daybook. 'Now. How can I help?'

'Lamont, James Lamont, I work with Kenzie, Mister Jardine, at the docks.' James showed his warrant card. 'Port Security. He was brought in here after a shooting at Cairnryan.'

'Ah right, yes.' She clicked the computer keyboard. 'Yes, he's in the post-operative ward.'

'Which is?'

'The Eilean Dà Bhàrr Wing, but Mrs. Jardine is with him now.'

'Faye?'

'Mrs Jardine, yes. We're only allowing one visitor at a time and family takes priority.'

'As they should. Can you just tell me how he is and pass a message on from me please?'

She looked again at the computer screen and spoke to a nearby nurse. 'Nurse Powell, could you just...?' The receptionist tapped the screen.

Nurse Powell looked at the computer then up at James. 'Mr. Jardine has come through the operation very well, is awake and comfortable but still drowsy.'

James stood in silence for a second or two. 'That it?'

'That's all we can share at present Mr...?'

'Lamont.'

'Mr. Lamont.'

'Right… OK, well can you just let him know I was here asking after him and that Cashman…' the nurse raised a quizzical eyebrow, 'His dog…'

The door to the reception area burst open and two men supporting a third between them staggered through. Blood was flowing freely from an ugly wound to his neck as, like a hooker and two prop-forwards, they lurched scrum-like towards the desk as one of the men shouted out, 'Get a doctor somebody, he's been glassed!'

The nurse slipped round the desk to assist, clamping a hand to the man's wound to staunch the flow. 'Doctor! Security please!'

Within seconds a doctor, two nurses and a burley security man were amongst the trio, guiding the ruck to seats and triage.

She forced a smile as she passed James. 'You'll have to come back Mister…?'

'Lamont.'

'Lamont. As you can see, we're a little busy at the moment.'

~

As he approached the lane Arnold took out his mobile and was surprised to see bars showing a signal. He stopped dead and held up his palm.

'Hold on Jasper; sit.' The terrier sat. 'I need to make the most of this. If I move a step it'll go…' He clicked on a favourite and waited… 'Pat? Yeah. No, still at the hit-and-run site … What news? Out here? You're joking, right? … What, both! Who? … Well good for him, saves the taxpayer a fortune in prison bills, send him our thanks and a bottle of The Balvenie on me … Oh, good work … Arnue? Excellent choice. Good at the detail is Mister Cho. Keep me posted … His name's Jasper.' He glanced down at the sitting terrier. 'Struggling but making the best of what he's got. You got a call from Amoya, the WPC here? … Good, and bear her in mind for a transfer Pat, she's a keeper.

Right, let me flesh things out a little. I've now found our victim's campsite, or rather the dog did. There's been outside interest shown ... An American, Alabamian, Aiden Steerholm-Youngman III, get in touch with immigration, check visas ... Right, can you spare Debbie and Phil? I'd like them over here as back-up when Jay does the first sweep. Excellent, and look, the signal here's crap. If you so much as sniff it's gone, so can you ring Anita for me? Jay'll probably be en route to here by now, so ask her to rustle up the forensics team and get them over here... yeah, whole team, tell her why. Debs and Phil can act as liaison with HQ. Anything further on that lady, the one on the train? ... Where? Are you sure? ... Christ, Brightwick keeps comin' back like a bad smell. Right, his housekeeper, yeah, get one of the team and someone from uniform ... whoever's available.' Archie heard Pat call out, '*Mary!*' as he continued, 'Yeah, Mary's a good choice. Get them across to take a statement from her, and tell Mary to use the chance to put Brightwick on notice that we want a word ... I don't care what the Super will say ... no, nor his secretary. I want that meeting set up ... Minister of the Crown or not you tell them from me this is a murder inquiry and someone on his staff is a person of interest ... CIC can kick up all he wants, Pat. We need to fight this fire with a flamethrower! Sorry Pat, don't mean to shout ... Oh, and I'm gonna want a security team set up to cover Lin, Miss Lea, until we know all the detail ... Not sure yet, her flat's still out commission so I'll let you know as soon as I do, but hand-pick 'em Pat, I want top-of-the-range but discreet.' Archie paused, looked at the sitting dog and sighed. 'Look Pat, are you alright with this heavy-duty stuff coming at you? ... No, I know, it's just, I'm here swanning round the countryside and you're ... Thanks, you're the best ... yeah. Be in touch.'

'Tch-tch! Come on Jasp, we've got stuff to do.'

~

Quinn re-entered the makeshift interview room at the hospital, pocketed his mobile and held Brightwick's gaze, smiling slightly. Brightwick made to wind things up. 'Ah...Right, we've just got time for one more. Erm... yes, you.'

Karen Pritchard, political features writer for The Independent nodded her thanks. 'Minister, is it possible this shooting could have been difficult to investigate because of the drop in police numbers? Even according to the government's own figures, the last six months have seen a rise in violent crime of seventeen percent which, coincidentally, matches the reduction in the force since your government took office; seventeen percent.'

Brightwick stared hard at Karen before answering. 'No, I don't...Pritchard, is it?' She knew he knew, and Karen smiled back and nodded. 'Can I say I think, in the present circumstances, your question and its tone are insensitive to say the least. Here...' Karen attempted to justify but Brightwick talked over her, 'Here we have a brave policewoman fighting for her life in this hospital, in this very wing. A policewoman who was just doing her job, and all that seems to matter to you is using it as an opportunity to snipe at the government.' Karen tried once again, but Brightwick continued to talk her down. 'I would think you would be better served concentrating on this lady's ordeal and that of her parents.'

'Are they here?'

Brightwick answered the shouted question from one of the other reporters. 'I believe...' he looked across at Quinn who shook his head. 'I believe they are on their way here and when they do arrive, I'm sure you will all respect their privacy.' He held up a hand. 'Now, I'm sorry, but that's all we've time for. The hospital was kind enough to allow us use of this room but only for a few minutes.' He indicated the starched bouncer, Sister Bray, who was standing with arms folded. 'I can see hospital forces gathering at the door, so thank you all again.'

Brightwick turned from the table and signalled to Quinn who began to sheepdog the journalists out of the room. 'Thank you all for your time; the Minister will have a written statement for release later today, yes, thank you... Thank you...'

Gradually the room emptied and Brightwick joined Quinn at the door. Quinn gave a fixed smile as he called out, 'Thank you so much for your help with this, nurse, it's much appreciated.' Stony silence bade them farewell.

In the sparsely-occupied corridor Brightwick leaned towards Quinn. 'You looked pleased when you came back in. Good news I trust?'

Quinn did a quick sweep before answering. 'The Irish contingent...both dead.'

'Both! Excellent!'

'Security chappie was hospitalised with gunshot wounds but is expected to live.'

'And what does he know?'

'Nothing, and anything he does know is unconnected to us. Just a couple of bad people who ran into the wrong man.'

Brightwick frowned. 'I imagine the police will eventually join them up with the shooting at the flat?'

'Undoubtedly, but all this just neatly moves it further afield, certainly further away from us.'

'Yes. Good.'

'The spotlight's on him. He's the story, him and his dog.'

'Dog?'

Quinn nodded. 'Yes. Dead by all accounts, shot by one of the felons.'

'Good. A tearful pet drama to occupy the red tops. Prepare a line for me. Always good to play the Beatrix Potter card.'

'Already done Sir. The Mail is running it as their lead.'

'Good. Could this be a talking point for my appearance on the television?'

'It could Sir.'

'Indeed. Work on it Quinn and also, make sure I get a résumé of any of the probable questions beforehand. Look them over then ensure the Cabinet Secretary has been briefed and any statements cleared with the PM's PPS.'

'Yes, Sir.'

'All working out well, we just have the return visit of our Chinese friends to contend with before then. Where are we with that?'

'I have yet to get full confirmation from Lamb Sir.'

'Has he found other competition?'

'I believe he's been quite busy Sir, so...'

'Get him on to it! We need a replacement Quinn. The Chinese are expecting it and I'll not disappoint them. Is that clear?'

'Yes, Sir.' Quinn's mobile rang as Brightwick spotted Mr. York and moved purposefully towards him.

'Ah Desmond. Glad I got to see you before we left. Off to see your star patient? I could see what excellent care she was getting when I popped my head round her door.' He took York's arm and steered him along the corridor towards Kanjara's room. 'I trust you'll keep me abreast of any changes in the health of Ms. Desai and also update Quinn on any conversations she may have, with the press in particular, hmm? You have his number?'

As they reached the ward doorway and the awaiting Sister Waldeck, Desmond freed his arm and turned towards Brightwick. 'Yes I do, and rest assured Larry, firstly the press will have no access to her during her stay, and second, Randal will be the first to know should Ms. Desai decide she wants to share anything with anyone...outside of her immediate family and her medical team that is.'

Brightwick smiled thinly. 'Of course.'

They were joined by Quinn brandishing his mobile phone. 'Apologies Mister York. Sir, it's Lord MacGrady from Defra, wants a word.'

'Sorry Desmond, no peace for the wicked eh? I have to take this.' He held out a hand for the phone. 'Let's not forget, about dinner.'

'No, let's not.'

Brightwick and Quinn moved towards the lift. 'Reggie! What can I help with...?'

York watched him for a few seconds before turning towards Kanjara's room and a grinning Sister Waldeck standing nearby. 'He who sups with the devil... Good luck with that one then Sir.'

He returned her smile. 'I'm certain surgery will beckon. My wife was aware of his visit before I was and left me to face the flak, but I'm sure she'll be able to plan an escape route from the invitation.' They entered Kanjara's room. 'Ah, Miss Desai. I trust the visit from our representative of government wasn't too taxing?'

Kanjara smiled weakly, shook her head and spoke quietly. 'No, but be careful of that oil slick on the floor, you might slip on it.'

Sister Waldeck grinned. 'I'll have the cleaners come in with a mop right away.'

Mister York reached the bedside. 'Right, enough chitchat. How are those wounds looking?' Sister Waldeck took two pairs of surgical gloves from a box and passed one pair over, putting the other pair on before gently folding back the loose dressing on Kanjara's shoulder. 'Ah, excellent, just what we want to see.'

~

6 About fuckin' time too!' Chris' greeting at Aiden's arrival went unappreciated.

'I got held up...'

'Yeah, I'll bet.'

'By the police, they...'

Matt interrupted him. 'What? I said to go to the campsite! What the hell were you doin' sniffin' round the hit-and-run? You knew there were coppers there, they've been there all week!'

'I went to the campsite, that's where they were!' This stalled the conversation.

It was Chris who re-opened discussions. 'How th' hell did they manage that?' He turned to Matt. 'I told y' not to send him, the useless tosser!'

Aiden looked across at Chris. 'You wanna watch your mouth buddy, it'll likely get you into trouble one day.'

'Trouble?' Chris almost laughed. 'From who? You, y' fuckin' empty suit...'

Matt, who had been silently processing the information and its implications, stepped on the bickering. 'Shut up both of y'!' He turned to Aiden. 'The cops, where were they?'

'I said. In the woods.'

'Where?'

'On the grass-walk, two of 'em and the sister of that woman you ran over.'

Stunned silence followed until Matt spoke again. 'Is there anythin' else you want to share?'

Aiden shook his head. 'Aint that enough?'

'Don't let your gob get smarter than your head or I'll turn him loose on y'.'

Chris smiled. 'Say the word.'

'What'd they say?'

''Bout the hit-an'-run... Oh hey, I saw that dog, the one that bit y'all. Good lookin' terrier, neat.'

Once more, Matt spoke over Chris' attempted reply, except this time he moved very close to Aiden, holding his gaze as he placed the broom very particularly against the wall. 'Concentrate on me y' dipstick, not him. Now, what...did...they...say?'

All thoughts of a smart reply were doused. 'I told you, 'bout the hit-an'-run, how sad an' all... you know, the usual.'

'And you?'

'Agreed of course. I said it was a terrible thing and told 'em they'd need a search warrant if they reckoned on goin' any further.'

'You said what?'

'I told 'em they'd need a search warrant...' Aiden could see Matt was not amused by this and tried to justify it. 'They wanted to look round the woods an' I knew you'd not want that! What else could I say?'

'You mean apart from telling them there was stuff goin' on here we don't want them to find out about?'

'That's a heck of a jump there fella! I just said, what with the game birds an' all, it'd be best if they went through official channels; get in touch with His Lordship. It put 'em off too, they went on back to the road.'

Matt's reply matched Chris' expression. 'And you mean to say you think that's the end of it? That you've done this super job and solved all our problems, is that it?'

'A little gratitude for savin' your ass wouldn't come amiss.'

Chris could not hold it in any longer. 'Why you…!'

Matt pressed a hand on Chris' chest. 'Enough! Get y'self over there by that wall!' After a very long pause during which Aiden was left under no illusions as to how close he had come to obliteration, Chris grunted and Matt felt the pressure against his palm lessen. 'They went back to the lane. You're sure of that?'

'They left along the wall that backs up the wood so, yeah, I guess. I didn't wait to find out. Set off back here to let y'all know, fast as I could.'

Matt stared at the floor and rubbed his brow with his fingertips, his breath coming long and strained until he eventually summed up his feelings, beginning with an animal-like roar until it formed a screamed coherence. 'Jesus H Fuckin' Christ!'

Chris had been with Matt long enough to know when to remain in the shadows, but Aiden drew breath to speak. Chris fixed him with a stare of glacial proportions. 'Not now pal, not if you wanna stay in one piece.'

Matt retrieved his broom and handed it to Aiden without looking at him. 'You two get this finished and make a job of it, I've got calls to make.' He moved towards the doorway that led out to the yard. 'Sweep!' Matt tossed a key to Chris. 'And don't forget to lock up when you go!' He was gone.

Chris picked up the hose and began spraying down the recently disinfected floor.

Aiden looked across at him. 'Can we not use the pressure-hose?'

Chris spoke without looking up. 'Don't say another fuckin' word. Just sweep.'

~

'When you come out with the wall on your left, just move down the riding fifty yards or so to the right. Stay there. No one gets by you, understood? Not until Miss Cresson and the forensics team turn up.' The constable, his back to Arnold as he walked along the lane, lifted a hand in recognition without turning as Archie called out, 'It's now a crime scene, right?'

'Sir,' floated back, accompanied by that hand again.

Arnold looked down on the patiently waiting Jasper and spoke to the remaining constable. 'Right, me and the dog are gonna have a chat with Lin and the WPC. You just stick around here. I don't doubt Mister Millar will be along shortly and he may want help.'

'Sir.'

'Come on Jasp let's set this ball rollin'.' The terrier trotted alongside Archie as he called out to Lin and Amoya. 'Jasper was right, our American friend isn't kosher. I found Renata's campsite.'

This news, delivered straight-on, held sad relief for Lin. 'Knew it!'

'A double oven sunk in a small clearing; one half rabbit the other mushrooms. Supper for her and him.'

'Their last supper.'

Amoya put her hand gently on Lin's arm as Archie laid out his plan. 'Right, look, I'm gonna hang on here 'til Jay turns up. I need to get him up to speed and see to it that he's in the right spot. Amoya, you take Lin back to Penngorse and file this visit in the log. Before you go, three favours Lin. Will it be OK to keep Jasper with me for a while longer?'

'Of course. He's more your dog than anyone else's at present so yes, fine.'

'Thanks.'

'The second?'

'Where will you be?'

Amoya answered Lin's puzzled look. 'Your place will still be off-limits.'

'Oh yes, of course. Erm...well, probably the Red Lion then. Sarah will have gone back there by now. Can I be dropped there after Penngorse?'

Archie nodded. ''Course, and best you know now. I've briefed my team to set up a protection group for your safeguarding.' He saw Lin's reaction. 'Nothing for you to be alarmed about, you'll not know they're around. It's just belt-and-braces stuff until we know what we're dealing with. You also need to know that, given the lead in to all this, they'll be armed, so you need to brief the people you're closest to. Amoya, you'll have a reliable phone signal when you leave here so can you ring Pat again and let her know where you're taking Lin.' Amoya nodded in reply. 'Pat'll do the rest.' Lin still looked unsure. 'You OK with all this?'

'Yes...' Lin paused and thought before continuing. 'Yes, it's OK, I trust you. Number three?'

'The ID.'

'Of course, yes.'

'Sorry about that.'

'It's fine.' After a moment's silence Amoya turned and led Lin to her car.

Archie fished in his pocket as his mobile rang. 'Heck, a signal! Make the most of this!' He watched them go as he answered, 'Anita, hi. Am I on speaker ... are you driving on your own I mean? Good, I can talk freely then. Look, thanks again for rescuing me earlier, I owe you one ... Dinner? Er...yeah, sure ... You'll cook...? OK, yeah, that'd be great.' Archie raised a hand in farewell as Amoya swung the car in a three-point turn before driving back up the lane. 'So, the pellet from the dog, what did you glean from it? ... Ah-ha...mm... Only three? Read 'em out.

No... No... Black Feather! Wow! ...Well, believe it or not,' he took the cartridge from his pocket, 'I've just seen a Black Feather cartridge sitting in the front of a Land Rover not twenty minutes ago ... yeah, honest.' He dropped the volume of his voice. 'Look, would it help if you had a comparison cartridge, you know, to match against the pellet you've already got? ... Well I may be able to help, but only if you're willing to get in deep and swear not to tell Jay ...' He dropped his volume further, 'Because I stole one from out of an estate Land Rover earlier, that's why.' There was a full five seconds of silence before the conversation restarted. 'I know what you're thinking Anita ... no, I do, but because it's not admissible doesn't mean it won't matter ... I'll just use it as a conversation piece then, once I've got a confession, it'll be a moot point. After you've done with it, I'll chuck it ... I will! ... No, OK, I know, I shouldn't have taken it, I know that, but ... nor told you about it ... I know it makes you an accessory, yes ... but, now we have it, it'd be a pity for it to go to waste don't you think?' A further lengthy silence followed until Archie's face showed relief. 'Thanks Anita, you're a pal ... I'll hand it across to you asap, and I look forward to dinner and reminiscences. Thanks ... Yeah, I'm just waiting for Jay to roll up. He should be here pretty ... Oh hang on, talk of the Devil. OK, got to go. How long 'til you're here?' He waved at Jay, who had just stepped out of the car accompanied by two other people. 'Good. Your brilliance would be missed otherwise, and thanks again.' He closed off the conversation and went across to meet Jay.

'Hiya Jay. If you thought you were in for a cushy afternoon, think on.'

~

Silence had been the only accompaniment to the swish of bass brooms as Chris and Aiden finished up in the pigsties; for Chris the silence was easier, for Aiden safer. It was not until they had loaded the last of the kit into the back of the Land Rover that anything was said, and then it was only a grunted, 'Get in' from Chris which sounded less an invitation more a threat. Once settled and the first few yards of track covered, Aiden attempted to start a conversation.

'Where's all the hardware goin'?'

'Skip.'

'Cool.' Another short silence followed until Aiden tried again. 'Y'all be dealin' with those pups straight off, right?' There were better ways of breaking the silence, but Aiden was on solid ground now; this was his field of expertise and command, all of it backed up by the Gaffer. Chris knew it and his resentment showed in the tone of the reply.

'I know what I gotta do so fuck off.'

'Soon as we're back, right?'

Chris' hands gripped the wheel just a little tighter. 'Fuck. Off.'

'Just sayin' is all. Lordship wants no loose ends so just make it so.'

Chris slowed slightly as he continued to stare hard through the windscreen, but he enunciated clearly and precisely, 'Consider y'self lucky I'm busy drivin' 'cos that means you're not in traction. I'll drop you at your kennels and do my job, you do yours.'

Aiden breathed in to speak.

Chris changed gear roughly. 'Shut it.'

~

6 'Seems like years since I was last here, not hours.'

The Red Lion car park, never exactly full to bursting on any weekday, was particularly empty. Drawing up to the main entrance Amoya nodded in agreement. 'I can imagine.' She unclipped her seatbelt. 'I'll just see you in, if that's OK?'

Lin smiled. 'Yeah 'course, I think I'd be disappointed if you didn't. I just hope Sarah's back.'

'And that chap she was with.'

'Vaz, Vasiri.'

'Vasiri, that's him.'

As they stepped out onto the car park the pub door opened and Sarah and Vasiri came out to meet them. 'Lin! Thank goodness!' Sarah ran forward, grabbing Lin round the shoulders and hugging her tight. 'And if you ever scare us like that again I'm calling in your malt tab!' She paused then hugged Lin close again. 'I was so sorry to hear about Rene...about Rene's...'

'Murder. She was murdered Sarah.' Lin looked over Sarah's shoulder. 'Hi Vaz, not often you're up at this time of the day. You must be knackered.'

'Funny. You're really funny.' He smiled broadly. 'Jesus but you gave us a fright.' He nodded at the WPC standing by the car. 'Thanks for delivering her safe...?'

'WPC Williams.'

'Thank you, WPC Williams.'

Sarah released Lin and smiled across at Amoya. 'Yes, from me too. So, Rene really was murdered?'

Lin nodded. ''Fraid so.'

'Jesus...' Vaz was lost for words, not so Sarah.

'So are you in danger?' Sarah looked at Amoya. 'Is she?'

Lin shrugged her shoulders as Amoya spoke. 'We're not sure, that's why it's important that Lin's got friends around as support. Her flat's definitely out of bounds for all sorts of reasons, so until we can get a definite angle on this you all need to be vigilant and know also there'll be a police presence around the pub at regular intervals.'

Sarah smiled. 'That'll be lock-ins scuppered then.'

'Do you have any idea who?' asked Vaz.

'For the shootings?' Vas nodded and waited. 'We're still gathering information, it's an ongoing investigation so I don't want to compromise the outcome, and neither do I want any complacency setting in. Lin, you need to keep a low profile and you two, you need to make sure she does until the all-clear comes from DCI Arnold.'

'Who's he?' asked Sarah.

'The detective in charge of things.' Lin turned to Amoya. 'I should be helping Archie, detective Arnold, not stuck here in the pub.'

'DCI Arnold's got Jasper with him, remember?'

'Jasper?'

'Rene's terrier,' Lin could see Vaz's confusion, 'I'll tell you later. I just feel I need to be more involved.'

'And you will be. Archie's collecting you later for the ID.'

'Yes...'

'Oh, Lin. Really?' Lin nodded in reply to Sarah. 'Wow...' Sarah paused then moved towards the pub door. 'So, are all of us in the clear?'

'Yes. You seem worried, why?'

Sarah opened the door and called out, 'We're clear!'

After a few seconds Tim stepped out to join them and Amoya smiled. 'Ah right. You'll be the accomplice then?'

'Tim! Oh my goodness, Tim...!' Lin stepped rapidly across to him and took both his hands, Tim grinning widely in pleasure at the reunion. 'Are you alright? Did you get caught?' Lin turned sheepishly towards Amoya. 'Sorry, that sounds all wrong.'

'No harm done. Right, I need photos of you all to give to the security teams, is that OK? Lin and Tim, we already have yours so could I just...?' She took out her mobile and photographed Sarah and Vaz. 'Thank you. I'll get these across and they'll print off a strip for the team. Right, I'll leave you four to it, OK? You'll have a lot to discuss, and Lin, a lot to come to terms with. Please don't forget, if you have any suspicions, any at all no matter how insignificant they seem, report it to the officers who will be paying regular visits here and if they aren't about, phone Penngorse, you have the number Lin. OK?' They all muttered agreement as Amoya turned to Tim. 'I assume your belongings are still at Penngorse?'

'Yeah, I think so.'

'I'll ask one of the team to bring them across with the first visit. OK?'

Tim nodded. 'Thanks, thank you.'

Amoya returned to the car. 'Take care of each other.'

~

'How did you know my sister was here? Does Mister Quinn know you're here?'

'I doubt it. We showed our warrant cards when we asked one of the gardeners as we came in and he directed us to the kitchen door. Could we see your sister now?'

'Yes, yes. It's just that Mister Quinn likes to keep an eye on the comings and goings when his Lordship is absent. I'm amazed you got this far.'

'Because we're the police Madam.'

'Yes, of course. Sorry. I've only been here a few months so I'm still getting used to the level of fuss that happens here.' She paused. 'Right, I'll just give her a call, she's in the kitchen having a late breakfast.'

'Miss Connor?'

'Gemma, please.'

'Right. Gemma, look, if any of this makes you feel uncomfortable...'

'No no, I'm sure no one will mind, and it is a police matter so we need to help if we can.' Gemma left DS Beckett and PC Reddy on the step only to reappear almost immediately. 'So sorry, very rude. Would you like to come up? I've a pot of tea on.'

'That would be very welcome. Thank you.'

'Right. Tea for two.' Mary and Ameet followed Gemma into the huge kitchen. Sitting at a scrub-top table at its far end another woman of slightly younger age was seated, a plate empty of toast in front of her, a cup full of tea in her hand, a radio tuned to the local news babbling quietly in the background.

'Andrea? These are police officers. They want to talk about that do on the train, the one with the money and that girl, that coloured lass?'

Gemma quietened the radio as Andrea stood and turned to face them. 'Oh right, is everything alright?' Mary could see the family resemblance.

'Yes, Ms Connor.'

'Andrea.'

'Thank you, Andrea. I'm Detective Sergeant Mary Beckett and this is Constable Reddy.'

Andrea smiled at them both and took Mary's proffered hand. 'Good name for a policeman, Reddy.'

Ameet removed his hat. 'It's spelt R-e-d-d-y; no a, and too many d's.'

'Only teasing dear.'

'Oh yes, right...' Ameet coloured slightly and shifted his gaze. 'Big kitchen.'

Gemma nodded. 'Yes. Big house.'

Mary steered the concentration away from Ameet's blush. 'And this all belongs to Lord Brightwick, and Gemma you're the...?'

'House Cook. I do all the day-to-day meals for staff...'

'They all eat here?'

'Most of them, it's part of their perks. I also do for His Lordship and his business guests when he's here...shoot-day lunches, as well, and I help out at the banquets they have. They import a London chef for those.'

'Often?'

'Regular enough.'

'And does that bother you, someone else running your kitchen, I know I'd hate it?'

'No. Wouldn't want all that swanky stuff they cook, all that gold leaf and truffle nonsense. No room for any of that in a steak and kidney pudding, and if I may say, they don't run my kitchen, I do that. They import most of their own staff, sous chefs and such, use it, then clear off. We're just here to help them 'cos we know this space like the back of our hands, the quirks and such; they'd just be flailing about without us.'

'Us?'

'Me and three others.'

'Are they here at present?'

'No. Away in their rooms until lunch. Two are permanent kitchen staff, one's a helper from the room staff.'

'Right. And for special occasions they import people,' Mary turned to Andrea, 'so...you've come down to help?'

'Me? No. Smacks all too much of serfdom for me.'

'Andrea!'

'Well it does Gem, you know my views on it all, both here and at your last place. The grouse season there was always a bit hectic, but here, it seems non-stop.'

'Why's that?'

Gemma paused. 'Well...he's government isn't he, so lots of things go on here that have to do with that...and his other work, business meetings and such.'

'And you can cope with the staff you've got, they don't import cooks for those?'

'Oh no. His Lordship likes the grand occasions of course, but for the most part I cook traditional fare, all quite easy. It's with the Americans and the Chinese that the stress levels rise, them and the big evening do's, that's when they import staff...and the security levels rise too.'

'International then?'

'Oh yes. Once a month at least there's some session or other. We've got one coming up next week, another Chinese delegation, all very high-power.'

'Another?'

'Oh yes. The last lot that came over had their own bodyguards and everything, we had to cater for them too. When the formal meetings were going on they had nothing to do so they spent no end of time here, in the kitchen, cluttering up the place, getting under foot and all because they loved our tea and scones of an afternoon. Had no English of course, well not to speak of. Odd word, that was it.' Gemma paused for a moment. 'Dogs. That was one word they did have. Kept on about them. I said what dogs? No dogs in this kitchen I said, we keep it clean. Didn't understand me at all, waste of time. Was glad to see 'em gone truth be told...but I'm talking too much...'

'No, it all helps to build a picture. Can I just ask you...your sister, you didn't collect her from the station. Why was that?'

'Well I don't drive, and I had to be here for the evening.'

'No one else available to do it for you?'

'I wouldn't ask, I want no favours from here...'

Andrea cut in. 'And I wanted none either. I was quite happy being left to my own devices...'

'She's always been a bit of a loner has my sister.'

'Not a loner Gem, self-reliant is what I am, and it gave me a chance to look around, get a drink...'

Gemma reined in the conversation. 'And talking of drink, you've not come to gossip. Sit yourselves down and I'll sort out china.' Gemma laughed at her own joke. 'Ha! There's a thing, if only I could!'

She busied with crockery as Mary sat down next to Andrea. 'How did you know where to find me?' she asked.

'Your visit to the pub, the taxi firm you booked. Not often he delivers to here, so yours stuck in his mind.'

'Oh yes.'

'OK, right. What can you tell me about the train journey?'

Ameet opened his notebook...

... Andrea was well into the tale when the door opened swiftly and Quinn, bordering on breathlessness, entered the kitchen. 'Ah, there you are... Can I ask the nature of this interruption?'

'Interruption?' Mary turned in her chair to face him. 'You've got the wrong idea Sir, this is an official police interview, Mister...?'

'Quinn, Randal Quinn, I'm Lord Brightwick's PPS and it would have been politic to ask permission...'

'Ah yes, Randal Quinn. Your name's been noted at earlier meetings back at HQ.' This last threw Quinn, this mention of discussions about him that he was not party to. The chair legs scraped an announcement on the quarry-tiled floor as Mary stood to the full extent of her five foot four in stockinged feet and moved closer to Quinn who towered over her. 'I'm an officer of the law Mister Quinn. My name is Detective Sergeant Mary Beckett.' She brandished her warrant card. 'This is PC Ameet Reddy, and the last time I checked the duties of a police officer I wasn't aware I had to ask permission to interview Miss Connor or anyone else in pursuance of an investigation into a criminal act. However, to set your mind at rest, there are no interruptions being caused to the smooth running of this house by me interviewing someone who doesn't actually work here.'

Despite the size difference Quinn took a half pace back, fully aware of the balance of power but unwilling to surrender too much by way of ground. Composing himself he returned to his default setting of dismissive. 'Not permission exactly officer, poor wording on my part. More a courtesy call, to inform us of events.'

'I do believe one of our constables has already paid a visit here, to inform you of an incident that happened on this land.'

'That took place some way away from the hub, officer, and he wasn't seen by either myself or the Minister; I believe Carson the butler saw him.'

'That's as maybe Sir. We're not to be held responsible for staff shortcomings in the communications department of this house only for the information presented, recorded and documented by our officer.'

Quinn was cornered once more but pressed on. 'Semantics officer. Miss Connor's our cook's sister and naturally Connor here would want to support her sister in this ordeal.'

'Hardly an ordeal.' Mary indicated the table contents, 'This chat over tea.'

Quinn ignored it, determined to finish his reasoning. 'And this diversion means she would be absent from kitchen duties for the duration of the interview, and we have a very tight schedule to keep to.'

'So do we Mister Quinn, and I'm afraid our murder enquiry takes precedence over your canapés.' This firm statement of the police enquiry registered with Quinn, Mary could see it. 'Couple of things to bear in mind here Mister Quinn. We are interviewing a Miss Andrea Connor who is not a member of your staff, and I'm a Detective Sergeant, not just an officer. Remember those two things and we'll get along fine.'

'Then I would respectfully remind you Detective Sergeant that we are readying this house for a trade visit by a Chinese delegation. An event that will be attended by your Chief Superintendent Campbell and his immediate superior the Chief Commissioner.'

'Then in the interests of all concerned I would respectfully request that I'm allowed to swiftly complete my questioning here in the relaxed comfort of your kitchen, with your blessing but not your company, so that we can be out of your hair. That or we can ask Ms. Connor to join us at the station. I don't mind which, but I suspect Ms. Connor's sister might.'

Quinn could see how this game of Top Trumps was playing out and decided against playing any more cards. 'Yes of course. And do you need Ms. Connor's sister throughout or can we prize her back to her duties?'

'No, that'd be fine.'

'Excellent. Connor, I would be pleased to have your company in the butler's pantry in the next five minutes. We need to run the inventory for the required place settings for the twenty-first, together with Carson.'

Gemma had been silent throughout the exchanges between Quinn and Mary, her eyes gradually widening. It was the ringing of the hierarchy bell that stimulated her Pavlovian response. 'Yes, of course Sir.'

Quinn smiled at the pyrrhic victory, a smile that was quickly erased by Mary's next line. 'Oh, and whilst we have you here with us Mister Quinn, when would it be convenient for the detective in charge of this case, Detective Chief Inspector Arnold, to have a chat with Lord Brightwick? Tomorrow suit?'

Mary saw the effect of the question, Quinn's complexion blooding redder as he wrestled with this affront to his authority whilst being aware of the legalities. 'Tomorrow? Out of the question! His Lordship is in London all day. With a diary as full as His Lordship's we'll need at least two days' notice of any such arrangement.'

Mary was in fast. 'Also out of the question Mister Quinn. This is a murder enquiry. If he can't do tomorrow then how about later today? Is His Lordship at home?'

'His Lordship will be returning here later today, yes, but only very briefly.' Quinn waited. He sighed. 'Very well. I'll see if I can re-jig a couple of appointments, but it will only be a severely truncated meeting, we really are up against events.'

'As are we Mister Quinn.' Mary took out a card. 'This is our number, if you could ring in with a time?'

'Oh, I'm sure we have that on record, the Chief Constable is a good friend of His Lordship...'

'That's of little help to us Sir. This number will get you directly through to the Incident Room, and to me.'

Quinn took the card. 'Connor, I'll see you shortly.' He turned to Mary. 'In the meantime, I will do my best to support your enquiries, officer...'

'You do that, Sir...'

The door opened. 'Sorry to disturb. Mister Quinn?'

'Yes Willis, what is it?'

'This just came through.' He waved a folded piece of paper in Quinn's direction. 'More police business Sir. Hand delivered.'

Quinn scanned the faces. 'Well, this is turning into a busy day. Five minutes Connor...' He turned on his heel, snatching the paper from Willis as he left the kitchen.

Mary turned to Gemma. 'That went well. I hope I haven't made difficulties for you Ms. Connor?'

'Nothing I can't wade through. It's only his position that overshadows me, his person doesn't.'

Andrea picked up her mug. 'Pompous arse.'

Gemma smiled at her sister's remark. 'Would it be alright if I leave you to the delicate sensibility that is my sister?'

Mary smiled. 'Of course.'

'You'll pour Andrea?'

'I will.'

Gemma unhooked a striped apron from off the door and began to put it on as she left. 'Into the valley of death...'

Mary sat. 'Now Andrea, before we were so rudely interrupted you were saying about the car the two men drove off in. Any idea what make it was?'

'What was the paper, the one that Willis fella brought in? Quinn didn't seem pleased with it.'

'That? I suspect it was a search warrant for the woodlands Miss Connor, so no it'll not make his day. More stress for our overworked public servant.' Mary settled. 'Now, the car. Any idea of the make?'

~

J ay stepped beyond the blue and white taped line that encircled the newly discovered camp site and slipped off the hood of his white suit. 'Well it's a heck of a find Archie that's all I can say, heck of a find.'

Arnold, entry to the search site denied on account of his refusal to wear a suit, indicated Jasper whose gaze was transfixed on the tented area that had once been his late mistress' oven. 'Uh-uh Jay. I was just a passenger on this one, all down to this little chap, eh Jasper?' Unlike the terrier's gaze, his tail blinked, just the once, an outward sign the conversation had been logged. 'I think he still claims supper rights.'

'Well he'll get short shrift here I'm afraid, it's back to base for this lot.' Jay bent slightly and put out his hand. 'Sorry old fella.' Jasper's low growl and lifted lip said all there was to say on this subject and Jay pulled back instinctively. 'Feisty little chap isn't he?'

'Choosy rather. I think he finds the snowman look a bit scary, keeps thinking you'll fly off with him.' He swapped gum. 'Well, I'll leave you to it. It'll be alright for me to get along to you in a while with Lin will it, do that ID on her sister?'

'Ah yes, I was forgetting that.'

'Wish I could.'

'Yes, of course. We'll make sure all is ready, all is neat.'

'Thanks Jay. How soon can I get the results from here?'

'By the end of the day, there's little doubt about the pedigree of the remains and who put them there.'

'Certainly wasn't his Lordship. Is Anita about?'

'Of course, I'll just go and...' Anita exited the tent and made her way across to them. 'Ah, no need. Your timing as in all things is impeccable Ms. Cresson. Archie was just about to leave us. Are you about done?'

Anita slipped off her hood and nodded. 'Archie.' She turned to Jay. 'Yes, all but.' She raised the bagged and tagged ingredients she had carried from the tent, her action closely followed by Jasper's gaze. 'Rabbit and mushroom pie...' She saw Jasper, 'Oh sorry, that was unfair.'

Arnold smiled. 'You made it then? Getting here I mean, not the rabbit and mushroom pie.'

'I did. Maurice will finish up while I head back and write this up. You'll be along soon, Sir?'

Jay nodded. 'I will, I just want to pop back to the hit-and-run site. Those two uni bods will have finished their inspection by now, so I'll collect them and their information and we'll all be back before you can say knife.'

'Will they require office space?'

'A little.'

'I'll manoeuvre those boxes out of the annexe. Will they want kit?'

'No, they're self-contained. Apart from access to tea making and our notes they should be fine.'

'Right.' She turned to Arnold. 'You'll not forget dinner? My place?'

Jay shook his head. 'Fat lot of good my little talk did then.'

Anita coloured and Archie saw it. 'What talk?'

Jay covered. 'Nothing, nothing that should concern you anyway. I'll escort you back to the riding Miss Hood, there may be wolves about.'

The three of them walked in silence, each locked into their own thoughts. As they approached the ride, so the assembled forensic vehicles came into view and Jay turned to Arnold. 'Lot of tumult. I trust Lord Brightwick knows about all this?'

'As a courtesy only.'

'Shouldn't it have been more official, more personal, and with paper attached?'

'It's part of a murder enquiry Jay, how much more official or personal does it need to be?'

'You know what I meant. This chap has friends in high places, he expects due respect for that and he's not the sort you ignore or ride roughshod over.'

'If it makes you feel any easier Pat got the warrant delivered to his PPS.'

'How did he take it?'

'Don't know; with his hand?' Jay was not impressed. 'Jay, Pat only got the warrant signed off about twenty minutes ago.'

'You should have served it before we all turned up.'

'And give them advance warning, I think not.'

'Give who advance warning?'

'That American chap for one, the keepers for another. Early warning would've given them time to clear up here.'

'Why would they want to do that? That would be interfering with an official police site.'

Arnold looked at Anita. 'Such a trusting soul isn't he? Thinks he's still back in the nineteen fifties when you could go out and leave your doors unlocked. Because Jay, for one, that smart-mouthed American knows more than he's letting on and two, I don't make this sort of thing easy, not for anyone.'

'Well, far be it from me to be telling you your job DCI Arnold but you'd better be absolutely certain of your grounds for suspicion before you enter the arena that is a government minister; absolutely certain.' The measured pace of his words left Archie in no doubt as to how serious Jay was. 'If you get so much as a comma out of place with someone like him, with his connections and influence, he'll destroy you. Men like him take no prisoners; like at Agincourt, they execute them all.'

'Thank you for your history lesson and concern Jay; cave canem will be my watchword...' Arnold turned towards the distant purr of an approaching vehicle. Gliding along the ride was a black Range Rover and inside were two men. Archie smiled. 'Ah, your fears are unfounded; it would seem the warrant has got through to some level of the organisation. You'll have to do the walk back to the road on your own; these guys look as though they're not happy.' Archie stepped forward to meet the vehicle and noticed the bull-barred front. 'See that Jay?'

'I do.'

'On second thoughts, hang on here you two. Let's see if we can't get a measurement on that without alarming anyone. Ready?'

'As we'll ever be.'

'Just hold your ground Jay. I'll do the talking then introduce you.'

'Make sure you follow the rules then.'

'On my best behaviour Mister Millar.' Archie turned to Anita and whispered. 'See if you can get a photo of the front of his vehicle on your mobile.'

Jay heard this and looked across at Anita, making an all is lost gesture at her. The Range Rover whispered to a halt as Arnold shortened Jasper's lead and walked briskly towards the vehicle whilst reaching for his warrant card. The doors opened and the two men, one in a lounge suit the other in keepers' tweed, stepped out purposefully. In Matt's hand was a piece of paper and he spoke in a voice laced with controlled stress.

'Can I ask what the hell's goin'...?'

That was as far as he got with his opening speech. Jasper, already at the full stretch of the shortened lead lunged forward as the draught from the closing doors of the Range Rover reached him, carrying with it a scent of brutal familiarity. Standing on hind legs Jasper began yapping and barking, his nose and temper directed at Matt who swiftly stepped backwards. The keeper made his views known.

'You keep a tight 'old on that dog Mister, I don't want to 'ave to 'urt 'im.'

Archie was as surprised as anyone by Jasper's reaction but wasn't about to let such a statement go unchallenged. 'Good luck with that. I doubt you'll achieve it without significant bloodshed and not all of it his.' He flicked the lead. 'Jasper! Jasp! Enough!' It made no difference; Jasper was ready for a sort-out right then and there. 'Just hold on a minute.' Archie walked away dragging the highly agitated terrier with him, past Jay and Anita to the nearest police vehicle, a local force panda car. Shutting Jasper in it, his hysteria now lessened in volume if not in determination, Archie walked back to Matt. 'Sorry about that. Not often he takes against someone from the off.' He looked at the keeper. 'Could be the scent of death he's picked up.'

Matt disregarded the chat. 'Mad dog aside can I ask again, what the hell's goin' on 'ere?'

'You can, and you're addressing the right man to tell you. I'm Detective Chief Inspector Arnold, Northants Division.' He held up the warrant card. 'And this is part of a murder scene.'

'What murder?'

'Ah, bypassed you too has it? And here was me thinking the countryside was full of gossip. A hit-and-run on the lane over there, last week?'

'Oh yeah, heard something about it...yeah.'

'Oh good. Saves me having to go through it all again then. I can see you've got the search warrant with you. Excellent. And you are?'

'I'm Mister Lamb, His Lordship's head of operations and this is Mister Adderton, His Lordship's head keeper and the man whose livelihood you're trampling on.'

'You have my apologies for the intrusion Mister Adderton. We'll be as unobtrusive and as fast as we can, but as I said, this is part of a murder enquiry and although not strictly necessary we have duly obtained a search warrant from a county magistrate, the one you hold in your hand if I'm not mistaken.'

Matt bridled at the authority shown. 'How long are you gonna be 'ere on this...intrusion?'

Archie noted Matt's tone and his stance. Here was a man whose relaxed body language concealed an absolute readiness for action and Archie made a mental note. 'Ah well, you'll have to speak to the CSO about that.'

'CSO?'

'Crime Scene Officer.' Archie turned and indicated Jay as he winked at Anita. 'Jay, could you furnish Mister Lamb and Mister Adderton with the timings on this investigation please?' As Jay passed, Archie whispered to him. 'Move across to your right.'

Jay altered his line slightly as he approached the two men then halted, hand outstretched in greeting which caused the two men to clear the front of the Range Rover. 'Mister Lamb.' They shook hands. 'And Mister Adderton.' Adderton tipped his cap. 'I'm Jay Millar, Head of Forensics and CSO for this enquiry. As DCI Arnold has already said, we'll clear the area just as quickly as possible and with the minimum of disturbance, just as soon as our searches are complete.' As their conversation continued Archie moved slowly towards the front of the Range Rover until he stood to one side of the bull-bar.

'How long?' Matt's tone was flat.

Jay held his gaze. 'Should be gone by mid-afternoon at the very latest.'

'Good.'

Now Jay walked beyond them, waving a hand at the gathered police transport. 'Can I also say how sorry I am for these marks our vehicles have left on this well-kept riding. We will of course pay for any remedial work that has to be done should it be necessary.' The two men were forced to turn in order to face Jay, allowing Anita to snap away unseen as Jay continued, 'I assume that's the best way back?'

Adderton nodded. 'The only way.'

'Right. Well apologies in advance for the return marks as well then.'

'Just keep the speed down an' in first gear, an' when you turn round watch them ditches or we'll be havin' to bring a tractor to tow you out an' that'll mess these rides up even more, then I'll be even less happy.' Anita swiftly pocketed her phone as Adderton turned to Arnold. 'An' keep that dog well tethered. There's plenty of fox-wires around here to sort him out.'

'We'll be most careful Mister Adderton, won't we Detective Chief Inspector?' said Jay. 'Thank you.'

There was a short silence before Matt terminated the meeting. 'Right, well the quicker we leave the quicker will you.'

Matt moved back to his vehicle. Arnold, standing at the front end, nodded at it. 'Nice motor; come with the job?'

'No. It's mine.'

'Right. Must've cost you. In lovely condition. Not a mark on it.'

'Never has been never will be.'

'White seats. Hard to keep clean I'll bet. Show every mark, every stain?'

Adderton got into the vehicle as Matt brushed past on his way to the driver's door. 'Never a reason to get 'em dirty. Now if you'll just clear the front we'll get off...and mind that dog.'

'Noted.' Archie moved back to Anita as Matt started up the vehicle. 'Did you get some?'

Anita nodded. 'With you in it for the measurement.'

'Brill. I'll get Jasper.' The Range Rover purred out an effortless three-point turn and set off back down the riding as Arnold walked to the panda car. Like crimp marks on a pasty the frontispiece on the dashboard bore the teeth marks of what was still a very irate dog. Archie sighed. 'Ahhh, fuckit...'

'Problem?' Anita called to him.

'Sit. Jasper, sit!' He held up his palm and the terrier half-sat, tail and teeth telling two different stories. 'They've gone now.' Archie opened the door and made a quick grab for the lead as he answered Anita. 'Nothing the tax-payer can't handle. Whose car is this?' Jasper was still keen to visit the site where the Range Rover had been parked. 'Hang on Jasp. Sit.' The dog sat but it was a reluctant posture. 'Just...hang on. Whose car?'

Anita shook her head. 'Local? Don't know, I do know you'll not be popular.'

The trio gradually regrouped like eager mercury. 'Standard condition for me. That went well Jay. All denial-denial.'

'You do know those photos may not be admissible Archie?'

'Just like me scanning the bonnet for marks, I didn't ask Anita to get them as evidence, just as confirmation about the calculations you did.'

'Were there any?'

'No, it looked as clean as a whistle, but honestly? This dog gave me all I needed to know. If Lamb and Jasper haven't met before I'll give up chewing gum.'

'Ha! He certainly didn't want to make him a friend did he?'

'Not in this life. I'll text my measurements across to you Anita, unless you want to do them now?'

Jay held up his hand. 'Enough! We have further work to do before your cavorting begins; text them. We'll get measurements on the tyres from the grass where our visitor parked.'

Archie smiled at him. 'Is that allowed?'

'Absolutely. I'm CSO and this is still considered a crime scene; vehicle elimination process.'

'Now you're talking. Right, I'm gonna bugger off and get the checks on Mister Lamb started and I'll have a better chance of a signal on the lane. Then we're just gonna swing by that long driveway where I heard those dogs barking the other night, aren't we Jasp? Oh, and before you go...' He turned to Anita. 'That work you did on the shotgun pellet, the Black Feather? Let me shake your hand.' He did so, passing the virgin cartridge into her grasp with all the efficiency of a master magician. 'Outstanding, just remarkable.'

Anita closed her fist around it. 'My pleasure… Dinner, Archie?'

'Not forgotten. Can I bring the dog?' said Arnold.

'Of course.' said Anita.

'There'll be tears before bedtime.' said Jay.

~

6 'This way Mister Cho.' The nursing sister opened the door to the large side room. 'Mister Jardine? It's Sister Ó Faoláin.' The man lying in the bed turned from the window with difficulty, the dressed wounds on his upper chest and shoulder causing him to grimace. 'There's the police to see you, come all the way from Northampton he has.'

Arnue raised his hand in greeting. 'Don't bother to get up.'

Kenzie smiled and croaked back, 'Or wave.'

'You've fifteen minutes Mister Cho and not a moment more, I'll be back in twelve.'

The door closed and Arnue raised an eyebrow. 'No wriggle-room there then.'

'She's a stickler for protocols. Anything thwarts her and the Irish fills her cheeks.'

'I'll keep on the right side then. I'm DC Arnue Cho, Northants Serious Crimes' Squad.' He showed his warrant card.

'Kenzie Jardine, port security.'

'Bit more than that if tales are to be believed.' Arnue opened his attaché case and took out a notepad, a small tape recorder and a large bottle of The Balvenie single malt. 'Compliments of Northants SCS.'

Kenzie smiled. 'My favourite. How did you know? Thanks.'

Arnue looked towards the door. 'Shall we?'

Kenzie nodded. 'Sun's over the yardarm somewhere in the world.'

Placing pad and tape recorder on the bed, Arnue released two plastic water beakers from the dispenser in the corner of the room. He cracked open the seal, pulled the stopper out and poured two fingers of malt into each, placing the bottle on the side cupboard and sliding a chair to the bedside before sitting and handing one of the beakers to Kenzie. 'Here's to you.'

'And Cashman.'

'Cashman? That's your search dog?'

'Cash, yeah.'

'To you and Cashman.'

'Slàinte mhath.'

They both took a decent swig then Arnue picked up the pad. 'You'll know the drill?' Kenzie nodded. 'Thought so.' He switched on the tape recorder and placed it on the bed table. 'Right, let's get to it.' ...

... 'Anything else?'

Kenzie shook his head. 'That's the whole sequence.' He smiled. 'I just knew they were wrong 'uns from the off, so did Cash.'

Arnue sat back in his chair. 'Right, well that'll about do it. Have you got a mobile here?'

'Aye.' He nodded at the top drawer in the bedside cabinet. 'But can you get it out of the drawer, I'm a wee bit hampered, and have it in mind, Sister takes it away at night.'

'Seriously?'

'Oh yeah.' Kenzie put on a cod-Irish accent. 'I'll not be havin' my patients' sleep disturbed by these pesky machines. Nothing but ill comes of 'em.'

'Nice.'

'I tell y', get the wrong side of her and she'd have me tied to the gun carriage wheel, fifteen lashes and the salt rubbed in.'

'Ha! Can I text myself the number?'

'Yeah.' Arnue took out the mobile and sent the text then looked at his watch and the notes. 'Pretty full account I'd say.' He replaced the mobile.

'Things like that make an impression.'

'I'll bet, and sorry you had to relive some of them...'

The door opened. 'You wait there...' Sister Ó Faoláin swept into the room. 'You'll be near the finish then Mister Cho...'

All eyes fell on the bottle of malt and the two beakers decorating the cupboard as Arnue muttered. 'Oh, fuck.'

Sister Ó Faoláin stepped smartly across and snatched the bottle off the cabinet. 'And I'll be havin' that until after you're discharged Mister Jardine.' She turned to Arnue. 'Mister Cho! As a police officer I'd expect you to know the protocols we operate under in this and every hospital.'

Arnue nodded trying not to grin as he caught a glimpse of Kenzie smiling broadly. 'Yes Sister.'

She looked from one to the other as she lifted the bottle slightly. 'There is no comedy in this gentleman only heartbreak. Those rules Mister Cho, they make this hospital a society of care.'

'It was just a get-well drink from some colleagues.'

'And a fat lot of good that'll do to aid his recovery. If I'd have known this was your mission I'd have been in the sooner. Now, you'll be on your way, and judging by this, not before time.'

The two men exchanged the glance of guilty schoolboys as Arnue stood up and closed his notebook. 'Yes, thank you Sister. Sorry.'

'Apology rejected.' She turned to Kenzie. 'There's a regular stream of folk wanting to spend time with you Mister Jardine. I've told them you needed to rest; I'd not thought I'd have to tell them you'd need to get sober too. Mrs Jardine will be back very soon; I've sent all but one packing. He's a persistent one. I'm allowing him five minutes, as soon as Mister Cho leaves a space...'

The pause was fractional before Arnue spoke. 'Er, yes...of course. We're done here so I'll get out of your hair Sister.'

'That would be good of you.'

'Right, well...' Arnue smiled at Kenzie. 'Good to talk, I'll er...' He looked at Sister Ó Faoláin, her face implacable her folded arms still caressing the malt. 'Get yourself well Kenzie. I'll go and see your SCO and get the operational details from him. I'll give you a bell later, on my way back to Northants, if I need to fill in any gaps.'

'Aye sure, anytime...'

'Will these be calls made after dark Mister Cho?'

'Possibly Sister.'

'Then they'll wait 'til the morrow. I'll not have my patients' sleep disturbed by these pesky machines. Nothing but ill comes of 'em.' Arnue stifled a laugh as Sister Ó Faoláin unfolded her arms. 'You seem to find most things amusing, Mister Cho, and you're a long time taking to go.'

'Yes, sorry, well...bye.' Arnue opened the door revealing a man standing outside.

Kenzie saw him, smiled broadly and called out. 'Jimmie you rascal! Get yourself in here!'

'Good luck with that one,' whispered Arnue as they passed.

'You've five minutes Mister Lamont,' she held up an open hand, 'five.' Resting the bottle on the bottom of the bed she began to write notes on the clipboard hung on the rail.

James, smiling brightly, walked across to the bed. 'The things people do to get off overtime. How you feelin' hero?'

'Not like a hero that's for sure.'

'No, just sore I'll bet. Well this should help.' He held up the carrier bag. 'Some grapes and some oranges in there for you.'

Sister Ó Faoláin smiled. 'That'll be better.'

James spotted the bottle. 'That his medicine then?'

'Not in here Mister Lamont, all this will do is open the pores and allow misery in.'

'Oh, erm, right. Not what the doctor ordered then.' James took an envelope out of his inside jacket pocket. 'Got some photos I thought you ought to see. Here. Give you a bit of closure on it all.' He handed the envelope across and stood back a little as the Sister finished her writing, replaced the clipboard then picked up the bottle and beakers.

Kenzie took out the handful of photos, the first of which caused him an involuntary intake of breath and Sister Ó Faoláin looked up quickly. 'Mister Jardine, are you ailing?' There was nothing for several seconds as Kenzie flicked through the snaps, his cheeks flushing with colour his eyes brimming with unbidden tears. 'Mister Jardine?'

James answered for him. 'He's fine Sister, he just needed to see these sooner rather than later. They might even interest you, same profession sort of.'

Sister Ó Faoláin moved to the bedside and took one of the photos. A spaniel filled the frame, brightly lit and lying on its side, surrounded by gowned and masked people, a breathing tube in its open mouth. She took the next photo. The same spaniel, seemingly sleeping, intubated and with what looked like a large sticking plaster on the place where the front leg should be. The third photo was held tightly between the finger and thumb of Kenzie causing the Sister to look at it from there. In this photo the spaniel was half-lying, head up and looking to camera, the tail caught mid-wag. Covering the dog's body was a well-worn black t-shirt on which was a picture below which were printed the words, Rory Gallagher – Stage Struck. The dog's front right leg was through a sleeve, the other front leg missing.

'This is your dog Mister Jardine?'

It was several seconds before Kenzie replied. 'Cashman, yeah Sister...my lovely chap... How...?'

James smiled. 'After you went off in the ambulance, I went across to him, you know, like I said, to sort him out, bag him up like you'd asked. He was still bleeding a bit an' I did think at the time, I thought, that's odd, that should've stopped by now, him bein' dead an' all. Anyway, I bent down and put my hand on his head, say cheerio for you and I said, "Cash, you've no idea", and I patted his chest; little bugger wagged his tail! Could've knocked me flat with a pillow.'

'But...he was dead. I saw him get shot...' There was a long pause as the events replayed in Kenzie's head. Through his tears Kenzie choked, 'An' I left him...when all the time... Oh, Christ, that poor little lad.'

'Not your fault Ken, you'd enough to cope with.'

'No excuse Jimmie, I should've...'

Sister Ó Faoláin stepped in, her nursing side to the fore. 'Mister Lamont is right. The injuries you sustained could so easily have been so much worse; fatal even. The blood loss alone would have been sufficient to render you part senseless and look...' she tapped the photo Kenzie was still gripping, 'he's on the road to recovery so all turned out well.'

Kenzie stared at one of the photos for a while then pointed to Cash's shoulder. 'Is that a sticking plaster?'

The Sister shook her head. 'It's a fentanyl patch.'

'A what?'

'A strong painkiller, probably tramadol, administered at the site of the wound...' She looked at James, 'And some anti-inflammatories?' James nodded. 'Meloxicam?'

'I think that's what they said, yeah.'

She looked at Kenzie. 'Not much to choose between the two of you then. My guess is he'll be feeling a bit groggy with it all, but unlike yourself he'll not have been sippin' on the malt. He'll be back on what remains of his feet in no time and creatin' devilment, as all men are wont to do.'

James nodded. 'Oh, right. That's half the population sorted then. You know about dogs as well then?'

'I do. I come from farming stock Mister Lamont. I was used to workin' the sheepdogs back in Leitrim. Poor crop land but it homes some steep climbs and frisky sheep. I've had a dog snap a leg out herding and still want to work. Had to be forcibly carried back to get it set, but in two weeks he was back to bouncy and wantin' out on the lash before time...as all men are wont to do.'

Kenzie reached for a tissue from the box on the bedtable as James filled in the detail. 'Should've seen the escort he got Ken. I called across to the lads in the second ambulance, the one with the Irish chaps in. Nothin' was gonna save them bastards so I thought I'd give 'em some meaningful occupation.' He looked across at the Sister, 'No offence or anything.'

'None taken.' She offered back the photos. 'I know all about Mister Jardine's little adventure and I'll tell you now, I've no truck with gangsters and thugs Mister Lamont. I've spent enough time in the A&E in Belfast to wean me off that one.'

'I can't believe he survived it Jim.' Kenzie sifted through the photos again smiling, shaking his head. 'He's got some courage has that one.' His expression darkened a little. 'On three legs now. I wonder how he'll take to that.'

'In his usual style Ken. It'll take more than a lost limb to quell him; he'll not look back once he gets his balance. Vet says stitches out after a fortnight and he's gettin' massages twice a day.' James looked at the Sister. 'Much like here I'd say.'

'Ha!' was the Sister's only reply.

Kenzie looked from photos to James. 'Who treated him?'

'Ah well, there you have it...'

The Sister interrupted him. 'Enough Mister Lamont. You've had well over your time as it is.'

'Could he not just stay a few minutes longer, fill me in on the events? I'd like to know.' Kenzie lifted the photos. 'This is my partner, Sister, he saved my life.'

Sister Ó Faoláin looked at them both in turn then at her watch and sighed. 'Right. You've five further minutes Mister Lamont and then it really will be overtime. Mrs Jardine will be here for family visiting time, and her husband already looks like a ghost.'

'Right well, I'll get this done in less than five. Any excuse to spend time with the lovely Mrs. Jardine.'

Kenzie looked at the Sister. 'Yes, it is what you think. It really is lechery.'

She began to leave the room smiling broadly as James moved back to the bedside. 'Ah...' She returned to the foot of the bed and picked up the malt bottle. 'I'll just be havin' this with me.' Sister Ó Faoláin left, dropping the two plastic beakers in the bin on her way out.

James and Kenzie shook hands gently. 'Sick as a pig I was Ken, seein' you on that road.'

Kenzie nodded. 'I didn't feel great myself.'

'Well, just don't you ever do that again.'

'I'll try not to.' Kenzie gripped James' hand a little tighter. 'And thanks for savin' me and for giving me back my dog.'

'I did nothing for Cash apart from get him delivered to the medics and as for you, I wasn't prepared to let you die; you owed me a tenner.'

Kenzie half-laughed, 'Ha!' He immediately stifled it because of the jolt it gave to his shoulder. 'Ah, bugger... So, who did you say did the work on Cash?'

'University of Glasgow lads and they refused to charge for it as well...'

The door hissed to as a smiling Sister Ó Faoláin finally let it close.

Friday

‘Where are they?’

‘In a sack an’ in the incinerator.’

‘All of ’em?’

‘Yeah.’

‘All the scrap and cable from the fight site?’

‘In a pile back of the barn, tinkers are collectin’ tomorrow.’

Matt led the way along the line of empty kennels inspecting and talking as he went. ‘And you’ve sluiced and swept these lot clean?’

‘I have.’

‘Pressure-washed?’

‘Yeah. Do you want ’em stripped down?’

‘Nah. If the coppers come callin’ we’ll tell ’em they were for the Gaffer’s gun dogs, when he had any.’ As they reached the end kennel Matt indicated the wooden shed a few yards distant. ‘All the bowls and bedding gone?’

‘Er, yeah, all gone.’

Something in Chris’ manner caused Matt to repeat his question. ‘All bowls and bedding gone, yeah?’

‘Yeah, yeah…’

Matt faced Chris square on. ‘I don’t want any slip-ups here Chris. We’ve not shovels big enough if we get it wrong, y’know that, right?’

‘Yeah…’course.’

Matt looked back along the kennels. ‘Well, it looks like a tidy job. Did you clean out y’ Land Rover?’

‘Yeah.’

‘Properly cleaned it?’

‘Yeah!’ Chris made a move towards the vehicle. ‘Do you wanna have a look?’

Matt followed him and peered into the back of the vehicle. 'Looks OK. Did you sluice the back out?'

'With the hose and a broom, yeah.'

'Do it again, just to be sure. Have you cleared all the junk from the front?' Matt opened the passenger door. Everywhere was pristine. 'Neat. Right, well, sluice the back out again, use the pressure-washer this time.'

'Right. I still don't know why all them pups had to go when the big un's are still up with bloody Aiden.'

'Too much money spent for that. That's his breedin' pool and fighters rolled into one, and he's still got matches to do. You heard them Irish are dead now?'

'News just said two men were shot dead tryin' to board the Cairnryan-Belfast ferry, it said nothin' about them bein' our lads.'

'An' what are the odds, eh?'

'Yeah, and anyway, corpses make no complaints.'

'No, but we gotta reckon the plods will eventually work things out about their past, and those things will include they were dog-fighters.'

'Who'd know that?'

'We did for starters, and if we did then so did others, an' if others knew then plod will find out; they may be daft but they aint stupid. Things add up, can be pieced together, that's why them pups had to go.'

'Yeah,'s'pose.'

'No 's'pose about it. Adults we can explain away: estate guard dogs, terrorist threat, important government man and the rest. Pups were different.' Matt looked at his watch. 'Right, I'm away to sort out Aiden, make sure he's got the tale straight then see if I can find a replacement dog for them Chinky lot.'

Chris looked incredulous. 'What, Gaffer's still goin' on with it?'

'I said didn't I? We've still got matches to do.'

'But, where you gonna get another dog at such short notice?'

'I'm gonna try them gyppos out at Carlington, see what they can come up with, who they know.'

'Risky.'

'Only if I get caught, and anything will do to put on a show for the Chinks to bet on, give Derringer a bit of exercise.' Matt looked around at the kennelled silence. 'You've not forgotten we're to see the Gaffer at half past have y'?'

'As if.'

'Good. Right, see you up at the house. I'll do the talkin'.'

'Yeah.' Chris watched as Matt walked back to his Range Rover and drove away. He waited for a few seconds before moving quickly into the shed. At the back of it he raised the lid of one of the feed bins. The gap was immediately filled by Chipper as he scrabbled at the smooth side of the bin in an effort to get out. 'Steady Chip, you'll damage them claws if you keep that up.' Chris lifted the pup out by his scruff and closed the lid, cradling the crossbreed in his arms. 'Bloody hell, you weigh some don't y'?' The pup made efforts to scrape the whiskers off Chris' chin with his tongue and he pushed the pup's head gently away. 'Come on, enough of that. I've to get over to see the Gaffer in a short while, but I need you away from here and back to my place before then...and I've still to wash the back out again.'

He opened the shed door checked the coast was clear and scampered to his vehicle. Climbing in and placing the pup on the floor of the passenger side he set off to home.

~

'I will...'

'From all of us.'

'Yeah, from all of you.' With the phone on speaker Arnold was driving into one of the car parks at St. Margaret's Hospital.

'Oh, and some good news come through from Jay for you.'

'I could do with some. Tell me.'

'You haven't got to do the ID on Adam; Gabrielle's gonna do it.'

'Wow... Bless her heart. Can't say I'm not relieved to be spared that one. When was this decided?'

'Not sure. Jay rang through here; Marissa took the call.'

'That lass is an absolute star... Jesus, not a single bloody park...oh, hang on. Who's a lucky boy then, just hold that thought for a sec Pat...' Archie waited for the car to reverse out of the slot then swung into the vacant space. 'Excellent, eh Jasp?' The terrier wagged his tail as Archie switched off the engine, refreshed his gum and unclipped his seatbelt. 'Thanks for that Pat, that's a load off. I'll call Gabby later and thank her in person. OK so, our Mary. How did she leave it then?'

'For Mister Quinn to ring us the moment he'd got a time sorted, but by three regardless.'

'An' if he doesn't?'

'She'll be giving him a call toot-bloody-sweet.'

'Good.'

'Also, in other news.'

'I've been waiting for this. Don't tell me, the Gazette.'

'Correct. Go to the top of the class...'

'And jump off. What did he say?'

'Wants to meet. You'd said he could have an exclusive on the background if he'd just lay off the story until you gave the all-clear...and fulfil the promise of a radio chat?'

'I did.'

'Well, now the nationals have gone with it he's feeling just a little pissed that he wasn't at the party. Blames you for ripping up his invite.'

'Christ, he calls himself a reporter... The nationals have gone with the shootings, but not with the hit-and-run. We made sure the connections were kept closed, that's his exclusive angle.' Archie stopped talking for a few seconds. Pat could feel the tension in his voice and she gave him space. Eventually he sighed out loud. 'OK, look. Can you, Dougie and Marissa work out a strategy with our press office on the shootings that carries a local angle? Something that's got substance but lacks the full detail.'

'We'll try.'

'Give it to Beavis. That'll keep the pressure up on our friends at Bliss Bank, but it'll not come directly from me. Tell him I'll meet him later with the exclusive stuff I'm sorting for the radio clip, but only if he promises to give it front page treatment and lead with it on that ragbag he calls a radio show.'

'Crafty.'

'As a fox. If we can time that clip to come out around the same time as our meeting with Brightwick or just before we might get a reaction; that's why the meet needs to be today.'

'Mary left Quinn in no doubt about that.'

'I can imagine. You wouldn't want her at the breakfast table after a night's drinkin' would you?'

'Not my place to say. Who do you want with you for the interview?'

'Mary of course.'

'Yeah, I know Mary did the spade work, but Dougie's got his finger on the pulse concerning Brightwick's background, so...'

'He's also doing the Irish connection that's enough for him, and Mary's always champing at the bit for action...' Jasper, his paws on the door, wagged his tail and looked over his shoulder at Arnold before giving a single yap. 'Hang on Jasp...'

'Still got the dog then?'

'I have. He's good company, it's just every time we stop he thinks it's walkies...' Archie heard muttering in the background. 'Fucks' sakes...have I been on speaker?'

'You have.'

'Bugger.'

Collective laughter backed Pat's reply. 'Am I?'

'Yeah, and confusing the hell out of the dog. Oh, has Arnue fed his meeting with the security chap into the mix yet?'

'Yeah, some. He's on his way back, but he gave us a short briefing.'

'Which is?'

'We now have the gun and user pedigrees confirmed, we're just waiting for the Garda to get back to us with fuller details.'

'Form?'

'Like a race card.'

'Then you need to push them Pat.'

'Dougie's already on it.'

'Good, and that was my point; Dougie's got enough on. Where are we with those two rogues who work for Brightwick? I'd like to announce a desire to have a chat with them at that meeting, see how Brightwick reacts to that.'

'Matthew Lamb. Tartan past, lots of ragged-edge stuff, couple of affrays when he was a youngster... Spent a long time as a bookie.'

'Horses?'

'Dogs. Mixed with some rough stuff, er...London gangs mostly but a mix of foreigners too. Did a spell in Wellford Road.'

'Leicester. For what?'

'GBH, Section 20. Got five years, out after two and a half. Nasty business according to the reports, er...all three in hospital... multiple injuries...one lost the sight of an eye...'

'Three against one. What did he use?'

'Fists and feet.'

'Christ.'

'That was fifteen years ago. Since then he's been an upright citizen.'

'Yeah, sure. Colour me unconvinced, I've met him, remember. I thought he looked a handful then...wasn't wrong obviously. Right, I want names and pedigrees of those involved before I go to Bliss Bank, give what you get to Mary.'

'Workin' on it.'

'His compadre?'

'Bit more there.' Pages rustled in the background as Pat detailed the charge sheets. *'Christopher Phillips. Professional thug. Doorman-bouncer, prefers to smack 'em out of the door rather than ask 'em to leave. Been done twice, ABH then...er, oh, ABH again, second time went to Crown. Report on that one says he made a bit of a mess of the two fellas that lipped him, served nine months of an eighteen-month sentence. Model prisoner by all*

accounts...' Pat could hear the incredulity in Arnold's silence. *'I know, where's the sense in that? He was put onto duty at the prison's community petting zoo and it was the making of him... apparently. Loved being with the animals...er, spent all his spare time with them, feeding, brushing, fussing over them it says here.'*

'Just people he dislikes then.'

'Like the rest of us, it's just we don't go around whacking them into the gutter then on to hospital. Anyhow, according to his last probation worker he was just a soppy date with a short fuse.'

'There's lovely. I'm so looking forward to meeting him. And the American?'

'Aiden Steerholm-Youngman the Third.'

'The Yanks know how to name 'em don't they? What we got?'

'Alabamian. Shipped over by our gracious Lord. Listed as Estate Stockman on his visa.'

'Is everything in order on that?'

'Working for His Lordship? Whatever made you think otherwise? He was fast-tracked; essential employee status apparently.'

'Ha! Bollocks to that. Right well, kosher or not I'll want a further word with him too.'

'Before or after His Lordship and before or after the hired help?'

'After all of them. He seemed the cocky type so I'll put the word out via his boss that I want a chat. We'll let that sink in, let him sweat.'

'We've enough on him to question him at the nick if you want? There's his connection to the estate and also where you first met him.'

'No. I want them all jittery. Estate stockman you say?'

'Yeah.'

'That's what he said in the wood. Right, check what they farm there. Have they got cattle, racehorses, sheep, what? I want to know whether a stockman's needed.'

'OK.'

'And see if you can get anything from the American end. Get in touch with Montgomery PD. He was shifty with me so maybe there's a file on him somewhere.'

'Right.'

'And have Dougie get Mary up to speed with anything she's lacking for our meeting. Be good for her to see this through and she'll be a fearsome individual to have onside...don't tell her I said that.'

'I'm sure it'll filter back eventually...oh look, it has...You're still on speaker Boss, remember?'

'God...stupid.'

'Mary says she's over it for now, but she'll just be sure to bring it up in a seemingly unconnected discussion in about ten years' time.'

'Women; can't live with 'em, can't live with 'em.' The terrier yapped.

'Nor terriers it would seem.'

'Sorry Mary.'

Mary's distant voice came back. 'You're forgiven, not forgotten.'

Jasper yapped again. 'Jesus, if it aint one thing it's another. Look, I'm gonna have to go, he wants a walk and I've still to see Kanga yet.'

'You taking him into the hospital?'

'Ha!'

'Thought not. So...?'

'Leaving him in the car.'

'What, after his last little session?'

'Oh, you heard did you?'

'With three hundred and sixty quids' worth of damage to that panda car you think they'd stay silent? Broke their necks to get back here and tell.'

'Well, I reckon he'll be fine now he's got it out of his system. It was the company we were keepin' that made him mad. Does Campbell know, about the panda?'

'*Not yet, pro-forma's only just arrived.*'

'Hide it Pat. Marissa?'

Marissa's distant voice came again. '*Yes Archie.*'

'Get across and chat to Anita Cresson. Get all the details on the photos she took of that Range Rover before I meet up with Mary; I've sent her my measurements to make the comparisons... when you're over there ask her if she's finished her research on my present.'

There was a silence until Marissa's voice floated back. '*What research, what present?*'

'Just ask Anita. Mary?'

'*Yes, Archie?*'

'As soon as you've got the meeting time you let me know, right?'

'*Will do.*'

'And today, no excuses. Not from him or his oppo.'

'*It's in Quinn's mental diary; I underlined it for him.*'

Archie smiled. 'I'll bet. Right, I've to get on. Take me off speaker Pat.' He heard the set click to private. 'How are we for staff on this?'

'*Full stretch, and likely to lose some. That pile up on the M6 caused by that stray dog and now a missing person report...*'

'All we need...'

'*...also with a dog involved.*'

'Er...Is this local?'

'*No, M6 remember...*'

'Not that one, the missing person report.'

'*Oh, erm...yeah. Over at, Wynington, hang on...*' Archie heard the static as Mary stifled the mouthpiece, her muffled voice fogging through. '*Doug? Dougie!*'

A reply further afield answered, '*Yeah.*'

'*That missing person, what was the name...?*'

'And address.'

'*And address. What? For Archie, yeah...*' Archie heard the scrape of a removed hand from the phone. '*Stanley Mason, Penfore Close.*'

'Wynington?'

'*Yeah.*'

'And the dog?'

'*Dunno.*'

'Well get someone to check, I'll hold.'

A further silence ensued until, '*Hi Archie, it's Mary. The dog...*'

As she began to speak Archie butted in, 'Was a corgi.'

'*Yeah, how did you know?*'

'I just did.'

'*Ah, the woodland burial site.*'

'The same.' Mary could almost hear Arnold's brain working. 'OK, get someone onto Mason's background. You've got an hour, then get someone to meet me at the front of the hospital with whatever you've got.'

'*Do you want us round to Mason's place?*' Archie was silent for several seconds. '*You still there?*'

'Yeah Mary, yeah, just thinkin'...maybe... No...'

Nothing followed except a further silence. '*No or maybe?*'

'No. No one round to Mason's place; not yet. I've got an idea and the timing is all. Right, I really am away. Tell Pat no slouching on this.'

'*All over it Boss, see you later on today.*'

Archie hung up and swapped Jasper's harness for his lead. 'Right, quick trot for a piss, you not me, then it's back to the car for you...and if I come back to mayhem you'll be down the pound for the needle, got it?' Jasper yapped. 'Good.' Archie clipped the lead on, opened the door and the terrier hopped across the seats. 'Come on.'

~

Quinn, iPad under arm, was stood in the orangery next to Brightwick, the weak autumn sun warming the water-soaked quarry-tiled floor as they stared over the distant deer park.

'They sent it back Quinn, my bill...again. Sent it back in their game of bloody ping-pong!'

'Yes, sir, I heard from Reggie. He backed it?'

'Oh Reggie backed it. Min. of Ag. staff like their shooting too much not to. No, it was those lefties, that Labour lot, bleeding-heart Marxists the lot of them.'

'Not so easily controllable, the Commons, are they Sir?'

'As a sack of feral polecats.'

'The Parliaments Act?'

'Next session you mean? No. It'll run alongside the Breed Specific Legislation Bill the RSPCA reps are trying to push through.'

'But you support that Minister.'

'I do, but not so much that they get lumped together and my bill is watered down to make it fit in, or worse lost in the ether of their Bambi blubberings. There's a lot of influential people watching my bill, their lobbying time and fiscal input alone demands a separate time slot. No, they want their fifteen minutes and at the end of it they want this bill granted and underlined in bold.' Quinn nodded as Brightwick mulled things over. Eventually he voiced his thoughts out loud. 'Possibly get them to delay theirs further, use their slot?'

'You'll not make many friends if you do that.'

'I didn't go into politics to make friends Quinn. Even with the extra effort on my part I've already heard mutterings the Commie element are going to try to talk it out should it come back for a third reading. Whatever happened to democracy?'

'The public got hold of it Sir. By the time we'd wrestled it back off them it was ruined.'

This caused Brightwick to smile a little even though, inside, he was deeply annoyed at having his authority thwarted. 'Needs another war Quinn, thin the lower classes down, tilt the odds back in our favour.' They moved over to one of the benches dotted around and sat. 'Are we on track with the agenda for You.Gov?'

'We are. The show's producer has e-mailed us the list of expected questions, courtesy of Garland, and I've got Willis compiling any essential reading.'

'Yet more paperwork over the weekend.'

'Yes, Sir, but most of it you already know, and I've asked Willis to keep it to a minimum.'

'Good of you. And the Chinese Delegation reception here?'

'All progressing on time and target Sir.'

'Do we have a list of the ministers attending?'

'Not complete yet.'

'Needs to be soon. I need to know who I'll have here from the House so I can plan how to work on them for my bill.'

'Yes, Sir.'

'And all the ingredients for toasts and courses, are we still on track?'

'Up to a point Sir. The rhino horn powder arrived yesterday, but we're having a little difficulty with the tiger base for the Hŭbiān tāng. Over-zealous work from Sheerness Customs and Excise have stalled us a little.'

'I knew we should've cut their budget further.'

'I'm still hopeful we'll be able to source them, but at the present time absolute certainty is a little elusive I'm afraid. Do we have a fallback hors d´ oeuvre in case Sir?'

'Quinn, I want Hŭbiān tāng, they want Hŭbiān tāng, so, Hŭbiān tāng it will be.'

'Yes, Sir.'

'The tiger bone wine has been cut down to eighteen bottles because of local demand so I will not tolerate any further rationing, just shows bad form.'

'Yes, Sir.'

'Right.' There was a prolonged pause. Both men had been skirting round the elephant in the room but conversation on other events was now drained. Brightwick sighed. 'Right, the police today. Where are we with that?'

'You are to meet with...' Quinn opened his iPad, 'a Detective Chief Inspector Arnold and a Detective Sergeant Beckett at half-past. I tried to stall, but his assistant, Beckett, she was very insistent; very.'

'Was she! They get above themselves when you put them in uniform.'

'Yes...but these are plain clothes officers.'

Brightwick ignored it. 'Should never have given them the vote in eighteen; they got uppity the moment we capitulated. What's our brief?'

Quinn closed the iPad. 'Concern. Knowledge of the incident of course, it was on our doorstep after all. Apart from that, ignorance plus we will do everything in our power to help...the forces of law and order should be supported in the excellent job they do...a rerun of the hospital speech in fact, we just cross out dog and insert goldfish. I was wondering whether a call through to Commissioner Relphson would help.'

'Too soon Quinn. Low level, Lamb was right about that... However, a call to this detective's immediate superior mightn't come amiss, just a background check, words of caution etcetera. Save the big guns until later.'

'Yes, Sir.'

'Do we have any intelligence on their woodland search yet?'

'There is confirmation that the deceased lady did indeed lodge there.'

'Damn!'

'But there's nothing from that site that connects to here Sir.'

'Apart from them meeting with Youngman.'

'Apart from that.'

'And Lamb.'

'And Lamb, yes, Sir.'

Brightwick sighed and thought for a moment, his face laced with the uncertainty a lack of control bestows on someone so used to absolutes. 'We need have no concerns about how Lamb conducted himself but...Youngman?' He sighed again. 'Acquitted himself as well as can be expected I suppose.'

'Yes, Sir.'

'Can we really trust him to hold the line should they put him under pressure?'

'Ah, well...'

Brightwick looked in the general direction of the entrance to the orangery. 'The police will want to speak with Lamb and Phillips too I imagine. What time are they due here?'

'They should be here any moment.'

'We need to be a step ahead here Quinn. I don't want to be caught up in anything untoward. I can't afford it...neither can you, do you see?'

'Yes, Sir. Perfectly.'

'Good, let's keep it that way...'

~

Arnold's gentle knock on the door marked Mr. D. York – FRCS(Ed) was answered by a woman's voice.

'Hello? Yes, come in.'

Archie opened the door to a small office at one end of which was sat a picture-perfect, middle-aged lady hemmed in by a desk, a computer screen and a set of filing trays. On the colour-washed wall behind her hung a dry wipe board with dates and appointments written on it, next to it a large, framed print of The Anatomy Lesson of Dr. Nicolaes Tulp by Rembrandt.

The lady fixed Arnold with a stare. 'Can I help you Mister...?'

'Arnold. DCI Arnold. Archie.' He took out his warrant card. 'I was in the other day, the shootings?'

'Ah yes.' She stood and held out a hand. 'I'm Mrs York. Christina.'

Archie was puzzled for a second or two then it clicked. 'Oh right, sorry, you're his secretary. Bit slow, sorry. Your husband...'

'Desmond.'

'Mister York, he was the surgeon who did the work on Kanjara Desai.'

'He did.'

'You work together?'

'Yes, we are a team, he in theatre myself in admin; I lead he follows...' She stopped talking and stared hard at Archie. 'Forgive me, old habits...have you had any sleep over the past few days, only you look quite drawn?'

'Bits; naps...' He saw her look. 'No, not really.'

She smiled and Archie immediately felt secure in her company. 'Well, I know it's an impossible ask, but do try; lost sleep affects your decision-making processes, you know? Now, what is it I can do for you Detective Arnold?'

'Archie please. I was wanting to see Kanjara if that's possible?'

'Ah. I'm not au fait with such things I'm afraid, being just a secretary, and Desmond is away at clinic. Perhaps you would be better speaking to the ward Sister?'

'Sister Waldeck, is she on duty?'

'Ah, you know her. Well, she is indeed here. I sometimes think she never goes home.' Mrs York opened the office door and pointed up the slight slope to the right. 'Third door on the left. Knock and you shall be allowed entry. And can I say how very sorry I was to hear of the outcome for your colleague. Mister Reeve wasn't it?'

'Adam. No more than me.'

'I can imagine.'

Arnold recognised a fellow traveller and nodded. 'You've front line experience too. Can't hide it can you?'

'Not even slightly.' She smiled. 'But I feel sure there are better tidings concerning Miss Desai.'

'Thanks to your husband.'

'Not just Desmond, his whole team. They really are an extraordinary group.'

'They are. Well, thank you Christina. I'll get on and leave you in peace.'

'My pleasure, and do let me know if I can be of any further help. You have my number?'

'I do thanks, and I will...oh, and in case I miss him, pass on my regards to Mister York.'

'I will.' She closed the door leaving Archie to make his way up to Sister Waldeck's office.

~

'**H**ow right do you think you are?'

Anita Cresson took back one of the photos, taken in the wood, from DC Canning and looked at it again. 'On a scale of?'

'One to ten?'

Anita looked at the photo again. 'Ten. The coincidence of that bull bar and the measurements Archie sent me? This was the vehicle, that or its identical twin.'

'Evidence?'

'None. Archie had a chance to get up close; not a mark.'

'Starts to collapse doesn't it?'

'Only if you're picky. And you can't call in the vehicle?'

Marissa shook her head. 'Without due cause? If it'd been marked or if it was a street urchin's we'd risk it, but this one, given the calibre of the people involved and the fact it can't be the only one in the country, a magistrate wouldn't look at it. They'd need some sort of a buffer against the accusations of the snooper state that would inevitably follow. Brightwick's got the clout, and you're not gonna give me a buffer here-and-now are you?'

'Not yet, no, but watch this space.'

Marissa smiled at Anita's comment. 'So. Are we any more certain about the lead shot from the dog's gum?'

'The Black Feather?' Marissa nodded. 'There's lots of coincidences that join up easily...and a couple of unsupported leaps too.'

'Coincidences?'

'The pellet taken from the dog's gum and my research on its country of manufacture for starters; American pellet, the presence of an American on the estate.'

'Can we not trace a batch number, get a production date?'

'From the one pellet? That'd make our job too easy. No. All we do know is it was of US manufacture, possibly circa eighties, but it could've been purchased in the UK or anywhere, could be just an old batch in an attic, they were shipped all over.'

'Nothing closer on the date?' Anita shook her head. 'So, what's the odds?'

'Not the point Marissa. Dates of manufacture are inconclusive, as is place of origin. All we know is it came from somewhere, was manufactured sometime and could've been brought by anyone on or off that estate, could've just been a gift.'

'Just that one cartridge?'

'Yes. People collect them you know.'

'What, cartridges?'

Anita nodded. 'All the different types. They make framed collages out of them to hang on their walls.'

'Christ, they need to get out more. Do they fire them?'

'No. Use them and their value plummets.'

'Jesus... OK, let's have the unsupported leaps?'

'Need to be a bit circumspect there.'

Marissa's eyes narrowed slightly. 'How circumspect?'

'Like a lot?'

'Is this something I should know?'

'Yes...and no.'

'That'll help.' Marissa paused. 'OK, you've obviously been willing to compromise yourself and you're still in a job so, lay it on me.'

'I'm still in a job because no one other than myself and DCI Arnold know about this, and once spoken it can't be unheard. Are you sure?'

'No, but, go on.'

'Right. As an analyst, what I would need in order to verify the pedigree of the single lead shot taken from the dog's gum is a complete and unused cartridge. This would need to be discovered on a site connected to that where the original pellet was recovered, so as to compare the ingredients used to make the retrieved pellet and the shot taken from an unused cartridge...from that connected site...and then forge the link. Are you following this?'

'Just.'

'OK. That match, should the complete and unused cartridge provide one, would allow me to get an accurate reading on a date of manufacture. If I use the batch number from the whole cartridge I could also discover where it was purchased.' She paused to gauge Marissa's understanding again before repeating it. 'I'd need a complete, unused cartridge...' Anita lifted her hand, the Black Feather cartridge filched from the Land Rover gripped upright between thumb and forefinger. 'Like this one.'

Marissa's eyes widened. 'Where did you get that?'

'The fairies brought it here.'

'Is it from...?'

'Yes.'

Marissa's face registered understanding. 'It's Archie isn't it? Where did he...how?'

'Snaffled it from the Land Rover in the wood, the one the American was driving but which belongs to another member on the Bliss Bank staff.'

'Who?'

'Christopher Philips.'

'Bloody hell! Oh, hang on...what, Archie took it without asking?' Anita nodded. 'Well that's no bloody good, it's inadmissible as evidence.'

'It wasn't filched to be used for evidence, not yet anyway. Archie nicked it to help me get a match on the pellet taken from the dog, a match I'm just about to start working on. Might be a little late for his first interview, but it'll give him some leverage for any future questioning at Bliss Bank; an air of certainty.'

'Yeah, Archie says it always helps if the enemy think you know more than you actually do.'

'If my checks on this one run true it'll be more than supposition, and then he'll ask for another cartridge, but legally.'

Marissa considered for a few seconds before responding. 'This is all just too much of a coincidence isn't it?'

'Ah, now we're entering the realms of probability and I would say yes, that all these coincidences add up...' Both ladies turned towards the opening door as Jay walked in and Anita pocketed the cartridge without missing a beat in her speech. 'And we all know how DCI Arnold views the realm of coincidence.'

'With something less than fanaticism.' Jay joined them. 'Of what particular coincidence do we speak?'

'The Range Rover in the wood.'

'Ah...'

Marissa spoke after a glance at Anita. 'That and the campsite.'

'Ah yes, the scene of your latest observational triumphs Miss Cresson, and my brush with illegality.' Anita smiled as Jay continued. 'It would all seem to fit, all we need now is the small matter of usable evidence.'

'Or a confession,' said Marissa.

'I rather feel these kind of folk are a little more au fait with the workings of the world than your usual tea leaf or thug. There'll be no falling to their knees to offer a contrite, tear-stained testimony, these are the people who make the rules not follow them. Their mantra is never to apologise as it makes them look weak, and never confess to your sins. Confession is for Catholics, as they say.'

'Well if anyone can wheedle a false admission out of them it'll be Archie.'

'With the right information to help him.' added Anita.

Jay looked hard at Marissa. 'In an attempt to remain topical, are you riding shotgun?'

'No. Mary is, DS Beckett?'

'Ah yes, know her by reputation.' Jay nodded sagely. 'I have said as much to Archie earlier in the investigation, but it bears repeating...for all the notice he'll take. Before he opens up negotiations with His Lordship he needs to know exactly why he's in that arena because if they feel even the slightest bit threatened, truth or not, they'll not stop until they've destroyed that threat and anyone connected to it. These people play hard-ball DC Canning, make no mistake about that. You'd do well to make sure you reiterate this information to both DS Beckett and Archie.'

'I'll pass it on.' Marissa checked her watch. 'Right. Thanks for everything, I'd better be away. Archie's gone in to chat to Kanjara, see if she can recall anything else from the evening and I've got to pass this stuff on to Mary before their meeting. And... thanks for all the information Anita.'

'There'll be more, I'm sure.'

'Thanks, I'm sure Archie and Mary will make full use of it.'

'Make sure they do.'

Marissa left them, clutching photos, notes and Anita's parting words.

~

Brightwick dropped the sheets of paper onto the considerable pile on his desk. For a few moments he sat staring at them before rising from his chair and walking to the open door. 'Quinn! In here if you please!' Returning to his seat he picked up the last few sheets and flicked through them again.

'Yes Minister?'

'These questions from the You.Gov file.'

Quinn closed in on the desk. 'Possible questions Sir.'

'That's as maybe, but there's nothing in here that offers me an opportunity to comment on the forthcoming government initiative and my Chinese investment opportunities.'

'We had seen that Sir. I was just drafting a suggestions' sheet for Garland; do you want to have a look?'

'No I do not! I've done enough reading for the day, just make sure you leave no room for misinterpretation.'

'Yes, Sir, rest assured.'

'Can we not plant them amongst the audience?'

'I'm sure we can try.'

Brightwick looked at his watch. 'Lamb and Phillips are cutting it mighty close. That detective will be here in less than two hours and we've yet to gather a story line that fills all gaps, and he's sure to want to interview them to...' The intercom buzzer on the desk sounded. 'Yes?'

Willis answered, 'Sir. Lamb and Phillips are in the vestibule, do you want them sent straight up?'

'Yes. Now.' He cut the connection and turned to Quinn. 'Lamb's still not found a replacement for the rematch and this meeting will soak up yet more of his valuable scouting and fit-up time.' Brightwick sighed. 'I have an uneasy feeling about this, Quinn. I feel we, that is you and I, can handle all enquiries with certainty and Lamb knows how the deck is loaded, but Phillips? He's just stupid, liable to come out with whatever leaves what we laughingly refer to as his brain, and that makes me decidedly uneasy.'

'Yes, Sir.'

The door opened. 'Ah, there you are. We don't have much time, have you found another ring and another dog yet Lamb?'

~

Arnold removed the gum, wrapping and discarding it in the bin before squirting his hands with disinfectant gel in the corridor of the HDU. The walls were decorated with paintings by local artists, some decidedly average. Pausing at a watercolour panorama ambitiously entitled Low Tide at Hunstanton, Archie bobbed his reflection into view and ran his fingers through his flop of hair. *What do you look like? Jesus...* He opened the door to Kanjara's room. She turned in the bed, saw him and closed the book she was reading.

'Hello again Sir, Archie.'

'Hiya Kanga, how's tricks?'

'Good. You? How's the investigation going?'

'Moving forward. Got a result on the chaps who shot you and Adam.'

'Heard all about it.'

Archie glanced round the room and saw the blank screen. 'No newspapers and no TV blaring away, so...?'

'Not at present, no.' She indicated the bedside table and single book. 'I get the magazines that are left in the corridor; some fresh reading wouldn't come amiss, most of these are two or three years old. No, I got it from Sister Waldeck, she was in here earlier all smiles and triumph. The constable downstairs had told her.'

'Oh, right...they shouldn't really... So, hospital grapevine working well then.'

'Yes. Sister Waldeck said both of them were Irish.'

'Yeah, Garda said they had previous paramilitary experience going well back, and there's a strong suspicion about some nasty goings-on with dogs. That's being followed up, but whatever they were involved in, they aint no more.'

'Chap who got them not a regular shooter I heard.'

'Blimey, you're better informed than most of my team! No, he wasn't. An unarmed security guard at Cairnryan docks. Him and his dog took them both out.'

'Unarmed?'

'Yeah, He used the one fella's gun; karma.'

'Wow.'

'Yeah, wow. Last we heard the guard was recovering, like yourself.'

'Good. The dog?'

'Took a bullet I heard, so probably not good news.'

'Poor thing. So, unarmed and still he got a result.' Archie nodded. 'Puts me to shame then.'

Archie was in fast. 'Now just hold on there. No comparisons to be made here and don't you go searching for any. No one, and I mean no one, could have done anything about what happened to you and Adam other than what you did.'

'Which was to take two bullets and fall over a balcony. Easy.'

'You know full well what I mean. A door opens into a dark hallway and someone shoots. Even Adam had no time and he saw it.'

Her face shadowed and she held out her hand for Archie to take. 'I can't even begin to tell you how so very sorry I am for what happened. He was a friend of mine, but you two...?' The words caught in her throat and for a second or two neither said anything, their joined hands seeming to cover all conversation, her grip forcing meaning into his pores. Eventually Kanjara looked up from their clasped hands. 'I just wish...' She stopped, holding back her tears. Archie squeezed her hand.

'Hey... Hey, look, if wishes were horses then beggars would ride. These things...what you can't do is let them define you. What doesn't kill you makes you stronger.'

Kanga gave a spluttered laugh. 'Ha! Been reading the inspirational wall chart in the patient's lobby before you came in here have you?'

'No... OK yes, but I thought that was better than the, "Beware of Stupid People in Large Numbers" graffiti I saw scrawled on a wall outside.'

She looked directly at Archie and released his hand. 'They've been in.' Archie knew there was no reply needed. 'All of them. Mister York, you know him, Mister Penberry, he's the neurologist, Mrs Chasvinder, she's the orthopaedic surgeon, Mister Parkes, head of physiotherapy, in fact I'm surprised you could get in here without an appointment and letters after your name.'

Archie was silent for a few seconds before sighing and replying, 'So...what? Did they say anything?'

'About?'

'About anything.'

Kanjara decided to end the chess-play. 'Nice. Good effort, you need to work on your interview technique.' She held his gaze. 'About my mobility issues you mean. You knew didn't you, before you came in today, didn't you?'

'A bit before.'

'From when...? What, from when I was first admitted?'

'Yeah.'

'Wow.'

'Well...it was just...when you first came in, I had a chat with Mister York. There were suspicions...he suggested there might be problems.'

'Damn right.'

'Compromises then, but there was nothing definite. What I do know is we can beat this Kanga.'

'We? Oh, so you'll not be able to walk again either? Oh well, that's alright then, makes me feel, you know, that it's not just me...' Archie could see her grip on the sheet as she struggled to remain focussed. Her breathing was shallow, her concentration all-consuming. 'Sorry. Uncalled for, unfair.'

'No. Perfectly fair, but...'

'I can't feel them you know, my legs.' This stopped him short. 'Neither of them. They say that's not unusual given the time frame.'

He grasped at the chink of light in this seemingly darkening room. 'There you are then, see. Early days.'

'Yeah, early days.'

'And physio?'

'Yes, I'm already booked, starts next week.'

'Well then. On the road already.'

'Yes, but to what? They do it with everyone Archie; there's nothing special in what they say, no promises.'

Archie reached for her hand again, a look of determination on his face. Kanga could see it and shifted slightly to avoid the contact. 'They don't do these things to keep you positive Kanga, you know? They do it because they believe there's a chance they can sort it. I mean, OK, so there's a possibility you may not have the same amount of mobility you had before, but that doesn't mean life and love ceases here, in this room.' He saw her face. 'It doesn't! It just means it's altered the view, shifted your horizon... and when I said we, I meant me as well. I'll help all I can, if you'll let me.' He took her hand successfully this time, feeling the momentary resistance before she relaxed in his grip. 'Will you let me help?'

'Is this the agenda I think it is?'

'What?'

'That it was you who sent me to the flat.'

'How...?'

'Did I know what you were thinking?' Archie nodded. 'I can read you like a book.'

'Then I'd appreciate you not thumbing through the pages so fast; all the mystery will be gone.'

'Then you shouldn't be such a good read maybe? I just have a feeling you might be thinking that you owe me.' Her face softened a little, but her words had an edge to them. 'And it's something you can just stop right now, OK? If you say none of this is my fault then it's not yours either Archie.'

'OK, so the truth serum's working on both sides then.' Archie dragged his chair closer to the bedside. 'Kanjara, Kanga, I really like you. I mean really. From the very first, when Adam introduced us. Now, OK, I may be getting way ahead of myself here and I'm willing to be slapped down, but even if you do think that me being anything other than a friend is out of court, then just as a friend, I'd really like to help. No guilt, no agenda. Will you at least allow me that?'

Kanjara broke the long pause. 'Sorry, been a day. Yes, alright... You can start by pouring me some water please?'

'That's better.' Archie handed the filled beaker across.

'Thank you.' Kanjara's face took on a studied look and Archie could see she had come to a decision. 'OK. Right. Seeing as how we're into the confessional... Sister Waldeck mentioned something else yesterday.'

'About?'

'You. She was talking about how she'd seen you here before, but a while back. Something about a family member...' As she had been talking Kanjara could see the effect of her words. 'Sorry, I didn't mean to pry.'

'No, it's OK, fair exchange and all that.' Archie sighed and looked a little lost as he spoke almost to himself. 'What are the chances...ha!'

'Look, it's not my business, and Sister Waldeck shouldn't have said anything.'

He sat silently for a few moments then began, slowly. 'Adam, he knew the details; him and his sister Gabrielle, no one else. Then all this...the shooting, coming here again... God, I drag this stuff round with me like Marley's ghost...'

'Sister Waldeck said you came in, just the once during the whole time she was on duty here looking after a patient, and that was to identify the body. That was why she remembered you, 'cos you'd not visited 'til then.'

Archie looked out of the window for some seconds before replying. 'It was my wife, the patient.'

Kanjara stared at him for a few seconds. 'Your wife?'

'Long story short. Pamela, that was my wife's name, she was having an affair with a chap, Beavis...'

'What, that man from the Gazette, the Beavis Beat chap?'

'You know him?'

'Of him, yes. I told you, I try to keep up with the local stuff. I listen to his radio thingy occasionally...the Beavis Byline isn't it?' Kanga smiled. 'Big on alliteration, isn't he?'

'Suits his tabloid mentality. Well, we all knew each other, Adam and Gabrielle, my Pam, Beavis. We all sort of moved in the same social circle, our jobs and such, went out for the odd drink. Not often 'cos I was always working, well you know yourself. Anyway, the evenings out continued even when I wasn't available, but they just involved Beavis and Pam...' Archie paused.

'Did you know about it?'

'Erm, yeah. I did.'

'Did they know you knew?'

'They'd been an item for about three months. I found out about it after the second month, but I stayed shtum, trying to figure out if anything could be salvaged... Anyway, this one night, she'd said she was going across to see her Aunt Lily, spend the night with her. I knew she'd been ill and I was working late, again, on a people-smuggling case with Adam as it happens, so I was all fine with it, good company for Pam I thought, and her Aunt... Then I got the call, that's how Adam knew, and through that Gabrielle of course.' He smiled thinly. 'Pam was driving, they were involved in a head-on. Not her fault. Driver of the other vehicle was three times over the limit. Pam and Beavis were both unconscious when the emergency crews arrived, but because they were in our car the ANPR search threw me up as the owner and they knew who to call. Beavis busted his arm and lost an eye, Pam was in a bad way, well, in a coma; she died four days later, never regained consciousness.'

'Lord... And you never came to see her?'

'No. No I didn't. Hard enough fashioning a narrative for it all to myself let alone see the results. Just a coward really.' He paused, partially drained but also searching. 'Hard to explain how I could do that... That's why Sister Waldeck recognised me. I figured she'd made me when I first came here to see how you were, guessed she'd rumbled me right then.' It was several seconds before Archie broke the moment with false bonhomie. 'And talking of guessing, guess where I'm off to now?' Kanjara shook her head. 'To see Mister Beavis. Lucky me eh?'

Her eyes widened. 'Really?'

'Really.'

'Can't someone else do it?'

'Adam. He'd have done it.' Archie shrugged. 'No, it's OK. Probably about time and the visit isn't about reconciliation. The information coming from Forensics set me to thinking and I want to see if a well-placed word or two on the radio can bait a trap for a missing person.'

Kanjara waited. Nothing followed. 'Is that it?'

'For now, yes.'

'Well that's not very fair.'

'If I go around telling everyone it ceases to be a trap, so don't go talking to that constable.'

'From in here? Really?' She could see there was no leeway so she changed tack. 'Can't you take someone with you then, to dilute it a little.'

'No dilution. He takes it neat this time.' He smiled. 'I'll be fine.'

'Yeah, right.' Kanjara shook her head. 'Men. No wonder they die earlier than women.'

'There's a claim that needs discussion...' Archie looked up at the clock, 'But another time, I've got to go. There's Beavis to see then I'm over with Lin, Miss Lea, to do a formal ID on her sister, then on to interview the noble Lord.'

'Your day just keeps on giving doesn't it?'

'It does. Plus, I'm about to go down to my car and find it shredded.'

'By?'

'Jasper, the victim's terrier.'

'You've got her dog?'

'On loan.'

'Why?'

'Because he doesn't like cars, I guess.'

'No, idiot, I meant why have you still got him?'

'He's been useful in the investigation...' He stopped abruptly. 'Enough. I've got an appointment with a hack and you've got an appointment with some rest. If York finds me in here and sees your face...'

'My face?'

'You look tired; lovely but worn, if you get my meaning.' She smiled. 'Didn't quite come out as I wanted.' He patted the bed. 'You just concentrate on getting better.' He stood and replaced the chair. 'Take care you.' He was at the door before Kanjara spoke.

'You'll come to see me again?'

'What else is there for me here, eh? Every day, I promise.'

She smiled. 'I feel myself getting better already.'

'Excellent. See y' tomorrow.' Archie stepped out of the room, and taking fresh gum from his pocket, he walked along the corridor smiling out loud...

... He was surprised to see Dougie parked outside the hospital entrance. 'Bloody hell, I thought I said to send someone else?'

Dougie stayed sat in the car, the door opened to its furthest. 'And a good day to you too.'

'No, not like that. I'd already said you'd enough on your plate without this little errand. Where's Marissa, or Mary for that matter?'

'All just as busy as everyone else.' Dougie shrugged. 'Needs must Archie.'

'Does no one take me seriously?'

'Depends on the subject. Take search warrants for instance...' Both men smiled and Dougie got out of the car, a thin file in his hand. 'Here, all we could get in the time.'

Archie scanned the contents and after a few moments he nodded. 'Good stuff. Who put it together?'

'Marissa, Phil and a bit of Mary, the sweary bit.'

'Thought I recognised her hand. What's this about fly-tipping?'

'Yeah. Mister Mason reckoned it was travellers doin' it. As self-appointed neighbourhood watch chief, or nosey parker depending on who you speak to at the council, he saw it as his duty to get evidence and present it to them so they'd prosecute and move them on.'

'What did he have?'

'Diaries I'm told, or so the council said. Written observations, dates, timings and such.'

'Were there any clues as to which particular band of travellers?'

'Not really, but you know the Northants, Bucks and Oxon areas. Prime gypsy counties they are, all bound up with their history and such. They set up camp, councils try and move 'em on, they dig in, wait for the bailiffs, pack up at the last minute and move to the next county, set up camp, councils try and move 'em on...round it goes.' Archie sighed and nodded. 'You'll want further enquiries made with all the councils?'

Archie closed the folder. 'Yup. Get back in touch, see where the flashpoints were...are. Get a map and locations then spread the workload...' He paused and looked Dougie in the eye. 'Spread it Dougie, understand?'

'Yeah. And what about Mason's place?'

'Here's the thing; I've been thinking...' Archie took out a sheet of paper and resting it on the car's roof, wrote a few words on it then gave it to Dougie. 'When you get back to base give Pat this. Tell her to tune in and when she hears those words on Beavis' radio show to send round a scout to Mason's place. No cavalry just a scout, understand?' Dougie nodded. 'Uniform would be good, I want a copper to be seen, someone who knows a bit about the case...'

'Reddy?'

'Yeah him, but just him, just for a sniff. Tell him to do an inspection tour, like we would any first visit, but tell him I want no heroics, just a snoop and a report back to Pat on what he sees.'

'Will there be a need for any heroics?'

'Shouldn't think so...later maybe.'

'That it?'

'For now, yeah. Tell Pat it'll explain itself, she'll know what I mean. And good work all round Dougie. Is it still Mary with me when I go to see the Lord?'

'Yeah...' Dougie's face spoke volumes. 'You'll need to keep a tight leash on that one.'

'No, let her have her head. By all reports Brightwick and his secretary need a humility transplant. Mary's just the back-up you want in what could turn into a bit of a verbal pub brawl.'

'Right.' Dougie got back into his car. 'I'll have them draw up your retirement papers soon as I get back.'

'Thanks for that, the spur to prick the sides of my intent...' Archie tapped the roof of the car with his flattened palm and Dougie drove away.

On the walk back to his vehicle Archie heard it before he saw it, the high-pitched yap of a decidedly irate dog. When he first saw the car he figured the terrier was in the middle of a fit and he increased his stride in concern; it soon became obvious, as he got closer, that what was in Jasper's mouth was not froth but foam.

'Oh, f' fuck's sake! You little...shit.'

Having seen Archie approaching, Jasper increased his tail-wag momentum and yapped ever quicker, spitting out the seating foam to help with volume. Archie clicked the lock and stepped back a little as Jasper bounced off the window yapping and wagging, his face split wide by a grin of welcome, and only now could Archie see the full devastation that could be wrought by seven kilos of seriously pissed-off terrier; the passenger seat was distributed round the car's interior like old bedding from a badger sett.

'Jasper...! F' Chrissakes!' He opened the driver's door and the terrier bounced into his arms forcing Archie to catch him, whereupon Jasper whipped his tongue across Archie's face in continuous, ecstatic greeting. Looking beyond the dog he surveyed the wreckage and as annoyed as he was, he could not help but be overwhelmed by the dog's greeting. 'Yeah, yeah... alright, calm down... Jesus, Jasp, look at the state of this, it's like the wreck of the Hesperus! What the hell am I gonna tell transport, eh? Twice you've done this now, twice!' Archie popped the terrier onto the back seat. 'Here... Just stay there, sit and stay.'

Jasper sat, still unable to control his tail as Archie gathered the shredded remains of the passenger seat, talking to the terrier throughout. 'Jesus, dog... I've got to collect Lin in a bit. How do you think she's gonna react when she sees this and has to sit on that metal frame? Technically she's your next of kin y'know, if she turns you down 'cos of this you'll be across to that dog pound faster than you can bark.'

With his arms full of stuffing, Archie looked around for a rubbish bin. Nothing. 'Right. Stay, stay there you.' Leaving the driver's door open Archie walked to the back of the car watched all the way by Jasper. He opened the boot and flipped the seat debris into it, slamming it shut before climbing back into the car. Turning round to face the dog Archie lifted a stern finger.

'Right you. We're gonna see a chap about a radio report and this time you're coming in with me. Once we're in there one step out of line and I'll sell you down the river, and when we meet Lin it'll be you that tells her what's happened here. Understand?' He started the engine. Jasper, after a moment's hesitation, jumped from back to front, landing on what remained of the passenger seat before putting his paws up on the dashboard and yapping just the once.

'Oh no, if you're in the front this goes on.'

Archie clipped the lead to the collar then to the seat adjuster as Jasper looked at him, grinning widely. 'Do you know no shame, eh?'

~

6 'And you think the dog will give a good account of itself?'

Matt nodded. 'Good as any on short notice Gaffer, but they want their retainer up front.'

'Do they indeed? How much?'

'Five hundred.'

Brightwick raised his eyebrows. 'Very steep Lamb.'

'Cheap compared to some of 'em, but if you want the Chinese gig to go ahead that's what it'll cost.'

'Quinn?'

Brightwick's PPS held back for a few seconds, weighing up the chances of either upsetting his master with a negative answer, upsetting his reputation by agreeing to the match and having it go wrong, or garnering kudos should it turn out to be a success. 'Well Sir, I would say we have to weigh up the cost-benefits of such a venture.' He turned to Matt and Chris. 'Has a new space been sorted out yet?'

'Workin' on it, been busy Quinn. Just tryin' to find space in me diary's a challenge.'

Quinn shrugged slightly and turned to Brightwick. 'Then it would seem, should Lamb fail in his quest, we may not be able to accommodate the whims of our Chinese friends Sir. If we were forced to cancel how would that factor into your plans?'

'It wouldn't Quinn, you know it wouldn't, so why ask?' Quinn coloured a little as Brightwick addressed the three as if it were a cabinet meeting with lesser ministers which, in effect, it was. 'Let me explain to you all. This is the culmination of a number of years of work and a considerable amount of my money. There should be sufficient clues as to why timing is of the essence, even for such as you, but in order to forestall any misunderstandings let me make myself crystal clear. The expansion of the China-end of my livestock businesses launched at the same time as the China Trade Bill means my whole venture looks fortuitous and complimentary; launched separately it smacks of opportunism. Do you see?' Nodded agreement followed. 'Good.' He turned full face to Matt. 'We have nowhere?'

'Well when I say nowhere, I'm lookin' at payin' Valley Farm a visit, but that's it.'

'Valley Farm? We looked at that originally and turned it down because of its distance from the house, Lamb. It's on the very edge of the estate, highly inconvenient.'

Quinn butted in. 'Four miles distant Sir.'

'There Lamb, four miles. Is there nowhere closer?'

Matt tried to keep his growing frustration hidden. 'Gaffer...I...' He sighed. 'Valley Farm's still for sale and empty. The old milking parlour just might convert in the time I've got to satisfy your clients. If not, then I'm struggling. The immediate arrival of our boys in blue aint helping me neither...'

Brightwick broke from the group. 'Oh, this is intolerable!'

'Gaffer, you an' your guests will be wanting a bit more than a shed, that's why I'm struggling...'

Brightwick's patience now ran out completely and his voice boomed out. 'I. Don't. Care! You will find somewhere Lamb! Valley Farm is only to be used if all other avenues fail! I will not have the success of this visit circumscribed by your shabby handling of the details, shabby handling that will make me look incapable in the eyes of people who see any sign of weakness as a reason to withdraw their support. Do you understand?'

Chris and Matt were both taken aback by Brightwick's vehemence and it was a few seconds before Matt could reply. 'Yes Gaffer. And the coppers?'

'What about them?'

'Now they've found that campsite on our land they'll be sniffin' all round here. We only have to make one slight mistake...'

'Then don't, and leave the police angle to me, I'll make some calls. You have very little time in which to discover and prepare a site fit for both dogs and delegation so I would suggest you'll have more than enough to occupy you. Mister Youngman has prepared the home competition, which I'll be visiting later, so all that remains is for you to do the job you're paid for. Now, no more. Other things are pressing.' He turned to Quinn. 'The Connor sisters. Do we know the content of their Q&A with the police?'

'Most of it Sir. Nothing that will reflect back here.'

'We need to be sure of it Quinn. I would be grateful if you would return to Miss Connor and remind her who it is she works for and that permissions are requested before she speaks to the police again.'

Quinn nodded and was about to speak when Chris, unable to contain his silence and feelings any longer, spoke up. 'Never mind them two dummies, are we as sure about Youngman?'

Brightwick fixed him with a stare of sheep-slaughtering proportions. 'Meaning, Phillips?'

Matt attempted to quell it. 'Chris...'

'No Matt, fuckit, this has t' be said. Gaffer you're just wastin' time on them women. One of 'em slices cabbage for a livin' and the other's a stranger on a short visit. Youngman, he knows all the background to them Irish. He delivered the car, sorted the money, collected the car, sluiced the old fight stalls down with me earlier, and he's best friends of that gang of lads who nick dogs for him to use as trainin'. If the shit hits the fan are we sure we can trust him with all that information, that he won't sell us down river?'

'You doubt him?'

'He's got a big head with a loose tongue in it Gaffer, an' he's a Yank.'

'Hardly a compelling argument.'

'Gaffer, they aint like us, they've got no sense of honour! I say ship him back. When it all calms down then think about bringin' him back, him or another, 'til then lose him, I say.'

Brightwick paused for a long time. Whatever opinion he had of Chris this speech certainly had merit and needed consideration. The dogs were trained so apart from entering them at the forthcoming Chinese session, a job Chris could do if pushed, Youngman was indeed bordering on surplus for the immediate demands. 'You make your point succinctly Phillips. If Mister Youngman was unavailable for the event could you step up and do the set?'

All three men were taken completely off-guard by this, particularly Chris. After a pause he straightened slightly. 'Yes Gaffer, if it helps.'

'Well done Phillips. It may not come to that, but your agreement is noted. Does anyone else have anything to add on this? No? Good.' Brightwick focussed on Quinn. 'Have the police requested an interview with Lamb and Phillips?'

'Not as yet Sir, but I wouldn't imagine it'll be long before they do.'

'Well, there you are Lamb, there's the space in your diary you were searching for, use it well and get me what I want. Right. Storyline for our officers of the law Quinn, you have an outline I believe?' Quinn opened a notepad. 'Make it short, Lamb and Phillips need to be away...'

~

The reception foyer of Radio NorthOx-Xtra was all chrome with just enough smoked glass to make it seem mysterious. Arnold figured it was much like the vast majority of media broadcasting reception foyers the country over, a facade full of ego, conjecture and promise. At the rear of the front counter, behind a half-frosted glass frontage, were the blurred outlines of desks, each one misted with this glazed self-importance. The foyer was bathed in faux professionalism, with just a soupçon of arrogance and lift muzak.

'Sit and stay.' Jasper obeyed, aware throughout the journey that he was not exactly best-in-show at present.

Sydney Orme, the thin and decidedly anaemic twenty-something receptionist, looked up as a gum chewing Archie leant against the counter. He stood and peered over at the terrier sat neatly at Arnold's feet. Jasper curled his lip slightly and let out a low rumble causing Sydney to sit back down quickly.

'Can I help?'

'Bob Beavis please.'

'Is he expecting you?'

'That's why I'm here.'

'And the dog?'

'Him and me both.'

Orme's slightly officious tone was coupled with a glance at the foyer clock. 'He's on-air in twenty-five minutes Mister...?'

Archie took out his warrant card. 'Detective Chief Inspector Arnold, and this will only take ten of them...if we hurry.'

If Jasper's reaction wasn't sufficient the sight of the warrant card and Archie's look was. Sydney scuttled into what shimmered as an office at the far end of the open-plan area. After a few seconds he reappeared with another man at his side. Even with his hazed view Archie recognised Beavis and an involuntary sigh left him. 'Right.' He looked down at the terrier. 'You behave.' Jasper blinked and lolled his tongue. 'I've got to concentrate.'...

... 'So let me get this straight. You want this information about this man...'

'Missing man.'

'...Missing man, Mason, and his missing dog...'

'And his extensive woodland photo collection gathered as part of his Neighbourhood Watch duties about fly tipping. Most important that.'

'Yes, that as well, you want this information linked to the sob story about the terrier, and have me put it out on my show this afternoon with no verification, just taking your word for it that it's true, that it's a scoop.'

'Yeah.'

'Your word.'

'Not gonna be hard. I've even written it out for you.' Archie indicated the sheet of paper on Beavis' desk. 'A handwritten scoop.'

'And the dog?' He motioned towards Jasper sitting quietly at Arnold's side.

'Is the only witness to the hit-and-run, like I said, so a great angle to run with, tears already embedded.'

In spite of it all Beavis had to admit it rolled well. He glanced over the words, tilting the page slightly to take advantage of his one good eye. 'It's got all the hooks, I admit...' Beavis shook his head. 'So, what's the catch?'

'There isn't one. It's as it seems.'

'With us? Our history? You know what they say, if something sounds too good to be true...?'

'Not this one.' Archie paused for a second or two then looked at the clock. 'Look, as your vampiric front desk op told me, you're on-air in what, eleven minutes from now, so let's just cut to the chase. As difficult as it may seem our past has nothing to do with this; nothing. You want to go over old ground? Fine, we'll do that. We'll book a table or a boxing ring and come to an agreement over lunch or blows about fault and blame, whatever suits, just not now. OK? This information is unavailable to anyone else until tomorrow, then it ceases to be a scoop, so it needs to be out on your show today to qualify. And yes, it'll be doing me a favour, but most of all it'll help a group of people come to terms with what's just happened to them. We lost one officer, had one seriously injured and a lady lost her twin sister. This is bigger than our backstory right now and that's the truth.'

'Fair play.' Beavis seemed and sounded moved. 'I was really sorry to hear about Adam. Really. How's Gabrielle taking it?'

The conversation softened; the edge dulled by a shared understanding. 'You not been in touch?'

Beavis shook his head.' Wasn't sure how it would be received...y' know?'

'Never stopped you before... Sorry; uncalled for. You should try; give her a call...time's passed. She's staying with Jay and his missus until the funeral.' Arnold scribbled a note on the paper block on the desk. 'That's Jay's number. God knows what she'll do after that, but one thing for certain, she'll need a lot of support.'

'When's the funeral?'

'Not got clearance from the coroner yet, could be a fortnight or more...with your help, maybe less.'

'Would it be OK for me to attend?'

'Not my place, you'd need to approach Gabrielle about that, you've got the number there, that's your excuse.'

'Yeah, OK, thanks, I will. And from you?'

Archie stopped chewing and looked long and hard at Beavis before replying. 'Yeah sure, why not? Shit husband I may have been but I'm not vindictive. So, the announcement, you'll do it?'

Beavis re-read the page of script. 'Will it be alright to change a couple of words?'

'As long as the central information about the photo collection isn't altered, yeah.'

'Just to make it more radio friendly, and can I get a photo of the dog, for the website and the paper?'

'Yeah sure. When?'

'On your way out? Last desk in the line, Chris King, she'll sort it.'

'OK.' Archie used the clock as a prop. 'Right, come on Jasper, we'll leave you to get back to work, and...thanks.'

He got up and moved to the door. Beavis' voice followed him. 'You still chew gum then? You know she never liked that about you, don't you?'

Archie stopped and turned back to Beavis. 'Then she should have said somethin' shouldn't she.'

'She would've if you'd ever been at home for longer than the space of a meal.'

'And what would you have done if I had've been?' With that Archie left, aware he was shaking slightly.

~

6 Your sister, has she left already Connor?'

Gemma looked up from her pastry making and shifted her concentration away from the radio which was tuned to the incessant, opinionated blabbing with occasional musical interlude that was the daily fodder of Radio NorthOx-Xtra. 'Yes, Mister Quinn. She left this morning, early train. Why, did you want to see her before she left?'

Quinn approached the table. 'No, no. It was you I wanted to see. I was just...' He stalled slightly. 'A pie I see. For tonight?'

Gemma looked from Quinn to pastry board then back. 'Yes, a pie...chicken in a tarragon sauce with wild mushrooms...' She stopped her culinary sideshow. 'What was it you wanted Mister Quinn?'

'Well it was really about whether you felt at all awkward?'

'About?'

'About the visit by the police yesterday.'

'In what way Mister Quinn?'

'Well, you know, it must have felt tricky, them asking all sorts of questions.'

'Not really. It was my sister they wanted to talk to so, no, I didn't feel anything.'

Quinn gave her a dead-eyed smile. 'Indeed, yes, of course. So they had little to ask you then?'

'Well, in what way? I mean, what would they need to ask me when Andrea was there?'

'So they didn't ask you anything about events here then?'

'What events Mister Quinn?'

Quinn was not sure whether Gemma was being very thick or very clever, but whichever it was, he was being drawn in to make comments he would rather not. 'Oh, you know, our guests and such. Their activities.'

'I'm sure I don't know what you're suggesting Sir.' Gemma put down the knife she was holding and leant on the table. 'I was told, when I first came for interview here, I was told that one of the prerequisites of the job was to keep my own counsel and I have done Sir; always. As far as anyone else is concerned this is just the home of a man who happens to work for the government. What happens here is of no concern to anyone else but His Lordship and his immediate circle, certainly not for outside consumption.'

'Absolutely as it should be. I think his Lordship would be very upset should he hear anything to the contrary.'

'He'll have nothing to fear from me Sir.'

Gemma was subjected to a long silence and stare from Quinn before he finally spoke. 'Quite right Connor. Absolutely. So, no enquiries...of any sort...?'

Gemma raised her voice a little. 'Mister Quinn, I've already said...'

She would have continued but was aware that Quinn was not listening. Rooted to the spot his focus was on the radio and the voice of Beavis emanating from it and she too tuned in to the words.

'*...the missing man was believed to be a regular visitor to the woodland which is on the estate owned by the Conservative spokesperson for Business, Trade and Industry in the House of Lords, Lord Brightwick de Roazhon. Mister Mason and his dog, believed to be a Pembroke corgi, were well known in the* district. As a keen Neighbourhood Watch supporter he'd already reported several incidents of fly-tipping in the woodlands around the area and had gathered significant photographic evidence of such behaviour and of those responsible which he was about to present to the Council and local police. Mister Mason and his dog haven't been seen for several days now and the police are keen to have contact with family members or friends who may have knowledge of his whereabouts.

Now, as regular listeners will know we've covered fly-tipping around the county's more out-of-the-way and picturesque areas before, so if you'd like to contact us with your experiences on this behaviour which is blighting our countryside, then we'd love to hear from you. The number to ring is zero-one-eight-six-five...

The number to ring fell on deaf ears, Quinn was already out of the kitchen door.

~

The Land Rover bobbed and weaved its way across the estate road, Chris steadying himself via the steering wheel, Matt via the dashboard, the radio dulled into the background of general vehicle noise.

'You'd think, with all his money, he'd sort out these bloody tracks.'

Chris looked across at Matt. 'That's why he's got so much, he doesn't spend it.'

'Yeah...watch out!' Chris snatched at the wheel avoiding yet another sizeable pothole. 'Christ, I'll be glad to get back into mine.'

'What, an' get some of this muck on it? That'll be a...'

'Shut up Chris!'

'What?'

'Shut up and pull over!' Matt rolled the volume knob on the radio up and leant forward in concentration as Chris juddered the vehicle to a halt.

'What is it?'

'Shut it will y'; listen!'

'*...Mister Mason and his dog, believed to be a Pembroke corgi, were well known in the area. As a keen Neighbourhood Watch supporter, he had already reported several incidents of fly-tipping in the woodlands around the area and had gathered significant, photographic evidence of such behaviour and of those responsible which he was about to present to the Council and local police. Mister Mason and his dog haven't been seen for several days now and police are keen to have contact from family members or friends who may have knowledge of his whereabouts...*'

Matt snapped the radio to silent and looked across at Chris. 'We didn't find any photos! Christ, this gets worse. You saw nothing?'

Chris shook his head. 'No!'

'You looked all over?'

'I may not be much use at a lot of things Matt, but I can search an 'ouse, it's been a hobby of mine for years; I found no photos.'

'Well we've lucked out according to this radio fella.'

'Beavis.'

'Who?'

'The Beavis Beat, he does this radio programme...'

'I aint interested in him! We missed this bloke's album of photos! Christ alone knows what he's got on 'em... I'll bet there's some of us amongst 'em, that's why he turned up at the sties that day...to confront us!'

'That adds up.'

'Jesus, what a fuckin' mess this is.'

'We gonna go back and search?'

'Fuck searchin', we need to sort it before them cops find anything.'

'How do you know they 'aven't already?'

''Cos you an' me would be in separate interview rooms right now if they had. No, we need to be on top of this. We need to trigger that fire...you need to trigger that fire.'

'How come me?'

'Because I've got a fight site to put together, you heard him! All you've got to do is slip in, pull that plug in the hose, flick that master switch then slope off. Right?' Chris nodded. 'An' don't hang about neither, that cable joiner'll go pretty quick, you'll have three minutes tops.'

'I thought they were slow-burn capacitors?'

'They were ten years ago; just don't hang about.'

Chris sighed. 'Right.'

'An' just make sure you keep a low profile.'

'I 'ave done this before, y'know.'

'Well just don't let this be the first one you fuck up. Drop me back at the yard so's I can collect me motor, I'll let the Gaffer know, you get over an' torch that bungalow.'

~

Lin and Archie had just left the car and were making their way across the car park of Three Counties Forensics, Lin still processing the amount of damage inside the car as Archie tried to justify the wreckage.

'I'm just sorry you had to travel in the back. It's my fault, I should never have left him in the first place; at least the perpetrator had to suffer the discomfort of his deed on the way over to Penngorse.'

'It was fine, it was like being chauffeur driven complete with guard dog.'

'I thought he'd be OK for that short a time, shows how capable I am of owning a dog.'

'A dog yes, Jasper's a different matter altogether.' The seemingly light-hearted conversation was a welcome diversion from what was ahead of them. 'How long did you leave him in for?'

'Forty, forty-five minutes tops.'

'Wow.'

'Yeah. Wow. Look at the bloody steering wheel.'

Lin almost laughed. 'Teeth marks must help with the grip though.'

'Nice...and no, it doesn't. I've not been back to the fleet garage with this one yet 'cos they've already got one car he's buggered up. Wait 'til my Super hears about this one.'

'Well at least he'll do little damage in the cell he's housed in now.'

'Don't be so sure. A metal bunk bed, stainless steel pan and sink will be no match.'

'He'll be fine. Very sensible to drop him off there.'

'I just hope the leather chew keeps him occupied 'til we get back.'

They had reached the main entrance and Lin slowed her pace suddenly. 'Would you stay with me, when I go in I mean?'

'Yes of course, if you want.'

'I do.'

'Well alright then.' He opened the smoked glass door for her and they stepped into an airy vestibule where Anita and Jay were waiting. 'Lin this is Anita Cresson, Senior Forensic Pathologist, and Jay Millar, Chief Forensic Officer for our fair counties. Anita, Jay, this is Miss Linden Lea.'

Jay stepped forward. 'Miss Lea. So sorry to meet you under such circumstances.' They shook hands.

'Thank you, Mister Millar.'

'Jay please.'

Anita stepped forward and held out her hand. 'And call me Anita.'

'Thanks Anita, I'm Lin.'

Jay looked expectantly at Archie. 'I'll return to my office if that's alright. No need for me to intrude.'

'Yeah, sure. Er, can I just have a word Jay?'

'Yes, of course.'

'Just away a bit.'

Jay and Archie stepped aside. 'Gabby, the ID; what was that all about?'

'Ah, yes. Well, it came about because she's staying with us... No great mystery. I said I'd asked you to do the ID and Gabrielle just came out with it. Why not let me, I'm here, spare Archie the turmoil; that kind of thing...well, you know yourself what she's like.'

'I do; she's far more a woman than I'll ever be a man. Will she be at yours this evening?'

'Yes, from about six she said.'

'Let her know I'll give her a call will you?'

'Of course.'

'Thanks Jay.' The two men moved back to Lin and Anita.

'All very clandestine,' said Anita.

'Not at all,' replied Jay.

Archie slipped the gum from his mouth and wrapped it in a handkerchief then rested his hand on Lin's arm. 'Right, we need to do this. You good?' Lin nodded.

'If you have any questions Lin you are in the safe, highly knowledgeable hands of Miss Cresson, my Girl Friday. She's cared for your sister since her arrival here and I can think of no one better. I'll be on hand for your return should you need me.'

'Thanks again Jay.'

Anita led the way across the vestibule, through a set of solid wooden doors and along a corridor to halt at a door marked Viewing. She turned to Lin. 'Have you done anything like this before?'

'Erm... Mum and Dad...and elephants.'

Anita paused at this then continued. 'Oh. Well, here it's in semi-darkness with central, overhead lighting. You'll be separated by a double-glazed screen from the room, but the distance between you is quite short to ease the identification process. I'll make sure you're settled then I'll go in and remove the upper part of the sheet, is that alright?'

'Can I go in?'

Lin's question took Anita a little by surprise. 'What, in-in?'

Lin nodded. 'And Archie too.'

'Erm...well, yes, yes of course, if that's what you want, but it'll also have to be with me.'

'It is and that's fine. She's my sister, mina...and I love her.'

Anita put her hand on the door handle. 'We've done as right by your sister as we're able, but you'll notice some bruising on the cheek and forehead for which I apologise.' She opened the door. 'After you Lin, Archie.'

As they entered the dimmed room Lin took Archie's arm and he could feel emotion's constrictor in her grip.

~

This detective, you've been in touch?'

'Yes Minister, as you directed. I spoke to his superior officer and used the forthcoming international trade talks as an excuse to check on the local force's arrangements for policing the capital and what effect that might have on the Chinese delegation's visit here. Then I veered off into the number and suitability of senior officers tasked with controlling these things.'

'Good. Who did you speak to?'

'A Chief Superintendent James Campbell.'

'Hmm. Know him a little, met him at a couple of soirées held by the Lord Lieutenant. I know his superiors better of course. The detective's name?'

'Arnold Sir. Archibald Arnold.'

'What do we know?'

'Some.' Quinn opened a thin file and read selected highlights. 'High-flyer...case-solving rate well above average. Bit of a loose cannon when it comes to the rules and regs of everyday policing though.'

'Useful.'

'Yes, Sir. Been on the carpet on several occasions, mainly procedural, but he's very much under review.'

'Then I think we need to underline our conversations and undermine his position.'

'Yes, Sir. I'll get back to them.'

'No, leave it to me. I'll have Willis get Commander Strathallen on the phone, it's time I did a little preparation for our interview, and the radio report was somewhat disquieting. Do we not know where Lamb is?'

'No, he's not picking up, but to be fair if he's hunting the area for a site then he could well be out of signal.'

Brightwick thought for a moment or two. 'Neither Lamb nor Phillips mentioned anything about photos which means they missed them completely...'

'Which means a sloppy search.'

'Or they did find them and intend to use them as insurance.'

'Phillips is too dumb for such as that, but, Lamb? Surely not Sir.'

'One thing I've learnt as I've gone through this life Quinn is to never trust anyone. I have knowledge on him, he knows that, but I'd put nothing past him.' Brightwick's eyes narrowed. 'Let's say they did miss them. If the police had searched the house and found them, they would've acted on it by now.'

'But there's nothing that connects to you, to us; of that I'm sure.'

'There is if he's taken photos! No, there's something not right about this, Quinn, not right. Did he have a camera when he blundered into the sties?'

'I'm not sure, everything happened so fast... Neither Lamb nor Phillips commented when we first discussed the matter and there was nothing in Lamb's written notes concerning the corpse's removal from under the tin.'

'Hmm. We must be proactive in this. I'll get on to Strathallen, you get a message to Lamb somehow. I want that bungalow searched again and properly this time, is that clear?'

'Yes, Sir.'

~

They were making their way across the car park when Archie's phone rang. He handed the keys to Lin then stood still to concentrate as she made her way back to the car.

'Hi Pat ... No, just done it ... Yeah, laugh a minute ... No, not a lot. She held it together really well; she's a toughie ... Yeah, another job jobbed. All good with the radio broadcast? And he said the script? ... Excellent, is Ameet on his way there now? ... More excellent. Well done Pat, thanks ... Because if there's been prior police presence we've a legitimate reason to apply for a fast-track search warrant ... Yes, very funny. If I had a pound...' Archie clicked off the mobile, made his way to the car and got in. 'Sorry Lin, just stuff.'

'Progress?'

'Of a sort.' Lin lapsed into silence and Archie glanced across at her. 'I've just told my second in command, you're a toughie, y'know that? The way you handled yourself in there.'

'Case of having to.'

'No, it's more than that. An inner steel is what it is; it humbles me.'

'Not intentional. Plenty tears been cried out, as Mum used to say. I've still got to contact Momma Lesedi and Khanyisile about all this.'

'That's the midwife and her daughter?'

'Yes, good memory Detective Arnold.'

'Like an elephant's. You've not done it yet then?'

'Cowardy custard.'

'Not at all, I don't blame you. How long since they've heard from you?'

'Not sure...four maybe five years. Momma Lesedi's very old now, but Khanyisile will be able to explain it to her.'

'After a gap like that they'll know it's not a social call, and I also remember you saying something about they'd know already.'

'They will, they do. I can hear Momma Lesedi now. "Be strong, buhle", she'd say, "no more cry".'

'For good or ill it's part of your story Lin, and Renata's. Cherish the pain, it's her paying you a visit.'

Archie took out some fresh gum and offered one to Lin who looked at him for a few seconds before shaking her head. 'No thanks. How did you become the police?'

'Eh?'

'You. You seem like you're from a different time zone, a different nation almost.' She could see Archie was foxed by this. 'Never mind, not important.' Lin released a huge sigh. 'Only became real in there. The world seems an emptier place now, like someone's misted our mirror...do you understand?'

'Mine was smashed, but, yeah, I understand.'

'You have hidden depths Archie.'

'Hidden shallows more like.'

'You undersell yourself; you know that? "There's no passion in playing small".'

Archie smiled. 'Marianne Williamson.'

'See? Top marks, well remembered.'

'Like an elephant, I said. One of these days, when we have the time, maybe then we'll talk.'

'That's why Anita's so stricken with you.'

'What stricken? You make me sound like a disease.'

'To her you are.' Archie laughed. 'Smitten then. You're an enigma.'

Archie snorted with volume. 'Yeah, right...'

'No, you are to her.'

'But not you?'

'No. You're a cat's cradle to me.'

'Not sure what that means, and I think you'll find Anita is the sort of person who doesn't do smitten or enigma, trust me.'

346

'Since when did you get all knowledgeable about women. You can't even see it when one of them has the hots for you.'

Archie coloured slightly and said smilingly. 'This conversation stops right now. You're undermining the dignity of the office.'

'You do that every time you chew that gum of yours. What is it with you and gum?'

'Habit.'

'Well it's not an endearing one.'

'Yeah, I've been told that before...just not by the right people at the right time.' Lin was about to reply when Archie cut across her. 'Later, eh? Not to be rude, but, time and place, y'know? We've got a police station to rescue from a terrier before I drop you pair back at the Red Lion, so...' Arnold mounted his mobile on the hands-free holder and turned the key. The engine fired and they lapsed into a silence of intrigue and secret histories.

~

As quickly and as surreptitiously as the broken ground would allow and using the scattered scrub as cover, Chris made his undetected way to the rear of thirty-six Penfore Close. Slipping through the fractured fence he quickly moved to the back door before pausing to listen in stooped concentration. All quiet. He eased the door from its blu tack embrace and entered the kitchen...

~

PC Reddy slowed the car, checking numbers out loud as he went. 'Twenty-four, twenty-six, twenty-eight, thirty...two, four, six.' He pulled up at the front gate. A look along the road revealed suburban life at its dullest. A black and white cat walked across the road ahead. He smiled. *There it goes, the possibility of some indeterminate luck. Today's excitement over in a flash.* Having got out of the car he adjusted his hat, standing just long enough for anyone who was a member of the Penfore Close net-twitch group to get a glimpse, before moving down the path to the bungalow's ridge-glazed front door...

... *Now where th'...? Ah, there...* The gas feed pipe had slipped off the cooker's splash guard and slithered behind it to the floor. Chris lifted the pipe, pulled out the bung and balanced it back on the cooker top, the gas hissing away nicely. 'Right, now then...' The knock at the front door sent Chris across and behind the kitchen wall...

... After knocking Amit cupped his hands round his eyes, pressing the palm edges to the glass and peering through in search of movement beyond. Nothing. He leant back and rapped on the door again...

... A loud scraping sound came from the metal and rubber pipe as it clattered down the back of the cooker once more, finally coming to rest on the tiled kitchen floor with a loud clunk...

... *What the...?* Amit pressed his ear against the glass seeking an aural second opinion...

... Chris winced through the noise, peering through the crack between door and frame at the disjointed, frozen figure of PC Reddy. *Fuckit...*

... Poised for several seconds Amit eased away and shrugged. *Cats? No, he's supposed to have a dog.* Looking along the window line he saw all was sealed. *Back door...*

... The shadow slipped away and Chris breathed a sigh of relief. After a few seconds he peered round the door. *Right, I want away from here, it's gettin' far too busy...*

... Amit pushed against the back gate and the rust-fastened weatherboard gave way. *Nice. Really safe that, especially for a Neighbourhood Watch veteran.* Along the short alley he turned along the back of the house...

... Chris moved across to the kitchen mains box. *Switch down and away...*

... Ameet moved toward the kitchen door. *Ah, there we are. Hmm, no cat-flap so not a cat.* He put his hand on the door handle...

... Chris switched the power on.

Old, tired and fed up of waiting, the capacitor was good to go.

The first stress wave of the massive explosion sucked in all the kitchen's air, causing a vacuum of a nanosecond's duration as every molecule of available oxygen inside and outside of Chris was gobbled up by the missile-like burn rate. Chris' body cavities and lungs were collapsed then rapidly over-expanded as the shear waves followed quickly on as, at the same instant, the positioned chemicals covered Chris in their napalm-like greed and the force of the explosion slammed him up and back, into the wall-mounted cupboard and its liberated crockery.

The searing pain of being burned alive would have made Chris scream, but he was already dead.

Point four of a second later the contents of the kitchen, its windows and door were launched, like shrapnel, out and across the backyard, taking PC Amit Reddy with them.

~

Brightwick, hands behind back, paced gently round the immaculately kept indoor training arena, stopping every now and then to inspect the spotless exercise paraphernalia dotted around the walls. He looked at his watch then turned towards the door as it opened and Aiden strode in. With him was Derringer, at full stretch on a thick leather lead which was attached to the dog's chest harness. Leaning back in an effort to keep the black and brindle Staffordshire cross American pit bull to hand, it was all Aiden could do to keep from being pulled off his feet by the dog's sheer muscular power. If ever there were a Kennel Club breed standard for such as these then Derringer was the epitome of it; a magnificent specimen of canine endeavour, a tribute to the care and time lavished on him.

The dog saw Brightwick and moved towards him with a purpose, a low rumble escaping his panted grin. Aiden leant back a little more.

'Best step back a-ways, behind the judge's barrier would be best, and close the door.'

Brightwick did as instructed, stepping behind a thick wooden gate set in a waist-high brick wall that offered both separation and refuge from the arena. Aiden wrestled Derringer into one of the corners where a horizontal metal bar was bolted to the wall. Swapping the long leather lead for a shorter, thicker one, he clipped the dog, via a carabiner, to a metal ring that moved freely along the length of the bar, and hung the long lead on a meat-hook just to the side.

Derringer was bouncing left and right in anticipation, his eyes and grin holding no sign of amusement. Across from him, in the opposite corner, Aiden put on a pair of scarred cricket pads then reached behind a flat wooden board and retrieved a fur-covered cylinder some fourteen inches in diameter and eighteen inches long. At the centre of this cylinder was a facsimile of a dog's head, jaws agape and set with rounded wooden teeth. The painted eyes gleamed, the leather ears laid flat on the head and the mock-up face and short neck joining it to the cylinder were fur covered. Two thick legs, fur covered and stuffed with wood wool, were attached under the neck and set in front of a barrel chest to which two long metal handles were attached to control this copy-cat challenger.

Throughout Aiden's preparations Derringer recognised the drill, knew what was coming and he started to growl ever louder, his tongue projecting slightly from his mouth as he tested the strength of the metal fixings against his own determined efforts.

'You'll see how ready he is Boss. There's no competition will give him any trouble.'

Using the dummy set-up much like a battering ram and letting out a continuous roar of aggression, Aiden pushed it at Derringer, bobbing, feigning and dodging in actions as near to another dog's attack as could be achieved. For his part, and restricted as he was by the short leash, Derringer also dodged and weaved, trying his best to lay hold of the dummy, until eventually the dog managed to side-step Aiden's lunge and get a grip on the side of the dummy's neck and shoulder. Flipping his head from side to side, Derringer began to destroy the head as he snarled and grizzled his way to victory by grim determination. When the head was finally dislodged the dog could give it the full treatment, which he did.

Aiden smiled. 'Consider him match-ready. Do we have a site yet, a challenger?'

Brightwick, still safely ensconced behind the barrier, applauded. 'I would say you were right Mister Youngman. Excellent preparation. A site? Not yet no, but I feel Lamb will come through.'

'Good luck with that then.' Aiden collected up the remains as Brightwick's mobile rang and the letter Q came up on the screen.

'I need to take this.'

'OK.' Aiden left with the shattered remains of the dummy. 'I'll just tip these away Boss.'

After a brief but animated conversation Brightwick shut down the mobile and called out, 'Youngman! I have to get back immediately.'

Aiden walked back into the arena. 'Boss?'

'Listen to my instructions and act on them, no questions and no delay. You're going home; Alabama. Kennel Derringer then go and pack, essentials only, your future depends on your speed.' Brightwick could see the confusion on Aiden's face. 'No questions, I'll get Willis to drop you at the airport and give you money. Tickets will be at the airport check-in; Willis is seeing to it now. Quinn will explain how the system works. You haven't a moment to lose...we haven't a moment to lose.'

Aiden could see consternation writ large in the look. 'Somethin' wrong Boss?'

Brightwick exited from the barrier leaving the gate ajar. 'Yes... I fear Phillips has been involved in an incident.'

Aiden half-smiled. 'What incident?'

'Not now. I have to go. Just do as asked.'

'But Boss, the dogs, the match...'

'Least of our worries right now Youngman, I assure you. Lamb will see to their well-being until you return, and you will. This is just a little hiccup; things can be resurrected once the dust settles. Now leave!'

With that Brightwick crossed the pit and was gone.

~

Dougie leant against the framework of the glass partition around Mary's desk, arms folded, grin on his face. '...And I'm telling you, that's what he said!'

'Well he's wrong the cheeky bugger. You carry no more and no less of the burden than anyone else here and I'll tell him that when I see him in...' Mary checked the clock, 'thirty minutes. Now,' she slipped her coat on and brushed past Dougie, 'if you'll excuse me I'll be on my way to try and make up for my obvious shortfall as a team member.' She called across the room. 'Pat!' DI Kershaw poked her head above her partition. 'I'm away to Bliss Bank to meet Archie. Take this smug bastard through the staff operations board and down a peg or two while I'm away, will you?'

'You causing trouble Dougie?'

'No. Just repeating the praise heaped on me by our beloved boss.'

Mary laughed out loud. 'Ha!'

DC Martha Carron burst through the main office door that led from the front office, her face ashen. Her appearance was so sudden and her expression so arresting that it caused everyone to stand silently, expectantly.

'It's the Mason place.' She scanned the room. 'A bomb...'

Seconds elapsed before Pat asked the communal question. 'Ameet?'

Martha shrugged, shook her head. 'Don't know...'

~

Brightwick replaced the telephone receiver. After a brief pause, he looked towards the sound of an opening office door. 'Quinn! In here!'

'Yes, Sir. Further information?'

'There is. From what we know it's most likely Phillips, and my chat with Commander Strathallen has only served to confirm the sense of my strategy.'

'And the police interview?'

'I've stalled it for a couple of hours, used the incident as leverage. Strathallen was most accommodating. Get over to Youngman's now...'

'He is packing though isn't he?'

'As we speak. Willis will drive him to the airport, but I want you to explain how things work in these circumstances. I've already sourced money and Willis has arranged tickets and boarding. I want them off the premises within the next thirty minutes.'

'Phillips, is it bad?'

Brightwick stood up from the desk and moved towards the door. 'He's dead, that bad enough? Come on, I'll walk you.' They left the office. 'It seems Lamb underestimated his equipment. Willis has fast-tracked Youngman on the next available flight.

He's used my VIP clearance and the company account to pay for it. I've transferred five thousand into his bank as of immediately.' He saw Quinn's reaction. 'I used the blind account.'

'Yes, Sir. Does this mean there'll be no dog match for the delegation?'

'Not since my conversation with Strathallen, no. Recognise which way the wind is blowing and trim the sails accordingly Quinn, that's how you stay afloat.' They had reached one of the vehicles and Brightwick opened the door, the faster to be rid of Quinn. 'That's enough for the time being. Shouldn't take Willis more than a couple of hours, traffic willing. I'll fill you in about how I intend to organise Lamb as soon as you're back.' Brightwick closed the door and Quinn sped away, the gravel and dust forming a smokescreen for the deed.

~

⁶Can I come in? Is that sister about?' Kenzie turned stiffly in the bed to face the door and James' scared-rabbit stare as he leant round the part-opened door.

'No. Yeah, come in... No, she's not, not long done the drug round.'

James smiled. 'Damn, missed the ketamine did I?'

'You did. Good to see you. Have you heard any more about Cashman, how is he, have you seen him?'

'Better than that.' James opened the door fully to reveal Faye standing behind a wheelchair which had a bundle of blankets on it. 'If Mohammed can't come to the mountain...'

Like a poor man's David Copperfield, Faye pulled the blankets to one side to reveal the t-shirt-wearing Cashman dressed in his working harness and sitting in the chair. 'Ta-da!' It took a couple of seconds before Cashman could focus on the room then the dog locked onto Kenzie and his tail rev rate increased exponentially.

'Cash! Cashman!'

Staying the spaniel with a firm grip on the lead, Faye pushed the wheelchair into the room and up to the bedside, the whines of ecstasy escaping Cash's mouth in a series of short yaps. Faye steadied the wheelchair and with a little help from James the spaniel was transferred onto the bed, where, with delinquent tongue he washed Kenzie's tearful face. 'Cash...oh my lad, my boy...'

After a prolonged greeting and with gentle commands from Kenzie, Cash eventually lay on the bed, relieving the stress on his one sound front leg. As he ran his hand over the spaniel, so Cash rolled onto his back to allow a tummy tickle.

'How the hell did you two smuggle him in here under that?'

Faye smiled and nodded at James. 'He works in the trade remember. It was like a heist movie, up in the lift and everything.'

'And no one stopped you?'

'Nope...he looked like my nan under that blanket...' Cashman flicked up onto his front leg and let out a deep bark.

'Mister Jardine! Mister Jardine, what on earth...?' Sister Ó Faoláin stood at the threshold, 'Mister Lamont, you rapscallion, have you been leading Mrs Jardine astray with your subterfuges?' She looked James square in the eye. 'Of you I expect no better...and that dog!'

Cashman barked again as Kenzie spoke. 'Sister Ó Faoláin, Cashman; Cash, Sister Ó Faoláin. Say hello Cash, speak.' Cashman barked again.

'Don't you come on with your sweet-talking in here my man, tryin' to get round me with your tricks.'

Kenzie looked directly at Cashman, taking hold of each side of his head gently in his hands. 'She's wise to you fella, but good effort.'

'Not good enough. Mrs Jardine you're welcome to stay, but you, I want you and that dog out right away... Now Mister Lamont if you please!'

~

Archie turned into the street. 'I'm really sorry about this Lin. I'll have a car drop you off just as soon as we get sorted.'

'Only if it suits, and I'm sure Jasper will be safe at the station. Whatever damage he could do will have been done by now.'

'No doubt... Oh, OK, we're here; Penfore Close.' The constable lifted the line of tape allowing access and Arnold drove slowly along the street, the signs of activity growing with each yard covered. Pulling up behind a wall of fire engines and ambulances he got out then leant back into the car. 'You'll have to stay here for a bit Lin, sorry.'

'No that's OK, I understand. Is there anything I can do?'

Archie smiled at her. 'Here? No, that's very kind, but no; all police business from here on... Oh hang on, tell you what, ask the officer who gives you a lift to go via the police station and you could collect Jasp. That'd be a real help.'

'Yeah sure. And bring him to you?'

'Er... Could he go back to the Red Lion with you?'

'Yes, of course. You shouldn't be feeling responsible for him you know.'

'No, but I just...'

'Feel responsible?'

Archie nodded. 'A bit yeah; does it bother you?'

'No...' she smiled, 'and I'm sure Rene would approve.'

'Thanks. Feel as though I've got the seal of approval... Bugger.'

'What is it?'

Archie indicated the vehicle drawing up behind them, the logo declaring it was an outside broadcast truck from BBC Look East. 'Just something I could rather have done without, summat that's gonna go down like a cup of cold sick in certain quarters.' He looked out towards the busy firemen. 'Give me a few minutes, I'll organise a driver.' As he walked between the fire engines, warrant card to hand, he met Melanie Brooke, the fire crew manager, discussing details with two of her team. Behind them, the full panorama of the incident spread before him.

Smoke was still rising from the remains of the bungalow. The road was snaked with hoses that looped round the various police cars and gas and power vehicles, all of them grouped around the afterbirth of the explosion. An ambulance crew, together with DC's Granger and Truman, were gathered round a gurney. Sitting on it was Amit and Archie raised a hand and whistled, attracting the attention of Deborah who turned and waved back as he called across. 'Debriefing in five?'

'Yup!' Deborah called back, nodding towards the OB truck. 'You seen what's just arrived?'

'Yeah, perfect timing. I'll be over to see the invalid in a few minutes.' Arnold switched his attention back to the crew manager. 'Hi Melanie.'

'Hi Archie.' She turned back to the firemen. 'No, I think if we let Northants stand down we should be able to cope with the clean-up. Just do a roll call, watch them off site and then report back, OK?' The two firemen nodded and moved away as Melanie turned back to Archie and they shook hands. Melanie held on to Archie's after the initial greeting. 'Can I say how truly sorry I was to hear about DC Reeve Archie; truly.'

Archie smiled. 'Thanks Mel. Yeah, us too. Had you met him?'

'Just the once and it was a pleasure.'

'Yeah, others felt the same.'

'I'm sure. When's the funeral?'

'No date yet. Coroner's still holding the body, ongoing investigation and all that.'

'OK, well can you keep us informed? We'd like to send a delegation, if that fits in with the family of course.'

'Gabrielle, his sister, and I'm sure she'd welcome the support; be deeply touched by it.'

'Good, thanks.'

Archie indicated the general scene. 'OK, so what can you tell me about this little lot...?'

~

The front-page mock-ups of next day's Gazette were spread across the office desk as Beavis and Andrew Millman, the paper's Editor, pored over the details. Millman pointed to the headline. 'The font size?'

'Yeah, that's good, leaves the space open for last minute updates.'

'Will there be any?'

'Don't know, I just want to be sure I milk this scoop-cow for all it's worth, it cost me enough.'

'I don't want any antagonism coming back our way through this, y'know?'

'And there won't be.'

'He's that reliable?'

'He is. And if any concern about conflict of interests comes your way, the paper's not his target. That'll be for me.'

'And all this ties in with your radio broadcast of earlier?'

'It does.'

Millman inspected the photo of Jasper. 'And no one's aware of the connection of this dog to the hit-and-run victim?'

'Not yet, not until we publish. No, we're ahead of the curve with this one.' He smiled.

'Nice exclusive.' Millman peered closer. 'Colour's good; dog stands out well, and the addition of the question mark on the whiteboard behind him, nice. Your idea?'

'I wish. No, that was Arnold's. He always did have a feel for the dramatic.'

'He looks reasonable in the photo.'

'You don't know him.'

'You go back a bit I understand...?' Millman's query was cut short by the at-speed arrival of Sally Aston from Traffic Report Desk. 'Problem Sally?'

Sally nodded, speaking directly to Beavis. 'That radio broadcast you did? It got results.'

She led the way to the wall-mounted television screen in the main office around which were gathered several of the reporting staff all locked onto the news report on Look East about an explosion at a bungalow which had claimed the life of one person. A talking head, DCI Archie Arnold's to be precise, was detailing the story so far in answer to reporters' questions.

... *'And do you think these incidents may be connected?'*

'It's too early to say...'

'But they could be?'

'Well yes, of course. This incident coming so close to the recent hit-and-run tragedy, the known interest the man living at this address had in that woodland, and the incident north of the border with port security may well be linked. We'd be foolish to disregard that possibility.'

'And the black terrier you mentioned, the one belonging to the hit-and-run victim. Where's it being kept at the minute?'...

Millman and Beavis exchanged glances as Millman leant into him and spoke under the continuing television coverage. 'Reliable source? Now we're behind the bloody curve.'

Beavis almost smiled at the screen. 'Touché Arnold...bastard.'

~

Matt put the phone to his ear. 'C'mon Chris, where th' fuck are y'?' He looked at the screen as if, by his annoyed stare, it would be answered...

'Nothing takes this long...' He fast dialled the number again and it repeated number unobtainable. 'Right.' Matt shut down the phone and climbed into his Range Rover. 'Can't spend any more time on it, he'll just have to sort things out himself.' He opened his notebook and scanned the list. *'Big house first, find out why that bloody Quinn keeps phonin' then collect the Valley Farm plans, sod what Lordy wants, then over to see where that bloody Chris has got to, can't possibly take this long to get back from that bungalow...Big House...hmm; maybe see Gemma, buy her some flowers...? Yeah, flowers...'*

On his drive across the immaculately manicured parkland Matt became calmer. He drove through the stunning vista of the deer park set above the valley lake which, in turn, led the eye across the park grounds dotted with browsed hardwoods, a rivulet of woodland hemming the edges; Capability Brown at his finest. Matt almost smiled. Out through one of the gate-housed entrances, he drove into the local village and pulled up at the Nisa store, the village's general shop and post office. He collected a bunch of chrysanthemums from a bucket outside and a box of chocolates from within, placed them on the counter and waited to be served, gazing idly round. The ubiquitous wall-mounted television screen, placed strategically in order to distract customers from the interminable wait at the post office counter, was set to rolling news and muted. The picture showed the latest news about the arrival of the Chinese trade delegation; it was the ticker-tape strip of information scrolling along the bottom that attracted Matt's attention: 'Gas Explosion at Bungalow Kills One and Injures Police Officer in Sleepy Oxfordshire Village' it read.

Matt was out the shop and well on the way back to his vehicle at a near run as the voice reached him,

'Sir! Your flowers...!'

~

Moving away from the TV crew who were already well into packing and leaving mode, Arnold moved across to the gurney now loaded into the ambulance. Stepping up into the back he raised a hand. 'Amit. How you feelin' buddy?'

Amit, a bandage around his head, a scratched face, an arm in a sling and his uniform well soiled, raised his good hand in greeting. 'Never better Sir, raring to get back out there.' He smiled.

'That'll not be happening for a few weeks yet. Put all your energies into getting better.' Pleasantries over Archie switched tack. 'You've given a full report to Martha?'

360

'Yes, Sir, what there is to tell. All happened a bit fast.'

'I'll bet. Right, I'll let these two take you to hospital. Someone will be along to get a tidy-up from you later.' Archie stepped off the ambulance. 'And well done, you did exactly what was asked.'

'I didn't do anything 'cept get blown up.'

'It got folks' attention, I'll put money on it.' Archie smiled at Amit and raised a hand in farewell as the crew closed the doors and drove away then he re-joined Phil and Martha. 'Right, let's have a look, fill me in on the way...'

~

Sat at his desk, Brightwick waved a dismissive hand. 'That'll be all Willis.' He swivelled in his chair to face Quinn and Matt standing respectfully nearby. 'This whole episode... What on earth were you thinking sending Phillips to do this?'

'Because there was nothing to it Gaffer. Just the flick of a switch and a few minutes later the place goes up. He should've been long gone before then. Christ, even Chris was capable of that...summat must have gone badly wrong.'

'That, Mister Lamb, is an understatement. We're sure he's dead?'

Quinn was in fast. 'All reports speak of one fatality.'

Matt shook his head. 'Poor sap.'

Brightwick swivelled his chair to look out across the parkland and gathered deer herd before he eventually turned back to the desk. His expected raised voice of frustration never came; quite the opposite in fact, much to the surprise of Quinn and Lamb. 'Well there we are. Nothing to be done. This will mean cancelling the entertainment for our Chinese friends Lamb.'

Something was off balance here, but Matt could not quite get a fix on it. 'Er...yeah, 'fraid so Gaffer. We're gonna be swamped with coppers just as soon as they discover who he worked for and that'll not take much of a stretch.'

'I fear you're correct Lamb. Quinn?'

Quinn looked from one to the other as he spoke, seeking to make things ambiguous and the decision not quite made. 'I know how much this means to you Sir, but yes, it would seem that to cancel is the correct way forward. What we have to be sure of is that all avenues have been explored. Is there no way round it Lamb?'

Matt stiffened a little, fully aware of Quinn's footwork. He began speaking very carefully as he traversed the minefield of their agendas. 'I think we can all agree holding a match anywhere near here would be real dodgy, a real risk for everybody...it'd only take a slipped word or a poor decision and we could all end up in big trouble, and we don't want that, do we Gaffer?' Brightwick shook his head but said nothing. He knew exactly Matt's meaning. 'If I know the coppers they're gonna want a long chat with me and that leaves little room for manoeuvre. Two things for sure, we need to delay it for as long as we can, and I need to get my story straight...for everyone's benefit.'

'Yes, absolutely.' Brightwick was once again seemingly fixated by the view through the huge Georgian window that backed his desk. After what was only seconds, but which felt like minutes to Matt, he swivelled back to face the room again. 'No. This is grossly unfair; we can do much better. You say it would be safer, for everyone's benefit, if we delayed your appearance for interview Lamb and I agree.'

'In a perfect world, yeah, but... Why? You got summat in mind?'

'I have. Do you still have dog contacts in London?'

'I do. Not seen 'em for a long while now 'cos we do our own thing here, but, yeah.'

'We do our own thing yes, but in circumstances such as these...'

'Needs must?'

'Needs must, precisely Lamb. Enormous favour to ask. If we put the match back by say, three days, to the latter end of their visit, do you think, through your good offices and contacts, you could salvage something for the Chinese delegation by way of entertainment, but away from here? It would be helping me out of a hole for which I would be in your debt.'

Once again Matt was on high alert. Brightwick had never, in all the years he had worked for him, ever been pleasant when giving an instruction for something he wanted. This was a man who considered everything should be his as of right; that the world, its peoples, and its resources were there only to serve his lifestyle and his demands; a man who considered every request an order. Matt answered with circumspection. 'What, sort out a match in London you mean?' Brightwick nodded as Matt considered for some moments, thinking on his feet. 'Well...yeah. I could make some calls, yeah.'

'Not calls, Lamb, meetings.'

Once again Matt was perplexed. 'What, go there you mean? When?'

'Now.'

'What, now?'

'Now. The quicker you're away from here the safer for you, and the greater the chance of you being able to arrange things, d'you see?'

'I do Gaffer. I mean, no promises, but it could be worth a punt, an' like you said it gets me legally out of the way.'

'Then might I suggest you pack an overnight bag and set off straight away. And go by train.'

'By train?'

'Yes.' Brightwick leant forward. 'As you have explained, the police have seen your vehicle in the woods. Should you travel by road your vehicle will be easily picked out by the CCTV cameras that litter our country. Leave the keys in your kitchen, I'll have Willis pop round and park it in the barn at the back of the old milking shed on Home Farm after he's dropped you at the station.'

'But...'

'I know how proud you are of it; don't worry, we'll take extra care with it.

'Well...is he even back yet?'

'Just. Quinn will furnish you with fake ID from our stock before you leave. Use that name for the booking which we'll make for you. Can't be too careful, can we?'

'Er...right Gaffer. Yeah...'

'Leave the handling of the police to us Lamb. The quicker you leave the more convincing our story.'

'Which is?'

'That your journey was planned some while ago, family matters. Quinn will book you into Claridge's.' Brightwick turned to Quinn. 'Make it a suite, Lamb needs to make a good impression, make the potential customers feel valued. Spoil them Lamb, this needs to succeed.'

'The police will still want to talk to me when I get back.'

'They will, but this will give me just a little more space in which to formulate a defence, talk to my contacts in the police force.'

'What about gettin' Derringer down to the smoke, if I can find a match that is? He'll be off the training regime and...'

Brightwick stepped in with a conciliatory tone. 'Let us worry about that Lamb. I saw Derringer earlier and I feel he and we will rise to the challenge. Correct Quinn?'

A bewildered Quinn answered. 'Oh, yes, Sir, of...of course.'

'So nothing to concern you back here Lamb. Just you concentrate on doing a good job with your friends.' Brightwick stood up but he could see Matt was preoccupied. 'Yes, what is it?'

'Don't mean to make difficulties for your plans Gaffer, but...if I'm to be arranging matches at short notice I'll be...'

'Needing funds?'

'Yes Gaffer.'

'Not a difficulty Lamb, a business necessity. I'll see to it that my private banker in London delivers any extra amount to your room, but will five thousand be sufficient to get guarantees?'

'For starters, yeah.'

'Then consider it done. Quinn, see to it that Lamb has the funds to go with him. There'll be a wall safe in the suite, keep the money in there until you need it, one can never be too careful, but pick a set of four numbers you can remember easily. There would be nothing more embarrassing than you having the clientele on site and being unable to open the safe; make a very bad impression.'

'Good point, Gaffer. One four, four four.'

'Which is?'

'Registration of my motor, four-wheel drive, four doors; always use it.'

'Very good. Now I suggest you pack and leave, and when you travel do so discreetly, keep your face muffled, it's cold enough. I'd like you to be London bound within the next half hour if that's possible.'

'Right Gaffer.' Matt looked at his watch. 'Forty-five minutes max.'

'Good. Willis will collect.' Brightwick's expression told them both the conversation was at an end, and Matt, after a quick look across at Quinn, left the room. After a few seconds had elapsed Quinn turned to the Minister. 'Claridge's Sir...a suite?'

Brightwick was already on his mobile and he held up a hand to halt conversation as the call was connected. 'Hello. Could I speak to Taras Vladkov please? ... it's Larry de Roazhon.' Brightwick put his hand over the mouthpiece and spoke to Quinn. 'Charge the hotel bill and the corresponding hospitality expenses to the off-shore account...Taras! Yes, it's about our chat of earlier; that possible unearthing of surprising details? ... Good. Look, I'm on the bit here, so if it's not too rude of me can I come straight to the point? Good. I'm now in possession of fuller information concerning that good canine friend of ours. Yes, still rankles ... yes ... Well, history does have a way of being exhumed ... No, I'd rather we meet. Delicate conversations need to be done face-to-face. Would you? Excellent. That'll be fine ... Six-thirty this evening then.' Brightwick closed the call.

Quinn was fast in. 'You're not going to let Lamb arrange a dog match with Mister Vladkov surely.'

'The dog match was cancelled the minute I spoke to Strathallen earlier, the details he gave me about the explosion saw to that. We'll find alternative entertainment. As soon as Willis leaves with Lamb I want you to collect his vehicle and drive it over to the Loveridge's yard.'

'But, you said...?'

'I want Lamb's vehicle crushed today. Take a chisel and hammer with you and remove the number plates and ID strips before it goes into their yard, no need for niceties, then bring them back here for disposal.' Quinn's face registered genuine surprise that quickly gave way to understanding. 'And stay there until it's done. I don't want those rogues keeping back even so much as a wheel nut from it, understand?'

'Yes, Sir.'

'Tell them I also want them over here to remove all the training gear today. Tell them I want it disassembled and stacked in the grain store.'

'What, all of it?'

'All of it. And get them to drain the training pool too. Give them five hundred in cash, that should be sufficient to buy their labour.'

'And their silence about the car?'

'The car was deemed unsafe to drive after dropping through a cattle grid, it is a danger, what's to tell? And when you go over there, go via the back roads. No cameras that way. Walk back by the same route. Call Willis when you set off, have him meet you somewhere.'

'But...Lamb, Minister, he's not going to appreciate...'

'The loss of his vehicle when he returns?'

Quinn nodded. 'That and the wild goose chase he's been sent on.'

'Why do you think I sent him to Claridge's with fake ID and covered the bill from one of our blind accounts? You have to do what needs to be done when the family pet is ailing Quinn.'

~

The reek of damp destruction permeated the shrubbery and leaf-strewn lawns of Penfore Close and clung to the clothing of all those involved in deciphering the explosion's storyline. For any tree within a dozen yards of the blast's centre the shock wave had given the slow leaf stripping of autumn a hurry-up, scattering the already frosted foliage in a single direction away from the bungalow. Anything closer was in a state no spring could ever breathe life into.

Archie, Phil and Martha converged on the suited forensic team who were busy sifting debris around the cordoned off area, Archie laying out logistics as they walked. 'No, not you Phil, you're wanted here. Just get a uniform to drop her off.' DC Grainger left to go in search of a driver for Lin. 'Jay? Jay!' Millar turned at Arnold's call and joined them at the tapeline. 'Some party.'

'Indeed. Am I to assume this will all form part of your investigation?'

'Correct. This is the home of that chap from the shallow grave in the wood.'

'Mister Mason?'

'The same.'

'According to your gut, yes, but I deal in positives. DNA will tell...when we find some.' Jay turned and looked afresh at the devastation. 'And if those remains do belong to Mister Mason then someone's gone to an awful lot of trouble to punish an already dead man.'

'Not an accident then?'

'According to the expert, no.' The threesome was joined by Naomi Prentiss, Chief Fire Investigating Officer for Northants, Bucks and Beds. 'Let me introduce you to that expert. CFIO Naomi Prentiss, DCI Archie Arnold and DC Martha Carron. I'll leave you in knowledgeable hands and return to my searches.' Jay began to leave then turned back. 'He's a bit of a mess I'm afraid, but Ms. Cresson has inputted the DNA on our portable tester; if he's on record we should have it within the next twenty minutes.'

Jay returned to his searches as Arnold's voice followed him. 'The wonders of modern science. OK Jay, thanks. Can you do the same for Mason?'

'We can, but finding evidence of him is somewhat harder.'

'Well, we know for sure it isn't Mason that got toasted.'

Jay turned back again. 'Indeed, but unaccustomed as you are, a wait will be necessary, albeit a short one. As to the how, Naomi will give you chapter and verse.'

Naomi slipped under the tape. 'Gas explosion brought on by a doctored electrical supply to a socket.'

'Deliberate. You're sure of that?'

'Absolutely.'

'So the initial detonation fractured the gas main?'

'Simpler still.' As Phil joined them Naomi produced a short length of rubber hose. 'Funny how, even amongst such devastation, the nuts and bolts of the event are often perfectly preserved.' Naomi held out the pipe for all to see pointing to a rip in the casing. 'This smooth edge here? A knife did that. Probably plugged with a small bung to act as a seal until required. That's gone of course, and no hope of finding it, but see these ragged bits here?' Archie nodded. 'Glue remains. Jay will test it, but there's little doubt in my mind.' She indicated various parts of the blasted space as she talked. 'See the flare mark up the wall there, the blackened area? That was the result of the blast and accelerant, not the direct result of a fractured gas supply.'

'Why do you say that?'

'When gas goes up the blast and shock waves are, important word here, instantaneous. Everything is affected at one and the same time, no time gaps and no secondaries because the blast is all-consuming, hence instantaneous.' Naomi pointed to the blackened wall. 'Isolate that and you get a fuller picture of the explosion's initial progress, momentary though it was.' The three officers were fully engaged as Naomi held up the rubber pipe again. 'The gas was let out after the plug's removal, but the ignition of it was caused by the malfunctioning of the electric supply igniting a strategically positioned accelerant, hence that scorched wall caused by its initial burn, just before it ignited the escaping gas. One thing can go on your report right now, none of this was the result of an accident.'

'Do you know what it was caused the electrics to go?'

'A shorting device, possibly a low-rate capacitor.'

'And the accelerants?'

'Lack of darker scorch marks at the socket site indicate a fast burner so, lighter fuel, thinners, something like that, possibly held in some form of fluid-tight bag that was obliterated on the first burn. As for the propellant? We've found the remains of a plastic bottle of drain cleaner.'

'Well it's a kitchen, so...'

'Yes, it's a common kitchen chemical, a highly flammable one. Where we start to get suspicious is that, along with the fragments from the drain cleaner bottle, we also found glass fragments from an overlarge bottle; first indications are that it probably contained acetone.'

'What, like nail-polish remover?' said Arnold.

'Yup, and that makes me very suspicious. My guess is it was put there as insurance by the arsonist, because according to your information this was the home of a single man.'

'Could be a very gay single man, a transvestite...?' Naomi gave Phil an old-fashioned look and clocked the rolled eyes of both Archie and Martha. 'What? Just saying...'

Naomi shook her head. 'Meanwhile, back in the twenty-first century... Those two together? The drain cleaner and possible nail polish remover placed right against the initial cause of the conflagration? That's when I smell a rat.'

'The DNA result on the victim will help...'

It was then that Anita joined them, laptop with DNA sequencer attached, balanced on her extended arm. She nodded a greeting. 'News from the oracle or, as we know it now, the internet.'

'The victim?'

'One Christopher Phillips.'

A ripple of recognition ran through the gathered detectives, Martha voiced it. 'Oh, sweet...employee of the month, hoisted by a petard of his own making possibly?'

'How certain are we Anita...?'

The arrival of a constable cut across the discussion. 'Sir, we think we've found the vehicle the victim might have travelled in. A battered Land Rover parked two streets from here partway across someone's driveway; they hailed a passing panda with a complaint...'

Martha smiled and once again voiced the collective opinion. 'The wonders of modern science coupled with a bit of careless parking.'

'Licence number?'

The constable read from his notebook. 'B eight four one PMW, registered to Bliss Bank Estates.'

Archie smiled. 'That's the kiddie; did you look inside?'

'Just a peek. Nothing in there.'

Archie cast a quick glance at Anita. 'No shotgun cartridges then?'

'Spotless.'

'Figures.' Archie looked up to where Jay was directing the collection of the remains from amongst the debris and he rubbed his brow. 'OK, let's just pause here.' He turned to Anita. 'We're sure about the ID?'

Anita moved closer, turning the laptop so Archie could see the screen. They were both very close to one another now and Archie leaned in and whispered to her. 'Our one chance at legality gone then, anything on the stolen one yet?'

Anita pointed at the screen as cover. 'No. Would've been but I got called away to this lot.'

Archie nodded. 'Sorry about that. Well, fast as you can, I'm on to Brightwick next.' He moved slightly away. 'That sure?'

'As sure as our DNA sequencer and the National Database can be, yes.'

'Error rate?'

'Miniscule.'

'Close enough.' He called across, 'How far are you off finishing Jay?'

'Us? Twenty minutes, maybe a half hour.'

'Can I split your team, steal some of them? Another search site, well two actually.'

Jay moved back to them. 'Yes, and thank you for asking.'

'Land Rover of the victim's been found. Seems like it's been spring-cleaned, but worth a sweep anyway.'

'Right.' Jay turned to his team. 'I'll get Maurice and Beverly over there, wherever there is. You know this will slow our process here.'

'Yeah, but I know you'll work doubly hard to make up for it.' Archie smiled at Jay's flat-faced look and talked on. 'This constable will show your lot where. Martha, get round there with them. Feed the results back in through the team at HQ. Whoever's there will collate then complete the circle.'

Two of the forensic team were now removing the black-bagged remains of the victim as Jay distributed staffing. 'Right. I'll turn the vehicle site over to Ms. Cresson to head up...if that's permissible?'

Anita closed up the laptop. 'Of course.' She smiled at Archie before returning to collect her bag. 'On with the motley.'

Jay, moving back to disseminate further information, was met by one of his team. A short conversation passed between them before he turned back. 'Archie? Is this anything you need to be aware of? Beverly found it in what's left of the victim's jacket pocket.' Jay approached them holding out a set of keys and a slightly charred netsuke.'

Arnold's eyes widened as he reached across and took it from Jay. 'Jesus H. Christ... I know where your double is!' Archie turned to Phil. 'Oh bollocks... Phil, you sent Lin off.'

'Er yeah, with a PC like you asked...'

'Get her back.' Phil looked confused. 'Get her back, get the driver to turn round and get her back here!' Phil moved swiftly to a squad car to use the radio as Archie flipped open his phone. 'Brilliant work Jay, top drawer. Just hang on there a sec.' The call connected. 'Pat? Yup. I want that work-up on Christopher Phillips completed, and get someone round to his place as soon as you have an address. I've let Jay know what's what, he'll send a team across as soon as you give him a location...' Archie closed his hand over the mouthpiece. 'Will it be Anita?'

'No. She's got the Land Rover to complete yet.'

'Send Maurice then, once they've done the initial sweep of it.' Without waiting for a reply Archie returned to his phone call. 'It'll be Maurice, Pat. Yeah...' He palmed the phone again. 'Fast as you can Jay, yes?'

Jay sighed and nodded. 'Right... I used to run my own department once upon a time.'

Archie ignored him and spoke back into the phone, moving away from the group. 'Maurice, yeah. You lead Pat, bring Arnue and Dougie with you. Phil will deliver the keys then send him back to me. A warrant ... no, I'm sure you weren't Pat ... you'll not need a warrant, he's a deceased criminal...ah; hang on, no, all that talk of warrants has just set me to thinking. Is Mary there? Good, pass me on ... Mary, big ask; have you still got your legal contacts in Bedford? ... Excellent. No, I'll talk it through later, at our meeting with Brightwick.'

~

The terraces of Probert Street had sat through many a police visit, this was just one more ignominy heaped on the shoulders of an already shabbily treated part of town.

'One seventy...there, that's the place.'

'Locals are here I see.' DC Dougie Brand pointed to the gathered police cars. 'Pull over there Arnue.'

DC Cho swung the car into a space between others and they got out to meet DC Carron as Phil also pulled up, handed the keys across then set off back.

Pat addressed the gathered officers. 'Forensics not here yet?'

Sergeant Nathan Lander stepped forward. 'No Ma'am.'

'Right.' Pat looked at the group, one of whom carried a steel battering ram. 'Won't be needing that today, sorry to ruin your sport.' She held up and jingled the fire-stained set of keys. 'In the victim's pocket.'

Lander spoke for the group. 'Is there anyone to consider?'

'Nope. Lived alone, no relatives traced as yet.' A tall, solid-sided van pulled up and Maurice, followed by two other people, spilled out. 'Ah excellent, our wardrobe arrives.'

Silence followed as the group donned plastic gloves and overshoes. When all were suitably attired Pat opened the door just a crack then drew back swiftly, closing the door as the smell and the sound of a barking dog reached them. 'Right stand down folks.' The crew relaxed. 'Dougie, get on to the RSPCA and have them send someone over, but now. I'll phone Archie, he's gonna love this...'

~

Like a matched pair of Boutet duelling pistols the netsuke boasted identical quality and cosseting.

'Can I keep it?' Lin's question to Archie was half spoken, half whispered.

'You can, but not yet. It's evidence.'

Lin nodded and handed it back. 'Of course, and I didn't mean straight away, I meant later, you know...'

'Yep, but I'm gonna have to borrow yours too, if that's in order.'

'Oh...'

'Only for an hour or two, just so's photos can be taken, then you can have yours back straight away, and Rene's too when we close this down.'

'OK...' She removed and handed over her netsuke with a certain amount of reluctance. 'This'll be the first time I've been without it for more than an hour since I was...God...twenty.'

'I'll guard them with my life.'

'See that you do.'

Arnold's phone rang. 'Excuse me Lin, I need to take this.' Archie stepped away. 'Hi Pat ... What? A what? Jesus, another one? RSPCA, right ... Brixworth? What, the dog pound by Pitsford Reservoir you mean? What about it? ... In five days... Jesus, what happened to seven days ... a what? A dangerous breed? I thought you said it was a pup ... no we can't! Well, if that's what they do then that's what they do, bugger-all I can do about it. Right, I'm across to meet Mary now. It's definitely Phillips, he had Rene's netsuke in his pocket ... Yup, dead ringer; with the emphasis on dead.' Archie snapped off the call and looked across at Lin who was smiling at him. 'Nothing good comes of listening in to conversations that don't concern you.'

'Another dog?' Archie nodded. 'Well, never say never I say.'

'And I said no. Now, I'll get these netsuke to Anita for photos and indexing, you back to base and me across to see His Lordship, see what he knows. Anita?'

Anita looked up from her search. 'Yes Archie, what is it?'

'Can I just have a word? Just excuse me a second Lin, least heard the better.' Archie walked over to Anita. 'Small favour to ask.'

Anita's eyes narrowed a little. 'Ye-es...?'

'Here's the pair of netsuke for photos...can we have that one back asap please?' Archie stopped and Anita sensed the conversation was not at a close.

'And...?'

'Erm...have you got any official notepaper with you?'

'Jesus, Archie...'

~

$\mathbb{P}$at Kershaw looked up from the call, turned to her busy-busy crew and called out as the RSPCA warden led the grappled, yapping Chipper past her. 'DCI Arnold, he say no!'

'Yeah, right...'

'He sounded pretty adamant.'

The jumbled chorus came back. 'Ha!' 'No he won't.' 'Fiver anybody?' 'You're on!' 'Easy money!'

~

$\mathbb{Q}$uinn opened the door. It was obvious that as far as he and Brightwick were concerned the meeting was at an end. If anyone was left in any doubt, Brightwick's closing lines made that very plain. 'No, I'm sorry Detective Arnold...'

'Detective Chief Inspector.'

'Yes, well, I'm sorry Detective Arnold, but I can be of no further help and I do have a six o'clock, so...' He looked pointedly at his wristwatch, smiling thinly.

Archie felt he was being railroaded and did not appreciate it. 'A six o'clock?' He too looked at his wristwatch...but ostentatiously. 'Well that gives us another two hours Sir.' Archie caught Mary's glance followed by her steely look at both Quinn and the Minister.

Brightwick's face hardened, his syrupy tone scarcely a veneer for his annoyance. 'Unfortunately, that's two hours I cannot spare. The affairs of state I oversee afford me no such luxury and I have much to plan, I'm sorry.' He waved an inviting yet dismissive hand toward the door. 'And...do give my regards to the Commissioner the next time you're together.'

'Tell me Sir, do you supply your staff with shotgun cartridges?'

This question from Arnold was so left-field that for a few seconds Brightwick and Quinn wore expressions of complete puzzlement. Eventually Brightwick answered, thinking on his feet as the conversation developed. 'I...I beg your pardon Detective?'

'Cartridges for shotguns; do you supply them to your personal staff?'

Brightwick looked hard at Arnold before answering, sensing an elephant trap but not knowing whereabouts it was. 'No Detective I do not. To my keepers, yes of course, we have a monthly order with Eley, but certainly not to my general employees. I pay them at a sufficiently high level for them to afford to buy their own, should they need ever them.'

'And do they?'

'Ever need them?'

'Buy their own.'

'Best ask them Detective...'

Not for the first time since their conversation had started did Archie get the feeling that, when Brightwick smiled, as he was doing now, it was akin to staring out a shark. *The eyes, they're dead, that's what it is*, he thought as he squared his frame to take in both men. 'So your personal staff would supply their own cartridges?'

'I have said so, yes.'

'And they come from?'

'Wherever they buy them from... Look, I'm sorry Detective, but what has this to do with anything?'

'So they could come from America?'

'America? Now you've lost me completely and I've no time to waste on riddles.'

'Your stockman Mister Youngman, he's American, right?'

'He is.'

'Would he have brought his own cartridges with him from America?'

Brightwick's mask of patience cracked. 'I have no idea Detective! I have more on my mind than where my employees obtain their munitions from.'

'Your affairs of state.'

'Indeed.'

'Well, putting your affairs of state and the fact that this investigation is inconvenient to one side Sir...'

'You are perfectly correct on that Detective it is inconvenient! My schedule for today alone would make your head spin. These affairs of state you so glibly dismiss involve us in preparations that require military accuracy, affairs of state that will bring in much-needed currency to pay for our public servants, yourself included.'

Archie sensed the emphasis on the word servants but could also sense he had rattled Brightwick's cage. He kept his voice level and matter of fact in order to emphasise who was in control. 'That's as maybe Sir, but I'm afraid such things are going to have be put on hold until I, and no doubt the Commissioner too, are satisfied that we're all fully aware of the seriousness of this situation and the need for this interview.'

'Oh, this is intolerable...!'

Quinn stepped in. Working for a man totally unused to the word 'no' meant the ability to diffuse such language difficulties was a skill constantly called upon. 'The Minister, Detective, is fully aware of your situation, but nothing can or will stand in the way of his schedule for today. Is that clear enough?' He smiled, but Quinn's edge went unappreciated.

'Forgive me Mister Quinn, but I don't think the Minister is fully aware, or you for that matter.' Before either of them could respond Archie talked on, removing the door from Quinn's grip. 'Whatever else your calendar tells you Sir, I have to remind you that we have three dead bodies, all of whom have links to this address. Now...' The door clicked shut. 'The cartridges.'

Brightwick cut across, almost snarling. 'And I've told you Detective Arnold that these events have nothing to do with me!'

'Due respect, Sir, the fatal hit-and-run took place on your estate; the victim's campsite was on your land; a burial site found in your woodland was of a man still missing but who owned the burnt out bungalow that Christopher Phillips was killed at; Phillips worked for you, and if this isn't sufficient to concentrate your minds, on Mister Phillips' person was found a very distinctive artefact belonging to the hit-and-run victim... full circle?'

Brightwick reined in his temper and remained calm in the face of this list of disclosures. 'I have no knowledge of the poor lady, I neither visit nor am familiar with the area where this bungalow is situated, and I am not Mr Phillips' keeper. He worked here on this estate; surely it's not beyond the bounds of possibility that he just found the artefact you're referring to? But all that aside, I don't know why Mr Phillips was in the vicinity of the bungalow when it exploded, tragic as it was, and I resent any such implication to the contrary.'

'These aren't accusations Sir, these are merely the enquiries we have to make in such circumstances. You were aware of Phillips' past?'

'Yes Detective, of course. I'm a Minister of the Crown. I do not take on employees here without a thorough knowledge of their background, but...' Archie was about to interject but Brightwick held up a hand and talked on, 'but their background should not predetermine what chances they are offered in life, do you not think?' He paused just long enough for Archie to not be able to answer. 'Whatever their circumstances, I try my best to give a helping hand to those less fortunate than myself. I was aware Phillips had come from a troubled background, but still I considered he should be given every chance to prove himself. I believe people make their own futures, Detective, and will behave in an adult fashion if treated as such. Now it seems, in Phillips' case, I misread an individual. These things happen... but truth be told, what my workers do in their spare time is their own affair. I'm not answerable to you or anyone else for that.'

'And Mister Lamb?'

'As I told you Detective, Mister Lamb asked for and was given compassionate leave yesterday, family problems. I didn't probe beyond assuring him I would help in any way I could.'

'And you have no idea where he might be?'

'I do not. Birmingham possibly, but that's just a guess. Could be Manchester or York for all I know.'

'Nor for how long he'll be away?'

'Indefinite leave Detective, that's what was asked for and, as a considerate employer, that's what I granted. However, rest assured as soon as Mister Lamb gets in touch you will be the very first person to know.'

There was a short silence which underlined Arnold's next comment. 'Mister Lamb, Sir, did he drive to his destination?'

Brightwick had not spent twenty-five years in the muck heap that was modern-day politics without knowing when someone was baiting a verbal rat trap. Knowing when to speak and when to shut up is a fundamental skill he had picked up when he served in the Whip's Office, that and the ability to create thinking time. He smiled. 'Detective...?'

Archie repeated his query. 'Did Mister Lamb drive to his destination?'

Brightwick's face took on a 'like I could give a fuck' expression but his voice held studied concern. 'Do you know Detective; I didn't think to ask. Oh dear, do you think I should have?'

'Is Mr Lamb's Ranger Rover, ML14 BLR, still on the premises?'

'If he didn't use it to travel to wherever he has gone then yes, it is.'

'Then you'll not mind if I have a look for it will you?'

'Not without a warrant Detective.'

'And why's that Mister Quinn?'

Brightwick took over. 'Given the sensitive nature of my work here I would insist on a warrant, for security reasons if nothing else. You do see that don't you?' Brightwick's question was framed in such a way that, even given the circumstances, Archie could not help but admire the skills on display here.

'Very well Sir. Thank you. Your obstruction is noted.'

'Not obstruction Detective, sensitivity.'

'Yes, Sir, sensitivity, of course. Apologies. And Mister Youngman?'

'As I said Detective, he was called back to America only yesterday, family crisis I'm afraid.'

'Another one.'

'Indeed. Always the way. You wait for one and two come along at once, isn't that what they say? Quinn organised the whole trip didn't you Quinn?' Quinn nodded. Brightwick smiled that smile again, his next words slick with concern. 'The very least we could do, given the seriousness of his recall. We organised priority boarding and tried to ensure the whole, difficult venture ran as smoothly as possible.'

Mary looked across at Archie as she tossed out her comment like a hand grenade. 'I'll bet you did. Families, eh?'

Brightwick's expression shifted instantly as he gave Mary a withering glance. 'Yes Detective, families.' He smiled at her and it made Mary feel grubby. 'Of course, had you thought ahead, informed us that you wanted to speak to Youngman and Lamb then I'm sure they would've been only too pleased to help with your enquiries, indeed I would've insisted on it...even though you got off to a poor start, or so they both informed me.'

'Mister Youngman was on the verge of obstructing an investigation Sir...'

'Then why was he not arrested?' Brightwick's tone remained calm and assured. 'May I remind you that Youngman, as any judge in the country would be quick to point out, was legally safeguarding my interests and my property from an illegal intrusion.'

'I was accompanied by a uniformed officer and that woodland was an official crime scene...'

'Not when you first met him it wasn't Detective; I believe that discovery was made later, ergo, you were found on estate land without a warrant...something I believe you are quite adept at.'

Archie just caught the fast-cleared smirk on Quinn's face and looked long and hard at Brightwick before speaking. 'Can I ask what you mean by that Sir?'

'I am merely referring to locker-room gossip Detective. Why, is it something you would dispute?'

Mary's sharply delivered declaration beat Archie to the punch. 'I'm sorry Sir but how did you come by that information? What you've just quoted is from interdepartmental briefings, never has and never would have been in the public domain, not in the locker room either.' The silence that followed was deafening.

Archie looked across at her but spoke to Brightwick. 'This has been a long and difficult investigation, Sir, in which we have lost one of our own officers and had two badly wounded...'

Brightwick ambushed them. 'Detective Constable Adam Reeve, WPC Kanjara Desai and PC Amit Reddy. Yes, I know Detective. When I last spoke to the Commissioner, about many things, I nominated Detective Reeve to be the recipient of a National Police Bravery Award, posthumous but nonetheless deserved. I have visited WPC Desai in order to offer her my best wishes for a speedy recovery and my personal offer to the Chief Constable of any help, should she require it, particularly in the supply of enabling devices, and although I have yet to contact PC Reddy I will do so once this interview releases me. Now...' Brightwick looked at his watch once more, his timing coinciding perfectly with the opening of the door and the appearance of Willis. 'Yes Willis, what is it?'

'Apologies Minister, gentlemen...and ladies. Sir, I have the Police Commissioner on the line for you and your six o'clock appointment has just telephoned asking if your meeting could be brought forward.'

'To?'

'As soon as is practicable Sir.'

Brightwick looked at Arnold. 'Those pesky affairs of state Detective, what? Quinn, can we reschedule the six o'clock for this afternoon?'

'I'll need to consult the diary Minister, but yes, I think it can be done.'

'Get back on to Nicholas, Willis, and suggest, four thirty...?' Quinn nodded. 'Four thirty then, and tell the Commissioner to hold. I'll be there very shortly.'

'Yes, Sir.'

'Leave the door, our guests are just going.' He pivoted slowly back to Arnold. 'I do believe we're about finished here Detective, and my next appointment is now twenty minutes away, as you just heard.'

He had been outplayed; Archie knew it. All he could offer by return was. 'For now, Sir, yes. I'll obtain the warrant, then I'll probably want to talk to you again.'

'And I will be very willing to talk to you Detective, providing it's something I'm connected to and you have the correct paperwork in place for it...and rest assured, I'll be informing the Commissioner of your visit shortly, tell him how dedicated and persistent you've been.' After a pause Archie and Mary left the room, Brightwick ahead of them, Quinn following, along the passageway that led to both inner sanctum and outer courtyard. 'I wish you good fortune with your investigations Detective.' Before Archie could reply Brightwick was into another conversation, 'Willis...!'

A voice came from one of the offices further along the corridor. 'Sir?'

'Switch Commissioner Strathallen's call through to my private quarters, would you?'

'Yes, Sir.'

Brightwick was round the dogleg in the passageway and gone, leaving Quinn to sheepdog the two detectives out of the door, Quinn leaning on its jamb and watching them cross the gravel yard as if they were trade.

'Tell you summat Mary, if that bastard Brightwick didn't pull the trigger of the gun that killed Adam then he sure as hell paid for someone else to. Right. I'm gonna ring Jay, you phone through to HQ and tell Pat of events here and get her to start a CCTV search to locate Lamb's Range Rover. Anita's got photos of it on her mobile; tell Pat to use that as the starter.'

'OK.'

'And tell her I want passenger manifests of all flights to the US from yesterday, asap. Tell her to get onto the Met and start a search for Lamb; that bugger's gone to London I'm certain of it.' As both officers opened their mobiles Archie turned back towards Quinn and waved ostentatiously. Quinn pointedly closed the door.

After making their calls Archie looked back towards the house. 'Well Mary, there you have it. An object lesson in how not to conduct an interview. Jesus...like a rookie in there I was, sorry. I really buggered that up, the slithy fuck.'

'Too clever for his own good that one, but we'll have him yet.'

'Yeah, there's more ways of killin' a cat than chokin' it on cream... They knew it y' know, the timing. That phone call, the Commissioner? If that wasn't stage managed for our benefit, then I don't know what was. They knew before we said it, got it all rehearsed before we'd even got here. What's that lawyer thing about never asking a question that you don't already know the answer to?'

'You think they were that well prepped?'

'The Commissioner on the phone just then, all that detail on me, on the others, the changing of the appointment, for whose benefit if not ours? My guess is we can expect a call back into the office very soon Mary, both of us. Sorry.'

'We did it all by the book. I'll look forward to it.'

'No bouncing you is there?' Archie smiled at her. 'What we need is to throw a snake into Brightwick's pit of complacency.... and we need a search warrant for the yard and buildings.'

'After Brightwick's chat with the CC...? We'll not get one will we?'

'Doubtful, but...I've also done a little prep work, our phone chat of earlier, about your Bedford court contacts.'

'Yes, Lucy Armitage, she's still a chair in Ampthill.'

'And is the legal advisor there friendly?'

'Sandy Cork, yeah... What're you thinking?'

'I figured there might be a log jam about the search so, long trek at short notice I know, but if I write out an authorisation can you get it to them?'

'Wow... Yeah, OK, I'll call ahead, give Lucy fair warning.'

'We've got the grounds, tentative ones I know, but I don't want to incriminate you further...it's an oath thing, an "I swear by Almighty God" thing, y'know?'

'Yeah I know, I have done them before. It's fine, anything to get that smug bastard netted.'

They got into the car, Archie to the driver's seat Mary to the back. 'Sorry about the front seat.'

'You've already said, it's fine, honest, my own chauffeur.' As Mary opened her phone Archie opened the glove box and took out several sheets of headed notepaper. 'Where'd you get those from? I thought we were going to have to go back to HQ or summat.'

'You're not the only one with friends.' Archie began to write, leaning across onto the open glove box. 'I'll scribble this out for you, then we'll skip over to the bungalow...oh, hang on. Before your Bedford call, ring Dougie and tell him to wait for you there, he can give you a lift back, then do Bedford, then on to Pat. Tell her I'll be in touch shortly.'

'You not want to ring her?'

'I've a feeling the less contact I have with HQ the less chance there'll be of me being called back in.'

'Good point.'

'Pat'll question you, just say the fewer people know the better and that I'll call her at a more convenient time.'

'On it.'

'Let's see if we can't shake some fruit loose.'

~

Pat Kershaw opened the door to the incident room and the gathered crew could see from her expression that she was annoyed. 'That was my one and only session with the CC, via the ACC, handed down by our CS.'

'Obviously not worthy of an audience in person then.'

'No, just an insignificant cog am I.' She paused and drew breath. 'In a nutshell, from here on in, we're to leave Brightwick alone.' There was an immediate silent reaction. 'We're not to pester him, pay him spurious visits, whatever that means, and if we do have anything that needs direct contact it's all to go through our Chief Super, who'll refer up.'

The silence continued until Marissa voiced the groups' considered reply. 'Well that's bollocks.'

'Bollocks it may be Mari but that's the word,' Pat scanned the room, 'and it goes for everyone.'

'Even Archie?'

'Especially Archie.'

DC Grainger shook his head. 'Fuck me, he's gonna love that.'

'Love it or loathe it he's into the Chief Super's office as soon as he gets back.' Pat dropped her voice level. 'Do we know where he is?'

Martha sat up slightly, their conversation shifting in volume to reflect who and what was under discussion. 'Mary rang in and asked for you, but you were, you know...elsewhere. She said Archie was suspicious about the replies he got so he wanted Brightwick's outside buildings turned over for Lamb's motor and the work-up on him intensified. He also asked that the fire report be collated and the flight manifest's search for the American completed asap so, in your absence, we got on with it.'

Pat nodded. 'As you should. If Archie wants the Bliss Bank job done, then he's gonna need to apply for a warrant. Past transgressions aside, did he give any indication?' Silence greeted Pat's query and she sighed. 'Right, so just relax on that until I can talk to him.' Pat loaded her next question, enunciating loudly and clearly. 'Do you think DCI Arnold will have a network signal where he is Martha?'

'Er, no Pat, I doubt it.'

'Well give it a try will you please?' Martha opened her phone as Pat continued, quietly again, 'Post my chat with the CS things have shifted slightly. The official line now is we're all going to comply with what is a direct order from our commanding officer, got it?' There were nods all round as Pat turned to Martha. 'Any luck?'

Martha closed her phone and shook her head. 'No sorry, must be out of signal, it's pretty spartan out that way.'

'Try it again a little later.' Pat moved to the centre of the group. 'As far as I'm concerned no one, Commissioner or otherwise, is going to steer me away from pursuing enquiries, wherever they lead and whoever they implicate. But. We have to be secure in everything we do. We do it by the book; no half measures, no short cuts, no one going rogue and no gut feelings, full paperwork and everything run past either Archie or me before it's acted on, got it?' Nods of agreement again preceded Pat's private mobile ringing on her desk; she saw it was Archie. 'Erm, hold on everyone, just got to take this, my mum...' Pat went out into the corridor, returning after several minutes and erasing the call details as she gathered the crew together again. 'That was the man from Del Monte...he say, amongst other things, our man from the ministry plays hard ball if he feels at all threatened.' Pat smiled. 'Good thing is, we've got us. From now on nothing we discuss about this case goes outside this room, not to anyone. Not friends, not colleagues, no one. If we go off half-cock or aim too high and miss, we'll be history in this force and two victims will receive no justice. Anyone feeling uneasy about this leave now.' No one flinched. 'Good. Right, Dougie? Archie's info from Brightwick about the Yank, is it accurate?'

Dougie picked up the story. 'Partially. Family crisis unknown but a possibility, all private so no details. Youngman definitely boarded a flight from Heathrow to New York at,' he checked his screen, 'eleven forty yesterday morning.'

'When did he book it?'

'He didn't. It was organised for him on the day so that fits the story. Ticket collected at the desk, purchaser paid cash.'

'Brightwick?'

'Yeah. His VIP pass was surety, all doors were opened and he was fast-tracked through, priority boarding the lot. We could ask US Homeland Security to seek and detain. Send him back on a return flight?'

'On what?'

'Well him being at the campsite for one.'

'You're fishing Dougie. No one saw him at the campsite, just in the wood...and if the CS gets a whiff of this we'll only get to hear of his displeasure as we carry our belongings past his office and out of the building.'

'But...'

Pat addressed them wholesale again. 'Guys, this is serious, and the CS wasn't kidding; he's under the cosh too. Anything we do has to be watertight; it has to be flawless. The last thing I want is to be presiding over the wholesale demolition of this department and the careers of those involved in it, Archie'd never forgive me for one.' Pat turned to Dougie. 'Like you, I hate to see smug bastards like Brightwick get one over on us, but he's got all the tricks, all the contacts. No, let's leave our American friend for the while and concentrate on Matt Lamb. That's a local thing so we can sidestep the Commissioner's friendship with Brightwick and come at it sideways because of our involvement with the bungalow blast.'

'Excellent name for a rock band that.'

Pat ignored Martha. 'Where are we with that Mari?'

DC Canning wafted her notes. 'I followed up on the London end, Phil did the biog, I chipped in here and there. Phil?'

DC Grainger quoted from his notes. 'Matthew Brian Lamb. Wide boy and all-round law shuffler. Been with Brightwick for four years. Met each other out dog racing, paired up and he's been a model citizen ever since.' Collective snorts of disbelief followed. 'Sometime bookie and enforcer. Dog man mostly; greyhounds, flapper and registered tracks...oh, and some live hare coursing, his name came up courtesy of a raid in...two thousand and five at Nethersholt, that's Norfolk. The local bobbies were called out for a suspected contravention of the two thousand and four Hunting Act where they broke up an illegal meet.'

Pat frowned. 'His name came up?'

'As the supposed organiser. Nothing came of it.'

Marissa chipped in. 'Too much trouble by all accounts. Budgets slashed.'

Phil picked up the story again. 'Our Mister Lamb was one step removed from the event by all accounts, which was a pity as those involved could have used his persuasive skills when the RSPCA and uniform turned up.'

Dougie smiled across at Phil. 'Trouble was there?'

'I do believe sticks were in evidence.' This created a room-round smile. 'But this is where it gets interesting. His greyhound past wasn't his only dog related interest.' The gathered squad concentrated. 'Not sure how reliable all this is, there's never much honour among thieves, but there were rumours he was a pit arranger, y'know, dog fights, back in his London days and not for the traveller community and their scrapyard grudge matches either.'

'Like them Loveridge lot y' mean?'

'Yeah. That gaggle are too low down the pecking order for our Mister Lamb. No, the rumour puts him in with dogs raised specifically and at great cost for the purpose by moneyed men; big money and big reputations at stake. Notables mixing with gangsters, getting a thrill by slumming it. Mister Lamb was the supposed fixer. Some of the chancers mentioned were on the Met's radar as well, and we all know what I mean when I say chancers.'

Pat asked the group question, 'Anything firmed up?'

'Is there ever? I did some Q&A's with a few of the Met's animal welfare and wildlife section, chatted to the RSPCA dog bods.' Phil shook his head. 'Nothing.'

'No names?'

'Possibility of foreign involvement; Eastern Europeans, Americans, some Chinese...rumours. Strong ones, but...'

Pat sighed. 'Right...it would seem our Mister Lamb isn't just a pretty face then. Knows the game and keeps a low profile. Follow up what you can, I'll let Archie know, but be discreet. Mari, the London angle?'

'Cold.'

'Nothing?'

'Nope.'

'His vehicle?'

'Nope. Not on a single camera. Nada.'

'CCTV at travel outlets?'

'Same.'

'Wow... OK, well...talk of warrants might not be premature.'

'He'll not get one will he, Archie, not with the CS on his mate's case?'

'Just...drop that for a while, Phil.' Phil made a puzzled face as Pat continued. 'Anything from the Met Mari?'

'Same old same old. Got the description across to them, vehicle number, photos the works, but nothing's come to light yet. I did hear mutterings of underfunding quoted.'

'As if we aren't. They know the background to this do they, about Adam and Kanga?'

Marissa paused and sighed. 'Yeah, and they're just as keen as we are, but...'

Pat waited then asked. 'What Marissa?'

'I got the feeling they're on the Commissioner's radar too.'

The room gasped; Pat vocalised it. 'Are you serious?'

'Just a feeling you know, I might be maligning them so don't quote me. Anyhow, they said they'd look around, call's gone out, description etcetera, but we're not deemed as a priority for whatever reason. Spoke to an Alan Cooke...' Marissa turned towards Dougie, 'Mate of yours isn't he Doug?'

'From times past, yeah. How is he?'

'Asks to be remembered.' She turned back to the group. 'Anyhow, DC Cooke says they've enough on their hands dealing with the security surrounding this Chinese delegation shindig next week. Protests are expected over human rights abuses, the usual, so they're drafting in from the counties, he said we can expect our invites any day now.' There was a collective grunt of disapproval at this. 'Cooke says what they've done is the best they can do, but he seemed less than comfortable with the whole thing.'

'Things have changed since I knew him then, get him on the team of a dawn raid and he was like a bull in a china cabinet.'

Pat sighed and spoke more quietly now. 'OK, so that means it's a strong possibility Brightwick's been on to them via the CS, that means it's up to us. You've all got your lines of enquiry so get on with it, but discretion's the word. Dougie and Marissa, over to the bungalow...you'll be meeting up with Archie there, update him while I continue to avoid contacting him...Arnue?'

DC Cho looked up from his computer screen as Dougie and Marissa left the room. 'Yes Boss.'

'Can you spare me a minute?'

The rest of the room busied itself as Pat led Arnue into the locker room. After a quick glance around Pat closed in on Arnue and dropped her voice a little. 'Right Arnue, first things first. If at any time you aren't comfortable with what I'm about to say then tell me and I'll redirect, OK?' Arnue nodded. 'OK. Word's come across from Archie. He's put in for a search warrant for Brightwick's place, not the house just the farm buildings around it, places where the Range Rover might be stashed.'

'Chief gets to hear he'll block it won't he?'

'With a vengeance. Mary got onto it. It's borderline, sort of. She used her contacts to go outside the county for it; Bedfordshire.'

'Canny one aint she?'

'She is that. When it comes through, I've got to rustle up a search team for later today, and he wants you to head it.'

'Is Archie not coming in before then?'

'Not if he can help it.'

'He'll be lucky.'

'Yeah, like I said, it's up to us. So, are you good with this?'

There was a silence then Arnue nodded. 'I am Boss. Adam, Kanjara, Amit; they deserve no less. Career castration by the Chief Super is the least I can offer.'

'Thanks Arnue. OK, back in and get on with the everyday, and tell no one. As soon as the warrant's stamped and Archie gives the go, I'll haul you out. It'll be a new gang which I'll organise at the very last minute and that you'll collect from Penngorse, all locals and off patch so you'll need to stamp your authority on them. Good with that too?'

'Yup.'

'Good.' They left the locker room. 'Back to you in due course then.' Pat turned down the corridor as Arnue re-entered the bustling incident room. 'And thanks again Arnue.'

~

'Ah Taras, good to see you my friend, how are you?' The two men shook hands then embraced, Brightwick patting Vladkov on the shoulder. 'Do sit. I know you're in a hurry, but...a drink?'

Taras sat on the leather chesterfield and nodded. 'Thank you, Larry, and forgive me if my haste appears rude, you know how I value our friendship. It is just that I have pressing businesses that has thrown up unexpected problems and is demanding my input so, please to accept my apologies.'

'No need Taras, I fully understand how busy you are.' Brightwick poured two generous glasses of Glenfarclas, handed one across and sat next to Vladkov. 'I'll not keep you any longer than is necessary.'

'Thank you.' They chinked glasses and spoke together. 'Zdorov'ye.'

'Now Larry, what is it that couldn't wait?'

Brightwick leant forward slightly. 'I want to tell you a shaggy dog story and bring you a gift Taras...'

~

'How sickening is that? I shopped that blouse from China, on the net. Eighty quid it cost and it looks like a plumber's tool bag on me, but on you and with just a pair of jeans...? Jealous isn't the word.'

'Don't be. After dedicated prosthetic reconstruction and nine hours in make-up anyone can look this good.'

'Ha! I see not so much as a blusher's worth. Natural light only serves to make you look beautiful; backlight only serves to make me look barely tolerable. You want coffee?'

'Yes please, and is there anything to eat, I'm starving?'

Sarah shook her head and laughed. 'God, you and food.'

'There's only so many variables with beans and bread.' Lin opened a wall cupboard and surveyed the contents. 'This is like having free-run in a supermarket sweep.' She rummaged around then lifted a large bottle of chilli and red pepper sauce off the shelf. 'Can I have this with some pasta, if you've got any...?' Lin started to open other cupboard doors haphazardly, tutting as she went. 'Do you not have saucepans, a plate...?'

Sarah moved across and took the bottle from Lin's hand. 'No, we just use the discarded foil trays we find at the back of the Indian... Here let me, before you wreck the place.' Sarah began to move around the familiarity that was the family kitchen, assembling the pasta and sauce requirements and chatting as she went. 'Do you want an onion in with it or garlic?'

'Both.'

She began peeling and chopping. 'I see events have made it into the paper.'

'I've not seen it yet.'

'That's 'cos you've spent the last God knows how many hours in the shower.' Sarah slid a copy of the Hertfordshire Gazette across the work surface. 'Here.'

'Just such a luxury, hot water on tap, food in store...' Lin looked at the photo then scanned the accompanying text before reading it out loud. 'By-Road Tragedy Makes Bee-Line Connection'? Fuck's sake... Is there not a newspaper anywhere in the land that can produce copy without reverting to infantile alliteration?'

'Language Lin.'

'Well...this is a person's life they're writing about, my sister's life!'

'It's just a rag with no commitment to anyone but its advertisers, just remember that; nice photo of Jasper though.'

'Only good thing about it.' Lin was about to fling the paper across the room when her eye was caught by another report and photograph at the bottom of the page. She read the headline out loud in a voice drenched with sarcasm; 'Do Animals Have Feelings? Local Politician to Debate on BBC.' Ha! This is the bastard who owns the land round where Rene was killed, this Brightwick fella.'

'Is it?'

'Yeah. How he's got the gall... As big a huntin'-shootin'-fishin' promoter as there is anywhere in this universe and he's the one they've got debating whether animals have feelings; fuck's sake...!'

'That's twice, I'm gonna install a jar... Butter or olive oil?'

'Oil, please.' Lin looked back at the paper. 'The face of privilege... Do your mum and dad know about everything that's been going on?'

'No, but when they learn to read there'll be hell to pay...'course they know, Mum in particular. She takes more interest in you than she does in me, her own daughter. Oh, and she knows about the cash and carry card too.'

Lin dropped the paper onto the table. 'You told her?'

'I had little choice Lin. Having the SAS gadding around the crime scene at your flat then over here...you getting dropped off by the cops, I could hardly say it was all about the Goddard boys could I?'

'OK, they suspected something was amiss, but why tell them about the card?'

Sarah sighed and paused in her onion chopping. 'You used it as fake ID, what did you expect?' Sarah stressed the point. 'Enquiries were made; you know, like, "This is Sarah Wilmott... no it's not"; that kinda thing?'

'Oh that.'

'Yeah. That.'

'Right, yeah... So...where do I stand with your mum?'

Sarah almost laughed. 'You? You're forgiven because of all this stress you've been under. Me? I'm on unpaid extra shifts in the bar this next week 'cos I lent it to you.'

'Sorry Sarah, truly. I never wanted any of this y' know? None of it...'

Putting the knife down Sarah moved across and rested her hand on Lin's shoulder. ''Course you didn't. I know.' Lin turned towards Sarah who could see the wrinkled face and the beginnings of tears. 'Oh Lin, love...don't, don't get all sad.'

'I'm not...' Lin moved Sarah's hand away, 'The onion, it's the onion on your hands...'

Sarah picked up the fumes and laughed. 'Oh bugger!'

'Blimey they're strong.'

'They're from Dad's allotment.' She passed Lin a tissue. 'Thank God for a sense of humour, eh?'

Lin wiped away her allium tears. 'Yeah, where would we be?' They both paused before Sarah went back to her culinary efforts. 'Your mum and dad. Are they in?'

Sarah loaded the hot pan with the onion, its gentle sizzle a strange comfort. 'Mum is, I think Dad's gone to his garden. Why?'

'Do you think it'd be alright if I went and chatted to her then? Apologise, tell her how things are?'

'Yeah, I think she'd appreciate that.'

'OK.' Lin moved across the kitchen to the door before stopping and turning back. 'Sarah...?'

'Yeah. What?'

'...Nothing.'

Sarah nodded. 'We're mates Lin, it's what we do. Go and see Mum, I'll give you a call when it's done, fifteen minutes tops.'

'Thanks.'

'Yeah. Now sod off.'

'I'm gonna tell our mum you said that.'

~

Brightwick placed his empty glass gently next to Vladkov's. 'And I don't want him found Taras, not ever.'

Vladkov smiled. 'Of course, Larry, it will be both my mission and pleasure. Under the name Fieldman you say?'

'Yes. First name Toby. The Mivart Suites.'

'A suite?'

'Yes, well...least one can do. I've assured Lamb that funds will be delivered to his room this evening. I suggest that pretext be used by your fellows to gain entry.'

'And the fee?'

'The five thousand. Lamb's taken it down with him.'

This caused Vladkov to smile broadly. 'Good of him to pay.'

'Yes, but the onus is on me. After harbouring Lamb and his secret all this time, the responsibility is mine.'

'Without knowing about it until now though Larry.'

'Yes...but it's the honourable thing to do.'

'And the kennel man who either turned a blind eye or was just stupid, Clarke wasn't it?

'Melvin. Nothing to be done there, he died of cancer last year.'

'Ah, pity.'

'Yes. And Lamb, I'm so sorry for the short notice...'

'Of course. I have a team always on standby for such emergencies. I will keep you informed as to progress and timings.' Vladkov stood up from the chesterfield and extended a hand which Brightwick took, no shaking just a squeeze of recognition. 'Now if you will now excuse me, I have a phone call to make then I must conclude other businesses. I will be in touch.'

'Of course, and thank you again Taras.'

Vladkov's face was stern, his eyes unblinking. 'My pleasure Larry, thank you for passing this information to me. Slippery Bob deserved to contribute so much more. To have him ended like that...' They walked across to the door which Brightwick opened. 'Oh, your meeting with the Chinese people...?'

'All on schedule. You received your invitation?'

'Yes, thank you.'

'I'm sure there'll be much you can discuss with them.'

'Indeed.'

They left the oak-panelled room to absorb their private conversation, as it had so many times before...

~

The bulk of the forensics team had gathered together as Jay handed out the clipboards. 'Right, final notes then we can all get back to homes or hostelry. Fill in the sheets and hand them to Ms. Cresson then disperse my children; fly, fly!'

Hoods were drawn back, gloves stripped off and pens were busied as each member of the team filled in the time sheet for their various tasks. One of their number questioned the procedure. 'Do you want the sweep of the Land Rover to be added to the bungalow times or kept separate Mister Millar?'

'Separate definitely, otherwise the fire service will be paying for the lot and I do believe they'll not be happy about that.'

Naomi Prentiss looked across. 'No, they won't.'

Heads were bowed again in earnest until, in quick succession, the clipboards and pens were piled onto Anita's outstretched arms. Jay watched them go. 'You'd think they were handing out ready money in the street wouldn't you?'

'Dedication personified.' Anita looked at the clipboards then at the remaining three team members who were in the process of finalising the search. Jay saw her look.

'Yes alright, I'll dismiss them as soon as they bag and tag the last exhibits. Satisfied?'

'I am now, unlike the CC will be when the overtime bill comes in.' She straightened the clipboard pile in her arms and took Jay's to add to it. 'Right, best get back and at least make a start on these reports.'

A vehicle drew up and Archie and Mary got out, their arrival quickly followed by a second vehicle as Marissa and Dougie pulled up behind them.

'Best shelve that thought Ms. Cresson, I do believe our erstwhile sleuth will want a word...and his cavalry. Why is it I always get a little frisson whenever he appears on the scene?' He looked across at Anita. 'That didn't come out well did it?'

'Not your finest work, no.'

'And to what do we owe this mob-handed pleasure DCI Arnold?'

Archie shook his head. 'I doubt you're going to find what follows a pleasure, but first thing's first Jay, if a phone rings, I'm not here, OK?'

Anita nodded, Jay just shook his head and sighed in resignation. 'Do I detect a lack of progress in the cooperation of our government minister?'

'Ha! Yeah, you could say that.'

'I recall past conversations of ours Detective Chief Inspector. Scientia est potestas?'

'You should have underlined it.'

'I tried to. So?'

'Brightwick's on the crest of a wave and I'm just hopeful the details you've got will go some way to salvaging our piss-poor attempts at paddling.'

'Precious little more than when you left I'm afraid. The who, the how and the where are still unchanged, although we do now have a definitive ID on the missing body in the woods, aided by Ms. Cresson and the wonders of portable DNA profiling; she's made a tentative match of the gentleman lately domiciled at the wreckage that stands before you.'

'Mason?'

'The same. Ms. Cresson...?'

Anita placed the clipboards on the ground. Moving back to the edge of the site she picked up her laptop, loading the details onto the screen as she approached them. The group of officers gathered round as she began. 'What I have to say before we all get too excited is the only available DNA sample was from a full thumbprint found on the inside front door handle.' Murmurings from Dougie and Marissa of, "Ooh, get her", and "Clever clogs", followed. Anita dismissed their joshing. 'Thank you. Using such material with such kit as this is still in the early stages of accuracy but it was all we could gather. So, from this somewhat shaky starting point and to be on the right side of legality, we've built in an inaccuracy percentage.'

'Of?' asked Marissa.

'Eighty-twenty.'

Archie shrugged. 'OK. Well, if I were betting on a dog race, I'd accept those odds.'

Anita lined up two samples on the screen. 'What makes things a little more certain is that we had a full match from the blood spots collected at the site of the burial in the woods, the site discovered by DCI Arnold.' She leant back slightly, her shoulder resting lightly on Archie's upper arm, thereby allowing the group to view the results more easily...and for her to snuggle slightly against him. 'That's it there, on the 'A' line. The 'B' and 'C' profiles are the comparisons collected from here and from the woodland, and hence the reason for the percentage figure.'

'Do you not need to see the whole string then?' Marissa asked.

'No, only the regions where the alleles are being matched.'

Archie broke from the group, disengaging the light touch between him and Anita. 'So, biology lesson aside, important thing is it's definitely Mason.'

Anita nodded. 'Eighty-twenty definite, but yes.'

Jay spoke up once more. 'The photographic evidence Mister Mason has gathered should help with discovering the whys of his ending up in the woodland, if we can ever find them amongst this debris of a life. Search as we have, they haven't come to light yet.'

Archie looked at Jay. 'What photographic evidence?'

Jay frowned. 'The photos Mister Mason took in the woodland. The ones mentioned by you to me...' Jay saw Archie's flat-line look. 'The ones that were central to the radio news report on The Beavis Beat and no doubt instrumental to the events here...'

'Ah, those photos.'

'Yes.'

Archie paused for a few seconds before replying. 'Nah. No such animal.'

'What?'

'Never were any photos Jay. I made it up to flush 'em out, worked too.'

Jay was livid. 'You made it up!'

Archie saw the faces of his trio of officers as Marissa muttered to Dougie, 'He said Jay wouldn't be pleased.'

None of them had ever witnessed this side of Jay and Archie's relationship, had certainly never seen Jay become so animated and Archie so openly matter of fact about something seemingly so damning. Archie squared his stance and shrugged his shoulders. 'Yeah, I made it up.'

'All of it?'

'Yeah. I needed to get them to break cover, which they did...'

'Nearly killing yet another police officer in the process, not to mention the destruction of a property and the death of an employee of the Brightwick estate! I've mentioned before how your cavalier attitude to law enforcement just locks us longer in purgatory, but do you not understand how it endangers others, threatens the integrity of the case and wastes, our, time?'

'How so? You were here anyway, and it got a result didn't it? Bit unexpected maybe but, bonus I'd say.'

'Archie... A man died here today!'

'Whoa there Jay! It's not my fault this guy decided to blow up a building to destroy evidence of a murder and got caught in the backdraught. He chose to do it and the cost was the loss of one of theirs, that's all.'

'And how do you propose to present this...this evidence?'

'It only needs to be true to me.' Archie shrugged his shoulders again and waved a hand at the wreck. 'And as for this? What goes around comes around.'

Jay was dumbfounded and no one broke the silence. It was several seconds before he spoke. 'I'm going to try and pretend I didn't hear that Detective.'

'Don't.' All eyes fixed on Archie. 'I mean it Jay, don't pretend. Don't try to do anything other than accept it for what it was; the truth.'

'You really think this end justifies your means?'

'I do.' Archie scanned the group before the rest of his answer followed on, hard, uncompromising, complete with its jagged edges. 'You ask me, did I want PC Reddy to get injured? No, of course I didn't. But you ask if I'm concerned that the man who I believe was directly responsible for so much...brutality has been blasted into toast? The fuck I am.'

The silence settled as a blanket. Everyone took time to assimilate Archie's words. It was Jay who finally broke the group's introspection. 'I want no part in this side of your character, DCI Arnold.'

'Shame Jay 'cos I really like you.' He moved a step closer. 'This is me Jay and you should be pleased I show it you, think enough of you to be able to tell you; all of you.' He looked around at the gathered team. 'As you can probably tell, the game's changed slightly since Mary and I interviewed Brightwick and since the Commissioner and CS butted in. Jay, you told me I needed to be very sure of my ground before I walked into the arena that is Brightwick. Should've listened. Scientia est potestas, knowledge is power; you said it and you were right. Our friend Brightwick has it all and is as slippery as a shit-house rat. He knows how to play the system and only needed to use a few weapons from his considerable armoury in order to play me.' Archie paused, his gaze finally resting on the remains of the bungalow. 'Am I sorry about all this? I'll tell you. I'm only sorry I didn't get the chance to watch that bastard fry.' He took a fresh stick of gum from his pocket, concertinaed it into his mouth and begin chewing. 'He's gone, and if I have my way there's more to follow...and I'll get them any way I can.'

'Legality Archie. You have to be able to prove it.' Jay's voice almost held a plea.

'Right. Bonus truth time.' Archie turned to Mary and Marissa. 'You two already know a lot of the background on this, Dougie and Jay not so much so pay attention.' He turned to Anita and she knew what was to follow. 'OK?' She nodded without hesitation. 'The pellet taken from the dog's jaw and the ones from the cartridge I filched from the Land Rover in the wood, Anita ran them through a matching sequence for me.'

Anita looked at a wide-eyed, slack-jawed Jay. 'Can I share?'

Jay found his voice. 'Is this work you have carried out without my knowledge?'

Anita nodded. 'Yes, Sir, it is. I did the work at the request of DCI Arnold, but in the belief I would be helping the case; a belief I still hold.'

'How dare you compromise my department...!'

Archie stepped in. 'Jay, Jay! It was the right thing to do. Don't blame Anita, I pulled rank on her...'

'You think that'll work? It won't! In all things forensic I am Miss Cresson's immediate superior. She had a choice in this and is just as culpable as you; I should have been informed!'

'In the logics of all this you're right, but logic has no place where friendship's concerned. We act out of care, out of empathy as well as out of duty.'

Jay almost snorted his reply. 'Duty?'

'Yeah. Duty. I, owe, Adam, Jay!' Archie's voice cracked slightly. 'I owe him... And I'll not let this one go, not until the people who plotted, planned and murdered him and crippled Kanga are banged up and suffering the hell of what we laughingly call the English penal system. You think because those Irish fucks who pulled the trigger are dead the debt's paid? Think on. Brightwick and his coterie of muscle are in this up to their necks. There's one down here and one still missing, but up at that grand hall there's another two who're just as guilty, just as culpable as those who pulled the triggers, and if we stop, just for a second, we can hear them laughing. Fuck that, I aim to choke it off, and I'll do it in whichever way gets results.'

Jay cast a glance around at the gathered team. Support was etched on their faces. He sighed. 'The cartridge DCI Arnold used to consolidate this investigation is evidence obtained illegally;

you all know that don't you?' The team nodded in unison. 'Miss Cresson, you understand that too?'

'I do.'

'And pursuing this investigation on evidence knowingly obtained illegally makes you all accessories?' Jay shook his head at their determination. 'Very well. Once again DCI Arnold I find I'm accompanying you on the tightrope of legality. I am, first and foremost your friend but regardless of that, the position you've put me in says I should inform your superior officer of the conversation we've just had without delay...' Jay paused, looked, decided. '"We are so far steeped in blood...".'. Ms. Cresson, pray continue with the results of your pellet analysis, but Archie, you and I will talk later, and at length.'

'Of course, Jay.'

Anita addressed the group directly and immediately. 'The analysis says they're both from the same batch, like peas in a pod. The composite and trace elements from both pellets, from the dog's gum and unused cartridge, are as near an exact match in contents as makes no odds.'

'So Jay, how does that stand?' Archie asked.

'On shaky legs. When questions are asked by our masters concerning how this result came about, if we say anything other than the truth we will have, knowingly and with aforethought, lied. To admit to anything else will, on discovery, render the case and evidence invalid and those who sought to prosecute it in breach of their...'

Mary's mobile sounded. She opened the screen and made a general announcement. 'It's HQ front desk. I suspect they want to know why they can't reach you Archie. Super will want you to report back.'

'Ignore it; that or tell 'em I'm not here, either will do.'

'Pat will be getting stick.'

'She's a grown up, got broad shoulders.'

Mary raised her eyebrows at the others before closing her phone. 'I'll ignore it.'

402

Archie smiled at her. 'Good choice.' Jay sighed and Archie shrugged his shoulders. 'What Jay? What?'

'I'm going to return to my searches. This is turning into open rebellion and the more I hear the more implicated I become and the greater is my culpability for saying and doing nothing about it.'

Archie gently took his arm. 'A rebellion for the right reasons. All the Super wants to do is warn me off Jay, he's already put my team on notice, so, what? That's it? Close this down? Get me to back off Brightwick so's he can get a Christmas card from him? Not today, not ever. I refuse my consent.'

'Just don't forsake your empathy.' Jay returned to the wreckage as Archie turned back to the crew.

'There we have it folks. The only people who know these details are right here. You stay on, you stay shtum, OK?' Head nods were the only movement, hums of agreement the only sound. 'Anita, you still good with this?'

'I was signed up the minute I loaded the pellets into the gas chromatograph.'

'And you'd write that up and withhold the background?' Anita nodded. Archie called out. 'Jay!' Millar looked up from his note taking. 'We're about to incriminate you and your department, do you want to be here to defend yourself?'

'Will it do any good?'

'Probably not.'

'Then no, I'll just stay here and feel my ears burn.'

'Yeah, probably for the best.' Archie addressed the group again. 'New information for you all. The vehicle with the bull bars that we photographed belongs to Lamb, it's the vehicle that killed Renata Lea, right Anita?'

'Using the photos we took and your personal measurements as a template the match is perfect.'

'So, even though all the evidence gathered so far and which we're using to prove the case has, in the first instance, been gathered by means other than strictly legal, we can be almost certain that two employees of Brightwick were prime movers in events that have led us this far. Brightwick's story is that this is the work of a rogue employee, which is bollocks. He's the lynchpin for all of it, I'm certain, but to fix him to all this we need to find Lamb.'

'Then we can nail not only His Lordship, but Quinn too.'

'Noted Mary. Randal Quinn has all the hallmarks of a dud. So, there we have it, my vendetta itinerary, and I'll be chanting it until we get them.'

'How deep in with Brightwick is our Chief?' Marissa asked.

'They know each other, on first name terms, share broth and break bread together, but I'd say the Chief's got far more to lose. We've got some background on Brightwick, but it's Country Life stuff. What I want are the Penthouse papers. Look into the Chinese angle Mary. Dougie, I want you to follow up on Aiden Youngman. Got to be some paper on him somewhere, and we need more on his occupation at Bliss Bank. As for Mister Lamb, I gather the Met have been less than forthcoming?'

Dougie nodded. 'Pressure from Brightwick, we suspect.'

'Me too. If our enquiries don't uncover the Range Rover...'

'What enquiries?'

'Ah, sorry, best not ask Mari. The less you know the easier it'll be to deny when you're questioned. That goes for everyone. There's no way Lamb can have dodged all those CCTV cameras on his way to London. Anita, can you send the photos of Lamb's car across to the Met again with a short note; makes it look official, might jog their collective inertia.'

'Will do.'

Archie looked at her. 'Once again I'm in your debt.'

'I'll think of some form of recompense.' She closed the screen down and returned to her colleagues who were just about to wrap up their session.

'We all goin' back to HQ then?'

'Not me. I'll not get ten feet into the lobby before the summons comes. That'll make all this official and face me with the dilemma of lying or having the investigation closed down and my pension fucked. No, I'm going to stay away, run across to check on Kanga then get over to see Lin, collect that dog and give it a breath of air.'

Marissa's face held concern. 'You goin' back onto the estate then?'

'Yep.'

'Pushing your luck a bit aren't you? If Brightwick hears...'

'Who's to tell? Most of his staff have buggered off.'

'There's the keepers.'

'And I'm a copper in the middle of a murder investigation, we'll see who's got top trump if there's a discussion about it.'

Mary laughed. 'After our meeting today and the reaction of our Chief I think you'll find that Brightwick holds all the deck, so just don't get caught.'

Archie swapped old gum for new. 'I won't. Anyone asks from HQ tell 'em I'm doing a revisit on the hit-and-run site with a witness to get a handle on events and trying to help Jay out, so no signal, etcetera, etcetera...' He turned and called across, 'That alright Jay?'

'What?'

'Good, thanks.'

'For what?'

Archie blanked Jay's reply as the crew began to walk back to their respective vehicles. Mary shook her head. 'DCI Arnold, one of these days...'

'Feed me anything startling, but don't overdo it. Oh...and Mary?'

'I know, expect a call into the office.'

'You good with that?'

'I am.'

'Just give it straight, don't do anything fancy, OK?'

'Will do.'

'The rest of you, it'll not take much for department heads to notice all your activity, so be careful.'

Mary looked over the bonnet at Archie. 'Give our regards to Kanjara.' She opened the door then a thought struck her. 'Oh, talking of dogs, there's that one we found in Phillips' flat. What happens about that?'

Marissa and Dougie's earnest lean onto the car's roof was not missed by Archie and his eyes narrowed a little. 'Nothing happens about it. Why?'

'Nothing. It was just, you know, the RSPCA bods said it was classed as a dangerous breed...'

'What dangerous? It's a bloody pup! Only becomes dangerous if it's brought up wrongly.' Archie looked into the distance then back at Mary. 'Whoa...hang on.' His eyes widened. 'Phil, didn't you say something about Lamb being suspected as a dog-fight facilitator?'

'From the Met lads yeah, what Marissa got, but it was only hearsay.'

'No, no...there's something in this.' Dougie was about to speak but Archie held up his hand. 'Hang on, let me think... Marissa, those buildings on the OS map, how'd you get on?'

'Erm, OK I think, but other events took priority, so...'

'No I know, but were there any buildings that stood out?'

'A couple, yes.'

'Either of them near the hit-and-run site?'

'One was not too distant.'

'Can you get me the location?'

'The notes are on my desk so Pat can.'

'OK. Give her a bell and ask her to text the details to you and then you to me, that avoids direct contact.'

'What's this about Archie?' asked Mary.

'Just... Look, we know Brightwick likes killing stuff don't we?'

'I think obsessed would be the right description.'

'Well what if...what if he's also using Lamb's contacts to fix up dog fights?'

The silence from his team was palpable. Mary and Dougie spoke almost together. 'Are you serious? How...? More to the point, why?'

'I know, I know, big leap, but just think. When I went mooching on the evening the body was found I heard some dogs

406

barking up near some buildings that I think are part of the estate. A look at the OS map will confirm that.'

'It may have escaped your attention Boss, but dogs do bark and lots of people own them. With all he's involved in it's odds on Brightwick's got gundogs.'

'No, I'd swear this was young dogs barking. There was no depth to it, then we find this so-called dangerous pup in the home of one of Brightwick's staff, then we find out Lamb has possible links to dog fighting...no, there's a couple of loose links here, all we have to do is forge them together.' Archie turned to Dougie. 'How long did they say?'

'What?'

'The destruction of the pup.'

'Oh. Er, a week with normal stock but they said they'd euthanise this one pretty well straight away because...'

'It's a dangerous breed, yeah, I heard you.' Archie sighed and looked around, seemingly seeking inspiration. 'Right...I need to... 'Nuff said...don't just park here, you've got stuff to do, piss off and do it.'

Archie got into his car and drove off leaving Dougie to slide a five-pound note across the car's roof in Mary's direction.

~

6 Close the door Quinn.'

'Yes Minister.' The snap of the door's latch against the strike-plate gave a full stop to Quinn's arrival.

'Thank you, Taros. Yes, I'll be expecting it. Thank you.' Brightwick finished up his phone conversation then focussed on Quinn. 'Did all go as planned at the Loveridge's?'

'It did. I had to increase the crushing fee for Lamb's vehicle. Arlo said he'd do it, but only for an extra two hundred.'

'Arlo! Where on earth do they dream these names up?'

'From the celebrity gossip columns of course.'

'Stratton not there?'

'No, Arlo said his father was away on business, so he was the man in charge, and he was quite willing to use his position in order to extort.'

'But you paid him.'

'Of course. Last thing we need is a wrangle over small change.'

'Cash?'

'Of course.'

'Good. And the number and chassis plates?'

'Destroyed.' Quinn smiled. 'And, for future reference and with your permission, I suggest we keep an eye on young Arlo. He may be just the stopgap we need with Phillips out of the picture...'

'He seemed useful?'

'Looked the part, forthright but not insulting. Very self-assured.'

'Hmm. Yes, make a note then. So, all is progressing. What we need now...' One of the mobiles on Brightwick's desk rang and he glanced at the caller ID. 'Ah! Right on time, how obliging.'

Quinn motioned towards the door. 'Do you want me to...?'

'No no, stay, you may enjoy this.' Brightwick looked at his watch and opened the connection. 'Shouldn't take many moments... Lamb! Glad you called ... can I put you on speaker? Quinn's here, he'll need to hear what you have to say about arrangements so he can expedite matters at our end, time being of the essence... Good.' He flicked the speaker button and placed the phone on the desk cradle, glancing at Quinn as he did so. 'So, how are your searches going for alternative venues and competition?'

'*Not bad Gaffer. Things changed a bit over the years, but the same families are still in the business, couple of them even remembered me so knew I was a trusty.*'

'And you think you'll be able to organise something worthwhile and at such short notice?'

'*Yeah... Well, I think so, I'm meeting with a couple of them in the lounge bar tomorrow evenin' to discuss terms and suitable dogs, the Rearden Brothers. I remember them from way back, ran a couple of useful greyhounds.'*

'Heard of them; Harringay was it?'

'Yeah.'

'Thought so. And they seemed interested?'

'They did…well when I say that, I had to offer a sweetener Gaffer, keep 'em onside. I hope that was alright?'

'How much?'

'Seven thou appearance money plus five percent of the stake.'

There was a silence before Brightwick came back. 'You've got the five thousand with you?'

'Yeah, in the safe.'

'So you'll need an extra two plus five percent on the day; that's some sweetener Lamb. Do they know all the details?'

'No Gaffer, I'm not that daft! All they know is I want to arrange a scuffle at short notice, they don't know what for or who the audience will be. Thought it best to keep all this just amongst us until we're happy with the arrangements, you know, the venue, the pit quality, all the things I took care of before.'

'And the seven thousand; worth it?'

'Short notice an' beggars can't be choosers. I remember the Reardens used to run a useful fighter way back, Billycock I think he were called. Come out of an Irish connection, did some damage the couple of times I saw him in action, short bouts they were, bit of a brute. Anyway, they've kept his line goin'…'

'And how do you think Derringer will fare?'

'Well, I've not seen this 'un of theirs, but if he's anything like his relation Derringer should get topside. Theirs will probably be all cut-and-thrust. Derringer's a wily bugger, knows how to work it. I just worry a bit about his lack of preparation now the Yank's gone back.'

'We have people in mind for that, no need to worry Lamb. Now, because you mentioned that the five thousand was only for starters, I've arranged for a further five to be delivered today. You only need two of those, so use the rest for your entertainments tomorrow. Take the Reardens somewhere special for dinner, I suggest the Ledbury. I have a table, I'll ring ahead, book it for you; how many?'

'Er... Six Gaffer.'

'Six. Right. And the match, do you have dates in mind?'

'The first Sunday of the Chinese visit Gaffer, an' I reckon whatever goes on they'll have a bit of a show.'

'Good. That's what we want, isn't it Quinn.'

'Yes, Sir, it certainly is. Well done Lamb.'

There was a long silence as Matt processed this last remark. Eventually he spoke. *'Right, well, I'm gonna jump in the shower before...'* Faintly in the background the sound of a knock on the door was heard. *'Hello, who's that then?'*

Quinn exchanged a quizzical glance with Brightwick who raised a reassuring hand for silence. 'I think that may be the delivery of your payment.'

'Oh yeah, 'course...I'll just...' From the noises it was obvious Matt was moving across his hotel room, the phone cradled between chin and shoulder. *'I'll call you back when...'* The click of a latch preceded a gasp, a dull thud and the crashing sound of a dropped phone.

After a few seconds a different voice came on the line.

'Mister Brit-vick?'

'Wall safe, behind the picture over the bed; one four, four four.'

'Spasibo.'

'No, thank you.'

Brightwick closed the connection. 'I do believe Vladkov's chums have saved further expenditure, much of which, I have no doubt, was destined for Lamb's pocket.' Brightwick smirked. 'Silence is golden.'

~

6 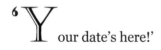 our date's here!'

'My what?' Lin, Jasper at heel, moved across the public bar of the Red Lion towards Sarah who had been clearing the vacant tables but was now staring out of the window, one knee resting on the bench seat.

'Your date. That copper, Arnold isn't it?'

Lin arrived at Sarah's side as Jasper hopped up onto the bench, popping his paws on the window sill to join in the convivial group scan, his tail wagging for no specific reason. Archie got out of his car, gum swapping as he went. 'He's not a date you cheeky madam.'

'You could do worse, apart from the gum thing that is.'

'Oh, I don't know, it's endearing. Doesn't matter anyway, he's too old for me.'

'Old-shmold. I'd give him six, maybe seven years on you and he's not old, he's experienced. Cut that hair of his and he might just scrub up as presentable.' Sarah's sales technique was interrupted as Jasper began to bounce on his rear legs and yap at the approaching detective. 'Someone else thinks he's a bit of alright too.'

Lin looked at the near-levitating dog. 'This is true, but he's a dog, so...' Lin turned to follow Jasper who had jumped down and was over by the bar door bouncing on all fours, a low whine escaping his tongue-challenged mouth. Lin opened the door and Jasper rushed out as Archie dropped to one knee to accept the greeting.

'Hello fella! Good lad Jasp...' The terrier lifted his front paws up onto Archie's bent knee. 'Steady, you'll have me over.' He scrubbed the terriers ears, losing balance against the dog's enthusiasm and dropping one hand to the ground as Jasper launched a face-licking attack. 'Good lad, steady, good lad.' He looked up at Lin and Sarah and smiled. 'Sorry, stealing him away from you.'

Lin shook her head. 'That's the most animated he's been since you left.'

Sarah joined in, 'True, really.'

'Just as well then as I've come to ask a favour.' Archie stood up, gently placing Jasper onto the ground. 'Can I borrow him, just for a short while?'

'Erm, yes.... Do I get to know why?'

'Yes and no... It's too complex to relate without taking up your next three weeks. It's just, there's someone I'd like to see in the frame if only I can gather enough damning evidence to do it.'

'Are we allowed to know who?'

Archie hesitated and smoothed back his wayward quiff. 'Not without me having to compromise a lot of the work we've done to date, no.'

'Oh, shame.'

'What I can say is that we're fast running out of perpetrators and it's nothing we've done; they seem to be doing it for us.'

'Running out?'

'Disappearing, well dying actually.'

'Oh... Mind you, that's helpful, saves the taxpayer having to pay prison fees.'

Lin smiled at Sarah's comment then at Archie. 'If you want pc you're barking up the wrong tree with Sarah.'

'Wrong forest even,' said Sarah.

Lin pursued the conversation. 'Can I come too?'

'I'm goin' back to the hit-and-run site Lin.'

'Oh, I see...'

'I mean yes, of course, I just didn't think you'd want the reminder.'

'I'm OK with it now, and a breath of air would do me good, away from here.'

'Thank you very much!' said Sarah.

'You know what I mean...'

Archie joined in. 'Look, I don't want to be the cause of upset...' His text alert sounded. 'Sorry, hang on...that'll be directions.' He moved away a little and opened the text from Pat. It contained the co-ordinates of the building Marissa had isolated together with a snapshot map. He moved back to Lin. 'So, you still want to come along?'

'Yes of course. Can I get a coat?'

'It's turning a little chilly, so my guess is you'll need one.'

'OK, I'll just pop inside.'

Sarah waved a hand towards the door and smiled. 'Don't stand out there in the cold, you a media star and all.' Archie made a puzzled face as he and Jasper followed Sarah into the pub. 'You not seen the local paper?' Archie shook his head. 'What, not at all?'

'Been a bit busy.'

'That I can understand.' Sarah turned to Lin as she came around the bar, coat slung over her shoulder. 'She has, seen the paper I mean.'

'And?'

'Chip paper shit is what it is,' replied Lin.

'Not fit for a budgie-cage, or so she told Mum.' Sarah moved behind the bar and retrieved a newspaper from the bin. 'Headlines.' She displayed the front page.

Archie nodded. 'Oh that. Yeah, I heard bits. I think my head of forensics was pretty pissed at me for some of my thoughts on the matter, Beavis too, I guess.'

'Makes three of us then.' said Lin.

'Seem to be making enemies all round this week.'

'Not you, I meant me, my reaction to the press and their willingness to play fast and loose with people's feelings!'

'That may well be, but Beavis' piece had the desired effect, especially the radio bit. I just didn't use it to proper advantage and now I'm paying for it.' Archie looked down at Jasper and smiled. 'Hopefully not you.'

Sarah placed the paper on the bar. 'You can do no wrong in his eyes.'

'We'll see.' Archie turned to Lin. 'Good to go?'

'The car; is the seat...?'

'Still knackered? Yeah, 'fraid so. I've put a seat cushion from my armchair on it.'

'What happened?' asked Sarah.

Lin and Archie answered together. 'He did.'

Lin collected her bag from the bar, the sight of the paper and its headlines reigniting her tirade of earlier. 'And then we're treated to listening to this...this snake.'

'Who?'

'Brightwick!' Lin picked up the paper and displayed the secondary headline. 'Him, preaching to us about how to treat animals. Him!' She threw the paper back on the counter.

'So that's why you were so animated back in the woodland when we met that Youngman fella.'

'Yeah, Mistral Pharmaceuticals, Brightwick's on their board of directors. That's a smug and very smackable face and I'd like to put myself forward to be the one to do it.'

'And I'd like to put myself forward as the one to tell you not to. Can I have that a minute?' Lin retrieved the paper and passed it to Archie who opened it at the correct page and laid it on the bar. 'Look at him Lin and know your enemy. This is coming from someone who's got first-hand knowledge of this particular noble Lord. This is in no way meant to denigrate your intellect, your passion or your accuracy, but I've recently been given a beating by him. He's got the right connections and the right vocabulary. I head up suspect interviews for a living, it's my job, but I went to interview him with insufficient background and he chopped me up.'

Lin sounded eager. 'He's the suspect then?'

Archie hesitated before answering. 'No...more a person of real interest and I don't want you doing anything that jeopardises our case or gets you into difficulty. Understand?' Lin nodded. 'Even if you think you've got everything tied up you haven't, not with him, so don't go near or he'll eat you alive.'

'Ha, you think?'

'I know. If you want proof, watch him in action on that TV programme. You'll see a professional politician at work and you'll know why I'm saying what I'm saying. Leave him be Lin. Now, we need to go.'

Archie walked to the door, Jasper trotting alongside him. Lin snatched up the paper, stuffed it into Sarah's hand and hissed. 'Brightwick's TV appearance, get me details.'

Archie had reached the door. 'I'll drop her back around four.'

'OK, thanks.' Sarah looked at Lin and mouthed. 'You'll get me into bloody trouble you will.' Then said aloud, 'If you're not back by nine the doors'll be bolted.'

'Yes Mum,' said Lin.

'Oh...hang on.' Archie took out his mobile. 'I've not got your number Sarah.'

'Lin's got it.'

'No phone Sarah, remember? I threw it away.'

Sarah sighed. 'Right.' She tore off a slip from the bar pad then tore that in two. 'I'll show you mine if you'll show me yours; mobile numbers that is.' She grinned at Archie as they swapped numbers.

Jasper whined in impatience at the delay and Archie looked at the terrier. 'And you, you just behave.' Jasper wagged his tail, grinned and barked just the once as Archie looked from dog to Lin. 'That goes for both of you.'

~

Pat's slow sweep of the room preceded her comment. 'Anyone heard from Archie yet?' Silence followed. 'Does anyone know where he is then?'

'When we left the bungalow he said he was off to collect the dog then go over to the hit-and-run site. That's the last we knew,' volunteered Dougie.

'Well we'll have to root him out soon. Chief Super's going barmy back there and this non-appearance lark is just making things worse...' Pat's warning was interrupted midstream as CS Campbell entered. 'Sir.'

'Is he here?'

'No Sir.'

'Then where?'

'Not sure Sir. We think out at the hit-and-run site...' she glanced round, 'where there's no signal.'

'Then you'll send a car to escort him back here Kershaw, and now.'

'Yes, Sir.'

'I've just had the CC on the phone to me for the second time today.' He noted the room's reaction. 'Yes, that's right, twice! He's had the Minister's private secretary onto him, a Mister Quinn, and the Justice Minister has also called me, in person. Both of them want to know why Lord Brightwick is being targeted by this department.'

'Targeted? I hardly think one visit can be classed as targeting anyone...'

'The Justice Minister's words not mine Kershaw, and you would do well to heed them! All of you!'

'Sir...'

'And it's more than one visit, you all know that.'

'We're investigating a double murder, one of them being a detective from this very department...' Pat could see she was off kilter as soon she started, and Campbell's stare was enough to check her.

'And you think I don't know that detective? I'm the one who faced his sister at the hospital!' The room reverberated with his volume then fell to silence. 'And now my direct superior, our boss, wants to know what's got into us when we treat a serving minister of the Crown as the prime suspect in the absence of anything tangible. We have been requested to cease targeting His Lordship and that is what we will do; understood?' Campbell began to leave. 'Now, get someone across to Arnold and tell him his future career in this force is at stake. I will not be placed in this intolerable position any longer, not by Arnold or anyone else!'

~

T he laptops, placed back to back on the Victorian bur oak writing desk in the private study, lit up the faces of Quinn and Brightwick, their broken conversation punctuated by the occasional click of a key. They stared at identical diary spreadsheets with the occasional peek over raised lids to make a point or underline a statement.

'...That may be difficult as you have the meeting with Lord Marstrand that lunchtime Sir.'

'Can we reschedule?'

'I'd advise against it Minister. His Lordship did support your wildlife bill and we've cancelled twice already.'

'Will it take long?'

'He wants to discuss the upcoming bill for the extension of licensing laws Sir, so...'

'Yes, yes, but I have to be back here at three to meet the Chinese Minister for Agriculture and Rural Affairs. My talks need to be completed with him prior to the arrival of other government members, that was the whole reason for getting him here early.'

'We could always swap the venue for your meeting with Lord Marstrand.'

'Where was it?'

'Members Room Sir.'

'Marstrand eats there every day.' Brightwick thought for a moment. 'Hmm...loves his food does Nigel...let's dangle a carrot. What about The Nut Tree? That will mean I can stay at home and do the meet there.'

'Just the two of you?' Brightwick nodded. 'I'll book an early table, say twelve-thirty? That'll give you plenty of time to salve his appetite and your conscience.'

'See to it.'

'Sir.' Scrolling silence was followed by Quinn's rapid typing. 'Have you had the final list for the Chinese visit Sir?'

'Willis has it.' Brightwick pressed the intercom button. 'Willis. In here if you will. Bring your laptop.'

A few seconds elapsed before Willis appeared, laptop balanced on extended arm. 'Minister?'

'The delegate list for the Chinese visit, you have it?'

'Yes, Sir...erm...' He placed his machine at right angles to those already decorating the desk. 'Ah, here.' He swivelled the laptop into their vision. 'Thirty-one in all Sir, including WAGS.'

Brightwick pointed at a name. 'Hua Furen? Remind me.'

'That's the wife of the Chinese Ambassador for Trade Sir, Pei Hua?'

'Ah, right...I'll need you on hand throughout Willis. I'll never remember all these names and titles.'

'Yes, Sir, of course.'

'And I understand we have all the banquet ingredients to hand now.'

Quinn nodded. 'We do Sir.'

'Good. Right. On to the Gov.UK agenda...' He looked up. 'You can go Willis.' Willis collected his laptop and left. 'What are the timings and where Quinn?'

'Studio A, at the Broadbrush Productions South facility.'

'They're in Oxford?'

'Yes, Sir. Banbury Road. The BBC outsource to them. The programme goes out live at nineteen hundred and runs for an hour. There's a truncated version which they use as part of the BBC Sunday Politics South show at twenty-one hundred the same evening, but with studio guests only, and a Q&A.'

'That'll not involve me will it?'

'No Sir, this is for the pundits to discuss.'

'Glad I'm out of it then. Last thing I want to be doing is to be sharing a platform with the trough-feeders.'

'Yes Sir. A car will collect you from the house at fourteen hundred...'

'That early?'

'Afraid so Sir. They need time to rehearse.'

'Rehearse what? It's a political panel show with a vetted and invited audience! Can they not get someone to stand in for me?'

'Afraid not. They did ask that all participants attend, something to do with the sighting of their fixed cameras, the lighting level and any make-up requirements.'

'Make-up! Oh, for God's sake...'

'A cross to be borne by all panel members I'm afraid Sir.'

Brightwick sighed in resignation. 'Who else will be on?'

'Confirmed are Hailey Cooper-Stern...'

'Just what I need, a fully-paid-up member of the Green Party-Cuddly Bunny brigade.'

'Yes, Sir, and Sir Reginald Bartley.'

'Another jumped-up union man riding on the gravy train of faux honours. Do they have no real people on these shows now?'

'Apart from yourself Sir? It would seem not.'

'Will I have anything pressing from the red boxes for the week-end?'

Quinn flicked though the electronic notepad on his phone. 'Er...you have the debate and vote on the third reading of the government's bill on housing on the Monday.'

'I'll be exhausted after the Sunday. I can be paired?'

'Yes, Sir. With the Member for Hailsham.'

'Fatty Chapman? Fine, see to it and I can stay at home. Is that all?'

'All that should concern you Sir.'

'Good.' Brightwick closed his laptop. 'Now, if we can dispense with diaries for the moment, I'd like to run through the likely questions coming up on the show, the ones Garland sent over for me.'

Quinn reached into a briefcase and took out a sheaf of papers. 'Good of him.'

'Yes, wasn't it? I expect my siding with the pharmaceutical industry will come under scrutiny from secondary questions and I need some strategies in order to deflect, particularly the licensing of D-Syne in the UK; that one could prove tricky. If anyone on the panel has done any diligent research they'll have linked the results from the US to it; last thing I want.'

'The bees.'

'Precisely, and with Mistral cooperating with the Chinese on their desire to license there could be awkwardness.'

'Do you think we can manipulate the session?'

'Let's see shall we.' Brightwick pressed the intercom button again. 'Willis!'

'Sir!'

'Get me Garland on the phone.'

~

Deserted now, crime scene no more, just a country lane facing November. Archie and Lin sat in snug silence wrapped in the heater's afterglow, their car parked in the space so recently occupied by the trysting couple, Allan and Turley. Several seconds passed, neither of them willing to break the moment, the only movement Arnold's rhythmic, silent chewing. It was Jasper, unsure of the lull's meaning, who fractured the moment with a whined yap, his head appearing through the gap between the front seats. Archie looked at Lin perched on the brown corduroy seat cushion.

'Was it even a little bit comfortable?'

'It was like riding one of those fairground bulls. You were lucky I didn't land in your lap when we turned off the main road, but apart from that, fine.'

'Sorry.' He turned to Jasper whose front paws were now balanced in line on the handbrake. 'Your bloody fault, you know that don't y'?' Jasper barked and slithered through, ending up with back paws on Archie's lap and his front paws on his chest, giving a lick in greeting. 'Jesus dog...get off!' Archie pushed the dog down gently, wiping his own mouth with the back of his hand. 'You only want the gum.'

'Cupboard love.'

'Yeah.' Archie sighed. 'Right, well we'd best get to it.' He brought up Pat's text and typed a short message. 'Just hope the signal is working.' He paused then the blip sounded. 'Bloody hell, will you look at that!' He turned the screen to Lin. 'It's gone!'

Lin read the text out loud. *'Thats a GO 4 Arnue.* All very cryptic.'

'Not really, just something that needed careful timing before being set in motion. Right, I just want to walk the space with Jasper if that's OK. Get my bearings and refresh.' The terrier reacted to Archie's movement and yapped again. 'Yes, you.' Archie clipped the lead on the dog and opened his door. Without waiting for the invite Jasper was out and at the extent of the lead in a trice. 'Summat tells me he needs to cock a leg.' The terrier immediately did so. 'Blimey, it's almost as if he does it to command, must've been bursting, poor chap. Once he's done and we've strolled a bit, I want us to go over to a farm building not far from here.'

'A building?'

'Yeah.'

'Why? Do you think it's connected?'

'In a way. Not the how, but I think it might have something to do with the why.' He smiled at Lin. 'Make yourself comfy.'

Lin watched them through the windscreen as they set off. He was, for all the world, a man out for a stroll with a dog that was intent on watering the entire woodland, but there was something in his manner, his scan of the surroundings that marked him out as totally tuned and balanced within the natural world. She had seen that ease of movement often enough in the bushmen she and Rene used to spend so much of their childhood with. *Only difference is he's white.* She smiled at Jasper now trotting alongside him on a loose lead, peeing every now and then, relaxed in his company. *Made for each other if ever two creatures were...*

On the lane, Arnold's phone blipped an incoming. *Cho&co onit. Car4u2HQ. CS command/demand. Comply? P*

Arnold typed *NFC,* hit the send button, closed the connection and looked down at Jasper. 'You and me we're in the shit Jasp.' Jasper yapped the once. 'Yeah, fuckit. Hung for a sheep as a lamb eh?' He switched the phone to silent then shut it down. 'Belt-and-braces, eh Jasp...'

~

Phil Grainger lifted his head above the computer screen. 'Is Arnue about?'

Mary looked across. 'Out...on an errand.'

'Oh, right... Where on an errand?'

Marissa slalomed over on her wheeled swivel chair. 'Jesus Phil, why don't you shout a bit louder, I don't think the Chief Super can hear you!'

'What? I only asked...'

'Where Arnue was! We know, we heard.'

'Well?'

'He's away with a search team, were you not at the briefing?'

'Which briefing?'

'The one in the staff locker room.'

'No, I was in records doing my job... Since when do we do briefings in the staff locker room?'

Marissa looked across at Deborah. 'Does he work here?'

'Who?'

'Him!' Marissa dropped her voice a little lower. 'Arnue's over to Brightwick's place, search and destroy mission.'

'Oh, yeah, now I get it.'

Marissa called across, 'He gets it now.'

Debbie spoke without raising her head. 'There's clever.'

Pat entered the room. 'By your beds, Chief Super's on his way, let me do the talk...' Pat closed down as CS Campbell entered.

'Do I have Arnold yet?'

'Car's on its way to escort him now Sir.'

'And he's still off range?'

''Fraid so. We've tried several times, but it keeps coming up unobtainable. Must be the tree cover.'

'This is just ridiculous. Does he not have a car radio?'

'Yes, Sir, but if he's not with his car...'

'Don't get facetious Kershaw, you're not out of the woods yet either...' He glanced round the room, 'None of you are.' He turned on his heel. 'Arnold to see me the second he walks through that door, understood?'

'Yes, Sir,' answered the room.

Pat addressed the crew. 'We just have to assume all is as it should be with Arnue and that Campbell really is as far out of the loop as he seems.'

'As usual.' Marissa wheeled herself back to her desk. 'Can we keep it up?'

Pat sighed. 'Case of having to. I just wonder how fast Brightwick will be on to the CS when he discovers Arnue on site. He'll call a halt as soon as he hears, you know that don't you?'

'Then we have to hope Cho kicks ass before our CS starts kissing it.'

Pat glanced at her computer screen. 'I've texted Archie and he's refused his consent, but with that car on the way I reckon we've got an hour, hour and a half at best to find some watertight positives before his meet with the CS, Archie will be relying on it.'

Phil shrugged. 'We need some stuff on Lamb; still no news?'

'Not a peep.' Marissa sighed. 'It's like he's vanished off the face of the earth.'

~

Like a water shrew that has had one stone shifted out of line from its stream-crossing pathway, creatures of habit dislike rearrangement; those reliant on a certain order of things bridle when others dictate placement. In human terms, many a war has found its beginnings in the kitchens of plenty.

The arrival of the paraphernalia, that preceded the arrival of the cooking professionals, that preceded the arrival of the selected guests at Bliss Bank Hall was seen, by Gemma Connor, as the first skirmish in a war she was never going to win, but she was prepared to fight a rear-guard action. To have her kitchen layout usurped by the stainless steel of modernism was one thing, but the rough handling of her wooden, scrub-top table out of the kitchen and into its anteroom really was the last straw.

Gemma stood her ground across the doorway and the two men had no choice but to put the table down and hear her out.

'No, I'm sorry but that won't do. Move it about yes, but I want it here, in the main kitchen. I still have meals to prepare until tomorrow and I'm damned if I'm going to be shoved out of my own kitchen to work in a corridor; this is not acceptable.' Gemma folded her arms, resolution dressing her face.

'Please, Mrs Connor...'

'Miss.'

'I apologise Miss Connor.' Armand, the kitchen arranger, flipped onto the plan on his MacBook. 'Here. This is what I have as layout. Look.' Gemma did so. 'Do you see space for your table?'

'No Armand...it is Armand isn't it?'

'Armand, yes.'

'No, there isn't a space for my table, but that still doesn't help me with the day-to-day feeding of this household until your chef de cuisine turns up full of position and empty of patience.'

'I can't help Miss Connor, I've only this plan...'

'The last time your man came here there was none of this. There was a willingness to accommodate the house needs.'

'This is a much bigger deal. Huge. That's why the day early, why it's me. Some of these foods need twelve hours to make. Chef will want all time and all room. Six sous chef and direct cook support too; we need the room; please...'

'Is there a problem?' Quinn had entered the kitchen.

Armand attempted to cover. 'No...'

Gemma stamped on it. 'Yes Mister Quinn there is. How am I supposed to run the house and staff meals if I'm banished to a corridor by this...this intruder!'

Quinn raised his eyebrows. 'Intruder? Connor...this gentleman is heading the preparatory group for the reception here that carries enough weight to bury us all should we get it wrong. Whatever is required see he gets it.'

'But...'

'No Connor, I will not have his efforts compromised because you want to make scones!' Quinn walked round the table to the doorway of the anteroom and flicked a quick glance at it. 'This looks to be plenty of room for your needs. If you feel it's not, then I suggest it will be you who informs the Minister that he and the house staff will be dining on take-outs.'

Gemma looked hard at Quinn before replying. 'Very well Mister Quinn. I'll make do with the space and bake smaller scones.' She turned and left the highly embarrassed Armand, brushing past Quinn as she entered the anteroom and closed the door.

Quinn smiled. 'Women...no ability to improvise have they?'

Armand, taken aback by the exchange, smiled nervously. 'Erm...Mister Quinn Sir, I hope I've not put Miss Connor into trouble.'

'No more than she has herself.' Quinn saw the puzzled look. 'Nothing to do with this or you...' Willis entered at a gallop, using the kitchen door frame as a brake. 'Yes Willis?'

'Sir, the Minister wants you...now.' He threw a glance at Armand, fixed Quinn with a stare and dropped the level of his voice. 'Some police are here...lots of them, with a warrant, and they're searching the grounds Sir.'

~

When Archie drew up to the woodland edge Jasper barked in readiness. Lin on the other hand was unsure.

'Is this it?'

Archie checked the segment of OS map on his mobile. 'Yup. We're here.'

'Where's here?'

'Through there, in through those Quercus...those red oaks.'

'Certain?'

'According to the map, but there's only one way to find out.' Archie clipped Jasper's lead to the collar again and opened his door. 'Let's go.' Stepping a short way along the road they reached an opening in the woodland's hedge and Archie drifted a little past it before moving back to Lin. 'This verge looks like an airport runway. Look at those depressions all along there, and this track's been well used.'

'Popular place.'

'Very. Why?'

'Couples having ubulili?'

'Ha! I know what you mean, I think, but, all these tracks? I think not. These tyre marks have been made by off-roaders, and I'm not talking scruffy Land Rovers either.'

'Well we know Lord Shit-Stain likes shooting things round here, don't we?'

'Too early in the year, they'll not start 'til late November early December I'll bet. No, this is a recently used entrance to gain access to that building for sure. Come on.'

With the indomitable Jasper leading the way Lin followed Archie as they entered the woodland via a long, narrow but definable track. Deep into the wood at the track's end a closed five-bar gate led into a wide, blue-bricked yard with a low building at its far end, the walls coloured a dark shade of history, its roof slate-tiled and moss-pocked. The first thing that struck Archie was that, as out-of-the-way and as unprepossessing as this building was, for some reason, someone had cared for it. Cared enough to clear the yard of its scrub growth and weeds... but not enough to cut back the overhanging tree branches that part concealed it from outside view. Enough to make sure the wooden door worked on oiled hinges...yet not enough to clean the windows. At this door Jasper yipped once then scratched at its frame before backing up and yapping again, tongue and tail wagging. Archie paused and turned to Lin. 'Can you hear something?'

Lin listened to the silence for a few seconds before shaking her head. 'No, can you?'

'I'm sure there's a crime being committed in there...I mean there's that busted padlock for starters.'

Lin saw the closed lock on the door's bolt. 'What busted lock? It looks OK to me.'

'Wait here.' Archie handed the lead to Lin and walked back down the track. After a few minutes he returned with the wheel-nut spanner from the car. Slipping the screwdriver end in between the lock and bolt he leant savagely onto it, parting the ironwork from the frame. 'That busted lock.'

Lin almost laughed. 'OK, but just to be sure, what happens if we're found in there?'

'Nothing. I'm the police in pursuance of a suspected crime. Anyhow, I reckon there'll be enough going on up at the big house to keep most folk busy right now.' Archie clicked the latch and the door surrendered.

'How do you know that?'

No answer came from Archie, he was too interested in Jasper's reaction to the opening of the door. 'There's something amiss here Lin. Look at him.' Lin looked down at Jasper who had taken another couple of steps backwards as the inside air rushed through the open door to greet them. Then Archie, too, took a step back. 'Bloody hell... Someone's been heavy-handed with the cleaning fluid in there.' He exchanged old gum for new and offered one to Lin. 'You might be glad of it.'

'I think I will.' She slipped the gum into her mouth and they entered the building's single room.

It was divided into two separate half-walled sections, both of them square with a concrete floor and serviceable, floor-mounted stone trough running along the rear wall. Archie nodded at them. 'Feed troughs; these are old pigsties.' He pointed to a low metal bar running along the side wall of each enclosure. 'Heaven-bar. Keeps the sow from crushing the piglets when she lies down or rolls over. See the gap in the middle?' Lin nodded. 'That's where they section them off.' He stood at the low wooden gate that opened onto the first sty and glanced around. 'Not been used for pigs for years so, why so clean?'

The smell of the cleansing fluid was all-pervading, and it took Archie and Lin several seconds to acclimatise. Jasper on the other hand had soon cancelled out the stench, discarding it to the periphery of his senses. Now he homed in on those background odours, the faint scents secreted within the building's surfaces that would tell a tale. Archie felt the tightening of the lead and unclipped the terrier. Opening the gate he spoke quietly. 'Off you go then Jasp, get on!'

The terrier scuttled away, inhaling the aromas that laid out a story despite the attempts of secrecy-by-hygiene. Archie followed him, beginning a careful inspection, using his own primary sense in order to piece together the building's secrets. Lin watched him from the door, something akin to a physical barrier denying entry. She shuddered, not knowing why.

All was scrubbed, all was clean, but just as dew-draped cobwebs shine in the sun the odd deep gouges that no amount of scrubbing could hide showed up on the front of the troughs. Archie bent to gain a better view of the marks. 'These're new, scrubbed with a vengeance by the looks.' It was then he noticed Jasper.

The terrier had nosed his way round the pen then re-circled to the wall containing the door. Nose buried deep in the scour between doorpost and floor Jasper huffed and snorted, every now and then pulling back to decompress his nose and instigate a paw search.

'What's he found?'

'Not sure. Jasper. Jasp? What you got, eh?' The terrier dropped onto front paws and fixed the gap with a stare. Archie went on hands and knees alongside the dog. 'What? In there?' He bent low, folding back the quiff, and peered in. 'There's summat in there.' Archie leant back and pulled the spanner from his pocket. He tried it in the gap, but it was too narrow. 'Is there a stick about, something thin?'

Lin left the sty and rummaged around the space. 'There's this.' She held up a short piece of electricity cable. 'Will this do?'

Archie took it. 'Yeah perfect...' then he stared at it. 'Where'd you find this?'

'Over there, on the floor by the door.'

Archie turned it over in his hand. 'This looks very new.' He looked at the wires contained within the outer sheath. 'Brown and blue. This is up to date wiring, post two thousand and six and definitely out of kilter with the building.' He considered out loud, 'Fresh-out-the-box cabling.' He looked at the door. 'And the hinges are new and greased... Odd thing to replace in an unused plot like this, wiring. And hinges, they're usually a rat's nest of baler twine.' He switched his concentration back to Jasper whose gaze was still fixed to the gap. 'Right fella, let a dog see the rabbit.' Archie stripped back the outer grey casing with his teeth to expose the inner wiring then bent back two of the wires. Sliding the single remaining wire into the gap Archie windscreen-wiped the space and flicked out an off-white object. Jasper dabbed at it. 'Leave that Jasp!' The dog hesitated long enough for Archie to pick it up.

'What is it?'

After a long stare, during which he twirled the object round, Archie shook his head and sighed. 'Jeez... It's a tooth Lin, a front canine...a dog's I think.' He inspected further. 'Not a puppy tooth, an adult one.' He stood and looked back at the scratched trough front, the thought process on his face clearly visible. He motioned around the sty with his hand. 'And this, if I'm not much mistaken, is the crime scene.'

'What, someone hit a dog and knocked a tooth out?'

'Not a person, another dog.'

'What, it got into a fight you mean...?' Realisation glimmered, 'Oh, bloody hell...is this a dog fight venue?'

Archie nodded and sighed. 'The main suspects have got form Lin, so why not?' He scanned the room slowly, speaking as he turned around. 'This is Lamb's doing, got to be. He's got previous and the signs of a clean-up are clear. Can Brightwick not have known about this? I mean, I can't believe a bloke that's got his thumb on the throat of politics and a team to keep him abreast of all the little nuances in his life knows nothing about this...' Jasper stood on his hind legs and put his front paws on Archie's knee, it was the contact that triggered the thought. 'Oh shit! The dog!'

'The one with the missing tooth?'

'No, no, the one they found at Phillips' place! The RSPCA said they'd have to put it down 'cos it was a dangerous breed. This is them, they've got breeding stock!' Archie pulled his mobile from his pocket, fired it up and opened the screen in preparation to make a call. The vibrations came thick and fast. 'Fuck.' He turned the phone so Lin could see the list of eleven missed calls and six texts. He looked down at the terrier. 'I told you we were in trouble.' He turned the sound back on and keyed in the saved number. 'Got a signal... Hello? Yes, you can. This is DCI Archie Arnold, Northants and Beds police. You had a dog, a puppy, brought in by one of my officers ... DC Brand, yes. There was talk of the dog being classed as a dangerous breed and having to be put down, that's not happened yet has it? Good, I need to see it ... yes, so you'll have to keep it there. When I'm done you can keep it on and re-home it...' Archie looked at Lin and rolled his eyes as he listened and repeated the salient words. 'Overstocked ... legal reasons ... responsibility to the rules of the charity...' He held up his hand. 'No, OK, I get the point, no ... Right, but this is police business, so ... Yes, it's evidence ... OK, put mine down for it. Yes, DCI Arnold. Keep it there until you hear from me next ... I'm a serving police officer, that should be enough surely ... hello...? Shit, signal's gone.' He gave the phone a hard stare and looked at Lin, 'Have you still got that gum wrapper?'

'Yes, here.' Lin took the crumpled silver paper out of her pocket and gave it to Archie who enclosed the tooth before pocketing it.

'Jay's gonna love me.'

'Why?'

'Never mind.' He bent to the terrier. 'You're a bit too clever for your own good, you know that?' He scrubbed the dog's ears. 'Good lad Jasp, good find.' Archie opened the gate and allowed the terrier out then opened the second sty. 'Have a sniff. Get on. Just cast a glance in that sectioned-off space will you Lin, see what's what?' Jasper and Archie entered the second sty where the metal bar showed distinct signs of recent abrasion along its length. Jasper returned to his side. 'Nothing, eh? Lin! Anything?'

Lin called out. 'You might want a look yourself.'

In the room were all the signs of hurried deconstruction. Shelf supports, clean painted and cobweb free, were denuded of shelves, a sizeable hole went through the wall and the floor, in all this seeming destruction, was spotless. Archie looked around. 'Blimey. This has got all the marks of having been some set up. Look at that outline on the wall. Some sort of heater been fixed there at one time...' He looked back into the sty area. 'Home comforts for an audience to the bloodletting; Christ, what a way to get your kicks, bastards. Abbot Amalric had it right, "Kill 'em all, let God sort 'em out", or something like that. But, as the abbot's not about, that means it's up to me.'

Lin was paused in thought. 'Hang on...' She went back into the main space followed by Archie and Jasper. 'These light fittings above us, and that wiring in there...what powered them? I mean, I doubt there's mains electric laid on out here is there?'

'No, good point. A generator?' He walked to the door. 'Let's see...'

Out in the yard the trio walked along the wall then round to the rear of the building, Lin and Archie looking for signs, Jasper looking for sport. Archie indicated the hole in the wall. 'This is the other side of that alcove...' A cursory glance revealed the marks where a draw bar had been dropped onto the blue-brick floor. 'Generator, sizeable one probably, brought here by a tractor, unhooked there, stood here...see?' Archie inspected the wall. 'Here, look.' He rubbed the wall with his hand and showed Lin the staining. 'Exhaust ash, so most likely facing that way...' His mobile notified another incoming text. 'Fuckit...' Archie ignored its summons and continued to look around the yard.

The repeat came and Lin prompted him. 'You not going to answer that?'

'No need, I know who it is.'

'Could be important.'

Archie sighed, 'Right.' He opened the phone. 'Oh no, good news. It's from that Scottish fella who did for those Irish blokes... That sounded a bit blunt.'

'Not a bit of it. Thank him from me will you? Why's he calling?'

'I got in touch earlier, to see how he was.'

'Oh, good. What's his name?'

'Jardine, Kenzie Jardine.'

'It was his dog got killed?'

'Shot, yeah, and apparently minus a leg but plus a life.'

'Even better news then.'

Archie tapped out a reply and sent the text. As they retraced their steps he mulled things over out loud. 'Well, I've seen enough here to qualify for another warrant. All that effort for no pigs, this has gotta be Lamb...' The growl from Jasper as they walked back round the building and into the courtyard alerted them all and they followed the dog's throaty gaze to the yard's entrance as Archie put a hand on the terrier's collar and took out the lead. 'Steady now lad.' Seconds later estate Head Keeper Adderton walked into the yard, halting at its threshold. 'Mister Adderton.' Archie raised a hand in greeting, Jasper raised his hackles.

'What's happenin' here then?'

'Just following up on our enquiries, the hit-and-run?'

Adderton cast a wary glance round. 'Here?'

'I know, seems strange, but yes, here also.'

'Does His Lordship know?'

Archie clipped the lead onto Jasper's collar then pressed his hand against the spanner nestling insecurely in his back pocket. 'I'm not sure...possibly.'

'You got a warrant?'

'Yes, we used one in the woodland remember?'

'A warrant for here I mean, all sites need a separate warrant.'

'Know your law then.'

'I'm a keeper, I have to, so, have you got one?'

'Not at present.'

'I see. That your car parked on the lane back there?'

'It is.'

'Then I suggest you clear off in it until you've sorted the paperwork. These are private grounds belonging to His Lordship, I think you know that. Any uninvited visits only serve to make the pheasants nervous, me too.' He turned sideways and swept a hand at the gateway. 'So until that all-important warrant's obtained I'd be grateful for your absence.'

'Yes fine, just going.' Archie flicked the lead. 'Let's go.'

Lin followed Archie, and as they approached Adderton, so Jasper's growl increased in volume and depth, sufficient to make the keeper take a step away as they passed him. 'Hasn't got any more friendly has he?'

'Depends on who he's supposed to be friends with.' As they walked through the gate Adderton took out his mobile and Archie added helpfully. 'Signal's a bit iffy round here.'

'Really.'

'Yeah,' replied Archie. 'At least, that's my story and I'm sticking to it.'

Along the path both Lin and Archie were acutely aware of Addison's stare boring into their backs and heard his fading voice. 'Hallo, Willis? Adderton here. Put me on to Mister Quinn will y'...'

Archie took Lin's arm and quickened his pace as he leant towards her. 'Bit of distance between us and him would be good; that padlock.'

Lin fell in step. 'Good point.' Up ahead a siren sounded. 'The cavalry's here.'

Archie smiled. 'Not the cavalry Lin, that's the arrival of the Plains Indians and this is my Little Big Horn.'

~

Cashman shifted his weight slightly, not from discomfort just from his lack of familiarity concerning life with a missing limb.

'He's gettin' ready for home love, and a bit of dinner maybe.'

Faye smiled at Kenzie. 'You're getting bored of my company you mean.'

'Not a bit of it, no...but you've been here a couple of hours. I'll bet you've enough waiting back home without wasting time on me.'

'Don't be a martyr.'

'A tom-ata you mean.' They both smiled. 'No seriously hen, I'm fine. Healin' well. Nurse Ratched says they're looking to discharge me by next weekend, then you'll have me back home and sick of the sight of me in no time.'

Faye rested a hand on his. 'Never sick of y' Kenzie Jardine.' She looked at the wall clock. 'Right, well if y' want rid I'll be off... oh, I dropped a text to the police in Northampton, their detective there, Arnold?'

'What about?'

'That other detective who came to see you, Arnue Cho. When he was here, he said his boss would like to know how things were going along, left me the number so I let him know. He texted back and said he'd like to meet when you feel up to it.'

'Where, here?'

'Yeah. He said he was due a holiday.'

'Right. Well that'd be good, put a face to a name.' Faye stood and Cash rose easily to his three feet. 'You look after Mum Cash, hear me?'

Cash barked once. 'He will. Getting on famously with it all he is, loves all the attention, and the fuss at the vets too.'

'When's he back in?'

'Monday. They're taking out half the stitches in his shoulder and all the ones in his ear and top lip. He'll be glad to see 'em gone I'm sure.'

'Aye...'

Faye picked up on the tone and sat again. 'What's up Ken?'

'Eh? Nothing hen, just...'

'What?'

'I keep thinking about how different it all could've been but for him.' Kenzie took Faye's hand. 'All of this, y'know?' He nodded at Cashman stood by the chair, eyes expectant, tail more so.

'I do, you've no need to convince me.'

'I really thought I'd lost him Faye, even said my goodbyes in head and heart. Plays on my mind does that, pains me.'

'What?'

Kenzie tapped his chest. 'Right here.'

'And what? You'd rather he'd have died there, on that road?'

''Course not, no. It's just...oh, I don't know what it is.'

'Try. Tell me.'

Kenzie stared at the dog for several seconds before squeezing Faye's hand and letting it go. 'Nothing.'

'No, that's not going to work Kay-Jay, not this time.' She retook his hand. 'Now, you tell me what's going on in that pea whizzing round the vacuum that's the inside of your head.'

Kenzie could see her determination and began speaking slowly. 'I know what it's gonna feel like...when he goes I mean, and I don't wanna face it, not again.'

'Oh Kenzie...' Faye placed her palm to his cheek and she felt the weight of him as he sought the contact. She thought for a long time before speaking. 'Then what you do is make whatever time he's got left with us mean something, and that means you getting well and him getting back to saving the lives of other puppies. The chance he gives them, that'll be his legacy.'

'Yeah. I know you're right, I just...' Kenzie closed down. All he could do was stare at Cash.

Faye worked at lifting the mood. 'You can see how well he's managing. This is just a little setback, you'll see.' She removed her hand and stood again. 'Now, no more morbid thoughts or you'll give him a complex.' Cashman barked again at this sudden flurry of activity. 'See, raring to go.'

Kenzie smiled. 'Aye, he is that. Good lad Cash.' He held out his hand and Cashman nuzzled it before sitting back on his haunches, then with immaculate balance the dog reared slightly and put his one front paw onto the bed before releasing a tongue. Sister O'Faoilan chose this very moment to enter the room.

'Now what have I told you? This is no way to behave. Trouble so you are.' She approached the bed and brushed at Cashman's paw. 'Off now y' devil an' take that grin with y'.' The spaniel dropped easily to the floor and stood looking up at the sister. Kenzie saw it and recognised both the look and stance.

'Have you been feeding him titbits Sister?'

'I have not!' She smiled at Faye. 'He's lookin' better wouldn't y' say Mrs Jardine? Y' man, not the dog.'

'Yes I would, and all thanks to you Sister.'

'Me and a few of the doctors. Mind, it's been a battle at times. Doesn't take to being ordered about very well does he?'

'He can be tricky, yes.'

'Not too old for a smack Mrs Jardine, none of them are, remember that. I come from a family of five brothers, leave him with me a fortnight and I'll send you back a changed man.' Faye laughed at the thought. 'But indeed, I do detect a little healthy colour in those cheeks, although that could just be down to embarrassment at being found once more enticing this poor animal onto the bed.'

'Is there a chance he'll be home next weekend?'

'There is providing he behaves and the wounds carry on their good work. Him and that dog of his.'

'We can hear you Sister, we're both in the room, remember?'

Sister O'Faolian dismissed Kenzie's comment with a wave of her hand. 'We're talking about y' not to y'.'

Cashman still had his gaze fixed on the sister and Kenzie smiled. 'Bit of something nice was it, the bribes?'

'None of your concern Mister Jardine. Now, visiting times are nearly up and I'm sure Mrs Jardine has enough concerns on her mind than to be frettin' about your sorry backside.'

'I'll have you know I'm a saint to her, just ask!'

'I will when we're alone, then I'll have the truth of it. Now enough. Mrs Jardine, I'll walk yourself and that mobile fleabag out the building, we'll take a short cut by the kitchens...' she turned to Kenzie, 'It's liver tonight.'

~

Arnue walked along the row of empty kennels, stopping at one and pushing open the unlocked door, causing it to swing away and bang against the inner wall. *All this for no dogs? Doesn't make sense.*

A sergeant and a constable exited the large tractor barn and, after another look along the kennels, Arnue joined them. 'Anything?'

The sergeant shook his head. 'No. Spotless. Not a thing out of place...odd for a farm shed. Everything put away, nothing on the floor, no oil stains or leftovers. Spotless.'

'Just like these kennels.' Arnue cast a glance around the yard. 'Like everything here.' He pointed to the chain-link-fenced concrete yard. 'We been into there?'

'No Sir. It's just a yard and even from this distance we can see there isn't a Range Rover in it. It looks like everywhere else looks round here...'

'Spotless. Yeah.' Arnue shook his head. 'I've heard of tidy but this? Nothing in the other outbuildings?'

'No Sir. Everyone else has come up blank as well.'

'Right. Well...' Arnue stopped as a Jeep pulled into the yard. Willis stepped out of it, mobile phone in hand.

'Are you Detective Cho?' Arnue nodded. 'I have your Chief Superintendent, James Campbell, on the phone, he wants a word.' He held out the mobile.

After a long look at Willis, Arnue took it and answered slowly, 'Hello? ... It is, yes, Sir...'

~

⁶I thought it was me in trouble when I saw the cop car pull in, so did Mum. Where's your date gone?'

Lin smiled at Sarah. 'Taken back to his HQ, I think he's the one might be in a bit of trouble, and he's not my date.'

'What for? He's doing his job isn't he?'

'Far as I can tell, yes.'

Sarah nodded at Jasper. 'I see he's not completely lost it though?'

'What?

'Left you the dog.' Sarah bent down to stroke the terrier and Jasper half lifted a lip. Sarah withdrew her hand. 'Nothing changed with him while you were away then, still a little shit.'

'Just a bit distrustful really, you can't blame him, can you?'

'I can. I've taken you both in off the streets.' Sarah walked behind the bar muttering as she went, 'The least he could do is offer a paw.'

Lin looked round the empty room. 'Quiet again.'

'Yeah, probably the curse of you.' She laughed and began to rearrange the stock of spirits on the mirrored back of the bar. 'Oh, Mum wants a word, something about whether you'd like to help out this evening.'

'In here?'

'Quiz night tonight, always a good few for that.'

'Well then, yeah, sure. Behind the bar you mean?'

'If you're up for it. I'll give you a quick rundown on how things work, although the amount of time you've spent in here...'

'Drinking's different from serving, so I'm told.'

'A little, yes. So, you'll do it?'

'Yeah, sure.'

'Good, Vaz and crew will likely turn out, be good for you to see them.'

'From the dark side this time though.'

'Now you'll know what I have to put up with. Right, given your recent past we'll need to make it legal...'

'Ha! Hysterical, really funny.'

'Go and have a chat with Mum and put the paperwork in place. She's upstairs.'

As Lin moved behind the bar and towards a set of stairs leading up to the pub's living quarters, she picked up the local paper. 'Did you manage to find out anything else about this Gov. UK bullshit?'

'I looked on my laptop. Only confirms what's already in there. Time, date, place. There was a bit about it on the local news too, but that's it, read it yourself.'

'Can't be arsed.' Lin dropped the paper back and strolled nonchalantly the final few paces to the foot of the stairs then paused. 'Oxford's what, twenty-five, thirty miles from here?'

Sarah looked up from her sorting. 'What...? Erm, yeah, about forty minutes away, bit less maybe; why...?'

'Nothing. Just wondered.'

'Thinking of going to university are you?'

'Funnier and funnier... No, just idle curiosity.'

'And it killed the cat. You've been there often enough, why ask?'

'Not that often, lack of transport and lack of money, things may have altered since.'

Sarah almost laughed. 'Not the distance, it's still forty minutes. Now, are you going to see Mum or not?'

'Yes yes. There's not a deadline is there?'

'There is as far as Mum's concerned. She saw you pull up.'

'Yeah OK, going. She'll not be cross will she, with all this?' Lin started up the stairs as Sarah's voice followed her.

'With you? Now there is funny.' Sarah listened to Lin's footsteps before going back to bottle re-arrangement. After a few seconds she picked up the newspaper, ostensibly to discard it...

~

The rise and fall of muffled conversation drifted smoke-like down the short corridor stretching from CS James Campbell's office to Incident Room Two. No words were decipherable, but the timbre of the conversation, rising and falling in volume, was easily discernible. The vigorous exchange had begun almost as soon as Archie had crossed the threshold, kicking off with a firm and well enunciated, 'Close the door Arnold.' The discussion had been relentless ever since and every now and then the hum of dialogue reached a crescendo, sending a Mexican wave of anxious looks around the concentrated faces of the incident team. It was into this tense and silent gathering of detectives that DC Cho entered. He listened before finally speaking.

'That Archie in there?' Nods gave confirmation. 'How long's he been back?'

Pat looked at her watch. 'Twenty minutes?'

'How long in there?'

'Nineteen minutes fifty-five seconds?'

'Wow... Right. You'll all have heard then, about my recall?'

Dougie left the eavesdropping group and moved back to his desk. 'We did. CS came down here demanding to know who'd organised it. We all played shtum, but he knew anyway. I think you may be next up, after Mary.'

'How'd the CS hear?'

'Brightwick, had to be, and must have been on his private line 'cos it didn't go through the switchboard, they'd 'ave given us a heads-up. He came down here like Taz, never seen him so animated. I really thought he was going to explode, after sacking us all that is.'

'Wow.'

Mary joined them. 'Yeah, wow.'

'And you and me next then.'

'He'll want a debrief with you both if nothing else.' Pat moved across to them. 'Just stick to the lines, both of you; Archie's taking the brunt. We think he'll be lucky to escape this one entire, very lucky.'

'What, like suspended you mean?' said Arnue.

'Possibly by his goolies. When Dougie says the CS was animated he wasn't kidding. Came in here roarin' about Archie breaking into some premises, violating yet another search warrant legality; he snapped off a padlock apparently.'

'What, Archie did?'

'Well, he was there and there was a busted padlock, so...'

'Christ. If that's true what'll happen to us?'

'I reckon it'll be a reprimand, nothing more. You know Archie, the only thing he got to say before he was whisked in there was, "Tell Arnue and Mary they're not to fret and to give it straight". My guess is, right now, he's shouldering the blame for the lot.'

'Is there nothing we can do?'

Dougie laughed. 'Huh... No Mary, not unless we all want to commit group hara-kiri...sorry, that may have sounded a bit racist Arnue.'

'Not a bit, it's Japanese.'

'That's a relief. No, Archie will tough it out and we'll let him.'

The door opened and voices reached them. '...And that means now Arnold; with immediate effect.'

'Yes, Sir.'

Archie closed the door and began to walk down the short corridor to the incident room, his approach causing human confetti as the team dispersed to desks and peripherals, all busy in their aimless shuffling of embarrassment. Archie's expression was fixed as he walked past the team to his sectioned-off desk and began to empty the middle drawer into a plastic carrier bag taken from the bin. This action caused an audible in-breath from the room as gradually, one by one, his team gathered. It was Pat who opened the inquest.

'So?'

Archie looked up before continuing his desk clearance. 'So what?'

'What happened in there?'

'Blood bath.'

'Why're you emptying your desk drawers?'

'Suspended, oh, and call off the watch teams at the Red Lion too.'

'You what?' 'Jesus...' 'Bastard...' 'Suspended?' came from the collective.

'Suspended? For how long?' asked Dougie.

'A month, while the internal goes on.'

Mary kicked off. 'Internal! The mealy-mouthed, lickspittle of an excuse... F' fuck's sake Archie, is there nothing we can do?'

'Mary...' Archie paused. 'Thank you for your thoughts on the matter, but I've got you into enough trouble already; Campbell said he's got a couple of phone calls to make...'

'I wonder who to?'

'...A couple of phone calls to make, then I do believe you're in Mary, swiftly followed by Arnue. I'd be very careful what you say, true though it may be. As far as he's concerned you were both following a direct order. Arnue, you protested against it, the search went ahead, I overrode your concerns; Mary, you were under the direct control of your superior officer.'

'Jesus, Archie...'

'But what about the results from your searches in the building, the dog stuff?'

'Broken into, invalid.'

Arnue's eyes were wide. 'So you did?'

'Yup. Makes no odds now anyhow. All cancelled. Harassment.'

'I should never have gone round there...I knew it. When the help came at me with the phone, I knew I was in the wrong place.'

Archie stopped packing. 'You did the right thing Arnue, you and Mary followed a direct order. That's what I told Campbell and it's what you'll both tell him as well when he asks...which he will and very shortly; understood? Mary? Arnue? Understood?' They both nodded. 'Good. It won't clear you of everything just most of it, and I'm really sorry to have caused this. And the rest of you? As far as both the CS and the CC are concerned, I'm the guilty party and the matter of the murders of DC Reeve and Renata Lea were solved when our Scottish friend shot those two Irish lads.'

'That's bollocks for a start...!'

'Mary...' Archie sighed. 'Look...I've been officially informed by our commanding officer that the investigation is to close down. I'm telling you lot the same and I'm sure he'll underline it.' Then his tone changed slightly. 'Should you choose not to do that, choose to make further discreet enquiries, then that's your prerogative, I have no control over that as I'm no longer your immediate superior.' Archie placed the carrier bag onto his desk before picking up a notebook and a full A4 file, popping them into the bag before smiling at them. 'Just some retirement reading.'

With that Archie left, the team parting at the doorway to allow him a dignified exit.

Saturday

Lin leant against the bar, phone in one hand glass cloth in the other. 'Jenni? Hi, it's Lin...'

'Oh goodness, Lin, I've just been thinking about you, haven't seen you in ages.'

'Yeah, long time. Sorry, been a bit tied up. You'll have heard then, about Rene?'

'Yes I did. I did try and ring but got no reply, is your phone broken?'

'Something like that... Long story Jen.'

'I'm just so sorry Lin; bit late now, but if there's anything I can do...'

'Not late Jen, I know you've got a life that's permanently on fast forward, but...there may be something you can do for me. Are you busy this weekend?'

'Er, no. We're still in dry rehearsals so make-up's the last thing on their mind. I'm not needed until test shooting starts. Why?'

'Rather not say over the phone. Can I call round?'

'Yeah. When?'

'Tomorrow afternoon?'

'Oh... Yeah, sure. What time?'

'I've got to ask the boss here, but about three I'd think.'

'The boss?'

'Well, Sarah.'

'Who, Wilmott you mean? At the Red Lion? That Sarah?'

'The very same.'

'You're working there? Since when?'

'Like I said Jen, long story.'

'Then I'll want to hear all about that as well.'

'Right. Three o' clock it is.'

'*Yup. Bye Lin.*'

Lin replaced the handset and wiped up the few straggler glasses from the previous night as Sarah appeared from the stairway. 'Who were you talking to?'

'No one...myself, I wanted an intelligent conversation.'

'Ha!'

'No, just getting some things straight in my head, y'know?'

Sarah laughed. 'Take more than a conversation with yourself to do that. You'd need a dozen shrinks for that job.'

'Thanks. With a friend like you... No wonder I've got low self-esteem.'

'You'll thank me for it one day. Demotivation means you don't try so you don't fail.' Sarah smiled at Lin. 'About last night...'

'Yeah?'

'You did really well. Mum was mightily impressed, says the increase in takings was all down to you...mind you, I think she'd be mightily impressed if all you did was turn up.'

'Stop it Sarah. She loves you too, you know she does. You just say these things to wind me up.'

'Next time you see her, ask. I swear if you torched the place she'd blame the match company.'

'Yeah right.' Lin picked up another glass and began to wipe. 'Sarah, can I ask a favour?'

'You want Mum to adopt you?'

'No! I could just use a little time off, if that's OK?'

'Time off! You've hardly been here ten seconds and here you are wanting a break from it all. I thought you were strong?'

'Aroma not ability. No, I want to go and see a friend, let her know about Rene. She doesn't know yet.'

'She's a hermit then?' Sarah saw Lin's puzzled look. 'Well, it's been in all the local press, the radio...'

'Ah. No, she lives out in the sticks a bit and she's always away somewhere or other, always very busy. I just figure it'd be best coming direct from me, y'know, rather than have her hear it third hand?'

Sarah softened, making Lin's little white lie turn huge and black. 'Of course Lin, of course. Sorry. I didn't mean... Yes. When do you want to go?'

'Tomorrow afternoon? About half two-ish?'

'I'll check with Mum, see if she'll cover, which is a bit like asking if Santa's got any reindeer. There's times when I forget about things, about Rene. Sorry, Lin.'

Lin stared at the floor. 'It's OK Sarah, I do too...sometimes.' This fibbing thing was becoming way too easy. She turned away and busied herself with an already dry glass.

'Premature senility creeping in?'

'What?'

'They're done.'

'Oh yeah, right, yeah... Well Boss, what's to do next?'

'Mad as a cut snake you are. Right, I've got a couple of barrels to swap so this'll be a good time to show you how it's done, yeah?'

'Yeah, sure.'

Sarah lifted the trapdoor that led to the cellar. 'Walk this way.'

'If I could walk that way I'd be up at Jericho and earning a fortune.'

'Cheeky bugger.' Sarah stopped on the top step of the downward flight. 'Lin?'

'Yeah.'

'Do you want me to go with you, you know, when you meet this friend and tell her?'

Lin wrinkled inwardly but her face held true. 'No Sarah, no... thanks for asking. It'll be fine. I just need to see her on my own, you understand?'

''Course, yeah. You would ask though wouldn't you, if it would help?'

'You'd be the first.'

'Good.' Sarah rested her palm on the edge of the trapdoor and ducked under it. 'Watch your head on the edge there, these steps were made for the seven dwarfs and you're no Snow White!'

446

Lin, cheeks still burning, followed Sarah into the cellar's gloom.

~

'I told him the evidence was damning, he said it was far from conclusive; I said the proof was staring us in the face, he said it was coincidental and conjecture... I just think he likes alliteration.' Archie's closing words brought a smile to both Anita and Jay's faces, but there had been precious little to smile about from his tale up to then.

'But...the ballistics evidence alone should have concentrated his thinking and...'

'Didn't want it pursued Anita.'

'...an investigation would have determined it.'

'Didn't want it pursued Anita. He saw every connection of the Irish lads to the murder of Adam, saw every connection of Lamb and Phillips to the Irish lads, but saw no connection back to Brightwick. With Phillips dead and Lamb missing he wasn't prepared to have us clump into the life of a respected government minister on what he considered were the flimsiest of reasons.'

Jay considered for a few moments before speaking. 'I hate to say I told you so, but...'

Anita was cross. 'Due respect Mister Millar, but that helps no one.'

'I'm not in favour of the Commander's playing style any more than you are...'

'And that's exactly why it needs to be challenged!'

'It does, but not like that. Not like our Detective Arnold tried.' He looked apologetically at Archie. 'Sorry, but I did warn you.'

'That you did Jay, that you did. He's right Anita. The thing is...there's people dead here Jay and not just people, my friend.'

'And to paraphrase an old chestnut, you've been at this long enough to know there's no room for sentiment in policing.'

Archie looked at Jay for a long while then said simply, 'I forgot.'

The realisation was there, Anita and Jay could see it in his face and neither of them had anything to quell or assuage the obvious hurt on display. The only thing to do was to change the conversation which Anita did. 'So, if you're off the books. Does this mean we'll not be having dinner then?'

Jay rolled his eyes as Archie stumbled on. 'Erm...dinner... yes, yes, 'course we're having dinner. No work to get in the way now is there?'

'Oh good. How about tomorrow? Sunday. I've a day off.'

Jay's interjection gave Arnold breathing space. 'Since when?'

'Since I did that last sixteen-hour day at the bungalow site.'

'But we have the fine debris from it to sift through.' Jay looked at Archie who shook his head.

'Not for me you don't. I'm stood down, remember?'

'Thanks Archie.'

'My pleasure.'

Anita's expression hardened. 'And I'm not doing it. That last session took my quota of hours to well over the European directive. My time off in lieu is rolling into three figures as it is, and if I don't start using some we'll be into next year and I'll lose them.'

'This is the job Ms. Cresson...'

'It is Mister Millar, but I can work for myself for nothing, and quite frankly, after working three Sundays on the trot I think I've earned the break.'

Archie turned to leave. 'I'll just duck out of this little domestic.'

Anita took hold of his coat sleeve. 'Tomorrow Archie.'

'Yes, of course...you sure? I'm persona non grata now.'

'I'm sure.'

'OK. Where?'

'Mine. I'll text the address. Seven thirty?'

'Yeah, OK...sorry Jay.'

'You could possibly be.'

~

Glum faces filled the incident room. Inertia had overtaken the crew, inertia and disbelief tinged with anger.

'Thing is,' said Pat, 'now we aren't sure which way to tread.'

'Landmines to the left of them, landmines to the right,' added Marissa.

'There are. Our compromised commanding officer thinks the people responsible for the death of one of our own are on a mortuary slab in Glasgow and we know different, but as far as our illustrious leader's concerned, that's a pat on the back and case closed.'

'What was it Archie said when he left; make further discreet enquiries if you want? Well, why don't we?'

Phil stood up and began to put on his coat. 'Because our compromised commanding officer's told us not to; that not good enough Mary?'

'No.'

Pat also stood and began to tidy the files on her desk. This late of a Saturday evening was not the time to start such discussions and it showed in her tone. 'Mary...'

'Well it isn't... Look, sorry everyone. I know you're further up the chain than us Pat and so privy to stuff we don't know about.' Mary looked round at them all. 'And I know that all you lot wanna do is go home and forget all about it, me too, but how can we? Huh? What we all know is Brightwick's leant on our boss and he's caved in because, when it comes down to it they all piss in the same pot. Well I for one would like to tip that pot over Brightwick's head.' There was a silence. These words of Mary's were like skewers. The gathered group exchanged looks. 'OK yes, we know for certain it was those two Irish fellas did for Adam and shot Kanga. We also know, probably to a certainty, that it was Phillips and Lamb who ran over Renata, but what we don't know is who gave the order 'cos it wasn't either of them. Look at their history! There's not a working brain can be fashioned from the four of 'em, certainly not one that could green-light this little lot...but...there's one we know who could.'

'OK Mary, I'll give you Lamb and Phillips, but those two Irish guys? We've made no connection to Brightwick apart from a dabbling in dogs...'

'And the site Archie found concurs with that Pat.'

'No it doesn't. As far as anyone's concerned it's just a well-tended building that a police officer forced entry into without the necessary paperwork thereby rendering the search and discovery invalid. Proof's required Mary, proof, and we've come up with nothing concrete that passes as that. Marissa and Phil did the background checks, right guys?'

Phil nodded. 'We did. There really was nothing Mary.'

Mary shook her head dismissively. 'Then you've missed something Phil, you and Marissa.' Marissa was about to speak but Mary cut across her. 'This isn't about looking for blame Mari, not on you or Phil. Look...I was there when Archie interviewed Brightwick, him and Quinn. They're clever, I mean really smart, but it also makes them think they've got it sewn up, consider themselves untouchable, above it all. They're not. There's a chink in the armour.'

'Now that is a bit racist.' Mary looked across at Arnue who was smiling at her. 'Move on; where's the chink?'

Mary scanned them all then addressed Pat directly. 'Brightwick's temper.'

'Bad?'

'Enough. It comes a close second to his arrogance. He takes the word "no" and anything that imputes his status very personally. I reckon, if we can poke the bear...'

'He'll come out and bite all our fuckin' heads off,' said Marissa. 'Mary, I'm all for nailing this bastard to the shed door, but this is sedition we're talking about here Pat; y'know? Jobs will be on the line, not the least of which will be yours.'

'I know.' Pat sighed. 'OK...so what if we decided, each in our own way, to do a little light research. How do we go about it? What are the lines?'

Mary shrugged. 'I only know one thing; whatever we decide to do we can't do it from here.'

Pat considered as she glanced round the room. 'Well, no one's left to go home yet so from that I guess there's no dissension in the ranks?' Nods and murmurings followed. 'OK, here's what I suggest. Who's on duty tomorrow?' Phil held up his hand. 'Poor sod, another Sunday gone. OK Phil, you're the one who'll coordinate. You've got the completed file on mainframe and access to others should they be needed. The rest of you, get copies but take home only what you're allowed to. Don't run the risk of being hauled out for removing case-sensitive material. OK? That'll give you tonight and all of Sunday. Run through stuff as though it's the first time. If you want anything extra Phil's ideally placed to discreetly add to your knowledge. Right Phil?' He nodded. 'The watchword here is discreetly Phil. I know a visitation from the CS on a Sunday is as rare as rocking horse shit but do things in the belief that he'll be leaning over your shoulder at any moment. Will that work Mary?'

'Yes Pat, thanks.'

'I want us all back here on Monday morning with a list of lines of pursuit.'

'Can I give us all a starter for ten?'

'You kicked this off, so yeah I think some sort of incentive would be good.'

'Not really an incentive more an insight into the kind of scum we're after. He's on the telly on Sunday.'

Pat snorted. 'Who Brightwick! Christ, the shit that gets on TV these days.'

'What's he on?' asked Marissa.

'That politics show, UKGov is it?'

'Gov.UK you mean.'

'Yeah that's it, Gov.UK. He's on that.'

Pat crossed to her desk and picked up a copy of the Daily Telegraph. She folded it to the weekend TV listings. 'What channel?'

'BBC.' Mary circled the programme blurb with a pen. 'Here.' The newspaper was passed round drawing the odd comment from the crew. 'It'll just give us a detailed look at him. As Archie's always saying, know your enemy. I suggest we all tune in.'

After a short silence Pat closed the paper. 'Right, we all have our homework and it's late. Let's get the copying done then it's home time children.' The team moved to their respective desks, collecting up paperwork and converging on the photocopier. 'Phil, you're point man tomorrow.'

'I am.'

'And Mary?' Mary looked across at Pat. 'You were right. Well done.'

Sunday

Archie poured a second mug of tea, idly flicking the Sunday paper from its centre spread of fashion must-haves to the sports pages; it was displacement activity, he knew it. He sighed, looked at the kitchen clock, back at the report of England's latest score against the West Indies then back at the clock again. *Ten fifteen. They'll be open now, definitely by the time I drive over there.* He closed the paper and wandered, mug in hand, to the living room. At the threshold, he scanned the room for no reason. Nothing had changed, not for three years. Everything was in its place, only the top layer of dust was new. He sipped his tea, brushed his forelock back and walked over to the sofa where an array of framed photos adorned the wall behind it. Arnold's history in all its sun-faded glory, demonstrated forcibly that everyone had seen better days, just like the buttermilk paintwork that formed its backdrop. He slowly inspected each picture in the array until finally, inevitably, his eyes rested on the centremost photo. The couple depicted were in dance pose, bodies facing one another, his arms round her waist, hers over his shoulders, heads to camera, a smile of shared intimacy on their faces and, as it did on every occasion, the image cut him to the quick. *Got that wrong, eh Pam? Well, you got it wrong, I got it spectacularly wrong. Never one to do things by halves was I?* He sipped again, sighed, and sat in an armchair. Opening his mobile, he keyed the pre-dialled number and waited for the ringtone.

'Hi, you're through to the Beavis Beat. I'm sorry but Bob's unable to answer. Leave a short message after the tone and he'll call you back at the earliest opportunity. If you wish to re-record your message, please press star at any time.'

'Hi Robert...Er...DCI Arnold here...Erm, I just wanted to apologise, and to thank you for the radio broadcast and piece in the Gazette. Had the desired effect...well, a bit more than that really as you'll no doubt have heard, so...thanks...really. Er, that's it I guess, thanks...Oh, you may also have heard, but just to confirm, it's no good trying to reach me at Northants HQ. I'm on leave, so...OK, well...see y'.' He closed the phone and spoke across to the photo.

'Don't say I don't try Pam, OK?'

He got up and walked back to the kitchen. Taking a last swallow of tea he placed the mug on the table, picked up his car keys and a pack of gum and moved towards the front door. *Just get them to give it a stay of execution that's all, it's evidence... yeah, it's evidence...*

~

⁶ Sarah!'

'Yeah.'

'I'm away now alright?'

'Yeah sure.'

'And can I borrow your parka?'

'Which one?'

'You've got more than one parka?'

'Doesn't everyone? Which one?'

'The one with the fur trim hood?'

'Christ, it's not that cold out, you'll look like Nanook of the North.'

'Long as I don't look like Eskimo Nell. So, can I?'

'Yeah, yeah sure, and are you certain you don't want to leave Jasper here?'

'No, he'll be a useful prop, like for a memory thing, even though I know he'd rather be with that detective than either here with you or out with me.'

'Don't take it personal, I don't.'

Lin clipped the lead to Jasper's collar. 'Could you just...?' She passed the lead to Sarah, slipped the parka on and picked up a large canvas tool bag. 'Thanks. Good boy Jasp.'

'So, are you gonna do a bit of plumbing at your friend's house while you're there?'

Lin glanced down at the bag. 'What? Oh this? No no, just easier...for the few things, some personal stuff, reminders, for her...to take with me...'

'For your friend, yeah, you said. Jasper doesn't mind you using his safe space then?'

'Safe space?'

'When I passed by your room the door was open and I saw you feeding him in it, scraps or something?'

'Oh that...yes, safe space, yes. I was, it is. He took a shine to it, makes him feel...safe, so...' Lin's voice tailed off in uncertainty. She had been amazed at how easily the terrier had accepted the confines of the bag. Those minutes spent enticing him into it with pork scratchings and beef scraps from the pub roast had paid off and now he was perfectly willing to enter it on command, well, command and a slice of underdone beef.

'Yeah, I can understand that. Trauma does strange things to a body doesn't it, poor little mite.' said Sarah, 'And you two will be back for the evening shift will you?'

'Erm, possibly not...well, we might be a bit late, will that be alright? I think I ought to stay for a little bit, not just give the news then rush off out.'

Sarah stared at Lin for a few seconds before replying. 'Yeah 'course.' She paused. 'Are you OK Lin?'

'Yes of course, yes.'

'Only, you seem a bit on edge.'

Jasper looked up at Lin and whined quietly. 'Do I? Yes, OK Jasp... Look, we really do have to go...sorry Sarah.'

'No, you go. Hope it all goes well.'

'Thanks.' Lin paused, shouldered the bag and made a determined exit. 'Come on Jasp.'

Sarah watched them leave and stood looking at the empty space for a few seconds before turning back into the bar. 'Summat not right with those two...'

~

Nicky Colbert smiled the smile she had smiled a thousand times at a thousand other prospective owners who she realised had felt the sudden chill of reality at the last minute. *A penny for every promise,* she thought.

Archie recharged his gum. 'I have to go to the hospital first so that'd prove tricky. But I will come back, promise.'

'Oh OK, so we can hold him for you until...? When will that be exactly?'

'I don't know.'

'Well, you saw for yourself we're at overload here, and the pup your colleagues brought in is stretching both room and legality.'

'I said I'd look out for him, see what I can find. My job means I'm out all hours, y'know?'

'And you'll also know that his chances of finding a home are slim to non-existent given the breed he is.'

'Oh, come on, he's just a pup. Surely he'll melt someone's heart.'

'Getting rid is easy, but getting rid in the right place...? Like I said, slim to none.'

'OK, I really will see what I can do.'

'Right, we'll hold off the five-day destruction order until...'

'I thought you said you kept them indefinitely?'

'Not borderline dogs we don't; we can't. We just haven't the space...'

'Christ.'

'Nor the money. Once our kennels here are full, which they are, and the volunteer homes we've got are full, which they are, there really is nothing else. The last thing we want to do is put healthy animals to sleep, it's not in our brief, but sometimes, like with your pup in there...'

'He's not my pup.'

'No OK, but with that pup in there, with him the decision is kind of made for us.'

'So you do put down healthy animals then?'

Nicky thought for a long time before answering. 'Yes. Yes we do.' She sighed. 'We have to.' Her eyes held the same expression Archie had seen in Lin's when she told him about the discovery of the slaughtered cow elephant. 'Five maybe six months after Christmas, that's the worst time. They come in from every direction, we get swamped, do you see? From rubbish tips, dustbins, tied to signposts, fly-tipped on side roads, from sacks in canals, some shot, some beaten, nearly all starved, all of them rejected; inundated we are...you have no idea. A lot of them are way past our help, anybody's help really, but we do our best by them, treat them humanely...and that includes sometimes putting them to sleep.'

Archie sighed. 'Look...I didn't want to get into stuff that obviously troubles you... I'm sure it's heart-breaking, you do something I sure as hell couldn't, really.' He paused, checking the landscape of their conversation before he spoke. 'I went to a place yesterday, part of our investigation, a place where they pitch one dog against another, you know for sport? A place where they clip their ears, their tail, sometimes their teeth then shoot them after a life of torture. Coupled with what you've just described and walking down your line of kennels...?'

Nicky's expression gradually changed to one of a connection with Archie. 'Brings it close doesn't it, makes it real?'

'You betcha...' Archie shook his head then looked Nicky in the eye. 'But, even given the difficulties, you'll hold on to him 'til I come back?'

She nodded. 'Yes, OK.'

'Thanks Nicky, really.' Archie moved toward the exit. 'I won't let you down.'

Nicky's voice, as she turned back to the kennel yard and its yaps of confusion, followed him. 'Not me; him...'

~

The foyer of the television studio glistened, the high-gloss mock-marble flooring reflecting the self-regard etched into the surroundings. At the half moon smoked-glass reception desk three security guards and two reception clerks held court. Discreetly housed in the overhang of the counter-top the four CCTV screens relayed the comings and goings of all who entered this inner sanctum, all watched and commented on by the security men. On either side of this trio of voyeurs, the two reception clerks sat at regularly ringing telephones, their clipped speech indicating purely by tone whether the call was internal-important or external-circumspect. Conversation between these five was infrequent, and when dealing with outsiders, phrases so often used in their day-to-day took on a form of shorthand, a kind of civil rudeness. It was into this sanctuary of the sanctimonious that Brightwick, preceded by Quinn, entered via the revolving central door. Once inside both men marched with purpose up to the reception desk and all three security heads lifted above their parapet as they drew near. Glynis Maldon stood up, clipboard in hand. Quinn reached the desk, Glynis smiled as he approached.

'Yes, Sir. Can I help?'

'Lord Brightwick, Gov.UK show. I am his PPS, Randal Quinn.'

Glynis glanced at the list and ran her finger down it. She knew full well who this was and why they were here; they were expected, but this was just her way of maintaining control, of showing who was in charge of the proceedings. Quinn knew it too, recognised it, smiled at it. After a short stall she looked up. 'Ah yes, here we are. Lord Brightwick, for Mister Garland.'

'Anthony, yes.'

'Just one moment Sir.' She picked up one of the handsets, punched in numbers and sat back, a thin-lipped smile directed at Quinn as she waited. 'Ah Miriam, Glynis here. I have a Lord Brightwick and his PPS in reception for Mister Garland ... For tonight I believe...?' She covered the mouthpiece and addressed Quinn, 'It is for tonight's show?'

'Yes. Tonight.' He smiled, reptilian.

'Yes Miriam, for tonight ... you will? Excellent, you're a love ... Thank you, I'll let them know.' Glynis replaced the handset. 'They're sending someone down to show you the way to the green room very shortly. Mister Garland has been informed you're here. Would you like to take a seat?'

For the first time Brightwick spoke, 'Will they be long?'

Glynis recognised the tone. 'No Sir, no time at all.'

'Then we'll stand.'

A rustle of servile respect shivered along the staff behind the desk...

... 'Lawrence, how are you?' Anthony Garland strode across to Brightwick, his hand out in greeting.

'Tony.' They shook hands. 'You know Quinn, my PPS?'

'I do yes, hello Randal.'

'Mister Garland.'

'Are you being looked after Lawrence?'

'I could've done without the early start.'

'Ah yes, that's television for you I'm afraid. You've been briefed about the format?'

'A little yes. I know it's live and I know there's an audience.'

'Invited but tame.' Garland leant in. 'You received my information sheet, the question line up?'

'Yes Tony, thank you for that, most instructive.'

'Not at all. Can't have any surprises voiced by some unprincipled commie, can we?'

'Would do nothing to serve democracy would it?'

'Not at all...'

Barbara Craddock, Floor Manager for Gov.UK, complete with clipboard, in-ear headset and American accent joined them. 'Hi Mister Garland, afternoon everyone. My name is Barbara and I'll be walking you through the rehearsal this afternoon. Lord Bright-wick?'

Quinn stepped forward. 'Brittick.'

'Pardon?'

'It's pronounced, Brittick.'

'Oh, I'm most sincerely sorry Your Lordship.'

'Him not me.'

'Excuse me?'

'This is Lord Brightwick, I'm Randal Quinn, his Secretary.'

'Oh my, I'm having a car crash of a day today. Forgive me Sir.' She consulted her clipboard. 'Now we haven't much time so if we can go into the studio and I can give you a brief rundown of events?'

Brightwick stepped forward, his voice dripping faux enthusiasm. 'Please do.' He cast a look at Garland who shrugged his shoulders.

'Theatre protocols I'm afraid Larry, not my department. Right, well, I'll leave you in the capable hands of Barbara here and see you in the studio for rehearsals.'

Barbara smiled broadly at them both, her array of pristine, perfectly formed teeth dazzling in their brilliance. 'You all want to follow me then and we can get this show on the road.'

~

Even though she had been to visit Jenni before, Lin never ceased to marvel at the difference between here and her own abode. It was strange that the same word could have two completely juxtaposed interpretations; take the word 'flat'.

Flat fifteen Mayflower Rise, Lin's one-time address now major crime scene, was a flat. Eleven, Stentson Gardens, Borden was also a flat. And yet, as a visitor from outer space, you could be forgiven for not seeing any connection between the two. Mayflower Rise was all fast-food cartons and expletives. Here in Borden, on the outer reaches of the town, all was peace and prosperity; clipped, vandal-free hedges and money-scented flowers, the whole area wearing the high-gloss sheen of success, just like the people who lived here.

Lin had Jasper in tow, the terrier endeavouring to water as many shrubs and bushes as he could and she had not passed a single boarded up residence, broken window, stained net curtain or stray dog turd; not a one. *These aren't flats, they're apartments.* She pressed the doorbell and looked at Jasper. 'And you, be on your best behaviour. No pissing in the kitchen or biting Jenni, OK?' Jasper gave her the look of an experienced disobeyer then growled at the door and the shadowed approach of a challenge. 'Just bloody behave...' the door opened. 'Hi Jenni, how's you?'

'Hi stranger...' Jenni made a move to give Lin a hug, but was forestalled in her action by the continued, low but perfectly audible growl from Jasper. 'Oh, hello. I didn't know you had a dog Lin.'

'I didn't...don't, long story, Jasper shut up.'

'Jasper? Excellent name! Where's he from...come in,' she stepped back, 'come in, come in, I want to hear all about it...'

~

The doorway, distant but still clearly sealed and banded, bragged its specialness. Archie's hand rested on the car's front wing, his gaze fixed on the front door of flat fifteen Mayflower Rise. He was almost in awe of the place and its surroundings, its utter careless neglect courtesy of strapped-for-cash councils. He shifted his gaze slowly along the balcony, past the odd boarded up plot, many with graffiti emblazoned across their walls, the nineteen seventies precursor to social media. A couple of doors down from number fifteen an elderly, dressing-gowned lady stepped out and lit up a cigarette. Archie watched her with ill-disguised dislike. *Why? Eh? Why wasn't it you with y' fags and y'...uselessness, eh?* He looked around. *Such a shitty place to meet your end Adam, you deserved better than this.* The woman spotted him looking up and waved. Archie, without thinking, waved back. He sighed. *That thought was unworthy Arnold. She no more deserves to live here than Adam deserved to die here...* He turned and got back into the car. Opening his mobile, he searched, selected, then waited.

'Hello, Glasgow Infirmary? ... Yes hello, erm, could you put me through to a Mister Kenzie Jardine, please? ... Not sure. He was in intensive care, gunshot victim? ... Yeah, that's him ... No, a friend, Detective Chief Inspector Arnold, Northants CID ... Yes thanks, I'll hold...'

~

The disembodied voice of programme producer Richard Laine floated into the studio, 'Right. that'll be all for now thank you, and thank you, panel, for being so patient.'

The microphone linked to the studio clicked off and Barbara Craddock scuttled over, all placations and assurances. The guests began to leave their desks as Quinn tried to intercept her stratagems, but she arrived just a fraction before him at Brightwick's side. 'That went very well Minister, did you think? Sound all good for you, not too hot under the lights?'

Brightwick's gravitas showed through. 'This is not my first appearance in such circumstances Ms. Craddock, having done Question Time on four separate occasions, but thank you for your concern.'

The look told Barbara she was dismissed and after a glance at Quinn she turned towards the other three panellists and began her fussing where it would be better appreciated. Brightwick turned to Quinn. 'I still have misgivings about being seen with these people, and if I'd have known Pritchard was here...'

'Last minute cancellation I'm afraid Sir, couldn't be avoided.'

'Who cancelled?'

'Lord Lavery.'

Brightwick winced. 'There we are, see? The only friendly face on the panel and who do they get to replace him? The toady gossip monger Karen-bloody-Pritchard!'

Lady Hayley Cooper-Stern moved across to them all smiles. 'You were very forthright on the test question Lawrence. Is this a sample of what's to be expected this evening?'

Brightwick leant across and air-kissed her proffered cheek. 'Hayley my dear, why ever would you think that?'

'Call it female intuition.'

'Well rest assured, I shall take each question on its merits. That tester was obviously there to help with sound levels so I obliged, but it has to be said, when asked forthright questions such as, "What is the role of government organisations in the protection of the rural environment?", they deserve forthright answers. No shilly-shallying or sitting on fences.'

'Well I think Karen was a little taken aback.'

'She's a big girl Hayley, like yourself. I have every confidence that, should the opportunity arise, you'll be taking no prisoners yourselves.'

'Yes, but I'd like to think there'll be a little more finesse involved.'

'Finesse begets misunderstandings Hayley; say what you mean and mean what you say.' He looked over at Karen Pritchard, who was being talked at by Barbara, waved a tentative hand then looked back at Hayley. 'I do believe an incomplete coven is awaiting?' Hayley followed his look.

'Unkind Lawrence, unkind.' She turned. 'I'll leave you to your schemes.'

Brightwick invited her away. 'And to yours; upon the heath.' He switched back to Quinn. 'Oh dear, nearly a hissy fit from Pritchard and now a rap on the knuckles by that limp lettuce from the Green Party.' He rubbed his hands together. 'Both on the back foot; excellent! Ah Tony. Super rehearsal, well done!'

Garland stepped over to shake Brightwick's hand. 'Yes, not too painful was it?'

'Not at all, and an interesting panel choice; stimulating.'

'We thought so. Sorry we sprung Karen on you.'

'You have a schedule to keep.'

'We do.' Garland looked at the studio clock. 'We've got just over three hours before the half Larry, how about a spot of early dinner?'

'Not some pie and chips outlet I hope?'

'Good Lord no. I was wanting a word with you and it was too late to book for the Wild Rabbit, so I took the liberty of reserving a table for two at The Partridge in Kingham. You know it?'

'I do.' Brightwick turned to Quinn. 'Right Quinn, get on to Willis and sort out any House business which needs to be in place for next week and I'll see you back here at...?' he turned to Garland.

'Oh, I think six thirty will be plenty early enough.'

'Six thirty then.'

'Yes. You'll find an excellent canteen just along the corridor there Randal.' Garland waved a hand in the general direction of the studio door. 'All manner of goodies on sale there.'

The two men turned away chatting, Garland leading the way out through a separate side door and leaving Quinn alone in the now empty studio.

~

'God Lin, I'd no idea... I mean, I'd heard the reports just like everyone, but I'd no idea of the details. You must feel dreadful.'

Lin broke off a section of her digestive biscuit, dipped it quickly into her tea and offered it to Jasper who took it with a snatch, swallowing it whole. 'To be honest Jenni it's only just recently sinking in. Everything was so full-on, the cop chase, the arrest, the sessions with the detective...the ID.'

'So sorry, Lin. That must have been harrowing for you, and he sounds like a keeper.'

'Ha! Yeah, right. You're not the first to say that...he's a really nice guy, but he's carrying a bit too much baggage for me.'

'Sounds to me like you've assessed him quite carefully.'

'That's not...no, look, I'm not here for idle girlie chat. What I came here for was some expert advice and help.'

Jenni could see Lin was in earnest. 'OK, no more love advice, how can I help?'

'I want another make-up job from you...sort of now?'

'Oh, erm...OK. For what?'

'The man who arranged to have Rene killed, he's on the TV tonight, a politics show, Gov.UK...'

Lin paused just a little too long for Jenni's comfort.

~

'How's the duck?'

'Excellent with the lingonberries, very innovative. Your cod?'

'Very good, excellent sauce.' Garland rested his knife and fork on either side of his plate, picked up his wine glass and leant back slightly in his chair. 'This bill you've got going through Parliament Larry, the exotic animal hunting bill isn't it?'

'The Rare and Exotic Animals Research Bill Tony; distinct difference in the nomenclature.'

'Yes, well, is it something that'll get through before recess?'

'I have every hope.'

'Been sent back though hasn't it?'

'Twice.'

Brightwick's tight-lipped reply did nothing to dissuade Garland from pursuing further. 'So there's a chance it may get lost in the ether then?'

'I'd say not. It has cross-party support...'

'Minority cross-party support.'

'...Cross-party support of a sufficient diversity to see it onto the books. It just needs a final push. Why the interest Tony, can you help?'

'Might be so. We have a few friends coming over for dinner next week, Thursday to be precise. Maybe it would help the cause if you were there too?'

Brightwick leant forward. 'Ah... And the guest list consists of...?'

~

'But you've worked there though?'

'Well yes...'

'So you know the layout?'

'Bits, yes...' Jenni drew breath, her mind working on the permutations. 'We used it as a try-out space for the make-up, you know, for the cameras and lighting and such when I did that sci-fi movie the year before last.'

'The one with that thingy-monster in it...a Gingardoo wasn't it?'

'You remembered! Yes.'

'Stupid name like that, hardly forget would you? It was great make-up you did though.'

'Yes, I was pleased with it, the prosthetics too.'

'That was the sort of mask-like thing with the boils and such?'

'Yeah.'

'The ones that leaked pus.'

'Good wasn't it?'

'Very realistic, sick-making really.'

'Worked then.' Jenni took a sip from her tea. 'But you've already said you're not here to interview me for a possible Oscar. The Broadbrush studios in Oxford, what of it?'

'Can you keep a secret?'

Jenni moved forward in her chair. 'Erm...yes, I can...I think, depends on the revelation.'

Lin also leant forward, her movement giving false hope to Jasper that a walk was imminent. She looked down at him. 'In a bit, Jasp, we'll go for a walk in a bit...' The dog settled again. 'You can't tell anyone Jenni.'

'I live here on my own Lin, who am I going to tell?'

'Good point. OK. Well, I'm going to surprise Brightwick at that show tonight.'

'You've managed to get a ticket?'

'No, not exactly...'

'What's that supposed to mean? You either have or you haven't. There's no way you'll get through security in the lobby without one, that front desk is like the buzz-doors into Alcatraz.'

'OK, but...is there another way in? You know, one that avoids Alcatraz?'

~

At the barrier Archie tugged the ticket resentfully from the grip of the machine and stashed it in his pocket. *Paying to visit the sick...Jesus, what a country.* A space was empty at the far end of the first row and Archie guided his car into it then, once inside St. Margaret's Hospital, he followed the signs along the corridor that led to the HDU. Part-way along there was a WHSmith outlet and he went in, browsing along the magazine shelves until his eye finally alighted on a copy of Asian Voice alongside a copy of that month's issue of Asian Wedding magazine. *Oh, OK...I think they'll be alright...* He took them down, collected a copy of the i newspaper, picked up a packet of plain Hula Hoops, a bar of mint chocolate, and a box of mixed grapes from the chiller cabinet and walked to the checkout.

The young lady at the till, wearing a badge just above her right breast which read 'Sophie', began to reckon up and smiled. 'Covering all the bases?'

Archie took out a ten-pound note from his wallet and smiled at the assortment. 'Yup. Should be able to appease all-comers with this little lot.'

'That'll be fourteen pounds thirty please.'

There was a stunned silence from Archie until eventually he said. 'How much?'

'Fourteen pounds thirty. This one...is seven eighty-five on its own.'

'That's more than the entire cost of my first wedding.'

'Whatever, it's still fourteen pounds thirty.' Archie took out his debit card. 'Into the slot, key in the pin when it says to.'

'I've done this before you know.'

'With your level of surprise at the cost of everything I began to wonder.' She gave him a cheeky smile.

Archie saw the payment go through and sighed. 'Let's hope it'll be worth it.'

'With that sort of outlay, how could anyone resist?' She gave him the receipt.

'Anyone tell you, Sophie, that you're very sparky?'

'My mum, my husband...'

Archie turned and left. 'They were right.'

~

The walk from The Partridge to Garland's vehicle was mercifully short as the clouds gathering in the west threatened heavy rain. Indeed, both Brightwick and Garland could feel the odd spot as they climbed in.

'Timed that just right Larry, what?'

Brightwick opened his overcoat and fastened his seatbelt. 'Yes. Nothing worse than a soaking when there's no change of clothes to be had. Are we straight back to the studio?'

'We are.' Garland looked at his watch. 'Sundays are lighter for traffic, but we never seem to get an open road round here; I blame the Chipping Norton effect. Leaving now means we'll be in good time, give you a chance to catch up with your PPS.'

'Quinn, yes. It was good to get away, even for that short lunch break; thank you for that Tony, very thoughtful.'

'Least I could do.' He started the car and began the drive back. 'So, to be clear, you'll have a word with the PM, get you both on my Sunday Politics Show, give you a chance to explain this Chinese trade deal in a fuller fashion. That'll give yourself and the government a welcome fillip and me an exclusive.'

'I certainly will Tony; I'm sure it can be arranged...least I can do...'

~

'Well, yes there is, but this is left field even for you Lin.'

'Don't know what else to do to help.'

'Is that how your detective friend will see it, as help?'

'Don't know.'

''Cos I doubt it. Isn't this interfering in an investigation or some such legal thingy?'

'No. It's a one girl protest so not his concern.'

'Isn't it?'

'No. He's got no foreknowledge of it, he's not invited, I've had no contact with him about this so no one can accuse him of subterfuge or me of coercion.'

'Well I think you're on thin ice.'

Lin looked at Jenni for several seconds before she replied. 'OK then, we agree to differ, but will you help? Please? This is the only way I can give meaning to the life of Rene, Jen...the death of Rene. I've done precious little up to now and that Brightwick creep, he's a dog fighter and sister killer.'

'Has it been proved?'

'There's enough to make it highly probable.'

'Probability isn't proof Lin.'

Jasper, having realised no more dunked biscuits or walks were coming his way, whined his disapproval at the continuing conversation. Lin looked down at him 'Yes OK Jasp, in a minute. Please Jen... Please?'

Jenni sighed. 'Is there any way I can get dragged into this?'

'Not even slightly. I'm in there on my own, no one knows we're friends, well no one connected to this anyway, so no.'

'The make-up?'

'I'll say I did it, just like I did with the bee thing.'

'Right...' Jenni looked round the room. "Cos I'd hate to swap all this for a prison cell, y'know?'

'No one will know Jenni; I give you my word on that.'

'You'd better be right... OK, apart from the make-up you want a way into the studio that avoids the front desk...' Jenni thought for a moment then her eyes widened. 'Oh...erm, yes, there is. It's where they keep the bins at the back of the building, where the OB trucks are parked when they're not in use. The cast used to go out there and have a smoke, but...you'd have to go through the main gate to get to it... Unless...'

'Unless what?'

'Hang on, let me think... The parking area at the back is a cinder floor and I think there's a chain-link fence round it, quite tall, with an overhang that backs onto an industrial estate. It's surrounded by units, places that do car repairs and make bread...' Jenni stopped in her description. 'You're not thinking of going in that way, are you?'

'If that's the only other way, yes. After you've done the make-up job I'll definitely not get in the front.'

'But the climb...' Jenni looked at Jasper. 'And him?'

Lin lifted the canvass bag, tipped out the contents and smiled. 'He'll be in here, then we'll see.'

'Are you serious?' Lin nodded. 'This just gets crazier.'

'Crazier than the bee stunt?'

'Much.' Jenni looked at the scattered, distressed clothing Lin had tipped out of the bag. 'Is that your costume?'

'It will be if you can use your artistic bent to add a few more rips, scuffs and bloodstains, yeah.'

'Lin...?'

Lin pre-empted Jenni's concern. 'I've never been surer Jen, and I've nothing else to lose.'

'Except your freedom.' Jenni sighed in decision. 'OK, I'll help with the make-up and stuff, but you're on your own for the break-in.'

'Wouldn't have it any other way.'

Jenni walked into a back room and returned with a large, tired looking tool case. 'God, I haven't opened this old thing in years. Most of what we need is supplied on site and I only take that little thing with me these days.' She pointed to a small vanity case on a desk at the far end of the room. 'This is from my early days, my am-dram times, so I'm not even sure what's in here nor whether it all still works.' She opened the lid and folded out the trays. 'You want to look like you've been in an accident?'

'A high speed hit-and-run, yeah.'

'Jenni sighed and began to sift through the box's contents. 'Right...so...wounds...bruises... I've not got access to the modern stuff so...' She went into the kitchen and came back with a first-aid kit. Opening it she took out a couple of rolls of bandage and some cotton wool then went to a cupboard and took out a large bottle of Copydex. 'Necessity is the mother of invention: I haven't done wounds with this sort of stuff for years. Hope I can make it all work.' She removed a large and tired-looking plastic bottle from the box. 'Is blood required?'

'Yeah, face and hands, but can you supply me with extra? I'll put it into a different bottle, so not yours, and use it later.'

'To do what with?'

'To...you know...to pour over me, at the last second... otherwise it'll dry out and I'll lose the impact.'

'Well good luck with that then 'cos the stuff I've got in here is old. What I use now is really good, but this...it really doesn't wash out well at all, leaves a blush that lasts for ages.'

'Makes no odds to me, once I'm in there I want to really stand out.'

'If you ever get that far you'll do that...oh, hang on...' Jenni opened a desk drawer and took out a plain clipboard with pad and pen attached. 'Take these in with you, hold it like so, keep the hood up you might get away with it.'

'Thanks Jen, you're a real mate.'

'Yeah, as long as I don't become a cell-mate.' Jenni took a cloth loop from her vanity case and scraped Lin's hair back off her forehead, slipping the cloth in place to pin it back from her face. Jasper, seeing a further wait was on the cards, took himself off to the settee, hopped up on it and curled up for a doze. Jenni took a cotton wool pad from the box, doused it in cleansing fluid and began to gently wipe Lin's face. She paused. 'My God but you are beautiful, you know that? Your bone structure... it's a crime to disfigure you, even in play.'

Lin smiled. 'Just...just shut up and get on with it.'

'Alright Little Miss Mardy; hold still.'...

... 'Well, that's as good as I can do in the time and with the kit. Have a look, there's a mirror in the hallway.'

Lin walked out to stand in front of the oval wall mirror and even though she had been the recipient of the work the sight reflected back made her gasp. Her forehead was rainbow-coloured with slashes from a gaping wound striping it crosswise. Both her eyes were sunken somehow, the colouring surrounding them reminiscent of a Goth look gone wrong, and whilst her right cheek was bloodied and scraped of skin her left cheek hung slashed and torn in a fold of drooping skin which exposed her painted jawbone and teeth. Her chin was gouged and torn, the strips of damaged skin hanging loosely, swinging obscenely. The sight, ghoulish and shocking though it was, brought with it a skipped heartbeat and choked throat as Lin looked into Rene's reflection. 'Jesus...'

'You alright, Lin. Not too much, is it?'

Lin looked again into the mirror. 'No Jenni, it's...it's brilliant. Cruel but brilliant.' She looked at her hands, the bruising and scraped skin seeming so real that she almost felt the pain. 'Christ, no wonder you're always in demand.' She came back into the room and her entrance woke Jasper from his nap; the change in him was instant, sharp and terrifying. From curled, snoozing indifference to tuft haired, snarling concentration, Jasper twisted over and half jumped, half fell from settee to floor, his bark given extra impetus the instant his front paws hit the deck. Jenni stepped back with a gasp as Lin spoke out in firm but calming tones.

'Jasper...! Hey, Jasp. It's me, it's Lin... 'S'alright, just me in some funny make-up...good boy, it's OK...' She squatted down and held out a seemingly brutalised hand towards the terrier who was all confusion and scare. 'It's me, Lin...good boy...here.' She bent forward slightly and Jasper leant in to sniff her flattened palm, 'See? Nothing to frighten you here...'

'Wow Lin, he might be small but he's scary as shit when he lets rip.'

Jasper, having taken a good sniff, had lowered his ruff and was looking from Lin's hand to her face. 'He's got the heart of a lion.' She smiled at the dog. 'And there's no side to him, is there boy? Eh, Jasp?'

There was silence before Jenni spoke. 'Do you think he...?'

'Saw Rene? I suppose so, yes.' She looked round the room, at her hand, at Jasper and finally at Jenni. 'I keep catching myself in the midst of all this, you know? Like waking up in a foreign land and having no recollection of ever having travelled to it. I'm just...here, in the now, d'you understand?' Jenni nodded. 'It's like that.'

Having satisfied himself as to the provenance of Lin, Jasper sat down and Lin snapped off another section of biscuit and gave it to the terrier. For a while the only sound was his determined scrunching until Lin cleared her throat. 'Ha-hum! Erm, couple more favours?'

Jenni sighed. 'What?'

'Nothing dreadful...'

'I'm sure. What else?'

'Could you sketch out a rough map of the studio for me, the corridor layouts and where the main broadcast area is?'

'It's been a while since I've been there, it could have all been turned round.'

'Nah, they'd never spend shareholder's money on such a thing.'

'You think? The BBC spend it on Strictly...' Jenni thought for a moment. 'Yes, OK, but it'll just be a rough one and you'll have to draw it. I'm not having anything to connect me to this.'

'No, 'course. And talking of driving...'

'Were we?'

'We are now. Is there any chance you can drop me round the back, on the factory estate?' Lin saw Jenni's reaction. 'It's just that it's too far to walk, and I can't go by bus looking like this...'

'"You think the chamber's empty but there's always one for you".'

'What's that?'

'A line one of the characters says in this new film I'm doing; she says it to a gun.' Jenni sighed. 'OK, I'll drop you, but that's it Lin. I know it sounds harsh, but I really can't risk being caught up in all this, honourable though it is.' Jenni closed the make-up box with finality and picked up the discarded and ravaged clothing. 'Right, let's get these clothes distressed a little more and you dressed in them. If you're going to make the Lord Mayor's Show, we need to get on...'

~

Once back in the warmth of the studio, Brightwick and Garland went their separate ways, Garland to speak to the programme's producer and Brightwick to catch up on postprandial events with Quinn. With just over an hour to go to the start of the broadcast Brightwick felt he needed to re-run some of the questions and formulate his replies...

~

V alerie Wilmott stepped round and behind the bar, tidying as she went. 'Is there any chance she'll be back this evening?'

'Mum... I don't know, I've said.'

'But did she say where she was going?'

'No, just across to see some friend of hers.'

'Where?'

'Other side of town.'

'What, you mean Silford and Borden way?'

'They're both on the other side so yes, I suppose... I'm here you know? Your real daughter? Me?'

Valerie forced a laugh and began to re-arrange the shorts' bottles. 'What do you mean?'

'Mum... You've practically adopted her over the last few days. I'm just waiting to be kicked out of my bedroom.'

'Don't be silly Lin...Sarah.'

'See!'

'Sarah, I meant Sarah. You two are just confusing me.' She picked up the local newspaper from where it had been left it on the bar. 'And what's this?'

'Local paper. Some of the regulars like to have a read.'

'Let them buy their own then.' She tossed it in the bin. 'Over Borden way you say?'

'What?'

'Where Lin's gone.' Valerie saw Sarah's look. 'It's just that she's gone through a lot just recently, I just want to be reassured she's alright.'

Sarah shrugged. 'Yes, you're right Mum, and I've been helping her all I can, you know that.'

'I know you have dear. Let me know when she's back.' She was gone.

'Yeah. Right.' Sarah mooched along the bar and retrieved the newspaper. Casting a surreptitious look up the stairs, she smoothed it out on the counter. 'Let them have a free read, miserable sod...' Her eye alighted on the headline low down on the front page: Local Politician to Debate Animal Welfare on BBC. A look of realisation came into Sarah's eyes as she re-ran earlier conversations. *How far is it to Oxford...? Oh, my, God... Borden, that's where Jenni... The bees, it's the bees... She wouldn't...*

Continuing to read, Sarah slowly reached out and picked up her mobile. Keying in the address book she scrolled down until the name Jenni-Borden came on screen. She pressed the connect button and waited for the ring out, biting her bottom lip, her breath, like her expression, concentrated.

~

Archie gently opened the door to Kanjara's private room and peered round it. 'This a good time?'

Kanjara sat up, switching off the wall-mounted television with the handset. 'Oh, hello Archie...yes, fine. Come in.'

'I bought you some goodies.' He piled the magazines, fruit and sweets on to the bed table. 'How's tricks?'

'Thank you, that really is very kind. OK...erm, physio's going well, early days, but they seem to be pleased with progress and I also seem to be repairing on schedule...' She slowed, holding up the copy of Asian Voice. 'This I understand, thoughtful if not a little typecasting, but this?' She swapped it for the copy of Asian Wedding. 'Do you know something I don't?'

'No. I just thought it would be an interesting read, you know...just...I don't know.'

Kanjara shook her head. 'You should've been in half an hour ago. Mum and Dad were here, if she'd seen this on the table she would've been part way through the planning stage before she left.'

'Really? I just bought it because I thought you would enjoy the read.'

'No ulterior motive then?'

This stalled Archie completely and it was some time before he could formulate a reply as he moved a step closer to the bed. 'Erm...would you like there to be?'

The silence between them was crowded with possibilities that neither had the courage to interpret. It was Kanjara who broke the impasse. 'OK...let's just... How's the case going?'

Off the hook for the time being, Archie, to a chorus of Kanjara's surprised comments, sat at the bedside and explained the recent events...

~

Sarah clipped the connection closed and stood rooted to the spot, her mind in overdrive. 'Mum?' She moved quickly to the foot of the stairs. 'Mum!'

Valerie appeared at the top of the stairs, barefooted, a bath towel wrapped round her body, her hair loosely tied up. 'What? And stop shouting.'

'Can you come down here a minute please?'

'Like this? I'll catch my death; I was just going to shower and wash my hair.'

'This is important Mum. It's about Lin.'

Valerie immediately began to descend the stairs. 'What? What about Lin...?'

~

'So, as you can guess, I've got some time on my hands; it may be you'll be seeing a bit more of me...if that's OK?'

'That would be lovely, really.'

'Good.' Archie looked at the magazines and half laughed. 'Huh... Next time I'll just bring flowers.'

'Just bring yourself.'

He smiled and pulled the chair closer to the bedside. 'Now you. What have the docs said?'

'Not so happy there.'

'I thought physio said you were making good progress.'

'They did, it's progress to what that's concerning me.'

'Why? What have they said?'

Kanjara looked out the window for a few seconds before replying, 'Let's say the prognosis isn't all it could be.'

'The full recovery thing you mean?'

'Yes... They think, or at least my orthopaedic surgeon thinks, that full recovery may well be beyond current technology...and possibly beyond my skeletal capabilities.'

'For now.'

She smiled at him. 'Sweet... Yes OK, for now, but I prefer to be more realistic and substitute 'for now' with 'for ever'.'

'Have they said that?'

'They don't need to.'

'You're the expert in all this are you?'

'When it comes to my body and how it feels, yes.'

'But they haven't said so.'

She smiled and shook her head slightly. 'No... No Archie, they haven't.'

'So, we need to see what the future brings.'

'We?'

'Yes. We.'

'Want to spend time with a cripple then do you?'

'Ouch.' Archie took in a deep breath, then took hold of her hand. 'I want to spend time with you Kanga... There, I've said it.

I want to spend time with you, no matter the outcomes, spend time with you.' He stopped abruptly as he saw Kanjara's expression. 'I've gone a bit too far now haven't I? Bugger...'

~

The voice followed quickly on from the door knock. 'Five minutes Lord Brightwick; thank you.'

Quinn looked toward the door then his concentration returned to the folder on his lap. 'The only other possible surprise question we need to consider is one surrounding the government's stance on ivory Sir.'

'Do you think that'll arise?'

'It's not on the list Garland furnished us with, but I think we would do well to consider it a possibility, revise it, certainly after the Development Minster's evasive answer to that reporter at the G7 conference.'

'She should never have been put in that position, exposed like that and having to either answer with something not cleared or keep shtum and look stupid.'

'Forgive me for saying Sir, but she managed to do both; spectacularly. I blame her PPS, that and her briefing team.'

'What's our official line?'

Quinn shuffled papers. 'Ah well, that's where it could play to our benefit.' He scanned the papers. 'Er...ah, here. "A ban on all ivory products is in the pipeline... A year away, eighteen months possibly... The government, under the umbrella of Defra, will set out plans to help protect elephants for future generations," da, da, da...ah, here, "the British government wishes to underwrite a research project properly monitoring the health and well-being of the present herds, their safety and longevity".'

'And that welds neatly into the sampling aspects of my bill... Excellent!'

'Yes, I think it can be said that, with the timely introduction of your bill, you're showing global leadership in this.'

'Then this question should be brought in from the shadows Quinn.'

Quinn stood up and moved to the door. 'I'll see to it straight away.'

~

'Do you really think she'll do it?'

'After going to all that trouble? Even Jenni said the make-up was spectacular, and with the clothes...? Well, you know Lin, Mum.'

Valerie sighed. 'That girl... And Jennifer said she'd dropped her at the studio?'

'At the back of it yes.'

'What on earth was she thinking.'

'Jenni said Lin was really insistent, and you know what that means.'

'Then you must phone that detective.'

'But that'll be telling on Lin...'

'I don't care about your street loyalty, Sarah. I'll not have one of my girls...'

'One of your girls?'

'As good as; I'll not stand by and watch her get deeper into trouble and do nothing to stop it. Now, do you have his number?'

Sarah could see there was no sidestepping this one. 'Yes; he gave it to me before he and Lin went off crime hunting.'

'Then phone him. Now! She'll be in real trouble with this, this is serious!'

Sarah scrolled the address book to the Arnold-Cops label. She keyed the autodial, Valerie hovering at her elbow...

~

Kanjara gave a raised-eyebrow smile. 'I'll tell you when it's too far.' She slid her hand out of his, picked up Asian Wedding and smiled broadly at him. 'Like this. This is borderline too far.'

'Sorry... Might get me in good with your mum though.'

She laughed. 'Ha! You'd be her golden boy, trust me.'

'Then I've not got a flat refusal?'

Now Kanjara took Archie's hand. 'Not a flat refusal no, but just so's you know what you're letting yourself in for, I've got a short temper and won't take to this...little local difficulty kindly. OK?' Archie nodded. 'I don't do self-pity; I don't do sycophancy and I definitely don't appreciate verbal tranquillizers. If we can use that as a foundation then no, you've not got a flat refusal.'

'OK, well, to avoid doing that we need to get you off your fat arse as frequently as possible whether you like it or not then.'

Once again Kanjara laughed and with it the accompanying expression that had captivated Archie back at the hit-and-run site when he had first been introduced to her. 'Think you might have gone too far the other way now.'

'Yeah.' Archie tightened his grip. 'Whatever needs to be done Kanga...' His mobile rang out. 'Bugger...sorry...'

'It'll not be from the office, not after what you've just told me.'

'No chance.' He opened the phone and saw the label. 'Oh, it's Sarah, her from the pub. Sorry Kanga, can I just take this?'

"Course, busy man, in demand.' Kanjara watched as Archie took the call and snapped out his replies.

'She's what? ... You think so? Oh shit! ... What? ... Oh, shit! ... Are you sure? ... Right... OK, I'm on it ... no Sarah, leave it with me, I'll get over there ... Yes, now ... No, your mum was quite right, you did the right thing, absolutely. Tell her I'm on my way over there now ... I will ... promise.'

Archie clipped the phone shut and looked at Kanjara. 'I'm really sorry, but I have to go.'

'That important huh?'

Archie nodded. 'Yeah.' He took her hand again. 'Look, can we pick up where we left off when I come back in?'

'You'll be coming back then? I've not frightened you off with my list of idiosyncrasies?'

'Not even slightly, and it won't all be one way, trust me, it's just...this case...'

'You're suspended.'

'If I don't sort this out I will be...from a gibbet.' Letting go of her hand he moved towards the door. 'See y' in a while, all things being equal...' He was gone.

Kanjara looked at the door for a few seconds before picking up the copy of Asian Wedding. 'Wow...'

~

Walking across the concrete desert of the haulage yard, the bag slung carelessly across one shoulder the fur hood pulled up and zipped tight, Lin hugged the outline of the buildings. As soon as she had left Jenni's car she had popped Jasper into the bag and he had settled in with a further scrap of meat and the lasting aroma of previous feasts, trusting in Lin's gentle progress and their confidence in each other. The only person Lin had seen on her journey from the drop-off point was an elderly man some distance away walking a Labrador and a pug. She had pressed her hand onto the top of the bag and reassured Jasper, whose nose was just visible through the gap left in the tie top, that all was well and no threat was imminent. She paused and surveyed the land ahead. Left and right of her were warehouse buildings, their roller doors and tall entrances locked for the weekend. Ahead she could see, just as Jenni had described, the chain-link fence that backed onto the television studio, a gap of thirty yards separating it from the rear of the building. A long look round gave her an all-clear and she scampered over to where the fence met another at right angles. She spoke to the bag.

'You stay there now Jasp. We're going over the fence just stay where you are until I'm done with the climb; stay...' She pinpointed two CCTV cameras. One was fixed to the rear wall of the studio complex, its field of vision focussed on a huge roller door with a standard size doorway cut into it. A number of large green rubbish bins on wheels were parked in haphazard fashion a little away from it. The other camera took in what looked like a wide sweep of the compound. Lin studied the cameras' angles and decided she had about a three-foot alley of operation close to the fence where the one camera would most likely fail to pick her up. The one facing the roller door was trickier to avoid, but Lin figured she could use the bins as cover and would pass as one of the hoped-for fag-smoking staff if she was quick in the door. 'Stay Jasp.'

She began the climb, and with the help from the fence's acute right angle, easily reached the top. The overhang was more difficult to conquer but she did it, only once having to tell Jasper to stay still when the bag snagged on the fence top. The downward climb was completed in record time, and once on the yard, Lin opened the bag a little more and Jasper poked his head out, snuffling the air.

'Good lad.'

Trusting that she had read the camera angles correctly, Lin sidled along the fence towards the roller door and bins. As she drew nearer so she saw the tell-tale remnants of the smoking brigade scattered like confetti. *Let's hope someone's desperate for a fix...*

~

'And we've got time for just one more question. Yes, the gentleman with the red tie, middle row...yes, what's your question for the panel?'

The man glanced at his paper before speaking.

'A question for the Minister, Lord Brightwick.' Brightwick sat forward a little. 'Given the government's present strategy on the sale of ivory, does the Minister think that the bill being put forward by him...'

Brightwick spoke over him. 'My Rare and Exotic Animals Research Bill, is that the one you're referring to?'

'Yes. Does the Minister think that bill will be a help or hindrance to the safeguarding of elephant numbers?'

'I'm really pleased this question has come up. My bill...'

~

Traffic had been trickier than he thought it would be and Archie was relieved to get to the studio. At the front barrier he flashed his warrant card and was allowed immediate access to the car park. The speed he entered through the revolving doors alerted the staff behind the reception desk and Glynis Maldon stood tall.

'Yes, Sir, can we help?'

Archie took out his warrant card again. 'DCI Arnold, Northants Serious Crime Squad. You have a broadcast going out live at the moment?'

Even the usually unruffled Glynis was thrown by this. 'Northants? But, this is...'

'Do you!'

'Erm...Yes we do, the Gov.UK Show. Is there a problem?'

'Not sure, could be. Is there someone connected to the show I can talk to?'

'Yes, yes...' She looked across at the two security men. 'Richard? Could you put a call out for Barbara please...?'

'An urgent call,' added Archie.

'An urgent call,' repeated Glynis.

Richard Llewelyn opened the channel. 'Urgent call for Barbara Craddock...' There was a short hiatus then the radio crackled back.

'Barbara.'

'Miss Craddock it's front desk here. Could you come out and have a word?'

'Now? I'm still on air.'

'Yes Miss, I know, but this is urgent; the police are here, something to do with the show.'

There was a heartfelt sigh followed by Barbara's clipped response, 'Yes. Right.'

Richard put the handset down. 'On her way Sir.'

Archie took out and wrapped his stale gum. 'Good.'

~

'I don't know why we've bothered to watch it, just another load of promises never fulfilled...and as for that twat in the blue suit...'

Dougie looked across at his fiancée Claire. 'AKA Lord Brightwick, Minister of the Crown. He's my homework, and it's almost over now...'

~

Mary closed the notebook and laid it and the pen next to her on the settee. *God, if ever there needs to be a definition for a smug bastard, then Brightwick, you're it.* She picked up her wine glass and pressed the mute button on the handset. At least I don't have to listen to you...

~

Marissa poured Deborah another glass of red and sat back down on the settee next to her.

'Some Sunday, huh?'

'Yes, it's been so worthwhile. How much longer?'

Marissa looked at her watch. 'Ten minutes or so. You in a hurry to get away?'

'Am I ever?'

Marissa smiled. 'Not often no. You want to say the night?'

'Again? This is becoming serious.'

'Problem?'

Deborah leant across and kissed Marissa on the cheek. 'I'll let you know when it is.'

~

The door opened and Lin, tucked neatly in the shadow of the bins just six feet away, dropped down on her haunches, laying a gentle hand on the bag to still Jasper's quiet growl. *There's lucky...*

Fags alight, the two girls chatted quietly, dragging back on their cigarettes in concentrated fashion until one of them dropped and squished it with the sole of her flat shoe.

'Best get back, almost finished.'

Her friend took a final, deep drag then copied her. 'Yeah, sooner the better.'

They disappeared from sight, but before the door closed Lin ran across and held it, banging the frame with her hand to make it sound like it had shut. After a short pause she slipped into the corridor and took out the paper sketch. Unzipping a side pocket in the bag she took out the clipboard. 'We're in Jasp; nearly showtime...'

~

6

So my bill will ensure species longevity through the selling of this ivory to replenish conservation funds, thereby giving a higher level of protection to the elephants of Africa, indeed to the wildlife of all nations; a level of protection never before available to them. I truly believe this bill will ensure the continued survival of our most endangered species.'

Garland looked out into the audience. 'I trust that answers your question?'

An audience member put up his hand. 'Up to a point...'

'Well, we are running out of time and the panel members have yet to make their closing statements, so...'

Brightwick cut across Garland. 'Oh, I think my time in the House has prepared me for supplementary questions Anthony.' He smiled broadly at the man. 'Go ahead, shoot.'

The man sat up a little more. 'Well, that's actually my point. That you shoot.'

'I do. It's not illegal, not to my knowledge.'

'No, it's not, but I just wondered, isn't that the design behind your bill, to allow you to continue to hunt and kill wild animals?'

Brightwick saw the route the man was taking and decided to divert him straight away. 'Can I just say that's very emotive language you're using. The method detailed in my bill is for regular, scientific population sampling to take place...'

~

Quinn yawned loudly, almost spilling the mug of tea in his hand. He looked across at Baariq, the researcher who had been assigned to Brightwick. 'All going to plan. You must get very bored.'

'Not at all. I prefer it this way, it means we've done our job right.'

~

Carefully avoiding a couple of people in the corridor, hood still pulled up and clipboard to the fore, Lin navigated her way along the route without incident. She checked Jenny's sketch again. The heavy brown door with a red-green light over it beckoned, the red light gently flashing both welcome and warning. Lin stood next to it but could hear nothing. *Soundproofed...good for us all.* She opened the door slightly and the dulcet tones of someone holding forth reached her. She let the door close, lifting Jasper out of the bag and clipping on his lead as she shushed him and put the bag down. Unzipping the parka and dropping the hood, she took the two-pint, plastic milk container of fake blood from one of the pockets and a wide-brimmed beaker from the other, speaking softly to Jasper.

'Quiet you. Nothing 'til it all kicks off; you'll know when.'

The terrier wagged his tail and began to pant at the expectation that was drenching Lin's voice. Pouring the blood into the beaker she reopened the door, the discussion reaching her clearly now as she stepped into the confines of the studio, the curtaining behind the dais shrouding her and Jasper nicely...

~

'Hello, I'm Barbara Craddock, floor manager for the Gov. UK show? How can I help?'

Archie utilised his ID card again. 'DCI Arnold, Northants Serious Crime Squad. You have a live event going out today, now?'

'Going out and almost over...' She checked her stopwatch. 'Twelve minutes to titles.'

'OK, well, I believe there's a possible threat to one of the members on the panel so I want access to the studio, discreetly of course, in order to identify if that possible threat is present and if it is to nullify it.'

'A threat?' Archie nodded. 'What kind? Is it a bomb or...?'

'No no, not at all, no. I don't want any alarm spreading or anything like that. I just think there might be some kind of disturbance and I'm trying to pre-empt it. So...?'

'Just you?' Barbara looked at the security men. 'Do we need support?'

'That won't be necessary.' This last from Arnold brought a look of relief to their faces. 'Just allow me to scan the audience so I can put everyone's mind at rest.'

'OK, but I need you to be very quiet, we're still on air.' She indicated the flashing red light above the studio door. 'This way.' As Archie walked towards the door Barbara leant back to the desk and whispered, 'Call the police,' before quickly joining Archie and opening the door which led to a pitch-black vestibule...

6   ~

So, as I'm sure you can appreciate, a great deal has gone into the formulation of this bill. It has been far from cobbled together, as some of my critics have said, Mister...?'

'Nick. Just Nick. But you do admit it'll allow animals to continue to be shot for sport.'

'For research.'

'Have it your way, all the same to the animal. Shot for sport, shot for research; still dead, and by people such as you.'

'Yes... Erm, you have homed in on this aspect but...'

'Because it's integral to it.'

'Yes, it is but it's about far, far more than that. It's about bringing prosperity to an underdeveloped area through licensed hunting revenues; it's about regimented crop protection, it's about revitalising jobs and hope; it's about giving a boost to the third-world economy. People are prepared to spend considerable sums of money to hunt, and this money would go towards safeguarding that wild population and the people linked to it so that...'

'So that blokes like you can go out and shoot some more of them.'

'Yes. It's called environmental economics, something you seem woefully ignorant about...'

Garland stepped on the escalating disagreement. 'As interesting as all this is I'm afraid we're reaching the end of our broadcast. Thank you for your question and I'm sure it'll be one we'll return to. Now, before our panel members make their short closing statements, can I just remind you that if you want to comment on the programme you can find us at...'

~

Tina Evritt, RVS representative and ward assistant was leaning round the door. 'Do you want a cup of tea dear?'

Kanjara looked across from the TV. 'Hi Tina. Yes that'd be lovely, thank you.'

'What you watchin', the football?'

'Ha! No, a discussion show, politics, y'know?'

'Can't be doin with all that. Liars, the lot of 'em.' She smiled.

'They are, it's just someone I've heard about is on, and...' Kanga could see Tina's eyes were glazing over. 'Never mind.'

'White and no sugar?'

'It is, thanks...oh, don't drown it in milk though, please.'

'Just a spot. Back in a minute...'

~

Round the back of the dais Lin saw the shaft of light knifing though the join in the backdrop. Jasper was all concentration, his ears pricked at the conversations and sounds.

Placing down the two containers Lin slipped the parka clear, letting it fall to the floor and fully revealing her shredded, tattered clothing and the fullness of the gruesomely brutal, highly detailed make-up. She picked up the full beaker, poured some of it over her head and topped it up. 'Jasper?'

The terrier looked up at her.

'We're on.'

Jasper yapped, just the once, but it was enough to alert the attention of a stagehand stood in the shadows some distance away from Lin. His urgent, whispered call reached her.

'Hey! Hey...you...!'

Archie followed Barbara into the studio through the second soundproof door. The runway between the raked seating to the left and right of him led arrow straight to the dais and panel, Brightwick being positioned neatly in the centre. In mid flow, Garland was winding up the session.

Barbara leant across and whispered hoarsely, 'Is the person you want here?'

Archie didn't answer. His undivided attention was focussed on the sound he had heard above Garland's closing remarks. 'Was that a bark...a dog?'

'In here...?'

Archie made determined progress along the aisle as Barbara called out in a hissed, panic-drenched whisper, 'Sir! Please Sir...! You can't go down there, we're still on air... Sir!'

~

Dougie sat up and retrieved the TV handset from between cushion and seat arm. 'Well, that was all very enlightening.'

'Glad you thought it was. And that's the bloke you've all been censured over then?'

'Yeah, and we've not been censured.'

'Put on notice then.' Claire got up from the settee. 'Do you want a drink?'

'Of?'

'There's some of that white left in the kitchen.'

'Yeah, that'd be good.'

~

Lin knew she had been rumbled so made a determined step through the curtain and up onto the dais directly behind Brightwick. The ripple of an audible gasp followed by the odd pocket of nervous laughter accompanied her entrance, but the four members of the panel were still unaware as to the reason for the audience's reaction. It was not until they saw Garland's open-mouthed look of horror did they realise that whatever it was, it was behind them. Jasper, low to the ground as he was, remained unseen.

Archie, his view of the space masked by cameras and sound engineers, heard the gasp too, but was unable to pinpoint the reasons for it. He turned and looked up into the seating on both sides which gave Barbara enough time to catch up with him.

'Sir...Mister policeman, you cannot go on there...'

It was by following the nearest camera's line of focus that Archie now saw the apparition that was Lin. Barbara saw it too and she let out an audible gasp. 'Oh, my, Lord...' She snapped on her intercom. 'Security!'

~

Sitting bolt upright in his chair, Quinn gawped at the screen. After a couple of seconds for reality to kick in he threw the mug onto the table and rushed to the door, snapping at a highly startled Baariq as he did so.

'Quickest way to the stage! To the stage! WHICH WAY?!'

~

Sarah slipped back upstairs to try and catch a little more of the Gov.UK show. The pub had been busier than usual, and with Lin missing the workload for them was considerable. She entered the room just in time to see Camera One, placed side-on to the stage, pick up a creature directly out of a Michael Jackson video, accompanied by a jet black and seemingly very aggressive terrier.

'Oh, fuck... Mum! Mum! Come up here quick! MUM!'

~

The constant barking confirmed to Archie that it was Lin just as Garland shouted out, 'What do you think you're doing? How dare you...!'

Lin kept a tight hold of Jasper who was, by now, hysterical at the strangeness of the surroundings and the aggressive reaction to his mistress. She lifted the container of fake blood up high.

A gasp went out from those audience members closest to the action.

~

Marissa, in the kitchen collecting further refreshment, nearly dropped the bottle as she heard the yell from Deborah.

'Bloody hell...! Mari! In here! This is all going tits...!'

~

Arnold waved his warrant card and shouted above the studio noise.

'This is the police and you're all safe. Could you please remain where you are!'

The volume and authority in his voice registered, the tension relaxed. On the dais the four panellists were now facing Lin and Jasper. Lin pointed at Brightwick and began to talk loudly and clearly at him, her voice picked up by the ambient microphones above the stage, the previously applied blood streaking her face and dripping onto the floor.

'What's it like to murder someone Brightwick? Well, you'd know, wouldn't you?' Lin moved away from the curtain drawing closer to Brightwick who backed up until the desk barred further movement. Seeing that he was the target, his other three panellists slipped away to the side. 'Well? Wouldn't you?' She talked past Brightwick now, addressing the audience, the skin flaps created by Jenni flapping obscenely. 'This miserable excuse for a man who thinks it's OK to spend his leisure time shooting wild animals, who's trying to trick us all into believing he means them no harm, this is the man who killed my sister!' Now the whole room was fixed on the unfolding drama. 'Got some friends of his to run her over, make it look like a hit-and-run. She looked just like this when his thugs, under his orders, had finished with her.' Lin opened her arms slightly giving all house cameras an excellent view of her state; they made the most of it. 'All that she left behind was this dog and my broken heart.' Jasper had now ceased barking, a low slow growl escaping bared teeth.

Archie slowly walked to the edge of the dais and into camera view...

~

Jenni, holding her wineglass like a statuette, spoke at the screen. 'I'd like to thank the members of the Academy...'

~

Kanjara, cup to mouth but not drinking, slowly lowered it to the saucer without taking her eyes off the screen.

'Archie...?'

~

Archie paused on the edge of the dais. 'Lin? Lin. What the hell are you doing?'

Brightwick looked across at him. 'You?'

Two stagehands appeared in the curtain's gap and Archie, warrant card in hand, snapped out a command. 'I'm police! Stay exactly where you are!' They froze.

Lin looked over at Archie, surprised to see him, puzzled even. 'Archie?' Brightwick saw the opening and tried to slither along the desk and away to Lin's left and she stepped in line with him. 'Brightwick! You stay right where you are you fucker! Archie leave me, please. I have to do this, for Rene.'

'Do you know what you're doing; I mean really know?'

'I do Archie.' She looked down at the terrier. 'Could you... please? Please?' Archie stood for stretched seconds.

The two front desk security guards arrived alongside Barbara. 'Police have just arrived.'

'Get them in here,' she snapped. 'Now!'

Archie scanned the immobility of the curious gawking audience and spoke loudly. 'Everyone just stay where you are. I'm Detective Inspector Arnold, Northants CID and there's no need to be concerned. OK, Lin, let me help...' Archie stepped around the desk towards the wag and grin of Jasper. Everyone was fixed to the spot, the drama unfolding to its seemingly inevitable conclusion.

Archie stopped just beyond Brightwick. To Brightwick's surprise, Lin dropped the lead, Arnold squatted, and the terrier yapped and jumped up into his awaiting arms. He stood up.

'All yours Lin.'

Archie moved to the rear of the dais as three more of the stagehands came through the curtain. 'Not now! I'm ordering you to stand back.'

Lin fixed Brightwick with the stare of a mongoose at a cobra. 'This is what it's like to be alone Brightwick, just like my sister was when your thugs left her in a ditch to die and left her dog, that dog, to watch.' Lin poured more of the fake blood over her head. The stream of red ran down her face and clothing to splash onto the floor to the gasp of the audience. 'The freshness and beauty of her life seeping out as you planned how to sell your next slaughter mission.' She launched the remaining liquid in a graceful arc towards Brightwick before dropping the beaker on the floor.

~

Sarah and Valerie both screamed out together...

~

Marissa grabbed Deborah's hand. 'Oh Jesus, Debs...she's fucked it now...'

'And Archie's career with it.'

~

'Wow! Headlines in the Sun tomorrow Dougie.'

Dougie looked on spellbound. 'In all of 'em...'

~

Arriving at full tilt through the backdrop, Quinn tap danced onto the dais and made a determined effort to reach Lin. Archie saw his motivation and, snuggling Jasper a little more tightly, stepped in front of Quinn and felled him with a single, short-arm jab to the jaw with his free hand.

~

'Oh no!' Kanjara's cup and saucer clattered onto her chest then crashed to the floor.

~

Deborah looked across at Marissa. 'What career?'

~

After a short pause the door opened; Tina saw the shattered crockery and Kanga's wide-eyed, mouth agape stare.

'I said it'd be hot with so little milk in it...'

~

The fake blood completed its graceful journey, drenching Brightwick and drawing a roar of approval from the fully engaged audience before it splashed over set and guests alike.

'Get off me you crazy woman!' Brightwick lunged at Lin. This was as far as he got with both speech and movement. Dropping Jasper and releasing his lead, Archie stepped forward and caught Brightwick's two hands in his then pushed him backwards onto the edge of the desk.

'Stay back Minister or your next move will be to the hospital.'

Jasper, now free to join in and wanting to protect his friend, took hold of Brightwick's trouser leg and shook it.

'Go to a black-out card! Now!'

The assistant producer's yell in the studio was heard even through the supposedly soundproof smoked glass of the control room. What was missed was the snapped but hissed reply by the show's producer.

'Not on your life, this is great TV!'

Brightwick was incandescent with embarrassed rage. A sharp shake of his leg dislodged Jasper but tore his trousers as he turned on Archie, wresting the detective's hands free. 'How dare you! You're finished! I'm a Minister of the Crown, a member of Her Majesty's government and I'll see to it that you're finished!' Lin snatched up the lead as the stagehands, after their initial stunned reaction, closed in and grabbed her. The other traumatised guests were hustled away from the fracas.

Brightwick turned to the technical crew all dutifully doing their jobs. 'And turn those cameras off. Now!' Garland rushed over to offer support to the hyperventilating Brightwick, but his attempt to wipe away the blood served only to smear it further. Four constables entered the space and endeavoured to restore order as Archie moved over to the staff who were restraining Lin.

'OK lads, OK, leave her be. She's fine now. That right Lin?'

Lin smiled broadly, 'I am now.'

They released her as the constables approached. Archie showed his warrant card. 'Detective Chief Inspector Arnold, Northants Division.'

Brightwick reared up and pointed to Archie and Lin in turn. 'He is not your superior officer he is a suspended officer and I want him arrested and charged with assault; her too! Do it now, or like him you'll have no jobs tomorrow!'

The constables looked at each other, at Archie, at Brightwick, then back to Archie. Archie smoothed back his forelock. 'Best do it, he's not got a sense of humour that one.'

A groan came from the floor as, like the kraken, Quinn woke up and attempted, unsuccessfully, to stand. Archie was over to him.

'Steady a bit there.' He dragged over a chair. 'You'll need to sit for few minutes...OK? Sorry about that, had to be done.' A still dazed and glazed Quinn took the steadying arm and sat gratefully. 'Just sit there, breathe deeply and you'll be fine.' He turned to one of the constables. 'Get a first aid kit will you please? That's gonna need an ice pack at the very least.'

Slapping Garland's ministering hands away, Brightwick was having none of it. 'Never mind Quinn, arrest that man!' His voice now rose to a shriek. 'Arrest him!'

Archie took Lin's arm and she smiled at him. 'Thank you, ndugu.'

Brightwick screamed over to his still-dazed PPS. 'Quinn! Quinn, get me the Commissioner on the phone, now!'

Archie and Lin, accompanied by a still-growling Jasper, left with two of the officers as the two remaining constables attempted to sort the disarray into a coherent whole.

~

Kanjara shook her head. 'No Tina, the tea was fine. I've just seen what unemployment looks like, that's all.'

~

The phone rang in Anita's apartment and she looked at the caller ID. *'What the hell? This time on a Sunday; really?'* She picked up the receiver.

'Hello Jay.'

'Ah, Miss Cresson.'

'Has something important come up? Only...'

'*You are awaiting the arrival of your dinner date?*'

'Yes, he's a bit late but...'

'*Might I suggest you turn on your television set, BBC One?*'

'Why?'

'*Just...turn it on and we'll talk tomorrow. Goodnight.*'

'Goodnight...?'

Anita put the receiver down, went into the sitting room and turned on her television set. Picking up the handset, she sat in one of the two armchairs...

Monday

The focus of the gathering in the Serious Crimes' Office was mixed. On the one hand the events of the previous evening were the central point of comment, on the other the business of the day demanded action. To that end and with mugs of coffee or tea in hand, those members present were gathered around a plot chart as DI Pat Kershaw detailed the latest intelligence surrounding their ongoing investigation into a network of cigarette smuggling operations.

'We know the level of dealing and receiving has been partially choked off since two members of the Carter family were nailed in the joint operation of Northants and Oxon forces, but as is always the way with these things, suppression in supply leads to an increase in price and an upsurge in efforts to cash in on that. Phil, where are we with intelligence from the Port of Tilbury Police?'

'Slow.'

'Why?'

'Because interdepartmental cooperation stumbles when it comes to budget.'

Marissa almost laughed. 'So, this isn't about how secure a collar this might be nor what it means in terms of crime reduction, it's just about whose budget it comes out of. Fuck's sake Pat, it's a bloody joke.'

Pat nodded. 'Right, I'll have a word with the Chief Super, see if we can't get budget oversight on this...' She caught a movement out the corner of her eye and stiffened a little. 'OK, stall that. I think we're about to get an announcement.'

Into the office walked Chief Superintendent James Campbell followed by two other officers.

'Good morning.'

A grunted, 'Morning Sir,' greeted him.

'I assume you are all acquainted with the events of last evening?'

'Sir.'

'Good, that makes what I have to say pertinent and you will listen without interruption. Late last night and again this morning I received representations from senior members of our police force and Her Majesty's government. The debacle at the television studios in Oxford has resulted in Detective Chief Inspector Arnold's immediate and indefinite suspension from the force. He and this whole department, after having acted contrary to my direct instructions, are under investigation for the deliberate and persistent harassment of the staff and servants of Lord Brightwick, a serving minister of the Crown. You'll have noticed that Detectives Cho and Beckett are also absent from these proceedings. This is because they, too, have been put on indefinite suspension following the legally untenable search of the Bliss Bank property and the questionable interview procedures used on Lord Brightwick and his staff.' He pre-empted any dissent, 'No matter who gave those orders!' He indicated the two men alongside him. 'Now, I expect this department to afford DCIs Carngrove and Merryman every courtesy in their internal investigation.' He fixed Pat with a stare. 'DI Kershaw, as senior officer, at present, you'll be held responsible for seeing this happens. They'll require full access to all material appertaining to the Brightwick affair to be delivered to room Twelve B, where all recorded interviews will be conducted. This case is now closed, need I add.'

Campbell left the room as the two investigating officers faced the collective stares of the Serious Crime Unit.

Wednesday

Red is an insistent almost incorrigible colour. Like the remains of porridge oats in a saucepan after the wash, you think you have got it all and then, as you wipe that freshly-laundered tea towel round the inside, you feel it drag...but it's too late. Not that anyone present at the reception for the Chinese Delegation at Bliss Bank Hall would have done anything to draw attention to it. That would be frightfully bad form, but still, there it was, like a bogey on a moustache, a red streak acting as a beacon to history.

Apart from Brightwick's slightly ruddy appearance the event had gone perfectly; just like clockwork. The welcoming toast of champagne laced with powdered rhino horn was savoured and commented on by the Ambassador and Pei Yuan; each course at dinner was perfection, particularly the Hŭbiān tāng, which resulted in the chef being called from the kitchen for applause by the Chinese contingent. Now, as the guests mingled in the great hall arranging meetings and swapping stories and diary notes, the feeling was more relaxed, more informal.

Seeing Brightwick in the far corner of the room dispensing orders to Willis, Taros made his way over, malt in hand. 'Lawrence. A word?'

Brightwick dismissed Willis and collected his glass of Remy Martin as he joined Vladkov. 'Taros. Sorry, poor host, haven't had any time to spend with you this evening, guidance needed throughout. I trust you've been made comfortable, made some new friends?'

'Yes I have Larry, most instructive.'

'Good.'

There was a short but significant pause before Taros spoke, 'I was made aware of the unfortunate events of Sunday evening.'

Brightwick stiffened a little. 'Yes, yes, all very unfortunate, but all sorted now. The required result is set in motion and will be achieved, etcetera, etcetera.' He paused. 'You didn't see it then?'

'No. I do not watch television. It was your Noel Coward who said, I think, television is for the appearing on not for the watching.'

Brightwick frowned. 'Not on Sunday it wasn't.'

'No, so I gathered. And tell me, the mobile phones...?'

'In the audience?' Taros nodded. 'No. One of the things the company did do right. The invited audience were told mobiles had to be switched off, so trial by makeshift media was mercifully curtailed. I feel sure someone will leak it at some time, just not at the moment, and I'll have a carefully prepared government-sanctioned line when it does.'

Taros moved in close. 'Is there anything I can do? To... resolve the situation?'

Brightwick shook his head slowly. 'Thank you no, Taros. You are a good friend and rest assured, should anything be required then you would be the person I would turn to, but I have put the problem to rest myself.'

'The girl? She is to be charged?'

'With the full force of the law, I've seen to that.'

'And the policeman?'

'Out of work, certainly for the foreseeable future. I also believe, should he ever be taken back, that it will be with a significant demotion.'

'But that is unlikely to happen?'

'That he is taken back?' Vladkov nodded. 'Very unlikely if my conversations with his superiors are anything to go by.'

'Because, if it should become likely I would be most happy to...'

'You are most kind Taros, but no. Best to let sleeping dogs lie. I feel I've filled enough headlines for a lifetime.' Vladkov smiled and shrugged his shoulders. 'And I'm still in your debt for your efficient handling of Mister Lamb.'

'That? That was nothing; a favour to an old friend, for instructive informations.'

'Well, I trust the connections you make here will be some small recompense for that.' He took a sip of brandy and held Taros' gaze for a second or two before clearing his throat. 'Ahem... Mister Lamb...?'

'Do you really want to know?' Brightwick paused then shook his head. 'Good choice.'

'Enough of this maudlin talk.' He took Taros by the arm. 'Come, let me introduce you to the Chinese Minister for Commerce. With your banking interests you should have much in common...'

~

The light from Inspection Room Two attracted Jay's attention as he left his office, coat on, briefcase in hand. Walking down to the light source he peered through the box window to see Anita, clipboard at her side, transferring data onto a computer. After a combined long pause and indrawn breath he gently opened the door.

'Evening Mister Millar.'

'Ah, semper erecti. Can I ask, if it's not too impolite, why you're still here at...' he checked his watch, 'nineteen forty-five? Do you have no home to go to?'

'I do, but it's empty.'

'As is this place, or will be very shortly when I leave.'

'Cadavers for company.'

'Oh dear, bad as that?'

Anita looked up from the screen. 'A bit.'

'Well, if I'm not being too light with it all, you'll be pleased to hear that while you were locked into the monthly figures the funeral directors have collected both Miss Lea and Detective Reeve; cases closed.'

'Why do you think I was locked away in here?'

'You knew?'

'I did.'

'Not much gets by you does it?'

'Not much. There's funeral dates then?'

'For Ms Lea it's next Monday, for Detective Reeve we have yet to be informed. Gabrielle, his sister?' Anita nodded. 'She has yet to make clear her arrangements.'

'He was from Shropshire originally, wasn't he?'

'Ludlow, yes. I did have a chat when Gabrielle came in. She was unclear as to what was expected, here or there. All a bit daunting, there being no arrangements made by the deceased.'

'He wasn't expecting to die quite yet.'

'No indeed.'

'She has no immediate family to call on?'

'No. Both parents are passed. There's an uncle, her mother's brother...she's returning to update him on the story to date as we speak, so...'

'All very sad.'

'Indeed, but that's outside our remit now. All will go through the coroner, the funeral home and Gabrielle... Not looking forward to the invite to that one.'

'Sorry Jay.'

'For...?'

'Leaving it all to you, a bit unfair.'

'Fully understandable in light of recent circumstances.'

Anita gave Jay a blank look. 'What circumstances?'

'You force my hand Ms. Cresson. I hesitate to ask, but, Archie...?'

'No, it's not that...' She saw Jay's expression. 'Well yes, a little bit, but it's more...' She sighed. 'You sure you want to do this?'

Jay placed his briefcase on the floor, took his coat off and sat opposite her. 'Absolutely.'

'Now?'

'Absolutely.'

'Liar.'

'No. For true. If it ever became known to Mrs Millar that I'd left one of my staff in a blue funk in order to get home to dinner I'd be in very hot water. So, tell me.'

Anita smiled at him. 'Capo dei capi.'

'I'm sure, just don't tell Mister Brando. So...?'

'Oh... I look at my life. I'm thirty-eight, unmarried... Ha, there's a joke, I'm not even close. So here I am, spending my evenings in an office of the dead transferring fatality figures for the month onto a database with this...' she picked up a part-finished pack of Hula Hoops, 'as my definition of fine dining.' Anita glanced round the room. 'Some would say I'm wallowing in self-pity and they'd be right, because this last fortnight...it's been shitty Jay.'

'We are of one mind. I'd hate to stir things up any further by branding these feelings as part of a "women and relationships" discussion, but the cancelled appointment by Detective Arnold on Sunday last?'

'She shrugged. 'Let's just say it was the blue touch paper that lit the thought process.'

'Ah...'

'And before you say I told you so, don't. I know you did.'

'Pity our woodland conversation didn't bear fruit then.'

'Thing is, really...he didn't promise anything, it was me loading him with expectation. I let myself down.'

'That's a bit harsh.'

'Honest not harsh. My desire to form a relationship, any relationship, is a two-way street and I lost sight of that.'

'Now that is very honest, very grown up. The pity is, as far as the heart is concerned, the street of love often leads to a cul-de-sac.'

Anita gave Jay a long look of surprise. 'That was very profound Mister Millar.'

'A partial diet of classics when at university often makes uninvited intrusions into the everyday.' He smiled at her. 'Poor recompense I know, but what say I phone ahead, warn Mrs Millar of a fourth for dinner, and you join us this evening?'

'A fourth? I thought you said Gabrielle had gone home?'

'She has, it's my son, he's back from his sojourn in Inverness.'

'Oh, right. What's he been doing there?'

'He's a marine biologist, did you not know?'

'Well no, I mean, I knew you had a son...'

'And daughter.'

'Yes, Marianne. We've met, remember, at the summer open day? She was still at university then, doing her PhD.'

'Ah yes. Memory failing. Well, she's completed that now and working for Kellogg.'

'The corn flake people?'

'The oil exploration people.'

'Ah. And your son?'

'Nathan. He's working for the salmon fishery board on the Cromarty Firth, looking into changes of the migration patterns of wild salmon caused by marine pollution. The river Ness is of particular value, apparently, and with the closeness of the oil industry... Thirty-five and still messing about on the river; where did I go wrong?'

'So she's mining it and he's guarding it. That must be fun.'

'Yes. When they're both at home you can imagine the conversation when we gather for evening meals.'

'I'll bet. Where's Marianne working now?'

'Orlando, so no risk of fallout this evening, should you say yes of course.'

'Well, I've not planned meals for this evening,' she held up the Hula Hoops pack again, 'as you can see, and as I've not met Nathan before and not seen Mrs Millar for a good while, not since that open day in fact...I'd be delighted, thank you.'

'Our pleasure. How long will you be here?'

'Another twenty minutes?'

'Perfect. I'll slip back to the office and make the call then spend the time until you're ready closing up the hit-and-run file for Renata Lea.'

508

Nine Days Later

'You sure about this?'

Lin nodded. 'Seeing as how it was for me you lost your job.'

The breeze picked up as Archie and Lin walked across the hospital car park. 'I got suspended, I'm not dead.'

'Luckily.' Lin glanced around. 'I'm surprised there's no paparazzi chasing us.'

'After all this time? Maybe it's just that we're not as important as we think we are.'

'Chip-paper legends.' Lin thought for a little. 'You think they'll let you back in, to the force I mean?'

'Ha! Over the CS's dead body.' Archie stepped back to allow Lin into the vestibule of the HDU. 'And thanks for coming, I know Kanga will be pleased to see you.'

Their journey along the corridor was interrupted by the appearance of Sister Waldeck. 'Ah, Detective Arnold, and if I'm not mistaken Miss Linden Lea.'

Lin smiled. 'Fame or notoriety?'

'Bit of both according the papers...and the slight staining.'

'And here was me thinking my skin tones would conceal it after this time.'

'It does a pretty good job. Tell me, that fake blood...it was fake wasn't it?'

Lin laughed. 'Ha! Yes, more's the pity, it should've been his.'

'Oh, I think your gallant hero was more in danger of spilling that blood than you.' She turned to Archie. 'So, back in to see Ms Desai?'

'I am, we are...'

'Well I've got news for you. She's been moved to a room in the Brittain Wing; Mary Seacole Ward, room eight. Transferred yesterday.'

'So she's...?'

'Go and see for yourself, but you'll need to hurry as visiting time closes in half an hour.'

'Thanks, and thanks for...you know, for other stuff.'

Sister Waldeck smiled and nodded. 'What happens in HDU stays in HDU.'

There was a long look between Archie and Sister Waldeck. Lin picked up on it but could not quite decipher the meaning. 'Nice to meet you...?'

'Sister Waldeck, Jenny.'

'Jenny.'

They returned along the corridor and back down the flight of stairs...

... The Brittain Wing was easy to find and the vestibule of the Seacole ward was large, light and airy even on this November evening. A relaxed atmosphere prevailed with vending machines decorating the walls and a small RVS outlet filled the centre; all the offices were open plan.

'All I'm saying is, seeing as how you say you've only been in that shop once before you must have made quite an impression on that young lady.'

'For all the wrong reasons, trust me.'

Lin, flowers in hand, held back as they approached the door and Archie turned slightly, aware she was no longer at his side. She stopped and nodded at the door. 'No, you go. I'll come in after; after you've, you know... Give you time to announce me.'

'OK, if you want. Do you require trumpets?'

'Not trumpets, a red carpet would be good though.'

'Consider it forgotten.' He turned and looked in through the small window near the top of the door. 'Oh, wow... Here. Look at this!'

Lin looked through the door's circular window. The room was large, and the view was out onto what had once been the walled kitchen garden of the old mansion, now redesigned into a sensory area and lit with wall and paving lights. The bed was empty and in a wheelchair at its side sat Kanjara, looking out into the panorama.

Lin smiled. 'That nurse was right. This is just brill.'

'Bloody excellent.'

'Right, in you go. I'll go and fetch a coffee and follow on in a few minutes...go on!' Archie was about to recharge his gum when Lin took the fresh stick from his hand and shook her head. 'Uh-uh. Not this evening. Spit out what you've got,' she held out a tissue, 'here.' Archie did so. 'Thank you. Now, I'll get coffee... do you want one?'

'Yeah, coffee would be good.'

'Right, see you in five.'

Archie eased the door open. 'Well look at you! When did all this happen?'

Kanjara pressured the one wheel backwards to turn the wheelchair. 'Oh hi, how lovely! Erm...yesterday morning. My physio said my progress was good enough for me to be moved to a ground floor ward. so I'd be easier to exercise...makes me sound like a dog!'

'A bitch surely?'

'Careful, I'm in a delicate state, so I'm told.'

'Yeah. Sorry I've not been in much, been a bit hectic.'

'I can imagine. Anyway, we've talked on the phone in between whiles...' She smiled but it seemed a little forced. Archie picked up on it.

'So, what's wrong with all this?' He waved a hand at the room and wheelchair.

Kanga raised her eyebrows, smiled. 'I'm told any sort of recovery will take months.'

'But there will be one.'

'Yes, but still...'

Archie nodded. 'I can understand how frustrating that seems right now, but put you a month and half down that road and you'll see the destination much more clearly and know the journey was worth it.'

'Those inspirational quotes again?' She sighed. 'Sorry, ungrateful little minx aren't I?'

'Impatient not ungrateful; the jury's still out about the minx bit.' Archie walked across to her. 'I can't tell you how good it is to see you.'

'And you. You mentioned, last time you were in, about the press bother. Has it all subsided now?'

'It was over a week ago now, Kanga, you know the papers. Storm in a teabag.'

'A bit more than that.' She smiled and winked at him. 'Quite a short-arm jab you gave him.'

'He deserved it.'

'How is the lady in question?'

'You'll be able to ask her yourself, she's here to see you.'

Kanjara looked towards the door. 'Here?'

'Yeah, just gone to get us coffee.'

'Is she as pretty as she looked on the TV?'

'Good make-up wasn't it?'

'It was. Did she do it herself?'

Archie winced a little. 'Best not go there. If I admit to it then it'll just involve another person. So, what's been done and said with you, that's new?'

'Clunky change of subject there... OK, it's very early days remember, very, but yesterday...I stood, on my own!'

'Oh, Christ Kanga, that's...that's great, that's amazing! For how long?'

'For about ten seconds, and with lots and lots of help to get up in the first place, but, stood on my own.'

'Oh blimey, good vibes from your minders then?'

'Ah well, that's where it gets a little sticky.' Archie pulled up a chair. 'What they've said is although I may be able to stand...'

'That's great...!'

'You need to rein it in a little Archie, OK?' Archie could see the seriousness in her face and nodded. 'They said although I may be able to stand, occasionally and for short periods, they're of the collective opinion that I'll be wheelchair-dependent, certainly for the foreseeable future.'

'But you stood up today! That's gotta count for something.'

'Yes it has.'

'Well then.'

'And they've also said they expect to see a steady improvement in my general condition and that they'll be on my case for a long while yet, so...'

'NHS...doesn't get any better than them, does it?'

'Nope.' There was a short silence before Kanjara spoke again. 'OK, if you won't, I will. What about you? Back in the thick of it before long?'

'As a Constable, yeah, if at all.'

'Really? They'll be that harsh?'

'By the time Brightwick's finished with me. Yeah.'

'You'll appeal though.'

'Ha! Unlikely.'

'Got it sewn up that tightly have they?' Archie nodded. 'And Lin? What about her?'

'She's pleaded guilty. Probation couldn't prepare reports on the day, so her case comes up early January.'

'Happy New Year.'

'Yeah. Brightwick's been pushing for the whole shtick but she's got a clean record, suffered documented personal trauma... A lot depends on the magistrates. She might get the book thrown at her or get away with a fine or some community service. Like I say, it depends on how sympathetic the court and the reports are.'

'As if she's not got enough on her plate. And now there's you.'

'And now there's me.'

'What's the charge sheet?'

'Assault; bringing the department into disrepute; dereliction of duty; wilful disregard of a direct order; endangering the public; destruction of private property...' Arnold shrugged. 'I'm up before the court and then the Chief Comm and his committee next month too, and I'll be lucky if I come out of there with my testicles intact. Brightwick wants the CPS to prosecute me for ABH, but that depends on whether the CPS are satisfied with the verdict of the internal hearing. If they are, I'll probably just get the departmental punishment, which'll be substantial.'

'You'll not go back in then?'

'Nah, don't think so.' He smiled, 'Not even if they pleaded with me to.'

'Like that is it? Well, you seem very relaxed about it.'

'Funnily enough I am. I mean, I enjoyed the job but not the politics of it. Maybe this is nature's way of telling me to quit, to move on to the next chapter of my life.' He slipped out of the chair, squatted down in front of Kanjara and took her hand, 'Which will hopefully involve you?'

Kanga put her hand on his. 'Archie...'

The door opened and Lin came into the room. She saw Archie's position and took a slight step back. 'Oh shit, were you...? Shit, sorry, I don't want to interrupt anything...' She held out a waxed paper cup of coffee. 'I brought this in before it went cold, really sorry...'

'No no, come in.' Archie stood up quickly and took the coffee. 'Nothing as dramatic, we were just trading notes. Linden Lea, meet Kanjara Desai, Kanga, meet Lin.'

Lin held out a hand. 'Hello Kanjara, it's really good to meet you at last.'

'So you're what all the fuss was about.'

Lin faltered a little. 'I guess so...yes.'

Kanga smiled at her. 'Sorry Lin, that came out all wrong. What I meant was that Sunday night session, not the events at your flat... Oh Lord, got that wrong too...'

'It's fine, really, and I know what you meant.'

'Can I say how sorry I am about your sister, and I was so sorry I couldn't get to her funeral.'

'I understand, Archie was there as your representative, the cremation was all a cremation should be and now she's going home.'

'Yes, Archie mentioned something about that when he phoned the other day, about her journey. What was that about?'

'She's on her way back to our village...'

'The container is?'

'Yes, along with our connector.' Lin looked across at Archie. 'He paid for that.'

Kanga nodded. 'I'd expect nothing less. Connector?'

Lin untied the netsuke from her wrist and handed it across. 'One of a set of triplets.'

'Oh, this is beautiful,' Kanga turned it over in her hand, 'Just exquisite. Reminds me a lot of the stories my gran told me. "When Elephants Did Fly" was one, and er...oh, "The Elephant and the Jackal", tales like that.' She handed the netsuke back. 'And how about you? Will you go back?'

'When I can. Khanyisile will hold onto our sister until then, wait for me to complete the circle...' There was a short pause before Lin broke the moment by holding out the brilliant yellow chrysanthemums. 'I hope these're OK.'

'They're lovely, and you shouldn't have.'

Lin looked round the room at the collection of six flower-filled vases and smiled. 'Maybe. Is there a vase left in the hospital?'

'My mother's to blame for most of these,' she looked at Archie, 'Mum and your lot.'

'I may no longer be their boss, but they're still my team. Have your folks been back in then?'

'Yesterday.' Kanga fixed Archie with a look. 'They'll be back in tomorrow too...you should meet them; they're coming for afternoon visiting.'

'Er, yeah, OK. I've got some time off, so... Ha! There's an understatement.' He looked at his watch and then at Lin. 'I figure we're gonna get chucked out soon...'

'Bell's not gone yet.'

'No, I know, but I don't want to be held responsible for you not being rested, or of being the subject of ire for the nursing staff.'

Kanjara pointed to a chair. 'Right. Drag that over here Lin and you can give me the proper version of that Sunday night.'

Lin put the flowers in the sink, ran some water to join them then moved the chair across. Archie nodded at her. 'Your story Lin, you tell it.'...

... 'I still can't believe you got in that easily...'

'Honestly, neither can I.'

'And with the dog in a bag! Well, if nothing else you'll have served the BBC notice on the quality of the security systems in place at their...what did you call it?'

'Outsourcing studio.'

'Yes, there.'

Archie smiled. 'And their terrorist threat-handling procedure too.'

'You and Lin should go into the security business together, advise these conglomerates on the weak spots in their organisations.'

'After what we got the BBC to broadcast? I doubt we'd get past the front gate ever again, either of us,' said Archie.

'No need, Lin here can always be relied on to find a back-way in.'

All three chuckled then Lin stood up. 'Right you two, I'm away.'

'Oh, do you have to go now?'

'I do, Kanga, trust me. I've got a group of friends, a small terrier and a large bar tab waiting for me back at the Red Lion.' Archie also stood, but Lin talked on, 'no, you stay, I'll cab it back.'

'Cab it? It'll cost a fortune. No, visiting time's almost over, and I did want to chat to you.'

'Oh, OK.'

'Can you just give me five minutes and I'll drop you back.'

'OK. I'll just wait out there. Lovely to meet you Kanga. Is it OK if I visit again?'

'Yes, I'd like that.'

Lin bent, kissed Kanjara on the cheek and whispered in her ear, 'Snap him up before someone else does.' She stood and smiled at Archie. 'See you in five.'

The door closed behind her and Archie turned to Kanga. 'Why do I have the feeling that something just happened?'

'It's your suspicious nature. She is really pretty Archie...I mean really.'

'Yes, she is, almost as pretty as you.'

'Oh, that was also a bit clunky too, but welcome all the same.' Archie gave another look at the door then at Kanga who fixed him with a penetrating gaze. 'You were saying?'

'What?'

'Nothing as dramatic?'

'Oh, that.'

'Yes, that.'

Archie folded the flop of hair back and sat again. 'Well, maybe...' He took in a deep breath. 'I'm just hoping my future will include more of you.'

'What sort of future are we talking about? As a Sunday lunch visitor or...?'

'Or. Definitely talking or.'

This time she took his hand. 'If I'm honest, you've figured in my thoughts these last few days, a lot, and not always for the right reasons.' Archie made a puzzled face and she motioned the wheelchair. 'This.'

'The wheelchair?'

'Yes. This elephant in the room. This is serious Archie. My next few months are going to be no picnic.'

'And you think what? That I'm doing this out of guilt or pity or...?'

'No, you made that very plain the last time it came up. I just... I don't want to hold you back from being the best you can be.'

Now it was Archie's turn to fix Kanga with a look of real concentration. 'That won't happen if you're with me; I knew that from the very first time we met...felt things that've been strangers to me for years.' Archie put his hand on his heart. 'In here.'

For a few seconds all Kanga could do was blink and stare. 'Wasn't expecting that.'

'What, the truth? Can't work on anything less, and know this. I want to support you in any way you want me to, that way you can be the best you can be as well.'

Kanjara glanced round the room, her eyes finally resting on the wheelchair. 'Can't say I'm not frightened.'

'OK, then let's be frightened together.'

'You'll have to run the gauntlet of my parents. My dad can be very protective, definitely when he sees my affection is for a white boy.'

'Then I'll practice my elegance and charm...and get under a sun lamp.'

'The sun lamp's a bit racist and you don't have long enough to develop the elegance and charm, they're here again tomorrow.'

'Cheeky...' The end-of-visiting bell sounded. 'Saved by it.' Archie got up. 'I'm away. See you tomorrow.' He leant forward to kiss Kanga on the cheek, but she altered her position and their lips touched, lightly at first, but with slightly more pressure as the seconds ticked by until Archie gradually caressed her cheeks in his palms.

They parted and Kanga looked at him, her eyes alive with meaning. 'That was...perfect. Thank you.'

'Willingly done and beautifully returned. First of many...'

Their conversation was halted by the arrival of Staff Nurse Collins. 'Still here? Bell's gone; did you not hear it?'

Archie straightened. 'Er, yes...sorry, I was just...'

'Going...?'

'Occupied.' He turned to Kanga. 'See...?'

Staff Nurse Collins talked over him. 'Not here you aren't. Another big day with the physiotherapist tomorrow so it would be helpful if you could make yourself scarce and this young lady can get her rest...much like that fella needed to on the BBC.' She saw his expression. 'Oh yes, all the night staff saw it. You're quite the film star round here, you and that young lady sitting out there.'

'Well...' Archie looked at her badge, 'Staff Nurse Collins, I'll do as I'm told. Last thing I want is to cause any slowdown in the young lady's recovery.' He took Kanga's hand. 'I'll see you tomorrow...you've just made an old man very happy.'

~

Sarah pulled the last pint of Summer Blush and stood it alongside the other four.

'You sure about this, Sarah?'

'Absolutely, Mum said, and after Lin's TV appearance and I think we should toast the cause of that event.' They picked up their glasses. 'To Granny Betty; she made Lin the woman she is today.'

There was laughter and a chorus of 'Granny Betty.' They drank and Tim was the first to speak when glasses were down.

'I have to say, it was made all the more remarkable by having the dog there. Where is he now?'

'Up with Mum. Prefers the company of older people when Lin's not around.'

'And talking of Lin, do we know when she'll be gracing us with her presence?'

'Later this evening so she said.' Sarah took another pull on the pint.

'You went to the hearing?'

'I did Vaz. I hardly had time to blink. She came up from the cells, said her name, confirmed her address and pleaded guilty.'

'Did she say the Lion?'

'She did, Mum insisted. They set the date for the next hearing, beginning of January, got bail and she was gone.'

Pitter-pattering down the stairs and on through the group came Jasper. Disregarding the calls of 'Hi Jasp,' and 'Hello boy,' the terrier tail-wagged his way to the entrance door then stood alert and expectant.

'What's up with him, does he need a walk?' asked Lisa.

'Shouldn't think so, he's only just been out and done one.' Sarah squatted down. 'Come here Jasper. Come on...' Rooted to the spot, gaze fixed on the handle of the outer-door, Jasper ignored her sweet tones. 'Oh well up to you, just watch out for that door.'

They turned back to their conversations as Jasper maintained his vigil. After a few minutes the terrier stood, bounced a couple of times and barked. Sarah looked across. 'What is it Jasper?' After a short pause the door opened and Lin came in, closely followed by Archie. 'How the hell did he know that?'

Lin bent to fuss the overjoyed dog as he bounced around her then moved on to Archie who also dished out a greeting before asking, 'Know what?'

'That you two were on your way? He's been by that door for ages before you arrived.'

'Has he?' Lin scrubbed his ear. 'Who's a clever chap then, eh?'

'He is,' said Archie as he stood up. 'OK, delivered back safe and sound as promised. I'm gonna head off...'

Lin took his arm. 'Stay and have a drink with us.'

Archie looked round the gathered group. 'I fear I'd cramp your style.'

Sarah stepped forward. 'No you wouldn't. Nothing being discussed here that an officer of the law can't hear, is there?'

There was a mumbled half-agreement of this, and Archie looked from them to Sarah. 'Vote of no confidence there Ms Wilmott, obvious even to an ex police officer.'

'Thanks a lot for that, I'll just have those drinks back.'

'Don't be hard on them, and I really ought to be on my way. So it's OK then, Lin? What we discussed in the car.'

'Jasper? Yes, but only if you tell me why.'

'I'm going across to the RSPCA Centre at Brixworth.'

Tim looked at the bar clock. 'What, at this time of night?'

Archie looked decidedly sheepish. 'Yeah. Nicky, the lady who runs it, she's going to meet me there. I phoned earlier.'

'They have a night shift?'

'Have to apparently, insurance thing. Anyway, she said she'd pop back and meet me.'

'Why are you going there?' asked Lin.

'Er...just something I feel I ought to do, and that's why I need to borrow this wee fella for a bit.'

'OK. I'll fetch his collar and lead. When will you bring him back?'

'It'll be late by the time I'm finished will tomorrow morning do?'

'Yes, fine.' Lin fetched Jasper's collar and lead.'

'Right. I'm away.' He scanned the group. 'And, if you're driving home...just make sure you've got a car.'

He and Jasper turned and left, the terrier giving not so much as a backward glance.

~

⁶**H**i Nicky, got your message, what's up?'

Nicky Colbert walked into the office, a bag over her shoulder and one under each eye. 'Just a customer coming in.'

'At this time of night?'

'Yeah, long story. Could you do me a favour Rick and fetch that pup we got from Probert Street, the dangerous dog callout? Bring him into a holding pen for me.'

'Yeah sure. Is he re-homed then?'

'Think so, yeah.'

'Do they know what he is?'

'Not they, he, and he's a copper.'

Rick Barnes, night watchman and one of the general kennel staff, stared. 'Wow. Really?' Nicky nodded. 'Blimey...right, I'll go and fetch the lucky sod.'

Rick went out to the kennels, setting off a round of barks as each inmate tried desperately to join his pack. Nicky listened to the noise, its meaning not lost on her, and she closed the door in an attempt to stifle their calls for help; it failed. She sat at the desk and flicked idly through the paperwork, seeing but not reading the words typed on each sheet of canine woe; there was no need, she knew them all by heart. She sighed and closed the file. 'Jeez...'

'All done. He's a perky little chap isn't he?'

Nicky's face brightened a little. 'Yeah, a perky chap that just might escape the long drop.' As she said this the outer door opened and Archie walked in, Jasper cradled in his arms. 'Talk of the Devil...' she saw the terrier. 'And who's this, an exchange?'

'Ha! Not on your life, this is Jasper, my test dog.'

Nicky got up and moved towards Archie. 'Hello Jasper.'

The terrier yapped once, and Archie could feel his tail wagging as he stretched forward to accept the fuss. 'Well there's a first. He can smell it on you I guess.'

Nicky smiled thinly. 'What, death?'

'Hope.'

'Sorry.' She indicated the desk-bound files. 'Shouldn't be reading report sheets this time of night.'

'No. If it's any consolation I feel the same about old cases that got away from me.'

'Well this time maybe it'll be better.'

'Let's see. I figured I ought to at least give it a try, give him a try I mean, does he have a name?'

'Un-chipped. No sign of a name in the house I suppose?'

'Nothing, and the owner's no longer with us. What've you called him?'

'Eight seventy-four. How do you want to do this?'

'Let's see how the pup is with Jasper here. He's not naturally trusting, doesn't go lookin' for trouble but can handle himself if it's offered. If that pup's aggressive he'll soon be served notice.'

'Your dog, your rules.'

'Not my dog, but I have permission. Shall we...?'

'Yes OK. Can you just sign this?'

Archie took the sheet and looked it over. 'Oh...right.'

'You shouldn't be surprised. If he does become aggressive then we'll not be liable for any injuries sustained, by any party.

OK?' Archie nodded. 'And understand this also, if that pup does become aggressive, he'll be on the Friday list for the vet.'

'Yeah, you said when I phoned, so no pressure.' He put Jasper on the floor, signed the paper then slipped the lead over his hand. 'Let's just hope he behaves then, shall we?'

'Let's. Rick, can you man the office for me?'

'For all the rush we'll be getting at this time of night, sure.'

Nicky led the way out and onto a concrete corridor which had wire-fronted cages left and right of it. All of them were empty except the one on the end. In it a slightly leggy brindle puppy bounced at their approach, then, as they got closer and the pup spied the approaching terrier its excitement was tempered by wariness. All four pads on the ground, Chipper whined quietly in suspicious confusion. Jasper too was alert, his pull on the lead increasing as they drew near.

Nicky sighed. 'Here we go. Just let them have a sniff through the wire.'

'Yeah, but I'll let him off if that's OK. I don't want Jasp to feel he's restrained in any way, that he can't do what might need to be done.'

Nicky nodded. 'Yeah sure...'

He bent to the terrier. 'And you, just show some manners here, OK?' Archie slipped the lead and Jasper trotted over to the kennel, neck-ruff and ears on high alert. As he approached so Chipper backed away slightly accompanied by a low rumble.

'Just be ready to shift your dog away if there's a lunge.'

'Will do.'

Jasper, not one to be fazed by anything, moved right up to the wire and barked once at the pup. Dropping front paws and chest to the floor, Chipper moved back then pounced forward with a bark, his snipped tail wagging as well as it could. Up against the wire the two dogs met face to face, Jasper half grin-half snarl, Chipper all grin.

'It's obvious they both know who's in charge.' Archie gave a relieved sigh. 'Can I let them together?'

'Yes, OK.'

As Nicky moved to the door to unclip the latch so Chipper clocked the event and was there waiting, Jasper was more aloof but still focussed. As soon as the kennel door opened Chipper was out, bouncing round Jasper then Nicky, then Archie, Jasper, Nicky, Archie, Jasper...

'Lots of energy here, and there's a bit of socialising gone on; it might just save him.' Archie smiled at the pup's delight at all this attention, Jasper taking the brunt of it, the pup licking his face and rolling over onto his back only to flick himself upright and begin his circuit of the two humans again before returning to face-wash the terrier. After the pup's fourth visit Jasper showed his tolerance level had been breached. With a snarl and air-snap millimetres away from the pup's face he continued growling quietly in admonition. Chipper went instantly floppy then rolled upright into a semi-prone position and flicked a tongue into thin air, a puppy whine escaping his mouth.

'Lesson number one,' said Archie.

'Will they be together all the time?'

'Not all the time no, but I suspect they'll be seeing quite a bit of each other. Right, Nicky, how do you want to progress with this? What's the damage for starters?'

'That's really your call. We ask for a donation, that's it really.'

'What's the average?'

'Fifty, sixty pounds.'

'OK, well, a hundred should cover it.' Nicky was about to speak but Archie stalled her. 'Really, worth every penny for what you lot do here.'

'Well, thank you.'

'My pleasure. Now, if he can just hang on here until tomorrow, I'd like to sort out stuff for him back at home, bed and feeding bowl, before he moves in.'

'We can provide all that.'

'No...thank you. No, I'd like to do it myself. I could do with some feeding rules though. You know, what he's on now, how much, how often, that kind of thing.'

'Sure, yeah. Let's go back into the office and we can sort out the paperwork.' The two dogs were now sniffing their way along the empty kennels on an inspection run, Chipper following in Jasper's wake. 'I'll just pop him back in the holding kennel...'

'He'll not appreciate that.'

'Maybe, but it's a happy ending for this fella so he'll just have to put up with it 'til tomorrow.'

Five Weeks Later

Archie sat alongside Kanga in her wheelchair as they chatted through the various bits of news.

'And I got a reply from Faye, about how his spaniel's back at work and ripping the place up now he's mastered the three-legged race.'

The door to the room opened and Nurse Danjuma came in. 'Kanga...?' She saw Archie. 'Oh, sorry.'

'Hi Onyedi, it's fine, just small talk.'

'Oh good. Just to let you know your physio time's been put back until twelve o'clock. Something about a faulty heating system, it's like Siberia in there I'm told. Engineers are in and fixing it now, but they've had to reshuffle all appointments and wait for it to warm up a bit; is that OK?'

'Yes of course. Not much choice really.'

'Sorry...so, back to collect you in twenty-five minutes.'

'Thanks, Onyedi.' The door closed. 'Oh well, that gives us a little extra time. What about the dog you rescued?'

'Clip, nee eight seventy-four?'

'Yes...and why Clip?'

''Cos he had a close clip with the needle and he needed a name; taken to it quite well all-in-all. He's still in training, phase one, but doing alright for a mutt. Phase two is I'm gonna try and get him and Jasper out together, with Lin's permission. Take 'em round the country park at Brixworth, the old gravel pits?'

'Oh yes, know of them.'

'You not been there?'

'No.'

'Right, we'll book a date, good place to go to...no excuses either, they're wheelchair friendly.'

'You don't reckon you'll be seeing me jogging round there in the foreseeable future then?'

'Not in the next couple of months no, but soon, and if not jogging then walking.'

'Yeah right.'

'Stop it.'

She smiled at him and there was a companionable silence before Archie spoke again. 'So OK, is there anything you'll need by my next visit?'

Kanga cast a look round the room. 'No more flowers?'

'Your mum?' Kanga nodded. 'She means well.'

'I know, she just...'

'Swamps you a bit?'

'Yeah, for all the right reasons I'm sure... She likes you.'

Archie shrugged. 'I've no idea why, but it's reciprocated. Your dad's a bit...'

'Distant?'

'Yeah.'

'Just his way, don't read anything into it. Accept that no one is ever going to be good enough for his only daughter and you'll get on fine.' There was a further silence then Kanga tentatively opened the conversation. 'What's the word on the court case?'

'I wondered when that would come up. You read the opinion piece in the Mail then?'

'Hatchet job you mean. All that stuff about search warrants... and what was it, your cavalier...'

Archie joined in with her to finish the quote, 'Attitude to policing and the rule of law.'

'They made you seem incompetent.'

'Yeah. Bit one-sided wasn't it?'

'A bit? All that personal stuff about Pamela and that terrible accident. Who was 'the source' they got it all from?'

'Campbell...or Brightwick via Campbell. My internal files for sure, that amount of detail could only have been gleaned from them.'

'Well they had no right! Can you prove any of that?'

'Ha! I wish. I'm only glad you'd heard it from me first.' I'm just glad they didn't get the Beavis-Pamela link; that could have been really shitty.

'But what's it got to do with them anyway. It's just so unfair Archie.'

'Fair aint in it. These are professionals Kanga. They'd destroyed my credibility and proved me an unreliable individual even before I've opened my mouth.' Archie looked out of the window and spoke under his breath to the middle distance. 'Millar was dead right on that one.'

'Jay Millar?'

'Yeah... It's nothing.'

'And now there's the court case to get through, when did you say?'

'I didn't, we got side-tracked putting the world to rights.' He smiled at her. 'I'm up before the beak on the twenty-eighth.'

'For?'

'Common assault on Brightwick and Quinn. Brightwick pushed for ABH for them both, but the CPS wouldn't allow it, said it violates the statutory procedures.'

'So it'll be handled in the Magistrates' Court.'

'Yeah.'

'Good. Bet that pissed him off.'

'Not privy to that, but I'd like to think so. Small victory.'

'And the internal?'

'Three days after that.'

'Bit arse-wise isn't it, internal after the Magistrates' Court? I thought...?'

'Brightwick's doing. Not legal just procedural. Wanted to make sure he got his pound of flesh so probably swung it with the CC and the CPS to doctor the dates.'

'You think?'

'Yeah. Brightwick's got the CC by the ball-sack and more friends in the law-game than I've got pounds in the bank, so that'll be me for the highest penalty on all counts.'

'But Lin only got a fine.'

'I'm a servant of the crown don't forget, plus my Super will bend to it so, between the two of them, I'll be out of a job permanently by the beginning of February.'

She smiled at him. 'I must say you don't look fazed by it.'

'Nah, not really... I'm just sorry for Arnue and Mary.

'You said, about Arnue taking a demotion back to uniform. What was the final outcome for Mary?'

'She decided for herself... I believe that, at the end of her interview, she said, and I quote; "I'm not taking any more of this shit, you can stuff your job where the squirrel stuffs his nuts." Case closed.'

Kanga smiled. 'Wow! What's she going to do now then?'

'Not sure, but she's too good a copper not to utilise her skills somehow.'

'And you?'

'It's time for a change, I said, which I'll get when the verdict comes in... but then, I've got you, so my wishes are granted.'

She took his hand. 'A life sentence with me.'

'Yeah, I'd get less for murder...'

Nurse Danjuma appeared round the door again. 'They're coming to get you Kanga.'

'Wasn't there a song about that? "They're coming to take you away", or summat?' Onyedi flat-lined him.

'S'alright Onyedi, he's stopped taking his medication.'

Onyedi smiled at her. 'He's not going to join you in physiotherapy then?'

Archie raised an eyebrow. 'He's here, he can hear you.'

'Then I can tell him to his face that it's time for his companion to do her exercises and for him to leave.' The door closed.

'What is it with nurses eh? They swan about like they own the place.' He stood, bent forward and kissed Kanga on the cheek. 'How about, as soon as you, your health and the doctors allow, how about we go up to Scotland and meet Kenzie and Faye? You, me and Clip, let them see what all the fuss was about?'

'That'd be great. Can Lin and Jasper come too?'

He looked at her. 'Er, yeah, if you like. You sure about that?'

'Of course, it'd be good to get it all signed off, another bit of closure for Lin.'

'OK, I'll make the calls, fix it up and await your release. See you tomorrow.'

'Not later today?'

'No sorry, got errands to run.'

'Man-of-mystery is it?'

Archie folded back his forelock. 'No not at all. I'm going across to see Jay and Anita, I've not seen them since my suspension...I think I owe them an apology, then I'm over to see Lin so I'll mention about your idea for Scotland.' He kissed her on the cheek again. 'See y' tomorrow, keep taking the tablets and doin' the exercises.'

'Yup. I'll be here.'

The door opened and a white coated physiotherapy nurse came in. Archie nodded to him on his way out. 'Good luck with that one.'

~

'Hi Lin, you look busy.'

'Oh, hi Archie!' Lin got down from the set of steps. 'Fancy seeing you.'

'Yeah, I know, point taken. Sorry not to have been in touch recently; lot of stuff been going on with Kanga.'

'I thought as much, no need to apologise, that opening was very cruel of me.'

'No, it's valid.'

'Well, I've only managed to get in and see her twice so I've no room to talk. How is she?'

'Doing all the right things, just has to be a patient patient.'

'Not her strong suit?'

'Not by a country mile. She sends her love.'

'And by return. Will it be OK for me to call in tomorrow and see her?'

'Yeah, she'll be thrilled. You may even bump into me.'

'Oh, I wanted girl-talk time.'

'Don't worry, I'll give you both space.'

'Meeting arranged then.'

'Yup. So, what did you want to see me about?'

'Oh, yeah...I'm applying for a job with the British Trust for Conservation Volunteers...'

'Window cleaning at the Red Lion not to your taste then?'

'Never make a career out of it, but it's helping me pay off my council tax arrears, living here now, cheaply, and the bar work. So, for the job, could you be my referee, please?'

'Absolutely. When do you want it for?'

'I'll have the application form finished tonight, post it tomorrow, so if they like me, I guess some time in the next ten days or so.'

''Course they'll like you! They'll snap you up.'

'Yeah, right.'

'They will! And, talking of snapping, how do you fancy getting Clip and Jasper together again sometime next week, get them into the park, do a bit of recall work?'

'Still not got the hang of it then?'

'Not really, does it when it suits.'

'Yeah, OK... if I can prize him away from Valerie.'

'I was gonna say where is he? Like that is it?'

'A bit, yeah. She keeps feeding him treats from the pub roast, he goes into that tool bag at the first sound of meat being moved anywhere in the building.'

'He'll not be rushing down to greet me then?'

'Open a tin of corned beef, yeah; other than that...'

'There was a time...'

'I know, for me too.'

'Talking of greetings, how did your conversations with Khanyisile go?'

'Oh, OK. It was her having to tell Momma Lesedi that was my main concern. I sent her all the information I could, press cuttings and such, so she could explain it all fully, but from this distance what else are you supposed to do? Still working on it... Anyway, to what do I owe this visit of yours?'

'Couple of things. First, something that may help. I'd like you to have this.' He handed across a small, thick, brown paper bag.

Lin began to open it. 'What is it?'

'That tiepin I showed you, remember? In the police station when we first met up. It's what intrigued me, way back at the very start of all this.'

She held it up. 'Then you have it, as a memento.'

'No, it'll be of more use to you. That's not white gold Lin, it's platinum, and that's a real diamond in there, the jeweller told me that.'

'But, won't there be someone out there who's lost it?'

'It's done the statutory six weeks, more than, and that makes it free-to-finder.'

'But, a tie pin, what would I do with it?'

'You're asking me? Sell it; just don't take less than a grand for it.'

Lin's eyes widened. 'Thank you, Archie, I don't know what to say...'

'Nothing. If anyone deserves it, it's you. Right, let me say hi to Jasp and I'll bring you up to date with my legalities and Kanga's suggested trip to Scotland...'

Three Weeks Later

6'T̶hird reading of The Rare and Exotic Animals Research Bill. Lord Brightwick.'

Brightwick stood up from the buttoned, red leather bench seat, a sheaf of notes in hand. 'My Lords, I beg to move that this bill be read for the third time, a bill that will prove to be a milestone in the safeguarding of endangered species. Never has there been a more active threat to the world's wildlife than now. To delay the progress of this bill any longer simply allows the hands on the clock of their extinction to move closer to midnight.'

'Hear-hear...'

'I thank my Honourable Friend the Baroness Clarisston for her comments and agree with her that the sensible, legal harvesting of ivory from carefully guarded elephant stocks would prove a mainstay in the protection of any such species. Such a statement dovetails neatly into the very reason for this timely bill. Anyone who understands the natural world as I do, and has scrutinised my bill, will understand such a safeguarding policy is central to the bill's operating maxims. Only by maintaining a healthy population of such creatures, from which surplus animals can be harvested for research by paying sportsmen, will that species' future be safe...

'...and this would open up heretofore sealed-off tracts of land for the native population to graze their beasts and collect much needed fuel without fear of encountering or affecting the wild creatures in their vicinity. To upgrade and consolidate the longevity of such creatures, this bill offers a brighter future to all wildlife through the sampling of what would be well guarded populations, utilising that sampling process as a form of scientific and fiscal harvesting which would, I believe, be of enormous benefit to wildlife and humankind alike.'

Brightwick sat down as the Lord Speaker stood.

'The question is that this bill be read for the third time.'

Lord MacGrady stood. 'My Lords it is a great pleasure to speak in this debate. I congratulate the noble Lord for bringing to the House this very timely bill which I wholeheartedly support...'

Lord Kitter stood. 'My Lords it is with considerable pleasure that I add my full support to this timely bill. I have known the noble Lord for many years and know him to be a steadfast and doughty champion for the wildlife of Africa...'

Lord Brightwick stood. 'My Lords, I thank all noble Lords who have supported this bill for their valuable and knowledgeable contributions to this debate. I greatly appreciate their strong support. Some in the Chamber remain unconvinced as to the efficacy and scrupulousness of both my research when compiling this bill and the trustworthiness of its intent, so I would like to take a moment to address these concerns...

'...In conclusion to this debate on the third reading of The Rare and Exotic Animals Research Bill can I reiterate this is an important, dare I say vital bill. My sole reasons for bringing it before the House have been obvious from the outset; to safeguard and protect these wild creatures and their natural habitat. I can do no better at this point than quote the words of His Royal Highness the late King George the sixth and use them as my vade mecum on all things natural: "The wildlife of today is not ours to dispose of as we please. We have it in trust. We must account for it to those who come after". The adoption of this bill will offer nothing less than salvation for these creatures. Can I also say that the House's comments, from whatever quarter, have done much to improve this bill. Their contributions will serve to make it a significant step in the safeguarding of our global natural heritage...

'...I would ask that your Lordships give this bill a third reading and I beg to move.'

The Lord Speaker stood. 'The question is that this bill now be read a third time. As many of that opinion will say Content.'

'Content!'

'To the contrary, Not Content.'

'Not Content!'

'Clear the Bar.'

~

'Very well. Detective Chief Inspector Arnold, is there anything you wish to add to today's proceedings by way of mitigation before the panel retire to consider their ruling?'

Archie looked at their faces and the words *Done-Deal* went through his head. 'Not so much mitigation Sir, more explanation.'

Chief Superintendent James Campbell looked along the line of the three fellow officers who all nodded their consent. 'Very well.'

Archie was silent as he framed his thoughts, his flop of hair partially hiding his face. 'What I don't seek to do is excuse my behaviour at the television studio that Sunday, nor do I want to use the job as the litmus test for it. We all suffer from the pressure that goes with being a serving police officer, more so since the government cuts have taken so many out of the trade leaving their workload to settle on the shoulders of already overstretched staff. But, it has to be said that these things are factors in how much of an impact certain events may have had on an already stretched team as well as on an individual.'

'An observation?'

Archie looked at Divisional Commander Foreston. 'Yes, Sir.'

'There's no mention in any report of the details surrounding this enquiry of a deficiency in mental aptitude or cognisance on your part. Are we to understand that you are now introducing a decreased mental capacity into the evidence?'

'No Sir, far from it. I knew exactly what I was doing throughout.'

'Ah right. Good. Continue.'

'Thank you, Sir. What I meant was that the case leading up to the assault...'

'You admit that then?' Campbell was in fast.

'The assault? Of course. Could hardly do otherwise, not after it being witnessed by three million people, and definitely not after yesterday's verdict in the Magistrates' Court.'

'But to this committee you admit the offence?'

'Yes, it was an assault; I did it. It was a résumé of the case and the events leading up to it that I wanted to cover here Sir.'

Campbell scribbled notes as he spoke. 'Very well.'

'Thanks. Er... I think the various sites of evidence we found during the investigation, the murder of an innocent bystander, Renata Lea, of one of our serving officers, Adam Reeve my colleague and friend, and the probable murder of a third, an elderly resident, Stanley Mason, laid the foundations for an investigation that was not without emotion. When coupled with the near-fatal injuries caused to WPC Kanjara Desai, Customs Officer Kenzie Jardine and Constable Ameet Reddy, notwithstanding the death of at least one dog and the serious injuries sustained to at least two others, all these events built the subsequent findings into a volcano that finally erupted in that television studio. But more than that. These people, the ones mentioned, they're humans. They know why they're there, what they're doing, what the dangers and risks are. But the animals involved? They're just serving at the whim of their masters. They don't question, procrastinate or evaluate; their obedience and their commitment to us, their life-companions, is absolute, unflinching and total. The terrier that stood guard over his dead mistress for three days and tried to protect me in the television studio; the sniffer spaniel who took a bullet in his endeavours to protect his master, losing a leg in the process; the puppy I subsequently took on who was, I fully believe, destined to be a fighter that would've lived "a life nasty, brutish and short". All these animals suffered at the behest of men with nothing but brutality and kudos on their minds. On Bliss Bank estate, behind this gated community of privilege, were all the trappings to make these things real, complete with a purpose-built arena in which to test it; an arena decorated with the claw-marks of desperation enforced by a master fully prepared to cheer on those confrontations in order to enhance his personal standing in, and profit from, the world; that master was Brightwick.'...

~

The four tellers bowed and moved to the back of the clerk's chair. The Lord Ebbw Vale was handed a slip of paper by the clerk and a murmur went round the chamber. Moving along the centre benches he bowed and placed the paper onto the book held by the Deputy Speaker who bowed by return then read out loud.

'There have voted. The Contents three hundred and fifty-four. The Not Contents two hundred and thirty-five. So the Contents have it.' The Lord Stoneham stood.

'I beg to move that this House adjourns.'

The Deputy Speaker nodded in acceptance. 'The Question is that this House do now adjourn during pleasure until eight o'clock. As many of that opinion will say Content.'

'Content!'

'To the contrary, Not Content... The Contents have it.'

Brightwick, along with the vast majority of other Lords, scuttled out of the doors and away to afternoon tea. As he passed through the main door, he was joined by Reginald MacGrady who patted him on the back.

'Well done Larry.'

'Thank you, Reggie, longest twenty-eight minutes I've spent for a many a day.'

'Result was never in doubt, was it?'

'Always a doubt, Reggie.'

'But a good day all round.'

'Twice over if things go as planned.'

'Ah yes, your policeman's case. What punishment was handed down?'

'Not enough. Should have gone to Crown. His defence used his so-called exemplary record, his team's character statements and the personal events as mitigation. A fine of one thousand pounds; paltry. Still, we managed to manipulate his appearances, so I hope for greater things from his disciplinary hearing today.'

'You've not heard yet?'

'Not yet. Quinn will feed me the result sometime this afternoon, but I fully expect all that is required from this one will be achieved.'

'Good show. Not so welcome news on her though I gather. I heard she was treated very lightly.'

Brightwick's annoyance showed through. 'Should have been ABH and gone to Crown.'

'Ah, the fickleness of the judiciary.'

'And the idiocy of the CPS.'

'But justice was done?'

'Of a sort. I had paid for it after all.'

MacGrady smiled. 'Yes you had. You'll pursue of course.'

Brightwick paused and shook his head. 'Er...no, I think not. I feel the lady in question has learned her lesson. It would be unfair of me to expose an unfortunate such as her to any further punishment; let sleeping dogs lie I think.'

'Well that's magnanimous of you Larry. In that case let's skip tea and let me buy us a late lunch in celebration of your bill getting through and your obvious fellow-feeling for those less fortunate. You can tell me all the gory details.'

'Most kind Reggie.'

'House food I'm afraid. I'm due back in at eight.'

'The Waste Recycling Bill of Lady Mary's?'

'The same.'

'Then let me treat us to a good Claret, you'll need something to help you sleep.'

Laughing softly the two Lords walked across the main lobby towards the restaurant.

~

Campbell emphasised his point by stabbing the desktop with his finger. 'Something you have absolutely no proof about.'

'But which, if I'd been left to conclude the case, I would have got.'

'Are you suggesting, Arnold, that there's been some form of collusion between the forces of law and order and the cessation of enquiries into the behaviour of Lord Brightwick?'

'Yes.'

Chief Superintendent Campbell leant forward on the desk, fixing Archie with a gimlet eye. 'And may I say, this is exactly the sort of wild behaviour that I've had cause to reprimand you over in the past, reprimands that are on record and have been seen by this panel. Behaviour that I've done my best to find reasons for, given your detection rates...'

'Are you saying that I wasn't told to drop the case Sir?'

'You were, but only because the case had been closed!'

'In your opinion.'

'And that of my immediate superior, and I followed his direct order. But it would seem that, once again, when you received a direct order from me, your immediate superior, you chose to disregard it!'

'I did Sir, but only because I considered your reasoning to be flawed.'

Norman Palliston, Head of Internal Investigations, followed on. 'And this supposed superior intellect of yours caused you to leap, mistakenly, to the conclusion that somehow Lord Brightwick, a peer of the realm and Member of Parliament no less, was involved in all these sordid events?'

'Still do Sir, Sunday red tops proved that.'

This stopped Palliston in his tracks. After a long silent look at Archie and a glance at his colleagues he spoke, 'By showing a total lack of understanding, not a hint of remorse for your actions, dispensing wild accusations and having scant regard for those in high office you are not doing your case any favours Detective Inspector Arnold.'

'Will it make any difference if I do; show remorse I mean?' The panel was silent. 'Didn't think so, that's why there isn't any; I did it then, I'd do it now...' Campbell tried to speak but Archie talked over him. 'And can I say for the record that Brightwick's a wrong'un; rotten as a pear and what's worse, you all know it. The investigation's closed now, you've all seen to that, so I'll not have the chance to prove it...but let me tell you, there's a lot of people and a lot more animals that'll rue this day, and it's all thanks to you lot.'

The panel reacted and Campbell gave Archie a venomous look. 'Are you quite finished?!'

'If I wasn't before I am now.'

Two Years Later

Archie stood in the doorway, tea towel in hand. 'What time did Faye say they'd be here?'

The muted television flashed images of entertainment into the room, adding to the firelight and table lamp illumination gracing Kanga's face. 'She reckoned about seven, but you know the traffic this time of year.'

'December twenty third, hardly the best day to travel is it?'

'No. And Gabrielle?'

'Not until nine she said, something about a work's do.'

'Oh, right. Do you think Faye will bring both dogs?'

'Well, she sort of said as much, so...' Archie looked towards the window etched with the promise of cold. 'Bit of frost moving in, at least Lin and Tim have only got a short drive over here. All he's got to do is remember the car.'

'Ha! Yeah. He's clever not sensible.'

'Silly as a sheep.'

'Is he going with Lin for the sister ceremony thing now she's finally committed to going back?'

'I'm not sure. When I saw her at that BTCV open day the week before last...'

'The one I couldn't go to because of physio.'

'The same, sorry.'

'No, that was a good day. Did nearly a hundred yards, and I really am feeling stronger each time I go. It's the chance of losing that wheelchair for good that keeps me going.'

'That's because you're a fighter, knew it all along. Another few months and we'll be entering you in a pentathlon.'

'Ha! So, Lin and Tim...?'

'Oh, yeah. Well, Lin said it might be difficult for him to get time off but that she was definitely going in the middle of March, with or without him; sixteenth, I think. I just wish she'd have let me spot her for the travel fares last year, put it towards that tiepin I handed over.'

'She sold it, you said.'

'She did, and then used it to pay off her debts and back tax but she'd still a bit left. I suggested I make up the difference, but you know how stubborn she is.'

'Not stubborn, she's her own lady; power to her.' Kanga tapped the chair's arm to underline it. 'The job at the BTCV's going well, she's full-time in conservation, got that promotion...'

'She did.'

'And that's because she's good at it, and she's also good for the fare now; owes no one but herself.'

'Yeah, you're right, and it'll be a good thing when it happens, she'll be able to draw the whole thing to a close, that part of it anyway.'

'It's going to be a difficult trip whatever, so let's make her few days here really festive.'

'Yeah.' Archie fixed Kanga with a stare. 'You're sure about this, the invasion again I mean?'

'Bit late now ex-detective Arnold, wouldn't you say?'

Archie sat on the arm of the adjacent chair. 'You know what I mean ex-WPC Desai. This is the second year we've done this.'

She smiled at him. 'It's a reunion to counter the group's annual Christmas melancholy, and you, you're prepared to put up with my parents on New Year's Eve, so quid pro quo.'

'Bit different really, in-laws are family. This is a gang of five on Christmas Day plus James and Megan on Boxing Day again.'

'And I said, I'm fine with it.'

'They'll all be gone by the thirtieth anyhow. Hogmanay at home for the Scots lot, Gabby across to Jay's...'

'Oh, that reminds me. I'm OK to reply with a yes for Anita and Nathan's engagement party at the end of January, aren't I?'

'Wouldn't miss it, pity they couldn't join us this year.'

'Too much to plan, Anita said.'

'I guess. They seemed to really enjoy it last year.'

'There'll be plenty of others. Now, what were you saying?'

'Nothing important, just reeling off the visitors, their destinations. Gabby across to Jay's, Lin, Tim and her tribe over with Sarah and her mum and dad at the Lion.'

'Well then. It's only for a couple of days and I do love having lots of folk around, especially that lot, and the year's not been bad has it?'

'No. No one was more sceptical than me when you suggested starting up this security business, but as things are...'

'Lin pushed it, and I'm glad she did. Without wanting to tempt fate we've done really well this year, and that three-year contract we got with Rocksteady Promotions...'

'You got.'

'Whatever, that'll be a nice little earner.'

'I just hope we like the music.'

'You and Mary will be there to oversee the security of their clientele, not go dancing in the aisles. All we have to do is for me to keep up the pressure for new work and for you pair to keep doing things right when we get it.'

No pressure then. Right... Do you want a cuppa before they get here?'

'Please.'

Archie sat for a few seconds then sighed. 'I suppose I'll have to get up and make it then?'

'If you want it hot, yeah. You know how long it takes me to make one, juggling with this stick...'

'I think you slot back into that mode on purpose.' He stood up and folded back his flop of hair. A prone and snoozing Clip lifted his head up from the rug in front of the fire, let out a huge sigh then flopped it back down again. 'No, don't get up, don't trouble y'self...' The dog's stump-tail twitched a couple of times before a stretch of front legs and a closing of eyes completed his relaxation routine. As he walked round the back of Kanga's chair Archie stroked her hair and she let out a contented sigh.

'I love you Mister A.'

Archie smiled. 'Right back at y'.' He looked at the television. 'Do you want that left on?'

'Yeah, the news is just starting. Let's at least try and not shut ourselves off from the world completely, eh?'

'Yeah, s'pose...'

'Where's the remote?'

Archie reached down the side of her chair, retrieving it from between cushion and the arm. 'Down here, where you hid it.'

Archie went into the kitchen to shuffle tea making into life.

Kanga unmuted the TV just as the news started.

"...and we'll go live to our Africa Correspondent, Marcus Gerber... Marcus, first reports in say this incident happened during a rest day; is that correct? What can you tell us?"

"...Yes Patrick. I've been covering the African Trade Talks in Gaborone where leaders of the industrialised nations have gathered for discussions surrounding the refunding of the region's mining and agricultural assets, called after the country defaulted on payments to the World Bank made to shore up the country's degraded economy earlier this year. Yesterday and today were rest days after a week of six sessions of gruelling and sometimes fractious negotiations. A small number of the delegates took the opportunity to fly out and attend an organised tour of a sanctuary...

'Archie... Oh, Lord... Archie! You need to come and see this...'

"...for elephants orphaned by the continued poaching in...

'Archie!'

Clip opened an eye as Archie appeared in the doorway.

"...the region. At fifteen thirty local time the leader of the Botswana delegation, Limdaba Mabatene, called a press conference where we were given as yet unconfirmed information that a serious incident had taken place at the Iranti ti Erin sanctuary after an elephant overturned a vehicle carrying a number of the delegates.

Archie looked at Kanga. 'Is that...?'

'Yes! Shush!'

"...and we can go across to speak to the head of the Forest Rescue Department, Mtabe Molongo, who's been overseeing the recovery operation. Mister Molongo, this has been a tricky and quite harrowing rescue.

'Just wait 'til Lin gets here...'

"Can you firstly confirm for us if there are any fatalities...?"

The doorbell sounded. 'Talk of the devil.' Archie went to the door closely followed by Clip. 'Oh, decided to get up now have y'? Turn it up Kanga...' Archie tried to open the front door, but Clip pressed up against it in his eagerness to greet his friends. 'Jesus dog...will y' just let me...'

Pulling the door open sufficiently to allow Clip's exit only meant giving Jasper sufficient room to enter and the two dogs began an immediate and extravagant greeting as, to Archie's delight, Cashman, demonstrating his three-legged skills, slalomed round them both and scampered in to Kanga, swiftly followed by Jasper and Clip. Archie opened the door fully to reveal Lin, Tim, Kenzie and Faye.

'Hi you guys.' Archie saw the sixteen-week-old black and white Cocker Spaniel pup in Faye's arms. 'Oh, you brought her along. Excellent! Kanga will be thrilled.'

The greetings fell one on the other. 'Hi Archie.' 'Merry Christmas.'

'Hi Kenzie...good journey?'

'Aye, not bad.'

He stepped back. 'Come in come in, no fuss, go through, Kanga's watching some interesting news...'

'Something's happened hasn't it, Archie? Something big... I knew it.' Archie stared at Lin as she moved rapidly into the sitting room. 'What is it Kanga?'

'You're not going to believe this Lin...'

Archie pecked Faye on the cheek as she and Kenzie passed him. Tim took Archie's hand and held on. 'She's been like that for the past twenty minutes.'

'Like what?'

'Like she's on glass stilts. On the way over here, she suddenly grabbed me by the arm and shouted out, like she'd been stabbed. Scared the bejesus out of me. Then she took hold of that netsuke of hers like it was life itself, hasn't let it go since.' Archie stared at Lin as they gathered in the large sitting room to watch the news unfold with ever-growing astonishment.

... *"Thanks, Derek. That was our Deputy Political Editor Derek Sawbridge. We can now return to our Africa Correspondent. Marcus?"*

"Patrick, yes. The details as to what happened are clearer now. The incident was sparked when the vehicle carrying four of the delegates became blocked behind another that had apparently stalled. This put a barrier between the matriarch elephant here and one of the calves. This herd leader has lived on the reserve since she was an orphaned baby some thirty plus years ago, and she reacted in the only way an elephant can when it feels one of the herd, particularly a calf, is being threatened. Moving to the vehicle she pushed it across the roadway where it plunged thirty feet into a ravine, all this in a matter of seconds. We can go across and talk again to Mtabe Molongo. Mr Molongo, firstly can you give us an update on events?"

"Yes. The German finance minister, Mara Fischer, was in the vehicle and is being cared for at the Central Hospital..."

"Yes yes, a lucky escape from this tragic accident, and can you now confirm that two of the three fatalities were members of the British delegation?"

"Yes. A Lord Brightwick and a Mister Randal Quinn..."

The reaction that ran through the group gathered in the firelit sitting room was palpable.

"...the third fatality was the Chinese Ambassador for Trade, Xhio Lin Hua..."

On the television, in the background, a woman appeared behind the reporter smiling broadly. A small, barely discernible wave exposed a flash of something white in her hand. After a short pause she moved away out of shot.

'Oh, shit.'

All eyes turned to Lin as Archie spoke, 'What Lin? What is it?'

'What's this on?'

'Er...BBC News...'

'No, I mean is it on a box-thingy.'

Kanga held up the remote. 'A set-top box? Yes.'

'Pause it can you Kanga?' Kanjara pressed the pause button and the picture blinked once then froze. 'Send it back a bit, I'll say when... That'll be enough. Now play it.'

"*... of the three fatalities were members of the British delegation?*"

"*Yes. A Lord Brightwick and a Mister Randal Quinn, the third fatality was the Chinese Ambassador for Trade, Xhio Lin Hua...*"

The woman appeared centre shot again. 'There. Stop there!' The picture froze and Lin moved a little closer to the screen.

Faye looked across. 'Lin, is that...?'

After a long pause Lin turned to them. 'Khanyisile? Yes. Let it run again until I say.' Kanga restarted the broadcast as the group locked intently on to the screen. 'Stop!' The playback froze again and Lin moved closer to the screen and placed her finger on it. 'Recognise them Archie?'

Lin released the netsuke from her closed fist as Archie closed in on the screen too. 'The twins?'

Lin held up her netsuke. 'The triplets.'

Lin looked once more at the screen. 'Let it play, Kanga.'

Kanga released the frozen picture and once again the lady in the background left the shot.

"*Thank you Mister Molongo. I believe you also have the warden of the Iranti ti Erin reserve who was driving the vehicle that stalled and who, I believe, has the elephant responsible for the incident with her. Can we speak to her?*"

The camera crew moved slowly across to the lady standing alongside a full-grown elephant. The tip of its trunk, caressing the woman's hands which cradled the two netsuke, lifted momentarily to mumble on the microphone before returning to the woman's hands and gripping them gently. Alongside a one-month old calf was slowly, nonchalantly whisking the floor with a wisp of grass held in its trunk.

"*Warden Khanyisile. Does the elephant have a name?*"

"*This elephant is Amahle.*"

The whole room stared open mouthed at Lin.

'*And this is her calf?*'

'*Yes; this is Rene.*'

"*Well, even from this distance I must say Amahle and Rene look extremely calm. What can you tell us about what might have prompted her reaction?*"

Khanyisile turned slightly and looked straight to camera...

The Memory of an Elephant

Hello Reader,

I wanted to add a personal note to this novel, but first, thank you very much for purchasing a copy of *The Memory of an Elephant*. For writers such as me who work as a one-man-band and run on a shoestring budget it really means a great deal; I hope it didn't disappoint. Thank you.

There may be some who are already familiar with my work and have read and commented on my previous two novels, *Ladies of the Shire* and *The Quarry*, or who have made contact with me through my web page and social media sites to discuss like-minded topics, for which I also thank you. From my work and other interests, readers will have a grasp on how the natural (and sometimes unnatural) world has figured, both in my writing and in my everyday living.

For as long as I can remember, since my dad introduced me to the wonders of nature when I was six or so years old, my fascination and involvement with our natural environment has educated and influenced my employment, philosophy and social conscience. Close contact with creatures, both domesticated and decidedly undomesticated, has broadened my understanding, underlining just how fragile and interconnected this earth and its inhabitants are.

Most of us know, either through study or default, the level of threat facing both the natural environment and the creatures living in and dependent on it; the vexing question is what can we, as individuals, do about it? As you'll know by now, definitive answers are hard to come by (and sometimes harder to enforce) but there are measures each of us can take, as well as facts we have to acknowledge, in order to lessen our impact on the earth and help safeguard the creatures who live with us; only by doing this can we ensure our and their survival.

1) **Recognise and act on the truth: It's up to us.** There's no magic wand, no miracle-cure and no silver bullet. (As you can see, like DCI Arnold in the story, I've been reading the inspirational quotes in the vestibule.) We have to take responsibility for our planet and act on that responsibility, or no one will. It'll take time and effort on our part, and we really will have to go without some of the things we've been told, mostly by advertisers, we cannot live without. But the investment of us taking responsibility will pay our children and grandchildren back with interest.

2) **Understand and embrace the fact: We're interdependent.** Every time an individual creature, piece of vegetation, watercourse or body of water is corrupted, the ripples stretch right back to us. There really is a balance in nature and it's a delicate one; very. Every living creature, no matter how disconnected they may seem to us, has an impact on those around them; enforced changes, brought about by either bad management or wilful ignorance, affect others.

3) **Know that, although one person can make a difference, a large group can effect real change: Join an organisation.** Whichever one seems to suit your purpose or interest, do your research on them carefully. Get to understand the goals and ideologies of the different organisations, find out how they spend their money; once you're satisfied (and only then) support them with either your money, your voluntary expertise, or your voluntary labour (or all three).

4) **Know for certain: Every purchase we make is a vote for the kind of world we want to live in and the kind of people we want to help us run it.**

About the Author: Born in Wolverhampton, and so a true Black Country Lad, I've had a varied career; rock drummer, zoo and game keeper, gundog trainer, conservation officer, writer, actor, director, designer and theatre production manager. I now live in Cornwall with my wife, Marjorie, and our Bedlington x whippet, Milo. This is my third novel, following on from the international success of *Ladies of the Shire* (2009) and *The Quarry* (2014)

~

Thank you for purchasing *The Memory of an Elephant* and I hope you enjoyed your time in this story as much as I did when writing it. If you did enjoy the tale then tell others and post your thoughts on Facebook or Twitter and your reviews on Amazon. I'm very happy to discuss my work with book clubs and writing groups and welcome discussion and feedback on my work from readers. Please contact me directly through my Facebook page, Peter Webb-Writer, or via my webpage, www.peter-webb.com

Lightning Source UK Ltd.
Milton Keynes UK
UKHW011139111220
374996UK00001B/50